Minette Walters lives in Hampshire with her husband and two children. She has worked as a magazine editor but is now a full-time writer.

With her debut, *The Ice House*, she won the Crime Writers' Association John Creasey Award for the best first crime novel of 1992. Rapidly establishing a reputation as one of the most exciting crime novelists writing today, her second novel, *The Sculptress*, was acclaimed by critics as one of the most compelling and powerful novels of the year and won the Edgar Allan Poe Award for the best crime novel published in America in 1993.

In 1994 Minette Walters achieved a unique triple when *The Scold's Bridle* was awarded the CWA Gold Dagger for best crime novel of the year. Her following novels, *The Dark Room*, *The Echo* and *The Breaker*, were also published to further critical acclaim.

BBC TV has adapted all five novels with huge success, most recently *The Dark Room* starring Dervla Kirwan and James Wilby.

By the same author

MINETTE WALTERS

THE
Scold's Bridle
&
THE
Dark Room

PAN BOOKS

For Jane, Lisanne, Maria and Hope
and
For Colleen
&
In memory of my father

The Scold's Bridle first published 1994 by Macmillan.
First published in paperback 1995 by Pan Books and reissued 1998.
The Dark Room first published 1995 by Macmillan.
First published in paperback 1996 by Pan Books.

This omnibus first published 2006 by Pan Books
an imprint of Pan Macmillan Ltd
Pan Macmillan, 20 New Wharf Road, London N1 9RR
Basingstoke and Oxford
Associated companies throughout the world
www.panmacmillan.com

ISBN-13: 978-0-330-44682-2
ISBN-10: 0-330-44682-7

1 3 5 7 9 8 6 4 2

A CIP catalogue record for this book is available from
the British Library.

Printed and bound in Great Britain by
Mackays of Chatham plc, Chatham, Kent

THE
Scold's Bridle

'Scold *skold,* n. a rude clamorous woman or other'
                                    Chambers English Dictionary

'Branks *brangks,* (Scot.) n.pl., rarely in sing., a scold's bridle; an instrument of punishment used in the case of scolds, etc., consisting of a kind of iron framework to enclose the head, having a sharp metal gag or bit which entered the mouth and restrained the tongue.'
                                    Oxford English Dictionary

'Create her child of spleen, that it may live
And be a thwart disnatur'd torment to her!
Let it stamp wrinkles in her brow of youth;
With cadent tears fret channels in her cheeks;
Turn all her mother's pains and benefits
To laughter and contempt; that she may feel
How sharper than a serpent's tooth it is
To have a thankless child!'

Shakespeare, *King Lear*

'Forty-two!' yelled Loonquawl. 'Is that all you've got to show for seven and a half million years' work?'

'I checked it very thoroughly,' said the computer, 'and that quite definitely is the answer. I think the problem, to be quite honest with you, is that you've never really known what the question is . . . Once you know what the question is, you'll know what the answer means.'

Douglas Adams, *The Hitch-Hiker's Guide to the Galaxy*

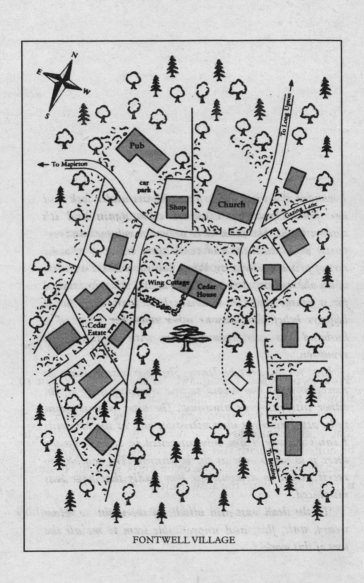

FONTWELL VILLAGE

I wonder if I should keep these diaries under lock and key. Jenny Spede has disturbed them again and it's annoying me. She must have opened a volume inadvertently while dusting, and reads them now out of some sort of prurient curiosity. What does she make, I wonder, of an old woman, deformed by arthritis, stripping naked for a young man? A vicarious lust, I am sure, for it beggars belief that anyone other than her brute of a husband has ever regarded her with anything but revulsion.

But, no, it can't be Jenny. She's too lazy to clean so thoroughly and too stupid to find anything I say or do either interesting or amusing. The later volumes seem to be attracting the most attention but, at the moment, I can't see why. I am only interested in beginnings for there is so much hope at the beginning. The end has no merit except to demonstrate how badly that hope was misplaced.

'In the dead vast and middle of the night ... How weary, stale, flat, and unprofitable seem to me all the uses of this world.'

1

Who then? James? Or am I going senile and imagining things? Yesterday I found Howard's offer open on my desk, but I could have sworn I put it back in the file. 'O judgement, thou art fled . . .'

The pills worry me more. Ten is such a round number to be missing. I fear Joanna is up to her wretched tricks again, worse, I wonder if Ruth is going the same way. Blood will always out . . .

One

DR SARAH BLAKENEY stood beside the bath and wondered how death could ever be described as a victory. There was no triumph here, no lingering sense that Mathilda had abandoned her earthly shell for something better, no hint even that she had found peace. The dead, unlike the sleeping, offered no hope of a re-awakening. 'You want my honest opinion?' she said slowly, in answer to the policeman's question. 'Then no, Mathilda Gillespie is the last person I'd have expected to kill herself.'

They stared at the grotesque figure, stiff and cold in the brackish water. Nettles and Michaelmas daisies sprouted from the awful contraption that caged the bloodless face, its rusted metal bit clamping the dead tongue still in the gaping mouth. A scattering of petals, curling and decayed, clung to the scraggy shoulders and the sides of the bath, while a brown sludge below the water's surface suggested more petals, waterlogged and sunk. On the floor lay a bloodied Stanley knife, apparently dropped by the nerveless fingers that dangled above it. It was reminiscent of Marat in *his* bath, but so much uglier and so much sadder. Poor Mathilda, thought Sarah, how she would have hated this.

The police Sergeant gestured at the pitiful grey head. 'What in God's name is *that* thing?' His voice grated with repugnance.

Sarah waited a moment until she felt her own voice was under control. 'It's a scold's bridle,' she told him, 'a primitive instrument of repression. They were used in the Middle Ages to curb the tongues of nagging women. It's been in Mathilda's family for years. I know it looks awful like that, but she kept it downstairs in the hall over a pot of geraniums. As a decoration it was rather effective.' She raised a hand to her mouth in distress and the policeman patted her shoulder awkwardly. 'They were white geraniums and they poked their heads through the iron framework. Her coronet weeds, she always called them.' She cleared her throat. 'She was rather fine, you know. Very proud, very snobbish, very intolerant and not overly friendly, but she had a brilliant mind for someone who had never been trained to do anything more than keep house and she had a wonderful sense of humour. Dry and incisive.'

'Coronet weeds,' echoed the pathologist thoughtfully. 'As in:

"There with fantastic garlands did she come,
Of crowflowers, nettles, daisies, and long purples,
That liberal shepherds give a grosser name,
But our cold maids do dead men's fingers call them:
There, on the pendent boughs her coronet weeds – "'

'*Hamlet*,' he explained apologetically to the policeman. 'Ophelia's end. I had to learn it for O level. Amazing what you remember as you get older.' He stared at the bath. 'Did Mrs Gillespie know *Hamlet*?'

Sarah nodded unhappily. 'She told me once that her entire education was based on learning chunks of Shakespeare by heart.'

'Well, we're not going to learn much by standing staring at the poor woman,' said the policeman abruptly. 'Unless Ophelia was murdered.'

Dr Cameron shook his head. 'Death by drowning,' he said thoughtfully, 'while of unsound mind.' He glanced at Sarah. 'Was Mrs Gillespie depressed at all?'

'If she was, she never gave any indication of it.'

The policeman, decidedly more uncomfortable in the presence of death than either of the two doctors, ushered Sarah on to the landing. 'Many thanks for your time, Dr Blakeney. I'm sorry we had to subject you to that but as her GP you probably knew her better than most.' It was his turn to sigh. 'They're always the worst. Old people, living alone. Society's rejects. Sometimes it's weeks before they're found.' His mouth turned down in a curve of distaste. 'Very unpleasant. I suppose we're lucky she was found so quickly. Less than forty hours according to Dr Cameron. Midnight Saturday, he estimates.'

Sarah leant her back against the wall and stared across the landing towards Mathilda's bedroom where the open door showed the old oak bed piled high with pillows. There was a strange sense of ownership still, as if her possessions retained the presence that her flesh had lost. 'She wasn't that old,' she protested mildly. 'Sixty-five, no more. These days that's nothing.'

'She looks older,' he said matter-of-factly, 'but then she would, I suppose, with all the blood drained out of her.' He consulted his notebook. 'A daughter, you say, living in

London, and you think a granddaughter at boarding school.'

'Don't Mr and Mrs Spede know?' She had caught a glimpse of them in the library as she came in, grey faces curiously blank from shock, hands clasped tightly together like petrified children. 'They've been coming in twice a week for years. He looks after the garden and she cleans. They must know more about her than anyone.'

He nodded. 'Unfortunately we've had nothing but hysterics out of them since Mrs Spede found the body. We'll be asking round the village, anyway.' He looked towards the bedroom. 'There's an empty bottle of barbiturates on her bedside table beside the remains of a glass of whisky. It looks like a belt and braces job. Whisky for courage, sleeping pills, then the Stanley knife in the bath. Do you still say you wouldn't have expected her to kill herself?'

'Oh, lord, I don't know.' Sarah ran a worried hand through her short dark hair. 'I wouldn't have prescribed barbiturates if I thought there was a chance she'd abuse them, but one can never be certain about these things. And anyway, Mathilda had been taking them for years, they were commonly prescribed once. So yes, I would rule out suicide from what I knew of her, but we had a doctor–patient relationship. She had severe pain with her arthritis and there were nights when she couldn't sleep.' She frowned. 'In any case, there can't have been many of the sleeping pills left. She was due for another prescription this week.'

'Perhaps she was hoarding them,' he said unemotionally. 'Did she ever open her heart to you?'

'I doubt she opened her heart to anyone. She wasn't the type. She was a very private person.' She shrugged. 'And I've only known her – what? – twelve months. I live in Long Upton, not here in Fontwell, so I haven't come across her socially either.' She shook her head. 'There's nothing in her records to suggest a depressive personality. But the trouble is—' She fell silent.

'The trouble is what, Dr Blakeney?'

'The trouble is we talked about freedom the last time I saw her, and she said freedom is an illusion. There's no such thing in modern society. She quoted Rousseau at me, the famous rebel-cry of students in the sixties: "Man was born free, and everywhere he is in chains." There was only one freedom left, according to Mathilda, and that was the freedom to choose how and when to die.' Her face looked bleak. 'But we had conversations like that every time I saw her. There was no reason to assume that one was any different.'

'When was this conversation?'

Sarah sighed heavily. 'Three weeks ago during my last monthly visit. And the awful thing is, I laughed. Even that wasn't a freedom any more, I said, because doctors are so damn scared of prosecution they wouldn't dream of giving a patient the choice.'

The policeman, a large detective nearing retirement, placed a comforting hand on her arm. 'There now, it's nothing to fret about. It was slitting her wrists that killed her, not barbiturates. And the chances are we're looking at murder anyway.' He shook his head. 'I've seen a few suicides one way and another, but I've yet to see an old

7

woman turn herself into a flower arrangement in her bath. It'll be money that's behind it. We all live too long and the young get desperate.' He spoke with feeling, Sarah thought.

An hour later, Dr Cameron was more sceptical. 'If she didn't do it herself,' he said, 'you'll have the devil's own job proving it.' They had removed the body from the bath and lain it, still with the scold's bridle in place, on plastic sheeting on the floor. 'Apart from the incisions in her wrists there's not a mark on her, bar what one would expect, of course.' He pointed to the lividity above and around the wrinkled buttocks. 'Some post mortem hypostasis where the blood has settled but no bruising. Poor old thing. She didn't put up any sort of a fight.'

Sergeant Cooper leaned against the bathroom doorjamb, drawn to look at the poor grey body, but deeply repulsed by it. 'She couldn't if she was drugged,' he murmured.

Cameron peeled off his gloves. 'I'll see what I can find out for you back at the lab, but my advice is, don't hold your breath. I can't see your Chief Super wasting too much time and resources on this one. It's about as neat as anything I've seen. Frankly, unless something pretty unusual shows up in the post mortem, I'll be recommending a suicide verdict.'

'But what does your gut tell you, Doctor? The nettles are telling mine it was murder. Why would she deliberately sting herself before she died?'

'Self-reproach, probably. Good God, man, there's no logic to this kind of thing. Suicides are hardly in their right mind when they top themselves. Still,' he said thoughtfully,

'I am surprised she didn't leave a note. There's so much of the theatre about this headdress that I'd have expected something by way of explanation.' He began to tuck the plastic sheet about the body. 'Read *Hamlet*,' he suggested. 'The answer's in there, I expect.'

Mr and Mrs Spede hovered in the library like two squat spectres, so unprepossessing and shifty in their appearance that Cooper wondered if they were quite normal. Neither seemed able to meet his gaze and every question required unspoken consultation between them before one would offer an answer. 'Dr Blakeney tells me Mrs Gillespie has a daughter living in London and a granddaughter at boarding school,' he said. 'Can you give me their names and tell me where I can contact them?'

'She kept her papers very neat,' said Mrs Spede eventually, after receiving some sort of permission to speak from her husband. 'It'll all be in the papers.' She nodded towards the desk and an oak filing cabinet. 'In there some place. Very neat. Always very neat.'

'Don't you know her daughter's name?'

'Mrs Lascelles,' said the man after a moment. 'Joanna.' He tugged at his lower lip which drooped oddly as if it had been tugged many times before. With a petulant frown his wife smacked him on the wrist and he tucked the offending hand into his pocket. They were very childlike, thought Cooper, and wondered if Mrs Gillespie had employed them out of compassion.

'And the granddaughter's name?'

'Miss Lascelles,' said Mrs Spede.

'Do you know her Christian name?'

'Ruth.' She consulted with her husband behind lowered lids. 'They're not nice, either of them. The Mrs is rude to Mr Spede about his gardening and the Miss is rude to Jenny about her cleaning.'

'Jenny?' he queried. 'Who's Jenny?'

'Jenny is Mrs Spede.'

'I see,' said Cooper kindly. 'It must have been a terrible shock for you, Jenny, to find Mrs Gillespie in her bath.'

'Oh, it was that,' she howled, grabbing her husband's arm. 'A terrible, terrible shock.' Her voice rose on a wail.

With some reluctance, because he feared an even louder outburst, Cooper took the polythene bag containing the Stanley knife from his pocket and laid it across his broad palm. 'I don't want to upset you any more, but do you recognize this? Is it a knife you've seen before?'

Her lips puckered tragically but she stopped the wailing to nudge her husband into speech. 'The kitchen drawer,' he said. 'It's the one from the kitchen drawer.' He touched the handle through the bag. 'I scratched an h'aitch on it for "house". The one I keep in the shed has a gee on it for "garden".'

Cooper examined the crude 'h' and nodded as he tucked the bag back out of sight into his pocket. 'Thank you. I'll need the one from the garden for comparison. I'll ask an officer to go out with you when we've finished.' He smiled in a friendly way. 'Now, you presumably have keys to the house. May I see them?'

Mrs Spede drew a string from around her neck, revealing a key that had lain within the cleft of her bosom. 'Only me,' she said. 'Jenny had the key. Mr Spede didn't need one for the garden.' She gave it to Cooper and he felt the warmth of her body seeping into his hand. It repelled him because it was damp and oily with sweat, and this made him feel guilty because he found them both deeply unattractive and knew that, unlike Mrs Gillespie, he could not have tolerated them about his house for even half an hour.

Mathilda Gillespie's nearest neighbours lived alongside her in a wing adjoining the house. At some stage Cedar House must have been one residence, but now a discreet sign indicated the door to Wing Cottage at the western end of the building. Before Cooper knocked on it, he walked along a gravel path to the rear corner and surveyed the patio at the back, neatly bordered by tubs of everlasting pansies, beyond which a clipped box hedge separated this garden from the expanse of lawn and distant trees that belonged to Cedar House. He felt a sudden envy for the occupants. How drear his own small box was by comparison, but then it was his wife who had chosen to live on a modern estate and not he. He would have been happy with crumbling plaster and a view; she was happy with all mod. cons and neighbours so close they rubbed shoulders every day. It was a policeman's lot to give in to a wife he was fond of. His hours were too unpredictable to allow him to impose his own yearning for isolation on a woman who had tolerated his absences with stoical good humour for thirty years.

He heard the door open behind him and turned, producing his warrant card from his breast pocket, to greet the fat elderly man who approached. 'DS Cooper, sir, Dorset police.'

11

'Orloff, Duncan Orloff.' He ran a worried hand across his wide, rather pleasant face. 'We've been expecting you. Dear me, dear me. I don't mind admitting Jenny Spede's howling is a little difficult to take after a while. Poor woman. She's a good soul as long as nothing upsets her. I can't tell you what it was like when she found Mathilda. She came rushing out of the house screaming like a banshee and set her wretched husband off in sympathy. I realized something dreadful must have happened which is why I phoned your people and an ambulance. Thank God they came quickly and had the sense to bring a woman with them. She was really quite excellent, calmed the Spedes down in record time. Dear me, dear me,' he said again, 'we live such a quiet life. Not used to this sort of thing at all.'

'No one is,' said Cooper. 'You've been told what's happened, I suppose.'

He wrung his hands in distress. 'Only that Mathilda's dead. I kept the Spedes here until the police car arrived – thought it best, really, what with them collapsing in heaps about me – mind you, I wasn't going to let my wife downstairs till it was safe – one can't be certain about things – anyway the uniformed chaps told me to wait until someone came to ask questions. Look, you'd better come in. Violet's in the drawing-room now, not feeling too well in the circumstances, and who can blame her? Frankly, not feeling a hundred per cent myself.' He stood aside to let Cooper enter. 'First door on the right,' he said. He followed the policeman into a cosy, over-furnished room with a television on low volume in the corner, and bent over the prostrate figure of his wife on the sofa. 'There's a Sergeant to see us,' he said, raising her gently to a sitting position with one hand and using the other to swing her legs to the floor. He lowered his large bulk on to the sofa beside her and gestured Cooper towards an armchair. 'Jenny kept screaming about blood,' he confided unhappily. 'Red water and blood. That's all she said.'

Violet shivered. 'And Jesus,' she whispered. 'I heard her. She said Mathilda was "like Jesus".' She raised a hand to her own bloodless lips. 'Dead like Jesus in blood red water.' Her eyes filled. 'What's happened to her? Is she *really* dead?'

'I'm afraid she is, Mrs Orloff. It's only approximate, but the pathologist estimates the time of death between nine o'clock and midnight on Saturday.' He looked from one to the other. 'Were you here during those three hours?'

'We were here all night,' said Duncan. He was clearly drawn between his own perceived good taste of not asking questions and an overwhelming need to satisfy a very natural curiosity. 'You haven't told us what's happened,' he blurted out. 'It's much, much worse if you don't know what's happened. We've been imagining terrible things.'

'She hasn't been *crucified*, has she?' asked Violet tremulously. 'I said she's probably been crucified, otherwise why would Jenny have said she looked like Jesus?'

'I said someone had tried to clean up afterwards,' said Duncan, 'which is why there's red water everywhere. You hear about it every day, old people being murdered for their money. They do terrible things to them, too, before they kill them.'

'Oh, I do hope she wasn't *raped*,' said Violet. 'I couldn't bear it if they'd raped her.'

Cooper had time to feel regret for this elderly couple who, like so many of their peers, lived the end of their lives in terror because the media persuaded them they were at risk. He knew better than anyone that statistics proved it was young men aged between fifteen and twenty-five who were the group most vulnerable to violent death. He had sorted out too many drunken brawls and picked too many stabbed and bludgeoned bodies from gutters outside pubs to be in any doubt of that. 'She died in her bath,' he said unemotionally. 'Her wrists were slit. At the moment the pathologist is inclining towards suicide and we are only asking questions to satisfy ourselves that she did in fact take her own life.'

'But Jesus didn't die in his bath,' said Violet in bewilderment.

'She was wearing a scold's bridle on her head with flowers in it. I think perhaps Mrs Spede thought it was a crown of thorns.' It made no sense otherwise, he thought.

'I *hated* that thing. Mathilda was always *very* peculiar about it.' Violet had a habit, Cooper noticed, of emphasizing words she thought important. 'It must have been suicide, then. She wore it when her arthritis was bad. It took her mind off the *pain*, you know. She always said she'd kill herself if it got so bad she couldn't stand it.' She turned tear-filled eyes to her husband. 'Why didn't she call out to us? I'm sure there's *something* we could have done to help.'

'Would you have heard her?' asked Cooper.

'Oh, yes, especially if she was in the bathroom. She could have rattled the pipes. We'd certainly have heard *that*.'

Cooper transferred his attention to Mr Orloff. 'Did you hear anything at all that night?'

Duncan gave the question long and thoughtful consideration. 'Our days are very uneventful,' he said apologetically. 'All I can say is that if we had heard something, we'd have acted' – he spread his hands in a gesture of surrender – 'like this morning when Jenny started screaming. There was nothing like that on Saturday.'

'Yet you both assumed she'd been murdered by a gang. You mentioned "they".'

'It's difficult to think straight when people are screaming,' he said, reproaching himself with a shake of the head. 'And to be perfectly honest, I wasn't at all sure the Spedes themselves hadn't done something. They're not the brightest couple as you've probably discovered for yourself. Mind you, it wouldn't have been intentional. They're foolish, not dangerous. I assumed there'd been some sort of accident,' he spread his palms on his fat knees, 'I've been worrying that I should have gone in to do something, saved her perhaps, but if she died on Saturday . . . ?' His voice tailed off on a query.

Cooper shook his head. 'You couldn't have done anything for her. What about during the daytime? Did you hear anything then?'

'On Saturday, you mean?' He shook his head. 'Nothing that leaps to mind. Certainly nothing unsettling.' He looked at Violet as if seeking inspiration. 'We notice if the bell rings in Cedar House, because it's very rare for Mathilda to have visitors, but otherwise' – he shrugged helplessly – 'so little happens here, Sergeant, and we do watch a lot of television.'

'And you didn't wonder where she was on Sunday?'

Violet dabbed at her eyes. 'Oh, dear,' she whispered, 'could we have saved her then? How *awful*, Duncan.'

'No,' said Cooper firmly, 'she was certainly dead by three o'clock on Sunday morning.'

'We were friends, you know,' said Violet. 'Duncan and I have known her for fifty years. She sold us this cottage when Duncan retired five years ago. That's not to say she was the *easiest* person in the world to get on with. She could be very cruel to people she didn't like, but the trick with Mathilda was not to *impose*. We never did, of course, but there were those who did.'

Cooper licked the point of his pencil. 'Who for example?'

Violet lowered her voice. 'Joanna and Ruth, her daughter and granddaughter. They *never* left her alone, always complaining, always demanding money. And the vicar was shocking.' She cast a guilty glance at her husband. 'I know Duncan doesn't approve of tittle-tattle but the vicar was always pricking her conscience about the less well off. She was an *atheist*, you know, and very rude to Mr Matthews every time he came. She called him a Welsh leech. To his face, too.'

'Did he mind?'

Duncan gave a rumble of laughter. 'It was a game,' he said. 'She was quite generous sometimes when he caught her in a good mood. She gave him a hundred pounds once towards a centre for alcoholics, saying there but for the grace of her metabolism went she. She drank to deaden the pain of her arthritis, or so she said.'

'Not to excess, though,' said Violet. 'She was never *drunk*. She was too much of a lady ever to get drunk.' She blew her nose loudly.

'Is there anyone else you can think of who imposed on her?' asked Cooper after a moment.

Duncan shrugged. 'There was the doctor's husband, Jack Blakeney. He was always round there, but it wasn't an imposition. She liked him. I used to hear her laughing with him sometimes in the garden.' He paused to reflect. 'She had very few friends, Sergeant. As Violet said, she wasn't an easy woman. People either liked Mathilda or loathed her. You'll find that out soon enough if you're planning to ask questions of anyone else.'

'And you liked her?'

His eyes grew suddenly wet. 'I did,' he said gruffly. 'She was beautiful once, you know, quite beautiful.' He patted his wife's hand. 'We all were, a long, long time ago. Age has very few compensations, Sergeant, except perhaps the wisdom to recognize contentment.' He pondered for a moment. 'They do say slitting the wrists is a very peaceful way to die, although how anyone knows I can't imagine. Did she suffer, do you think?'

'I'm afraid I can't answer that, Mr Orloff,' said Cooper honestly.

The damp eyes held his for a moment and he saw a deep and haggard sadness in them. They spoke of a love that Cooper somehow suspected Duncan had never shown or felt for his wife. He wanted to say something by way of consolation, but what could he say that wouldn't make matters worse? He doubted that Violet knew, and he wondered, not for the first time, why love was more often cruel than it was kind.

17

I watched Duncan clipping his hedge this afternoon and could barely remember the handsome man he was. If I had been a charitable woman, I would have married him forty years ago and saved him from himself and Violet. She has turned my Romeo into a sad-eyed Billy Bunter who blinks his passion quietly when no one's looking. Oh, that his too, too solid flesh should melt. At twenty, he had the body of Michelangelo's David, now he resembles an entire family group by Henry Moore.

Jack continues to delight me. What a tragedy I didn't meet him or someone like him when I was 'green in judgement'. I learnt only how to survive, when Jack would, I think, have taught me how to love. I asked him why he and Sarah have no children, and he answered: 'Because I've never had the urge to play God.' I told him there was nothing godlike about procreation — doglike perhaps — and it's a monumental conceit that allows him to dictate Sarah's suitability as a mother. 'The vicar would say you're playing the devil, Jack. The species won't survive unless people like you reproduce themselves.'

19

But he is not an amenable man. If he were, I would enjoy him less. 'You've played God for years, Mathilda. Has it given you any pleasure or made you more content?'

No, and I can say that honestly. I shall die as naked as I was born . . .

Two

A WEEK LATER the receptionist buzzed through to Dr Blakeney's office. 'There's a Detective Sergeant Cooper on the line. I've told him you have a patient with you but he's very insistent. Can you speak to him?' It was a Monday and Sarah was covering afternoon surgery in Fontwell.

She smiled apologetically at the pregnant mother, laid out like a sacrificial offering on her couch. She put her hand over the receiver. 'Do you mind if I take this call, Mrs Graham? It's rather important. I'll be as quick as I can.'

'Get on with you. I'm enjoying the rest. You don't get many opportunities when it's your third.'

Sarah smiled at her. 'Put him through, Jane. Yes, Sergeant, what can I do for you?'

'We've had the results of Mrs Gillespie's post mortem. I'd be interested in your reactions.'

'Go on.'

He shuffled some papers at the other end of the line. 'Direct cause of death: loss of blood. Traces of barbiturates were discovered in her system, but not enough to prove fatal. Traces also discovered in the whisky glass, implying she dissolved the barbiturates before she drank them. Some alcohol absorbed. No bruising. Lacerations on the tongue where the rusted bit of the scold's bridle caused the surface to bleed. Nothing under her fingernails. Slight nettle rash on her temples and cheeks, and minor chafing of the skin beneath the bridle's framework, both consistent with her donning the contraption herself and then arranging it with the nettles and daisies. No indications at all that she put up any sort of struggle. The scold's bridle was not attached to her head in any way and could have been removed, had she wished to do so. The wounds to the wrists correspond precisely with the Stanley knife blade discovered on the bathroom floor, the one on the left wrist made with a downward right-handed stroke, the one on the right with a downward left-handed stroke. The knife had been sub-merged in water, probably dropped after one of the inci-sions, but there was an index fingerprint, belonging to Mrs Gillespie, one-point-three centimetres from the blade on the shaft. Conclusion: suicide.' He paused. 'Are you still there?' he demanded after a moment.

'Yes.'

'So what do you think?'

'That I was wrong last week.'

'But surely the barbiturates in the whisky glass trouble you?'

'Mathilda hated swallowing anything whole,' she said apologetically. 'She crushed or dissolved everything in liquid first. She had a morbid fear of choking.'

'But your immediate reaction when you saw her was that she was the last person you'd expect to kill herself. And now you've changed your mind.' It sounded like an accusation.

'What do you want me to say, Sergeant? My gut feeling remains the same.' Sarah glanced towards her patient who was becoming restless. 'I would not have expected her to take her own life, but gut feelings are a poor substitute for scientific evidence.'

'Not always.'

She waited, but he didn't go on. 'Was there anything else, Sergeant? I do have a patient with me.'

'No,' he said, sounding dispirited, 'nothing else. It was a courtesy call. You may be required to give evidence at the inquest, but it'll be a formality. We've asked for an adjournment while we check one or two small details but, at the moment, we aren't looking for anyone else in connection with Mrs Gillespie's death.'

Sarah smiled encouragingly at Mrs Graham. *Be with you in a minute,* she mouthed. 'But you think you should be.'

'I learnt my trade in a simpler world, Dr Blakeney, where we paid attention to gut feelings. But in those days we called them hunches.' He gave a hollow laugh. 'Now, hunches are frowned on and forensic evidence is God. But forensic evidence is only as reliable as the man who interprets it and what I want to know is why there are no nettle stings on Mrs Gillespie's hands and fingers. Dr Cameron began by saying she must have worn gloves but there are no gloves in that house with sap on them, so now he thinks the water must have nullified the reaction. I don't like that kind of uncertainty. My hunch is Mrs Gillespie was murdered but I'm an Indian and the Chief says, drop it. I hoped you'd give me some ammunition.'

'I'm sorry,' said Sarah helplessly. She murmured a goodbye and replaced the receiver with a thoughtful expression in her dark eyes.

'It'll be old Mrs Gillespie, I suppose,' said Mrs Graham prosaically. She was a farmer's wife, for whom birth and death held little mystery. Both happened, not always conveniently, and the whys and wherefores were largely irrelevant. The trick was coping afterwards. 'There's talk of nothing else in the village. Awful way to do it, don't you think?' She shivered theatrically. 'Slitting your wrists and then watching your blood seep into the water. I couldn't do that.'

'No,' agreed Sarah, rubbing her hands to warm them. 'You say you think the baby's head has engaged already?'

'Mm, won't be long now.' But Mrs Graham wasn't to be side-tracked so easily and she'd heard enough of the doctor's end of the conversation to whet her appetite. 'Is it true she had a cage on her head? Jenny Spede's been hysterical about it ever since. A cage with brambles and roses in it, she said. She keeps calling it Mrs Gillespie's crown of thorns.'

Sarah could see no harm in telling her. Most of the details were out already, and the truth was probably less damaging than the horror stories being put about by Mathilda's cleaner. 'It was a family heirloom, a thing called a scold's bridle.' She placed her hands on the woman's abdomen and felt for the baby's head. 'And there were no brambles or roses, nothing with thorns at all. Just a few wild flowers.' She omitted the nettles deliberately. The nettles, she thought, *were* disturbing. 'It was more pathetic than frightening.' Her probing fingers relaxed. 'You're right. It won't be long now. You must have got your dates wrong.'

'I always do, Doctor,' said the woman comfortably. 'I can tell you to the minute when a cow's due but when it's my turn,' she laughed, 'I haven't time to mark calendars.' Sarah linked arms with her to pull her into a sitting position. 'Scold's bridle,' she went on thoughtfully. 'Scold, as in a woman with a vicious tongue?'

Sarah nodded. 'They were used up until two or three centuries ago to shut women up, and not just women with vicious tongues either. Any women. Women who challenged male authority, inside the home *and* outside.'

'So why do you reckon she did it?'

'I don't know. Tired of living perhaps.' Sarah smiled. 'She didn't have your energy, Mrs Graham.'

'Oh, the dying I can understand. I've never seen much sense in struggling for life if the life isn't worth the struggle.' She buttoned her shirt. 'I meant why did she do it with this scold's bridle on her head?'

But Sarah shook her head. 'I don't know that either.'

'She was a nasty old woman,' said Mrs Graham bluntly. 'She lived here virtually all her life, knew me and my parents from our cradles, but she never acknowledged us once. We were too common. Tenant farmers with muck on our shoes. Oh, she spoke to old Wittingham, the lazy sod who owns Dad's farm, all right. The fact he's never done a hand's turn since the day he was born, but lives on his rents and his investments, made him acceptable. But the workers, rough trade like us – ' she shook her head – 'we were beneath contempt.' She chuckled at Sarah's expression. 'There, I'm shocking you. But I've a big mouth and I use it. You don't want to take Mrs Gillespie's death to heart. She wasn't liked, and not through want of trying, believe me. We're not a bad lot here, but there's only so much that ordinary folk can take, and when a woman brushes her coat after you've bumped into her by accident, well, that's when you say enough's enough.' She swung her legs to the floor and stood up. 'I'm not much of a church-goer, me, but some things I do believe in, and one of them's repentance. Be it God or just old age, I reckon everyone repents in the end. There's few of us die without recognizing our faults which is why death's so peaceful. And it doesn't really matter who you say sorry to – a priest, God, your family – you've said it, and you feel better.' She slipped her feet into her shoes. 'I'd guess Mrs Gillespie was apologizing for her vicious tongue. That's why she wore her scold's bridle to meet her Maker.'

Mathilda Gillespie was buried three days later beside her father, Sir William Cavendish MP, in Fontwell village churchyard. The coroner's inquest had still to be held but it was common knowledge by then that a verdict of suicide was a foregone conclusion, if not from Polly Graham, then from a simple putting two and two together when the Dorset police removed their seals from Cedar House and returned to headquarters in the nearby coastal resort of Learmouth.

The congregation was a small one. Polly Graham had told the truth when she said Mathilda Gillespie wasn't liked, and few could be bothered to find time in their busy lives to say goodbye to an old woman who had been known only for her unkindness. The vicar did his best in difficult circumstances but it was with a feeling of relief that the mourners turned from the open grave and picked their way across the grass towards the gate.

Jack Blakeney, a reluctant attendant on a wife who had felt duty-bound to put in an appearance, muttered into Sarah's ear: 'What a bunch of whited sepulchres, and I am not referring to the tombstones either, just we hypocrites doing our middle-class duty. Did you see their faces when the Rev referred to her as "our much loved friend and neighbour"? They all hated her.'

She hushed him with a warning hand. 'They'll hear you.'

'Who cares?' They were bringing up the rear and his artist's gaze roamed restlessly across the bowed heads in front of them. 'Presumably the blonde is the daughter, Joanna.'

Sarah heard the deliberate note of careless interest in his voice and smiled cynically. 'Presumably,' she agreed, 'and presumably the younger one is the granddaughter.'

Joanna stood now beside the vicar, her soft grey eyes huge in a finely drawn face, her silver-gold hair a shining cap in the sunlight. A beautiful woman, thought Sarah, but as usual she could admire her with complete detachment. She rarely directed her resentment towards the objects of her husband's thinly disguised lust, for she saw them as just that, objects. Lust, like everything in Jack's life apart from his painting, was ephemeral. A brief enthusiasm to be discarded as rapidly as it was espoused. The days when she had been confident that, for all his appreciation of another woman's looks, he wouldn't jeopardize their marriage were long past and she had few illusions left about her own role. She provided the affluence whereby Jack Blakeney, struggling artist, could live and slake his very mundane cravings, but as Polly Graham had said – *there was only so much that ordinary folk could take*.

They shook hands with the vicar. 'It was kind of you both to come. Have you met Mathilda's daughter?' The Reverend Matthews turned to the woman. 'Joanna Lascelles, Dr Sarah Blakeney and Jack Blakeney. Sarah was your mother's GP, Joanna. She joined the practice last year when Dr Hendry retired. She and Jack live at The Mill in Long Upton, Geoffrey Freeling's old house.'

Joanna shook hands with them and turned to the girl beside her. 'This is my daughter Ruth. We're both very grateful to you, Dr Blakeney, for all you did to help my mother.'

The girl was about seventeen or eighteen, as dark as her mother was fair, and she looked anything but grateful. Sarah had only an impression of intense and bitter grief. 'Do you know why Granny killed herself?' she asked softly. 'Nobody else seems to.' Her face was set in a scowl.

'Ruth, please,' sighed her mother. 'Aren't things difficult enough already?' It was a conversation they had clearly had before.

Joanna must be approaching forty, thought Sarah, if the daughter was anything to go by, but against the black of her coat, she looked only very young and very vulnerable. Beside her, Sarah felt Jack's interest quicken and she had an angry impulse to turn on him and berate him publicly once and for all. How far did he think her patience would stretch? How long did he expect her to tolerate his contemptuous and contemptible indifference to her beleaguered pride? She quelled the impulse, of course. She was too trammelled by her upbringing and the behavioural demands of her profession to do anything else. *But, oh God, one day* . . . she promised herself. Instead she turned to the girl. 'I wish I could give you an answer, Ruth, but I can't. The last time I saw your grandmother she was fine. In some pain from her arthritis, of course, but nothing she wasn't used to or couldn't cope with.'

The girl cast a spiteful glance at her mother. 'Then something must have happened to upset her. People don't kill themselves for no reason.'

'Was she easily upset?' asked Sarah. 'She never gave me that impression.' She smiled slightly. 'She was tough as old boots, your grandmother. I admired her for it.'

'Then why did she kill herself?'

'Because she wasn't afraid of death perhaps. Suicide isn't always a negative, you know. In some cases it's a positive statement of choice. I will die now and in this manner. "To be or not to be." For Mathilda "not to be" would have been a considered decision.'

Ruth's eyes filled. '*Hamlet* was her favourite play.' She was tall like her mother but her face, pinched with cold and distress, lacked the other's startling looks. Ruth's tears made her ugly where her mother's, a mere glistening of the lashes, enhanced a fragile beauty.

Joanna stirred herself, glancing from Sarah to Jack. 'Will you come back to the house for tea? There'll be so few of us.'

Sarah excused herself. 'I'm afraid I can't. I have a surgery in Mapleton at four thirty.'

Jack did not. 'Thank you, that's very kind.'

There was a small silence. 'How will you get home?' asked Sarah, fishing in her pocket for her car keys.

'I'll beg a lift,' he said. 'Someone's bound to be going my way.'

One of Sarah's colleagues dropped in as evening surgery was finishing. There were three partners in a practice serving several square miles of Dorset coast and countryside, including sizeable villages, scattered hamlets and farmhouses. Most of the villages had small self-contained surgeries, either attached to the doctors' houses or leased from patients and, between them, the partners covered the whole area, boxing and coxing in neat rotation. Mapleton was Robin Hewitt's home village but, like Sarah, he spent as much time out of it as he did in. They had so far resisted the logic of pooling their resources in one modern clinic in the most central of the villages, but it was doubtful if they could resist for much longer. The argument, a true one, that most of their patients were elderly or lacked transport, was far outweighed by the commercial pressures now existing inside the health service.

'You look tired,' said Robin, folding himself into the armchair beside her desk.

'I am.'

'Trouble?'

'Only the usual.'

'Domestic, eh? Get rid of him.'

She laughed. 'And supposing I told you, as casually, to get rid of Mary?'

'There's a small difference, my darling. Mary is an angel and Jack is not.' But the idea was not without a certain appeal. After eighteen years, Mary's complacent self-assurance was so much less attractive than Sarah's troubled seeking after truths.

'I can't argue with that.' She finished writing some notes and pushed them wearily to one side.

'What's he done this time?'

'Nothing, as far as I know.'

Which sounded about right, thought Robin. Jack Blakeney made a virtue of doing nothing while his wife made a virtue of supporting him in idleness. Their continuing marriage was a complete mystery to him. There were no children, no ties, nothing binding them, Sarah was an independent woman with independent means, and she paid the mortgage on their house. It only required the services of a locksmith to shut the bastard out for ever.

She studied him with amusement. 'Why are you smiling like that?'

He switched neatly away from his mild fantasy of Sarah alone in her house. 'I saw Bob Hughes today. He was very put out to find me on duty and not you.' He fell into a fair imitation of the old man's Dorset burr. ' "Where's the pretty one?" he said. "I want the pretty one to do it." '

'Do what?'

Robin grinned. 'Examine the boil on his bum. Dirty old brute. If it *had* been you, he'd have come up with another one, presumably, lurking under his scrotum and you'd have had the fun of probing for it and he'd have had the thrills while you did it.'

Her eyes danced. 'And it's completely free, don't forget. Relief massage comes expensive.'

'That's revolting. You're not telling me he's tried it on before.'

She chuckled. 'No, of course not. He only comes in for a chat. I expect he felt he had to show you something. Poor old soul. I bet you sent him away with a flea in his ear.'

'I did. You're far too amenable.'

'But they're so lonely some of them. We live in a terrible world, Robin. No one has time to listen any more.' She toyed with her pen. 'I went to Mathilda Gillespie's funeral today and her granddaughter asked me why she killed herself. I said I didn't know, and I've been thinking about that ever since. I *should* know. She was one of my patients. If I'd taken a little more trouble with her, I *would* know.' She flicked him a sideways glance. 'Wouldn't I?'

He shook his head. 'Don't start down that route, Sarah. It's a dead end. Look, you were one person among many whom she knew and talked to, me included. The responsibility for that old woman wasn't yours alone. I'd argue that it wasn't yours at all, except in a strict medical sense, and nothing you prescribed for her contributed to her death. She died of blood loss.'

'But where do you draw the line between profession and friendship? We laughed a lot. I think I was one of the few people who appreciated her sense of humour, probably because it was so like Jack's. Bitchy, often cruel, but witty. She was a latterday Dorothy Parker.'

'You're being ridiculously sentimental. Mathilda Gillespie was a bitch of the first water, and don't imagine she viewed you as an equal. For years, until she sold off Wing Cottage to raise money, doctors, lawyers and accountants were required to enter by the tradesman's entrance. It used to drive Hugh Hendry mad. He said she was the rudest woman he'd ever met. He couldn't stand her.'

Sarah gave a snort of laughter. 'Probably because she called him Doctor Dolittle. To his face, too. I asked her once if it was by way of a job description and she said: "Not entirely. He had a closer affinity with animals than he had with people. He was an ass."'

Robin grinned. 'Hugh was the laziest and the least able doctor I've ever met. I suggested once that we check his medical qualifications because I didn't think he had any, but it's a bit difficult when the bloke in question is the senior partner. We just had to bite the bullet and hang on for his retirement.' He cocked his head on one side. 'So what did she call you, if she called him Dr Dolittle?'

She held the pen to her lips for a moment and stared past him. There was a haunting disquiet in her dark eyes. 'She was obsessed with that wretched scold's bridle. It was rather unhealthy really, thinking about it. She wanted me to try it on once to see what it felt like.'

'And did you?'

'No.' She fell silent for a moment, then seemed to make up her mind to something. 'She called her arthritis her "Resident Scold" because it caused her so much nagging pain' – she tapped the pen against her teeth – 'and in order to take her mind off it, she used to don the bridle as a sort of counter-irritant. That's what I mean about her unhealthy obsession with it. She wore it as a sort of penance, like a hair shirt. Anyway, when I took her off that rubbish Hendry had been prescribing and got the pain under some sort of manageable control, she took to calling me her little scold's bridle by way of a joke.' She saw his incomprehension. 'Because I'd succeeded in harnessing the Resident Scold,' she explained.

'So what are you saying?'

'I think she was trying to tell me something.'

Robin shook his head. 'Why? Because she was wearing it when she died? It was a symbol, that's all.'

'Of what?'

'Life's illusion. We're all prisoners. Perhaps it was her final joke. My tongue is curbed for ever, something like that.' He shrugged. 'Have you told the police?'

'No. I was so shocked when I saw her that I didn't think about it.' She raised her hands in a gesture of helplessness. 'And the pathologist and the policeman latched on to what I said she always called the geraniums inside the beastly thing. Her coronet weeds. It comes from the speech about Ophelia's death and, what with the bath and the nettles, I thought they were probably right. But now I'm not so sure.' Her voice tailed off and she sat staring at her desk.

Robin watched her for several seconds. 'Supposing she *was* trying to say that her tongue was curbed for ever. You realize it has a double meaning?'

'Yes,' said Sarah unhappily, 'that someone else curbed it. But that doesn't make sense. I mean, if Mathilda knew she was going to be murdered she wouldn't have wasted time donning the scold's bridle in the hall when all she had to do was run to the front door and scream her head off. The whole village would have heard her. And the murderer would have taken it off anyway.'

'Perhaps it was the murderer who was saying, "Her tongue is curbed for ever".'

'But that doesn't make sense either. Why would a murderer advertise that it's murder when he's gone to so much trouble to make it look like suicide?' She rubbed her

34

tired eyes. 'Without the scold's bridle, it would have looked straightforward. With it, it looks anything *but*. And why the flowers, for God's sake? What were they supposed to tell us?'

'You'll have to talk to the police,' said Robin with sudden decision, reaching for the telephone. 'Dammit, Sarah, who else knew she called you her scold's bridle? Surely it's occurred to you that the message is directed at you.'

'What message?'

'I don't know. A threat, perhaps. You next, Dr Blakeney.'

She gave a hollow laugh. 'I see it more in terms of a signature.' She traced a line on the desk with her fingertip. 'Like the mark of Zorro on his victims.'

'Oh, Jesus!' said Robin, putting the receiver back. 'Maybe it's wiser not to say anything. Look, it was obviously suicide – you said yourself she was unhealthily obsessed with the damn thing.'

'But I was fond of her.'

'You're fond of everyone, Sarah. It's nothing to be proud of.'

'You sound like Jack.' She retrieved the telephone, dialled Learmouth Police Station and asked for Detective Sergeant Cooper.

Robin watched with gloomy resignation – she had no idea how the tongues would wag if they ever got wind of Mathilda's nickname for her – and wondered disloyally why she had chosen to tell him before anyone else. He had the strangest impression that she had been using him. As a yardstick by which to measure other people's reactions? As a confessor?

DS Cooper had already left for home and the bored

voice at the other end of the wire merely agreed to pass on Sarah's request to speak to him when he arrived the next morning. There was no urgency, after all. The case was closed.

How I detest my arthritis and the cruel inactivity it imposes. I saw a ghost today but could do nothing about it. I should have struck it down and sent it back to Hell whence it came, instead I could only lash it with my tongue. Has Joanna brought him back to haunt me? It makes sense. She has been plotting something since she found that wretched letter. 'Ingratitude, thou marble-hearted fiend, more hideous when thou show'st thee in a child than the sea monster.'

But to use James of all people. That I shall never forgive. Or is it he who is using her? Forty years haven't changed him. What loathsome fun he must have had in Hong Kong where I've read the boys dress up as girls and give paederasts the thrill of pretended normality as they parade themselves and their disgusting perversion before a naïve public. He looks ill. Well, well, what a charming solution his death would be.

I made a 'most filthy bargain' there. They talk glibly about cycles of abuse these days but, oh, how much more complex those cycles are than the simple brutality visited by parent on child. Everything comes to him who mates . . .

37

Three

JACK WAS WORKING in his studio when Sarah's key finally grated in the lock at around eleven o'clock. He looked up as she passed his open door. 'Where have you been?'

She was very tired. 'At the Hewitts'. They gave me supper. Have you eaten?' She didn't come in, but stood in the doorway watching him.

He nodded absent-mindedly. Food was a low priority in Jack's life. He jerked his head at the canvas on the easel. 'What do you think?'

How much simpler it would be, she thought, if she were obtuse, and genuinely misunderstood what he was trying to achieve in his work. How much simpler if she could just accept what one or two critics had said, that it was pretentious rubbish and bad art.

'Joanna Lascelles presumably.'

But not a Joanna Lascelles that anyone would recognize, except perhaps in the black of her funeral weeds and the silver gold of her hair, for Jack used shape and colour to paint emotions, and there was an extraordinary turbulence about this painting, even in its earliest stage. He would go

39

on now for weeks, working layer on layer, attempting through the medium of oils to build and depict the complexity of the human personality. Sarah, who understood his colour-coding almost as well as he did, could interpret much of what he had already blocked in. Grief (for her mother?), disdain (for her daughter?), and, all too predictably, sensuality (for him?).

Jack watched her face. 'She's interesting,' he said.

'Obviously.'

His eyes narrowed angrily. 'Don't start,' he murmured. 'I'm not in the mood.'

She shrugged. 'Neither am I. I'm going to bed.'

'I'll work on the jacket tomorrow,' he promised grudgingly. He made a living of sorts by designing book jackets, but the commissions were few and far between because he rarely met deadlines. The disciplines imposed by the profit motive infuriated him.

'I'm not your mother, Jack,' she said coolly. 'What you do tomorrow is your own affair.'

But he was in the mood for a row, probably, thought Sarah, because Joanna had flattered him. 'You just can't leave it alone, can you? No, you're not my mother, but by God you're beginning to sound like her.'

'How odd,' she said with heavy irony, 'and I always thought you didn't get on with her because she kept telling you what to do. Now I'm tarred with the same brush, yet I've done the exact opposite, left you to work things out for yourself. You're a child, Jack. You need a woman in your life to blame for every little thing that goes wrong for you.'

'Is this babies again?' he snarled. 'Dammit, Sarah, you knew the score before you married me, and it was your

40

choice to go through with it. The career was everything, remember? Nothing's changed. Not for me, anyway. It's not my fault if your bloody hormones are screaming that time's running out. We had a deal. No children.'

She eyed him curiously. After all, she thought, Joanna must have been less accommodating than he had hoped. Well, well! 'The deal, Jack, for what it's worth, was that I would support you until you established yourself. After that, all options were open. What we never considered, and for that I blame myself because I relied on my own artistic judgement, was that you might *never* establish yourself. In which circumstance, I suspect, the deal is null and void. So far, I have kept you for six years, two years before marriage and four afterwards, and the choice to marry was as much yours as mine. As far as I remember we were celebrating your first major sale. Your only major sale,' she added. 'I think that's fair, don't you? I can't recall your selling a canvas since.'

'Spite doesn't suit you, Sarah.'

'No,' she agreed, 'any more than behaving like a spoilt brat suits you. You say nothing's changed, but you're wrong, everything's changed. I used to admire you. Now I despise you. I used to find you amusing. Now you bore me. I used to love you. Now I just feel sorry for you.' She smiled apologetically. 'I also used to think you'd make it. Now I don't. And that's not because I think any less of your painting, but because I think less of you. You have neither the commitment nor the discipline to be great, Jack, because you always forget that genius is only one per cent inspiration and ninety-nine per cent sheer, bloody graft. I'm a good doctor, not because I have an especial talent for

41

diagnosis, but because I work my fingers to the bone. You're a rotten artist, not because you lack talent, but because you're too damn lazy and too damn snobbish to get down on your hands and knees with the rest of us and earn your reputation.'

The dark face split into a sardonic grin. 'Hewitt's doing, I suppose? A cosy little supper with Cock Robin and his wife, and then it's dump on Jack. Jesus, he's a greasy little toad. He'd be in your bed quicker than winking if sweet little Mary and the kiddiwinkles weren't guarding his door.'

'Don't be absurd,' she said coldly. 'It's your doing entirely. I ceased having any feelings for you whatsoever the day I had to refer Sally Bennedict for an abortion. I draw the line at being asked to approve the murder of your bastards, Jack, particularly by a selfish bitch like Sally Bennedict. She enjoyed the irony of it all, believe me.'

He stared at her with something like shock, and she saw that for once she had scored a direct hit. He hadn't known, she thought, which was something in his favour at least. 'You should have told me,' he said inadequately.

She laughed with genuine amusement. 'Why? You weren't my patient, Sally was. And, sure as eggs is eggs, she wasn't going to go to term with your little bundle of joy and lose her chance with the RSC. You can't play Juliet six months pregnant, Jack, which is what she would have been when the run started. Oh, I did my bit, suggested she talk it through with you, suggested she talk it through with a counsellor, but I might have been pissing in the wind for all the good it did. She'd have preferred cancer, I think, to an unwanted pregnancy.' Her smile was twisted. 'And let's face it, we both knew what your reaction would be. It's the only time I've felt confident that the wretched foetus, were it born, would be rejected by both parties. I passed the buck on to the hospital and they had *her* in and *it* out within two weeks.'

He swirled his brush aimlessly around the colours on his palette. 'Was that the reason for the sudden move down here?'

'Partly. I had a nasty feeling Sally would be the first of many.'

'And the other part?'

'I didn't think the wilds of Dorset would appeal to you. I hoped you'd stay in London.'

'You should have told me,' he said again. 'I never was very good at taking hints.'

'No.'

He put the palette and the brush on a stool and started to wipe his hands with a kitchen towel dipped in turpentine. 'So how come the year's grace? Charity? Or malice? Did you think it would be more fun to cast me adrift down here than in London where I'd be assured of a bed?'

'Neither,' she said. 'Hope. Misplaced, as usual.' She glanced at the canvas.

He followed her gaze. 'I had tea with her. Nothing more.'

'I believe you.'

'Why so angry then? I'm not making a scene because you had supper with Robin.'

'I'm not angry, Jack. I'm bored. Bored with being the necessary audience that your ridiculous ego requires. I sometimes think that was the real reason you married me, not for security but because you needed somebody else's emotion to stimulate your creativity.' She gave a hollow laugh. 'In that case you should never have married a doctor. We see too much of it at work to play it all out again at home.'

He studied her closely. 'That's it then, is it? My marching orders? Pack your bags, Jack, and never darken my door again.'

She smiled the Mona Lisa smile that had first bewitched him. He thought he could predict exactly what she was going to say. *It's your life, make your own decisions.* For Sarah's strength and her weakness was her belief that everyone was as confident and single-minded as she was.

'Yes,' she said, 'that's it. I made up my mind that if you ever went near Sally again I'd call it quits. I want a divorce.'

His eyes narrowed. 'If this was about Sally, you'd have given me an ultimatum two weeks ago. I made no secret of where I was going.'

'I know,' she said wearily, staring at the painting again. 'Even your betrayals demand an audience now.'

He was gone when she came downstairs the next morning. There was a note on the kitchen table:

Send the divorce papers c/o Keith Smollett. You can find yourself another solicitor. I'll be going for a fifty-fifty split so don't get too attached to the house. I'll clear the studio as soon as I've found somewhere else. If you don't want to see me, then don't change the locks. I'll leave my key behind when I've retrieved my stuff.

Sarah read it through twice then dropped it in the rubbish bin.

Jane Marriott, the receptionist at the Fontwell surgery, looked up as Sarah pushed open the door of the empty waiting-room. Sarah covered Fontwell on Monday afternoons and Friday mornings and, because she was more sympathetic than her male colleagues, her sessions were usually busy ones. 'There's a couple of messages for you, dear,' said Jane. 'I've left them on your desk.'

'Thanks.' She paused by the desk. 'Who's first?'

'Mr Drew at eight forty-five and then it's hectic until eleven thirty. After that, two home visits, I'm afraid, but I've told them not to expect you before midday.'

'Okay.'

Jane, a retired teacher in her sixties, eyed Sarah with motherly concern. 'No breakfast again, I suppose?'

Sarah smiled. 'I haven't eaten breakfast since I left school.'

'Hm, well, you look washed out. You work too hard, dear. Doctoring's like any other job. You should learn to pace yourself better.'

Sarah put her elbows on the desk and propped her chin on her hands. 'Tell me something, Jane. If heaven exists, where exactly is it?' She looked for all the world like one of the eight-year-olds Jane had once taught, puzzled, a little hesitant, but confident that Mrs Marriott would know the answer.

'Goodness! No one's asked me a question like that since I stopped teaching.' She plugged in the kettle and spooned coffee into two cups. 'I always told the children it was in the hearts you left behind. The more people there were who loved you, the more hearts would hold your memory. It was a devious way of encouraging them to be nice to each other.' She chuckled. 'But I thought you were a non-believer, Sarah. Why the sudden interest in the afterlife?'

'I went to Mrs Gillespie's funeral yesterday. It was depressing. I keep wondering what the point of it all is.'

'Oh dear. Eternal truths at eight thirty in the morning.' She put a cup of steaming black coffee in front of Sarah. 'The point to Mathilda Gillespie's life might not emerge for another five generations. She's part of a line. Who's to say how important that line might be in years to come?'

'That's even more depressing,' said Sarah gloomily. 'That means you have to have children to give meaning to your life.'

'Nonsense. I haven't any children but I don't feel it makes me any less valuable. Our lives are what we make them.' She didn't look at Sarah as she spoke, and Sarah had the feeling that the words were just words, without meaning. 'Sadly,' Jane went on, 'Mathilda made very little of hers. She never got over her husband running out on her and it made her bitter. I think she thought people were laughing at her behind her back. Which, of course, a lot of us were,' she admitted honestly.

'I thought she was a widow.' How little she really knew about the woman.

Jane shook her head. 'Assuming he's still alive, then James is her widower. As far as I know they never bothered with a divorce.'

'What happened to him?'

'He went out to Hong Kong to work in a bank.'

'How do you know?'

'Paul and I took a holiday in the Far East about ten years after he and Mathilda separated, and we bumped into him by accident in a hotel in Hong Kong. We'd known him very well in the early days because he and Paul went through the war together.' She gave a quirky little smile. 'He was happy as Larry, living amongst the other expatriates, and quite unconcerned about his wife and daughter back home.'

'Who was supporting them?'

'Mathilda was. Her father left her very well provided for, which was a shame, I sometimes thought. She'd have been a different woman if she'd had to use that brain of hers to keep the wolf from the door.' She tut-tutted. 'It's bad for the character to have everything handed to you on a platter.'

Well, that was certainly true, thought Sarah, if Jack was anything to go by. Fifty-bloody-fifty, she thought wrathfully. She'd see him in hell first. 'So when did he leave her? Recently?'

'Good heavens, no. It was about eighteen months after they married. Well over thirty years ago, anyway. For a year or two we had letters from him, then we lost touch. To be honest, we found him rather tiresome. When we met in Hong Kong he'd taken to the bottle in a big way and he became very aggressive when he got drunk. We were both rather relieved when the letters dried up. We've never heard from him again.'

'Did Mathilda know he'd written to you?' Sarah asked curiously.

'I really couldn't say. We'd moved to Southampton by then and had very little to do with her. Mutual friends mentioned her from time to time, but other than that we lost touch completely. We only came back here five years ago when my poor old chap's health broke down and I took a decision that fresh Dorset air had to be better for him than the polluted city rubbish in Southampton.'

Paul Marriott suffered from chronic emphysema and his wretched wife agonized over his condition. 'It was the best thing you could have done,' said Sarah firmly. 'He tells me he's been much better since he came home to his roots.' She knew from past experience that Jane wouldn't be able to let the subject drop once she'd embarked upon it and contrived to steer her off it. 'Did you know Mathilda well?'

Jane thought about that. 'We grew up together – my father was the doctor here for many years and Paul was her father's political agent for a time – Sir William was the local MP – but I honestly don't think I knew Mathilda at all. The trouble was I never liked her.' She looked apologetic. 'It's awful to say that about someone who's dead but I refuse to be hypocritical about it. She was quite the nastiest woman I've ever met. I never blamed James for deserting her. The only mystery was why he married her in the first place.'

'Money,' said Sarah with feeling.

'Yes, I think it must have been,' Jane agreed. 'He was very much poor gentry, heir to nothing but a name, and Mathilda was beautiful, of course, just like Joanna. The whole thing was a disaster. James learnt PDQ that there were some things worse than poverty. And being dictated to by a virago who held the purse strings was one of them. He *hated* her.'

*

One of the messages on Sarah's desk was from Ruth Lascelles, a short note, presumably put through the surgery door the previous evening. She had surprisingly childish writing for a girl of seventeen or eighteen. 'Dear Dr Blakeney, Please can you come and see me at Granny's house tomorrow (Friday). I'm not ill but I'd like to talk to you. I have to be back at school by Sunday night. Thanking you in anticipation. Yours sincerely, Ruth Lascelles.'

The other was a telephoned message from Detective Sergeant Cooper. 'Dr Blakeney's call drawn to DS Cooper's attention this morning. He will contact her later in the day.'

It was nearly three o'clock before Sarah found time to call in at Cedar House. She drove up the short gravel drive and parked in front of the dining-room windows which faced out towards the road on the left-hand side of the house. It was a Georgian building in yellowy-grey stone, with deep windows and high-ceilinged rooms. Far too big for Mathilda, Sarah had always thought, and very inconvenient for a woman who, on bad days, was little better than an invalid. Her one concession to poor health had been the introduction of a stair-lift which had allowed her continued access to the upper floor. Sarah had once suggested that she sell up and move into a bungalow, to which Mathilda had replied that she wouldn't dream of any such thing. 'My dear Sarah, only the lower classes live in bungalows which is why they are always called Mon Repos or Dunroamin. Whatever else you do in life, *never* drop your standards.'

Ruth came out as she was opening her car door. 'Let's

talk in the summer-house,' she said jerkily. She didn't wait for an answer but set off round the corner of the house, her thin body, dressed only in tee-shirt and leggings, hunched against the biting north wind that was swirling the autumn leaves across the path.

Sarah, older and more susceptible to the cold, retrieved her Barbour from the back seat and followed. Out of the corner of her eye, she caught a glimpse of Joanna watching her from the dark depths of the dining-room. Had Ruth told her mother she'd asked Sarah to call, Sarah wondered, as she tramped across the lawn in the girl's wake. And why so much secrecy? The summer-house was a good two hundred yards from Joanna's listening ears.

Ruth was lighting a cigarette when Sarah joined her amongst the litter of art deco cane chairs and tables, relics from an earlier – happier? – age. 'I suppose you're going to lecture me,' she said with a scowl, pulling the doors to and flopping on to a chair.

'What about?' Sarah took another chair and folded the Barbour across her chest. It was bitterly cold, even with the doors closed.

'Smoking.'

Sarah shrugged. 'I'm not in the habit of lecturing.'

Ruth stared at her with moody eyes. 'Your husband said Granny called you her scold's bridle. Why would she do that if you didn't tick her off for nagging?'

Sarah looked out of the windows to where the huge cedar of Lebanon, after which the house was named, cast a long shadow on the grass. As she watched, the blustery wind drove a cloud across the sun and wiped the shadow away. 'We didn't have that sort of relationship,' she said, turning back to the girl. 'I enjoyed your grandmother's company. I don't recall any occasion when a ticking-off would have been appropriate.'

'*I* wouldn't have liked being called a scold's bridle.'

Sarah smiled. 'I found it rather flattering. I believe she meant it as a compliment.'

'I doubt it,' said the girl bluntly. 'I suppose you know she used the bridle on my mother when my mother was a child?' She smoked the cigarette nervously, taking short, rapid drags and expelling the smoke through her nose. She saw Sarah's disbelief. 'It's true. Granny told me about it once. She hated people crying, so whenever Mum cried she used to lock her in a cupboard with that thing strapped to her head. Granny's father did it to her. That's why she thought it was all right.'

Sarah waited but she didn't go on. 'That was cruel,' she murmured.

'Yes. But Granny was tougher than Mum and, anyway, it didn't matter much what you did to children when Granny was young, so being punished by wearing a bridle was probably no different from being thrashed with a belt. But it was awful for my mother.' She crushed the cigarette under her foot. 'There was no one to stand up for her and take her side. Granny could do what she liked whenever she liked.'

Sarah wondered what the girl was trying to tell her. 'It's an increasingly common problem, I'm afraid. Men, under stress, take their problems out on their wives. Women, under stress, take theirs out on their children, and there's nothing more stressful for a woman than to be left holding the baby.'

'Do you condone what Granny did?' There was a wary look in her eyes.

'Not at all. I suppose I'm trying to understand it. Most children in your mother's position suffer constant verbal abuse, and that is often as damaging as the physical abuse, simply because the scars don't show and nobody outside the family knows about it.' She shrugged. 'But the results are the same. The child is just as repressed and just as flawed. Few personalities can survive the constant battering of criticism from a person they depend on. You either crawl or fight. There's no middle way.'

Ruth looked angry. 'My mother had both, verbal and physical. You've no idea how vicious my grandmother was to her.'

'I'm sorry,' said Sarah helplessly. 'But if it's true that Mathilda was also punished brutally as a child, then she was as much a victim as your mother. But I don't suppose that's any consolation to you.'

Ruth lit another cigarette. 'Oh, don't get me wrong,' she said with an ironic twist to her mouth, 'I loved my grandmother. At least she had some character. My mother has none. Sometimes I hate her. Most of the time I just despise her.' She frowned at the floor, stirring the dust with the toe of one shoe. 'I think she killed Granny and I don't know what to do about it. Half of me blames her and the other half doesn't.'

Sarah let the remark hang in the air for a moment while she cast around for something to say. What sort of accusation was this? A genuine accusation of murder? Or a spiteful sideswipe by a spoilt child against a parent she disliked? 'The police are convinced it was suicide, Ruth.

They've closed the case. As I understand it, there's no question of anyone else being involved in your grandmother's death.'

'I don't mean Mum actually did it,' she said, 'you know, took the knife and did it. I mean that she drove Granny to killing herself. That's just as bad.' She raised suspiciously bright eyes. 'Don't you think so, Doctor?'

'Perhaps. If such a thing is possible. But from what you've told me of your mother's relationship with Mathilda, it sounds unlikely. It would be more plausible if it had happened the other way round and Mathilda had driven your mother to suicide.' She smiled apologetically. 'Even then, that sort of thing doesn't happen very often, and there would be a history of mental instability behind the person who saw suicide as their only escape from a difficult relationship.'

But Ruth wasn't to be persuaded so easily. 'You don't understand,' she said. 'They could be as unpleasant as they liked to each other and it didn't matter a damn. Mum was just as bad as Granny, but in a different way. Granny said what she thought while Mum just went on chipping away with snide little remarks. I hated being with them when they were together.' Her lips thinned unattractively. 'That was the only good thing about being sent to boarding school. Mum moved out then and went to London, and I could choose whether to come here for my holidays or go to Mum's. I didn't have to be a football any more.'

How little Sarah knew about these three women. Where was Mr Lascelles, for example? Had he, like James Gillespie, run away? Or was Lascelles some kind of courtesy title that

Joanna had adopted to give her daughter legitimacy? 'How long did you and your mother live here, then, before you went away to school?'

'From when I was a baby to when I was eleven. My father died and left us without a bean. Mum had to come crawling home or we'd have starved. That's her story at least. But personally I think she was just too snobbish and too lazy to take a menial job. She preferred Granny's insults to getting her hands dirty.' She wrapped her arms about her waist and leaned forward, rocking herself. 'My father was a Jew.' She spoke the word with contempt.

Sarah was taken aback. 'Why do you say it like that?'

'It's how my grandmother always referred to him. *That Jew*. She was an anti-Semite. Didn't you know?'

Sarah shook her head.

'Then you didn't know her very well.' Ruth sighed. 'He was a professional musician, a bass guitarist, attached to one of the studios. He did the backing tracks when the groups weren't good enough to do them themselves, and he had a band of his own which did gigs occasionally. He died of a heroin overdose in 1978. I don't remember him at all, but Granny took great delight in telling me what a worthless person he was. His name was Steven, Steven Lascelles.' She lapsed into silence.

'How did your mother meet him?'

'At a party in London. She was supposed to get off with a deb's delight but got off with the guitarist instead. Granny didn't know anything about it until Mum told her she was pregnant, and then the shit hit the fan. I mean, can you imagine it? Mum up the spout by a Jewish rock guitarist with a heroin habit.' She gave a hollow laugh. 'It was a hell

54

of a revenge.' Her arms were turning blue with cold but she didn't seem to notice it. 'So, anyway, they got married and she moved in with him. They had me and then six months later he was dead after spending all their money on heroin. He hadn't paid the rent for months. Mum was a widow – before she was twenty-three – on the dole with a baby and no roof over her head.'

'Then coming back here was probably her only option.'

Ruth pulled a sour face. 'You wouldn't have done it though, not if you knew you'd never be allowed to forget your mistake.'

Probably not, thought Sarah. She wondered if Joanna had loved Steven Lascelles or if, as Ruth had implied, she had taken up with him simply to spite Mathilda. 'It's easy to be wise after the event,' was all she said.

The girl went on as if she hadn't heard. 'Granny tried to change my name to something more WASP – you know, White Anglo-Saxon Protestant – to erase the Hebrew in me. She called me Elizabeth for a while but Mum threatened to take me away, so Granny gave in. Other than that and her refusal to let Granny put the bridle on me when I cried, Mum let Granny dictate terms on everything.' Her eyes flashed scornfully. 'She was so wet. But it was easy to stand up to my grandmother. I did it all the time and we got on like a house on fire.'

Sarah had no desire to be drawn into a domestic squabble between a mother and daughter she barely knew. She watched the long shadow creep across the lawn again as the sun emerged from behind a cloud. 'Why did you ask me to come here, Ruth?'

'I don't know what to do. I thought you'd tell me.'

Sarah studied the thin, rather malicious face and wondered if Joanna had any idea how much her daughter disliked her. 'Don't do anything. Frankly, I can't imagine what your mother could have said or done that would have driven Mathilda to kill herself and, even if there were something, it would hardly be a chargeable offence.'

'Then it should be,' said Ruth harshly. 'She found a letter in the house last time she was down here. She told Granny she'd publish it if Granny didn't change her will immediately and move out of the house. So Granny killed herself. She's left everything to me, you see. She *wanted* to leave everything to me.' Now there was definite malice in the immature features.

Oh God, thought Sarah. *What were you trying to tell me, Mathilda?* 'Have you seen this letter?'

'No, but Granny wrote and told me what was in it. She said she didn't want me to find out from my mother. So, you see, Mum did drive her to it. Granny would have done anything to avoid having her dirty linen washed in public.' Her voice grated.

'Do you still have the letter she wrote to you?'

Ruth scowled. 'I tore it up. But that one wasn't important, it's the one Mum found that's important. She'll use it to try and overturn Granny's will.'

'Then I think you should find yourself a solicitor,' said Sarah firmly, drawing her legs together under her chair preparatory to getting up. 'I was your grandmother's doctor, that's all. I can't get involved between you and your mother, Ruth, and I'm quite sure Mathilda wouldn't have wanted me to.'

'But she would,' the girl cried. 'She said in her letter that

56

if anything happened to her I was to talk to you. She said you would know what to do for the best.'

'Surely not? Your grandmother didn't confide in me. All I know about your family is what you've told me today.'

A thin hand reached out and gripped hers. It was icy cold. 'The letter was from Granny's uncle, Gerald Cavendish, to his solicitor. It was a will, saying he wanted everything he had to go to his daughter.'

Sarah could feel the hand on hers trembling, but whether from cold or nerves she didn't know. 'Go on,' she prompted.

'This house and all the money was his. He was the elder brother.'

Sarah frowned again. 'So what are you saying? That Mathilda never had any rights to it? Well, I'm sorry, Ruth, but this is way beyond me. You really must find a solicitor and talk it through with him. I haven't a clue what your legal position is, truly I haven't.' Her subconscious caught up with her. 'Still, it's very odd, isn't it? If his daughter was his heir, shouldn't she have inherited automatically?'

'No one knew she was his daughter,' said Ruth bleakly, 'except Granny, and she told everyone James Gillespie was the father. It's my mother, Dr Blakeney. Granny was being fucked by her uncle. It's really sick, isn't it?'

Joanna came to visit me today. She fixed me with that peculiarly unpleasant stare of hers through most of lunch — I was reminded of a terrier Father once had which turned vicious after a beating and had to be put down; there was the same malicious gleam in his eyes just before he sank his teeth into Father's palm and ripped the flesh from the bone — then spent most of the afternoon searching about in the library. She said she was looking for my mother's book on flower arranging, but she was lying, of course. I remember giving that to her when she moved back to London. I did not interfere.

She looked very tarty, I thought — far too much make-up for a trip to the country and in a ridiculously short skirt for a woman of her age. I suspect some man brought her down and was abandoned to forage for himself at the pub. Sex, to Joanna, is a currency to be used quite shamelessly in return for services rendered.

Oh, Mathilda, Mathilda! Such hypocrisy!

Do these men realize, I wonder, how little she cares for and about them? Not through contempt, I think, but through sheer indifference to anyone's feelings but

*her own. I should have taken Hugh Hendry's advice
and insisted on a psychiatrist. She's quite mad, but then,
so, of course, was Gerald. 'The wheel is come full circle.'*

*She came out of the library with his idiotic will held
in front of her like some holy relic and cursed me in the
most childish and absurd way for stealing her inheritance. I wonder who told her about it . . .*

Four

WHEN SARAH ARRIVED home that evening, she made a bee-line for Jack's studio. To her relief, nothing had been moved. She passed the canvas on the easel without so much as a glance, and started rummaging feverishly through the portraits stacked against the far wall. Those she recognized, she left; those she didn't, she lined up side by side, facing into the room. In all, there were three paintings she had no recollection of ever having seen before. She stood back and gazed at them, trying to decipher who they were. More accurately, she was trying to isolate one that might strike a chord.

She hoped quite earnestly that she wouldn't find it. But she did, of course. It screamed at her, a violent and vivid portrayal of bitterness, savage wit and repression, and the whole personality was encaged in a rusted iron framework that was all too clearly the scold's bridle. Sarah's shock was enormous, driving the breath from her body in a surge of panic. She collapsed on to Jack's painting stool and closed her eyes against the jeering anger of Mathilda's image. *What had he done?*

The doorbell rang, jerking her to her feet like a marionette. She stood for a moment, wide-eyed with shock, then, without consciously rationalizing why she was doing it, she seized the picture, turned it round and thrust it amongst the others against the wall.

It crossed DS Cooper's mind that Dr Blakeney wasn't well. She looked very pale when she opened the door, but she smiled a welcome and stepped back to let him in, and by the time they were settled on chairs in the kitchen some of the colour had returned to her cheeks. 'You telephoned last night,' he reminded her, 'left a message saying you had more information about Mrs Gillespie.'

'Yes.' Her mind raced. *She said you would know what to do for the best.* But I don't! I DON'T! 'I've been worrying about why she wore the bridle,' she said slowly. 'I've come to the conclusion that she was trying to tell me something, although I must emphasize that I don't know what that something could have been.' As clearly as she could, she repeated what she had told Robin Hewitt the night before about Mathilda's nickname for her. 'It's probably just me being fanciful,' she finished lamely.

The Sergeant frowned deeply. 'She must have known you'd make a connection. Could she have been accusing you, perhaps?'

Sarah showed an unexpected relief. 'I hadn't thought of that,' she admitted. 'You mean a slap over the knuckles to bring me down a peg or two. Doctors can't cure unhappiness, Sarah. Something along those lines?'

He found her relief puzzling. 'It's possible,' he agreed. 'Who else knew that she called you her scold's bridle, Dr Blakeney?'

She folded her hands in her lap. 'I don't know. Whoever she mentioned it to, presumably.'

'You didn't tell anyone?'

She shook her head. 'No.'

'No one at all? Not even your partners or your husband?'

'No.' She forced a light chuckle. 'I wasn't altogether sure that she meant it as a compliment. I always took it as such because it would have strained our relationship if I hadn't, but she might have been implying that I was as repressive and tormenting as the instrument itself.'

He nodded thoughtfully. 'If she killed herself, then you and I will be puzzling over the significance of this for the rest of our lives.' His eyes watched Sarah's face. 'If, however, somebody else killed her, and that person knew she called you her scold's bridle, then it does seem to me that the message is very direct. Namely, I have done this *for* you, Dr Blakeney, or *because of* you. Would you agree with that?'

'No,' she said with a spark of anger. 'Of course I wouldn't. You can't possibly make assumptions like that. In any case I was under the impression that the inquest verdict was a foregone conclusion. The only reason I felt I should tell you all this was because it's been worrying me, but at the end of the day I'm probably reading far more into it than Mathilda intended. I suspect the pathologist was right, and that she simply wanted to deck herself out like Ophelia.'

He smiled pleasantly. 'And, of course, you may not have been the only person she used the nickname on.'

'Well, exactly.' She plucked a hair from the front of her jacket. 'May I ask you something?'

'By all means.'

'Does the pathologist's report come down firmly in favour of suicide or is there any room for doubt?'

'Not much,' the policeman admitted. 'He's unhappy about the absence of a letter of explanation, particularly in view of the rather dramatic way she killed herself, and he's unhappy about the flower arrangement.'

'Because the nettles stung her?'

'No. If she was set on killing herself the way she did, a few nettle stings wouldn't have worried her.' He tapped his pencil on the table top. 'I persuaded him to do some experiments. He's been unable to reproduce the arrangement she came up with without assistance.' He drew a quick diagram in his notebook. 'If you remember, the Michaelmas daisies were set upright in the forehead band, which incidentally is so rusted it can't be tightened, and the nettles hung down like a veil over her hair and cheeks. The stems were alternate, a nettle down, a daisy up, completely symmetrical all the way round. Now that is impossible to achieve without help. You can hold half the arrangement in place with one hand but the minute you get beyond the stretch of the fingers, the flowers start to drop out. It's only when three-quarters of the arrangement is in place that the gap between the frame and the head has reduced enough to retain the other quarter without dropping them, assuming the same circumference head as Mrs Gillespie. Do you follow?'

She frowned. 'I think so. But couldn't she have used cotton wool or tissues to pad the gap while she put in the flowers?'

'Yes. But if she had, then something in that house would have had rust marks on it. We searched it from top to bottom. There was nothing. So what happened to the padding?'

Sarah closed her eyes and pictured the bathroom. 'There was a sponge on the bathrack,' she said, remembering. 'Perhaps she used that and then washed it in the bath.'

'It does have particles of rust on it,' he admitted, 'but then the bath was full of them. The sponge could have picked them up when it was soaked by the water.' He pursed his lips in frustration. 'Or, as you say, it could have been used as padding. We don't know, but what worries me is this: if she did it herself, then she must have sat at her dressing-table to do it. It's the only surface where we've discovered any sap.' He made a vague gesture with his hand. 'We picture it something like this. She placed the flowers on the dressing-table, sat down in front of the mirror and then set about arranging them in the framework on her head, but she wouldn't have discovered she needed padding until she was half-way round, at which point the natural thing to do would have been to reach for some Kleenex or some cotton wool, both of which were there in front of her. So why go to the bathroom for the sponge?' He fell silent for a moment or two. 'If, however, someone else killed her and arranged the flowers after she was in the bath, then the sponge would have been the obvious thing to use. It's a far more logical scenario and would explain the absence of nettle rash on Mrs Gillespie's hands and fingers.'

'You said the pathologist's report mentioned nettle rash on her cheeks and temples,' said Sarah apologetically. 'But she'd have to have been alive for her skin to react to the stings.'

65

'It was only slight,' he amended. 'The way I see it, her killer didn't wait till she was dead – you don't hang about when you're murdering someone – he or she shoved the nettles in while she was dying.'

Sarah nodded. 'It sounds plausible,' she agreed, 'except—' She didn't finish the sentence.

'Except what, Dr Blakeney?'

'Why would anyone want to murder her?'

He shrugged. 'Her daughter and her granddaughter had strong enough motives. According to the will, the estate is to be divided equally between the two of them. Mrs Lascelles gets the money and Miss Lascelles gets Cedar House.'

'Did they know?'

He nodded. 'Mrs Lascelles certainly did because she showed us where to find the will – Mrs Gillespie was very methodical, kept all her papers and correspondence in neat files in a cabinet in the library – but whether *Miss* Lascelles knew the precise terms, I don't know. She claims her grandmother intended her to have everything and is very put out to discover she is only going to get the house.' His face assumed a somewhat ironic expression. 'She's a greedy young woman. There's not many seventeen-year-olds would turn their noses up at a windfall like that.'

Sarah smiled slightly. 'Presumably you've checked to find out where they were the night she died?'

He nodded again. 'Mrs Lascelles was at a concert in London with a friend; Miss Lascelles was thirty miles away under the watchful eye of a housemistress at school.'

She forced another smile. 'Which puts them out of the picture.'

'Maybe, maybe not. I never set much store by alibis and someone had to get into Cedar House.' He frowned. 'Apart from Mrs Spede and Mrs Gillespie herself, the Lascelles women were the only other ones with keys.'

'You're determined to make it murder,' protested Sarah mildly.

He went on as if she hadn't spoken. 'We've questioned everyone in the village. Mrs Spede was at the pub with her husband and, as far as friends are concerned, we can't find anyone who was on calling terms with Mrs Gillespie, let alone at around nine o'clock on a Saturday night in November.' He shrugged. 'In any case, her neighbours, Mr and Mrs Orloff, say they would have heard the bell ringing if someone had come to her door. When Mrs Gillespie sold them their part of the house, she simply had the bell moved from the kitchen, which is now theirs, to the corridor outside which remained hers. I tested it. They couldn't have missed it if it was rung that night.'

Sarah caught his eye. 'Then it seems fairly obvious that it must have been suicide.'

'Not to me, Dr Blakeney. In the first place, I intend to put those two alibis under a microscope and, in the second place, if Mrs Gillespie's murderer was someone she knew, they could have tapped on the windows or the back door without the Orloffs hearing them.' He closed his notebook and tucked it into his pocket. 'We'll get them eventually. Probably through their fingerprints.'

'You're going on with it then? I thought your boss had decided to drop it.'

'We raised a number of fingerprints in that house which don't belong to Mrs Gillespie or the three women who had keys. We'll be asking everyone in the village and outsiders like you, who knew her, to let us take prints for comparison purposes. I've persuaded the Chief to find out who else went in there before he draws a line under this one.'

'You seem to be taking Mrs Gillespie's death very personally.'

'Policing's no different from any other job, Doctor. The higher up the ladder you are the better the pension at the end.' His amiable face grew suddenly cynical. 'But promotion has more to do with empire-building than ability, and to date my light has always been hidden under some other sod's bushel. I do take Mrs Gillespie's death personally. It's my case.'

Sarah found this bleakly amusing. She wondered how Mathilda would feel about a policeman benefiting from her death, assuming, of course, he could prove it was murder and then convict the murderer. She might have felt happier if she wasn't so convinced that he was going to score on both counts.

'Keith? It's Sarah. Sarah Blakeney. Has Jack been in touch with you, by any chance?' She toyed with the telephone wire while she listened to the sound of Cooper's car fading into the distance. There were too many shadows in this hall, she thought.

'Not recently,' said Keith Smollett's pleasant voice. 'Should he have been?'

There was no point beating about the bush. 'We had a row. I told him I wanted a divorce and he's gone off in a huff. He left a note saying I could contact him through you.'

'Oh, good God, Sarah! Well, I can't act for both of you. Jack will have to find himself another solicitor.'

'He's opted for you. I'm the one who has to find someone else.'

'Bugger that,' said Keith cheerfully. '*You're* my client, sweetheart. The only reason I've ever done anything for that lazy good-for-nothing is because you married him.' He and Sarah had been friends from university days and there had been a time, before Jack entered the frame, when Keith had had designs on Sarah himself. Now, he was happily married with three strapping young sons, and only thought about her on the rare occasions when she telephoned.

'Yes, well, that's a side issue at the moment. The main issue is that I need to talk to him rather urgently. He's bound to contact you so will you let me know where he is as soon as he does. It's desperately important.' She glanced towards the stairs, her face a pale glimmer in the reflected light from the kitchen. Far too many shadows.

'Will do.'

'There's something else. What's my legal position with regard to a police investigation into a possible murder?' She heard his indrawn breath. 'I don't mean I'm involved or anything but I think I've been given some information that I really ought to pass on. The police don't seem to know about it, but it's incredibly sensitive stuff and very second-hand, and if it doesn't have any bearing then I shall be betraying a confidence that's going to affect quite a few lives really badly.' She drew to a halt. *Why had Ruth told her about the letter and not Cooper? Or had she told Cooper as well?* 'Does any of that make any sense?'

'Not much. My advice, for what it's worth, is don't withhold anything from the police unless it's confidential medical information on a patient. Force them to go through the proper channels for that. They'll do it, of course, but you'll be squeaky-clean.'

'The person who told me isn't even a patient.'

'Then you don't have a problem.'

'But I could ruin lives by speaking out of turn,' she said doubtfully. 'We're talking ethics here, Keith.'

'No, we're not. Ethics don't exist outside church and ivory towers. We're talking big, bad world, where even doctors go to prison if they obstruct the police in their enquiries. You won't have a leg to stand on, my girl, if it turns out you withheld information that could have resulted in a conviction for murder.'

'But I'm not sure it *is* murder. It looks like suicide.'

'Then why is your voice quivering about two pitches higher than normal? You sound like Maria Callas on a bad night. It's only a snap judgement, of course, but I'd say you're one hundred per cent certain that you're looking at murder and ninety-nine per cent certain that you know who did it. Talk to the police.'

She was silent for so long that he began to wonder if the line had been cut. 'You're wrong about the ninety-nine per cent,' she said at last. 'Actually, I haven't a clue who might have done it.' With a muted goodbye, she hung up.

The telephone started to ring before she had removed her hand from the receiver, but her nerves were so shot to pieces that it was several moments before she could find the courage to pick it up.

The following morning, Saturday, a solicitor drove from Poole to Fontwell with Mathilda's will in his briefcase. He had telephoned Cedar House the previous evening to introduce himself and to unleash his bombshell, namely that all Mathilda's previous wills were rendered null and void by the one she had signed in his office two days before she died. He had been instructed by Mrs Gillespie to break the news to her daughter and granddaughter in person as soon as convenient after her funeral, and to do it in the presence of Dr Sarah Blakeney of Mill House, Long Upton. Dr Blakeney was free tomorrow. Would eleven o'clock be convenient for Mrs and Miss Lascelles?

The atmosphere in Mathilda's drawing-room was icy. Joanna stood by the french windows, staring out over the garden, her back to both Sarah and her daughter. Ruth smoked continuously, darting malicious glances between the rigid back of the one woman and the obvious discomfort of the other. No one spoke. To Sarah, who had always loved this room with its mish-mash of beautiful antiques: Georgian corner cabinets, old and faded chintz covers on the Victorian sofa and chairs, nineteenth-century Dutch watercolours and the Louis XVI Lyre clock on the mantelpiece, this unwelcome and unwelcomed return was depressing.

The sound of car tyres on the gravel outside broke the tension. 'I'll go,' said Ruth, jumping up.

'I can't even remember what he said his name was,' declared Joanna, turning back into the room. 'Dougall, Douglas?'

'Duggan,' said Sarah.

Joanna frowned. 'You know him, then.'

'No. I wrote his name down when he phoned last night.' She fished a piece of paper from her pocket. 'Paul Duggan of Duggan, Smith and Drew, Hills Road, Poole.'

Joanna listened to her daughter greeting someone at the door. 'My mother seems to have had considerable faith in you, Dr Blakeney. Why was that, do you suppose? You can only have known her – what? – a year?' Her face was impassive – schooled that way, thought Sarah, to preserve her youthfulness – but her eyes were deeply suspicious.

Sarah smiled without hostility. She had been placed in a very invidious position, and she wasn't enjoying the experience. She had considerable sympathy for Joanna, one way and another, and she was becoming increasingly troubled by Mathilda's memory. Their relationship, a light-hearted one at best, was turning oppressive in retrospect, and she resented the old woman's assumption that she could manipulate her doctor after her death and without prior permission. It was neither Sarah's business nor her wish to act as mediator in an acrimonious legal battle between Joanna and her daughter. 'I'm as much in the dark as you are, Mrs Lascelles, and probably just as annoyed,' she said frankly. 'I've a week's shopping to do, a house to clean and a garden to take care of. I'm only here because Mr Duggan said if I didn't come then he would have to postpone this meeting until I could. I thought that would be even more upsetting for you and Ruth' – she shrugged – 'so I agreed to it.'

72

Joanna was on the point of answering when the door swung open and Ruth walked in, followed by a smiling middle-aged man carrying a video recorder with a briefcase balanced on top of it. 'Mr Duggan,' she said curtly, flopping into her chair again. 'He wants to use the television. Would you believe, Granny's made a frigging video-will?'

'Not strictly true, Miss Lascelles,' said the man, bending down to place the recorder on the floor beside the television. He straightened and held out a hand to Joanna, guessing correctly that she was Mathilda's daughter. 'How do you do, Mrs Lascelles.' He moved across to Sarah, who had stood up, and shook her hand also. 'Dr Blakeney.' He gestured to the chairs. 'Please sit down. I'm very aware that all our time is precious, so I don't intend to take up more of it than I need to. I am here as one of the joint executors of the last written will and testament of Mrs Mathilda Beryl Gillespie, copies of which I will give you in a few minutes, and from which you may satisfy yourselves that it does in fact supersede any previous will or wills made by Mrs Gillespie. The other joint executor is Mr John Hapgood, currently manager of Barclays Bank, Hills Road, Poole. In both instances, of course, we hold our responsibilities as executors on behalf of our firms so should either of us cease employment with the said firms, then another executor will be appointed in our place.' He paused briefly. 'Is all that quite clear?' He glanced from one to the other. 'Good. Now, if you'll bear with me for a moment, I'll just connect the video to the television.' He produced a coil of coaxial cable like a magician from his pocket and plugged one end into the television and the other into the video recorder. 'And now a power socket,' he murmured, unrolling a wire and a plug from the back of the video. 'If I remember correctly, it's above the skirting board to the right of the fireplace. Ah, yes, here we are. Splendid. And just in case you're wondering how I knew, then let me explain that Mrs Gillespie invited me here to make an inventory of all her possessions.' He beamed at them. 'Purely to avoid acrimonious arguments between the relative parties after the will has been read.'

Sarah was aware that her mouth had been hanging open since he entered the room. She shut it with a conscious effort and watched him deftly tune the television to receive the signal from the recorder, then open his briefcase and remove a video cassette which he inserted into the recorder before standing back to let Mathilda speak for herself. You could have heard a pin drop, she thought, as Mathilda's face materialized on the screen. Even Ruth sat as if carved in stone, her cigarette temporarily forgotten between her fingers.

The well-remembered voice, with its strident upper-class vowels, spoke confidently from the amplifier.

'Well, my dears,' Mathilda's lips thinned scornfully, 'I'm sure you're wondering why I insisted on bringing you together like this. Joanna, I have no doubt, is cursing me quietly under her breath, Ruth is nursing yet another grievance and Sarah, I suspect, is beginning to wish she had never met me.' The old woman gave a dry laugh. 'I am, by now, impervious to your curses, Joanna, so if there is awareness after death, which I doubt, they won't be troubling me. And, Ruth, your grievances have become so tiresome recently that, frankly, I'm bored with them. They won't be troubling me either.' Her voice softened a little. 'The irritation, however, that I am sure Sarah is feeling at my unilateral decision to involve her in my family's affairs *does* concern me. All I can say is that I have valued your friendship and your strength of character, Sarah, during the time I've known you, and I cannot think of anyone else who could even begin to support the burden that I am about to place on your shoulders.'

There was a brief pause while she consulted some notes on her lap. To Sarah, whose uncritical affection now appeared naïve in the face of the universal dislike which Mathilda had inspired in those who knew her, the old woman's eyes were uncharacteristically cruel. Where, she wondered, had her humour gone?

'I wish to make it absolutely clear that Joanna is not James Gillespie's daughter, but the daughter of my uncle, Gerald Cavendish. He was my father's elder brother and . . .' she sought for the right words to express herself, 'the liaison between us began some four years after he invited me and my father to live with him in Cedar House following the death of my mother. My father had no money of his own because the estate had been settled on the elder son, Gerald. My mother's money reverted to her family when she died, apart from a small inheritance which was left in trust for me. Without Gerald's invitation to live with him in Cedar House, my father and I would have been homeless. To that extent I was grateful. In every other respect I despised and loathed the man.' She smiled coldly. 'I was a child of thirteen when he first raped me.'

Sarah was shocked – not just by what Mathilda was

saying, but by the way she was saying it. This was not a Mathilda *she* recognized. Why was she being so brutal, so coldly calculating?

'He was a drunken monster, like my father, and I hated them both. Between them, they destroyed any chance I might ever have had of forming a lasting and successful relationship. I have never known if my father knew what Gerald was doing but, even if he did, I am in no doubt whatsoever that he would have let it continue for fear of Gerald evicting us from Cedar House. My father was an intensely lazy man who scrounged off his wife's family until she died, and then scrounged off his brother. The only time I ever knew him to work was later, when he stood for election to the House of Commons, and then only because he saw membership as an easy route to a knighthood. Once elected, of course, he reverted to what he truly was – a contemptible man.' She paused again, her mouth turned down in bitter remembrance.

'Gerald's abuse of me continued on and off for twelve years when, in desperation, I told my father about it. I cannot adequately explain why it took me so long, except to say that I lived in constant terror of both of them. I was a prisoner, financially and socially, and I was brought up to believe, as many of my generation were, that men held natural authority within a family. I thank God those times are passing because I see now that natural authority belongs only to those who earn the respect to exercise it, be they male or female.' She paused for a moment. 'My father, of course, blamed me for what had happened, calling me a disgusting slut, and was disinclined to do anything. He preferred, as I knew he would, to maintain the status quo at my expense. But he was vulnerable. He was now a Member of Parliament, and in desperation I threatened to write to the Conservative Party and the newspapers in order to expose what sort of family the Cavendishes really were. As a result of this, a compromise was reached. I was allowed to marry James Gillespie who had declared an interest in me, and in return I agreed to say nothing. Under these conditions, we made some attempt to resume our lives although my father, fearing perhaps that I would go back on my word, insisted that my marriage to James take place immediately. He secured James a position at the Treasury, and packed us off to a flat in London.'

There was a longer silence this time while she turned to another page of her notes, adjusting her glasses as she did so. 'Unfortunately, I was already pregnant, and when Joanna was born less than five months after our marriage, even James, by no means the brightest of men, realized the baby couldn't possibly be his. Life became very difficult after that. Not unreasonably, he resented us both, and this led to bouts of violence whenever he had too much to drink. We continued in this unhappy vein for another eighteen months until, mercifully, James announced that he had secured a job abroad and would be sailing the next day without us. I have never regretted his departure or cared one iota what happened to him. He was a very unpleasant piece of work.' The old eyes stared straight out of the screen, arrogant and disdainful, but for Sarah at least there was a sense of something withheld. Mathilda, she thought, was not being quite honest.

'It is tedious now to recall the difficulties of those months after his departure. Suffice it to say that money was short.

Joanna experienced similar problems herself when Steven died. The difference was that my father refused to help me – he had by now received his knighthood and enough water had passed under the bridge to mitigate my threats of exposure – while *I* did help *you*, Joanna, although you have never thanked me for it. In the end, when it was clear that eviction was becoming a real possibility, I wrote in desperation to Gerald and asked him to support his daughter. This, I gather, was the first he knew of Joanna's existence,' she smiled cynically, 'and my letter prompted him into the one honourable act of his life. He killed himself with an overdose of barbiturates. The pity is he didn't have the decency to do it sooner.' Her voice was brittle with dislike. 'A verdict of accidental death was recorded, but I cannot believe the two things were unrelated, particularly in view of the letter he sent to his solicitor, making Joanna heir to all his property.'

She turned to what was obviously the last page of her notes. 'I now come to what has prompted me to make this film. Joanna first. You threatened me with exposure if I refused to leave Cedar House immediately and make the property over to you. I have no idea who suggested you look for your father's letter, although,' she smiled grimly, 'I have my suspicions. But you were very misinformed about your rights. Gerald's absurd will could not break the trust whereby his father granted him a life interest in the property after which it passed to the nearest male relative, namely my father. By dying, Gerald merely conferred on his brother and his brother's heirs a permanent interest in the Cavendish wealth. He knew it, too. Please don't imagine that his pathetic codicil was anything more than a weak man's atonement for sins of commission and omission. Perhaps he was naïve enough to believe that my father would honour the obligation, perhaps he just thought that God would be less harsh if he showed willing to make amends. Either way he was a fool. He did, however, have the sense to send me a copy of the codicil and, by threatening to go to court with it in order to challenge the trust, I was able to use it to influence my father. He agreed to finance you and me in London while he remained alive and to make the property over to me on his death which he was entitled to do. As you know, he was dead within two years, and you and I moved back to Cedar House.' Her eyes, staring fixedly into the lens, picked out her daughter. 'You should never have threatened me, Joanna. You had no reason to, whereas I had every reason to threaten my father. I have made some very handsome settlements on you, one way and another, and feel that I have discharged all my obligations towards you. If you haven't already taken me to court when you see this, then I urge you not to waste your money after I'm gone. Believe me, I have given you more than the law ever entitled you to.

'Now, Ruth.' She cleared her throat. 'Your behaviour since your seventeenth birthday has appalled me. I can find no way to account for it or excuse it. I have always told you that the property would be yours when I died. I was referring to Cedar House but you assumed, without any prompting from me, that the contents and the money would be yours, too. That was a false assumption. My intention was always to leave the more valuable contents and the money to Joanna, and the house to you. Joanna, I assumed, would not wish to move from London, and you would have had the choice either to sell up or stay but you would have sold, I'm sure, because the house would have lost its charms once the estate was approved. What little remained to the property would never have satisfied you because you're as greedy as your mother. In conclusion, I can only repeat what I said to Joanna: I have made some very handsome settlements on you and feel that I have more than discharged my obligations to you. It may be the fault of inbreeding, of course, but I have come to realize that neither of you is capable of a decent or a generous thought.' Her eyes narrowed behind her glasses. 'I therefore intend to leave everything I own to Dr Sarah Blakeney of Mill House, Long Upton, Dorset, who will, I am confident, use her windfall wisely. In so far as I have ever been capable of feeling fondness for anyone I have felt it for her.' She gave a sudden chuckle. 'Don't be angry with me, Sarah. I must have died without changing my mind, or you wouldn't be watching this. So remember me for our friendship and not for this burden I have laid on you. Joanna and Ruth will hate you, as they have hated me, and they will accuse you of all manner of beastliness, just as they have accused me. But "what's done cannot be undone", so take it all with my blessing and use it to promote something worthwhile in my memory. Goodbye, my dear.'

'When sorrows come, they come not as single spies but in battalions.' I am afraid that Ruth's behaviour is becoming compulsive but am reluctant to tackle her about it for fear of what she might do to me. She is not above taking a stick to an old woman who annoys or frustrates her. I see it in her eyes, an awareness that I am more valuable to her dead than alive.

It was truly said: 'He that dies pays all debts.'

If I knew where she was going every day, it would help, but she lies about that as she lies about everything. Could it be schizophrenia? She is certainly the right age for it. I trust the school will do something about it next term. I am not strong enough for any more scenes nor will I be blamed for what was never my fault. God knows, there was only one victim in all this, and that was little Mathilda Cavendish. I wish I could remember her, that loving lovely child, but she is as insubstantial to me now as memories of my mother. Forgotten wraiths, both of them, unloved, abused, neglected.

Thank God for Sarah. She convinces me that like Shakespeare's sad old man 'I am more sinned against than sinning . . .'

Five

PAUL DUGGAN switched off the television set and spoke into the silence. 'The video recording, of course, has no legal standing which is why I referred to Mrs Gillespie's last *written* will and testament.' He reached into his briefcase and produced some sheaves of paper. 'These are photocopies only but the original is available for inspection at my office in Hills Street.' He handed a copy to each of the women. 'Mrs Gillespie felt you might try to contest this document, Mrs Lascelles. I can only advise you to consult a solicitor before you do so. As far as Dr Blakeney is concerned' – he turned to Sarah – 'Mr Hapgood and I will need to discuss details with you as soon as possible. We can offer you three mornings next week. Tuesday, Wednesday or Thursday. In my office for preference, although we will come to Long Upton if necessary. You understand, however, that executors are entitled to charge for expenses.' He beamed encouragingly at Sarah, waiting for an answer. He appeared to be completely unaware of the brewing hostility in the room.

Sarah gathered her scattered wits together. 'Do I have any say in this at all?'

'In what, Dr Blakeney?'

'In the will.'

'You mean, are you free to reject Mrs Gillespie's bequest?'

'Yes.'

'There's an alternative provision which you will find on the last page of the document.' Joanna and Ruth rustled through their copies. 'If for any reason you are unable to take up the bequest, Mrs Gillespie instructed us to sell her entire estate and donate the proceeds to the Seton Retirement Home for donkeys. She said, if you couldn't or wouldn't have her money, then it might as well go to deserving asses.' He was watching Sarah closely and she thought that, after all, he wasn't quite so complacent as he seemed. He was expecting that remark to strike a chord. 'Tuesday, Wednesday or Thursday, Dr Blakeney? I should point out that an early meeting is essential. There is the future of Mrs Lascelles and her daughter to be considered, for example. Mrs Gillespie recognized that they would be in residence at Cedar House when the will was read and had no wish that we as executors should demand their immediate vacation of the property. It was for this reason, and without any offence intended,' he smiled amiably at the two women, 'that a full inventory of the contents was made. I'm sure the last thing any of us wants is a battle royal over just what was in the house at the time of Mrs Gillespie's death.'

'Oh, bloody fabulous,' said Ruth scathingly, 'now you're accusing us of theft.'

'Not at all, Miss Lascelles. It's standard procedure, I assure you.'

Her lip curled unattractively. 'What's our future got to

do with anything, anyway? I thought we'd ceased to exist.' She dropped her cigarette butt deliberately on to the Persian carpet and ground it out under her heel.

'As I understand it, Miss Lascelles, you have another two terms at boarding school before you take your A levels. To date, your grandmother paid your fees but there is no provision in the will for further expenditure on your education so, in the circumstances, whether you remain at Southcliffe may well depend on Dr Blakeney.'

Joanna raised her head. 'Or on me,' she said coolly. 'I am her mother, after all.'

There was a short silence before Ruth gave a harsh laugh. 'God, you're a fool. No wonder Granny didn't want to leave her money to you. What are you planning to pay with, Mother dear? No one's going to give you an allowance any more, you know, and you don't imagine your sweet little flower arrangements are going to produce four thousand a term, do you?'

Joanna smiled faintly. 'If I contest this will then, presumably, things will continue as normal in the meantime.' She looked enquiringly at Paul Duggan. 'Do you have the authority to give the money to Dr Blakeney if I, too, am laying claim to it?'

'No,' he admitted, 'but, by the same token, you will receive nothing either. You are putting me in a difficult position, Mrs Lascelles. I was your mother's lawyer, not yours. All I will say is there are time limits involved and I urge you to seek independent legal advice without delay. Things will not, as you put it, continue as normal.'

'So in the short term Ruth and I lose either way?'

'Not necessarily.'

She frowned. 'I'm afraid I don't understand.'

Ruth flung herself out of the sofa and stormed across to the window. 'God, why do you have to be so obtuse? If you behave nicely, Mother, Dr Blakeney may feel guilty enough about inheriting a fortune to keep subsidizing us. That's it, isn't it?' She glared at Duggan. 'Granny's passed the buck of trying to create something decent out of the Cavendishes to her doctor.' Her mouth twisted. 'What a frigging awful joke! She warned me about it, too. Talk to Dr Blakeney. She'll know what to do for the best. It's so unfair.' She stamped her foot. 'It's so bloody unfair.'

Joanna's face was thoughtful. 'Is that right, Mr Duggan?'

'Not strictly, no. I will admit that Mrs Gillespie's reading of Dr Blakeney's character was that she would honour some of the undertakings Mrs Gillespie made to you and your daughter, but I must stress that Dr Blakeney is not obliged to do so. There is nothing in the will to that effect. She is free to interpret your mother's wishes any way she chooses, and if she believes that she can promote something worth-while in Mrs Gillespie's memory by ignoring you and building a clinic in this village instead, then she is entitled to do so.'

There was another silence. Sarah looked up from a prolonged study of the carpet to discover all their eyes upon her. She found herself echoing Ruth's words. *What a frigging awful joke.* 'Thursday,' she said with a sigh. 'I'll come to your office on Thursday and I shall probably bring my own solicitor with me. I'm not happy about this, Mr Duggan.'

'Poor Dr Blakeney,' said Joanna with a tight smile. 'I do believe you're finally beginning to realize what a ruthless bitch my mother was. From the moment she seduced Gerald, she had her hands on the Cavendish purse strings and she kept them there, through threats and blackmail, upwards of fifty years.' A look of compassion crossed her curiously impassive face. 'And now she's appointed you to carry on her tyranny. The dictator is dead.' She gave a small, ironic bow. 'Long live the dictator.'

Sarah stood by Paul Duggan's car as he packed the video recorder into the boot. 'Have the police seen that film?' she asked him as he straightened up.

'Not yet. I've an appointment with a Sergeant Cooper in half an hour or so. I'll give him a copy then.'

'Shouldn't you have shown it to them straight away? Mathilda didn't sound to me like a woman who was about to commit suicide. *I must have died without changing my mind* . . . She wouldn't have said that if she was planning to kill herself two days later.'

'I agree.'

His moon face beamed at her and she frowned her irritation. 'You're very relaxed about it,' she said tartly. 'I hope, for your sake, DS Cooper understands why you've delayed producing it. I certainly don't. Mathilda's been dead two weeks and the police have been tying themselves in knots trying to find evidence of murder.'

'Not my fault, Dr Blakeney,' he said amiably. 'It's been with the film company who made it for the last two weeks, waiting to have titles and music added. Mrs Gillespie wanted Verdi playing in the background.' He chuckled. 'She chose *Dies Irae* – The Day of Wrath. Rather appropriate, don't you think?' He paused briefly, waiting for a reaction, but she was in no mood to oblige. 'Anyway, she wanted to vet it afterwards and they told her to come back in a month for a viewing. These things can't be hurried, I gather. They were very put out to hear from me that she was already dead. All of which lends weight to your argument, that she wasn't planning to kill herself.' He shrugged. 'I wasn't there when she made it, so I didn't know what was in it. As far as I was concerned it was a message to her family. I saw it for the first time last night, at which point I rang for an appointment with the boys in blue.' He glanced at his watch. 'And I'm going to be late. I'll see you on Thursday, then.'

Sarah watched him drive away with a horrible feeling of insecurity chewing at the pit of her stomach. She should have guessed, prepared herself a little. *Talk to Dr Blakeney. She will know what to do for the best.* And what about Jack? Had *he* known?

She felt suddenly very lonely.

Sarah was raking up leaves when DS Cooper arrived that afternoon. He picked his way across the grass and stood watching her. 'Hard work,' he murmured sympathetically.

'Yes.' She propped the rake against a tree and thrust her hands into her Barbour pockets. 'We'd better go in. It's warmer inside.'

'Don't worry on my account,' he said. 'I'd just as soon stay out and have a smoke.' He fished a crumpled pack of Silk Cut from inside his coat and lit up with obvious enjoyment. 'Disgusting habit,' he murmured, eyeing her warily. 'I'll give it up one day.'

Sarah lifted an amused eyebrow. 'Why are smokers always so consumed with guilt?'

'Cigarettes reveal the weakness of our character,' he said morosely. 'Other people give up, but we can't. To tell you the truth I've never understood why society treats us like pariahs. I've yet to meet the smoker who's beaten his wife after one too many fags or killed a child while in charge of a car, but I could show you a hundred drunks who've done it. I'd say drink is a far more dangerous drug than nicotine.'

She led him to a bench seat beside the path. 'The moral majority will get round to condemning the drinkers, too, eventually,' she said. 'And then the whole world will be jogging around in its vest and pants, bristling with good health, eating vegetables, drinking carrot juice and never doing anything remotely detrimental to its health.'

He chuckled. 'Shouldn't you applaud that, as a doctor?'

'I'll be out of a job.' She leant her head against the back of the seat. 'Anyway, I have a problem with the moral majority. I don't like it. I'd rather have free-thinking individuals any day than politically correct mobs who behave the way they're told to because somebody else has decided what's socially acceptable.'

'Is that why you liked Mrs Gillespie?'

'Probably.'

'Tell me about her.'

'I can't really add anything to what I've told you already. She was quite the most extraordinary person I've ever met. Completely cynical. She had no respect for anyone or anything. She didn't believe in God or retribution. She loathed mankind in general and the people of Fontwell in particular, and she considered everybody, past and present, beneath her. The only exception to that was Shakespeare. She thought Shakespeare was a towering genius.' She fell silent.

'And you *liked* her?'

Sarah laughed. 'I suppose I enjoyed the anarchy of it all. She put into words what most of us only think. I can't explain it any better than that. I always looked forward to seeing her.'

'It must have been mutual or she wouldn't have left you her money.'

Sarah didn't answer immediately. 'I had no idea what she was planning,' she said after a moment or two. She thrust a hand into her hair, fluffing it skyward. 'It's come as a nasty shock. I feel I'm being manipulated and I don't like that.'

He nodded. 'According to Duggan, Mrs Gillespie instructed the two executors to keep the whole thing secret.' He examined the glowing tip of his cigarette. 'The trouble is, we can't be sure that she herself didn't tell someone.'

'If she had,' said Sarah, 'she would probably still be alive. Assuming she was murdered, of course.'

'Meaning whoever killed her didn't know you were the beneficiary but thought they were?'

She nodded. 'Something like that.'

'Then it must have been the daughter or the granddaughter.'

'It depends what was in the previous will. She may have made other bequests. People have been murdered for far tinier amounts than Joanna or Ruth were expecting to get.'

'But that's assuming she was murdered for her money. It's also assuming that neither you nor anyone dependent on you murdered her.'

'True,' she said unemotionally.

'Did you murder her, Dr Blakeney?'

'I wouldn't have done it that way, Sergeant. I would have taken my time.' She gave a light chuckle. A little forced, he thought. 'There was no hurry, after all. I've no outstanding debts and I certainly wouldn't want to link her death so closely to a will changed in my favour.' She bent forward, clasping her hands between her knees. 'And it would have looked very natural, too. Doctors have a built-in advantage when it comes to committing the perfect murder. A period of illness, followed by a gentle death. Nothing so dramatic or traumatic as slitting the wrists while wearing an instrument of torture.'

'It might be a magnificent bluff,' he said mildly. 'As you say, who would suspect a doctor of doing something so crass within hours of an old lady making over three-quarters of a million pounds?'

Sarah stared at him with undisguised horror. 'Three-quarters of a million?' she echoed slowly. 'Is that what she was worth?'

'More or less. Probably more. It's a conservative estimate. Duggan's valued the house and its contents at around four hundred thousand, but the clocks alone were insured for well over a hundred thousand and that was based on a ten-year-old valuation. I'd hate to guess what they're worth now. Then there's the antique furniture, her jewellery and, of course, Mrs Lascelles's flat in London, plus innumerable stocks and shares. You're a rich woman, Dr Blakeney.'

Sarah put her head in her hands. 'Oh, my God!' she groaned. 'You mean, Joanna doesn't even own her own flat?'

'No. It's part of Mrs Gillespie's estate. If the old woman had had any sense she'd have made it over to her daughter in annual dollops to avoid anyone having to pay inheritance tax on it. As it is, the Treasury's going to have almost as big a windfall as you're getting.' He sounded sympathetic. 'And it'll be your job to decide what has to be sold off to pay the bill. You're not going to be very popular with the Lascelles women, I suspect.'

'That must be the understatement of the year,' said Sarah bleakly. 'What on earth was Mathilda thinking of?'

'Most people would see it as manna from heaven.'

'Including you?'

'Of course, but then I live in a very ordinary house, I've three grown-up children who touch me for money whenever they can, and I dream about retiring early and taking the wife on an extended cruise round the world.' He glanced about the garden. 'In your shoes, I'd probably react as you are reacting. You're not exactly short of a bob or two, and your conscience will stop you spending it on yourself. She was right when she said she was laying a burden on your shoulders.'

Sarah digested this for a moment or two in silence. 'Does that mean you don't think I murdered her?'

He looked amused. 'Probably.'

'Well, thank God for small mercies,' she said dryly. 'It's been worrying me.'

'Your dependants, however, are a different matter. They stand to benefit just as much as you do from Mrs Gillespie's death.'

She looked surprised. 'I don't have any dependants.'

'You have a husband, Dr Blakeney. I'm told he's dependent on you.'

She stirred some leaves with the toe of her wellington boot. 'Not any more. We're separated. I don't even know where he is at the moment.'

He took out his notebook and consulted it. 'That must be fairly recent then. According to Mrs Lascelles, he attended the funeral two days ago, went on to Cedar House afterwards for tea and then asked her to drive him back here at around six o'clock, which she did.' He paused to look at her. 'So when exactly did the separation begin?'

'He left some time that night. I found a note from him in the morning.'

'Was it his idea or yours?'

'Mine. I told him I wanted a divorce.'

'I see.' He regarded her thoughtfully. 'Was there a reason for choosing that night to do it?'

She sighed. 'I was depressed by Mathilda's funeral. I found myself exploring that old chestnut, the meaning of life, and I wondered what the point of *her* life was. I suddenly realized that my own life was almost as pointless.' She turned her head to look at him. 'You probably think that sounds absurd. I'm a doctor, after all, and you don't enter medicine without some sort of vocation. It's like police work. We're in it because we believe we can make a difference.' She gave a hollow laugh. 'There's an awful arrogance in a statement like that. The presumption is that we know what we're doing when, frankly, I'm not sure that we do. Doctors strive officiously to keep people alive, because the law says we must, and we talk grandly about quality of life. But what *is* quality of life? I kept Mathilda's pain under control with some sophisticated drugs but the quality of her life was appalling, not because of pain, but because she was lonely, bitter, intensely frustrated and very unhappy.' She shrugged. 'I took a long hard look at myself and my husband during the funeral, and I realized that the same adjectives could be applied to the two of us. We were both lonely, both bitter, both frustrated and both unhappy. So I suggested a divorce, and he left.' She smiled cynically. 'It was as simple as that.'

He felt sorry for her. Nothing was ever that simple, and it sounded to him as if she had tried to bluff a hand at poker, and lost. 'Had he met Mrs Lascelles before the funeral?'

'Not as far as I know. *I* hadn't, so I can't imagine how he could have done.'

'But he knew Mrs Gillespie?'

She looked out across the garden, playing for time. 'If he did, then it wasn't through me. He never mentioned meeting her.'

DS Cooper's already lively interest in the absent Jack Blakeney was growing. 'Why did he go to the funeral?'

'Because I asked him to.' She straightened. 'I hate funerals but I always feel I have to go to them. It seems so churlish to turn your back on a patient the minute they're dead. Jack was very good about lending support.' Unexpectedly, she laughed. 'To tell you the truth, I think he rather fancies himself in his black overcoat. He enjoys looking satanic.'

Satanic. The Sergeant pondered over the word. Duncan Orloff had said Mathilda liked Blakeney. Mrs Lascelles had described him as 'a peculiar man who said very little and then demanded to be taken home'. Ruth had found him 'intimidating'. The vicar, on the other hand, had had a great deal to say when Cooper had approached him about the various members of the funeral congregation. 'Jack Blakeney? He's an artist though not a very successful one, poor chap. If it wasn't for Sarah, he'd be starving. Matter of fact, I like his work. I'd buy a canvas if only he'd lower his sights a little, but he knows his worth, or says he does, and refuses to sell himself cheap. Did he know Mathilda? Yes, he must have done. I saw him leaving her house one day with his sketchpad under his arm. She'd have been a wonderful subject for his type of work. He couldn't have resisted her.'

He took the bull by the horns. 'The Reverend Matthews tells me your husband was painting a portrait of Mrs Gillespie. He must have known her quite well to do that.' He lit another cigarette and watched Sarah through the smoke.

She sat for a long time in silence, contemplating a distant cow in a far field. 'I feel inclined to say I won't answer any more questions until my solicitor's present,' she murmured at last, 'except that I have a nasty feeling you'd regard that as suspicious.' He didn't say anything, so she glanced at him. There was no sympathy in the pleasant face, only a patient confidence that she would answer in the affirmative, with or without a solicitor. She sighed. 'I could deny a portrait quite easily. They're all in the studio, and there isn't a chance in a million you'd recognize Mathilda's. Jack doesn't paint faces. He paints personalities. And you have to understand his colour-coding and the way he uses dynamics in shape, depth and perspective to interpret what he's done.'

'But you're not going to deny it?' he suggested.

'Only because Jack won't, and I'm not particularly keen to perjure myself.' She smiled and her eyes lit with enthusiasm. 'Actually, it's brilliant. I think it's probably the best thing he's ever done. I found it yesterday just before you came.' She pulled a wry face. 'I knew it would be there because of something Ruth said. According to her, Jack mentioned that Mathilda called me her scold's bridle.' She sighed again. 'And he couldn't have known that unless Mathilda had told him, because I never did.'

'May I see this painting?'

She ignored the question. 'He wouldn't have murdered her, Sergeant, not for money, anyway. Jack despises materialism. The only use he has for money is as a guide to the value of his genius. Which is why he never sells anything. His own valuation of his art is rather higher than everybody else's.' She smiled at his frown of disbelief. 'Actually, it makes sense in a funny sort of way, but it's irritating because it's so conceited. The argument goes something like this: your average prole is incapable of recognizing genius so he won't be interested in buying your picture whatever price you put on it. While a Renaissance man, on the other hand, will recognize genius and will pay handsomely for it. Ergo, if you're a genius, you put a high price on yourself and wait for the right person to come and discover you.'

'If you'll pardon the language, Dr Blakeney, that is bullshit.' He felt quite angry. 'The man's conceit must be colossal. Has anyone else said he's a genius?'

'No one said Van Gogh was a genius either until after he was dead.' Why, she wondered, did Jack's single-minded view of himself always put people's backs up? Was it because, in an uncertain world, his certainty was threatening? 'It really doesn't matter,' she said calmly, 'what sort of an artist Jack is. Good, bad, indifferent. I happen to think he's good, but that's a personal opinion. The point is he would never have killed Mathilda for her money, assuming he knew she'd made the will in my favour, which I doubt. Why should she have told him when she never told me?'

'Except that he thought you were going to divorce him and push him into the cold.'

'Hardly. That would leave me enjoying the loot all by myself, wouldn't it? How could he get his hands on the inheritance if he and I were divorced?' *I'll be going for a fifty-fifty split* . . . She pushed that thought away. 'And in any case, two weeks ago when Mathilda died, he didn't know I wanted to divorce him. How could he? I didn't know myself.'

Cooper took that with a pinch of salt. 'These things don't happen out of the blue, Dr Blakeney. He must have had an inkling that the marriage was in difficulties.'

'You're underestimating Jack's egotism,' she answered with a somewhat bitter irony. 'He's far too self-centred to notice anyone else's unhappiness unless he's painting them. Believe me, my decision *did* come out of the blue. For him, anyway.'

He puffed thoughtfully on his cigarette. 'Do you expect him to come back at all?'

'Oh, yes. He'll want to collect his paintings if nothing else.'

'Good. Some of the fingerprints we lifted may well be his. It will help if we can eliminate them. Yours, too, of course. There'll be a team taking prints in Fontwell on Wednesday morning. I assume you've no objections to giving yours? They'll be destroyed afterwards.' He took her silence for assent. 'You say you don't know where your husband is, but can you think of anyone who might be in contact with him?'

'Only my solicitor. He's promised to let me know the minute he hears anything.'

The Sergeant dropped his cigarette end on to the damp grass and stood up, drawing his mackintosh about him. 'No friends he might have gone to?'

'I've tried everyone I can think of. He's not been in touch with any of them.'

'Then perhaps you'll be so kind as to write out your solicitor's name and phone number while I take a look at this painting.' He grinned. 'In view of what you've said, I'm fascinated to see if I can make anything of it.'

Sarah found his careful appraisal of the picture rather impressive. He stood for a long time without saying anything, then asked her if Jack had done a portrait of her. She fetched hers from the drawing-room and placed it alongside the one of Mathilda. He resumed his silent study.

'Well,' he said at last, 'you're quite right. I would never have guessed that this was a portrait of Mrs Gillespie, any more than I would have guessed that that was a portrait of you. I can see why no one else considers him a genius.'

Sarah's disappointment surprised her. But what had she

expected? He was a country policeman, not a Renaissance man. She forced the polite smile to her lips that was her customary response to other people's often rude comments on Jack's paintings and wondered, not for the first time, why she was the only person who seemed able to appreciate them. It wasn't as if she were blinded by love – rather the reverse in fact – and yet, to her, the portrait of Mathilda was extraordinary and brilliant. Jack had worked layer on layer to bring a deep golden translucence into the heart of the painting – Mathilda's wit, she thought, shining through the complex blues and greys of cruelty and cynicism. And round it all the browns of despair and repression, and the rusted red of iron, shorthand in Jack's work for backbone and character, but moulded here into the shape of the scold's bridle.

She shrugged. After all, perhaps it was a mercy the Sergeant couldn't see it. 'As I said, he paints personalities and not faces.'

'When did he paint the one of you?'

'Six years ago.'

'And has your personality changed in six years?'

'I shouldn't think so. Personalities change very little, Sergeant, which is why Jack likes to paint them. You are what you are. A generous person remains generous. A bully remains a bully. You can smooth the rough edges but you can't transform the core. Once painted, the personality should be recognizable for ever.'

He rubbed his hands together in anticipation of a challenge. 'Then let's see if I can work out his system. There's a lot of green in yours and your most obvious characteristics are sympathy – no – ' he contradicted himself immediately, 'empathy – you enter into other people's feelings, you don't make a judgement on them. So, empathy, honour – you're an honourable woman or you wouldn't feel so racked with guilt about this bequest – truthful – most people would have lied about this painting – nice.' He turned to look at her. 'Does niceness count as a personality trait or is it too flabby?'

She laughed. 'Far too flabby, and you're ignoring the unpleasant aspects. Jack sees two sides to everybody.'

'All right.' He stared at her portrait. 'You're a very opinionated woman who is confident enough to fly in the face of established fact, otherwise you wouldn't have liked Mrs Gillespie. A corollary to that is that you are also naïve or your views wouldn't be so divergent from everyone else's. You're inclined to be rash or you wouldn't be regretting your husband's departure, and that implies a depth of affection for hopeless causes which is probably why you became a doctor and probably, too, why you were so fond of the old bitch in this amazing painting next to you. How am I doing for a prole?'

She gave a surprised chuckle. 'Well, I don't think you are a prole,' she said. 'Jack would adore you. Renaissance man in all his glory. They are good, aren't they?'

'How much does he charge for them?'

'He's only ever sold one. It was a portrait of one of his lovers. He got ten thousand pounds for it. The man who bought it was a Bond Street dealer, who said Jack was the most exciting artist he'd ever come across. We thought our ship had come in, then three months later the poor soul was dead, and no one's expressed an interest since.'

'That's not true. The Reverend Matthews told me he'd

buy a canvas like a shot if they were cheaper. Come to that, so would I. Has he ever done a man and wife? I'd go to two thousand for me and the old girl over the mantelpiece.' He studied Mathilda closely. 'I take it the gold is her one redeeming feature of humour. My old lady's a laugh a minute. She'd be gold through and through. I'd love to see it.'

There was a sound behind them. 'And what colour would you be?' asked Jack's amused voice.

Sarah's heart leapt, but Sergeant Cooper only eyed him thoughtfully for a moment or two. 'Assuming I've interpreted these pictures correctly, sir, I'd say a blend of blues and purples, for hard-headed cynicism-cum-realism, common to your wife and Mrs Gillespie, some greens which I think must represent the decency and honour of Dr Blakeney because they are markedly absent from Mrs Gillespie's portrait,' he smiled, 'and a great deal of black.'

'Why black?'

'Because I'm in the dark,' he said with ponderous humour, fishing his warrant card from his inside pocket. 'Detective Sergeant Cooper, sir, Learmouth Police. I'm enquiring into the death of Mrs Mathilda Gillespie of Cedar House, Fontwell. Perhaps you'd like to tell me why she sat for you with the scold's bridle on her head? In view of the way she died, I find that fascinating.'

Arthritis is a brute. It makes one so vulnerable. If I were a less cynical woman, I would say Sarah has the gift of healing, though, frankly, I'm inclined to think anyone would have been an improvement on that old fool, Hendry. He was lazy, of course, and didn't bother to keep up his reading. Sarah tells me there have been huge advances in the field which he obviously knew nothing about. I am rather inclined to sue, if not on my own behalf, then on Joanna's. Clearly, it was he who set her on the path to addiction.

Sarah asked me today how I was, and I answered with a line from King Lear: *'I grow; I prosper. Now, gods, stand up for bastards.' She quite naturally assumed I was referring to myself, laughed good-naturedly and said: 'A bitch, possibly, Mathilda, but never a bastard. There's only one bastard I know, and that's Jack.' I asked her what he had done to deserve such an appellation. 'He takes my love for granted,' she said, 'and offers his to anyone who's foolish enough to flatter him.'*

How very flawed are human relationships. This is

not a Jack I recognize. He guards his love as jealously as he guards his art. The truth, I think, is that Sarah perceives both herself and him 'through a glass darkly'. She believes he strays, but only, I suspect, because she insists on using his effect on women as a criterion by which to judge him. His passions frighten her because they exist outside her control, and she is less adept than she thinks she is at seeing where he directs them.

I adore the man. He encourages me to 'dare damnation', for what is life if it is not a rebellion against death . . .

Six

VIOLET ORLOFF stood motionless in the kitchen of Wing Cottage, listening to the row that had broken out in the hall of Cedar House. She had the guilty look of an eavesdropper, torn between going and staying, but, unlike most eavesdroppers, she was free of the fear of discovery, and curiosity won out. She took a glass from the dishwasher, placed the rim against the wall, then pressed her ear to the base. The voices drew closer immediately. Perhaps it was a mercy she couldn't see herself. There was something indecent and furtive about the way she bent to listen, and her face wore the same expression that a Peeping Tom might wear as he peers through a window to see a woman in the nude. Excited. Leering. Expectant.

'. . . think I don't know what you do in London? You're a fucking whore, and Granny knew it, too. It's your bloody fault all this, and now you're planning to whore him, I suppose, to cut me out.'

'Don't you dare speak to me like that. I've a damn good mind to wash my hands of you. Do you think I care tuppence whether you get to university or not?'

'That's you every time. Jealousy, jealousy, fucking

JEALOUSY! You can't stand me doing anything you didn't do.'

'I'm warning you, Ruth, I won't listen to this.'

'Why not? Because it's true, and the truth hurts?' The girl's voice was tearful. 'Why can't you behave like a mother sometimes? Granny was more of a mother than you are. All you've ever done is hate me. I didn't ask to be born, did I?'

'That's childish.'

'You hate me because my father loved me.'

'Don't be absurd.'

'It's true. Granny told me. She said Steven used to moon over me, calling me his angel, and you used to fly into a temper. She said if you and Steven had got a divorce, then Steven wouldn't be dead.'

Joanna's voice was icy. 'And you believed her, of course, because it's what you wanted to hear. You're your grandmother all over again, Ruth. I thought there'd be an end of it once she was dead but I couldn't have been more wrong, could I? You've inherited every drop of poison that was in her.'

'Oh, that's great! Walk away, just like you always do. When are you going to face up to a problem, Mother, instead of pretending it doesn't exist? Granny always said that was your one true accomplishment, to brush every unpleasantness under the carpet, and then carry on as if nothing had happened. For Christ's SAKE' – her voice rose to a shout – 'YOU HEARD THE DETECTIVE.' She must have caught her mother's attention because her tone dropped again. 'The police think Granny was murdered. So what am I supposed to tell them?'

'The truth.'

Ruth gave a wild laugh. 'Fine. So I tell them what you spend your money on, do I? I tell them Granny and Dr Hendry thought you were so bloody mad they were thinking of having you committed? Jesus' – her voice broke – 'I suppose I might just as well be really honest and tell them how you tried to kill me. Or do I keep quiet because if I don't we won't have a hope in hell's chance of putting in a counter-claim for the money? You're not allowed to benefit from the murder of your mother, you know.'

The silence went on for so long that Violet Orloff began to wonder if they had moved to another part of the house.

'It's entirely up to you, Ruth. I've no compunction at all about saying you were here the day your grandmother died. You shouldn't have stolen her earrings, you stupid little bitch. Or, for that matter, every other damn thing your sticky little fingers couldn't resist. You knew her as well as I did. Did you really think she wouldn't notice?' Joanna's voice grated with sarcasm. 'She made a list and left it in her bedside drawer. If I hadn't destroyed it you'd be under arrest by now. You're making no secret of your panic over this idiotic will, so the police will have no trouble believing that if you were desperate enough to steal from your grandmother, you were probably desperate enough to murder her as well. So I suggest we both keep our mouths shut, don't you?'

A door was slammed so forcefully that Violet felt the vibrations in her kitchen.

Jack perched on his stool and rubbed his unshaven jaw, squinting at the policeman through half-closed lids. Satanic, thought DS Cooper, suited him well. He was very dark with glittering eyes in a hawklike face, but there were too many laughter-lines for a Dracula. If this man was a devil, he was a merry one. He reminded Cooper of an unrepentant Irish recidivist he had arrested on innumerable occasions over a period of twenty years. There was the same 'take-me-as-I-am' expression, a look of such startling challenge that people who had it were impossible to ignore. He wondered with sudden curiosity if the same expression had looked out of Mathilda Gillespie's eyes. He hadn't noticed it on the video, but then the camera invariably lied. If it didn't, no one would tolerate having their picture taken.

'I'll do it,' said Jack abruptly.

The policeman frowned. 'Do what, Mr Blakeney?'

'Paint you and your wife for two thousand pounds, but I'll string you up from a lamp-post if you tell anyone what you're paying.' He stretched his arms towards the ceiling, easing the muscles of his back. 'I'd say two thousand from you is worth ten thousand any day from the likes of Mathilda. Perhaps a sliding scale isn't such a bad idea, after all. It should be the dent in the sitter's pocket that sets the value on the painting, not my arbitrary pricing of my worth.' He raised sardonic eyebrows. 'What right have I to deprive impoverished vicars and policemen of things of beauty? You'd agree with that, wouldn't you, Sarah?'

She shook her head at him. 'Why do you always have to be so offensive?'

'The man likes my work, so I'm offering him a subsidized portrait of himself and the wife in blues, purples, greens and golds. What's offensive about that? I'd call it a compliment.'

He eyed Cooper with amusement. 'Purples represent your libido, by the way. The deeper they are, the randier you are, but it's how I see you, remember, not how you see yourself. Your wife might have her illusions shattered if I paint you in deep purple and her in pale lilac.'

Sergeant Cooper chuckled. 'Or vice versa.'

Jack's eyes gleamed. 'Precisely. I don't set out to flatter anyone. As long as you understand that, we can probably do business.'

'And presumably, sir, you need the money at the moment. Would your terms be cash in advance, by any chance?'

Jack bared his teeth in a grin. 'Of course. At that price you could hardly expect anything else.'

'And what guarantee would I have that the portrait would ever be finished?'

'My word. As a man of honour.'

'I'm a policeman, Mr Blakeney. I never take anyone's word for anything.' He turned to Sarah. 'You're a truthful woman, Doctor. Is your husband a man of honour?'

She looked at Jack. 'That's a very unfair question.'

'Sounds fair to me,' said Jack. 'We're talking two thousand pounds here. The Sergeant's entitled to cover himself. Give him an answer.'

Sarah shrugged. 'All right. If you're asking me: will he take your money and run? Then, no, he won't. He'll paint your picture for you, and he'll do it well.'

'But?' prompted Jack.

'You're not a man of honour. You're far too thoughtless and inconsiderate. You respect no one's opinion but your own, you're disloyal, and you're insensitive. In fact,' she gave him a twisted smile, 'you're a shit about everything but your art.'

Jack tipped a finger to the policeman. 'So, do I have a commission, Sergeant, or were you simply working on my wife's susceptibilities to get her to spill the beans about me?'

Cooper pulled forward a chair and offered it to Sarah. She shook her head so he sat in it himself with a faint sigh of relief. He was getting too old to stand when there was a seat available. 'I'll be honest with you, sir, I can't commission anything from you at the moment.'

'I knew it,' said Jack contemptuously. 'You're just like that slime-ball Matthews.' He aped the vicar's sing-song Welsh accent. 'I do love your work, Jack, and no mistake, but I'm a poor man as you know.' He slammed his fist into his palm. 'So I offered him one of my early ones for a couple of thousand, and the bastard tried to negotiate me down to three miserable hundred. Jesus wept!' he growled. 'He gets paid more than that for a few lousy sermons.' He glared at the Sergeant. 'Why do you all expect something for nothing? I don't see you taking a pay cut,' he flicked a glance at Sarah, 'or my wife either for that matter. But then the state pays you while I have to graft for myself.'

It was on the tip of Cooper's tongue to point out that Blakeney had chosen the path he was following, and had not been forced down it. But he refrained. He had had too many bruising arguments with his children on the very same subject to want to repeat them with a stranger. In any case, the man had misunderstood him. Deliberately, he suspected. 'I am not in a position to commission anything from you *at the moment*, sir,' he said with careful emphasis, 'because you were closely connected with a woman who may or may not have been murdered. Were I to give you money, for whatever reason, it would be extremely prejudicial to your chances in court if you were unfortunate enough to appear there. It will be a different matter entirely when our investigations are concluded.'

Jack eyed him with sudden fondness. 'If *I* paid *you* two thousand, you might have a point, but not the other way round. It's your position you're safeguarding, not mine.'

Cooper chuckled again. 'Do you blame me? It's probably empty optimism, but I haven't quite given up on promotion, and back-handers to murder suspects would go down like a lead balloon with my governor. The future looks a lot brighter if you make Inspector.'

Jack studied him intently for several seconds, then crossed his arms over his tatty jumper. He found himself warming to this rotund, rather untypical detective with his jolly smile. 'So what was your question? Why did Mathilda sit for me with the scold's bridle on her head?' He looked at the portrait. 'Because she said it represented the essence of her personality. She was right, too.' His eyes narrowed in recollection. 'I suppose the easy way to describe her is to say she was repressed, but the repression worked both ways.' He smiled faintly. 'Perhaps it always does. She was abused as a child and grew up incapable of feeling or expressing love, so became an abuser herself. And the symbol of her abuse, both active and passive, was the bridle. It was strapped to her and she strapped it to her daughter.' His eyes flickered towards his wife. 'The irony is that it was also a symbol of her love, I think, or those cessations from hostility that passed for love in Mathilda's life. She called Sarah her scold's bridle and she meant it as a compliment. She said Sarah was the only person she had ever met who came to her without prejudice and took her as she was.' He grinned amiably. 'I tried to explain that that was hardly something to applaud – Sarah has many weaknesses, but the worst in my view is her naïve willingness to accept everyone at his or her own valuation – but Mathilda wouldn't have a word spoken against her. And that's all I know,' he finished ingenuously.

DS Cooper decided privately that Jack Blakeney was probably one of the least ingenuous men he had ever met, but he played along with him for disingenuous reasons of his own. 'That's very helpful, sir. I never knew Mrs Gillespie myself, and it's important for me to understand her character. Would you say she was the type to commit suicide?'

'Without a doubt. And she'd do it with a Stanley knife, too. She found as much enjoyment in making an exit as she did in making an entrance. Possibly more. If she's looking at the three of us now, picking over the bones of her demise, she'll be hugging herself with delight. She was talked about in life because she was a bitch, but that's nothing to the way she's being talked about in death. She'd love every cliff-hanging moment of it.'

Cooper frowned at Sarah. 'Do you agree, Dr Blakeney?'

'It has an absurd sort of logic, you know. She *was* like that.' She thought for a moment or two. 'But she didn't believe in an afterlife, or only the maggot variety which means we're all cannibals.' She smiled at Cooper's expression of distaste. 'A man dies and is eaten by maggots, the maggots are eaten by birds, the birds are eaten by cats, the cats defecate on the vegetables and we eat the vegetables. Or any permutation you like.' She smiled again. 'I'm sorry, but that was Mathilda's view of death. Why would she waste her last, great exit? I honestly believe she would have prolonged it for all it was worth and, in the process, made as many people wriggle as she could. Take that video, for example. Why did she want music and credits added if it was only to be shown after she was dead? She was going to watch it herself, and if someone walked in while she was doing it, then so much the better. She meant to use it as a stick to beat Joanna and Ruth with. I'm right, aren't I, Jack?'

'Probably. You usually are.' He spoke without irony. 'Which video are we talking about?'

She had forgotten he hadn't seen it. 'Mathilda's posthumous message to her family,' she said, with a shake of her head. 'You'd have loved it, by the way. She looked rather like Cruella De Vil out of *The Hundred and One Dalmatians*. Dyed black wings on either side of a white streak, nose like a beak, and mouth a thin line. Very paintable.' She frowned. 'Why didn't you tell me you knew her?'

'You'd have interfered.'

'How?'

'You'd have found a way,' he said. 'I can't paint them when you bleat your interpretations of them into my ear.' He spoke in a mocking falsetto. 'But I like her, Jack. She's really very nice. She's not half as bad as everyone says. She's a softy at heart.'

'I never talk like that,' said Sarah dismissively.

'You should listen to yourself once in a while. The dark side of people scares you, so you close your eyes to it.'

'Is that a bad thing?'

He shrugged. 'Not if you want existence without passion.'

She studied him thoughtfully for a moment. 'If passion means confrontation, then yes, I prefer existence without passion. I lived through the disintegration of my parents' marriage, remember. I'd go a long way to avoid repeating that experience.'

His eyes sparkled in his tired face. 'Then perhaps it's your own dark side that scares you. Is there a fire in there waiting to blaze out of control? A scream of frustration that will topple your precarious house of cards? You'd better pray for gentle breezes and no strong winds, my angel, or you'll find you've been living in a fool's paradise.'

She didn't respond and the room fell silent, its three occupants curiously abstracted like the portraits round the walls. It occurred to DS Cooper, fixed in fascinated immobility upon his chair, that Jack Blakeney was a terrible man. Did he devour everyone in the way he was devouring his wife? *A scream of frustration that will topple your precarious house of cards.* Cooper had held his own scream in check for years, the scream of a man caught in the toils of rectitude and responsibility. Why couldn't Jack Blakeney do the same?

He cleared his throat. 'Did Mrs Gillespie ever tell you, sir, what her intentions were with regard to her will?'

Jack had been watching Sarah intently. He glanced now

114

towards the policeman. 'Not in so many words. She asked me once what I would do if I had her money.'

'What did you say?'

'I said I'd spend it.'

'Your wife told me you despise materialism.'

'Quite right, so I'd use it to enhance my spirituality.'

'How?'

'I'd blow the lot on drugs, alcohol and sex.'

'Sounds very materialistic to me, sir. There's nothing spiritual about surrendering to the senses.'

'It depends who you follow. If you're a Stoic like Sarah, your spiritual development comes through duty and responsibility. If you're an Epicurean like me, though I hasten to say poor old Epicurus probably wouldn't recognize me as an adherent, it comes through the gratification of desire.' He arched an amused eyebrow. 'Unfortunately, we modern Epicureans are frowned upon. There's something infinitely despicable about a man who refuses to acknowledge his responsibilities but prefers to fill his cup at the fountain of pleasure.' He was watching Cooper closely. 'But that's only because society is composed of sheep and sheep are easily brainwashed by advertisers' propaganda. They may not believe that the whiteness of a woman's wash is a symbol of her success, but they sure as hell believe that their kitchens should be as germ-free, their smiles as white, their children as well-mannered, their husbands as hard-working, and their moral decency as obvious. With men it's lager. It's supposed to persuade them they have balls, but all it really persuades them to do is wear a clean jumper, shave regularly, have at least three friends, never get drunk and talk amusingly in the pub.' His grim face cracked into a smile. 'My problem is, I'd rather be stoned out of my mind and rogering a sixteen-year-old virgin any day, particularly if I have to take off her gym slip slowly to do it.'

Christ, thought Cooper in alarm, feeling the weight of the other's gaze upon his bent head. Could the bastard read minds as well? He made a pretence of writing something on his notepad. 'Did you explain all that as graphically to Mrs Gillespie or did you just stick with the spending of her money if you had it?'

Jack glanced at Sarah, but she was staring at Mathilda's portrait and didn't look up. 'She had great skin for her age. I expect I said I'd rather be stoned and rogering a granny.'

Cooper, who was far more respectable than he realized, was shocked into looking up. 'What did she say?'

Jack was enjoying himself. 'She asked me if I'd like to paint her in the nude. I said I would, so she took her clothes off. If it's of any interest to you, the only thing Mathilda was wearing when I made my sketches of her was the scold's bridle.' He smiled, his perceptive eyes searching the policeman's. 'Does that excite you, Sergeant?'

'It does as a matter of fact,' said Cooper evenly. 'Would she also have been in the bath by any chance?'

'No. She was very much alive and lying on her bed in all her glory.' He stood up and went to a chest in the corner. 'And she looked bloody fantastic.' He took a sketchpad from the bottom drawer. 'There.' He flung the pad across the room and it fluttered to the floor at the policeman's feet. 'Be my guest. They're all of Mathilda. One of life's great individuals.'

Cooper retrieved the pad and turned the pages. They did

indeed show Mrs Gillespie, nude upon her bed, but a very different Mrs Gillespie from the tragic cadaver in the bath or the bitter harridan with the cruel mouth on the television set. He laid the pad on the floor beside him. 'Did you sleep with her, Mr Blakeney?'

'No. She never asked me to.'

'Would you have done if she *had* asked you?' The question was out before Cooper had time to consider its wisdom.

Jack's expression was unreadable. 'Does that have a bearing on your case?'

'I'm interested in your character, Mr Blakeney.'

'I see. And what would my accepting an elderly woman's invitation to sleep with her tell you? That I was a pervert? Or that I was infinitely compassionate?'

Cooper gave a small laugh. 'I'd say it was an indication that you needed your eyes testing. Even in the dark, Mrs Gillespie could hardly have passed for a sixteen-year-old virgin.' He fished his cigarettes from his pocket. 'Do you mind?'

'Be my guest.' He kicked the wastepaper basket across the floor.

Cooper flicked his lighter to the cigarette. 'Mrs Gillespie has left your wife three-quarters of a million pounds, Mr Blakeney. Did you know?'

'Yes.'

The Sergeant hadn't expected that. 'So Mrs Gillespie *did* tell you what her intentions were?'

'No,' said Jack, resuming his seat on the stool. 'I've just spent a delightful two hours at Cedar House.' He stared impassively at Sarah. 'Joanna and Ruth are labouring under

117

the misapprehension that I have some influence over my wife so they put themselves out to be charming.'

Cooper scratched his jaw and wondered why Dr Blakeney put up with it. The man was toying with her in the way a sleek cat playfully inserts its claws into a half-mangled mouse. The mystery was not why she had decided to divorce him so suddenly, but why she had tolerated him for so long. Yet there was a sense of a challenge unmet, for a cat only remains interested while the mouse plays the game, and Cooper had the distinct impression that Jack felt Sarah was letting him down. 'Did you know before that?'

'No.'

'Are you surprised?'

'No.'

'Do your wife's patients often leave her money then?'

'Not as far as I know.' He grinned at the Sergeant. 'If they have, she's never told me.'

'Then why aren't you surprised?'

'Give me a good reason why I should be. If you'd told me Mathilda had left her money to the Police Benevolent Fund or New Age Travellers, that wouldn't have surprised me either. It was hers to do with as she liked, and good luck to her. Mind you, I'm glad it's the *wife*,' he put an offensive emphasis on the word, 'who hit the jackpot. It'll make things considerably easier for me. I don't mind admitting I'm a bit short at the moment.'

Sarah raked him from head to toe with angry eyes. 'My God, Jack, if you knew how close I am to sinking my fist into your self-satisfied gut.'

'Ah,' he murmured, 'passion at last.' He stood up and

approached her, spreading his hands wide in an invitation to do it. 'Feel free. It's all yours.'

She took him by surprise and kneed him in the groin instead. 'Next time,' she said through gritted teeth, 'I'll break Mathilda's canvas over your head. And that would be a shame because it's probably the best thing you've ever done.'

'GODDAMMIT, WOMAN, THAT HURT!' he roared, clutching his balls and collapsing back on to the stool. 'I asked for passion not fucking castration.'

Sarah's eyes narrowed. 'It was supposed to hurt, you cretin. Don't even think about getting your hands on Mathilda's money. You're certainly not getting any of mine if I can help it. Fifty–fifty? Fat – bloody – chance. I'll sell up and give it to a cats' home before I see you living the life of Riley on the back of my hard work.'

He poked his fingers into his Levi's pocket and removed a folded piece of paper. 'My contract with Mathilda,' he said, holding it out to her with one hand while he fondled himself gingerly with the other. 'The silly old sod snuffed it before she paid me, so I reckon her executors owe me ten thousand and her heir gets the painting. Jesus, Sarah, I feel really sick. I think you've done me some severe damage.'

She ignored him to read what was on the paper. 'This looks kosher,' she said.

'It *is* kosher. Keith drew it up.'

'He never told me.'

'Why should he? It was none of your business. I just hope I've got a claim on the estate. The way my luck's running, the contract's probably invalid because she's dead.'

Sarah passed the paper to DS Cooper. 'What do you think? It would be a shame if Jack's right. It's his second major sale.'

She was genuinely pleased for the bastard, Cooper thought in surprise. What a peculiar couple they were. He shrugged. 'I'm no expert but I've always understood that debts have to be met out of an estate. If you'd supplied her with new carpeting, which she hadn't paid for, the bill would presumably be honoured. I don't see why a painting should be any different, particularly one where the subject is the deceased. It's not as though you can sell it to anyone else, is it?' He glanced at the canvas. 'Bearing in mind, of course, you might have a problem proving it's Mrs Gillespie.'

'Where would I have to prove it? In court?'

'Possibly.'

His eyes gleamed as he clicked his fingers for the contract. 'I'm relying on you, Sarah,' he said, tucking the paper back into his pocket.

'To do what?'

'Tell the executors not to pay, of course. Say you don't think it's Mathilda. I need the publicity of a court battle.'

'Don't be stupid. I *know* it's Mathilda. If the contract's legally binding on her estate, they'll have to pay.'

But he wasn't listening. He tossed his paints, brushes and bottles of turpentine and linseed oil into a hold-all, then released the canvas of Joanna Lascelles from the easel. 'I've got to go. Look, I can't take the rest of this stuff because I haven't found a studio yet, but I'll try and get back for it during the week. Is that okay? I only came for some clothes. I've been sleeping in the car and this lot's a bit rank.' He padded towards the door, slinging the hold-all over his shoulder and carrying the painting in his hand.

'One moment, Mr Blakeney.' Cooper stood up to block his path. 'I haven't finished with you yet. Where were you on the night Mrs Gillespie died?'

Jack glanced at Sarah. 'I was in Stratford,' he said coolly, 'with an actress called Sally Bennedict.'

Cooper didn't look up, merely licked the point of his pencil and jotted the name on his pad. 'And how can I contact her?'

'Through the RSC. She's playing Juliet in one of their productions.'

'Thank you. Now, as someone with material evidence, I must warn you that if you intend to go on sleeping in your car then you will be required to present yourself at a police station every day, because if you don't I shall be forced to apply for a warrant. We also need your fingerprints so that we can isolate yours from the others we lifted in Cedar House. There will be a fingerprinting team in Fontwell Parish Hall on Wednesday morning but if you can't attend, I shall have to make arrangements for you to come to the station.'

'I'll be there.'

'And your whereabouts in the meantime, sir?'

'Care of Mrs Joanna Lascelles, Cedar House, Fontwell.' He booted open the door into the hall and eased through the gap. It was clearly something he had done many times before to judge by the dents and scratches on the paintwork.

'Jack!' Sarah called.

He turned to look at her. His eyebrows lifted enquiringly.

She nodded to the portrait of Mathilda. 'Congratulations.'

He flashed her an oddly intimate smile before letting the door slam behind him.

The two, left behind in the studio, listened to his footsteps on the stairs as he went in search of clothes. 'He's a law unto himself, isn't he?' said Cooper, drawing thoughtfully on his cigarette.

'One of life's great individuals,' Sarah said, consciously echoing Jack's description of Mathilda, 'and very difficult to live with.'

'I can see that.' He bent down to stub the butt against the rim of the wastepaper basket. 'But equally difficult to live *without*, I should imagine. He leaves something of a vacuum in his wake.'

Sarah turned away from him to look out of the window. She couldn't see anything, of course – it was now very dark outside – but the policeman could see her reflection in the glass as clearly as if it were a mirror. He would have done better, he thought, to keep his mouth shut but there was an openness about the Blakeneys that was catching.

'He's not always like that,' said Sarah. 'It's rare for him to be quite so forthcoming, but I'm not sure if that was for your benefit or mine.' She fell silent, aware that she was speaking her thoughts aloud.

'Yours, of course.'

They heard the front door open and close. 'Why "of course"?'

'I haven't hurt him.'

Their reflected eyes met in the window pane.

'Life's a bugger, isn't it, Sergeant?'

Joanna's demands on my purse are becoming insatiable. She says it's my fault that she's incapable of finding a job, my fault that her life's so empty, my fault that she had to marry Steven and my fault, too, that she was saddled with a baby she didn't want. I forbore to point out that she couldn't get into the Jew's bed quick enough or that the pill had been available for years before she allowed herself to get pregnant. I was tempted to catalogue the hells I went through — the rape of my innocence, marriage to a drunken pervert, a second pregnancy when I'd barely got over the first, the courage it took to climb out of an abyss of despair that she couldn't begin to imagine. I didn't, of course. She alarms me enough, as it is, with her frigid dislike of me and Ruth. I dread to think how she would react if she ever found out that Gerald was her father.

She says I'm a miser. Well, perhaps I am. Money has been a good friend to me and I guard it as jealously as others guard their secrets. God knows, I've had to use every ounce of cunning I possess to acquire it. If shrouds had pockets, I'd take it with me and 'to hell, allegiance!'

It is not we who owe our children but they who owe us. The only regret I have about dying is that I won't see Sarah's face when she learns what I've left her. That would, I think, be amusing.

Old Howard quoted Hamlet at me today: 'We go to gain a little patch of ground that hath no profit but the name.' I laughed – he is a most entertaining old brute at times – and answered from The Merchant: *'He is well paid who is well satisfied . . .'*

Seven

VIOLET ORLOFF sought out her husband in the sitting-room, where he was watching the early evening news on the television. She turned down the volume and placed her angular body in front of the screen.

'I was watching that,' he said in mild reproof.

She took no notice. 'Those awful women next door have been screaming at each other like a couple of fishwives, and I could hear every word. We should have taken the survey-or's advice and *insisted* on a double skin with soundproof-ing. What's going to happen if it's sold to hippies or people with young children? We'll be driven *mad* with their row.'

'Wait and see,' Duncan said, folding his plump hands in his ample lap. He could never understand how it was that old age, which had brought him serenity, had brought Violet only an aggressive frustration. He felt guilty about it. He knew he should never have brought her back to live in such close proximity with Mathilda. It was like placing a daisy beside an orchid and inviting comparisons.

She scowled at him. 'You can be so infuriating at times. If we wait and see, it'll be too late to do anything. I think we should demand that something be done *before* it's sold.'

'Have you forgotten,' he reminded her gently, 'that we were only able to afford this house in the first place precisely because there was no soundproofing and Mathilda agreed to a five thousand pound discount when the surveyor pointed out the deficiency? We're hardly in a position to demand anything.'

But Violet hadn't come in to discuss demands. 'Fishwives,' she said again, 'screaming at each other. The police now think Mathilda was *murdered*, apparently. And do you know what Ruth called her mother? A whore. She said she knew her mother was a whore in London. Rather *worse*, in fact. She said Joanna was,' her voice dropped to a whisper while her lips, in exaggerated movement, mouthed the words, 'a *fucking* whore.'

'Good lord,' said Duncan Orloff, startled out of his serenity.

'Quite. And Mathilda thought Joanna was mad, and she tried to murder Ruth, and she's spending her money on something she shouldn't and, worst of all, Ruth was in the house the night Mathilda died and she took Mathilda's earrings. *And*,' she said with particular emphasis, as if she hadn't already said 'and' several times, 'Ruth has stolen other things as well. They obviously haven't told the police any of it. I think we should report it.'

He looked slightly alarmed. 'Is it really any of our business, dear? We do have to go on living here, after all. I should hate any more unpleasantness.' What Duncan called serenity, others called apathy, and the hornets' nest stirred up two weeks ago by Jenny Spede's screams had been extremely unsettling.

She stared at him with shrewd little eyes. 'You've known

126

it was murder all along, haven't you? *And* you know who did it.'

'Don't be absurd,' he said, an edge of anger in his voice.

She stamped her foot angrily on the floor. 'Why do you insist on treating me like a child? Do you think I didn't *know*? I've known for forty years, you silly man. Poor Violet. Only second best. Always second best. What did she tell you, Duncan?' Her eyes narrowed to slits. 'She told you *something*. I know she did.'

'You've been drinking again,' he said coldly.

'You never accused Mathilda of drinking, but then *she* was perfect. Even drunk, Mathilda was perfect.' She tottered very slightly. '*Are* you going to report what I heard? Or will I have to do it? If Joanna or Ruth murdered her they don't deserve to get away with it. You're not going to tell me you don't care, I hope. I *know* you do.'

Of course he cared – it was only Violet for whom he felt a numbing indifference – but had she no sense of self-preservation? 'I don't imagine Mathilda was killed for fun,' he said, holding her gaze for a moment, 'so I do urge you to be very cautious in what you say and how you say it. On the whole I think it would be better if you left it to me.' He reached past her to switch up the volume on the television set. 'It's the weather forecast,' he pointed out, gesturing her gravely to one side, as if tomorrow's atmospheric pressures across the United Kingdom were of any interest to a fat, flabby old man who never stirred out of his armchair if he could possibly avoid it.

*

Ruth opened the door to Jack with a sullen expression in her dark eyes. 'I hoped you wouldn't come back,' she said bluntly. 'She always gets what she wants.'

He grinned at her. 'So do I.'

'Does your wife know you're here?'

He pushed past her into the hall, propping the canvas of Joanna against a wall and lowering the hold-all to the floor. 'Is that any of your business?'

She shrugged. 'She's the one with the money. We'll all lose out if you and Mum put her nose out of joint. You must be mad.'

He was amused. 'Are you expecting me to lick Sarah's arse so that you can live in clover for the rest of your life? Forget it, sweetheart. The only person I lick arse for is myself.'

'Don't call me sweetheart,' she snapped.

His eyes narrowed. 'Then don't judge me by your own standards. My best advice to you, Ruth, is to learn a little subtlety. There is no bigger turn-off than a blatant woman.'

For all her outward maturity, she was still a child. Her eyes filled. 'I hate you.'

He studied her curiously for a moment, then moved off in search of Joanna.

No one could accuse Joanna of being unsubtle. She was a woman of understatement, in words, dress and action. She sat now in the dimly lit drawing-room, a book open on her lap, face impassive, hair a silver halo in the light from the table lamp. Her eyes flickered in Jack's direction as he entered the room, but she didn't say anything, only gestured towards the sofa for him to sit down. He chose to stand by the mantelpiece and watch her. He thought of her in terms of ice. Glacial. Dazzling. Static.

'What are you thinking?' she asked after several moments of silence.

'That Mathilda was right about you.'

There was no expression in her grey eyes. 'In which particular respect?'

'She said you were a mystery.'

She gave a faint smile but didn't say anything.

'I liked her, you know,' Jack went on after a moment.

'You would. She despised women but looked up to men.'

There was a lot of truth in that, thought Jack. 'She liked Sarah well enough.'

'Do you think so?'

'She left her three-quarters of a million pounds. I'd say that was a pretty good indication she liked her.'

Joanna leant her head against the back of the sofa and stared at him with a disconcertingly penetrating gaze. 'I assumed you knew Mother better than that. She didn't *like* anyone. And why ascribe such a mundane motive to her? She would have viewed a bequest of three-quarters of a million pounds in terms of the power it could buy her, not as a sentimental hand-out to someone who had done her a small kindness. Mother never intended that will to be her last. It was a piece of theatre, made for Ruth and me to find. Money buys power just as effectively if you threaten to withhold it.'

Thoughtfully, Jack rubbed his jaw. Sarah had said something very similar. 'But why Sarah? Why not leave it to a dogs' home? It would have achieved the same purpose.'

'I've wondered about that,' she murmured, her eyes straying towards the window. 'I think perhaps she disliked your wife even more than she disliked me. Do you imagine Ruth and I would have kept quiet if we'd seen that video while Mother was alive?' She stroked her hand rhythmically up and down her arm as she spoke. It was an extraordinarily sensuous action but she seemed unaware that she was doing it. She brought her head round to look at Jack again. Her eyes were strangely glassy. 'Your wife's position would have become untenable.'

'What would you have done?' asked Jack curiously.

Joanna smiled. 'Nothing very much. Your wife would have lost all her patients within six months once it got out that she had persuaded a rich patient to make over her entire estate. She'll lose them anyway.'

'Why?'

'Mother died in suspicious circumstances and your wife is the only person to benefit from her death.'

'Sarah didn't kill Mathilda.'

Joanna smiled to herself. 'Tell that to the people of Fontwell.' She stood up and smoothed her black dress over her flat stomach. 'I'm ready,' she said.

He frowned. 'What for?'

'Sex,' she said matter-of-factly. 'It's what you came for, isn't it? We'll use Mother's room. I want you to make love to me the way you made love to her.' Her strange eyes rested on him. 'You'll enjoy it far more with me, you know. Mother didn't like sex, but then I presume you discovered that for yourself. She never did it for pleasure, only for gain. A man's humping disgusted her. She said it reminded her of dogs.'

130

Jack found the remark fascinating. 'I thought you said she looked up to men?'

Joanna smiled. 'Only because she knew how to manipulate them.'

The news that Mathilda Gillespie had left Dr Blakeney three-quarters of a million pounds spread through the village like wildfire. The information surfaced after matins on Sunday, but precisely who started the fire remained a mystery. There was no doubt, however, that it was Violet Orloff who let slip the interesting snippet that Jack Blakeney had taken up residence at Cedar House. His car had remained on the gravel drive all Saturday night and looked like remaining there indefinitely. Tongues began to wag.

Jane Marriott was careful to keep her expression neutral when Sarah put in a surprise appearance at lunchtime on Wednesday. 'I wasn't expecting you,' she said. 'Shouldn't you be on your way to Beeding?'

'I had to give my fingerprints in the parish hall.'

'Coffee?'

'I suppose you've heard. Everyone else has.'

Jane switched on the kettle. 'About the money or about Jack?'

Sarah gave a humourless laugh. 'That makes life a lot easier. I've just spent an hour in a queue outside the hall, listening to heavy-handed hints from people who should have been diagnosed brain-dead years ago. Shall I tell you what the current thinking seems to be? Jack has left me to live with Joanna because he is as shocked as everyone else that I used my position as Mathilda's GP to persuade her to forget her duty to her family in favour of me. This being the same Jack Blakeney who, only last week, everyone loved to hate because he was living off his wretched wife.'

'Oh dear,' said Jane.

'They'll be saying next that I killed the old witch before she could change the will back.'

'You'd better believe it,' said Jane dispassionately. 'There's no point burying your head in the sand.'

'You're joking.'

Jane handed her a cup of black coffee. 'I'm serious, dear. There were two of them discussing it here in the waiting-room this morning. It goes something like this: none of the locals had reason to hate Mathilda more than usual in the last twelve months so none of them is likely to have murdered her. Therefore it has to be a newcomer, and you're the only newcomer with a motive who had access to her. Your husband, afraid for himself and Mrs Lascelles, has moved in to protect her. Ruth is safe because she's at school. And last, but by no means least, why did Victor Sturgis die in such peculiar circumstances?'

Sarah stared at her. 'You *are* serious, aren't you?'

''Fraid so.'

'Do I gather I'm supposed to have killed Victor as well?'

Jane nodded.

'How? By suffocating him with his own false teeth?'

'That seems to be the general view.' Jane's eyes brimmed with laughter suddenly. 'Oh dear, I shouldn't laugh, really I shouldn't. Poor old soul, it was bad enough that he swallowed them himself, but the idea of you wrestling with a ninety-three-year-old in order to ram his dentures down his throat' – she broke off to mop her eyes – 'it doesn't bear thinking about. The world is full of very foolish and very envious people, Sarah. They resent your good fortune.'

Sarah mulled this over. 'Do you think I'm fortunate?'

'Good lord, yes. It's like winning the pools.'

'What would you do with the money if Mathilda had left it to you?'

'Go on a cruise. See the world before it sinks under the weight of its own pollution.'

'That seems to be the most popular choice. It must be something to do with the fact that we're an island. Everyone wants to get off it.' She stirred her coffee then licked the spoon absent-mindedly.

Jane was dying of curiosity. 'What are you going to do with it?'

Sarah sighed. 'Use it to pay for a decent barrister, I should think.'

DS Cooper stopped at Mill House on his way home that evening. Sarah offered him a glass of wine which he accepted. 'We've had a letter about you,' he told her while she was pouring it.

She handed him the glass. 'Who from?'

'Unsigned.'

'What does it say?'

'That you murdered an old man called Victor Sturgis for his walnut desk.'

Sarah pulled a wry face. 'Actually, he did leave me a desk

and it's rather a nice one, too. The matron at the nursing home gave it to me after he died. She said he wanted me to have it. I was very touched.' She lifted weary eyebrows. 'Did it say how I murdered him?'

'You were seen suffocating him.'

'It makes a weird sort of sense. I was trying to prise his dentures out of his throat. The poor old boy swallowed them when he dozed off in his chair.' She sighed. 'But he was dead before I even started. I had a vague idea of trying mouth-to-mouth if I could unblock his airway. I suppose, from a distance, it might have looked as if I were suffocating him.'

Cooper nodded. He had checked the story already. 'We've had a few letters, one way and another, and they're not all about you.' He took an envelope from his pocket and handed it to her. 'This is the most interesting. See what you make of it.'

'Should I touch the letter?' she asked doubtfully. 'What about fingerprints?'

'Well, that's interesting in itself. Whoever wrote it wore gloves.'

She took the letter from the envelope and spread it on the table. It was printed in block capitals:

RUTH LASCELLES WAS IN CEDAR HOUSE THE DAY MRS GILLESPIE DIED. SHE STOLE SOME EARRINGS. JOANNA KNOWS SHE TOOK THEM. JOANNA LASCELLES IS A PROSTITUTE IN LONDON. ASK HER WHAT SHE SPENDS HER MONEY ON. ASK HER WHY SHE TRIED TO KILL HER DAUGHTER. ASK HER WHY MRS GILLESPIE THOUGHT SHE WAS MAD.

134

Sarah turned the envelope over to look at the frank mark. It had been posted in Learmouth. 'And you've no idea who wrote it?'

'None at all.'

'It can't be true. You told me yourself that Ruth was under the watchful eye of her housemistress at school.'

He looked amused. 'As I told you, I never set much store by alibis. If that young lady wanted to sneak out I can't see her housemistress stopping her.'

'But Southcliffe's thirty miles away,' Sarah protested. 'She couldn't have got here without a car.'

He changed tack. 'What about this reference to madness? Did Mrs Gillespie ever mention to you that her daughter was mad?'

She considered this for a moment. 'Madness is a relative term, quite meaningless out of context.'

He was unruffled. 'So Mrs Gillespie did mention something of the sort?'

Sarah didn't answer.

'Come on, Dr Blakeney. Joanna's not your patient so you're not giving away any confidences. And let me tell you something else, she's not doing you any favours at the moment. Her view is that you had to kill the old lady PDQ before she had time to change her will back, and she isn't keeping those suspicions to herself.'

Sarah fingered her wine glass. 'The only thing Mathilda ever said on the subject was that her daughter was unstable. She said it wasn't Joanna's fault but was due to incompatibility between Mathilda's genes and Joanna's father's genes. I told her she was talking rubbish but, at the time, I didn't know that Joanna's father was Mathilda's uncle. I imagine she was concerned about the problems of recessive genes but, as we didn't pursue it any further, I can't say for sure.'

'Inbreeding, in other words?'

Sarah gave a small shrug of acquiescence. 'Presumably.'

'Do you like Mrs Lascelles?'

'I hardly know her.'

'Your husband seems to get on with her well enough.'

'That's below the belt, Sergeant.'

'I don't understand why you're bothering to defend her. She's got her knife into you right up to the hilt.'

'Do you blame her?' She leaned her chin on her hand. 'How would you feel if in a few short weeks, you discovered that you were the product of an incestuous relationship, that your father killed himself with an overdose, that your mother died violently either by her own hand or someone else's and that, to cap it all, the security you were used to was about to be snatched away and given to a stranger? She seems remarkably sane to me in the circumstances.'

He took a drink from his glass. 'Do you know anything about her being a prostitute?'

'No.'

'Or what she spends her money on?'

'No.'

'Any ideas?'

'It's nothing to do with me. Why don't you ask her?'

'I have. She told me to mind my own business.'

Sarah chuckled. 'I'd have done the same.'

He stared at her. 'Has anyone ever told you you're too good to be true, Dr Blakeney?' He spoke with a touch of sarcasm.

She held his gaze, but didn't say anything.

'Women in your position drive their husband's car through their rival's front door, or take a chainsaw to the rival's furniture. At the very least, they feel acute bitterness. Why don't you?'

'I'm busy shoring up my house of cards,' she said cryptically. 'Have some more wine.' She filled her own glass, then his. 'It's not bad, this one. Australian Shiraz and fairly inexpensive.'

He was left with the impression that, of the two women, Joanna Lascelles was the less puzzling. 'Would you have described yourself and Mrs Gillespie as friends?' he asked.

'Of course.'

'Why "of course"?'

'I describe everyone I know well as a friend.'

'Including Mrs Lascelles.'

'No. I've only met her twice.'

'You wouldn't think it to listen to you.'

She grinned. 'I have a fellow-feeling with her, Sergeant, just as I have with Ruth and Jack. You don't feel comfortable with any of us. Joanna or Ruth might have done it if they didn't know the will had been changed, Jack or I might have done it if we did. On the face of it, Joanna appears the most likely which is why you keep asking me questions about her. I imagine you've quizzed her pretty thoroughly about when she first learnt who her father was, so you'll know that she threatened her mother with exposure?' She looked at him enquiringly, and he nodded. 'At which point, you're thinking, Mathilda turned round and said, any more threats like this and I'll cut you out altogether. So, in desperation, Joanna dosed her mother with barbiturates and slit the old lady's wrists, unaware that Mathilda had altered the will already.'

'What makes you think I don't feel comfortable with that scenario?'

'You told me Joanna was in London that night.'

He shrugged. 'Her alibi is very shaky. The concert ended at nine thirty which meant she had plenty of time to drive down here and kill her mother. The pathologist puts the time of death somewhere between nine p.m. on the Saturday night and three a.m. the following morning.'

'Which does he favour?'

'Before midnight,' Cooper admitted.

'Then her defence barrister will tear your case to shreds. In any case, Mathilda wouldn't have bothered with pretence. She'd have told Joanna straight out she'd changed the will.'

'Perhaps Mrs Lascelles didn't believe her.'

Sarah dismissed this with a smile. 'Mathilda always told the truth. That's why everyone loathed her.'

'Perhaps Mrs Lascelles just suspected that her mother might change the will.'

'It wouldn't have made any difference as far as Joanna was concerned. She was preparing to use her father's codicil to fight her mother in court. At that stage, it didn't matter a twopenny damn who Mathilda left the money to, not if Joanna could prove she had no right to it in the first place.'

'Perhaps it wasn't done for money. You keep wondering about the significance of the scold's bridle. Perhaps Mrs Lascelles was revenging herself.'

But Sarah shook her head. 'She hardly ever saw her

mother. I think Mathilda mentioned that she came down once in the last twelve months. It would be a remarkable anger that could sustain itself at fever pitch over such a lengthy cooling period.'

'Not if Mrs Lascelles is unstable,' murmured Cooper.

'Mathilda wasn't killed in a mad frenzy,' said Sarah slowly. 'It was all done with such meticulous care, even down to the flowers. You said yourself the arrangement was difficult to reproduce without help.'

The Sergeant drained his glass and stood up. 'Mrs Lascelles works freelance for a London florist. She specializes in bridal bouquets and wreaths. I can't see her finding a few nettles and daisies a problem.' He walked to the door. 'Good night, Dr Blakeney. I'll see myself out.'

Sarah stared into her wine glass as she listened to his footsteps echoing down the hall. She felt like screaming, but was too afraid to do it. Her house of cards had never seemed so fragile.

There was a conscious eroticism to every movement Joanna made and Jack guessed she had posed before, probably for photographs. For money or for self-gratification? The latter, he thought. Her vanity was huge.

She was obsessed with Mathilda's bed and Mathilda's bedroom, aping her mother's posture against the piled pillows. Yet the contrast between the two women could not have been greater. Mathilda's sexuality had been a gentle, understated thing, largely because she had no interest in it; Joanna's was mechanical and obtrusive, as if the same visual stimuli could arouse all men in the same way on every occasion. Jack found it impossible to decide whether she was acting out of contempt for him or out of contempt for men in general.

'Is your wife a prude?' she demanded abruptly after a long period of silent sketching.

'Why do you ask?'

'Because what I'm doing shocks you.'

He was amused. 'Sarah has a very open and healthy libido and far from shocking me, what you're doing offends me. I resent being categorized as the sort of man who can be turned on by cheap pornographic posturing.'

She looked away from him towards the window and sat in strange self-absorption, her pale eyes unfocused. 'Then tell me what Sarah does to excite you,' she said finally.

He studied her for a moment, his expression unreadable. 'She's interested in what I'm trying to achieve in my work. That excites me.'

'I'm not talking about that, I'm talking about sex.'

'Ah,' he said apologetically, 'we're at cross purposes then. *I* was talking about love.'

'How very twee.' She gave a small laugh. 'You ought to hate her, Jack. She must have found someone else or she wouldn't have kicked you out.'

'Hate is too pervasive,' he said mildly. 'It leaves no room for anything else.' With an idle flick of his fingers he tossed a torn page of his sketchpad towards her and watched it flutter to the bed beside her. 'Read that,' he invited. 'If you're interested, it's my assessment of your character after three sittings. I jot down my impressions as I go along.'

With a remarkable lack of curiosity – most women, he thought, would have seized on it with alacrity – she retrieved it and gave a cursory glance to both sides of the paper. 'There's nothing on it.'

'Exactly.'

'That's cheap.'

'Yes,' he agreed, 'but you've given me nothing to paint.' He passed her the sketchpad. 'I don't do glossy nudes and so far that's all you've offered me, bar a dreary and unremitting display of Electra complex, or more accurately demi-Electra complex. There's no attachment to a father, only a compulsive hostility towards a mother. You've talked about nothing else since I've been here.' He shrugged. 'Even your daughter doesn't feature. You haven't mentioned the poor kid once since she went back to school.'

Joanna got off the bed, wrapped herself in her dressing-gown and walked to the window. 'You don't understand,' she said.

'Oh, I understand,' he murmured. 'You can't con a conman, Joanna.'

She frowned. 'What are you talking about?'

'One of the most colossal egos I've ever come across, and God knows I should recognize one when I see it. You may persuade the rest of the world that Mathilda wronged you, but not me. You've been screwing her all your life,' he tipped a finger at her, 'although you probably didn't know until recently just why you were so damn good at it.'

She didn't say anything.

'I'll hazard a guess that your childhood was one endless tantrum, which Mathilda attempted to control with the scold's bridle. Am I right?' He paused. 'And then what? Presumably you were bright enough to work out a way to stop her using it.'

141

Her tone was frigid. 'I was terrified of the beastly thing. I used to convulse every time she produced it.'

'Easily done,' he said with amusement. 'I did it myself as a child when it suited me. So how old were you when you worked that one out?'

Her peculiarly fixed gaze lingered on him, but he could feel the growing agitation underneath. 'The only time she ever showed me any affection was when she put the scold's bridle over my head. She'd put her arms about me and rub her cheek against the framework. "Poor darling," she'd say, "Mummy's doing this for Joanna."' She turned back to the window. 'I hated that. It made me feel she could only love me when I was at my ugliest.' She was silent for a moment. 'You're right about one thing. It wasn't until I found out that Gerald was my father that I understood why my mother was afraid of me. She thought I was mad. I'd never realized it before.'

'Didn't you ever ask her why she was afraid?'

'You wouldn't even put that question if you'd really known my mother.' Her breath misted the glass. 'There were so many secrets in her life that I learnt very rapidly never to ask her anything. I had to make up a fantasy background for myself when I went to boarding school because I knew so little about my own.' She dashed the mist away with an impatient hand and turned back into the room. 'Have you finished? I've things to do.'

He wondered how long he could stall her this time before the demands of her addiction sent her scurrying for the bathroom. She was always infinitely more interesting under the stress of abstinence than she ever was drugged. 'Southcliffe?' he asked. 'The same school Ruth's at now?'

142

She gave a hollow laugh. 'Hardly. Mother wasn't so free with her money in those days. I was sent to a cheap finishing school which made no attempt to educate, merely groomed cattle for the cattle market. Mother had ambitions to marry me off to a title. Probably,' she went on cynically, 'because she hoped a chinless wonder would be so inbred himself he wouldn't notice the lunacy in me.' She glanced towards the door. 'Ruth has had far more spent on her than I ever had, and not because Mother was fond of her, believe me.' Her mouth twisted. 'It was all done to stamp out the Jew in her after my little faux pas with Steven.'

'Did you love him?'

'I've never loved anyone.'

'You love yourself,' he said.

But Joanna had already gone. He could hear her scrabbling feverishly through the vanity case in the bathroom. For what? he wondered. Tranquillizers? Cocaine? Whatever it was, she wasn't injecting it. Her skin was flawless and beautiful like her face.

Sarah Blakeney tells me her husband is an artist. A painter of personalities. I guessed he would be something in that line. It's what I would have chosen myself. The arts or literature.

'I have heard of your paintings too, well enough. God hath given you one face and you make yourselves another.' Funnily enough, that might have been written for Sarah. She projects herself as a frank and open person, with strong, decided views and no hidden contradictions, but in many ways she is very insecure. She positively loathes confrontation, preferring agreement to disagreement, and will placate if she can. I asked her what she was afraid of, and she said: 'I was taught to be accommodating. It's the curse of being a woman. Parents don't want to be left with spinsters on their hands so they teach their daughters to say "yes" to everything except sex.'

Times haven't changed then . . .

Eight

SARAH WAS WAITING outside the doorway of Barclays Bank in Hills Street when Keith Smollett arrived. She had her coat collar pulled up around her ears and looked pale and washed out in the grey November light. He gave her a warm hug and kissed her cold cheek. 'You're not much of an advertisement for a woman who's just scooped the jackpot,' he remarked, holding her at arm's length and examining her face. 'What's the problem?'

'There isn't one,' she said shortly. 'I just happen to think there's more to life than money.'

He smiled, his thin face irritatingly sympathetic. 'Would we be talking Jack by any chance?'

'No, we would not,' she snapped. 'Why does everyone assume that my equanimity depends on a shallow, two-faced skunk whose one ambition in life is to impregnate every female he meets?'

'Ah!'

'What's that supposed to mean?' she demanded.

'Just, ah!' He tucked her hand into his arm. 'Things are pretty bad at the moment, then?' He gestured towards the road. 'Which way to Duggan's office?'

147

MINETTE WALTERS

'Up the hill. And, no, things are not pretty bad at the moment. At the moment things are pretty good. I haven't felt so calm and so in control for years.' Her bleak expression belied her words. She allowed herself to be drawn out on to the pavement.

'Or so lonely, perhaps?'

'Jack's a bastard.'

Keith chuckled. 'Tell me something I don't know.'

'He's living with Mathilda Gillespie's daughter.'

Keith slowed down and eyed her thoughtfully. 'Mathilda Gillespie as in the old dear who's left you her loot?'

Sarah nodded.

'Why would he want to live with her daughter?'

'It depends who you listen to. Either because he feels guilty that I, his greedy wife, have deprived poor Joanna of her birthright, or he is protecting her and himself from my murderous slashes with a Stanley knife. No one appears to give any credence to the most obvious reason.'

'Which is?'

'Common-or-garden lust. Joanna Lascelles is very beautiful.' She pointed to a door ten yards ahead. 'That's Duggan's office.'

He stopped and drew her to one side. 'Let me get this straight. Are people saying you murdered the old woman for her money?'

'It's one of the theories going the rounds,' she said dryly. 'My patients are abandoning me in droves.' Dampness sparkled along her lashes. 'It's the absolute pits if you want to know. Some of them are even crossing the road to avoid me.' She blew her nose aggressively. 'And my partners

148

aren't happy about it either. Their surgeries are overflowing while mine are empty. If it goes on, I'll be out of a job.'

'That's absurd,' he said angrily.

'No more absurd than an old woman leaving everything she had to a virtual stranger.'

'I talked with Duggan on the phone yesterday. He said Mrs Gillespie was clearly very fond of you.'

'I'm very fond of you, Keith, but I don't intend to leave you all my money.' She shrugged. 'I probably wouldn't have been surprised if she'd left me a hundred quid or even her scold's bridle, but leaving me the whole caboodle just doesn't make sense. I didn't do anything to deserve it, except laugh at her jokes from time to time and prescribe a few pain-killers.'

He shrugged in his turn. 'Perhaps that was enough.'

She shook her head. 'People don't dispossess their families in favour of a slight acquaintance who turns up once a month for half an hour. It's completely crazy. Old men besotted with young girls might be foolish enough to do it, but not tough old boots like Mathilda. And, if she was that way inclined, then why didn't she leave it to Jack? According to him, he knew her so well she was happy to let him paint her in the nude.'

Keith felt unreasonably irritated as he pushed open the door of Duggan, Smith and Drew and ushered Sarah inside. There was, he thought, something deeply offensive about Jack Blakeney persuading a wretched old woman to strip for him. And why would she want to anyway? He couldn't get to grips with that at all. But then Blakeney's attraction, if it existed at all, was entirely lost on Keith. He preferred conventional types who told amusing anecdotes, bought their own drinks and didn't rock the boat by speaking or acting out of turn. He consoled himself with the idea that the story wasn't true. But in his heart of hearts he knew it must be. The real crippler about Jack Blakeney was that women *did* take their clothes off for him.

The meeting dragged on interminably, bogged down in technical details about the 1975 family provision legislation, which, as Duggan had warned Mathilda, might entitle Joanna, as a dependent, to claim reasonable provision for maintenance. 'She ignored my advice,' he said, 'and instructed me to draw up the will leaving all her assets at the time of her death to you. However, it is my considered opinion that in view of the allowance she was paying her daughter and the fact that Mrs Lascelles does not own her own flat, Mrs Lascelles has a good case in law for claiming maintenance. In which case a capital sum now, without prejudice, is worth consideration. I suggest we take counsel's opinion on it.'

Sarah lifted her head. 'You're jumping the gun a little. I haven't yet said that I'm prepared to accept the bequest.'

He could be very direct when he chose. 'Why wouldn't you?'

'Self-preservation.'

'I don't follow.'

'Probably because you haven't had a policeman parked on your doorstep for the last three weeks. Mathilda died in very mysterious circumstances and I'm the only person who

150

stands to gain by her death. I'd say that makes me rather vulnerable, wouldn't you?'

'Not if you didn't know about the bequest.'

'And how do I prove *that*, Mr Duggan?'

He smiled in his amiable way. 'Let me put it to you another way, Dr Blakeney, how will refusing the bequest prove that you didn't murder her? Won't everyone just say you've taken fright because your attempt to make it look like suicide didn't work?' He paused for a moment, but went on when she didn't say anything. 'And no one will applaud you for your magnanimity, you know, because the money won't go to Mrs Lascelles or her daughter but to a handful of donkeys. At least if you accept the bequest, they've a chance of a capital sum.'

Sarah stared past him towards the window. 'Why did she do it?'

'She said she was fond of you.'

'Didn't you question that at all? I mean, do you normally have rich old ladies turning up out of the blue, saying that they want to make new, secret wills which they don't wish their families to know about? Shouldn't you have tried to persuade her out of it? It might have been a spur-of-the-moment whim which we're all saddled with because she died on us. People are saying I used undue influence.'

He turned his pencil in his fingers. 'It wasn't spur-of-the-moment. She first approached me about three months ago and, yes, as a matter of fact I did try to persuade her out of it. I pointed out that, as a general rule, family money is best left with families however much one individual may dislike his or her children. I argued, with no success at all, that she should not regard the Cavendish wealth as hers but as a sort of inherited trust to be passed on to succeeding generations.' He shrugged. 'She wouldn't have it. So I tried to persuade her to discuss it with you first, but I'm afraid she wouldn't have that either. She was quite adamant that you were to inherit but weren't to know about it in advance. For the record, and as I told the police, I was satisfied there was no question of undue influence.'

Sarah was appalled. '*Three months*,' she echoed slowly. 'Have you told the police that?'

He nodded. 'They were also working on the theory that it was a sudden whim.'

She put unsteady fingers to her lips. 'I could just about prove I couldn't have known about it if she made the will two days before she died. There is no way I can prove ignorance if she'd been planning it for three months.'

John Hapgood, the bank manager, cleared his throat. 'It does seem to me, Dr Blakeney, that you are concentrating on entirely the wrong issue. The night Mrs Gillespie died was a Saturday if I remember correctly. Where were you that night, and what were you doing? Let's establish whether you *need* to prove your ignorance of the bequest.'

'I was at home on call. I checked when I learnt about the will.'

'And did you receive any calls?'

'Only one, shortly before eight o'clock. It was nothing serious so I dealt with it over the phone.'

'Was your husband with you?'

'No, he was in Stratford that weekend. No one was with me.' She smiled faintly. 'I'm not a complete moron, Mr Hapgood. If I had an alibi I'd have produced it by now.'

'Then I think you must have more faith in the police, Dr Blakeney. Despite what you read in the papers, they are probably still the best in the world.'

She studied him with amusement. 'You may be right, Mr Hapgood, but, personally, I have no faith at all in my ability to prove I didn't kill Mathilda for her money, and I have a nasty feeling the police know it.' She held up her fingers and ticked off point after point. 'I had motive, I had opportunity and I provided at least half the means.' Her eyes glittered. 'In case you didn't know, she was drugged with the barbiturates I prescribed for her before the incisions were made in her wrists. On top of that, I did twelve months in a pathology department because I was considering a career in forensic medicine before I became a GP, so if anyone would know how to fake a suicide it would be me. Now give me one good argument that I can quote in my defence when the police decide to arrest me.'

He steepled his fingers under his chin. 'It's an interesting problem, isn't it?' He beetled his white eyebrows into a ferocious scowl. 'What were you doing that Saturday?'

'The usual. Gardening, housework. I think I used most of that Saturday to prune the roses.'

'Did anyone see you?'

'What difference does it make whether anyone saw me or not?' She spoke with considerable irritation. 'Mathilda was killed some time during the night, and I certainly wasn't gardening in the dark.'

'What *were* you doing?'

Cursing Jack. Feeling sorry for myself. 'I was painting one of the bedrooms.'

'After doing the garden all day?'

'Someone had to do it,' she said curtly.

There was a short silence.

'You're obviously a workaholic,' said Mr Hapgood lamely. She reminded him of his wife, always on the move, always restless, never pausing long enough to work out where she was going.

Sarah gave a slight smile. 'Most women are. We can't shrug off the responsibility of the home just because we want a career. We got the worst of both worlds when we set out to storm the male bastions.' She pressed her thumb and forefinger to her tired eyes. 'Look, none of this is relevant to why we're here. As far as I can see Mathilda has put me in an impossible position. Whatever I do, I shall be saddled with guilt over her daughter and granddaughter. Is there no way I can simply side-step the issue and leave them to fight it out between themselves?'

'There's nothing to stop you giving it back to them in the form of a gift,' said Duggan, 'once it's yours. But it would be a very inefficient use of the money. The tax liability would be colossal.' He smiled apologetically. 'It would also be flying in the face of Mrs Gillespie's wishes. Whatever the rights and wrongs of it, she did not want Mrs Lascelles or Miss Lascelles to inherit her estate.'

Keith reached for his briefcase. 'Is there any hurry for Dr Blakeney to make her decision,' he asked reasonably, 'or can I suggest we put the whole thing on a back burner for another week or two until the police resolve this one way or another? I can't help feeling Dr Blakeney will find it easier to make her decision once the inquest has been held.'

And so it was agreed, although for Sarah it was simply the postponement of a choice already made.

Keith and Sarah had lunch in a small restaurant at the bottom of the hill. Keith watched her over the rim of his wine glass. 'Was that an act or are you genuinely afraid of being arrested?'

She shrugged. 'Does it matter?' He thought how deeply Jack's departure had affected her. He had never encountered Sarah's bitterness before.

'Of course it matters,' he said bluntly. 'If you're worried, then I suggest I come with you now to sort it out with the police. Where's the sense in tearing yourself apart over something that may never happen?'

She smiled faintly. 'It was an act,' she said. 'I got very tired of them discussing me as if I wasn't there. I might have been as dead as Mathilda. It's the money that excites them.'

Unfair, he thought. Both men had gone out of their way to sympathize with the difficult situation in which Sarah found herself but she was determined to see everyone as an enemy. *Including himself?* Impossible to judge. He turned his glass, letting the sober wall-lights gleam through the red wine. 'Do you want Jack back? Is that why you're so angry? Or are you just jealous because he's found someone else?'

'Can you be *just* jealous?'

'You know what I mean.'

She smiled again, a bitter smile that twisted her mouth. 'But I don't, Keith. I've been jealous for years. Jealous of

155

his art, jealous of his women, jealous of his talent, jealous of him and his ability to bedazzle every damn person he meets. What I feel now is nothing like the jealousy I've felt before. Perhaps it's there but, if it is, it's overlaid with so many other emotions that it's difficult to isolate.'

Keith frowned. 'What do you mean, his ability to bedazzle everyone he meets? I can't stand the man, never have been able to.'

'But you think about him. Mostly with irritation and anger, I expect, but you do think about him. How many other men do you dwell on with the compulsion with which you dwell on Jack? The policeman who's dogging my tracks put it rather well: he said: "He leaves something of a vacuum in his wake."' She held Keith's gaze. 'That's one of the best descriptions I've ever heard of him, because it's true. At the moment I'm living in a vacuum and I'm not enjoying it. For the first time in my life I do not know what to do and it frightens me.'

'Then cut your losses and formalize the separation. Make the decision to start again. Uncertainty is frightening. Certainty never is.'

With a sigh she pushed her plate to one side. 'You sound like my mother. She has a homily for every situation and it drives me mad. Try telling a condemned man that certainty isn't frightening. I doubt he'd agree with you.'

Keith beckoned for the bill. 'At the risk of blotting my copybook again I suggest you go for a long walk by the sea and blow the cobwebs out of your head. You're allowing sentiment to cloud your judgement. There are only two things to remember at a time like this: one, *you* told Jack to leave, not he you; and two, you had good reasons for doing so. It doesn't matter how lonely, how rejected or how jealous you feel now, it cannot affect the central issue, namely that you and Jack do not get on as man and wife. My advice is to get yourself a decent husband who'll stand by you when you need him.'

She laughed suddenly. 'There's not much hope of that. The decent ones are all spoken for.'

'And whose fault's that? You had your chance, but you chose not to take it.' He handed a credit card to the waitress, watched her walk away to the counter, then transferred his gaze to Sarah. 'I don't suppose you'll ever know how much you hurt me, not unless what you're feeling now is something like the hurt that I felt then.'

She didn't answer immediately. 'Now who's being senti-mental?' she said at last, but he thought he saw dampness in her eyes again. 'You've forgotten that you only found me truly desirable after you lost me, and by then it was too late.'

And the tragedy was, he knew she was right.

The door of Cedar House opened six inches in answer to Keith's ring. He smiled pleasantly. 'Mrs Lascelles?'

A tiny frown creased her forehead. 'Yes.'

'I'm Jack Blakeney's solicitor. I'm told he's staying here.'

She didn't answer.

'May I come in and talk to him? I've driven all the way from London.'

'He's not here at the moment.'

'Do you know where I can find him? It is important.'

She gave an indifferent shrug. 'What's your name? I'll tell him you called.'

'Keith Smollett.'

She closed the door.

Violet Orloff, sheltering by the corner of the house, beck-oned to him as he walked back to his car. 'I do hope you won't think I'm *interfering*,' she said breathily, 'but I couldn't help overhearing what you said. She's in a funny mood at the moment, won't talk to anyone, and if you've come all the way from London . . .' She left the rest of the sentence unsaid.

Keith nodded. 'I have, so if you can tell me where Jack is I'd be very grateful.'

She cast a nervous sideways glance towards Joanna's door, then gestured rapidly to the path running round the far corner of the house. 'In the garden,' she whispered. 'In the summer-house. He's using it as a studio.' She shook her head. 'But don't tell *her* I told you. I thought Mathilda's tongue was wicked, but *Joanna's* – ' she cast her eyes to heaven, 'she calls Mr Blakeney a homosexual.' She shooed at him. 'Quickly now, or she'll see you talking to me and Duncan would be *furious*. He's so afraid, you know.'

Somewhat bewildered by this eccentric behaviour, Keith nodded his thanks and followed the same route that Sarah had taken with Ruth. Despite the cold, the doors to the summer-house stood open and he could hear a woman singing a Cole Porter song as he approached across the lawn. The voice was unmistakable, rich and haunting, backed by a simple piano accompaniment.

158

Every time we say goodbye, I die a little,
Every time we say goodbye, I wonder why a little,
Why the gods above me, who must be in the know,
Think so little of me they allow you to go . . .

Keith paused in the entrance. 'Since when were you a
Cleo Laine fan, Jack? I thought Sarah was the aficionado.'
He pressed the eject button on the recorder and removed
the tape to read the handwritten label on the front. 'Well,
well. Unless I'm very much mistaken, this is the one I made
for her before you married. Does she know you've got it?'

Jack surveyed him through half-closed lids. He was on
the point of telling him to put his hackles down, his
customary response to Smollett's invariably critical opening
remarks, when he thought better of it. For once, he was
pleased to see the pompous bastard. In fact, he admitted to
himself, he was so damn pleased he could be persuaded to
change the habits of the last six years and greet him as a
friend instead of a marriage-breaking incubus. He stuck his
paintbrush in a jar of turpentine and wiped his hands down
the front of his jumper, producing a huge paint-smeared
palm as a peace-offering. 'I suppose Sarah's sent you.'

Keith pretended not to see the hand, instead eyed the
sleeping-bag, abandoned in a dishevelled heap in a corner,
then pulled forward a chair. 'No,' he said, folding himself
into it. 'I left her in Poole. She doesn't know I'm here. I've
come to try and talk some sense into you.' He studied the
portrait. 'Mrs Lascelles presumably.'

Jack crossed his arms. 'What do you think?'

'Of her or the portrait?'

'Either.'

'I only saw six inches of her through the gap in the door.' He cocked his head on one side to examine the painting. 'You've been pretty heavy-handed with the purples. What is she, a nymphomaniac? Or is that just wishful thinking on your part?'

Jack lowered himself gingerly into the chair opposite – the cold and the floorboards were wreaking havoc on the muscles of his back – and wondered if the gentlemanly thing was to bop Keith on the nose now or wait till the man was on guard. 'Not all the time,' he said, answering the question seriously, 'only when she's stoned.'

Keith digested this in silence for a moment or two. 'Have you told the police?'

'What?'

'That she's a user.'

'No.'

'Then I think it's better all round if you never told me and I never heard it.'

'Why?'

'Because I'm on the side of law and order and I don't have your freedom to behave as I like.'

'Don't blame your profession for your lack of freedom, Smollett,' Jack growled, 'blame yourself for selling out to it.' He nodded towards the house. 'She needs help and the best person to give it to her is the one she won't see. Sarah, in other words. What good would a policeman be to her?'

'He could prevent her murdering someone else.'

Thoughtfully, Jack rubbed his unshaven jaw. 'Meaning that because she's degenerate enough to use drugs, she's ipso facto degenerate enough to kill her mother. That's crap, and you know it.'

'It gives her a damn sight better motive than the one Sarah's been saddled with. It's expensive to feed a habit, not to mention the effect it has on the personality. If she didn't kill the old woman for money, then she's probably unpredictable enough to have done it out of sudden fury.'

'You'd have no qualms about briefing a barrister with that codswallop either, would you?' murmured Jack.

'No qualms at all, particularly if it's Sarah's neck that ends up on the line.' Keith turned the cassette in his fingers, then reached out to put it beside the recorder. 'You do know she's worried sick about losing her patients and being arrested for murder, I suppose, while you're here mooning over a drug-addicted nymphomaniac? Where's your loyalty, man?'

Was this Sarah talking? Jack wondered. He hoped not. 'Mooning' was not a word he recognized as part of her vocabulary. She had too much self-respect. He gave a prodigious yawn. 'Does Sarah want me back. Is that why you're here? I don't mind admitting I'm pretty fed up with freezing my balls off in this miserable dump.'

Keith breathed deeply through his nose. 'I don't *know* what she wants,' he said, bunching his fists in his lap. 'I came because I had an absurd idea that you and I could discuss this mess in an adult way without either of us needling the other. I should have known it was impossible.'

Jack squinted at the bunched fists, while doubting that Keith could ever be provoked into using them. 'Did she tell you why she wanted a divorce?'

'Not precisely.'

He linked his hands behind his head and stared at the

ceiling. 'She took against me when she had to arrange an abortion for my lover. It's been downhill ever since.'

Keith was genuinely shocked. *That* explained Sarah's bitterness all right. With a shake of his head, he pushed himself out of his chair and stood by the door, gazing out across the garden. 'If I wasn't so sure I'd lose, I'd invite you out there for a thrashing. You're a shit, Jack. JE-SUS!' he said, as the full import of what the man had said slowly dawned. 'You had the bloody nerve to make Sarah murder *your* baby. That is so damn sick I can hardly believe it. She's your wife, for God's sake, not some sleazy back-street abortionist slaughtering wholesale for money. No wonder she wants a divorce. Don't you have any sensibilities at all?'

'Clearly not,' said Jack impassively.

'I warned her not to marry you.' He turned back bludgeoning the air with his finger because he hadn't the courage to bludgeon Jack with a fist. 'I knew it wouldn't last, told her exactly what to expect, what sort of a man you were, how many women you'd used and discarded. But not this. Never this. How could you *do* such a thing?' He was almost in tears. 'Dammit, I wouldn't even turn my back on the baby, but to make your own wife responsible for its murder. You're sick! Do you know that? You're a sick man.'

'Put like that, I rather agree with you.'

'If I have my way you won't get a penny out of this divorce,' he said ferociously. 'You do realize I'm going to report this back to her, and make sure she uses it in court?'

'I'm relying on you.'

Keith's eyes narrowed suspiciously. 'What's that supposed to mean?'

'It means, Smollett, that I expect you to repeat every word of this conversation verbatim.' His expression was unreadable. 'Now do me a favour and take yourself off before I do something I might regret. Sarah's friendships are entirely her concern, of course, but I admit I've never understood why she always attracts domineering little men who think she's vulnerable.' He flipped the tape, pushed it back into the recorder and pressed the 'play' button. This time it was Richard Rodney Bennett's 'I never went away' that drifted in melancholy splendour upon the air.

No matter where I travelled to,
I never went away from you . . .
I never went away . . .

Jack closed his eyes. 'Now bugger off,' he murmured, 'before I rip your arms off. And don't forget to mention the sleeping-bag, there's a good chap.'

Duncan and Violet Orloff are the most absurd couple. They spent the entire afternoon on the lawn with Duncan fast asleep and Violet twittering non-stop drivel at him. She's like a manic little bird, constantly twitching her head from side to side for fear of predators. As a result she never once looked at Duncan and was quite oblivious to the fact that he wasn't listening to a word she said. I can't say I blame him. She was empty-headed as a child and age has not improved her. I still can't decide whether it was a good or a bad idea to offer them Wing Cottage when Violet wrote and said they'd set their hearts on spending their retirement in Fontwell. 'We do so want to come home,' was her appallingly sentimental way of putting it. The money was very useful, of course – Joanna's flat was a shocking expense, as is Ruth's education – but, on balance, neighbours should be eschewed. It's a relationship that can all too easily descend into forced intimacy. Violet forgot herself and called me 'love' last week, then went into paroxysms of hysteria when I pointed it out, beating her chest with her hands and ululating like some peasant

*woman. A most revolting display, frankly. I'm inclined
to think she's going senile.*

*Duncan, of course, is a very different kettle of fish.
The wit is still there, if somewhat slower through lack of
practice. Hardly surprising when it has been blunted
for forty years on Violet's plank of a brain. I wonder
sometimes how much they remember of the past. I worry
that Violet will twitter away to Joanna or Ruth one
day and let cats out of bags that are better confined. We
all share too many secrets.*

*I read back through my early diaries recently and
discovered, somewhat to my chagrin, that I told Violet
the week before her wedding that her marriage would
never last. If the poor creature had a sense of humour,
she could reasonably claim the last laugh . . .*

Nine

JOANNA SHOWED little surprise at finding Sarah on her doorstep at noon the next day. She gave the faintest of smiles and stepped back into the hall, inviting the other woman inside. 'I was reading the newspaper,' she said, as if Sarah had asked her a specific question. She led the way into the drawing-room. 'Do sit down. If you've come to see Jack, he's outside.'

This was a very different reception from the one Keith described having the previous evening, and Sarah wondered about Joanna's motives. She doubted that it had anything to do with the drug addiction Keith had harped on about, and thought it more likely that curiosity had got the better of her. It made sense. She was Mathilda's daughter and Mathilda had been insatiably curious.

She shook her head. 'No, it's you I've come to see.'

Joanna resumed her own seat but made no comment.

'I always liked this room,' said Sarah slowly. 'I thought how comfortable it was. Your mother used to sit over there,' she pointed to a high-backed chair in front of the french windows, 'and when the sun shone it turned her hair into a silver halo. You're very like her to look at but I expect you know that.'

Joanna fixed her with her curiously inexpressive eyes.

'Would it help, do you think, if you and I talked about her?'

Again Joanna didn't answer and to Sarah, who had rehearsed everything on the assumption that the other woman would be a willing party to their conversation, the silence was as effective as a brick wall. 'I hoped,' she said, 'that we could try to establish some sort of common ground.' She paused briefly but there was no response. 'Because, frankly, I'm not happy about leaving everything in the hands of solicitors. If we do, we might just as well burn the money now and be done with it.' She gave a tentative smile. 'They'll pick the bones clean and leave us with a worthless carcase. Is that what you want?'

Joanna turned her face to the window and contemplated the garden. 'Doesn't it make you angry that your husband's here with me, Dr Blakeney?'

Relieved that the ice was broken, though not in a way she would have chosen herself, Sarah followed her gaze. 'Whether it does or doesn't isn't terribly relevant. If we bring Jack into it, we'll get nowhere. He has a maddening habit of hi-jacking almost every conversation I'm involved in, and I really would prefer, if possible, to keep him out of this one.'

'Do you think he slept with my mother?'

Sarah sighed inwardly. 'Does it matter to you?'

'Yes.'

'Then, no, I don't think he did. For all his sins, he never takes advantage of people.'

'She might have asked him to.'

'I doubt it. Mathilda had far too much dignity.'

Joanna turned back to her with a frown. 'I suppose you know she posed in the nude for him. I found one of his sketches in her desk. It left nothing to the imagination, I can assure you. Do you call that dignified? She was old enough to be his mother.'

'It depends on your point of view. If you regard the female nude as intrinsically demeaning or deliberately provocative, then, yes, I suppose you could say it was undignified of Mathilda.' She shrugged. 'But that's a dangerous philosophy which belongs to the dark ages and the more intolerant religions. If, on the other hand, you see the nude figure, be it male or female, as one of nature's creations, and therefore as beautiful and as extraordinary as anything else on this planet, then I see no shame involved in allowing a painter to paint it.'

'She did it because she knew it would excite him.' She spoke the words with conviction and Sarah wondered about the wisdom of continuing – Joanna's prejudice against her mother was too ingrained for reasoned argument. But the offensiveness of the statement irritated her enough to defend Jack, if only because she had encountered the same sort of blinkered stupidity herself.

'Jack's seen far too many naked women to find nakedness itself a turn-on,' she said dismissively. 'Nudity is only erotic if you want it to be. You might just as well say that I get a thrill every time a male patient undresses for me.'

'That's different. You're a doctor.'

Sarah shook her head. 'It's not, but I'm not going to argue the toss with you. It would be a waste of both our times.' She ran her fingers through her hair. 'In any case your mother was too incapacitated by her arthritis, and in too much pain from it, to want to have intercourse with a virile man thirty years her junior. It's important to keep a sense of proportion, Mrs Lascelles. It might have been different if she had been sexually active all her life or even liked men very much, but neither was true of your mother. She once told me that the reason there were so many divorces these days was because relationships based on sex were doomed to fail. The pleasures of orgasm were too fleeting to make the remaining hours of boredom and disappointment worth while.'

Joanna resumed her study of the garden. 'Then why did she take her clothes off?' It was, it seemed, very important to her. Because she was jealous, Sarah wondered, or because she needed to go on despising Mathilda?

'I imagine it was no big deal, one way or the other, and she was interested enough in art for art's sake to help Jack explore the unconventional side of her nature. I can't see her doing it for any other reason.'

There was a brief silence while Joanna considered this. 'Do you still like her now that she's dead?'

Sarah clasped her hands between her knees and stared at the carpet. 'I don't know,' she said honestly. 'I'm so angry about the will that I can't view her objectively at the moment.'

'Then say you don't want the bequest. Let me and Ruth have it.'

'I wish it was that easy, believe me, but if I turn it down then you'll have to fight the donkeys' charity for it, and I honestly can't see how that will improve your chances unless, presumably, you can show that Mathilda never intended that will to be her last.' She looked up to find Joanna's pale eyes studying her intently.

'You're a very peculiar woman, Dr Blakeney,' she said slowly. 'You must realize that the easiest way for me to do that is to prove that my mother was murdered and that you were the one who did it. It fits so neatly, after all. You knew the will was just a threat to make me and Ruth toe the line, so you killed Mother quickly before she could change it. Once you're convicted, no court on earth will rule in favour of the donkeys.'

Sarah nodded. 'And if you can cajole my husband into testifying that I knew about the will in advance, then you're home and dry.' She raised an eyebrow in enquiry. 'But, as I suspect you're beginning to discover, Jack is neither so amenable nor so dishonest. And it wouldn't make any difference, you know, if you did manage to persuade him into bed with you. I've known him for six years and the one thing I can say about him is that he cannot be bought. He values himself far too highly to tell lies for anyone, no matter how much of an obligation they may put him under.'

Joanna gave a small laugh. 'You're very confident that I haven't slept with him.'

Sarah felt compassion for her. 'My solicitor phoned last night to say that Jack's camped out in your summer-house, but I was sure anyway. You're very vulnerable at the moment, and I do know my husband well enough to know he wouldn't exploit that.'

'You sound as though you admire him.'

'I could never admire him as much as he admires himself,'

171

she said dryly. 'I hope he's extremely cold out there. I've suffered for his art for years.'

'I gave him a paraffin heater,' said Joanna with a frown. The memory obviously annoyed her.

Sarah's eyes brimmed with sudden laughter. 'Was he grateful?'

'No. He told me to leave it outside the door.' She gazed through the window. 'He's an uncomfortable person.'

'I'm afraid he is,' Sarah agreed. 'It never occurs to him that other people have fragile egos which need stroking from time to time. It means you have to take his love on faith if you want a relationship with him.' She gave a throaty chuckle. 'And faith has a nasty habit of deserting you just when you most need it.'

There was a long silence. 'Did you talk to my mother like this?' Joanna asked at last.

'Like what?'

Joanna sought for the right words. 'So – easily.'

'Do you mean did I find her easy to talk to?'

'No.' There was a haunted look in the grey eyes. 'I meant, weren't you afraid of her?'

Sarah stared at her hands. 'I didn't need to be, Mrs Lascelles. She couldn't hurt me, you see, because she wasn't my mother. There were no emotional strings to be arbitrarily plucked when she felt like it; no shared family secrets that would lay me open to her vituperative tongue; no weaknesses from my childhood that she could exploit into adulthood whenever she felt like belittling me. If she'd tried, of course, I'd have walked away, because I've had all that from my own mother for years and there is no way I would put up with it from a stranger.'

172

'I didn't kill her. Is that what you came to find out?'

'I came to find out if bridges could be built.'

'For your benefit or mine?'

'Both, I hoped.'

Joanna's smile was apologetic. 'But I've got nothing to gain by being friendly with you, Dr Blakeney. It would be tantamount to admitting Mother was right and I can't do that, not if I want to contest the will in court.'

'I hoped to persuade you there were other options.'

'Every one of which is dependent on your charity.'

Sarah sighed. 'Is that so terrible?'

'Of course. I served forty years for my inheritance. You served one. Why should I have to beg from you?'

Why indeed? There was no justice in it that Sarah could see. 'Is there any point in my coming here again?'

'No.' Joanna stood up and smoothed the creases from her skirt. 'It can only make matters worse.'

Sarah smiled wryly. 'Can they *be* any worse?'

'Oh, yes,' she said with a twisted little smile. 'I might start to like you.' She waved dismissively towards the door. 'You know your way out, I think.'

DS Cooper was gazing thoughtfully at Sarah's car when she emerged from the front door. 'Was that wise, Dr Blakeney?' he asked as she approached.

'Was what wise?'

'Bearding the lioness in her den.'

'Do lionesses have beards?' she murmured.

'It was a figure of speech.'

'I gathered that.' She observed him with fond amusement. 'Wise or not, Sergeant, it was instructive. I've had my anxieties laid to rest and, as any doctor will tell you, that's the best panacea there is.'

He looked pleased for her. 'You've sorted things out with your husband?'

She shook her head. 'Jack's a life sentence not an anxiety.' Her dark eyes gleamed with mischief. 'Perhaps I should have paid a little more attention when my mother was making her predictions for our future.'

'Marry in haste, repent at leisure?' he suggested.

'More along the lines of "She who sups with the devil needs a long spoon". Which I, of course, countered with "The devil has all the best tunes".' She made a wry face. 'But try forgetting "Hey, Jude" or "Twenty-four hours from Tulsa". Like Jack they have a nasty habit of lingering in the memory.'

He chuckled. 'I'm more of a "White Christmas" man myself, but I know what you mean.' He glanced towards the house. 'So, if it's not your husband who's set your mind at rest it must be Mrs Lascelles. Does that mean she's decided to accept the terms of the will?'

Again Sarah shook her head. 'No. She's convinced me she didn't kill her mother.'

'And how did she manage to do that?' He looked very sceptical.

'Feminine intuition, Sergeant. You'd probably call it naïvety.'

'I would.' He patted her arm in an avuncular way. 'You really must learn not to be so patronizing, Doctor. You'll see things in a different light if you do.'

'Patronizing?' echoed Sarah in surprise.

'We can always call it something else. Intellectual snobbery or self-righteousness, perhaps. They cloak themselves just as happily under the guise of naïvety but, of course, naïvety sounds so much less threatening. You're a very decided woman, Dr Blakeney, and you rush in where angels fear to tread, not out of foolishness but out of an overweening confidence that you know best. I am investigating a murder here.' He smiled grimly. 'I don't pretend that I would ever have liked Mrs Gillespie because I'm rather inclined to accept the established view that she was an evil-minded old bitch who got her kicks out of hurting people. However, that did not give anyone the right to strike her down prematurely. But the point I want to stress to you is that whoever killed her was clever. Mrs Gillespie made enemies right, left and centre, and knew it; she was a bully; she was cruel; and she trod rough-shod over other people's sensibilities. Yet, someone got so close to her that they were able to deck her out in a diabolical headdress and then take her semi-conscious to the bath where they slit her wrists. Whoever this person was is not going to make you a free gift of their involvement. To the contrary, in fact, they will make you a free gift of their non-involvement, and your absurd assumption that you can tell intuitively who is or who is not guilty from a simple conversation is intellectual arrogance of the worst kind. If it was so damned easy – forgive my French – to tell murderers from the rest of society, do you not think by now that we'd have locked them up and confined unlawful killing to the oddities page of the history textbooks?'

'Oh dear,' she said. 'I seem to have exposed a nerve. I'm sorry.'

He sighed with frustration. 'You're still patronizing me.'

She opened her car door. 'Perhaps it would be better if I left, otherwise I might be tempted to return the insult.'

He looked amused. 'Water off a duck's back,' he said amiably. 'I've been insulted by professionals.'

'I'm not surprised,' she said, slipping in behind the wheel. 'I can't be the only person who gets pissed off when you decide to throw your weight about. You don't even know for sure that Mathilda was murdered, but we're all supposed to wave our arms in the air and panic. What possible difference can it make to anyone if I choose to satisfy myself that Mrs Lascelles hasn't disqualified herself from a cut of the will by topping the old lady who made it?'

'It could make a lot of difference to you,' he said mildly. 'You could end up dead.'

She was intensely scornful. 'Why?'

'Have you made a will, Dr Blakeney?'

'Yes.'

'In favour of your husband?'

She nodded.

'So, if you die tomorrow, he gets everything, including, presumably, what Mrs Gillespie has left you.'

She started the car. 'Are you suggesting Jack is planning to murder me?'

'Not necessarily.' He looked thoughtful. 'I'm rather more interested in the fact that he is – potentially – a very eligible husband. Assuming, of course, you die before you can change your will. It's worth considering, don't you think?'

Sarah glared at him through the window. 'And you say

Mathilda was evil-minded?' Furiously, she ground into gear. 'Compared with you she was a novice. Juliet to your Iago. And if you don't understand the analogy, then I suggest you bone up on some Shakespeare.' She released the clutch with a jerk and showered his legs with gravel as she drove away.

'Are you busy, Mr Blakeney, or can you spare me a few minutes?' Cooper propped himself against the doorjamb of the summer-house and lit a cigarette.

Jack eyed him for a moment, then went back to his painting. 'If I said I was busy would you go away?'

'No.'

With a shrug, Jack clamped the brush between his teeth and took a coarser one from the jar on the easel, using it to create texture in the soft paint he had just applied. Cooper smoked in silence, watching him. 'Okay,' said Jack at last, flipping the brushes into turpentine and swinging round to face the Sergeant. 'What's up?'

'Who was Iago?'

Jack grinned. 'You didn't come here to ask me that.'

'You're quite right, but I'd still like to know.'

'He's a character from *Othello*. A Machiavelli who manipulated people's emotions in order to destroy them.'

'Was Othello the black bloke?'

Jack nodded. 'Iago drove him into such a frenzy of jealousy that Othello murdered his wife Desdemona and then killed himself when he learnt that everything Iago had said about her was a lie. It's a story of obsessive passion and trusts betrayed. You should read it.'

'Maybe I will. What did Iago do to make Othello jealous?'

'He exploited Othello's emotional insecurity by telling him Desdemona was having an affair with a younger, more attractive man. Othello believed him because it was what he was most afraid of.' He stretched his long legs in front of him. 'Before Othello fell on his sword he described himself as "one that lov'd not wisely but too well". It gets misused these days by people who know the quote but don't know the story. They interpret "lov'd not wisely" as referring to a poor choice of companion, but Othello was actually acknowledging his own foolishness in not trusting the woman he adored. He just couldn't believe the adoration was mutual.'

Cooper ground his cigarette under the heel of his shoe. 'Topical stuff then,' he murmured, glancing towards the sleeping-bag. 'Your wife's not loving too wisely at the moment, but then you're hardly encouraging her to do anything else. You're being a little cruel, aren't you, sir?'

Jack's liking for the man grew. 'Not half as cruel as I ought to be. Why did you want to know about Iago?'

'Your wife mentioned him, said I was Iago to Mrs Gillespie's Juliet.' He smiled his amiable smile. 'Mind, I'd just suggested that if she were to die an untimely death you would make an eligible catch for someone else.' He took out another cigarette, examined it then put it back again. 'But I don't see Mrs Gillespie as Juliet. King Lear, perhaps, assuming I'm right and King Lear was the one whose daughter turned on him.'

'Daughters,' Jack corrected him. 'There were two of them, or two who turned on him, at least. The third tried to save him.' He rubbed his unshaven jaw. 'So you've got your knife into Joanna, have you? Assuming I've followed your reasoning correctly, then Joanna killed her mother to inherit the funds, found to her horror that Mathilda had changed her will in the meantime, so immediately made eyes at me to get me away from Sarah with a view to topping Sarah at the first opportune moment and then hitching herself to me.' He chuckled. 'Or perhaps you think we're in it together. That's one hell of a conspiracy theory.'

'Stranger things have happened, sir.'

He eased his stiff shoulders. 'On the whole I prefer Joanna's interpretation. It's more rational.'

'She's accusing your wife.'

'I know. It's a neat little package, too. The only flaw in it is that Sarah would never have done it, but I can't blame Joanna for getting that wrong. She can't see past her own jealousy.'

Cooper frowned. 'Jealousy over you?'

'God no.' Jack gave a rumble of laughter. 'She doesn't even like me very much. She thinks I'm a homosexual because she can't account for my irreverence in any other way.' His eyes gleamed at Cooper's expression, but he didn't elaborate. 'Jealousy over her mother, of course. She was quite happy loathing and being loathed by Mathilda until she discovered she had a rival. Jealousy has far more to do with ownership than it has with love.'

'Are you saying she knew about your wife's relationship with her mother before her mother died?'

'No. If she had, she would probably have done something about it.' He scraped his stubble again, his eyes narrowing thoughtfully. 'But it's too late now, and that can only make the jealousy worse. She'll start to forget her mother's faults, fantasize about the relationship she imagines Sarah had with Mathilda and torment herself over her own missed opportunities. Let's face it, we all want to believe that our mothers love us. It's supposed to be the one relationship we can depend on.'

Cooper lit another cigarette and stared thoughtfully at the glowing tip. 'You say Mrs Lascelles is jealous of your wife's intimacy with Mrs Gillespie. Why isn't she jealous of her daughter? According to the young lady herself she got on with her grandmother like a house on fire.'

'Do you believe her?'

'There's no evidence to the contrary. The housemistress at her boarding school says Mrs Gillespie wrote regularly and always seemed very affectionate whenever she went there. Far more affectionate and interested, apparently, than Mrs Lascelles who puts in infrequent appearances and shows little or no interest in how her daughter's doing.'

'All that says to me is that Mathilda was a magnificent hypocrite. You can't ignore her snobbery, you know, not without distorting the picture. Southcliffe is an expensive girls' boarding school. Mathilda would never have let the side down in a place like that. She always talked about "people of her sort" and regretted the lack of them in Fontwell.'

The Sergeant shook his head in disbelief. 'That doesn't square with what you told me before. You called her one of life's great individuals. Now you're saying she was pandering to the upper classes in order to make herself socially acceptable.'

'Hardly. She was a Cavendish and inordinately proud of

the fact. They were bigwigs round here for years. Her father, Sir William Cavendish, bought his knighthood by doing a stint as the local MP. She was already socially acceptable, as you put it, and didn't need to pander to anyone.' He frowned in recollection. 'No, what made her extraordinary, despite all the trappings of class and respectability which she played up to and tossed about in public to keep the proles in their place, was that privately she seethed with contradictions. Perhaps her uncle's sexual abuse had something to do with it, but I think the truth is she was born into the wrong generation and lived the wrong life. She had the intellectual capacity to do anything she wanted, but her social conditioning was such that she allowed herself to be confined in the one role she wasn't suited for, namely marriage and motherhood. It's tragic really. She spent most of her life at war with herself and crippled her daughter and granddaughter in the process. She couldn't bear to see their rebellions succeed where hers hadn't.'

'Did she tell you all this?'

'Not in so many words. I gleaned it from things she said and then put it into the portrait. But it's all true. She wanted a complete explanation of that painting, down to the last colour nuance and the last brush stroke, so' – he shrugged – 'I gave her one, much along the lines of what I've just told you, and at the end she said there was only one thing wrong, and it was wrong because it was missing. But she wouldn't tell me what it was.' He paused in reflection. 'Presumably it had something to do with her uncle's abuse of her. I didn't know about that. I only knew of her father's abuse with the scold's bridle.'

But Cooper was more interested in something he had

181

said before. 'You can't call Mrs Lascelles's rebellion a success. She lumbered herself with a worthless heroin addict who then died and left her penniless.' His gaze lingered on the portrait.

Jack's dark face split into another grin. 'You've led a very sheltered life if you think rebellion is about achieving happiness. It's about anger and resistance and inflicting maximum damage on a hated authority.' He lifted a sardonic eyebrow. 'On that basis, I'd say Joanna scored a spectacular success. If you're calling her husband worthless now, what on earth do you imagine Mathilda's peers said about him at the time? Don't forget she was a very proud woman.'

Cooper drew heavily on his cigarette and looked up towards the house. 'Your wife's just been to see Mrs Lascelles. Did you know?'

Jack shook his head.

'I met her as she was leaving. She told me she's convinced Mrs Lascelles didn't kill her mother. Would you agree with that?'

'Probably.'

'Yet you just told me that Mrs Lascelles's rebellion was to inflict maximum damage on the object of her hatred. Isn't death the ultimate damage?'

'I was talking about twenty-odd years ago. You're talking about now. Rebellion belongs to the young, Sergeant, not to the middle-aged. It's the middle-aged who're rebelled against because they're the ones who compromise their principles.'

'So how is Ruth rebelling?'

Jack studied him lazily from beneath his hooded eyelids. 'Why don't you ask her?'

'Because she's not here,' said Cooper reasonably, 'and you are.'

'Ask her mother then. You're being paid to meddle,' he cocked his irritating eyebrow again, 'and I'm not.'

Cooper beamed at him. 'I like you, Mr Blakeney, though God alone knows why. I like your wife, too, if it's of any interest. You're straightforward types who look me in the eye when you talk to me and, believe it or not, that warms my heart because I'm trying to do a job that the people have asked me to do but for which, most of the time, I get called a pig. Now, for all I know, one or other, or both of you together, killed that poor old woman up there, and if I have to arrest you I'll do it, and I shan't let my liking get in the way because I'm an old-fashioned sod who believes that society only works if it's bolstered by rules and regulations which give more freedom than they take away. By the same token, I don't like Mrs Lascelles or her daughter, and if I was the sort to arrest people I didn't like, I'd have banged them up a couple of weeks ago. They're equally malicious. The one directs her malice against your wife, the other directs hers against her mother, but neither of them has said anything worth listening to. Their accusations are vague and without substance. Ruth says her mother's a whore without principles, and Mrs Lascelles says your wife's a murderess but when I ask them to prove it, they can't.' He tossed his dog-end on to the grass. 'The odd thing is that you and Dr Blakeney, between you, appear to know more about these two women and their relationship with Mrs

Gillespie than they do themselves, but out of some kind of misguided altruism you don't want to talk about it. Perhaps it's not politically correct amongst gilded intellectuals to dabble their fingers in the seamy side of life, but make no mistake, without something more to go on, Mrs Gillespie's death will remain an unsolved mystery and the only person who will suffer will be Dr Blakeney because she is the only person who had a known motive. If she is innocent of the murder of her patient, her innocence can only be proved if someone else is charged. Now, tell me honestly, do you think so little of your wife that you'd let her reputation be trampled in the mud for the sake of not wanting to assist the police?'

'My God!' said Jack with genuine enthusiasm. 'You're going to have to let me do this portrait of you. Two thousand. Is that what we agreed?'

'You haven't answered my question,' said the policeman patiently.

Jack reached for his sketchpad and flicked through to a clean page. 'Just stand there for a moment,' he murmured, taking a piece of charcoal and making swift lines on the paper. 'That was some speech. Is your wife as decent and honourable as you are?'

'You're taking the mickey.'

'Actually, I'm not.' Jack squinted at him briefly before returning to his drawing. 'I happen to think the relationship between the police and society is drifting out of balance. The police have forgotten that they are there only by invitation; while society has forgotten that, because it chooses the laws which regulate it, it has a responsibility to uphold them. The relationship should be a mutually supportive one; instead, it is mutually suspicious and mutually antagonistic.' He threw Cooper a disarmingly sweet smile. 'I am thoroughly enchanted to meet a policeman who seems to share my point of view. And, no, of course I don't think so little of Sarah that I'd allow her reputation to suffer. Is that really likely?'

'You've not been out and about much since you moved in here.'

'I never do when I'm working.'

'Then perhaps it's time you left. There's a kangaroo court operating in Fontwell and your wife is their favourite target. She's the newcomer, after all, and you've done her no favours by shacking up with the opposition. She's lost a goodly number of patients already.'

Jack held the sketchpad at arm's length to look at it. 'Yes,' he said, 'I'm going to enjoy doing you.' He started to pack his hold-all. 'It's too damn cold here anyway, and I've got enough on Joanna to finish her at home. Will Sarah have me back?'

'I suggest you ask her. I'm not paid to meddle in domestic disputes.'

Jack tipped a finger in acknowledgement. 'Okay,' he said, 'the only thing I know about Ruth is what Mathilda told me. I can't vouch for its accuracy, so you'll have to check that for yourself. Mathilda kept a float of fifty pounds locked in a cash-box in her bedside table and opened it up one day because she wanted me to go to the shop and buy some groceries for her. It was empty. I said, perhaps she'd already spent the money and forgotten. She said, no, it's what came of having a thief for a granddaughter.' He shrugged. 'For all I know she may have been excusing her own memory lapse by slandering Ruth, but she didn't elaborate and I didn't ask. More than that I can't tell you.'

'What a disappointing family,' said the Sergeant. 'No wonder she chose to leave her money elsewhere.'

'That's where we part company,' said Jack, standing up and stretching towards the ceiling. 'They are Mathilda's creations. She had no business passing the buck to Sarah.'

*I had an appalling shock today. I walked into the
surgery, completely unprepared, and found Jane Marriott behind the counter. Why did nobody tell me they
were back? Forewarned would have meant forearmed.
Jane, of course, knowing our paths must cross, was as
cool as ever. 'Good morning, Mathilda,' she said.
'You're looking well.' I couldn't speak. It was left to
Doctor Dolittle, asinine man, to bray the good news
that Jane and Paul have decided to move back to Rossett
House following the death of their tenant. I gather Paul
is an invalid – chronic emphysema – and will benefit
from the peace and quiet of Fontwell after the rigours
of Southampton. But what am I to do about Jane? Will
she talk? Worse, will she betray me?*

*'Is there no pity sitting in the clouds, that sees into
the bottom of my grief?'*

*I would feel less desperate if Ruth had not gone back
to school. The house is empty without her. There are too
many ghosts here and most of them unlaid. Gerald and
my father haunt me mercilessly. There are times, not
many, when I regret their deaths. But I have high hopes*

*of Ruth. She is bright for her age. Something good will
come of the Cavendishes, I'm sure of it. If not, everything I have done is wasted.*

*'Hush! Hush! Whisper who dares! Mathilda Gillespie
is saying her prayers.' I have such terrible headaches
these days. Perhaps it was never Joanna who was mad,
but only I . . .*

Ten

RUTH, SUMMONED OUT of a chemistry lesson, sidled into the room set aside for Sergeant Cooper by her housemistress and stood with her back to the door. 'Why did you have to come back?' she asked him. 'It's embarrassing. I've told you everything I know.' She was dressed in mufti and, with her hair swept back into a tight bun, she looked more than her seventeen years.

Cooper could appreciate her embarrassment. Any school was a goldfish bowl but a boarding school peculiarly so. 'Police investigations are rarely tidy things,' he said apologetically. 'Too many loose ends for tidiness.' He gestured towards a chair. 'Sit down, Miss Lascelles.'

With a bad grace, she did so, and he caught a brief glimpse of the gawky adolescent beneath the pseudo-sophistication of the outer shell. He lowered his stocky body on to the chair in front of her and studied her gravely but not unkindly.

'Two days ago we received a letter about you,' he said. 'It was anonymous. It claimed you were in Cedar House the day your grandmother died and that you stole some earrings. Are either of those facts true, Miss Lascelles?'

189

Her eyes widened but she didn't say anything.

'Since which time,' he went on gently, 'I have been told on good authority that your grandmother knew you were a thief. She accused you of stealing money from her. Is that also true?'

The colour drained from her face. 'I want a solicitor.'

'Why?'

'It's my right.'

He stood up with a nod. 'Very well. Do you have a solicitor of your own? If you do, you may give your housemistress the number and ask her to telephone him. If not, I'm sure she will be happy to call the one the school uses. Presumably they will charge it to the fees.' He walked to the door. 'She may even offer to sit in herself to safeguard your interests. I have no objection to either course.'

'No,' she said sharply, 'I want the duty solicitor.'

'Which duty solicitor?' He found her transparency oddly pathetic.

'The one the police provide.'

He considered this during a prolonged and thoughtful silence. 'Would you be referring to duty solicitors at police stations who act on behalf of persons who have no legal representation of their own?'

She nodded.

He sounded genuinely sympathetic. 'With the best will in the world, Miss Lascelles, that is out of the question. These are harsh recessionary times, and you're a privileged young woman, surrounded by people only too willing to watch out for your rights. We'll ask your housemistress to contact a lawyer. She won't hesitate, I'm sure. Apart from anything else, she will want to keep the unpleasantness under wraps so to speak. After all, she does have the school's reputation to think of.'

'Bastard!' she snapped. 'I just won't answer your questions then.'

He manufactured a look of surprise. 'Do I gather you don't want a solicitor after all?'

'No. Yes.' She hugged herself. 'But I'm not saying anything.'

Cooper returned to his seat. 'That's your privilege. But if I don't get any answers from you, then I shall have to ask my questions elsewhere. In my experience, thieves do not confine themselves to stealing from just one person. I wonder what will happen if I call the rest of your house together and ask them en masse if any of their possessions have gone missing in the last year or so. The inference, surely, will be obvious because they know my only connection with the school is you.'

'That's blackmail.'

'Standard police procedure, Miss Lascelles. If a copper can't get his information one way, then he's duty-bound to try another.'

She scowled ferociously. 'I didn't kill her.'

'Have I said you did?'

She couldn't resist answering, it seemed. 'It's what you're thinking. If I was there I must have killed her.'

'She probably died during the early half of the night, between nine o'clock and midnight, say. Were you there then?'

She looked relieved. 'No. I left at five. I had to be back in time for a physics lecture. It's one of my A level subjects and I gave the vote of thanks at the end.'

He took out his pad. 'What time did the lecture start?'

'Seven thirty.'

'And you were there for the start?'

'Yes.'

'How did you manage to do that? You clearly didn't walk thirty miles in two and a half hours.'

'I borrowed a bicycle.'

He looked deeply sceptical. 'What time did you arrive at your grandmother's, Miss Lascelles?'

'I don't know. About three thirty, I suppose.'

'And what time did you leave the school?'

'After lunch.'

'I see,' he said ponderously, 'so you rode thirty miles in one direction in two hours, rested for an hour and a half with your grandmother and then rode thirty miles back again. You must be a very fit young woman. May I have the name of the person whose bicycle you borrowed?' He licked the point of his pencil and held it poised above the page.

'I don't know whose it was. I borrowed it without asking.'

He made a note. 'Shall we call a spade a spade and be done with the pretence? You mean you stole it. Like the earrings and the fifty pounds.'

'I put it back. That's not stealing.'

'Back where?'

'In the bike shed.'

'Good, then you'll be able to identify it for me.'

'I'm not sure. I just took the best one I could find. What difference does it make which bicycle it was?'

'Because you're going to hop on board again and I'm

going to follow closely behind you all the way to Fontwell.'
He looked amused. 'You see, I don't believe you're capable
of riding thirty miles in two hours, Miss Lascelles, but I'm
quite happy for you to prove me wrong. Then you can have
an hour and a half's rest before you ride back again.'

'You can't do that. That's just fucking – ' she cast about
for a word ' – harassment.'

'Of course I can do it. It's called a reconstruction. You've
just put yourself at the scene of a crime on the day the crime
was committed, you're a member of the victim's family with
easy access to her house and you thought you were going
to inherit money from her. All of which puts you high on
the list of probable suspects. Either you prove to my
satisfaction that you did go by bicycle, or you tell me now
how you really got there. Someone drove you, didn't they?'

She sat in a sullen silence, scraping her toe back and forth
across the carpet. 'I hitched,' she said suddenly. 'I didn't
want to tell you because the school would throw a fit if they
knew.'

'Was your grandmother alive when you left Cedar House
at five o'clock?'

She looked put out by the sudden switch of direction.
'She must have been, mustn't she, as I didn't kill her.'

'So you spoke to her?'

Ruth eyed him warily. 'Yes,' she muttered. 'I left my key
at school and had to ring the doorbell.'

'Then she'll have asked you how you got there. If you
had to hitch, she won't have been expecting you.'

'I said I had a lift from a friend.'

'But that wasn't true, was it, and, as you knew you were
going to have to hitch back to school again on a dark

November evening, why didn't you ask your grandmother to drive you? She had a car and, according to you, she was fond of you. She'd have done it without a murmur, wouldn't she? Why would you do something so dangerous as hitching in the dark?'

'I didn't think about it.'

He sighed. 'Where did you hitch from, Miss Lascelles? Fontwell itself, or did you walk the three miles along Gazing Lane to the main road? If it was Fontwell, then we'll be able to find the person who picked you up.'

'I walked along Gazing Lane,' she said obligingly.

'And what sort of shoes were you wearing?'

'Trainers.'

'Then they'll have mud from the lane squeezed into every seam and crevice. It was raining most of that afternoon. The boys at forensic will have a field day. Your shoes will vindicate you if you're telling the truth. And if you're not . . .' he smiled grimly, 'I will make your life a misery, Miss Lascelles. I will interview every girl in the school, if necessary, to ask them who you consort with, who's had to cover for you when you've gone AWOL, what you steal and why you're stealing it. And if at the end of it you have an ounce of credibility left, then I'll start all over again. Is that clear? Now, who drove you to your grandmother's?'

There were tears in her eyes. 'It's got nothing to do with Granny's death.'

'Then what can you lose by telling me?'

'I'll be expelled.'

'You'll be expelled far quicker if I have to explain why I'm carting your clothing off for forensic examination.'

She buried her face in her hands. 'My boyfriend,' she muttered.

'Name?' he demanded relentlessly.

'Dave – Dave Hughes.'

'Address?'

She shook her head. 'I can't tell you. He'd kill me.'

Cooper frowned at the bent head. 'How did you meet him?'

She raised her tear-stained face. 'He did the tarmac on the school drive.' She read censure in his eyes and leapt to defend herself. 'It's not like that.'

'Like what?'

'I'm not a slut. We love each other.'

Her sexual morality had been the last thing on his mind but it was clearly at the forefront of hers. He felt sorry for her. She was accusing herself, he thought, when she called her mother a whore. 'Does he own the house?'

She shook her head. 'It's a squat.'

'But he must have a telephone or you wouldn't be able to contact him.'

'It's a mobile.'

'May I have the number?'

She looked alarmed. 'He'd be furious.'

You bet your life he would, thought Cooper. He wondered what Hughes was involved in. Drugs? Under-age sex? Pornography? Expulsion was the least of Ruth's problems if any of these were true. He showed no impatience for the address or phone number. 'Tell me about him,' he invited instead. 'How long have you known him? How old is he?'

He had to prise the information from her with patient cajoling and, as she spoke and listened to herself, he saw the dawning confirmation of her worst fears: that this was not a story of Montagues and Capulets thwarting innocent love but, rather, a seedy log of sweaty half-hours in the back of a white Ford transit. Told baldly, of course, it lacked even the saving attraction of eroticism and Cooper, like Ruth, found the telling uncomfortable. He did his best to make it easy for her but her embarrassment was contagious and they looked away from each other more often than their eyes met.

It had been going on for six months since the tarmac crew had relaid the drive, and the details of how it began were commonplace. A school full of girls; Dave with an eye for the most likely; she flattered by his obvious admiration, more so when the other girls noticed he only had eyes for her; a wistful regret when the tarmac was done and the crew departed; followed by an apparently chance meeting when she was walking alone; he, streetwise and twenty-eight; she, a lonely seventeen-year-old with dreams of romance. He respected her, he loved her, he'd wait for ever for her, but (how big a word 'but' was in people's lives, thought Cooper) he had her in the back of his transit within a week. If she could forget the squalor of a blanket on a tarpaulin, then she could remember the fun and the excitement. She had crept out of a downstairs window at two o'clock in the morning to be enveloped in her lover's arms. They had smoked and drunk and talked by candlelight in the privacy of the parked van and, yes, all right, he wasn't particularly well educated or even very articulate, but that didn't matter. And if what happened afterwards had not been part of her gameplan, then that didn't matter either because, when it came to it (her eyes belied the words) she had wanted sex as much as he had.

Cooper longed to ask her, why? Why she valued herself so cheaply? Why she was the only girl in the school who fell for it? Why she would want a relationship with an illiterate labourer? Why, ultimately, she was so gullible as to imagine that he wanted anything more than free sex with a clean virgin? He didn't ask, of course. He wasn't so cruel.

The affair might have ended there had she not met him by sheer mischance (Cooper's interpretation, not hers) one day during the holidays. She had heard nothing from him since the night in the van, and hope had given way to depression. She was spending Easter with her grandmother at Fontwell (she usually went to Fontwell, she told Cooper, because she got on better with her grandmother), and caught the bus to Bournemouth to go shopping. And suddenly there was Dave, and he was so pleased to see her, but angry, too, because she hadn't answered his letter. (Sourly, Cooper imagined the touching scene. What letter? Why, the one that had got lost in the post, of course.) After which they had fallen into each other's arms in the back of the Ford, before Dave had driven her home and realized (Cooper reading between the lines again) that Ruth might be good for a little more than a quick tumble on a blanket when he felt horny.

'He took me everywhere that holidays. It was wonderful. The best time I've ever had.' But she spoke the words flatly, as if even the memory lacked sparkle.

She was too canny to tell her grandmother what she was doing – even in her wildest dreams she didn't think

Mathilda would approve of Dave – so, instead, like a two-timing spouse, she invented excuses for her absences.

'And your grandmother believed you?'

'I think her arthritis was really bad about then. I used to say I was going somewhere, but in the evening she'd have forgotten where.'

'Did Dave take you to his home?'

'Once. I didn't like it much.'

'Did he suggest you steal from your grandmother? Or was that your idea?'

'It wasn't like that,' she said unhappily. 'We ran out of money, so I borrowed some from her bag one day.'

'And couldn't pay it back?'

'No.' She fell silent.

'What did you do?'

'There was so much stuff there. Jewellery. Ornaments. Bits of silver. She didn't even like most of it. And she was so mean. She could have given me a better allowance, but she never did.'

'So you stole her things and Dave sold them.'

She didn't answer.

'What happened to Dave's job with the tarmac crew?'

'No work.' She shrugged. 'It's not his fault. He'd work if he could.'

Did she really believe that? 'So you went on stealing from your grandmother through the summer term and the summer holidays?'

'It wasn't stealing. I was going to get it anyway.'

Dave had indoctrinated her well – or was this Ruth herself speaking? 'Except that you didn't.'

'The doctor's no right to it. She's not even related.'

'Dave's address, please, Miss Lascelles.'

'I can't,' she said with genuine fear. 'He'll kill me.'

He was out of patience with her. 'Well, let's face it, it won't be much of a loss whichever way you look at it. Your mother won't grieve for you, and to the rest of society you'll be a statistic. Just another young girl who allowed a man to use and abuse her.' He shook his head contemptuously. 'I think the most depressing aspect of it all is how much money has been wasted on your education.' He looked around the room. 'My kids would have given their eye-teeth to have had your opportunities, but then they're a good deal brighter than you, of course.' He waited for a moment then shut his notebook and stood up with a sigh. 'You're forcing me to do it the hard way, through your headmistress.'

Ruth hugged herself again. 'She doesn't know anything. How could she?'

'She'll know the name of the firm that was employed to do the drive. I'll track him down that way.'

She wiped her damp nose on her sleeve. 'But, you don't understand, I have to get to university.'

'Why?' he demanded. 'So that you and your boyfriend can have a field day with gullible students? What does he deal in? Drugs?'

Tears flowed freely down her cheeks. 'I don't know how else to get away from him. I've told him I'm going to Exeter, but I'm not, I'm trying for universities in the north because they're the farthest away.'

Cooper was strangely moved. It occurred to him that this was very likely true. She did see running away as the only option open to her. He wondered what Dave had done to make her so afraid of him. Grown impatient, perhaps, and killed Mrs Gillespie to hasten Ruth's inheritance? He resumed his seat. 'You never knew your father, of course. I suppose it's natural you should have looked for someone to take his place. But university isn't going to solve anything, Miss Lascelles. You may have a term or two of peace before Dave finds you, but no more. How did you plan to keep it a secret? Were you going to tell the school that they were never to reveal which university you'd gone to? Were you going to tell your mother and your friends the same thing? Sooner or later there'd be a plausible telephone call and someone would oblige with the information.'

She seemed to shrink in front of his eyes. 'Then there's nothing I can do.'

He frowned. 'You can start by telling me where to find him.'

'Are you going to arrest him?'

'For what?'

'Stealing from Granny. You'll have to arrest me, too.'

He shrugged. 'I'll need to talk to your grandmother's executors about that. They may decide to let sleeping dogs lie.'

'Then you're just going to ask him questions about the day Granny died?'

'Yes,' he agreed, assuming it was what she wanted to hear.

She shook her head. 'He does terrible things to me when he's angry.' Her eyes flooded again. 'If you don't put him in prison then I can't tell you where to find him. You just don't understand what he's like. He'll punish me.'

'How?'

But she shook her head again, more violently. 'I can't tell you that.'

'You're protected here.'

'He said he'd come and make a scene in the middle of the school if I ever did anything he didn't like. They'll expel me.'

Cooper was perplexed. 'If you're so worried about expulsion, why did you ever go out and meet him in the first place? You'd have been expelled on the spot if you'd been caught doing that.'

She twisted her fingers in the hem of her jumper. 'I didn't know then how much I wanted to go to university,' she whispered.

He nodded. 'There's an old saying about that. You never miss the water till the well runs dry.' He smiled without hostility. 'But all of us take things for granted so you're not alone in that. Try this one: desperate diseases call for desperate remedies. I suggest you make a clean breast of all this to your headmistress, throw yourself on her mercy, so to speak, before she finds out from me or Hughes. She might be sympathetic. You never know.'

'She'll go mad.'

'Do you have a choice?'

'I could kill myself,' she said in a tight little voice.

'It's a very weak spirit,' he said gently, 'that sees cutting off the head as the only solution to a headache.' He slapped his hands against his knees. 'Find a bit of courage, girl. Give me Dave's address and then sort things out with your headmistress.'

Her lip wobbled. 'Will you come with me if I do?'

Oh, good grief, he thought, hadn't he had to hold his own children's hands often enough? 'All right,' he agreed, 'but if she asks me to leave I shall have to. I've no authority here as your guardian, remember.'

'Twenty-three, Palace Road, Bournemouth,' she whispered. 'It was my mother who told you I was a thief, wasn't it?' She sounded desperately forlorn, as if she realized that, for her, there was no one left.

'No,' said Cooper compassionately. 'More's the pity, but your mother hasn't told me anything.'

When Sarah pulled into her driveway later that Friday afternoon, she was greeted by the unexpected sight of Jack's car and Cooper's car nestling side by side against the wall in cosy intimacy. Her first inclination was to turn round and drive away again. She hadn't the stomach for a confrontation with either of them, even less for another baring of her soul in front of Cooper while her husband severed his remaining ties. But second thoughts prevailed. Dammit all – she banged her fist angrily against the steering wheel – it was *her* house. She was buggered if she was going to drive around for hours just to avoid her scumbag of a husband and a pompous policeman.

Quietly, she let herself in through the front door, half-thinking that if she tiptoed past the studio, she could possess herself of the kitchen before they knew she was there. As her mother had once said, slamming the kitchen door on Sarah's father: 'An Englishman's home may be his castle, but an Englishwoman's kitchen is where he eats his humble pie.' The sound of voices drifted down the corridor, however, and she knew they had possessed it before her. With a sigh, she fastened her dignity about her like armour plating, and advanced.

Jack, DS Cooper and Ruth Lascelles looked up from their glasses of wine with differing shades of alarm and embarrassment colouring their faces.

'Hi,' said Sarah into the silence. 'You found the '83 Cheval Blanc with no trouble then.'

'Have some,' said Jack, reaching for a clean glass off the draining board. 'It's good.'

'It should be,' she said. 'It's a St Emilion, Premier Grand Cru Classé, and it cost me a small fortune when I laid it down.'

'Don't be so stuffy, woman. You've got to try them from time to time, otherwise you'll end up with a collector's item that's totally undrinkable.' He filled the glass and pushed it across the table, his eyes bright with mischief. She felt a surge of affection for the randy bastard – love, she thought, was the most stubborn of all the diseases – but hid it under a ferocious glare. 'The consensus view amongst the three of us,' he went on cheerfully, 'is dark ruby colour, brilliant legs, and a very exotic nose – curranty fruit, cigar box and hints of herbs and spices.'

'It's a vintage wine, you moron. It's supposed to be savoured and appreciated, not drunk at five o'clock in the afternoon round the kitchen table. I bet you didn't let it breathe. I bet you just poured it out like Lucozade.'

Cooper cleared his throat. 'I'm sorry, Dr Blakeney. We did say we'd be happier with tea.'

'You pusillanimous rat,' said Jack with imperturbable good humour. 'You drooled when I waved the bottle under your nose. Well, come on, old thing, you might as well try it. We're all dying for second helpings but we thought it would be tactful to wait till you arrived before we opened another one.'

'Your life expectancy would be nil if you had,' she said, dropping her handbag and shrugging her coat to the floor. 'All right. Give it here, but I can tell you now it won't be drinkable. It needs another three years at least.' She sat in the vacant chair and drew the glass towards her, covering it with one hand and swirling it gently to release the bouquet. She sniffed appreciatively. 'Who smelt cigar boxes?'

'I did,' said Cooper nervously.

'That's good. The book says the bouquet should be smoky oak and cedar. Curranty fruit?'

Cooper indicated himself again. 'Me.'

'Have you done this before?' He shook his head. 'You should take it up. You've obviously got a nose for it.'

'Ruth and I sussed the herbs and spices,' said Jack. 'What's the verdict?'

Sarah took a sip and let the flavours play across her tongue. 'Spectacular,' she said finally, 'but you're bloody well not opening another bottle. The book says another three years, and I'm going by the book. You can use the wine box for refills. What are you all doing here anyway?' Her eyes rested on Ruth. 'Shouldn't you be at school?'

There was an uncomfortable silence.

'Ruth's been expelled,' said Jack. 'We're all wondering if she can live here with you and me until something more permanent is sorted out.'

Sarah took another sip of her wine and eyed him

thoughtfully. 'You and me?' she queried silkily. 'Does that mean you intend to inflict your company on me again?'

The dark face softened. 'That rather depends, my angel.'

'On whether or not I'm prepared to have you back?'

'No. On whether I come back on my terms or your terms.'

'My terms,' she said bluntly, 'or not at all.'

He gave a ghost of a smile. 'Shame,' he murmured.

Sarah held his gaze for a moment, then transferred her attention to Ruth. 'So why were you expelled?'

Ruth, who had been staring at her hands since Sarah came in, flicked a sideways glance at Cooper. 'The Sergeant knows. He can tell you.'

'I'd rather hear it from you.'

'I broke the school rules.' She resumed her study of her hands.

'All of them or one in particular?'

'Leaving school without permission.'

'Times haven't changed then. A friend of mine was expelled for sneaking down the fire escape and talking to some boys at the bottom of it. She was only caught because the rest of us were hanging out of the windows giggling. We were making such a row the housemistress heard us and expelled her on the spot. She's a barrister now. Rather a good one, too.'

'I've been sleeping with someone,' Ruth whispered, 'and the headmistress said I was a bad influence on the others. She said I was immoral.'

Sarah raised enquiring eyebrows at Cooper, who nodded. 'Ah, well, perhaps times have changed, after all,' she said matter-of-factly. 'I can't imagine any of us having the courage to do anything so daring, not after we'd had it firmly dinned into us that a prospective husband could always tell if a girl wasn't a virgin.' She gave a throaty chuckle. 'We knew a great deal about love bites and the bruising effects of frantic French kissing, and absolutely nothing about anything else. We were convinced we'd turn green or break out in pustules if we let a man loose below the neckline. It came as something of a shock to discover we'd been sold a lie.' She took another sip of her wine. 'Was it worth getting expelled for?'

'No.' A tear ran down the girl's face and on to the table. 'I don't know what to do. I want to go to university.'

'Surely the most sensible thing would be to go back to Cedar House and your mother. She'll have to find you another school.' Why had Cooper brought her here anyway? *Or was it Jack who'd brought her?*

Cooper rumbled into life. 'Her boyfriend's liable to cut up rough, once I've had a word with him, and Cedar House will be the first place he goes looking. It's an imposition, I know, but off-hand I couldn't think of anywhere else, not after the way the school dealt with her.' He looked quite put out. 'She was told to pack a suitcase while they ordered a taxi to take her home, so I said, forget the taxi, I'll take her. I've never seen the like of it. You'd think she'd committed a hanging offence the way they carried on. And the worst of it was, they wouldn't have known anything about it if I hadn't persuaded her to tell them herself. I feel responsible, I really do, but then I thought they'd give her some credit for being honest and let her off with a caution. It's what I would have done.'

'Does your mother know?' Sarah asked Ruth.

'Jack let me phone.'

'Is she happy about you staying here?'

'I don't know. All she said was she'd heard from Miss Harris and then hung up. She sounded furious.' Ruth kept her head down and dabbed at her eyes with a handkerchief.

Sarah made a wry face at Jack. 'You'll have to be the one to tell her then. I'm not exactly flavour of the month at the moment, and I can't see her being very pleased about it.'

'I've already tried. She hung up on me, too.'

It was on the tip of Sarah's tongue to ask why, before she thought better of it. Knowing Jack, the answer would be as teasingly illusive as the answer to life itself. What puzzled her more was the speed with which events, like the ball in a pinball machine, had taken such an unpredictable course. This morning she'd had only another solitary week-end to look forward to – *and now*? 'Well, someone's got to tell her,' she said irritably, isolating the one fact she could get to grips with. She looked at the Sergeant. 'You'll have to do it. I'm quite happy for Ruth to stay but only if her mother knows where she is.'

Cooper looked wretched. 'Perhaps it would be better if we involved social services,' he suggested, 'asked a third party to intercede, as it were.'

Sarah's eyes narrowed. 'I'm an extremely amenable woman on the whole but I do resent my good nature being taken advantage of. There is no such thing as a free lunch, Sergeant, and I'd like to remind you that you have just drunk some very expensive St Emilion of mine which, at a conservative estimate and allowing for inflation, costs well over seven pounds per glass. In other words, you owe me one, so you will not shuffle your responsibility and this child's future on to some overworked and underpaid social worker whose only solution to the problem will be to place her in a hostel full of disturbed adolescents.'

Cooper's wretchedness grew.

'You have also, by underestimating the old-fashioned ethics that still exist within girls' boarding schools, caused a young woman approaching the most important exams of her life to be expelled. Now, in a world where the renting out of a woman's womb is still the only reliable method that men have discovered to replicate themselves, the very least they can do in return is to allow their women enough education to make the life sentence of child-rearing endurable. To sit and stare at an empty wall is one thing; to have the inner resources, the knowledge and the confidence to turn that wall into a source of endless stimulation is another. And that's ignoring the positive influence that educated and intelligent women have on succeeding generations. Ruth wants to go to university. To do so, she must pass her A levels. It is imperative that Joanna finds another school to accept her PDQ. Which means someone' – she cocked her finger at him – 'namely *you*, must explain to her that Ruth is here, that she is here for a good reason, and that Joanna must come and talk it through before Ruth loses her opportunity to take her education as far as it can go.' She turned her gaze on the girl. 'And if you dare tell me now, Ruth, that you've given up on your future, then I'll put you through the first mangle I can find and, I promise you, the experience will not be a pleasant one.'

There was a long silence.

Finally, Jack stirred. 'Now you begin to see what Sarah's

208

terms consist of. There's no allowing for human frailty. I grant you, there are pages of subtext and small print dealing with the awful imperfections that most of us suffer from – namely, inadequacy, lack of confidence, seeing both sides and sitting on fences – but they are grey areas which she treats with insufferable patience. And, take it from me, you allow her to do that at your peril. It undermines what little self-respect you have left.' He beamed fondly at Cooper. 'I sympathize with you, old son, but Sarah's right as usual. Someone's got to talk to Joanna and you're the one who's run up the most debts. After all, you *did* get Ruth expelled and you *did* drink a glass of wine that cost over seven quid.'

Cooper shook his head. 'I hope Miss Lascelles can put up with the pair of you. I know I couldn't. You'd have me climbing the walls before you could say knife.'

The 'pair' wasn't lost on Sarah. 'How come you know so much more about my domestic arrangements than I do, Sergeant?' she asked casually.

He chuckled amiably, pushing himself to his feet. 'Because I never say never, Doctor.' He winked at her. 'As someone once told me, life's a bugger. It creeps up behind you and gets you where you least expect it every time.'

Sarah felt the girl start to tremble as she pushed open the door of the spare room and switched on the light. 'What's the matter?' she asked.

'It's downstairs,' she blurted out. 'If Dave comes, he could get in.'

'Not my choice. Geoffrey Freeling's. He turned the house upside down so that the reception rooms would have the best views. We're slowly turning it back again, but it takes time.' She pushed open a communicating door. 'It has its own bathroom.' She glanced back at the girl, saw the pinched look to her face. 'You're frightened, aren't you? Would you rather sleep upstairs in my room?'

Ruth burst into tears. 'I'm so sorry,' she wept. 'I don't know what to do. Dave will kill me. I was all right at school. He couldn't have got in there.'

Sarah put her arms about the other's thin shoulders and clasped them tightly. 'Come upstairs,' she said gently. 'You'll be safe with me. Jack can sleep in here.'

And serve the bastard right, she thought. *Ho, ho! For once, sod's law was on the side of the angels.* She had been toying with the ethics of medical castration but was prepared to compromise on a cold bed and a grovelling apology. It was a very partial compromise. She was so damn glad to have him back she felt like doing handsprings.

Joanna moved to the flat in London last week and for the first time since her abortive attempt at marriage I am in sole possession of Cedar House. It is a victory of sorts, but I have a sense of anticlimax. The game, I fear, was not worth the candle. I am lonely.

It occurs to me that in some strange way Joanna and I are necessary to each other. There is no denying the understanding that exists between us. We do not get along, of course, but that is largely irrelevant in view of the fact that we don't get along with anyone else either. There was some comfort in treading the mill of clichéed insults that trundled us quite happily through our lives, so worn and over-used that what we said to each other passed largely unnoticed. I miss the little things. The way she pursued Spede about the garden, taking the wretched man to task if he missed a weed. Her waspish remarks about my cooking. And oddly enough, as they always used to irritate me at the time, her long, long silences. After all, perhaps companionship is less to do with conversation than with the comfort of another human presence, however self-centred that presence might be.

211

I have a terrible fear that, by pushing her out to fend for herself, I have diminished us both. At least, while we were together, we checked each other's worst excesses. And now? The road to hell is paved with good intentions . . .

Eleven

IT WASN'T UNTIL late the following afternoon, a Saturday, that Sergeant Cooper felt he had enough information on Dave Hughes to make an approach viable. He was pessimistic about bringing charges of theft, but in respect of Mathilda's death there was some room for optimism. Ruth's mention of a white Ford transit had rung bells in his memory and a careful sifting of the statements taken in and around Fontwell in the days after the body was found had produced a gem. When asked if he'd seen anything unusual the previous Saturday, the landlord of the Three Pigeons, Mr Henry Peel, had said:

> I can't swear it had anything to do with Mrs Gillespie, but there was a white Ford transit parked on my forecourt that Saturday afternoon and evening. Had a young lad in it, as far as I could judge. Stayed ten minutes the first time then drove off towards the church and picked someone up. I saw it again that evening. I pointed it out to my wife and said some wretch was using our forecourt but not using the pub. I can't give you the registration number.

Underneath in a PC's handwriting was a short note:

Mrs Peel disagrees. She says her husband is confusing this
with another occasion when white vans were there twice in
one day, but her recollection is that the vans were different.
Three of our regulars drive white vans, she said.

Cooper talked the problem through with his Detective
Chief Inspector. 'I need to question Hughes, Charlie, so do
I take a team with me, or what? According to the girl, he's
living in a squat, so he won't be alone, and I don't fancy
trying to winkle him out from under a mob of squatters.
Assuming they let me in at all. It's bloody rich, isn't it?' he
grumbled. 'Somebody else's property and they can take it
over lock, stock and barrel. The only way the poor sod who
owns it can get it back is to pay through the nose for an
eviction order, by which time he finds they've turned the
place into a cess-pit.'

Charlie Jones's squashed face wore a permanently lugubrious expression which always reminded Cooper of a sad-
eyed Pekinese. He was more of a terrier, however, who,
once he got his teeth into something, rarely let go. 'Can we
charge him with theft on what Miss Lascelles has told you?'

'We could, but he'd be out again in a couple of hours.
Bournemouth have him on file. He's been brought in three
times and he's walked on each occasion. All similar offences
to this one, i.e. persuading youngsters to steal for him. It's
a clever scam.' He sounded frustrated. 'The children only
prey off their families and, so far, the parents have refused
to co-operate when they discover that Hughes's prosecution
will involve their daughters in a prosecution, too.'

'So how come he was brought in in the first place?'

'Because three indignant fathers have independently

accused him of forcing their daughters to steal and demanded that charges be brought. But when the girls were questioned, they told a different story, denied the coercion and insisted that the thieving was their own idea. It's a real honey, this one. You can't do him without the daughters, and the fathers won't have the daughters done.' He smiled cynically. 'Too much unpleasant publicity.'

'What sort of backgrounds?'

'Middle class, wealthy. The girls are all over sixteen, so no question of under-age sex. Mind, I'm sure these three and Miss Lascelles are only the tip of a very large iceberg. It sounds to me as if he's got the whole thing down to a very fine art.'

'*Does* he coerce them?'

Cooper shrugged. 'All Miss Lascelles said was, he does terrible things when he's angry. He threatened to make a scene at the school if she did anything he didn't like, but when I asked her about it in the car on the way to Dr Blakeney's, in other words after that particular threat had lost its sting because she'd already been expelled, she clammed up and burst into tears.' He tugged his nose thoughtfully. 'He must be using some form of coercion because she's terrified he's going to find her. I wondered if he makes videos of them but when I asked Bournemouth if they've found any equipment on him, they said no. Your guess is as good as mine, Charlie. He's got some hold on these girls, and it must be fear because they're desperate to get shot of him the minute they're found out. But precisely what's involved, I don't know.'

The Inspector frowned. 'Why aren't they afraid to name him?'

'Presumably because he's given them permission to shop him if they're caught. Look, he must know how easy it would be for us to track him down. If Miss Lascelles hadn't proffered the information, all I had to do was ask the headmistress for the tarmac firm and take it from there. I think his MO goes something like this: target a girl who's young enough and cosseted enough to warrant her parents' protection, win her over, then use some sort of threat to make sure she accuses herself along with him when she's caught. That way he's as sure as he can be that charges won't be brought and, if they are, he'll take her down with him. Perhaps his threat is as simple as that.'

The Inspector was doubtful. 'He can't make much out of it. How long before the parents notice what's going on?'

'You'd be amazed. One of the girls was borrowing her mother's credit card for months before the father queried the amount his wife was spending. It was a jointly held card, the balance was paid off automatically out of the current account, and neither of them noticed that it had increased by upwards of five hundred pounds a month. Or if they did, they assumed the other partner's expenditure was behind it. It's a different world, Charlie. Both parents working and earning a good screw, and enough money sloshing around in the coffers to obscure their daughter's thieving. Once they started looking into it, of course, they discovered she'd sold bits of silver, jewellery that her mother never wore, some valuable first editions of her father's and a five-hundred-pound camera that her father thought he'd left on a train. I'd say Hughes is doing very nicely out of it, particularly if he's running more than one of them at the same time.'

'Good grief! How much has Ruth Lascelles stolen then?'

Cooper took a piece of paper from his pocket. 'She made a list of what she could remember. That's it.' He put it on the desk. 'Same pattern as the other girl. Jewellery that her grandmother had forgotten about. Silver-backed hair-brushes from the spare room that were never used. China ornaments and bowls that were kept in cupboards because Mrs Gillespie didn't like them, and some first editions out of the library. She said Hughes told her the sort of thing to look for. Valuable bits and pieces that wouldn't be missed.'

'What about money?'

'Twenty pounds from her grandmother's handbag, fifty pounds from the bedside table and, a few weeks later, five hundred out of the old lady's account. Went to the bank as cool as cucumber with a forged cheque and a letter purport-ing to come from Mathilda, instructing them to hand over the loot. According to her, Mrs Gillespie never even noticed. But she did, of course, because she mentioned the fifty-pound theft to Jack Blakeney and, when I tackled her bank this morning, they told me she had queried the five-hundred-pound withdrawal on her statement, and they advised her that Ruth had drawn it out on her instructions.' He scratched his jaw. 'According to them, she agreed that it was her mistake and took no further action.'

'What date was that?'

Cooper consulted his notes again. 'The cheque was cashed during the last week in October, Ruth's half-term in other words, and Mrs Gillespie rang the bank as soon as she got the statement, which was the first week in November.'

'Not long before she died then, and *after* she'd made up her mind to change the will. It's a bugger that one. I can't get the hang of it at all.' He thought for a moment. 'When did Ruth steal the fifty pounds?'

'At the beginning of September before she went back to school. She had some idea apparently of buying Hughes off. She said: "I thought he'd leave me alone if I gave him some money."'

'Dear God!' said Charlie dismally. 'There's one born every minute. Did you ask her if Hughes put pressure on her to cash the five hundred at half-term?'

'I did. Her answer was: "No, no, no. I stole it because I wanted to," and then she turned the waterworks on again.' He looked very rueful. 'I've left the ball in Dr Blakeney's court. I had a word with her on the phone this morning, gave her the gist of what Hughes has been up to and asked her to try and find out why none of the girls will turn QE against him. She may get somewhere but I'm not counting on it.'

'What about the mother? Would Ruth talk to her?'

Cooper shook his head. 'First, you'd have to get *her* to talk to Ruth. It's unnatural, if you ask me. I stopped off last night to tell her the Blakeneys had taken her daughter in and she looked at me as if I'd just climbed out of a sewer. The only thing she was interested in was whether I thought Ruth's expulsion meant she'd killed her grandmother. I said, no, that as far as I knew there were no statistics linking truancy and promiscuous sex to murder, but there were a great number linking them to poor parenting. So she told me to eff off.' He chuckled happily at the memory.

Charlie Jones grunted his amusement. 'I'm more interested in friend Hughes at the moment, so let's break this down into manageable proportions. Have Bournemouth tried getting the three families together so that the girls gain strength from numbers?'

'Twice. No go either time. The parents have taken legal advice and no one's talking.'

Charlie pursed his lips in thought. 'It's been done before, you know. George Joseph Smith did it a hundred years ago. Wrote glowing references for pretty servant girls, then found them placements in wealthy households. Within weeks of starting work they would steal valuables from their employers and take them faithfully to George to convert into ready cash. He was another one with an extraordinary pulling-power over women.'

'George Smith?' said Cooper in surprise. 'I thought he did *away* with women. Wasn't he the brides-in-the-bath murderer?'

'That's him. Started drowning wives when he discovered how easy it was to get them to make wills in his favour upon marriage. Interesting, isn't it, in view of the way Mrs Gillespie died.' He was silent for a moment. 'I read a book about Smith not so long ago. The author described him as a professional and a literal lady-killer. I wonder if the same thing applies to Hughes.' He rapped a tattoo on his desktop with his knuckles. 'Let's pull him in for questioning.'

'How? Do I take an arrest warrant?'

Charlie reached for his phone. 'No. I'll get Bournemouth to pick him up tomorrow morning and hold him on ice till you and I get there.'

'Tomorrow's Sunday, Charlie.'

'Then with any luck he'll have a hangover. I want to see his expression when I tell him we have reason to believe he murdered Mrs Gillespie.'

Cooper was sceptical. 'Have we? The landlord's state-ment won't stand close scrutiny, not if his wife's claiming he was confused.'

A wolfish grin spread across the Inspector's features, and the sad Pekinese became a Dobermann. 'But we know he was there that afternoon because Ruth told us he was, and I'm inclined to be a little creative with the rest. He was using Mrs Gillespie's granddaughter to extort money. He has a history of ruthless exploitation of women, and he's probably feeding a habit because his outgoings far exceed his income. If they didn't, he wouldn't have to live in squats. I'd say his psychological profile runs something like this: a dangerously unstable, psychopathic addict, whose hatred of women has undergone a dramatic change recently and taken him from their brutal manipulation to their destruction. He will be the product of a broken home and inadequate education, and boyhood fear of his father will govern most of his actions.'

Cooper looked even more sceptical. 'You've been read-ing too many books, Charlie.'

Jones allowed himself a laugh. 'But Hughes doesn't know that, does he? So let's try and dent his charisma a little and see if we can't stop him using other people's little girls to do his dirty work.'

'I'm trying to solve a murder,' said Cooper in protest. 'That's what I want answers on.'

'But you've still to convince me it *was* a murder, old son.'

Ruth crept stealthily down the stairs and stood to one side of the studio doorway, watching Jack's reflection in her tiny hand mirror. Not that she could see him very well. He was sitting with his back to the window, working on a portrait but, because the easel was placed directly between him and the door, the canvas obscured all but his legs. From the bedroom window she had watched Sarah leave the house two hours ago, so she knew they were alone. *Would Jack notice when she slipped past the doorway?* She waited for ten minutes in panicky indecision, too afraid to take a step.

'If you want something to eat,' he murmured finally into the silence, 'then I suggest you try the kitchen. If you want someone to talk to, then I suggest you come in here, and if you're looking for something to steal, then I suggest you take Sarah's engagement ring which belonged to my grand-mother and was valued at two thousand pounds four years ago. You'll find it in the left-hand drawer of her dressing-table.' He leaned to one side so that she could see his face in her mirror. 'You might as well show yourself. I'm not going to eat you.' He nodded curtly as she came round the doorjamb. 'Sarah gave me strict instructions to be sympath-etic, patient and helpful. I'll do my best, but I warn you in advance I can't stand people who sniff into handkerchiefs and creep about on tiptoe.'

Ruth's cheeks lost what little colour they had left. 'Do you think it would be all right if I made myself a cup of coffee?' She looked very unattractive, damp hair clinging to her scalp, face puffy and blotched with crying. 'I don't want to be a nuisance.'

Jack returned to his painting so that she wouldn't see the flash of irritation in his eyes. Self-pity in others invariably brought out the worst in him. 'As long as you make me one, too. Black and no sugar, please. The coffee's by the kettle, sugar's in the tin marked "sugar", milk's in the fridge and lunch is in the oven. It will be ready in half an hour so, unless you're starving, my advice is to skip breakfast and wait for that.'

'Will Dr Blakeney be here for lunch?'

'I doubt it. Polly Graham's gone into labour and as Sarah agreed to a home-birth, she could be there for hours.'

Ruth hovered for a moment, then turned to go to the kitchen, only to change her mind again. 'Has my mother phoned?' she blurted out.

'Did you expect her to?'

'I thought—' She fell silent.

'Well, try thinking about making me a cup of coffee instead. If you hadn't mentioned it, I probably wouldn't have wanted one, but as you have, I do. So get your skates on, woman. This is not a hotel and I'm not in the best of moods after being relegated to the spare room.'

She fled down the corridor to the kitchen and, when she returned five minutes later with a tray and two cups, her hands were shaking so much that the cups chattered against each other like terrified teeth. Jack appeared not to notice but took the tray and placed it on a table in the window. 'Sit,' he instructed, pointing to a hard-backed chair and swinging his stool round to face her. 'Now, is it me you're frightened of, the boyfriend, men in general, Sarah not coming home for lunch, the police, or are you worried about what's going to happen to you?'

She shrank away from him as if he'd struck her.

'Me then.' He moved the stool back a yard to give her more room. 'Why are you afraid of me, Ruth?'

Her hands fluttered in her lap. 'I'm – you—' Her eyes widened in terror. 'I'm not.'

'You feel completely secure and at ease in my presence?'

'Yes,' she whispered.

'You have an odd way of showing it.' He reached for his coffee cup. 'How old were you when your father died?'

'I was a baby.'

'Since which time you've lived with your mother and your grandmother and, latterly, a bevy of women at boarding school.' He took a sip of coffee. 'Am I right that this Hughes character is the first boyfriend you've ever had?'

She nodded.

'So he's your only experience of men?'

She stared at her hands.

'Yes or no?' he demanded, the words whipping out impatiently.

'Yes,' she whispered again.

'Then you obviously require lessons on the male of the species. There are only three things to remember. One: most men need to be told what to do by women. Even sex improves when women take the trouble to point the man in the right direction. Two: compared with women, most men are inadequate. They are less perceptive, have little or no intuition, are poorer judges of character and, therefore, more vulnerable to criticism. They find aggression immensely intimidating because they're not supposed to and, in short, are by far the more sensitive of the two sexes. Three: any man who does not conform to this pattern should be avoided. He will be a swaggering, uneducated brute whose intellect will be so small that the only way he can give himself a modicum of authority is by demeaning anyone who's foolish enough to put up with him, and, finally, he will lack the one thing that all decent men have in abundance, namely a deep and abiding admiration for women.' He picked up her coffee cup and held it under her nose so that she had to take it. 'Now I don't pretend to be a paragon, but I'm certainly not a brute, and between you, me and the gatepost, I am extremely fond of my irascible wife. I accept that what I did was open to interpretation, but you can take it from me that I went to Cedar House for one reason only and that was simply to paint your mother. The temptation to capture two generations of one family was irresistible.' He eyed her speculatively. Almost as irresistible, he was thinking, as the temptation to capture the third generation. 'And if my much-put-upon wife hadn't chosen that precise moment to expel me, well,' he shrugged, 'I wouldn't have had to freeze on your mother's summer-house floor. Does all that set your mind at rest or are you going to go on quaking like a great jelly every time you see me?'

She stared at him with stricken eyes. She was beautiful after all, he thought, but it was a tragic beauty. Like her mother's. Like Mathilda's.

'I'm pregnant,' she said finally, exhausted tears seeping on to her cheeks.

There was a moment of silence.

'I thought – I hoped – my mother—' She dashed at her eyes with a sodden tissue. 'I don't know what – I ought to go – I shouldn't have told you.'

Somewhere in the recesses of his heart, Jack blushed for himself. Was the self-pity of a child under intolerable stress so despicable that he had to savage it? He reached across and took her hand, drawing her off the chair and into his arms, holding her tight and stroking her hair as her father would have done had he lived. He let her weep for a long time before he spoke. 'Your grandmother once said to me that mankind was doomed unless he learnt to communicate. She was a wise old lady. We talk a lot but we rarely communicate.' He eased her off his chest and held her at arm's length so that he could look at her. 'I'm glad you told me. I feel rather privileged that you felt you could. Most people would have waited until Sarah came home.'

'I was going—'

He stopped her with a chuckle and released her back on to her chair. 'Let me hang on to my illusions. Let me believe just once that someone thought I could be as easy to confide in as Sarah. It's not true, of course. There is no one in the world who can listen as well as my wife, or who can impart such sound advice. She'll look after you, I promise.'

Ruth blew her nose. 'She'll be angry with me.'

'Do you think so?'

'You said she's irascible.'

'She is. It's not so frightening. You just keep your head down till the saucepans stop flying.'

She dabbed frantically at her eyes. 'Saucepans? Does she—'

'No,' he said firmly. 'It was a figure of speech. Sarah's a nice person. She brings home wounded pigeons, splints their wings, and watches them die in slow and terrible agony with an expression of enormous sympathy on her face. It's one of the things they teach them at medical school.'

She looked alarmed. 'That's awful.'

'It was a joke,' he said ruefully. 'Sarah is the most sensible doctor I know. She will help you reach a decision about what you want to do and then take it from there. She won't force you to have the baby, and she won't force you not to have it.'

The tears welled again. 'I don't want it.' She clenched her hands in her lap. 'Is that wrong, do you think?'

'No,' he said honestly. 'If I were in your shoes, I wouldn't want it either.'

'But I made it. It was my fault.'

'It takes two to make babies, Ruth, and I can't see your boyfriend showing much enthusiasm when it's fully-fledged and bawling its head off. It's your choice, not his. Sperm comes two-a-penny and most of it gets washed down the sink. Wombs and their foetuses come extremely expensive. Sarah's right when she says it's a life sentence.'

'But isn't it alive? Won't I be murdering it?'

He was a man. How could he begin to understand the agony that women suffered because a biological accident has given them power over life and death? He could only be honest with her. 'I don't know, but I'd say it's only alive at the moment because you're alive. It has no existence as an individual in its own right.'

'But it could have – if I let it.'

'Of course. But on that basis every egg that any woman produces and every sperm that any man produces has the potential for life, and no one accuses young men of being murderers every time they spill their seed on the ground behind the bike sheds. I think for each of us our own life has priority over the potential life that exists inside us. I

226

don't for a moment pretend that it's an easy decision, or even a black and white one, but I do believe that you are more important at this moment than a life that can only come into being if you are prepared to pay for it, emotionally, physically, socially and financially. And you'll bear that cost alone, Ruth, because the likelihood of Hughes paying anything is virtually nil.'

'He'll say it isn't his anyway.'

Jack nodded. 'Some men do, I'm afraid. It's so easy for them. It's not their body that's been caught.'

She hid her face in her hands. 'You don't understand.' She wrapped her arms around her head. *To protect herself? To hide herself?* 'It might be one of the others'. You see I had to – he made me – Oh, God – I wish—' She didn't go on, only curled herself into a tight ball and sobbed.

Jack felt completely helpless. Her anguish was so strong that it washed over him in swamping waves. He could think only in platitudes – *there's nothing so bad that it might not be worse . . . it's always darkest before the dawn* – but what use were platitudes to a girl whose life lay in tatters before her? He put out an awkward hand and placed it on her head. It was an instinctive gesture of comfort, an echo of a priestly benediction. 'Tell me what happened,' he said. 'Perhaps it's not as bad as you think.'

But it was. What she told him in tones of abject terror rocked the foundations of his own humanity. So shocked was he that he felt physically sick.

Sarah found him in the garden when she came home at three-thirty after helping to deliver Polly Graham of a healthy baby daughter. He was forking industriously round some roses and scattering handfuls of fertilizer about the roots. 'It's almost December,' she said. 'Everything's dormant. You're wasting your time.'

'I know.' He looked up and she thought she saw traces of tears in his eyes. 'I just needed to do something active.'

'Where's Ruth?'

'Asleep. She had a headache so I gave her some codeine and packed her off to bed.' He brushed the hair from his forehead with the back of a muddy hand. 'Have you finished for the day?'

She nodded. 'What's happened?'

He leant on the fork and stared across the fields. The slowly fading light gave a misty quality to a landscape in which cows grazed and trees, shorn of their leaves, fingered the sky with dark filigree lacework. 'That's the England men and women die for,' he said gruffly.

She followed his gaze with a small frown creasing her forehead.

Tears glistened on his lashes. 'Do you know that poem by Rupert Brooke? "The Soldier". The one that goes:

"If I should die, think only this of me:
That there's some corner of a foreign field
That is for ever England. There shall be
In that rich earth a richer dust concealed;
A dust whom England bore, shaped, made aware . . ."'

He fell silent. When he spoke again, his voice shook. 'It's beautiful, isn't it, Sarah? England *is* beautiful.'

She wiped the tears from his face. 'You're crying,' she

said, her heart aching for him. 'I've never seen you cry before. What's happened, Jack?'

He didn't seem to hear her. 'Rupert Brooke died in 1915. A sacrifice of war. He was only twenty-eight, younger than you and me, and he gave his life with all the other millions, whatever country they came from, for the sake of other people's children. And do you know what breaks my heart?' His dark gaze slid away from her, looking into a private hell that only he could see. 'That a man who could write one of the most perfect pieces of poetry about his homeland that has ever been written should have sacrificed himself for the filth that England spawns today.'

'No one's all bad, Jack, and no one's all good. We're just human. The poor kid only wanted to be loved.'

He wiped a weary hand around his jaw. 'I'm not talking about Ruth, Sarah. I'm talking about the men who attacked her. I'm talking about the animal who taught her obedience by shutting her in a van with a group of low-grade scum who raped her one after the other for five hours to break her spirit.' He stared over the fields again. 'Apparently she objected when Hughes told her to start stealing from Mathilda, said she didn't want to do it. So he locked her in the van with his mates who gave her a graphic demonstration of what was going to happen every time she refused. I've had to give my word that I'm not going to repeat this to anyone except you. She is absolutely terrified they're going to find her and do it again, and when I said we should report it to the police I thought she was going to die on me. Hughes told her that if she was ever caught, all she had to do was say the stealing was her idea. As long as she does that and doesn't mention the rape, he'll leave her alone in the future.' His lips thinned. 'But if she talks, he'll send his goons after her to punish her, and he doesn't care how long he has to wait to do it. Police protection won't save her, marriage won't save her. He'll wait for years if he has to, but for every year her punishment is delayed, he'll add another hour to the final ordeal. She'd have to be a quite extraordinary person to talk to the police with a threat like that hanging over her.'

Sarah was too shocked to respond. 'No wonder she was frightened to sleep downstairs,' she said at last.

'She's hardly slept at all for weeks, as far as I can gather. The only way I could get her to take the codeine was to promise again and again that I wouldn't leave the house. She's paranoid about being caught unawares and she's paranoid about the police asking any more questions.'

'But the Sergeant knows there's something,' Sarah warned him. 'He phoned this morning and asked me to try and find out what it was. His word for it was coercion. Hughes must be using coercion, he said, but we can't do much unless we know what sort of coercion it is. Ruth's not the only one it's happened to. They know of at least three others and they think it's only the tip of the iceberg. None of them talk.'

'She's pregnant,' said Jack flatly. 'I said you'd know what to do. JE-SUS!' He threw the fork like a lance into the middle of the lawn, his bellow of rage roaring into the air. 'I-COULD-KILL-THE-FUCKING-BASTARD!'

Sarah put a hand on his arm to calm him. 'How many weeks is she?'

'I don't know,' he said, rubbing his eyes. 'I didn't ask. I wish to God you'd been here. I did my best but I was so damn useless. She needed a woman to talk to, not a clumsy sod who started out by telling her what nice people men are. I gave her a lecture, for Christ's sake, on male decency.'

She hushed him as his voice started to rise again. 'She wouldn't have talked to you if she hadn't felt comfortable with you. How long's she been asleep?'

He looked at his watch. 'A couple of hours.'

'Okay, we'll leave her a little bit longer, then I'll go and see her.' She linked her arm with his. 'I don't suppose you've eaten.'

'No.'

She drew him towards the house. 'Come on then. Things always look worse on an empty stomach.'

'What are we going to do, Sarah?'

'Whatever's best for Ruth.'

'And to hell with all the other wretched girls who get broken in the future?'

'We can only take one step at a time, Jack.' She looked desperately worried.

'O vile, intolerable, not to be endur'd!' Ruth is crying again and it is driving me mad. I simply cannot bear it. I want to take the wretched child and shake her till her teeth rattle, smack her, hit her, anything to stop this petulant whining. My anger never goes away. Even when she's silent, I find myself waiting for her to begin.

It is so unjust when I went through the same thing with Joanna. If she would only show some interest in her daughter, it wouldn't be so bad, but she does everything she can to avoid her. In desperation this morning, I tried to put the scold's bridle on Ruth's head, but Joanna convulsed at the sight of it. I called Hugh Hendry out again and this time he had the sense to prescribe tranquillizers. He said she was overwrought.

Would to God they had had Valium in my day. As always, I had to cope alone . . .

Twelve

DS COOPER'S CAR had barely drawn to a halt in Mill House driveway later that evening when Jack wrenched open the passenger door and folded himself on to the seat. 'Do me a favour, old son, reverse out slowly with as little noise as possible and drive me a mile or two down the road.' He nodded approval as Cooper eased into gear. 'And next time, phone first, there's a good chap.'

Cooper, apparently unconcerned by this somewhat disrespectful behaviour towards an officer of the law, manoeuvred backwards through the gate, pulling the wheel gently to avoid crunching the gravel. 'Doesn't she trust me?' he asked, changing to first gear and driving off in the direction of Fontwell.

'Not you personally. The police. There's a lay-by about half a mile ahead on the right. Pull in there and I'll walk back.'

'Has she said anything?'

Jack didn't answer and Cooper flicked him a sideways glance. His face looked drawn in the reflected light from the headlamps, but it was too dark to read his expression.

'You're obliged by law to assist the police in their enquiries, Mr Blakeney.'

'It's Jack,' he said. 'What's your name, Sergeant?'

'Just what you'd expect,' said Cooper dryly. 'Thomas. Good old Tommy Cooper.'

Jack's teeth gleamed in a smile. 'Rough.'

'Rough is right. People expect me to be a comedian. Where's this lay-by of yours?'

'A hundred yards or so.' He peered through the windscreen. 'Coming up on your right now.'

Cooper drew across the road and brought the car to a halt, placing a restraining hand on Jack's arm as he switched off the engine and killed the lights. 'Five minutes,' he said. 'I really do need to ask you some questions.'

Jack let go of the door handle. 'All right, but I warn you there is very little I can tell you except that Ruth is scared out of her wits and extremely reluctant to have anything more to do with the police.'

'She may not be given a choice. We may decide to prosecute.'

'For what? Stealing from a member of her family who didn't even bother to report the few trinkets that were taken? You can't prosecute Ruth for that, Tommy. And anyway, Sarah as legatee would insist on any charges being dropped. Her position's delicate enough without forcing a criminal record on the child she's effectively disinherited.'

Cooper sighed. 'Call me Cooper,' he said. 'Most people do. Tommy's more of an embarrassment than a name.' He took out a cigarette. 'Why do you call Miss Lascelles a child? She's a young woman, Jack. Seventeen years old and legally responsible for her actions. If she's prosecuted she will be dealt with in an adult court. You really shouldn't allow sentiment to cloud your judgement. We're not talking just trinkets here. She took her grandmother for five hundred pounds a month ago and didn't bat an eyelid while she was doing it. And on the day of the murder she stole some earrings worth two thousand pounds.'

'Did Mathilda report the money stolen?'

'No,' Cooper admitted.

'Then Sarah certainly won't.'

Cooper sighed again. 'I guess you've been talking to a lawyer, told you to keep your mouths shut, I suppose, and never mind what Hughes does to anyone else.' He struck a match and held it to the tip of his cigarette, watching Jack in the flaring light. Anger showed itself in every line of the other man's face, in the aggressive jut of his jaw, in the compressed lips and the narrowed eyes. He seemed to be exercising enormous self-control just to hold himself in. With a flick of his thumbnail Cooper extinguished the match and plunged the car into darkness again. Only the glow of burning tobacco remained. 'Hughes is working to a pattern,' he said. 'I explained as much of it as we have been able to find out to your wife this morning. In essence—'

'She told me,' Jack cut in. 'I know what he's doing.'

'Okay,' said Cooper easily, 'then you'll know how important it is to stop him. There'll be other Ruths, make no mistake about that, and whatever he's doing to these girls to force them to work for him will get more extreme as time goes by. That's the nature of the beast.' He drew on his cigarette. 'He does force them, doesn't he?'

'You're the policeman, Cooper. Arrest the sod and ask him.'

'That's exactly what we're planning to do. Tomorrow. But we'll have a much stronger hand if we know what to ask him *about*. We're stumbling around in the dark at the moment.'

Jack didn't say anything.

'I could get a warrant for Miss Lascelles's arrest and take her down to the station. How would she stand up to the psychological thumbscrews, do you think? You might not have realized it but she's different from the other girls Hughes has used. She doesn't have parents she can rely on to protect her.'

'Sarah and I will do it,' Jack said curtly. 'We're in loco parentis at the moment.'

'But you've no legal standing. We could insist that her mother was present during questioning and if it's of any interest to you the only thing Mrs Lascelles was concerned about last night was whether her daughter's expulsion had anything to do with Mrs Gillespie's murder. She'd break Ruth for us if she thought it would help her get her hands on the old lady's money.'

Jack gave a faint laugh. 'You're all piss and wind, Cooper. You're too damn nice to do anything like that, and we both know it. Take it from me, you'd have it on your conscience for life if you added to the damage that's already been done to that poor kid.'

'It's bad then.'

'I'd say that was a fair assumption, yes.'

'You must tell me, Jack. We won't get anywhere with Hughes if you don't tell me.'

'I can't. I've given my word to Ruth.'

'Break it.'

Jack shook his head. 'No. In my book a word, once given, cannot be taken back.' He thought for a moment. 'There's one thing I could do, though. You deliver him to me and I'll deliver him to you. How does that grab you as an idea?'

Cooper sounded genuinely regretful. 'It's known as aiding and abetting. I'd be kissing goodbye to my pension.'

Jack gave a low laugh. 'Think about it,' he said, reaching for the handle and thrusting open the door. 'It's my best offer.' The smoke from Cooper's cigarette eddied after him as he got out. 'All I need is an address, Tommy. When you're ready, phone it through.' He slammed the door and loped off into the darkness.

Violet Orloff tiptoed into her husband's bedroom and frowned anxiously at him. He was swathed in yards of Paisley dressing-gown and reclined like a fat old Buddha against his pillows, a mug of cocoa in one hand, a cheese sandwich in the other, the *Daily Telegraph* crossword on his knees. 'She's crying again.'

Duncan peered at her over his bifocals. 'It's not our business, dear,' he said firmly.

'But I can *hear* her. She's sobbing her heart out.'

'It's not our business.'

'Except I keep thinking, suppose we'd *done* something when we heard Mathilda crying, would she be dead now? I feel very badly about that, Duncan.'

He sighed. 'I refuse to feel guilty because Mathilda's

cruelties to her family, imagined or real, provoked one of them into killing her. There was nothing we could have done to prevent it then, and as you keep reminding me, there is nothing we can do now to bring her back. We have alerted the police to possible motive. I think we should leave it there.'

'But, Duncan,' Violet wailed, 'if we *know* it was Joanna or Ruth, then we must tell the police.'

He frowned. 'Don't be silly, Violet. We don't know who did it, nor, frankly, are we interested. Logic says it had to be someone with a key or someone she trusted enough to let into the house, and the police don't need me to tell them that.' The frown deepened. 'Why do you keep pushing me into meddling, anyway? It's almost as if you want Joanna and Ruth to be arrested.'

'Not *both* of them. They didn't do it together, did they?' She grimaced horribly, screwing her face into an absurd caricature. 'But Joanna *is* crying again, and I think we should do something. Mathilda always said the house was full of ghosts. Perhaps she's come back.'

Duncan stared at her with open alarm. 'You're not ill, are you?'

'Of course I'm not ill,' she said crossly. 'I think I'll pop round, see if she's all right, talk to her. You never know, she might decide to *confide* in me.' With an arch wave she tiptoed off again, and moments later he heard the sound of the front door opening.

Duncan shook his head in perplexity as he returned to his crossword. *Was* this the beginnings of senility? Violet was either very brave or very foolish to interfere with an emotionally disturbed woman who had, quite clearly, loathed her mother enough to murder her. He could only imagine what Joanna's reaction would be to his wife's naïve assertions that she knew more than she'd told the police. The thought worried him enough to force him out of his warm bed and into his slippers, before padding downstairs in her wake.

But whatever had upset Joanna Lascelles was destined to remain a mystery to the Orloffs that night. She refused to open the door to Violet's ringing and it wasn't until the Sunday at church that they heard rumours about Jack Blakeney returning to his wife and Ruth being so afraid to go home to Cedar House and her mother that she had chosen to live with the Blakeneys. Southcliffe, it was said, had asked her to leave because of the scandal that was about to break around the Lascelles family. This time the furiously wagging tongues centred their suspicion on Joanna.

If Cooper was honest with himself, he could see Dave Hughes's attraction for young middle-class girls. He was a personable 'bit of rough', handsome, tall, with the clean, muscular looks of a Chippendale, dark shoulder-length hair, bright blue eyes and an engaging smile. Unthreatening was the word that leapt immediately to mind, and it was only gradually in the confined atmosphere of a Bournemouth police interview room that the teeth began to show behind the smile. What you saw, Cooper realized, was very professional packaging. What lay beneath the surface was anyone's guess.

Detective Chief Inspector Charlie Jones was another where the packaging obscured the real man. It amused Cooper to see how seriously Hughes underestimated the sad Pekinese face that regarded him with such mild-mannered apology. Charlie took the chair on the other side of the table from Hughes and sifted rather helplessly through his briefcase. 'It was good of you to come in,' he said. 'I realize time's precious. We're grateful for your co-operation, Mr Hughes.'

Hughes shrugged amiably. 'If I'd known I had a choice, I probably wouldn't've come. What's this about then?'

Charlie isolated a piece of crumpled paper and spread it out on the table. 'Miss Ruth Lascelles. She says you're her lover.'

Hughes shrugged again. 'Sure. I know Ruth. She's seventeen. Since when was sex with a seventeen-year-old a crime?'

'It's not.'

'What's the hassle then?'

'Theft. She's been stealing.'

Hughes looked suitably surprised but didn't say anything.

'Did you know she was stealing?'

He shook his head. 'She always told me her granny gave her money. I believed her. The old bitch was rolling in it.'

'Was? You know she's dead then.'

'Sure. Ruth told me she killed herself.'

Charlie ran his finger down the page. 'Ruth says you told her to steal silver-backed hair brushes, jewellery and valuable first editions from Mrs Gillespie's library. Similar items, in fact, to what Miss Julia Sefton claims you told her to steal from her parents. Small bits and pieces that wouldn't be missed but could be disposed of very easily for ready cash. Who sold them, Mr Hughes? You or Ruth?'

'Do me a favour, Inspector. Do I look the sort of mug who'd act as a fence for an over-privileged, middle-class tart who'd drop me in it quick as winking the minute she was rumbled? Jesus,' he said with disgust, 'give me some credit for common sense. They only take up with me because they're bored out of their tiny minds with the jerks their parents approve of. And that should tell you something about the sort of girls they are. They call them slags where I come from, and thieving's in their blood along with the whoring. If Ruth says I set her up to it, then she's lying to get herself off the hook. It's so bloody easy, isn't it? I'm just scum from a frigging squat and she's Miss Lascelles from Southcliffe girls' school. Who's going to believe me?'

Charlie smiled his lugubrious smile. 'Ah, well,' he murmured, 'belief isn't really the issue, is it? We both know you're lying and that Ruth is telling the truth, but the question is can we persuade her to stand up in court and tell the *whole* truth? You made a bad choice there, Mr Hughes. She doesn't have a father, you see, only a mother, and you probably know as well as I do that women are far harder on their daughters than men ever could be. Mrs Lascelles won't protect Ruth the way Julia's father protected *her*. Apart from anything else, she positively loathes the girl. It would have been different, I suspect, if Mrs Gillespie were still alive, she would probably have hushed it up for the sake of the family's reputation, but as she isn't I can't see anybody championing Ruth.'

Hughes grinned. 'Well, go ahead then. Prosecute the thieving little bitch. It's no skin off my nose.'

It was Charlie's turn to look surprised. 'You don't like her?'

'She was okay for the odd screw, no great shakes but okay. Look, I told you, they only make out with me because they want to get back at their folks. So what am I supposed to do? Tug my forelock in gratitude for the use of their very ordinary bodies? I can get as good if not better down the nightclub of a Saturday.' He grinned again, a captivatingly wicked grin, guaranteed to melt female hearts but totally lost on Jones and Cooper. 'I do the business for them, give them their thrills, and I only complain when they try and lay their fucking thieving on me. It really gets up my nose, if you want the truth. You're such bloody suckers, you lot. A pretty face, a posh accent, a sob story, and, bingo, get Dave Hughes down here and give him the works. You just won't accept that they're slags, same as the prozzies on the streets in the red light district.'

Charlie looked thoughtful. 'That's the second time you've called Miss Lascelles a slag. What's your definition of a slag, Mr Hughes?'

'The same as yours, I guess.'

'A vulgar, coarse woman who sells her body for money. I wouldn't say that was a description of Miss Lascelles.'

Hughes looked amused. 'A slag's an easy lay. Ruth was so bloody easy, it was pathetic.'

'You said she was no great shakes as a screw,' Charlie carried on imperturbably. 'That's a very revealing admission, don't you think?'

'Why?'

'It says more about you than it does about her. Didn't she fancy you? Did you have to force her? What is it you like doing that she didn't like you enough to go along with? I find that fascinating.'

'I've had better, that's all I meant.'

'Better what, Mr Hughes?'

'Lovers, for Christ's sake. Women who know what they're doing. Women who handle themselves and me with more fucking finesse. Screwing Ruth was like screwing blancmange. It was me had to do all the work while she just lay there telling me how much she loved me. It pisses me off, that, it really does.'

Charlie frowned. 'Why did you bother with her then?'

Hughes smiled cynically at the all-too-patent trap. 'Why not? She was free, she was available, and I get horny like the next man. Are you going to charge me with doing what comes naturally?'

Charlie thought for a moment or two. 'Did you ever go into Cedar House?'

'The old biddy's place?' He shook his head. 'No way. She'd have done her nut if she'd got wind of who Ruth had hitched herself to. I don't go looking for trouble though you'd be amazed at the girls. Half of them think their parents are going to welcome me with open arms.' He mimicked the clipped diction of the upper classes. 'Mummy, Daddy, I'd like you to meet my new boyfriend, Dave.' The boyish grin again. 'They're so bloody thick, you wouldn't believe.'

'There've been a lot of these girls then. We thought there might have been.'

Hughes tilted his chair back, relaxed, complacent, unbelievably confident. 'I appeal to them, Inspector. It's a talent I have. Don't ask me where it comes from, though, because I couldn't tell you. Perhaps it's the Irish in me.'

'On your mother's side, presumably.'

'How did you guess?'

'You're a type, Mr Hughes. Probably the illegitimate son of a whore who screwed anything for money, if your extreme prejudice against prostitutes is anything to go by. You wouldn't have a clue who your father was because he might have been any one of fifty who shafted her during the week you were conceived. Hence your contempt and hatred for women and your inability to conduct an adult relationship. You had no male role model to learn from or emulate. Tell me,' he murmured, 'does getting it free make you feel superior to the sad, anonymous little man who paid to father you? Is that why it's so important?'

The blue eyes narrowed angrily. 'I don't have to listen to this.'

'I'm afraid you do. You see, I'm very interested in your pathological dislike of women. You can't speak about them without being offensive. That isn't normal, Mr Hughes, and as Sergeant Cooper and I are investigating an extraordinarily abnormal crime, your attitude alarms me. Let me give you a definition of psychopathic personality disorder.' He consulted the piece of paper again. 'It manifests itself in poor or non-existent job performance, persistent criminality, sexual promiscuity and aggressive sexual behaviour. People with this disorder are irresponsible and extremely callous; they feel no guilt over their antisocial acts and find it difficult to make lasting relationships.' He looked up.

'Rather a good description of you, don't you think? Have you ever been treated for this type of disorder?'

'No, I fucking well haven't,' he said furiously. 'Jesus, what is this garbage, anyway? Since when was thieving an abnormal crime?'

'We're not talking about thieving.'

Hughes looked suddenly wary. 'What are we talking about then?'

'The things you do to the girls.'

'I don't get you.'

Charlie leaned forward aggressively, his eyes like flints. 'Oh, yes, you do, you filthy little nonce. You're a pervert, Hughes, and when you go down and the rest of the prisoners find out what you've been banged up for, you'll learn what it's like to be on the receiving end of aggressive behaviour. They'll beat the shit out of you, urinate on your food and use a razor on you if they can get you in the shower alone. It's one of the oddities of prison life. Ordinary prisoners hate sex offenders, particularly sex offenders who can only get a hard-on with children. Whatever they've done themselves pales into insignificance beside what you and people like you do to defenceless kids.'

'Jesus! I don't do kids. I hate bloody kids.'

'Julia Sefton had just turned sixteen when you did her. She could almost have been your daughter.'

'That's not a crime. I'm not the first man who's slept with someone young enough to be his daughter. Get real, Inspector.'

'But you always pick young girls. What is it about young girls that gets you so excited?'

'I don't pick them. They pick me.'

'Do older women frighten you? That's the usual pattern with nonces. They have to make out with children because mature women terrify them.'

'How many times do I have to tell you? I don't make out with children.'

Abruptly Jones switched tack. 'Ruth stole some diamond earrings from her grandmother on Saturday, November the sixth, the same day that Mrs Gillespie killed herself. Did you take Ruth there that day?'

Hughes looked as if he was about to deny it, then shrugged. 'She asked me to.'

'Why?'

'Why what?'

'Why did she ask you to take her? What did she want to do there?'

Hughes looked vague. 'She never said. But I never went in the frigging place and I didn't know she planned to steal any frigging earrings.'

'So she rang you at your squat, asked you to drive all the way out to Southcliffe to pick her up, take her from there to Fontwell and then back to Southcliffe, without ever explaining why.'

'Yeah.'

'And that's all you did? Acted as her chauffeur to and fro and waited outside Cedar House while she went in?'

'Yeah.'

'But you've admitted you didn't like her. In fact you despised her. Why go to so much trouble for someone you didn't like?'

'It was worth it for a screw.'

'With blancmange?'

Hughes grinned. 'I felt horny that day.'

'She told my Sergeant she was absent from school for upwards of six hours. It's thirty miles from Southcliffe to Fontwell, so let's say it took you forty minutes each way. That leaves some four and a half hours unaccounted for. Are you telling me you sat in your van in Fontwell village for four and a half hours twiddling your thumbs while Ruth was inside with her grandmother?'

'It wasn't that long. We stopped on the way back for the screw.'

'Where exactly did you park in Fontwell?'

'Can't remember now. I was always waiting for her some place or another.'

Charlie placed his finger on the crumpled page of paper. 'According to the publican at the Three Pigeons your van was parked on his forecourt that afternoon. After ten minutes you drove away, but he saw you stop beside the church to pick someone up. We must presume this was Ruth unless you are now going to tell me you took a third party to Fontwell the day Mrs Gillespie killed herself.'

The wary look was back in Hughes's eyes. 'It was Ruth.'

'Okay, then what were you and Ruth doing for four and a half hours, Mr Hughes? You certainly weren't screwing her. It doesn't take four and a half hours to screw blancmange. Or perhaps it does for someone who suffers from a psychopathic personality disorder. Perhaps it takes you that long to get it up.'

Hughes refused to be needled. 'I guess there's no reason for me to protect the silly bitch. Okay, she asked me to drive her to this backstreet jeweller somewhere in Southampton. I didn't ask why, I just did it. But you can't do me for that. All I did was act as a taxi. If she stole some earrings and then sold them, I knew nothing about it. I was just the patsy with the wheels.'

'According to Miss Lascelles she gave the money to you as soon as she sold the earrings. She said it was six hundred and fifty pounds in cash and that you then drove her straight back to school in time for her physics lecture.'

Hughes didn't say anything.

'You profited from a crime, Mr Hughes. That's illegal.'

'Ruth's lying. She never gave me any money and, even if she did, you'd have to prove I knew she'd thieved something in the first place. She'll tell you it was all her idea. Look, I don't deny she funded me from time to time, but she said the money was hers and I believed her. Why shouldn't I? The old granny was rolling in it. Stood to reason Ruth would be as well.' He grinned again. 'So what if she did give me cash from time to time? How was I to know the silly bitch was stealing it? She owed me something for the petrol I wasted acting as her frigging chauffeur in the holidays.'

'But she didn't fund you that day?'

'I already said no, and no's what I mean.'

'Did you have any money on you?'

'A fiver, maybe.'

'What was the name of the backstreet jeweller in Southampton?' Charlie asked abruptly.

'No idea. I never went in the place. You'll have to ask Ruth. She just told me to go to a road and stop at the end of it.'

'What was the name of the road?'

'Don't know. She had a map, told me right, left, straight on, stop. I just did what I was told. You'll have to ask Ruth.'

'She doesn't know. She says you drove her there, told her which shop to go into, who to ask for and what to say.'

'She's lying.'

'I don't think so, Mr Hughes.'

'Prove it.'

Charlie thought rapidly. He had no doubt that Hughes was telling the truth when he said he hadn't entered Cedar House or the jewellers', not in Ruth's company anyway. The beauty of his scam was that he didn't handle the stolen goods himself, merely transported the girls and the goods to someone who would. That way, the only person who could ever implicate him was the girl, and she wasn't going to because, for whatever reason, she was too frightened of him. 'I intend to prove it, Mr Hughes. Let's start with an account of your movements after you dropped Ruth back at school. Did you go to this nightclub you mentioned? It'll be expensive, they usually are, and coke and ecstasy don't come cheap, both of which I suspect you're on. People will remember you, especially if you were throwing money about.'

Hughes saw another trap and giggled. 'I already said I hadn't got any money, Inspector. I drove around a bit and then went back to the squat.'

'What time was that?'

He shrugged. 'No idea.'

'So if I find someone who says a white transit van was

251

parked in the vicinity of a Bournemouth nightclub that night, you'll say it couldn't have been yours because you were just driving around.'

'That's about the size of it.'

Charlie bared his teeth in a predatory smile. 'I have to inform you, Mr Hughes, that you will be transferred shortly to Learmouth Police Station where you will be questioned at length about the murder of Mrs Mathilda Gillespie.' He gathered his notes together and thrust them back into his pocket.

'Shit!' said Hughes angrily. 'What crap are you trying to lay on me now? You said she killed herself.'

'I was lying. She was murdered and I have reason to believe you were involved in that murder.'

Hughes surged aggressively to his feet. 'I told you I never went in the fucking place. Anyway, the publican's my alibi. He saw me in his car park and watched me pick up Ruth. How could I murder the old lady if I was in my van the whole time?'

'She wasn't murdered at two thirty. She was murdered later that evening.'

'I wasn't there later that evening.'

'Your van was. The publican says you returned that evening and, as you yourself have just told us, you and your van have no alibi for the night of November the sixth. You were driving around, remember?'

'I was here in Bournemouth and so was the van.'

'Prove it.' Charlie stood up. 'Until you do, I'm holding you on suspicion of murder.'

'You're really out of order on this one. I'll get my brief on you.'

'Do that. You'll be allowed your phone call at Learmouth.'

'Why would I want to kill the old cow anyway?'

Charlie lifted a shaggy eyebrow. 'Because you have a history of terrorizing women. This time you went too far.'

'I don't bloody murder them.'

'What do you do to them?'

'Shag 'em that's all. And I don't short change 'em neither. I've never had a complaint yet.'

'Which is probably what the Yorkshire Ripper said every time he came home with his hammer and his chisel in the boot of his car.'

'You're way out of order,' said Hughes again, stamping his foot. 'I didn't even know the old bitch. I didn't *want* to know her. Jesus, you bastard, how could I kill someone I didn't even know?'

'You got born, didn't you?'

'What the hell's that supposed to mean?'

'Birth and death, Hughes. They happen at random. Your mother didn't know your father but you still got born. The not-knowing is irrelevant. You were there that day, you were using her granddaughter to steal from her and Mrs Gillespie knew it. You had to shut her up before she talked to us.'

'I don't work it that way.'

'How do you work it then?'

But Hughes refused to say another word.

I have brought Joanna and her baby home to live with me. I could not believe the squalor I found them in when I arrived in London. Joanna has given up all attempts at caring for the child or even practising elementary hygiene. She is clearly not fit to live alone and, while I abhorred that wretched Jew she married, at least while he was alive she had some pretensions to normality.

I am very afraid that the shock of Steven's death has sent her over the edge. She was in the baby's room this morning, holding a pillow over the cot. I asked her what she was doing, and she said: 'Nothing,' but I have no doubt at all that, had I entered the room a few minutes later, the pillow would have been across the baby's face. The awful part is that I saw myself standing there, like some ghastly reflection in a distorted mirror. The shock was tremendous. Does Joanna suspect? Does anyone, other than Jane, suspect?

There is no cure for inbred insanity. 'Unnatural deeds do breed unnatural troubles . . .'

Thirteen

JANE MARRIOTT MARCHED into Sarah's office in the Fontwell surgery the following morning after the last patient had left and deposited herself firmly in a chair. Sarah glanced at her. 'You're looking very cross,' she remarked as she signed off some paperwork.

'I feel cross.'

'What about?'

'You.'

Sarah folded her arms. 'What have I done?'

'You've lost your compassion.' Jane tapped a stern finger against her watch. 'I know I used to wig you about the length of time you spent on your patients, but I admired you for the trouble you took. Now, suddenly, they're in and out like express trains. Poor old Mrs Henderson was almost in tears. "What have I done to upset Doctor?" she asked me. "She hardly had a kind word for me." You really mustn't let this business over Mathilda get to you, Sarah. It's not fair on other people.' She drew an admonishing breath. 'And don't tell me I'm only the receptionist and you're the doctor. Doctors are fallible, just like the rest of us.'

Sarah pushed some papers about her desk with the point of her pencil. 'Do you know what Mrs Henderson's first words to me were when she came in? "I reckon it's safe to come back to you, Doctor, seeing as how it was that bitch of a daughter what done it." And she lied to you. I didn't have a *single* kind word for her. I told her the truth for once, that the only thing wrong with her is an acidulated spleen which could be cured immediately if she looked for the good in people instead of the bad.' She wagged the pencil under Jane's nose. 'I am rapidly coming to the conclusion that Mathilda was right. This village is one of the nastiest places on earth, peopled entirely by ignorant, evil-minded bigots with nothing better to do in their lives than sit and pass judgement on anyone who doesn't conform to their commonplace, petty-minded stereotypes. It's not compassion I've lost, it's my blinkers.'

Jane removed the pencil from Sarah's grasp before it could lodge itself in her nostril. 'She's a lonely old widow, with little or no education, and she was trying in her very ham-fisted way to say sorry for ever having doubted you. If you haven't the generosity of spirit to make allowances for her clumsy diplomacy then you are not the woman I thought you were. And for your information, she now thinks she is suffering from a very severe condition, namely acidulated spleen, which you are refusing to treat. And she's put that down to the cuts in the Health Service and the fact that, as an old woman, she is now considered expendable.'

Sarah sighed. 'She wasn't the only one. They're all cock-a-hoop because they think Joanna did it and I resent them using me and my surgery to score points off her.' She pulled her fingers through her hair. 'Because that's what today was all about, Jane, a sort of childish yah-boo-sucks at their latest victim, and if Jack hadn't decided to play silly buggers, then there wouldn't have been so much for them to gossip about.'

'Don't you believe it,' said Jane tartly. 'What they can't get any other way they make up.'

'Hah! And you have the nerve to haul me over the coals for cynicism!'

'Oh, don't assume I'm not just as irritated as you are by their silliness. Of course I am, but then I don't expect anything else. They haven't changed just because Mathilda's died, you know, and I must say it's a bit rich accusing Mrs Henderson of only seeing the bad in people when the greatest exponent of that has just left you a small fortune. Mrs Henderson's view of people is positively saintly compared with Mathilda's. *She* really did have an acidulated spleen.'

'All right. Point taken. I'll drop in on Mrs H. on my way home.'

'Well, I hope you'll be gracious enough to apologize to her. Perhaps I'm being over-sensitive but she did seem so upset, and it's not like you to be cruel, Sarah.'

'I feel cruel,' she growled. 'As a matter of interest, do you talk to the male doctors like this?'

'No.'

'I see.'

Jane bridled. 'You don't see anything. I'm fond of you. If your mother were here she would be saying the same things. You should never allow events to sour your nature, Sarah. You leave that particular weakness to the Mathildas of this world.'

Sarah felt a surge of affection for the elderly woman, whose apple cheeks had grown rosy with indignation. Her mother, of course, would say no such thing, merely purse her lips and declare that she had always known Sarah was sour at heart. It took someone with Jane's generosity to see that other people were diplomatically inept, or weak, or disillusioned. 'You're asking me to betray my principles,' she said mildly.

'No, my dear, I'm asking you to stand by them.'

'Why should I condone Mrs Henderson calling Joanna a murderess? There's no more evidence against her than there was against me, and if I apologize it's a tacit acceptance.'

'Nonsense,' said Jane stoutly. 'It's courtesy towards an old lady. How you deal with Joanna is a different matter altogether. If you don't approve of the way the village is treating her then you must demonstrate it in a very public way so that no one is in any doubt of where your sympathies lie. But,' her old eyes softened as they rested on the younger woman, 'don't take your annoyance out on poor Dolly Henderson, my dear. She can't be expected to see things as you and I do. She never enjoyed our liberal education.'

'I will apologize.'

'Thank you.'

Sarah suddenly leaned forward and planted a kiss on the other's cheek.

Jane looked surprised. 'What was that for?'

'Oh, I don't know.' Sarah smiled. 'Standing in for my mother, perhaps. I wonder sometimes if the stand-ins aren't rather better at the job than the real thing. Mathilda did it, too, you know. She wasn't *all* acidulated spleen. She could be just as sweet as you when she wanted to be.'

'Is that why you're looking after Ruth? As a sort of quid pro quo?'

'Don't you approve?'

Jane sighed. 'I don't approve or disapprove. I just feel it's a little provocative in the circumstances. Whatever your reasons for doing it, the village has put the worst interpretation on those reasons. You do know they're saying that Joanna's about to be arrested for the murder of her mother, and that's why Ruth has gone to live with you?'

'I hadn't realized it was quite that bad.' Sarah frowned. 'God, they're absurd. Where do they get this rubbish from?'

'They put two and two together and make twenty.'

'The trouble is' – she paused – 'there's nothing much I can do about it.'

'But, my dear, all that's required is an explanation of why Ruth is with you,' Jane suggested, 'and then you can knock these rumours on the head. There must be one, after all.'

Sarah sighed. 'It's up to Ruth to explain, and at the moment she's not in a position to do that.'

'Then invent one,' said Jane bluntly. 'Give it to Mrs Henderson when you see her this afternoon and it'll be all round the village by tomorrow evening. Fight fire with fire, Sarah. It's the only way.'

Mrs Henderson was touched by Dr Blakeney's apology for her bad temper in the surgery, thought it very handsome of her to take the trouble to come out to her cottage, and quite agreed that if you'd been up all night looking after a seventeen-year-old showing all the symptoms of glandular fever, you were bound to be shirty the next day. Mind, she didn't quite understand why Ruth had to stay with Dr Blakeney and her husband in the circumstances. Wouldn't it be more fitting for her to remain with her mother? Much more fitting, agreed Sarah firmly, and Ruth would prefer it too, of course, but, as Mrs Henderson knew, glandular fever was an extremely painful and debilitating viral infection, and because of the likelihood of its recurring if the patient wasn't cared for properly and bearing in mind this was Ruth's A level year, Joanna had asked Sarah to take her in and get her back on her feet again as quickly as possible. In the circumstances, what with Mrs Gillespie's will and all (Sarah looked suitably embarrassed), she could hardly refuse, could she?

'Not when you're the one what's got all the money,' was Mrs Henderson's considered retort, but her rheumy eyes clouded in puzzlement. 'Ruth going back to Southcliffe then, when she's better, like?'

'Where else would she go?' murmured Sarah unblushingly. 'As I said, it's her A level year.'

'Well, I never! There's some lies being told and no mistake. Who killed Mrs Gillespie, then, if it weren't you and it weren't the daughter?'

'God knows, Mrs Henderson.'

'Happen he does, too, so it's a shame He doesn't pass it on. He's causing a lot of bother by keeping the information to Hisself.'

'Perhaps she killed herself.'

'No,' said the old woman decidedly. 'That I'll never

believe. I don't say as I liked her very much but Mrs Gillespie was no coward.'

Sarah knew Joanna was in Cedar House, despite the stubborn silence that greeted her ringing of the doorbell. She'd seen the set white face in the shadows at the back of the dining-room and the brief flicker of recognition before Joanna slipped into the hall and out of sight. Rather more than her refusal to answer the door, it was her flicker of recognition that fuelled Sarah's anger. Ruth was the issue here, not Mathilda's will or Jack's shenanigans, and while she might have sympathized with Joanna's reluctance to open the door to the police, she could not forgive the barricading of it against the person Joanna knew was sheltering her daughter. Sarah set off grimly down the path that skirted the house. What kind of woman, she wondered, put personal enmity before concern for her daughter's welfare?

In her mind's eye, she pictured the portrait Jack was working on. He had trapped Joanna inside a triangular prism of mirrors, with her personality split like refracted light. It was an extraordinary depiction of confused identity, the more so because for each image there was a single image reflected back from the huge encompassing mirror that bordered the canvas. Sarah had asked him what the single image represented. 'Joanna as she wants to be seen. Admired, adored, beautiful.'

She pointed to the prism images. 'And what are they?'

'That's the Joanna she's suppressing with drugs,' he said. 'The ugly, unloved woman who was rejected by mother, husband and daughter. Everything in her life is illusion, hence the mirror theme.'

'That's sad.'

'Don't go sentimental on me, Sarah, or on her either for that matter. Joanna is the most self-centred woman I have ever met. I guess most addicts are. She says Ruth rejected her. That's baloney. It was Joanna who rejected her because Ruth cried whenever Joanna picked her up. It was a vicious circle. The more her baby cried the less inclined she was to love it. She claimed Steven rejected her because he was revolted by the pregnancy, but in the next sentence she admitted she couldn't stand the way he fussed over Ruth. It was she, I think, who rejected him.'

'But why? There must be a reason for it.'

'I suspect it's very simple. The only person she loves or is capable of loving is herself and because her swollen belly made her less attractive in her own eyes, she resented the two people responsible for it, namely her husband and her baby. I'll put money on the fact that she's the one who found the pregnancy repulsive.'

'Nothing's ever that simple, Jack. It could be something quite serious. Untreated post-natal depression. Narcissistic personality disorder. Schizophrenia even. Perhaps Mathilda was right, and she *is* unstable.'

'Maybe, but if she is, then Mathilda was entirely to blame. From what I can gather, she kowtowed to Joanna and Joanna's histrionics from day one.' He gestured towards the painting. 'When I said that everything in her life is illusion, what I meant was: everything is false. This is the fantasy she wants you to believe, but I'm ninety-nine per cent certain she doesn't believe it herself.' He laid his forefinger on the central triangle of the prism, which as yet contained nothing. 'That's where the real Joanna will be, in the only mirror that can't reflect her stylized image of herself.'

Clever stuff, thought Sarah, but was it true? 'And what is the real Joanna?'

He stared at the painting. 'Utterly ruthless, I think,' he said slowly, 'utterly and completely ruthless about getting her own way.'

The kitchen door was locked but the key that Mathilda had hidden under the third flowerpot to the right was still there and, with an exclamation of triumph, Sarah pounced on it and inserted it into the Yale lock. It was only after she'd opened the door and was removing the key to lay it on the kitchen table that she wondered if anyone had told the police that entry into Cedar House was that easy if you knew what was under the flowerpot. *She* certainly hadn't, but then she had forgotten all about it until the need to get in had jogged her memory. She had used it once, months ago, when Mathilda's arthritis was so bad that she hadn't been able to get out of her chair to open the front door.

Gingerly, she laid the key on the table and stared at it. Intuition told her that whoever had used the key last had killed Mathilda Gillespie, and she didn't need to be Einstein to work out that if their fingerprints had been on it she had just destroyed them with her own. 'Oh, Jesus!' she said with feeling.

'How dare you come into my house without asking,' announced Joanna in a tight little voice from the hall doorway.

Sarah's glare was so ferocious that the other took a step backwards. 'Will you get off your ridiculous high horse and stop being so pompous,' she snapped. 'We're all in deep shit here and the only thing you ever do is stand on your wretched dignity.'

'Stop swearing. I detest people who swear. You're worse than Ruth and she has a mouth like a sewer. You're not a lady. I can't understand how my mother put up with you.'

Sarah drew a deep angry breath. 'You're unreal, Joanna. Which century do you think you're living in? And what is a lady? Someone like you who's never done a hand's turn in her life but passes muster because she doesn't utter profanities?' She shook her head. 'Not in my book it isn't. The greatest lady I know is a seventy-eight-year-old Cockney who works with the down-and-outs in London and swears like a trooper. Open your eyes, woman. It's the contribution you make to society that earns you respect, not a tight-arsed allegiance to some outmoded principle of feminine purity that died the day women discovered they weren't condemned to a life of endless pregnancy and child-rearing.'

Joanna's lips thinned. 'How did you get in?'

Sarah nodded towards the table. 'I used the key under the flowerpot.'

Joanna frowned angrily. 'Which key?'

'That one, and don't touch it, whatever you do. I'm sure whoever killed your mother must have used it. Can I borrow the phone? I'm going to call the police.' She brushed past Joanna into the hall. 'I'll have to ring Jack as well, tell him

I'm going to be late. Do you mind? Presumably the cost will come out of your mother's estate.'

Joanna pursued her. 'Yes, I do mind. You've no business to force your way in. This is my house and I don't want you here.'

'No,' said Sarah curtly, picking up the phone on the hall table, 'according to your mother's will, Cedar House belongs to me.' She flicked through her diary for Cooper's telephone number. 'And you're only in it because I've balked at evicting you.' She held the receiver to her ear and dialled Learmouth Police Station, watching Joanna as she did so. 'But I'm rapidly changing my mind. Frankly, I see no reason why I should show you more consideration than you're prepared to show your own daughter. Detective Sergeant Cooper, please. Tell him it's Dr Blakeney and it's urgent. I'm at Cedar House in Fontwell. Yes, I'll hold.' She put her hand over the mouthpiece. 'I want you to come home with me and talk to Ruth. Jack and I are doing our best but we're no substitute for you. She needs her mother.'

A small tic flickered at the side of Joanna's mouth. 'I resent your interference in matters that don't concern you. Ruth is quite capable of looking after herself.'

'My God, you really are unreal,' said Sarah in amazement. 'You couldn't give a shit, could you?'

'You are doing this deliberately, Dr Blakeney.'

'If you're referring to my swearing, then, yes, you're dead right I am,' said Sarah. 'I want you to be as shocked by me as I am by you. Where's your sense of responsibility, you *sodding* bitch? Ruth didn't materialize out of thin air. You and your husband had a *fucking* good time when you made her, and don't forget it.' Abruptly she transferred her attention to the telephone. 'Hello, Sergeant, yes, I'm at Cedar House. Yes, she's here, too. No, there's no trouble, it's just that I think I know how Mathilda's murderer got in. Has anyone told you she kept a key to the kitchen door under a flowerpot by the coal bunker at the back? I know, but I forgot about it.' She pulled a face. 'No, it's not still there. It's on the kitchen table. I used it to get in.' She held the receiver away from her ear. 'I did not do it on purpose,' she said coldly after a moment. 'You should have searched a bit more thoroughly at the beginning then it wouldn't have happened.' She replaced the receiver with unnecessary force. 'We've both got to stay here until the police come.'

But Joanna's composure had abandoned her. 'GET OUT OF MY HOUSE!' she screamed 'I WILL NOT BE SPOKEN TO LIKE THIS IN MY HOUSE!' She ran up the stairs. 'YOU WON'T GET AWAY WITH IT! I'LL REPORT YOU TO THE MEDICAL COUNCIL! MUD STICKS. I'LL TELL THEM YOU MURDERED MR STURGIS AND THEN MY MOTHER.'

Sarah followed in her wake, watched her run into the bathroom and slam the door, then lowered herself to the floor and sat cross-legged outside it. 'Tantrums and convulsions may have worked a treat with Mathilda but they sure as hell aren't going to work with me. GODDAMMIT!' she roared suddenly, putting her mouth to the oak-panelled door. 'You're a forty-year-old middle-aged woman, you stupid cow, so act your age.'

'DON'T YOU DARE SPEAK TO ME LIKE THAT!'

'But you get up my nose, Joanna. I have only contempt for someone who can't function unless they're doped stupid.' Tranquillizers was Jack's guess.

No answer.

'You need help,' she went on matter-of-factly, 'and the best person to give it to you is based in London. He's a psychiatrist who specializes in all forms of drug addiction but he won't take you on unless you're willing to give up. If you're interested I'll refer you, if you're not then I suggest you prepare yourself for the long term consequences of habitual substance abuse on the human body, beginning with the one thing you don't want. You will get old very much quicker than I will, Joanna, because your physical chemistry is under constant attack and mine isn't.'

'Get out of my house, Dr Blakeney.' She was beginning to calm down.

'I can't, not till Sergeant Cooper gets here. And it's not your house, remember, it's mine. What are you on?'

There was a long, long silence. 'Valium,' said Joanna finally. 'Dr Hendry prescribed it for me when I came back here after Steven died. I tried to smother Ruth in her cot, so Mother called him in and begged him to give me something.'

'Why did you try to smother Ruth?'

'It seemed the most sensible thing to do. I wasn't coping terribly well.'

'And did tranquillizers help?'

'I don't remember. I was always tired, I remember that.'

Sarah believed her, because she could believe it of Hugh Hendry. Classic symptoms of severe post-natal depression, and instead of giving the poor woman anti-depressants to lift her mood, the idiot had effectively shoved her into a state of lethargy by giving her sedatives. No wonder she found it so difficult to get on with Ruth, when one of the tragic consequences of post-natal depression, if it wasn't treated properly, was that mothers found it difficult to develop natural loving relationships with their babies whom they saw as the reason for their sudden inability to cope. God, but it explained a lot about this family if the women had a tendency to post-natal depression. 'I can help you,' she said. 'Will you let me help you?'

'Lots of people take Valium. It's perfectly legal.'

'And very effective in the right circumstances and under proper supervision. But you're not getting yours from a doctor, Joanna. The problems of diazepam addiction are so well documented that no responsible practitioner would go on prescribing them for you. Which means you've got a private supplier somewhere and the tablets won't be cheap. Black market drugs never are. Let me help you,' she said again.

'You've never been afraid. What would you know about anything if you've never been afraid?'

'What were you afraid of?'

'I was afraid to go to sleep. For years and years I was afraid to go to sleep.' She laughed suddenly. 'Not any more, though. She's dead.'

The doorbell rang.

Sergeant Cooper was in very tetchy mood. The last twenty-four hours had been frustrating ones for him and not just because he had had to work over the weekend and miss Sunday lunch with his children and grandchildren. His wife, tired and irritable herself, had delivered the inevitable ticking-off about his lack of commitment to his family. 'You should put your foot down,' she told him. 'The police force doesn't own you, Tommy.'

They had held Hughes overnight at Learmouth Police Station but had released him without charge at lunchtime. After a persistent refusal the previous afternoon to say anything at all, he had reverted that morning to his previous statement, namely that he had been driving around aimlessly before returning to his squat. He gave the time for his return as nine o'clock. Cooper, dispatched by Charlie Jones to interview the youths who shared the squat with him, had come back deeply irritated.

'It's a set-up,' he told the DCI. 'They've got his alibi off pat. I spoke to each one in turn, asked them to give me an account of their movements on the evening of Saturday, the sixth of November, and each one told me the same story. They were watching the portable telly and drinking beer in Hughes's room when Hughes walked in at nine o'clock. He stayed there all night, as did his van which was parked in the road outside. I did not mention Hughes once, nor imply that I was at all interested in him or his blasted van. They offered the information gratuitously and without prompting.'

'How could they know he'd told us nine o'clock?'

'The solicitor?'

Charlie shook his head. 'Very unlikely. I get the impression he doesn't like his client any more than we do.'

'Then it's a prearranged thing. If questioned, Hughes will always give nine o'clock as the time he returns to the squat.'

'Or they're telling the truth.'

Cooper gave a snort of derision. 'No chance. They were scum. If any of them were tamely watching telly that night, I'm a monkey's uncle. Far more likely, they were out beating up old ladies or knifing rival football supporters.'

The Inspector mulled this over. 'There's no such thing as an alibi applicable in all situations,' he said thoughtfully. 'Not unless Hughes always makes a habit of committing crimes after nine o'clock at night, and we know he doesn't do that, because Ruth stole her grandmother's earrings at two thirty in the afternoon.' He fell silent.

'So what are you saying?' asked Cooper when he didn't go on. 'That they're telling the truth?' He shook his head aggressively. 'I don't believe that.'

'I'm wondering why Hughes didn't produce this alibi yesterday. Why did he keep mum for so long if he knew his mates were going to back him up?' He answered his own question slowly. 'Because his solicitor forced my hand this morning and demanded to know the earliest time that Mrs Gillespie might have died. Which means Hughes had already told him he was in the clear from nine o'clock, and hey presto, out comes his alibi.'

'How does that help us?'

'It doesn't,' said Jones cheerfully. 'But if it was the set-up you say it is, then he must have done something else that night that required an alibi from nine o'clock. All we have to do is find out what it was.' He reached for his telephone. 'I'll talk to my oppo in Bournemouth. Let's see what he can come up with on the crime sheet for the night of Saturday, November the sixth.'

The answer was nothing.

Nothing, at least, that remotely fitted the modus operandi of David Mark Hughes.

Hence Cooper's tetchiness.

He tut-tutted crossly at Sarah as he examined the key on the table. 'I thought you had more sense, Dr Blakeney.'

Sarah held on to her patience with an effort, remembering Jane's admonishment not to let events sour her nature. 'I know. I'm sorry.'

'You'd better hope we do raise someone else's fingerprints, otherwise I might be inclined to think this was a stunt.'

'What sort of stunt?'

'A way of leaving your fingerprints on it legitimately.'

She was way ahead of him. 'Assuming I was the one who used it to get in and kill Mathilda and had forgotten to wipe my fingerprints off it at the time, I suppose?' she said tartly.

'Not quite,' he said mildly, 'I was thinking more in terms of a Good Samaritan act on behalf of someone else. Who have you unilaterally decided is innocent this time, Dr Blakeney?'

'You're not very grateful, Cooper,' she said. 'I needn't have told you about it at all. I could have put it back quietly and kept my mouth shut.'

'Hardly. It has your fingerprints all over it and someone would have found it eventually.' He glanced at Joanna. 'Did you really not know it was there, Mrs Lascelles?'

'I've already told you once, Sergeant. No. I had a key to the front door.'

There was something very odd going on between her

and Dr Blakeney, he thought. The body language was all wrong. They were standing close together, arms almost touching, but they seemed unwilling to look at each other. Had they been a man and a woman, he'd have said he'd caught them in flagrante delicto; as it was, intuition told him they were sharing a secret although what that secret was and whether it had any bearing on Mrs Gillespie's death was anyone's guess.

'What about Ruth?'

Joanna shrugged indifferently. 'I've no idea but I wouldn't think so. She's never mentioned it to me, and I've only ever known her use her front door key. There's no sense in coming all the way round the back if you can get in through the front. There's no access on this side.' She looked honestly puzzled. 'It must be something Mother started recently. She certainly didn't do it when I was living here.'

He looked at Sarah who spread her hands in a gesture of helplessness. 'All I know is that the second or third time I came to visit her, she didn't answer the door, so I walked round to the french windows and looked into the drawing-room. She was completely stuck, poor old thing, quite unable to push herself out of her chair because her wrists had packed up on her that day. She mouthed instructions through the glass. "Key. Third flowerpot. Coal bunker." I imagine she kept it there for just that kind of emergency. She worried all the time about losing her mobility.'

'Who else knew about it?'

'I don't know.'

'Did you tell anyone?'

Sarah shook her head. 'I can't remember. I may have

mentioned it in the surgery. It was ages ago, anyway. She started responding very well to the new medication I gave her and the situation didn't recur. I only remembered it when I came round the back this afternoon and saw the flowerpots.'

Cooper took a couple of polythene bags out of his pocket and used one to inch the key off the table into the other. 'And why did you come round the back, Dr Blakeney? Did Mrs Lascelles refuse to let you in at the front?'

For the first time Sarah glanced at Joanna. 'I don't know about refusing. She may not have heard the bell.'

'But it was obviously something very urgent you needed to discuss with her or you wouldn't have been so determined to get in. Would you care to let me in on what that was? Presumably it concerns Ruth.' He was too old and experienced a hand to miss the look of relief on Joanna's face.

'Sure,' said Sarah lightly. 'You know my views on education. We were discussing Ruth's future schooling.'

She was lying, Cooper thought, and he was startled by the fluency with which she did it. With an inward sigh, he made a mental note to review everything she had told him. He had believed her to be an honest, if naïve, woman, but the naïvety, he realized now, was all on his side. There was no fool like an old fool, he thought bitterly.

But then silly old Tommy had fallen a little in love.

There is no truer saying than 'Revenge is a dish best eaten cold.' It is so much sweeter for the waiting, and my only regret is that I cannot broadcast my triumph to the world. Sadly, not even to James, who is duped but does not know it.

This morning I heard from my bank that he has cashed my cheque for £12,000 and has therefore by default agreed to the insurance settlement. I knew he would. Where money is concerned James has the intemperate greed of a child. He spends it like water because cash in hand is the only thing he understands. Oh, to be a fly on the wall and see how he's living, but I can guess, anyway. Drink and sodomy. There was never anything else in James's life.

I am £36,500 richer today than I was yesterday, and I glory in it. The cheque from the insurance company for the various items stolen from the safe over Christmas while Joanna and I were in Cheshire came to an astonishing £23,500, the bulk of which was for the set of diamond jewellery belonging to my grandmother. The tiara alone was insured for £5,500, although I imagine *it was worth more than that as I have not had it valued since Father's death. Extraordinary to have such a windfall for items I, personally, would not be seen dead in. There is nothing so ugly or heavy as ornate Victorian jewellery.*

By contrast, James's clocks are anything but vulgar, probably because it was his father who bought them and not James. I took them to Sotheby's to be valued and discovered they are worth more than double the £12,000 they were insured for. Thus, after paying James £12,000, I retain £11,500 from the insurance cheque and have effectively purchased from my contemptible husband a fine investment, valued at £25,000.

As I said, revenge is a dish best eaten cold . . .

Fourteen

EARLIER THAT afternoon, a tall, distinguished-looking man was shown into Paul Duggan's office in Poole. He gave his name as James Gillespie and calmly produced his passport and his marriage certificate to Mathilda Beryl Gillespie to prove it. Aware that he had dropped something of a bombshell, he lowered himself on to a vacant chair and clasped his hands around the handle of his walking-stick, studying Duggan with amusement from beneath a pair of exuberant white eyebrows. 'Bit of a shock, eh?' he said. Even from the other side of the desk, the smell of whisky on his breath was powerful.

The younger man examined the passport carefully, then placed it on the blotting-pad in front of him. 'Unexpected, certainly,' he said dryly. 'I had assumed Mrs Gillespie was a widow. She never mentioned a husband or,' he laid a careful stress upon the next syllable, '*ex*-husband still living.'

'Husband,' grunted the other forcefully. 'She wouldn't. It suited her better to be thought a widow.'

'Why did you never divorce?'

'Never saw the need.'

'This passport was issued in Hong Kong.'

'Naturally. Out there forty years. Worked in various banks. Came back when I realized it was no place to end my days. Too much fear now. Peking's unpredictable. Uncomfortable for a man of my age.' He spoke in clipped staccato sentences like someone in a hurry or someone impatient with social niceties.

'So why have you come to see me?' Duggan watched him curiously. He was striking to look at, certainly, with a mane of white hair and an olive complexion, etched with deep lines around his eyes and mouth, but closer examination revealed an underlying poverty beneath the superficial air of prosperity. His clothes had once been good, but time and usage had taken their toll and both the suit and the camel-hair coat were wearing thin.

'Should have thought it was obvious. Now she's dead – reclaiming what's mine.'

'How did you know she was dead?'

'Ways and means,' said the other.

'How did you know I was her executor?'

'Ways and means,' said the other again.

Duggan's curiosity was intense. 'And what is it that you wish to reclaim?'

The old man took a wallet from his inside pocket, removed some folded sheets of very thin paper and spread them on the desk. 'This is an inventory of my father's estate. It was divided equally amongst his three children on his death forty-seven years ago. My share was those items marked with the initials JG. You will find, I think, that at least seven of them appear on your inventory of Mathilda's estate. They are not hers. They never were hers. I now wish to recover them.'

Thoughtfully, Duggan read through the documents. 'Precisely which seven items are you referring to, Mr Gillespie?'

The huge white eyebrows came together in a ferocious scowl. 'Don't trifle with me, Mr Duggan. I refer, of course, to the clocks. The two Thomas Tompions, the Knibbs, the seventeenth-century mahogany long case, the Louis XVI Lyre clock, the eighteenth-century "pendule d'officier" and the crucifix clock. My father and grandfather were collectors.'

Duggan steepled his hands over the inventory. 'May I ask why you think any of these things appear on the inventory of Mrs Gillespie's estate?'

'Are you telling me they don't?'

The solicitor avoided a direct answer. 'If I understood you correctly you've been absent from this country for forty years. How could you possibly know what might or might not have been in your wife's possession the day she died?'

The old man snorted. 'Those clocks were the only things of value I had, and Mathilda went to a great deal of trouble to steal them from me. She certainly wouldn't have sold them.'

'How could your wife steal them if you were still married?'

'Tricked me out of them, then, but it was still theft.'

'I'm afraid I don't understand.'

Gillespie removed an airmail letter from his wallet and handed it across the desk. 'Self-explanatory, I think.'

Duggan unfolded the letter and read the terse lines. The address was Cedar House and the date was April 1961.

Dear James,

I am sorry to have to tell you that during a burglary here over Christmas much of value was stolen, including your collection of clocks. I have today received a cheque in settlement from the insurance company and I enclose their invoice, showing that they sent me a total of £23,500. I also enclose a cheque for £12,000 which was the insured value of your seven clocks. You bought my silence by leaving the clocks with me, and I am reimbursing you only because I fear you might return one day to claim them. You would be very angry, I think, to discover I'd cheated you a second time. I trust this means we will not need to communicate again.

Yours, Mathilda.

Duggan's amiable face looked up in bewilderment. 'I still don't understand.'

'They weren't stolen, were they?'

'But she gave you twelve thousand pounds for them. That was a small fortune in 1961.'

'It was fraud. She told me the clocks were stolen when they weren't. I accepted the money in good faith. Never occurred to me she was lying.' He tapped his walking-stick angrily on the floor. 'Two ways of looking at it. One, she stole the clocks herself and defrauded the insurance company. A crime, in my book. Two, other things were stolen to the value of twenty-three and a half thousand and she saw an opportunity to take the clocks off me. Also a crime. They were my property.' His ancient mouth turned down at the corners. 'She knew their value, knew they'd be the best asset she had. Been to Sotheby's myself. Rough estimate, of course, with only descriptions in the inventory to go by, but we're talking over a hundred thousand at auction, probably a great deal more. I want them back, sir.'

Duggan considered for a moment. 'I don't think the situation is quite as clear-cut as you seem to think, Mr Gillespie. There's a burden of proof here. First, you have to show that Mrs Gillespie deliberately defrauded you; second, you have to show that the clocks in Mrs Gillespie's estate are the precise clocks that were left to you by your father.'

'You've read both inventories. What else could they be?'

For the moment, Duggan avoided the question of how James Gillespie knew there was an inventory of Mathilda's estate or what was on it. Once broached, it was going to be a very unpleasant can of worms. 'Similar clocks,' he said bluntly. 'Maybe even the same clocks, but you will have to prove she didn't buy them back at a later stage. Let's say the collection was stolen, and she passed on the compensation to you as she was supposed to. Let's say, then, that she set out to replace the collection because she had developed an interest in horology. She could quite legitimately have used her own money to buy similar clocks at auction. In those circumstances, you would have no claim on them at all. There is also the undeniable fact that you had a duty, encumbent on you as the owner, to establish to your satisfaction that the money you were paid in 1961 represented a full and fair settlement by the insurance company for the theft of your goods. In accepting twelve thousand pounds, Mr Gillespie, you effectively did that. You abandoned the clocks to sail to Hong Kong, accepted handsome compensation for them without a murmur, and only wish to reclaim them now because after forty years you believe they might have been worth hanging on to. I will admit that this is a grey area, which will require Counsel's opinion, but off the top of my head, I'd say you haven't a leg to stand on. It's an old saying, but a true one. Possession is nine tenths of the law.'

Gillespie was not so easily intimidated. 'Read her diaries,' he growled. 'They'll prove she stole them off me. Couldn't resist boasting to herself, that was Mathilda's trouble. Put every damn thing on those miserable pages, then read them over and over again to remind herself how clever she was. Wouldn't have left out a triumph like this. Read the diaries.'

The younger man kept his face deliberately impassive. 'I will. As a matter of interest, do you know where she kept them? It'll save me the trouble of looking for them.'

'Top shelf of the library. Disguised as the works of Willy Shakespeare.' He took a card from his wallet. 'You're a solicitor, Mr Duggan, so I'm trusting you to be honest. That's where I'm staying. Expect to hear from you on this in a couple of days or so. Grateful if you'd treat it as a matter of urgency.' He levered himself to his feet with his walking-stick.

'I'd much prefer to deal through your solicitor, Mr Gillespie.'

'I don't have one, sir.' He spoke with a touching dignity. 'My pension won't allow it. I am relying on you being a gentleman. Presumably they still exist in this wretched country. Precious little else does.' He made his way to the door. 'Perhaps you think I treated Mathilda badly by deserting her and the child. Perhaps you think I deserved to be stolen from. Read the diaries. She'll tell you herself what really happened.'

Duggan waited until the door had closed, then reached for the telephone and dialled Learmouth Police Station.

The information about Mathilda's diaries was telephoned through to Cooper as he was about to leave Cedar House. He replaced the receiver with a frown. He'd been over that house from top to bottom, and he was as sure as he could be that there were no handwritten diaries in the library or anywhere else. 'Sorry, ladies, I shall have to trespass on your time a little longer. Will you come with me, please?'

Puzzled, Joanna and Sarah followed him across the hall and into the library.

'What are you looking for?' asked Joanna as he stood staring at the top shelf.

He reached up and tapped the thick mahogany ledge that ran, like its fellows, across the width of the wall. 'Do either of you see the collected works of William Shakespeare up here?'

'They're all over the place,' said Joanna dismissively. 'Which particular edition are you looking for?'

'The one that's supposed to be on this shelf.' He glanced at her. 'Your mother's diaries. I'm told she kept them on the top shelf, disguised as the works of William Shakespeare.'

Joanna looked genuinely surprised. 'What diaries?'

'Our information is that she kept a record of everything that happened to her.'

'I didn't know.'

'The informant was very positive.'

285

Joanna gestured helplessly. 'I didn't know,' she said again.

'Who's your informant?' asked Sarah curiously.

Cooper was watching Joanna as he spoke. 'James Gillespie,' he said. 'Mrs Lascelles's step-father.'

This time the look of surprise lacked conviction. It was left to Sarah to make the obvious response. 'I thought he abandoned Mathilda years ago,' she said thoughtfully. 'How would he know whether she kept diaries or not? Anyway, he's in Hong Kong, or that's what my receptionist told me.'

'Not any more, Dr Blakeney. According to Mrs Gillespie's solicitor, he's living in Bournemouth.' He addressed Joanna. 'We'll have to search the house again, and I'd prefer it if you were here while we did so.'

'Of course, Sergeant. I'm not planning to go anywhere. This is my house, after all.'

Sarah caught her gaze. 'What about Ruth? You can't just abandon her.'

'Ruth must learn to fend for herself, Dr Blakeney.' She gave an eloquent little shrug. 'Perhaps you should have considered the consequences a little more carefully before you persuaded Mother to change her will. You must see that it's quite impossible for me to support her as things stand at the moment.'

'It's emotional support she needs, and that won't cost you a bean.'

'There's nothing I could say to her that wouldn't make matters worse.' Joanna's pale eyes stared unwinkingly at Sarah. 'She's had more opportunities than I ever had and she's chosen to throw them away. You do realize she was stealing from Mother for months before this sordid little episode at school.' Her mouth thinned unpleasantly. 'You can't imagine the resentment I've felt since Miss Harris telephoned to explain why Ruth was being expelled. Have you any idea of the money that's been wasted on that child's education?'

'Miss Harris has given you a very one-sided view of what happened,' said Sarah carefully, aware that Cooper was all ears beside her. 'You must see that it's only fair to hear Ruth's side as well, at least give her the chance to demonstrate that what happened wasn't entirely her fault.'

'I've lived with my daughter on and off for nearly eighteen years, and I know exactly who's to blame. Ruth is quite incapable of telling the truth. You would be very foolish to assume otherwise.' She smiled very slightly. 'You may tell her that she knows where I am if she wants me, although please make it very clear that, unless this business of the will is settled satisfactorily, then she can expect no help from me either in terms of her continuing education or of her living expenses.'

This woman was using Ruth as a bargaining chip, thought Sarah in disgust, but she reminded herself that in her own way Joanna was as desperate as Ruth. She tried again. 'Money isn't the issue here, Joanna, the only issue is that your daughter would like to see you. She's too frightened to come to Cedar House because the man who persuaded her to steal knows this address and has made threats against her. Please, please, will you come with me to Mill House and talk to her there? She isn't lying, but she's deeply disturbed about everything that's happened and needs reassurance that you haven't rejected her. She has spent most of her time sitting by the telephone, hoping and praying that you would call. I don't think you have any idea how deeply she cares for you.'

There was the briefest of hesitations – *or was that wishful thinking on Sarah's part?* 'You took her in, Dr Blakeney, so I suggest you deal with her. I can't begin to condone anything she's done. Worse, I'm inclined to think it was she who murdered my mother. She's quite capable of it. Please don't be in any doubt about that.'

Sarah shook her head in disbelief. 'Ah, well, perhaps it's better this way. The one thing Ruth doesn't need at the moment is you downloading your hypocritical crap on her. You're tarred with exactly the same brush, or have you forgotten the mess you were in when Mathilda rescued you?' She shrugged. 'I'd made up my mind to turn the bequest down and let you and Ruth have a fair crack at convincing a court you had more rights than the donkeys. Not any more. You'll have to fight me for it now, and you'll be fighting your corner alone because I intend to put money in trust for Ruth so that she doesn't lose out whatever happens.' She walked to the door, flashing Cooper one of the sweet smiles that made his elderly heart race around like a young spring lamb. 'If it's of any interest to you, Sergeant, I am still of the opinion that Joanna did not kill Mathilda. Arthritis or no arthritis, Mathilda would have legged it for the hills the minute this bitch came near her.'

Well, well, Cooper thought, gazing after her as she stormed across the hall, there was passion in Dr Blakeney after all. But he wished he knew what had happened to Ruth that was making her and Jack so angry.

Cadogan Mansions, implying as it did something grand and impressive, was a misnomer for the shabby neglect of the purpose-built block that greeted Cooper the following morning. Sixties architecture, drab, square and unstylish, squeezed into a gap between two suburban villas and constructed solely to provide extra accommodation at minimum cost for maximum profit. How very different towns might look, Cooper always thought, if planners had been prosecuted instead of praised for their urban vandalism.

He climbed the utilitarian stairs and rang the bell of number seventeen. 'Mr James Gillespie?' he asked of the rugged old man who poked his nose round the door and gusted stale whisky in his face. Cooper flipped open his warrant card. 'DS Cooper, Learmouth Police.'

Gillespie's eyebrows beetled aggressively. 'Well?'

'May I come in?'

'Why?'

'I'd like to ask you some questions about your late wife.'

'Why?'

Cooper could see this conversation dragging on interminably. He opted for the direct approach. 'Your wife was murdered, sir, and we have reason to believe you may have spoken to her before she died. I understand that you have been living abroad for some years, so perhaps I should remind you that you are obliged by British law to assist us in any way you can with our enquiries. Now, may I come in?'

'If you must.' He seemed quite unruffled by the police-man's bald statement but led the way past a room with a bed in it to another room containing a threadbare sofa and two plastic chairs. There was no other furniture and no carpets, but a piece of net curtaining was draped in the windows to give a modicum of privacy. 'Expecting bits and pieces from Hong Kong,' he barked. 'Should arrive any day. Camping out meanwhile. Sit down.' He lowered himself on to the sofa, trying somewhat clumsily to hide the empty bottle that lay on the floor at his feet. The room was frowsty with whisky, urine and unwashed old man. The front of his trousers was saturated, Cooper saw. Tactfully, he took out his notebook and concentrated his attention on that.

'You didn't seem very surprised when I told you your wife was murdered, Mr Gillespie. Did you know already?'

'Heard rumours.'

'Who from?'

'My brother. We used to live in Long Upton once. He still knows people there. Hears things.'

'Where does he live now?'

'London.'

'Could you give me his name and address?'

The old man thought about it. 'No harm, I suppose. Frederick Gillespie, Carisbroke Court, Denby Street, Kensington. Won't help you, though. Doesn't know any more than I do.'

Cooper flicked back through the pages of his notebook till he came to Joanna Lascelles's address. 'Your step-daughter lives in Kensington. Does your brother know her?'

'Believe so.'

Well, well, well, thought Cooper. A panorama of intriguing possibilities opened up in front of him. 'How long have you been back in England, Mr Gillespie?'

'Six months.'

The bits and pieces from Hong Kong were eyewash, then. Nothing took that long these days to be freighted round the world. The old boy was destitute. 'And where did you go first? To your brother? Or to your wife?'

'Spent three months in London. Then decided to come back to my roots.'

Frederick couldn't put up with an incontinent drunk. It was guesswork, of course, but Cooper would put money on it. 'And you saw Joanna during that time and she told you that Mathilda was still living in Cedar House.' He spoke as if it were something he had established already.

'Nice girl,' said the old man ponderously. 'Pretty, like her mother.'

'So you went to see Mathilda.'

Gillespie nodded. 'Hadn't changed. Rude woman still.'

'And you saw the clocks. The ones she told you had been stolen.'

'Solicitor's talked, I suppose.'

'I've just come from Mr Duggan. He informed us of your visit yesterday.' He saw the old man's scowl. 'He had no option, Mr Gillespie. Withholding information is a serious offence, particularly where a murder has occurred.'

'Thought it was suicide.'

Cooper ignored this. 'What did you do when you realized your wife had lied to you?'

Gillespie gave a harsh laugh. 'Demanded my property

back, of course. She found that very amusing. Claimed I'd accepted money in lieu thirty years ago and no longer had an entitlement.' He searched back through his memory. 'Used to hit her when I lived with her. Not hard. But I had to make her frightened of me. It was the only way I could stop that malicious tongue.' He fingered his mouth with a trembling hand. It was mottled and blistered with psoriasis. 'I wasn't proud of it and I never hit a woman again, not until—' He broke off.

Cooper kept his voice level. 'Are you saying you hit her when she told you you couldn't have your property back?'

'Smacked her across her beastly face.' He closed his eyes for a moment as if the recollection pained him.

'Did you hurt her?'

The old man smiled unpleasantly. 'I made her cry,' he said.

'What happened then?'

'Told her I'd be putting the law on to her and left.'

'When was this? Can you remember?'

He seemed to become suddenly aware of the urine stains on his trousers and crossed his legs self-consciously. 'The time I hit her? Two, three months ago.'

'You went there at other times then?'

Gillespie nodded. 'Twice.'

'Before or after you hit her?'

'After. Didn't want the law on her, did she?'

'I don't follow.'

'Why would you? Doubt you saw her till she was dead. Devious, that's the only way to describe Mathilda. Devious and ruthless. Guessed I'd fallen on hard times and came here the next day to sort something out. Talked about a settlement.' He picked at the scabs on his hand. 'Thought I wouldn't know what the clocks were worth. Offered me five thousand to leave her alone.' He fell silent.

'And?' Cooper prompted when the silence lengthened.

The old eyes wandered about the empty room. 'Realized she'd pay more to avoid the scandal. Went back a couple of times to demonstrate how vulnerable she was. She was talking fifty thousand the day before she died. I was holding out for a hundred. We'd have got there eventually. She knew it was only a matter of time before someone saw me and recognized me.'

'You were blackmailing her.'

Gillespie gave his harsh laugh again. 'Mathilda was a thief. D'you call it blackmail to negotiate back what's been stolen from you? We understood each other perfectly. We'd have reached an agreement if she hadn't died.'

Cooper allowed his revulsion to get the better of him. 'It seems to me, sir, you wanted to have your cake and eat it too. You deserted her forty years ago, left her to fend for herself with a baby, snatched up what the clocks were worth in nineteen sixty-one, spent the whole lot' – he looked pointedly at the empty bottle – 'probably on booze, repeated the exercise with everything else you've ever earned and then came home to leech off the woman you'd abandoned. I'd say it's arguable who was the greater thief. If the clocks were so important to you, why didn't you take them with you?'

'Couldn't afford to,' said Gillespie dispassionately. 'Put together enough for my passage. Nothing left over to freight the clocks.'

'Why didn't you sell one to pay for the freight of the others?'

'She blocked it.' He saw the scepticism in Cooper's expression. 'You didn't know her, man, so don't make judgements.'

'Yet by your own admission you used to beat her to make her frightened of you. How could she stop you selling your own property? You'd have thrashed her.'

'Maybe I did,' he growled. 'Maybe she found another way to stop me. You think I was the first one to try blackmail? She was a past master at it.' He touched his lips again and this time the tremor in his hands was more marked. 'We reached an accommodation, the essence of which was no scandal. She'd let me leave for Hong Kong on the condition that there was no divorce and she kept the clocks. Mutual insurance, she called them. While she housed them, she could be sure of my silence. While I owned them I could be sure of hers. They were worth a bob or two, even in those days.'

Cooper frowned. 'What silence were you buying?'

'This and that. It was an unhappy marriage, and you washed your dirty linen in public when you divorced in those days. Her father was an MP, don't forget.'

She let me leave for Hong Kong . . . Strange use of words, thought Cooper. How could she have stopped him? 'Were you involved in something criminal, Mr Gillespie? Were the clocks a quid pro quo for her not going to the police?'

He shrugged. 'Water under the bridge now.'

'What did you do?'

'Water under the bridge,' the old man repeated stubbornly. 'Ask me *why* Mathilda had to buy my silence. That's a damn sight more interesting.'

'Why then?'

'Because of the baby. Knew who the father was, didn't I?'

Water under the bridge, thought Cooper sarcastically. 'You told Mr Duggan that your wife kept diaries,' he said, 'that they were on the top shelf of her library disguised as the collected works of William Shakespeare. Is that correct?'

'It is.'

'Did you see them when you went to Cedar House or did Mrs Gillespie tell you about them?'

Gillespie's eyes narrowed. 'You saying they're not there now?'

'Will you answer my question, please. Did you see them or are you relying on something Mrs Gillespie told you?'

'Saw them. Knew what to look for, see. I had the first two volumes bound for her as a wedding present. Gave her another eight with blank pages.'

'Could you describe them, Mr Gillespie?'

'Brown calfskin binding. Gold lettering on the spines. Titles courtesy Willy Shakespeare. Ten volumes in all.'

'What sort of size?'

'Eight inches by six inches. An inch thick or thereabouts.' He wrung his hands in his lap. 'They're not there, I suppose. Don't mind telling you, rather relying on those diaries. They'll prove she set out to defraud me.'

'So you read them?'

'Couldn't,' the old man grumbled. 'She never left me alone long enough. Fussed around me like a blasted hen.

But the proof'll be there. She'd've written it down, just like she wrote everything else.'

'Then you can't say for sure they were diaries, only that there were ten volumes of Shakespeare on the top shelf which bore a resemblance to some diaries you'd bought for her forty-odd years ago.'

He pursed his lips obstinately. 'Spotted them the first time I was there. They were Mathilda's diaries all right.'

Cooper thought for a moment. 'Did Mrs Lascelles know about them?'

Gillespie shrugged. 'Couldn't say. I didn't tell her. Don't believe in emptying the armoury before I have to.'

'But you told her you weren't her father?'

He shrugged again. 'Someone had to.'

'Why?'

'She was all over me. Wouldn't leave me alone. Pathetic really. Seemed wrong to let her go on believing such a fundamental lie.'

'Poor woman,' murmured Cooper with a new compassion. He wondered if there was anyone who *hadn't* rejected her. 'I suppose you also told her about the letter from her natural father.'

'Why not? Seemed to me she has as much right to the Cavendish wealth as Mathilda had.'

'How did you know about it? It was written after you left for Hong Kong.'

The old man looked sly. 'Ways and means,' he muttered. But he saw something in Cooper's eyes that caused him to reflect. 'There was talk in the village when Gerald topped himself,' he said. 'Word got about he'd written a letter which his brother managed to suppress. Suicide' – he shook his head – 'wasn't the done thing in those days. William hushed it up for the sake of the family. I heard the stories at the time and suggested Joanna look for the letter. Stood to reason what would be in it. Gerald was a sentimental half-wit bound to've mentioned his bastard. Couldn't've resisted it.'

'And perhaps you reached an accommodation with Mrs Lascelles as well. You'd testify in court to her real paternity if she kept you in clover for the rest of your life. Something like that?'

Gillespie gave a dry chuckle. 'She was a great deal more amenable than her mother.'

'Then why did you bother to go on negotiating with Mrs Gillespie?'

'Didn't rate Joanna's chances much, not against Mathilda.'

Cooper nodded. 'So you killed your wife to improve the odds.'

The dry chuckle rasped out again. 'Wondered when you'd pull that one out of the hat. Didn't need to. If she didn't kill herself, then rather think my step-daughter did it for me. She was mighty put out to discover that her mother played the tart with her great-uncle.' Abruptly, like some guilty secret he'd decided to unburden, he fished a full bottle of whisky from where it was tucked down behind the sofa cushions, unscrewed the cap and held it to his mouth. 'Want some?' he asked vaguely after a moment, waving the bottle in Cooper's direction before placing it between his lips again and half-draining it in huge mouthfuls.

The Sergeant, whose experience of drunks was considerable after years of plucking them out of the gutter in sodden heaps, watched in amazement. Gillespie's tolerance levels were extraordinary. In two minutes he had consumed enough neat spirit to put most men on their backs, and the only effect it seemed to have on him was to reduce the tremors in his hands.

'We're having difficulty establishing a motive for your wife's murder,' Cooper said slowly. 'But it seems to me yours is rather stronger than most.'

'Bah!' Gillespie snorted, his eyes bright now with alcoholic affability. 'She was worth more to me alive. I told you, she was talking fifty thousand the day before she died.'

'But you didn't keep your side of the bargain, Mr Gillespie. That meant your wife was free to reveal why you had to abscond to Hong Kong.'

'Water under the bridge,' came his monotonous refrain. 'Water under the bloody bridge. No one'd be interested in my little peccadillo now, but there's a hell of a lot'd be interested in hers. The daughter, for a start.' He raised the bottle to his mouth again, and the shutters went down.

Cooper couldn't remember when anyone or anything had disgusted him quite so much. He stood up, buttoning depression about himself with his coat. If he could wash his hands of this terrible family, he would, for he could find no saving graces in any of them. What's bred in the bone comes out in the flesh, and their corruption was as rank as the stench in that room. If he regretted anything in his life it was being on shift the day Mathilda's body was found. But for that, he might have remained what he had always believed he was – a truly tolerant man.

Unnoticed by Gillespie, he retrieved the empty bottle from the floor with his fingertips and took it with him.

Jack studied the address that Sarah had patiently cajoled out of Ruth. 'You say it's a squat, so how do I get him outside alone?'

She was rinsing some cups under the cold water tap. 'I'm having second thoughts. What happens if you end up in traction for the next six months?'

'It couldn't possibly be worse than what I'm suffering already,' he murmured, pulling out a chair and sitting on it. 'There's something wrong with the spareroom bed. It's giving me a stiff neck. When are you going to boot Ruth out and let me back where I belong?'

'When you've apologized.'

'Ah, well,' he said regretfully, 'a stiff neck it is then.'

Her eyes narrowed. 'It's only an apology, you bastard. It won't kill you. Stiff-necked says it all, if you ask me.'

He gave an evil grin. 'It's not the only thing that's stiff. You don't know what you're missing, my girl.'

She glared at him. 'That's easily cured.' With a swift movement she upended a cupful of freezing water into his lap. 'It's a pity Sally Bennedict didn't do the same.'

He surged to his feet, knocking the chair backwards. 'Jesus, woman,' he roared, 'will you stop trying to turn me into a eunuch!' He gripped her round the waist and lifted her bodily into the air. 'You're lucky we've got Ruth in the house,' he growled, twisting her sideways and holding her head under the running tap, 'otherwise I might be tempted to show you how ineffectual cold water is on a deprived libido.'

'You're drowning me,' she spluttered.

'Serves you right.' He set her on her feet again and turned off the tap.

'You asked for passion,' she said, dripping water over the quarry tiles. 'Don't you like it now that you've got it?'

He tossed her a towel. 'Hell, yes,' he said with a grin. 'The last thing I wanted was a wife who understood. I will not be patronized, woman.'

She shook her head in fury, splattering the kitchen with droplets. 'If one more person calls me patronizing,' she said, 'I will do them some damage. I am *trying* to be charitable towards some of the most useless and self-indulgent egotists it has ever been my misfortune to meet. And it's bloody difficult.' She rubbed her hair vigorously with the towel. 'If the world was made up of people like me, Jack, it would be paradise.'

'Well, you know what they say about paradise, old thing. It's heaven until the horned viper pops his head out from under the fig leaf and spots the moist warm burrow under the bushes. After that all hell breaks loose.'

She watched him pull on his old donkey jacket and take a torch from the kitchen drawer. 'What are you planning to do exactly?'

'Never you mind. What you don't know can't incriminate you.'

'Do you want me to come with you?'

His dark face split into a grin. 'What for? So you can stitch him back together again when I've finished with him?

You'd be a liability, woman. Anyway, you'd be struck off if we were caught, and someone's got to stay with Ruth.'

'You will be careful, won't you?' she said, her eyes dark with concern. 'In spite of everything, Jack, I am really very fond of you.'

He touched a finger to her lips. 'I'll be careful,' he promised.

He drove slowly up Palace Road, located number twenty-three and the white Ford transit outside it, made a circuit of the block and drew into a space which gave him an unobstructed view of the house but was far enough away from it not to attract attention to himself. Yellow lamplight gleamed along the street, throwing pools of shadow amongst the houses, but few people were abroad at eight o'clock on a cold Thursday evening in late November, and only once or twice did his heart jump at the unexpected appearance of a dark-clad figure on the pavement. An hour had passed when a dog emerged into a swathe of light ten yards from the car and began to rootle amongst some garbage by a dustbin. It was only after several minutes of watching that Jack realized it wasn't a dog at all but an urban fox, scavenging for food. So prepared was he for a long wait, and so entranced by the delicate scratchings of the fox, that he missed the door of number twenty-three opening. Only the noise of laughter alerted him to the fact that something was going down. With narrowed eyes, he watched a group of young men piling into the back of the van, saw the doors slam and a figure disappear round the side.

Impossible to tell if it was Hughes. Ruth had described him as tall, dark and handsome, but, as all cats are black in the night, so all young men look the same from thirty yards distant on a winter's evening. Jack, gambling on something else she had said, that the van was his and he always drove it, pulled out behind it as it drove away.

*The doctor has written 'heart failure' as the cause of
Father's death. I had difficulty keeping a straight face
when I read it. Of course he died of heart failure. We
all die of heart failure. Mrs Spencer, the housekeeper,
was suitably distraught until I told her I'd keep her on
while she looked about for another niche for herself.
After that she rallied with surprising speed. That class
has little loyalty to anything except money.*

*Father looked very peaceful in his chair, his whisky
glass still clasped in his hand. 'Taken in his sleep'
according to the doctor. How very, very true, in every
respect. 'He drank far more than was good for him, my
dear. I did warn him about it.' He went on to assure
me that I need have no fears about him suffering. I
made an appropriate response, but thought: What a pity
he hadn't. He deserved to suffer. Father's worst fault
was his ingratitude. James was really very lucky. Had I
realized how easy it was to get rid of drunks, well, well
. . . enough said.*

*Unfortunately, Joanna saw me. The wretched child
woke up and came downstairs just as I was removing*

303

the pillow. I explained that Grandpa was ill and that the pillow was to make him more comfortable, but I have the strangest feeling she knows. She refused to go to sleep last night, just lay looking at me with that very unnerving stare of hers.

But what possible significance could a pillow have for a two-year-old . . .

Fifteen

HALF AN HOUR later and well into the better side of
town, the van drew to a halt in the shadows of an expensive-
looking house to pick up the wide-eyed adolescent girl
waiting there. The hairs began to crawl on the back of
Jack's neck. He watched her climb with gawky eagerness
into the passenger seat, and he knew that she was as
unprepared as Ruth had been for the surprise that Hughes
had waiting for her in the back.

The van took the coast road east towards Southbourne
and Hengistbury Head and, as the traffic thinned, Jack
allowed the distance between it and him to lengthen. He
toyed with one possibility after another – should he stop to
call the police and risk losing the van altogether? – should
he ram the van and risk injuring himself and the girl? –
should he try to deter them by drawing in beside them
when they parked, at the risk of their driving off and giving
him the slip? He discarded each idea in turn, seeing only
their weaknesses, and suddenly felt a deep regret that he
hadn't brought Sarah with him. He had never wanted the
comfort of her friendship quite so desperately.

The van turned into a deserted car park on the sea front,

and more by instinct than design Jack killed his lights, thrust the gears into neutral and freewheeled to a stop beside the kerb some fifty yards behind it. Every detail of what happened next was lit by a cold, clear moon, but he knew what to expect because Ruth had described Hughes's MO in all too graphic detail. The driver, Hughes for a certainty, flung open his door and jumped out on to the tarmac, dragging the girl after him. There was the briefest of scuffles before he pinioned her in his arms and carried her, kicking and struggling, to the back of the van. He was laughing as he wrenched the rear door open and flung her like a sack of potatoes into the lit interior. The square of light shone out briefly before he closed the doors and strolled away towards the sea shore, lighting a cigarette as he went.

Jack could never explain afterwards why he did what he did. In retrospect he could only really remember his fear. His actions were governed entirely by instinct. It was as if, faced with a crisis, normal reason deserted him and something primeval took over. He focused entirely on the child. The need to help her was paramount, and the only method that presented itself was to open the van doors and physically remove her from danger. He eased into first gear and motored gently towards the transit, watching Hughes as he did so to see if he picked up the throb of the engine above the wash of the waves against the shore. Apparently not. The man stooped lazily to gather stones from the beach and send them spinning out across the black water.

Jack coasted to a halt behind the van and left the engine purring while he unbuckled his belt, drawing it from around his waist and wrapping the end about his fist. He took the heavy rubber torch in his other hand, clicked open the door and slipped out on to the tarmac, sucking in great draughts of air to still the thudding of his heart.

In the distance, Hughes turned round, took in the situation at a glance, and started to pound up the beach.

Adrenaline plays tricks. It floods the body to galvanize it into colossal and spontaneous effort, but the mind observes what happens in slow motion. Thus time, that most relative of phenomena, ceases to exist in any meaningful way, and what Jack would for ever insist took several minutes, in reality took seconds. He burst the van doors open and brought the torch down on the head of the man nearest him, bellowing like a bull. The startled white face of another youth turned towards him and Jack flicked the belt across it in a vicious backhand swipe, crooking his elbow round the first man's neck as he did so and pulling him backwards on to the tarmac. He released his hold and brought the torch round in a scything arc to smash under the chin of the face he'd whipped, toppling the youth off balance into thin air behind him.

The three men left in the van, two holding the girl down, the other bare-arsed on top of her, were frozen into shocked immobility. The violence of the onslaught was so extreme, the noise of Jack's continuous roaring so disorientating, that he was on top of them before they could register what was happening. He used the hand holding the belt to grip the hair of the bastard raping the girl, wrenched his head up and swung the torch in a mighty forehand smash into the wide-eyed, frightened face. Blood erupted from the broken nose in a stream, and the youth slithered sideways with a whimper of pain.

'GET OUT!' Jack shouted at the girl who was scrambling to her knees in terror. 'GET IN THE CAR!' He whipped the belt back and sliced it through the air into the eyes of a boy who was struggling to his feet in the corner. 'YOU BLOODY LITTLE SHITS!' he roared. 'I'M GOING TO KILL YOU.' He brought his boot down on the unprotected groin of the rapist and turned like a madman on the only youth he hadn't touched. With a cry of terror, the boy cowered away, his arms held protectively above his head.

Perhaps, after all, reason hadn't entirely deserted Blakeney. He abandoned the torch and the belt, flung himself precipitately out of the van, bundled into the car after the girl, and roared it into motion, tugging the door closed as he did so. He saw Hughes too late to avoid him as he careered across the tarmac, and caught him a glancing blow with the offside wing, bouncing him into the air like a rag-doll. Jack's anger was out of control, a red frenzy that pounded in his head like cannon-fire. Spinning the wheel, he turned the vehicle in a tight circle and headed back towards the crouching figure, switching on the headlights with a lazy flick of his fingers to catch Hughes's terrified face in the glare as he prepared to mow him down.

He had no idea what stopped him doing it. Perhaps it was the girl's screams. Perhaps his anger abated as rapidly as it had surged into life. Perhaps, quite simply, his humanity triumphed. Instead, he slewed the car to a screaming halt, slammed the door into the man's body and leapt out to wind his fist around the long hair and drag Hughes to his feet. 'Into the back, sweetheart,' he said to the girl, 'as fast as you can.' She was too terrified not to obey and slid in hysterics between the seats. 'Now, you, in,' he said, yanking down on the hair and shoving his knee into the small of Hughes's back, 'or, so help me, I'll break your filthy neck now.'

Hughes believed him. As the lesser of two evils, he allowed himself to be thrust face-down across the seat and sighed as Jack's heavy weight descended across his legs. The car raced into life again, screaming across the tarmac as Jack forced it into gear, the door slamming shut when it impacted against another flying figure. 'PUT YOUR SEAT BELT ON!' he yelled at the screaming girl. 'IF THIS BASTARD MOVES A MUSCLE I'M GOING TO PILE THE SIDE WHERE HIS HEAD IS INTO THE BIGGEST BRICK WALL I CAN FIND.' He changed up, swung out on to the road and set off at a blistering pace through Southbourne with his hand clamped over the horn. If there was any justice in this cess-pit of a world, someone would get the police out before the Ford transit caught up with him.

There was some justice left in the England Rupert Brooke died for. The local police received seventeen 999 calls in three minutes, twelve from elderly widows living alone, four from outraged men, and one from a child. They all reported the same thing. Joy-riders were turning the quiet tree-lined streets of their suburb into a death-trap.

Jack's car and the pursuing white transit were ambushed as they tore on to the main road leading into Bournemouth city centre.

*

The phone rang in Mill House at eleven thirty that night. 'Sarah?' Jack barked down the wire.

'Hi,' she countered with relief. 'You're not dead then.'

'No. I'm under sodding arrest,' he shouted. 'This is the one telephone call I'm allowed to make. I need help PDQ.'

'I'll come straight away. Where are you?'

'The bastards are going to charge me with joy-riding and rape,' he said furiously, as if she hadn't spoken. 'They're fucking *cretins* here, won't listen to a word I say. Goddammit, they've banged me up along with Hughes and his animals. The poor kid they were having a go at in the back of the van's completely hysterical and thinks I'm one of them. I keep telling them to contact Cooper but they're such bloody morons they won't listen to me.'

'Okay,' she said calmly, trying to make what she could of this alarming speech, 'I'll get Cooper. Now tell me where you are.'

'Some shit-hole in the middle of Bournemouth,' he roared. 'They're about to take swabs off my fucking penis.'

'The address, Jack. I need the address.'

'WHERE THE HELL AM I?' he bellowed at someone in the room with him. 'Freemont Road Police Station,' he told Sarah. 'You'll have to bring Ruth, too,' he said with regret. 'God knows, I never meant to involve her but she's the only one who knows what happened. And get Keith as well. I need a solicitor I can trust. They're all bloody fascists in this place. They're talking about frigging paedophile rings and conspiracies and Christ knows what else.'

'Calm down,' she said sternly. 'Keep your mouth shut

310

till I get there and, for God's sake, Jack, don't lose your temper and hit a policeman.'

'I already have, dammit. The bastard called me a pervert.'

It was well after two o'clock when Sarah, Cooper and Ruth finally arrived bleary-eyed at Freemont Road. The night Sergeant at Learmouth had been adamant in his refusal either to contact Cooper or to give Sarah his home phone number when she put through an urgent call requesting to speak to him. 'DS Cooper is not on duty, madam,' was his measured response. 'If you have a problem, you deal with me or wait until tomorrow morning when he will be on duty.' It was only when he was faced with her angry presence in front of his desk, threatening him with questions in Parliament and court action for negligence, that he was moved to contact the Detective Sergeant. The counter-blast from Cooper's end, not in the best of moods, anyway, after being woken up from a deep sleep, left him shaken. He grumbled away to himself for the rest of his shift. Sod's law said that it didn't matter how considerate a chap tried to be, he was always in the wrong.

Keith, even more irritable than Cooper to be dragged from the arms of Morpheus far away in London, perked up a little to hear that Jack was under arrest for joy-riding and rape. 'Good God,' he said with cynical amusement, 'I had no idea he was so active. I thought he preferred spectator sports.'

'It's not funny, Keith,' said Sarah curtly. 'He needs a solicitor. Can you come down to Bournemouth?'

'When?'

'Now, you oaf. They're taking swabs off him at this very minute.'

'Did he do it?'

'What?'

'The rape,' said Keith patiently.

'No, of course he didn't,' she spluttered angrily. 'Jack's not a rapist.'

'Then there's nothing to worry about. The swabs will prove he hasn't been in contact with the victim.'

'He says they think he's part of a paedophile ring. They may charge him with conspiracy to rape even if they can't charge him with the actual offence.' She sighed. 'At least I think that's what he said. He's very angry and it was all a bit garbled.'

'What on earth's he been up to?'

'I don't know yet,' she said through gritted teeth. 'Just get your arse down here, will you, and earn some of the fortune we've paid you over the years.'

'I'm not much of a criminal lawyer, you know. You might do better to get hold of a specialist from down there. I could give you some names out of the book.'

'He asked for you, Keith. He said he wants a solicitor he can trust, so – ' her voice rose ' – for God's sake will you stop arguing and get in your car. We're wasting time. He's at Freemont Road Police Station in Bournemouth.'

'I'll be there as soon as I can,' he promised. 'In the meantime, tell him to keep quiet and refuse to answer any questions.'

Easier said than done, thought Sarah ruefully, as she and Ruth were given chairs to sit on while Cooper was taken into an interview room. When the door opened, they heard

Jack in full spate. '*Look*, how many times do you have to be *told*? I was rescuing her from being raped, not bloody raping her myself. Jesus wept!' His fist pounded on the table. 'I will not talk to morons. Doesn't anyone in this piss-pot have a measurable IQ?' He gave a whoop of relief. 'Halle-lujah! Cooper! Where the hell have you been, you bastard?' The door closed again.

Sarah leant her head against the wall with a sigh. 'The trouble with Jack,' she said to Ruth, 'is he never does anything by halves.'

'He wouldn't be here at all if it wasn't for me,' the girl said wretchedly, washing her hands over and over in her lap. She was so nervous she could barely keep her breathing under control.

Sarah glanced at her. 'I think you should be rather proud of yourself. Because of you he obviously stopped someone else getting the treatment you were given. That's good.'

'Not if they think Jack was involved.'

'Cooper will set them straight.'

'Does that mean I won't have to say anything? I don't want to say anything.' The words came out in a rush. 'I'm so frightened,' she said simply, tears welling tragically in the huge dark eyes. 'I don't want anyone to know' – her voice shook – 'I'm so ashamed.'

Sarah, who had had to use a very heavy hand in the shape of emotional blackmail to get her this far, balked at using any more. The girl was in a highly emotional state already, desperately seeking to justify her mother's indifference because then she could justify her own indifference to the growing foetus inside her. But she couldn't justify it, of course, and that made her guilt about wanting an abortion all the stronger. There was no logic to human psychology, thought Sarah sadly. She had said nothing about her visit to Cedar House, merely offered to drive Ruth over to Fontwell. 'In fairness,' she had said, 'all your mother knows is that you've been expelled for going out to meet your boyfriend. I'm sure she'll be sympathetic if you tell her the truth.' Ruth shook her head. 'She wouldn't,' she whispered, 'she'd say I got what I deserved. She used to say it to Granny about her arthritis.' Her face had pinched in pain. 'I wish Granny hadn't died. I did love her, you know, but she died thinking I didn't.' And what could Sarah say to that? She had never come across three people so intent on destroying each other, and themselves.

She put her arm now around the girl's thin shoulders and hugged her tight. 'Sergeant Cooper will sort it out,' she said firmly, 'and he won't force you to say anything you don't want to.' She gave her throaty chuckle. 'He's far too nice and far too soft which is why he's never made Inspector.'

But the law, like the mills of God, grinds slow but exceeding small, and Sarah knew that if any of them emerged unscathed at the end of their brush with it, it would be a miracle.

'You realize, Dr Blakeney, we could charge you with being an accessory before the fact,' said an irate Inspector. 'You knew when you helped your husband get hold of Hughes's address that he planned to do something illegal, didn't you?'

'I wouldn't answer that,' said Keith.

'No, I did not,' said Sarah stoutly. 'And what's illegal

about preventing a brutal rape? Since when was rescuing somebody a chargeable offence?'

'You're in the wrong ballpark, Doctor. We're talking attempted murder, GBH, abduction, driving without due care and attention, assault on a police officer. You name it, it's down here. Your husband's an extremely dangerous man and you sent him off after Hughes, knowing full well that he was liable to lose control of his temper if confronted. That's a fair summary, isn't it?'

'I wouldn't answer that,' said Keith automatically.

'Of course it isn't,' she snapped. '*Hughes* is the extremely dangerous man, not Jack. What would you have done if you knew a young girl was about to be brutally attacked by five zombies who are so degenerate and uneducated they'll do anything their sadistic leader tells them to do?' Her eyes flashed. 'Don't bother to answer. I know exactly what you'd have done. You'd have crept off with your tail between your legs to the nearest telephone to dial nine-nine-nine, and never mind the damage that was done to the child in the meantime.'

'It's an offence to withhold information from the police. Why did you not inform us about Miss Lascelles's rape?'

'I really do advise you not to answer that question,' said Keith wearily.

'Because we gave her our word we wouldn't. Why on earth do you think Jack went out tonight if we could have told the police everything?'

Keith held up his hand to forestall the Inspector. 'Any objections to switching off the tape while I confer with my client?'

The other man eyed him for a moment then consulted

his watch. 'Interview with Dr Blakeney suspended at 3.42 a.m.' He spoke abruptly, then pressed the 'stop' button.

'Thanks. Now, will you explain something to me, Sarah?' Keith murmured plaintively. 'Why did you drag me all the way down here if neither you nor Jack will listen to a word I say?'

'Because I'm so bloody angry, that's why. They should be grateful to Jack; instead they're condemning him.'

'The Inspector's paid to make you angry. That's how he gets his results, and you're making this very easy for him.'

'I object to that remark, Mr Smollett. I am paid, among other things, to try and get at the truth when a criminal offence has occurred.'

'Then why don't you stop bull-shitting,' suggested Keith amiably, 'and deal in straightforward fact? I can't be the only one here who's bored stiff with all these idiotic threats of criminal prosecution. Of course you can charge Mr Blakeney if you want to, but you'll be a laughing-stock. How many people these days would have bothered to go in and do what he did with only a belt and a torch as protection?' He smiled faintly. 'We're a non-involvement society these days, where heroism is confined to the television screens. There was a case the other day where a woman was sexually assaulted by two men in full view of several taxi-drivers at a taxi rank, and not a single one of them lifted a finger to help her. Worse, they wheeled up their windows to block out her screams for help. Should I infer from your attitude towards Mr Blakeney that that is the sort of behaviour you approve of in our so-called civilized society?'

'Vigilante behaviour is just as dangerous, Mr Smollett.

For every case of non-involvement you cite, I can cite another where rough justice has been meted out on innocent people because a lynch mob decides arbitrarily who is or is not guilty. Should I infer from your attitude that you approve of the kangaroo-court approach to justice?'

Keith acknowledged the point with a nod. 'Of course not,' he said honestly, 'and had Mr Blakeney taken a private army with him I'd be on your side. But you're on very thin ice describing him as a lynch mob. He was one man, faced with an impossible decision – to act immediately to stop the rape or to abandon the girl to her fate while he drove off to summon assistance.'

'He would never have been there at all had he and his wife not conspired together to withhold the information about Miss Lascelles. Nor for that matter would Hughes and his gang have been able to subject the young lady Mr Blakeney rescued to the terror she was put through, for the simple reason that they would all have been under lock and key charged with the rape of Miss Lascelles.'

'But Miss Lascelles has told you categorically that she would have been too frightened to say anything to the police, assuming the Blakeneys had reported what she told them. She lives in terror of Hughes carrying out his threat to rape her again the minute he's set free, and there's no guarantee, even now, that she – or tonight's victim – will find the courage to give the evidence in court that will convict him. Your best bet, quite frankly, is Jack Blakeney's testimony. If he remains strong, which he will, Ruth will gain courage from his example, and if the other girl and her parents are made aware of just what they owe him, then she, too, may find the courage to speak out. By the same token, if you insist on pursuing these charges against Blakeney, then you can kiss goodbye to any co-operation from two terrified young women. Quite reasonably they will conclude that justice is on Hughes's side and not on theirs.'

The Inspector shook his head. 'What none of you seems able to grasp,' he said irritably, 'is that if we fail to charge Mr Blakeney we make the prosecution case against Hughes so much harder. His defence will have a field day in court pointing up the contrast between police leniency towards the *admitted* violence of a middle-class intellectual and police harshness towards the *alleged* violence of an unemployed navvy. Hughes was outside the van, remember, when the rape was taking place, and he's sitting there now claiming he had no idea what was going on. The lad who was raping the girl when your client burst into that van is only fifteen, a juvenile, in other words, who can be sentenced to detention but not to custody in an adult prison. The oldest boy there, if we exclude Hughes, is eighteen and his age will be taken into account at his trial. At the moment, they're all shell-shocked and fingering Hughes as the instigator and prime mover, but by the time they come to trial it will have become a bit of harmless fun that was the girl's idea and which Hughes knew nothing about because he had wandered off for a walk along the beach. The worst of it is, Mr Blakeney will have to testify to that in court because he saw him doing it.' He rubbed his tired eyes. 'It's a mess, frankly. God knows if we will ever succeed in bringing a conviction. Without clear evidence of intent I can see Hughes getting off scot-free. His MO is to manipulate youngsters into doing his dirty work while he stands aloof and collects the money, and once these boys realize how short their sentences are going to be because the law is relatively powerless against juveniles, they'll stop grassing him up. I'm so confident of that, I'd lay my last cent on it.'

There was a long silence.

Sarah cleared her throat. 'You're forgetting the girls,' she said. 'Won't their evidence carry weight?'

The Inspector's smile was twisted. 'If they're not too frightened to testify, if they don't collapse under cross-examination, if their stealing isn't used by the defence to blacken their characters, if the speed with which they were prepared to spread their legs for Hughes doesn't lose them the sympathy of the jury.' He shrugged. 'Justice is as fickle as fate, Dr Blakeney.'

'Then release him now and be done with it,' she said coldly. 'I mean, let's face it, it's going to be a damn sight easier to fill your productivity quota by prosecuting Jack than by having to put the counselling effort into bringing thieving little tarts up to scratch. Perhaps you should ask yourself why none of these girls felt confident enough to come to the police in the first place?' Her eyes narrowed angrily as she answered her own question. 'Because they believed everything Hughes told them, namely that *he* would always be acquitted, and *they* would always be left to fend for themselves. He was right, too, though I'd never have guessed it if I hadn't heard it from you.'

'He'll be charged and hopefully he'll be held on remand, Dr Blakeney, but what happens at trial is out of my hands. We can do our best to prepare the ground. We cannot, unfortunately, predict the outcome.' He sighed. 'For the moment, I have decided to release your husband without charge. I shall be taking advice, however, which means we may decide to proceed against him at a later date. In the meantime, he will be required to remain at Mill House in Long Upton and, should he wish to travel anywhere, he must advise Detective Sergeant Cooper of his intentions. Is that clear?'

She nodded.

'In addition, please note that if he ever involves himself again in similar activities to those he engaged in tonight, he will be charged immediately. Is that also clear?'

She nodded.

The Inspector's tired face cracked into a smile. 'Off the record, I rather agree with Mr Smollett here. Your husband's a brave man, Doctor, but I'm sure you knew that already.'

'Oh, yes,' said Sarah loyally, hoping that her expression was less sheepish than it felt. For as long as she'd known him Jack had always maintained the same thing. All men were cowards but it was only a few, like himself, who had the courage to admit it. She was beginning to wonder if there were other aspects of his character that she had misjudged so completely.

Father rang today to give me the inquest verdict on Gerald's death. 'They've opted for misadventure, thank God, but I had to pull every string in the book to get it. That damned Coroner was going to bring in suicide if he could.' Poor Father! He could never have shown his face in the House again if his brother had killed himself. Heaven forbid! What stigma is still attached to suicide, particularly amongst the upper classes. Nothing is so bad as the ultimate weakness of taking one's own life.

I am naturally delighted with the verdict, if somewhat piqued to have my brilliance overlooked. There is an extraordinary urge to confess, I find, if only to draw attention to what one has achieved . . . I won't, of course.

Gerald was putty in my hands when it came to writing the codicil because I told him he'd go to prison for raping his niece if he didn't. 'Lord, what fools these mortals be!' The only purpose of the codicil was to convince the idiot solicitor that Gerald had committed suicide when he discovered whose child Joanna really was. Once persuaded, he alerted Father to the fact that a document detailing Gerald's incest existed, and they both performed to perfection. They made such a song-

and-dance about pulling their various strings in order to suppress any hint that Gerald might have done away with himself that everyone, including the Coroner, was in no doubt that he had. It is all so very amusing. My only regret is that I had to involve Jane, but I am not unduly concerned about that. Even if she does have any suspicions, she won't voice them. She can't afford to, but in any case no one has questioned where Gerald acquired his barbiturates, or if they have I suspect Father has claimed them as his. He's so drunk most of the time, he probably believes they were.

Father's relief was short-lived. I told him I had a signed carbon copy of the codicil in my possession and he became apoplectic at the other end of the wire. He calls it blackmail. I call it self-preservation . . .

Sixteen

TWO FAXES were waiting on Cooper's desk when he arrived at the station later that morning. The first was brief and to the point:

> Fingerprints on Yale key, ref: TC/H/MG/320, identified as belonging to Sarah Penelope Blakeney. 22 point agreement. No other prints. Fingerprints on bottle, ref: TC/H/MG/321 agree in 10, 16 and 12 points respectively with prints located in Cedar House on desk (room 1), chair (room 1), and decanter (room 1). Full report to follow.

The second fax was longer and rather more interesting. After he had read it, Cooper went off in search of PC Jenkins. It was Jenkins, he recalled, who had done most of the tedious legwork around Fontwell in the days following Mrs Gillespie's death.

'I hear you've been busy,' said Charlie Jones, dunking a ginger biscuit into a cup of thick white coffee.

Cooper sank into an armchair. 'Hughes, you mean.'

'I'm going down there in half an hour to have another bash at him. Do you want to come?'

'No thanks. I've had more than enough of Dave Hughes and his fellow-lowlife to last me a lifetime. You wait till you see them, Charlie. Kids, for Christ's sake. Fifteen-year-olds who look twenty-five and have a mental age of eight. It scares me, it really does. If society doesn't do something to educate them and match a man's brain to a man's body, we haven't a hope of survival. And the worst of it is, it's not just us. I saw a ten-year-old boy on the telly the other day, wielding a machine gun in Somalia as part of some rebel army. I've seen children in Ireland throwing bricks at whichever side their bigoted families tell them to, adolescent Palestinian boys strutting their stuff in balaclavas, negro lads in South Africa necklacing each other because white police-men think it's a great way to get rid of them, and Serbian boys encouraged to rape Muslim girls the way their fathers do. It's complete and utter madness. We corrupt our children at our peril, but by God we're doing a fine job of it.'

Charlie eyed him sympathetically. 'Not just a busy night, obviously, but an exhausting one, too.'

'Forget *in vino veritas*,' said Cooper acidly. '*In insomnio veritas* is more like it. I wake up in the early hours of the morning sometimes and see the world as it really is. A bear garden, with religious leaders twisting souls on one side, power-corrupt politicians twisting minds on the other side, and the illiterate, intolerant masses in the middle baying for blood because they're too uneducated to do anything else.'

'Stop the world I want to get off, eh?'

'That's about the size of it.'

'Are there no redeeming features, Tommy?'

Cooper chuckled. 'Sure, as long as no one reminds me of Hughes.' He passed the first fax across the desk-top. 'Gillespie never left the sitting-room, apparently, and the key's a dead-end.'

Jones looked disappointed. 'We need something concrete, old son, and quickly. I'm being pushed to drop this one and concentrate on something that will get a result. The consensus view is that, even if we do manage to prove it was murder, we're going to have the devil's own job bringing a prosecution.'

'I wonder where I've heard that before,' said Cooper sourly. 'If things go on like this, we might as well pack it in and let the anarchists have a go.'

'What about the diaries? Any progress there?'

'Not really. The search was a wash-out, but then I knew it would be. I went through every book in the library the first time we searched Cedar House.' He frowned. 'I had a word with Jack and Ruth last night, but they're claiming ignorance as well, although Jack does remember Mrs Gillespie being in a paddy one day because she said her books were being disturbed.' He fingered his lip. 'I know it's hypothetical but, let's say the diaries did exist and that someone was looking for them, then that might at least explain why the books were disturbed.'

Charlie snorted. 'Hellishly hypothetical,' he agreed, 'and quite unprovable.'

'Yes, but if whoever was looking for them found them, then it might explain why they've been removed.' He took pity on Charlie's baffled expression. 'Because,' he said patiently, 'they could tell us who murdered her and why.'

Charlie frowned. 'You're clutching at straws. First, convince me they existed.'

'Why would James Gillespie lie?'

'Because he's a drunk,' said Charlie. 'You don't need any better reason than that.'

'Then why was Mathilda in a paddy because her books were being disturbed? Explain that, or are you suggesting Jack's lying, too?'

Charlie registered this second use of 'Jack' with an inward sigh. When would the silly fellow learn that it was his inability to keep his distance that scuppered his chances every time? *Unprofessional. Cannot remain objective*, was what Jones's predecessor had written on Cooper's last assessment. 'She must have guessed who it was,' he said. 'It's a narrow field in all conscience. Why didn't she tackle them about it?'

'Perhaps she did. Perhaps that's why she was murdered.' Cooper tapped the fax with his forefinger. 'The key complicates it, though. If whoever it was knew about that, then they could have let themselves in without her knowing. The field becomes much wider then.'

'I suppose you've considered that Gillespie's our man, and only mentioned the diaries to you because he thought everyone else would have known about them.'

'Yes. But why would he take them away and deny all knowledge if he's expecting them to prove she diddled him over the clocks?'

'Double bluff. He read them, discovered they proved the exact opposite, so destroyed them in order to keep his claim alive, then topped her to give himself a free run with Mrs Lascelles who he thought was going to inherit.'

326

Cooper shook his head. 'It's a possibility, I suppose, but it doesn't feel right. If he stole them himself because he knew they'd destroy his chances of any money, how could he be sure no one else had read them first? It's too iffy, Charlie.'

'It's *all* too iffy, frankly,' said the Inspector dryly. 'If the diaries existed – if the searcher *knew* they existed – if there was something incriminating in them – if he or she knew about the key . . .' He fell silent, dunking his biscuit again. 'There are two things I don't understand. Why did Mrs Gillespie leave all her money to Dr Blakeney and why did her murderer put the scold's bridle on her head and deck it out with nettles and daisies? If I knew the answers to those two questions, I could probably tell you who killed her. Otherwise I'm inclined to make do with a verdict of suicide.'

'I think I know why she left the money to Dr Blakeney.'

'Why?'

'I reckon it was a Pontius Pilate exercise. She'd done a lousy job herself bringing up her daughter and granddaughter, knew they'd destroy themselves with jealous infighting if she left the money to them, so passed the buck to the only person she'd ever got on with and respected. Namely Dr Blakeney. I think she hoped the doctor would succeed where she hadn't.'

'Sentimental twaddle,' said the Inspector amiably. 'And all because you're reasoning backwards, from the effect you see to the cause you imagine a normal person would wish to achieve. Try reasoning forwards. She was a bloody-minded, mean and vicious old woman, who not only acquired a fortune through blackmail and creative insurance scams but also loathed and despised everyone around her for most of her life. Why, having sown nothing but discord for sixty years, did she suddenly endow an easy-going, pleasant stranger with a fortune? Not for the sake of harmony, that's for sure.' The Inspector's eyes narrowed thoughtfully. 'I can go along with the scold's bridle as a sort of symbolic drawing attention to the final curbing of a peculiarly unpleasant tongue, but I cannot go along with the idea that the leopard suddenly changed its spots when it came to making the will.'

'You can't ignore the Blakeneys' view of her character, Charlie. According to them, she was a much pleasanter person than anyone else credited her with being. My guess is they gave her room to breathe, didn't demand anything and the real Mathilda blossomed.' He paused for a moment and took stock. 'Think about this. We've been dwelling on the symbolism of the scold's bridle, largely because of Ophelia's "nettles, daisies and long purples", but look at it in practical terms instead. They were used to keep women quiet, and perhaps the reason she was wearing it was as simple as that. Her murderer didn't want her alerting the next-door neighbours by screaming her head off, so shoved that contraption on her head and then adorned it with flowers to give it a mystical – but misleading – significance.'

Jones steepled his fingers under his chin. 'But she must have taken the barbiturates first or she'd have struggled when the bridle was put on and there'd have been scratches on her face. If she was so doped up that she didn't bother to fight it, then why put it on at all?'

'Do what you told me to do and reason forwards. You want to kill a woman by making it look like suicide, but the neighbours are too close for comfort so you need a method of keeping her quiet in case the barbiturates aren't as effective as you hope. A belt and braces job in other words. You can't use tape or Elastoplast because it'll leave a mark on the skin, and you're canny enough not to use a gag in case bits of fabric are found in the mouth during the post mortem, so you pitch on something you can leave in place which has its own significance to the victim, and you trust to luck that the police will put it down as a macabre example of self-condemnation. Then you carry her to the bath, clasp your hands over hers while you slit each wrist, drop the knife to the floor and leave her to die, knowing that even if she does struggle back to consciousness, the bridle will prevent her calling for help.'

Jones nodded. 'It sounds feasible, but why bother with the bath and the Stanley knife at all? Why not simply overdose her on sleeping pills and kill her that way?'

'Because there weren't enough, presumably, and even if there were, they're very unreliable. Supposing Ruth had come back the next morning and found the old lady still alive. It might have been possible to pump her out and revive her. Plus, of course, Ophelia drowned herself which may have inspired the idea.' He smiled self-consciously. 'I've read the play to see if there are any clues in it and a blood-thirsty piece it is, too. There's no one left standing by the end.'

'Did you find any clues?'

'No.'

'I'm not surprised. It was written four hundred years ago.' Jones tapped his pencil against his teeth. 'I can't see that any of this makes much difference, frankly. You're still describing someone who knew her intimately, which is what we've believed from the start. The only new pieces of information are the discovery of the key and the absence of the diaries. I admit the key may mean that her murderer came in uninvited, but it still had to be someone very close to her or she'd have screamed her head off. And there's so much intimate detail involved – the Stanley knife, the sleeping pills, her yen for Shakespeare, the scold's bridle. Whoever it was probably even knew there were nettles and daisies in her garden *and* where to find them in the dark. And someone *that* close means the Blakeneys, the Lascelles women or Mr and Mrs Spede.'

Cooper took the second fax from his notebook and spread it on the desk. 'According to the fingerprint tests we made, bearing in mind I told the lab to get a move on so these results will have to be double-checked for accuracy, they've made tentative identifications on four of the prints in that house, excluding Mrs Gillespie herself, Mrs Spede, the Blakeneys, Mrs and Miss Lascelles and now James Gillespie. The four are . . .' he ran his finger slowly down the page, 'the Reverend Matthews, matched in ten points with print located on hall mirror; Mrs Orloff, matched in sixteen points with print located on kitchen worktop and in fourteen points with print found on kitchen door; Mrs Spencer, matched in twelve points with print on hall door; and, lastly, Mrs Jane Marriott, matched in eighteen points with two prints on desk in library and one on stair newel post.' He looked up. 'Mrs Orloff is her neighbour. Mrs Spencer runs the local shop and Mrs Marriott is the receptionist at the Fontwell surgery. What's interesting is that the Reverend Matthews, Mrs Orloff and Mrs Spencer all admitted quite happily that they had been inside the house in the week before Mrs Gillespie died. Mrs Marriott didn't. According to Jenkins who interviewed her when he was going door to door, she said she hadn't been near Cedar House for years.'

With careless disregard for the restrictions placed on his movements by the Bournemouth police, Jack waited until Sarah had left for work then set off for Fontwell on the old bicycle that Geoffrey Freeling's next-of-kin had abandoned in the garage. His car was in the pound at Freemont Road and looked like remaining there indefinitely until a decision was reached on whether or not to prosecute him, but he was deeply suspicious about their motives for holding it. They had claimed it was material evidence, but he saw Keith's devious hand at work behind the Inspector. It's unreasonable to expect Dr Blakeney to guard her husband for you, so deprive Jack of his wheels, and he may stay put. For once he was grateful to Smollett's lingering partiality for his wife.

Ruth was dead to the world upstairs, worn out by the mental and physical stress that had taken its toll of her all too meagre reserves the previous night, but he left a note on the kitchen table in case she woke up and panicked to find him gone: 'You're quite safe with Hughes in the nick,' it read, 'but don't answer the door to anyone, just in case. Back soon, love Jack.'

'Mrs Marriott?' Cooper leant on the receptionist's counter in the empty surgery and held up his warrant card. 'DS Cooper, Learmouth Police.'

Jane smiled automatically. 'How can I help you, Sergeant?'

'I'd like a word or two in private, if that's possible.'

'It's private enough here for the moment,' she said. 'The only thing likely to disturb us is the telephone. Would you care for a cup of coffee?'

'Thank you. White, two sugars, please.'

She busied herself with the kettle.

'We've had some interesting results from our fingerprint tests,' said Cooper to her back. 'One way and another the evidence points to quite a few people visiting Mrs Gillespie before she died. You, for example.'

Jane became very still suddenly. 'I hoped you wouldn't find out,' she admitted after a moment, plucking invisible fluff from her jumper. 'And then, of course, you invited us all to give examples of our fingerprints. It was very difficult to know what to do then. Should I confess that I'd told a lie the first time or sit it out in the hopes I hadn't touched anything?'

'Why didn't you want us to know you'd been to Cedar House?'

'Because you'd have asked me my reason for going.'

He nodded. 'Which was?'

She turned back to the coffee cups and poured out the water. 'It had nothing to do with Mathilda's death, Sergeant. It was a very private matter.'

'I'm afraid that really won't do, Mrs Marriott.'

She pushed a cup across the counter and placed the sugar bowl and a spoon beside it. 'Will you arrest me if I refuse to tell you?'

He chuckled good-humouredly. 'Not immediately.'

'When?'

He sidestepped the question. 'If I say to you that, as long as what you tell me really does have no bearing on Mrs Gillespie's death, it will go no further than these four walls, will you trust me enough to keep my word?' He held her gaze with his. 'You've no idea of the sort of publicity you'll face if I have to take you in for questioning. Once the press have their teeth into you, they don't let go easily.'

Jane's plump homely face took on a very bleak expression. 'How Mathilda would adore this if she were still alive,' she said. 'She loved making trouble.'

'You knew her well then.'

'Too well.'

'And you didn't like her?'

'I couldn't bear her. I tried to avoid her as far as I could but that wasn't very easy once I started working here, what with phone calls demanding a doctor's visit and requests for repeat prescriptions.'

'Yet you went to see her?'

'I had to. I saw James coming out of her house the day before she died.' She held a hand to her bosom. 'It was such a shock. I thought he was in Hong Kong.' She fell silent.

'Tell me about it,' Cooper prompted gently.

'You wouldn't understand,' said Jane with conviction. 'You didn't know Mathilda.'

Jack was in a very bad mood by the time he reached Cedar House. He hadn't ridden a bicycle in years, and four miles along rutted country lanes on something that should have been condemned to the scrap heap years ago had given him

MINETTE WALTERS

sore balls and the sort of trembling thighs that would have
disgraced a nonagenarian. He abandoned the bicycle against
a tree in the Cedar Housing Estate, vaulted the fence and
ran lightly across the grass to the kitchen window. For
reasons of his own, he had no intention of announcing his
presence by approaching across the gravel or using the front
doorbell.

He tapped lightly but persistently on the window pane,
and after a minute or two, Joanna appeared in the doorway
that led from the kitchen into the hall. 'What do you want?'

He read her lips, rather than heard the words, and
gestured towards the back door. 'Let me in,' he mouthed,
his voice barely above a whisper.

Jane's eyes narrowed as she looked back down the corridors
of time. 'You see, you can't assess Mathilda on what people
tell you now. They've forgotten how beautiful she was as a
young woman, how witty she was and how many men
desired her. She was the most eligible girl around – her
father was the MP, her uncle was a wealthy bachelor – ' she
shrugged ' – she could have married anybody.'

'Then why didn't she?'

'At the time everyone assumed she was hanging on for
something better, a title perhaps, or a stately home with
acres, but I always thought there was more to it than that.
I used to watch her at parties and it was very clear to me
that, while she enjoyed flirting and being the centre of
attention, she couldn't bear men touching her.' She fell
silent.

'Go on,' Cooper prompted after a moment or two.

'It wasn't until ten years later when my husband and I met James in Hong Kong and he told us the truth about Joanna's parentage that it made sense.' She sighed. 'Not that I've ever really understood exactly what happened because, of course, child abuse and incest were kept under wraps in those days. James believed she encouraged Gerald, but I never did. It's the one area where I always felt sorry for her. She was emotionally crippled by it, I think.'

'So you've known for a long time that Mrs Lascelles wasn't James Gillespie's daughter?'

'Yes.'

'Did Mrs Gillespie know you knew?'

'Oh, yes.'

'Didn't that worry her?'

'She knew I wouldn't tell anyone.'

'How could she know?'

'She just did,' said Jane flatly.

What was it James Gillespie had called it? Mutual insurance.

Without warning, as the back door closed behind him, Jack's huge hand circled Joanna's throat and drove her through the kitchen and into the hall. 'Didn't what happened to Mathilda teach you anything, you silly bitch?' he said in a savage undertone.

Cooper took out a cigarette, remembered where he was and put it back again. 'Was it you who was friendly with Mr Gillespie, or your husband?' he asked Jane.

'Paul and he went through the war together, but I'd known him a long time as well.'

'Why did it shock you so much to see him coming out of Cedar House that day?'

'I'd always hoped he was dead.' She sighed. 'I know you've seen him. Sarah told me. Did he tell you anything?'

'About what, Mrs Marriott?'

She gave a tired smile. 'You'd know if he'd told you, Sergeant.'

'Then I don't think he can have done,' he said honestly. 'But you're obviously afraid he will, so wouldn't it be better coming from you? I presume it's something that only you, he and Mathilda were privy to. You were confident she wouldn't say anything because you could reveal the truth about Joanna's father, but he's a different matter. You have no hold over him, which is why you were so shocked to see him back in England and why you went to see Mathilda, to find out if he was going to spill the beans. Am I right?'

Joanna showed only the slightest flicker of alarm before she relaxed against the wall and stared into his eyes with a look of triumph. 'I knew you'd come back.'

He didn't say anything, just searched her beautiful face and marvelled again at its absolute perfection. It was the face of the Madonna in Michelangelo's Pietà, the face of a mother gazing down in quiet contemplation on the body of her adored son, a study of such simple purity that it had brought tears to his eyes when he first saw it. For years, he had wondered about the woman behind the Madonna. Was she real? Or was she something fabulous that Michelangelo had conjured from his own imagination? Until Joanna, he had believed she must have existed in the eye of her creator because only an artist could have made a thing of such immeasurable beauty. Now he held it beneath his hand and knew that its conception had been as random and as accidental as his own. He closed his eyes to stem the tears that threatened to well again.

Jane nodded unhappily. 'James blackmailed me for five years after we returned home from Hong Kong. In the end, I paid him over ten thousand pounds, which was all the money my mother left me.' Her voice shook. 'He stopped when I sent him copies of my bank statement which showed I had nothing more to give him, but he warned me he'd come back.' She was silent for a moment, striving for control. 'I never saw or heard from him again until that awful day when he came out of Cedar House.'

Cooper studied her bent head with compassion. He could only assume she'd had an affair that James and Mathilda Gillespie had found out about, but why was it so hard to confess to all these years on? 'Everyone has skeletons somewhere in their closet, Mrs Marriott. Mine still bring a blush to my cheeks when I think about them. But do you really think your husband would hold yours against you after thirty-odd years?'

'Oh, yes,' she said honestly. 'Paul always wanted children, you see, and I could never give him any.'

Cooper waited for her to go on but, when she didn't, he prompted her gently: 'What do children have to do with it?'

'Paul had an affair with Mathilda and Mathilda got pregnant. That's why James went to Hong Kong. He said it was the last straw, that he might have coped with Gerald's incestuous bastard but not with Paul's love child as well.'

Cooper was very taken aback. 'And that's what James was blackmailing you over?' But no, he thought, that didn't make sense. It was the adulterous husband who paid the blackmailer not the deceived wife.

'Not about the affair,' said Jane. 'I knew all about that. Paul told me himself after he resigned. He was Sir William's agent and used to stay with James and Mathilda in their flat in London whenever he had business in town. I don't think the affair was anything more than a brief infatuation on both their parts. She was bored with the tedious domestic routine of washing nappies and keeping house and he . . .' she sighed, 'he was flattered by the attention. You really must try to understand how captivating Mathilda could be, and it wasn't just beauty, you know. There was something about her that drew men like magnets. I think it was the remoteness, the dislike of being touched. They saw it as a challenge, so when she let her guard down for Paul, he fell for it.' She gave a sad little smile. 'And I understood that, believe me. It may sound odd to you but there was a time – when we were young – when I was almost as in love with her as he was. She was everything I always wanted to be and never was.' Her eyes filled. 'Well, you know how attractive she could be. Sarah fell in love with her, just the way I did.'

*

338

'Show me how much you love me, Jack.' Joanna's voice, soft and husky, was a lover's caress.

Gently his fingers smoothed the white column of her throat. How could someone so ugly be *so* beautiful? She made a mockery of the wonder of creation. He raised his other hand to the silver-gold hair and, with a violent twist, wrapped the strands around his palm and jerked her head backwards with his fingers still clamped about her throat. 'I love you this much,' he said quietly.

'You're hurting me.' This time her voice rose in alarm.

He tightened his grip on her hair. 'But I enjoy hurting you, Joanna.' His voice echoed through the emptiness of the hall.

'I don't understand,' she cried out, her voice rasping against his fingers on her larynx. 'What do you want?' She saw something in his eyes that brought the fear leaping into hers. 'Oh, my God. It was you who killed my mother.' She opened her mouth to scream but only a thread of sound came out as the pressure on her throat tightened.

'I'm sorry if I'm being particularly slow on the uptake,' said Cooper apologetically, 'but I don't quite see what hold James Gillespie could have had over you that would prompt you to pay him ten thousand pounds. If you already knew about the affair from your husband—' he broke off. 'It was something to do with the pregnancy, presumably. Did you not know about that?'

She compressed her lips in an effort to hold back tears. 'Yes, I did. It was Paul who never knew.' She drew another deep sigh. 'It's so awful. I've kept it secret for so long. I wanted to tell him but there was never a good time. Rather like the lie I told your constable. At what point do you come clean, as it were?' She touched her fingers to her lips in a gesture of despair. 'Being a father. It was all he ever wanted. I prayed and prayed that we would have children of our own, but of course we never did . . .' She tailed off into silence.

Cooper put a large, comforting hand over hers. He was completely at sea here, but was reluctant to press too hard in case she clammed up on him. 'How did you know about the pregnancy if your husband didn't?'

'Mathilda told me. She rang me and asked me to go to London, said if I didn't she'd make sure the whole of Fontwell knew about her and Paul. He'd written her some letters and she said she'd make them public if I didn't do what she wanted.'

'What did she want?'

It was some moments before she could speak. 'She wanted me to help her murder the baby when it came.'

'Good God!' said Cooper with feeling. And she must have done it, he thought, or James Gillespie would never have been able to blackmail her.

There was the sound of footsteps on the gravel outside and a ring on the doorbell. 'Joanna!' called Violet's high-pitched, nervous voice. 'Joanna! Are you all right, dear? I thought I *heard* something.' When she received no answer, she called again: 'Is someone with you? Do answer, please.' Her voice rose even higher. 'Duncan! Duncan!' she called.

'There *is* something wrong. I know there is. You must call the police. I'm going to get help.' Her footsteps skittered away as she ran towards the gate.

Jack stared down into Joanna's drawn and haunted face, then lowered her with surprising gentleness on to the nearest chair. 'You don't deserve it, but you were luckier than your mother,' was all he said, before walking off towards the kitchen and the back door.

Joanna Lascelles was still screaming when Duncan Orloff, in a state of complete panic, used a sledgehammer to break open the front door and confront whatever awaited him in the hall of Cedar House.

'And did you help her?' Cooper asked with a calm that belied his true feelings.

She looked wretched. 'I don't know – I don't know what she did – I can only guess.' She wrung her hands in distress. 'She didn't say anything in so many words. She just asked me to steal some sleeping pills – barbiturates – from my father's dispensary. She said they were for her because she couldn't sleep. I hoped – I thought – she was going to kill herself – and I was glad. I hated her by that time.'

'So you got her the pills?'

'Yes.'

'But she didn't kill herself.'

'No.'

'But you said she wanted you to help her kill the baby.'

'That's what I thought for ten years.' The long-held-back tears oozed slowly from between her lids. 'There was only Joanna, you see. The other baby might never have existed. I didn't think it had ever existed.' She held a shaking hand to her face. 'I thought I'd helped her kill it – and then in Hong Kong, James kept asking me how Gerald could have killed himself with barbiturates, because no doctor would have prescribed them for him, and I realized it was Gerald she'd wanted to kill all along, and I'd given her the means to do it.' She took out a handkerchief and blew her nose. 'I was so *shocked* that James guessed what I'd done. I think he'd always known, though. In many ways, he and Mathilda were very alike.'

Cooper sought desperately to break this down into manageable proportions. There were so many unanswered questions. 'Why would no doctor prescribe barbiturates for Gerald Cavendish? I've checked the coroner's report. There was no question of murder, only a choice between misadventure and suicide.'

'Gerald was . . .' Jane sought for the right word, 'feeble-minded, I suppose, like the Spedes, but today they call it educationally subnormal. It's why the property was kept intact for William. Mathilda's grandfather was afraid Gerald would give it away to anyone who asked for it. But I've never really understood how Mathilda came to sleep with him. He was a very pathetic person. I've always assumed her father forced her into it to protect his legacy somehow, but James said it was all Mathilda's idea. I don't believe that. James hated her so much he'd have said anything to blacken her.'

Cooper shook his head in bewilderment. How uneventful his own life had been, compared with the agonies of this grey-haired motherly soul who looked as if butter wouldn't melt in her mouth. 'Why did you visit James Gillespie in

Hong Kong if your husband had had an affair with his wife? There can't have been much love lost between the three of you in all conscience.'

'We didn't or at least not like that. We had no idea James had gone to Hong Kong. Mathilda never told us – why would she? – and we moved away from here after the affair and went to live in Southampton. I became a teacher and Paul worked for a shipping company. We put it all behind us, and then Paul had to go to Hong Kong on business and took me with him for a holiday.' She shook her head. 'And almost the first person we met when we arrived was James. The expatriate community was so small' – she raised her hands in a gesture of helplessness – 'we were bound to meet him. If we'd only known he was there, we'd never have gone. Fate is very cruel, Sergeant.'

He couldn't argue with that. 'Then why did you come back here to live, Mrs Marriott, knowing that Mrs Gillespie was in Cedar House? Weren't you tempting fate a second time?'

'Yes,' she said simply, 'but what could I do about it? Paul knows nothing of any of this, Sergeant, and he's dying – slowly – of emphysema. We kept our house here – it was his parents' house and he was too fond of it to sell it, so we let it out to tenants – and then five years ago, he was retired on health grounds and he begged me to let us come home.' Her eyes flooded again. 'He said I needn't worry about Mathilda, that the only thing he had ever felt for her was compassion, while the only woman he had ever loved was me. How could I tell him then what had really happened? I still thought his baby was dead.' She held her handkerchief to her streaming eyes. 'It wasn't until I went to Cedar

House and asked Mathilda about James that she told me she'd put the baby up for adoption.' She buried her face in her hands. 'It was a boy and he's still alive somewhere.'

Cooper pondered the sad ironies of life. Was it providence, God or random selection that made some women fertile and some barren? With a deep reluctance he took her back to the day Mathilda died, knowing there was little chance that what she told him could ever remain a secret.

I am pregnant again, sickeningly and disgustingly pregnant. Barely six months after giving birth to one bastard, I am carrying another. Perhaps James's drunken rages will achieve some good purpose by bringing on a miscarriage. He weeps and rants in turn, screaming insults at me like a fishwife, intent, it seems, on trumpeting my 'whorishness' to the entire building. And all for what? A brief, unlovely affair with Paul Marriott whose clumsy, apologetic gropings were almost past endurance. Then, why, Mathilda?

Because there are days when I could 'drink hot blood, and do such bitter business as the day would quake to look on'. Paul's priggishness annoyed me. He talked about 'dear Jane' as if she mattered to him. Mostly I think about death – the baby's death, James's death, Gerald's death, Father's death. It is, after all, such a final solution. Father connives to keep me in London. He tells me Gerald has sworn to marry Grace if I return. The worst of it is, I believe him. Gerald is so very, very frightened of me now.

I paid a private detective to take photographs of

James. And, my, my, what photographs they are! 'The fitchew nor the soiled horse goes to't with such a riotous appetite.' And in a public lavatory too. If the truth be told, I am rather looking forward to showing them to him. What I did was merely sinful. What James does is criminal. There'll be no more talk of divorce, that's for sure, and he'll go to Hong Kong without a murmur. He has no more desire than I to have his sexual activities made public.

Really, Mathilda, you must learn to use blackmail to better effect on Gerald and Father . . .

Seventeen

HUGHES, WHO WAS suffering from sleep deprivation and niggling doubts about the continued obedience of the youngsters he had so successfully controlled, was subdued when he faced Chief Inspector Charlie Jones across the table in the interview room at Freemont Road Police Station. Like Cooper, he was in pessimistic mood. 'I suppose you've come to stitch me up for the old cow's murder,' he said morosely. 'You're all the same.'

'Ah, well,' said Charlie in his lugubrious fashion, 'it makes the percentages look better when the league tables get published. We're into business culture in the police force these days, lad, and productivity's important.'

'That stinks.'

'Not to our customers it doesn't.'

'What customers?'

'The law-abiding British public who pay handsomely for our services through their taxes. Business culture demands that we first identify our client base, next, assess its needs, then, finally, respond in a satisfactory and adequate manner. You already represent a handsome profit on the balance sheet. Rape, conspiracy to rape, abduction, holding without

347

consent, conspiracy to hold without consent, assault, sexual assault, theft, conspiracy to commit theft, handling stolen goods, corruption, conspiracy to pervert the course of justice – ' he broke off with a broad smile – 'which brings me to Mrs Gillespie's murder.'

'I knew it,' said Hughes in disgust. 'You're gonna fucking frame me for it. Jesus! I'm not saying another word till my brief gets here.'

'Who said anything about framing you?' demanded Charlie plaintively. 'It's a little co-operation I'm after, that's all.'

Hughes eyed him suspiciously. 'What do I get in return?'

'Nothing.'

'Then it's no.'

Charlie's eyes narrowed to thin slits. 'The question you should have asked me, lad, is what do you get if you don't co-operate? I'll tell you. You get my personal assurance that not a stone will be left unturned until I see you convicted and sent down for the abduction and rape of a child.'

'I don't do children,' Hughes sneered. 'Never have done. Never will. And you won't get me for rape neither. I've never raped a girl in my life. I've never needed to. What those other punks did is their affair. I had no idea what was going on.'

'For an adult male to sleep with a thirteen-year-old girl is rape. She's under age and therefore too young to give consent for what's done to her.'

'I've never slept with a thirteen-year-old.'

'Sure you have, and I'll prove it. I'll work every man under me until he drops in order to turn up just one little girl, *virgo intacta* before you raped her, who lied to you about her age.' He gave a savage grin as a flicker of doubt crossed Hughes's face. 'Because there'll be one, lad, there always is. It's an idiosyncrasy of female psychology. At thirteen, they want to pass for sixteen, and they do. At forty, they want to pass for thirty, and by God they can do that, too, because the one damn thing you can be sure about the female of the species is that she never looks her age.'

Hughes fingered his unshaven jaw. 'What sort of co-operation are you talking about?'

'I want a complete run-down on everything you know about Cedar House and the people in it.'

'That's easy enough. Fuck all's the answer. Never went in. Never met the old biddy.'

'Come on, Dave, you're a pro. You sat outside in your van over the months, waiting while Ruth did her stuff inside. You were her chauffeur, remember, turned up day after day during the holidays to give her a good time. How did she know you were there if you couldn't signal to her? Don't kid me you weren't close enough to watch all the comings and goings in that place.'

Hughes shrugged. 'Okay, so I saw people from time to time, but if I don't know who they were, how's it gonna help you?'

'Did you ever watch the back of the house?'

The man debated with himself. 'Maybe,' he said guardedly.

'Where from?'

'If you're aiming to use this against me, I want my brief.'

'You're in no position to argue,' said Charlie impatiently.

'Where were you watching it from? Outside or inside the garden?'

'I sometimes used to park the van in the housing estate at the side. Ruth reckoned it was safer, what with all the yuppies living there. Wives commuting to work along with their husbands so no one in during the day,' he explained obligingly. 'There's some rough ground next to the fence round Cedar House garden, easy enough to hop over and watch from the trees.'

The Inspector took an ordnance survey map out of his briefcase. 'The Cedar Estate?' he asked, tapping the map with his forefinger.

Hughes sniffed. 'Probably. Ruth said the land once belonged to the house before the old lady sold it off for cash, though Christ knows why she didn't flog the rest while she was about it. What she want with a massive garden, when there's people living on the streets? Jesus, but she was a tight-fisted old bitch,' he said unwarily. 'All that frigging money and no one else got a bloody look-in. Is it true she left the lot to her doctor or was Ruth just spinning me a yarn?'

Charlie stared him down. 'None of your business, lad, but I'll tell you this for free. Ruth didn't get a penny because of what you forced her to do. Her grandmother took agin her when she started stealing. But for you, she'd have had the house.'

Hughes was unmoved. 'Shouldn't have been so quick to open her legs then, should she?'

Charlie looked at the map again, fighting an urge to hit him. 'Did you ever see anyone go in through the back door?'

'The cleaner used to sweep the step now and again. Saw the woman from next door pottering about in her bit and the old boy sunning himself on his patio.'

'I mean strangers. Someone you wouldn't have expected.'

'I never *saw* anyone.' He put unnatural emphasis on the verb.

'Heard then?'

'Maybe.'

'Where were you? What did you hear?'

'I watched Mrs Gillespie go out in her car one day. Thought I'd take a look through the windows, see what was there.'

'Was Ruth with you?'

He shook his head. 'Back at school.'

'Refusing to co-operate, presumably, so you had to find out for yourself what was worth stealing. You were casing the place.'

Hughes didn't answer.

'Okay, what happened?'

'I heard the old lady coming round the path so I dived behind the coal bunker by the kitchen door.'

'Go on.'

'It wasn't her. It was some other bastard who was nosing around like me.'

'Male? Female?'

'An old man. He knocked on the back door and waited for a bit, then let himself in with a key.' Hughes pulled a face. 'So I legged it.' He saw the triumph on Jones's face. 'That what you wanted?'

'Could be. Did he have the key in his hand?'

'I wasn't looking.'

'Did you hear anything?'

'The knocking.'

'Anything else?'

'I heard a stone being moved after the knocking.'

The flowerpot. 'How do you know it was a man if you weren't looking?'

'He called out. "Jenny, Ruth, Mathilda, are you there?" It was a man all right.'

'Describe his voice.'

'Posh.'

'Old? Young? Forceful? Weak? Drunk? Sober? Pull your finger out, lad. What sort of impression did you get of him?'

'I already told you. I reckoned it was an old man. That's why I thought it was *her* coming back. He was really slow and his voice was all breathy, like he had trouble with his lungs. Or was very unfit.' He thought for a moment. 'He might have been drunk, though,' he added. 'He had real trouble getting the words out.'

'Did you go round the front afterwards?'

Dave shook his head. 'Hopped over the fence and went back to the van.'

'So you don't know if he came by car?'

'No.' A flash of something – *indecision?* – crossed his face.

'Go on,' prompted Jones.

'I'd never swear to it, so it's not evidence.'

'What isn't?'

'I was listening, if you get my meaning. He gave me a hell of a shock when I heard him coming so I reckon I'd've heard a car if there'd been one. That gravel at the front makes a hell of a row.'

'When was this?'

'Middle of September. Thereabouts.'

'Okay. Anything else?'

'Yeah.' He fingered his shoulder gingerly where Jack's car door had slammed into it. 'If you want to know who killed the old biddy then you should talk to the bastard who dislocated my fucking arm last night. I sussed him the minute I saw his face in the light. He was forever sniffing round her, in and out that place like he owned it, but he made damn sure Ruth wasn't there at the time. I spotted him two or three times up by the church, waiting till the coast was clear. Reckon he's the one you should be interested in if it's right what Ruth told me, that the old woman's wrists were slit with a Stanley knife.'

Charlie eyed him curiously. 'Why do you say that?'

'He cleaned one of the gravestones while he was waiting, scraped the dirt out of the words written on it. And not just the once neither. He was really fascinated by that stone.' He looked smug. 'Used a Stanley knife to do it, too, didn't he? I went and read it afterwards . . . "Did I deserve to be despised, By my creator, good and wise? Since you it was who made me be, Then part of you must die with me." Some bloke called Fitzgibbon who snuffed it in 1833. Thought I'd use it myself when the time came. Kind of hits the nail on the head, wouldn't you say?'

'You won't be given the chance. They censor epitaphs these days. Religion takes itself seriously now the congregations have started to vanish.' He stood up. 'A pity, really. Humour never harmed anyone.'

'You interested in him now then?'

'I've always been interested in him, lad.' Charlie smiled mournfully. 'Mrs Gillespie's death was very artistic.'

Cooper found the Inspector enjoying a late pint over cheese and onion sandwiches at the Dog and Bottle in Learmouth. He lowered himself with a sigh on to the seat beside him. 'Feet playing you up again?' asked Charlie sympathetically through a mouthful of bread.

'I wouldn't mind so much,' Cooper grumbled, 'if my inside had aged at the same rate as my outside. If I felt fifty-six, it probably wouldn't bug me.' He rubbed his calves to restore the circulation. 'I promised the wife we'd take up dancing again when I retired, but at this rate we'll be doing it with Zimmer frames.'

Charlie grinned. 'So there's no truth in the saying: you're as old as you feel?'

'None whatsoever. You're as old as your body tells you you are. I'll still feel eighteen when I'm a bed-ridden ninety-year-old and I still won't be able to play football for England. I only ever wanted to be Stanley Matthews,' he said wistfully. 'My dad took me to watch him and Blackpool win the FA cup in 1953 as a sixteenth birthday present. It was pure magic. I've never forgotten it.'

'I wanted to be Tom Kelley,' said Charlie.

'Who's he?'

The Inspector chuckled as he wiped his fingers on a napkin. 'The photographer who persuaded Marilyn Monroe to pose nude for him. Imagine it. Marilyn Monroe entirely naked and you on the other side of the lens. Now, that really would have been magic.'

'We're in the wrong business, Charlie. There's no charm in what we do.'

'Mrs Marriott hasn't raised your spirits then?'

'No.' He sighed again. 'I made a promise to her, said we wouldn't use what she told me unless we had to, but I can't see at the moment how we can avoid it. If it doesn't have a bearing on the case, then I'm a monkey's uncle. First, Joanna Lascelles was not Mrs Gillespie's only child. She had another one thirteen, fourteen months later by Mrs Marriott's husband.' He ran through the background for Charlie's benefit. 'Mrs Marriott believed Mrs Gillespie killed the baby when it was born, but on the morning of the sixth, Mrs Gillespie told her it had been a boy and that she'd put it up for adoption when it was born.'

Charlie leaned forward, his eyes bright with curiosity. 'Does she know what happened to him?'

Cooper shook his head. 'They were screaming at each other, apparently, and that little tit-bit was tossed out by Mrs Gillespie as she closed the door. Mrs Marriott says Mathilda wanted to hurt her, so it might not even be true.'

'Okay. Go on.'

'Second, and this is the real shocker, Mrs Marriott stole some barbiturates from her father's dispensary which she says Mathilda used to murder Gerald Cavendish.' He detailed what Jane had told him, shaking his head from time to time whenever he touched on James Gillespie's part in the tragedy. 'He's evil, that one, blackmails everyone as far as I can judge. The wretched woman's terrified he's going to broadcast what he knows.'

'Serves her right,' said Charlie unsympathetically. 'What a corrupt lot they all were, and they say it's only recently the country started going to pot. You say she went to see Mrs Gillespie on the morning of the murder. What else did Mrs Gillespie tell her?'

'Murder?' queried Cooper with a touch of irony. 'Don't tell me you agree with me at last?'

'Get on with it, you old rogue,' said Jones impatiently. 'I'm on the edge of my seat here.'

'Mrs Gillespie began by being very cool and composed, told Mrs Marriott that the whole matter was out of her hands and that she wasn't prepared to pay the sort of money James was demanding from her. As far as she was concerned she didn't care any more what people said or thought about her. There had never been any doubt that Gerald committed suicide and if Jane wanted to own up to stealing drugs from her father, that was her affair. Mathilda would deny knowing anything about them.' He opened his notebook. '"I'm more sinned against than sinning," she said and advised Mrs Marriott that, in the matter of the baby, things would get worse before they got better. She went on to say that Mrs Marriott was a fool for keeping her husband in the dark all these years. They had a terrible row during which Mrs Marriott accused Mrs Gillespie of ruining the lives of everyone she had ever had contact with, at which point Mrs Gillespie ordered her out of the house with the words: "James has been reading my private papers and knows where the child is. It's quite pointless to keep quiet any longer." She then told Mrs Marriott it was a boy and that she'd put it up for adoption.' He closed the notebook. 'My bet is the "private papers" were the diaries and things were going to get worse because Mrs Gillespie had made up her mind to acknowledge her illegitimate child and spike James's guns.' He rubbed his jaw wearily. 'Not that that scenario really makes a great deal more sense than it did before. We'd more or less decided that whoever was reading the diaries was the same person who stole them and murdered the old lady, and I still say James Gillespie wouldn't have drawn our attention to the diaries if he was the guilty party. The psychology's all wrong. And what motive did he have for killing her? She was far more valuable alive as a blackmail victim. Let's face it, it wasn't just the business of the baby he could hold over her, it was her uncle's murder as well.'

'But he probably couldn't prove that, not so long afterwards, and you're making too many assumptions,' said Charlie slowly. '"I'm more sinned against than sinning",' he echoed. 'That's a line from *King Lear*.'

'So?'

'King Lear went mad and took to wandering in the fields near Dover with a crown of weeds on his head because his daughters had deprived him of his kingdom and his authority.'

Cooper groaned. 'I thought it was Ophelia who had the crown of weeds.'

'Hers were coronet weeds,' corrected Jones with idle pedantry. 'It was Lear who wore the crown.' He thought of the epitaph on the Fontwell tombstone. 'By God, Tommy, there's a lovely symmetry about this case. Jack Blakeney's been using a Stanley knife to clean inscriptions in Fontwell.'

Cooper scowled at him. 'How many pints have you had?'

Charlie leaned forward again, his keen eyes scouring Cooper's face. 'I studied *King Lear* at school. It's a hell of a play. All about the nature of love, the abuse of power, and the ultimate frailties of the human spirit.'

'Just like *Hamlet* then,' said Cooper sourly. '*Othello*, too, if it comes to that.'

'Of course. They were all tragedies with death the inevitable consequence. King Lear's mistake was to misinterpret the nature of love. He gave more weight to words than to deeds and partitioned his kingdom between two of his daughters, Goneril and Regan, whom he believed loved him but who, in reality, despised him. He was a tired old man who wanted to relinquish the burdens of state and live the rest of his life in peace and tranquillity. But he was also extremely arrogant and contemptuous of anyone's opinions but his own. His rash assumption that he knew what love was sowed the seeds of his family's destruction.' He grinned. 'Not bad, eh? Damn nearly verbatim from an essay I wrote in the sixth form. And I loathed the flaming play at the time. It's taken me thirty years to see its merits.'

'I came up with *King Lear* a few days ago,' remarked Cooper, 'but I still don't see a connection. If she'd divided her estate between Mrs Lascelles and Miss Lascelles there'd have been a parallel then.'

'You're missing the point, Tommy. *King Lear* was the most tragic of all Shakespeare's plays and Mrs Gillespie knew her Shakespeare. Dammit, man, she thought everything he wrote was gospel. There was a third child, don't forget, who was turned off without a penny.' He surged to his feet. 'I want Jack Blakeney in the nick in half an hour.

Be a good fellow and bring him in. Tell him your boss wants to talk to him about Mrs Gillespie's adopted son.'

What neither of them knew was that Jack Blakeney had been arrested at Mill House, half an hour previously, following the Orloffs' 999 call and Joanna Lascelles's hysterical assertions that he had not only tried to kill her but had admitted killing her mother.

The Inspector learnt of it as soon as he arrived back from lunch. Cooper was informed by radio and ordered to return post haste. He took time out, however, to sit for five minutes in depressed disillusion in a deserted country lane. His hands were shaking too much to drive with any competence, and he knew, with the awful certainty of defeat, that his time was over. He had lost whatever it was that had made him a good policeman. Oh, he had always known what his superiors said about him, but he had also known they were wrong. His forte had been his ability to make accurate judgements about the people he dealt with, and whatever anyone said to the contrary, he was usually right. But he had never allowed his sympathies for an offender and an offender's family to stand in the way of an arrest. Nor had he seen any validity in allowing police work to dehumanize him or destroy the tolerance that he, privately, believed was the one thing that set man above the animals.

With a heavy heart, he fired the engine and set off back to Learmouth. He had misjudged both the Blakeneys. Worse, he simply couldn't begin to follow Charlie Jones's flights of fancy over *King Lear* or comprehend the awful symmetry behind inscriptions and Stanley knives. Hadn't Mr Spede told him that the Stanley knife on the bathroom floor was the one from the kitchen drawer? The crown he thought he understood. Whoever had decked out Mrs Gillespie in nettles had seen the symbolic connection between her and *King Lear*. How then had Ophelia come to lead them up the garden path? *Coronet weeds,* he recalled, and Dr Blakeney's reference to them in the bathroom.

An intense sadness squeezed about his heart. Poor Tommy Cooper. He was, after all, just an absurd and rather dirty old man, entertaining fantasies about a woman who was young enough to be his daughter.

An hour later, Inspector Jones pulled out the chair opposite Jack and sat down, switching on the tape recorder and registering date, time and who was present. He rubbed his hands in anticipation of a challenge. 'Well, well, Mr Blakeney, I've been looking forward to this.' He beamed across at Cooper who was sitting with his back to the wall, staring at the floor. 'The Sergeant's whetted my appetite with what he's told me about you, not to mention the reports of your contretemps with the police in Bournemouth and this latest little fracas at Cedar House.'

Jack linked his hands behind his head and smiled wolfishly. 'Then I hope you won't be disappointed, Inspector.'

'I'm sure I won't.' He steepled his fingers on the table in front of him. 'We'll leave Mrs Lascelles and the Bournemouth incident to one side for the moment because I'm more interested in your relationship with Mrs Gillespie.' He looked very pleased with himself. 'I've deciphered the floral crown that she was wearing in her bath. Not Ophelia at all, but King Lear. I've just been looking it up. Act IV, Scene IV where Cordelia describes him as "Crown'd with rank fumiter and furrow weeds, With burdocks, hemlock, nettles, cuckoo-flow'rs". And then Scene VI, a stage direction. "Enter Lear, fantastically dressed with weeds." Am I right, Mr Blakeney?'

'It did occur to me that Ophelia was a very unlikely interpretation. I guessed Lear when Sarah described the scene to me.'

'And Lear certainly makes more sense.'

Jack cocked his irritating eyebrow. 'Does it?'

'Oh, yes.' He rubbed his hands in gleeful anticipation. 'It goes something like this, I think. Lear had two vile daughters, Goneril and Regan, and one loving daughter, Cordelia. Cordelia he banished because she refused to flatter him with hollow words; Goneril and Regan he rewarded because they were deceitful enough to tell lies in order to get their share of his wealth. For Goneril and Regan, read Joanna and Ruth Lascelles. For Cordelia, read the son Mrs Gillespie put up for adoption, i.e. the one she banished who never received a penny from her.' He held Jack's gaze. 'Now, in the play, Cordelia comes back to rescue her father from the brutality her sisters are inflicting upon him, and I think it happened in real life, too, though purely figuratively speaking of course. Neither Joanna nor Ruth were *brutal* to Mrs Gillespie, merely desperately disappointing.' He tapped his forefingers together. 'Cordelia, the adopted son whom Mathilda had long since given up on, reappears miraculously to remind her that love does still exist for her, that she is

not as embittered as she thought she was and that, ultimately, she has produced at least one person who has
qualities she could be proud of. How am I doing, Mr
Blakeney?'

'Imaginatively.'

Charlie gave a low laugh. 'The only question is, who is
Cordelia?'

Jack didn't answer.

'And did he come looking for his mother or was it pure
chance that brought him here? Who recognized whom, I
wonder?'

Again Jack didn't answer, and Charlie's brows snapped
together ferociously. 'You are not obliged to answer my
questions, Mr Blakeney, but you would be very unwise to
forget that I am investigating murder and attempted murder
here. Silence won't help you, you know.'

Jack shrugged, apparently unmoved by threats. 'Even if
any of this were true, what does it have to do with
Mathilda's death?'

'Dave Hughes told me an interesting story today. He
says he watched you clean a gravestone in the cemetery at
Fontwell, claims you were obviously so fascinated by it that
he went and read it after you'd gone. Do you remember
what it says?'

'"George Fitzgibbon 1789–1833. Did I deserve to be
despised, By my creator, good and wise? Since you it was
who made me be, Then part of you must die with me." I
looked him up in the parish records. He succumbed to
syphilis as a result of loose living. Maria, his wretched wife,
died of the same thing four years later and was popped into
the ground alongside George, but she didn't get a tomb-

stone because her children refused to pay for one. There's a written epitaph in the record instead and hers is even better. "George was lusty, coarse and evil, He gave me pox, he's with the devil." Short, and to the point. George's was ridiculously hypocritical by contrast.'

'It all depends who George thought his creator was,' said Charlie. 'Perhaps it was his mother he wanted to take to hell with him.'

Idly Jack traced a triangle on the surface of the table. 'Who told you Mathilda had an adopted son? Someone reliable, I hope, because you're building a hell of a castle on their information.'

Jones caught Cooper's eye, but ignored the warning frown. As Cooper said, their chances of respecting Jane Marriott's confidences were thin. 'Mrs Jane Marriott, whose husband was the boy's father.'

'Ah, well, a *very* reliable source then.' He saw the gleam of excitement in the Inspector's eyes and smiled with genuine amusement. 'Mathilda was not my mother, Inspector. If she had been I'd have been thrilled. I loved the woman.'

Charlie shrugged. 'Then Mrs Gillespie lied about having a son, and it's your wife who's Cordelia. It has to be one or other of you or she wouldn't have made that will. She wasn't going to make Lear's mistake and bequeath her estate to the undeserving daughters.'

Jack looked as if he were about to deny it, then shrugged. 'I imagine Mathilda told Jane Marriott it was a boy out of spite. She never referred to her by name, always called her that "prissy creature at the surgery". It was cruel of her, but then Mathilda was usually cruel. She was a deeply unhappy woman.' He paused to collect his thoughts. 'She told me about her affair with Paul after I'd finished her portrait. She said there was something missing from the painting, and that that something was guilt. She was absolutely racked with it. Guilt for having given up the baby, guilt for not being able to cope, guilt for blaming the second baby's adoption on Joanna's crying, ultimately, I suppose, guilt for her inability to feel affection.' Briefly he fell silent again. 'Then Sarah turned up out of the blue and Mathilda recognized her.' He saw the look of incredulity on Charlie Jones's face. 'Not immediately and not as the baby she'd given away, but gradually as the months went by. There were so many things that matched. Sarah was the right age, her birthday was the same day as the baby's birthday, her parents had lived in the same borough in London where Mathilda's flat was. Most importantly she thought she detected a likeness in Sarah's and Joanna's mannerisms. She said they had the same smile, the same way of inclining their heads, the same trick of looking at you intently while you speak. And from the start Sarah took Mathilda as she found her, of course, the way she takes everyone, and for the first time in years Mathilda felt valued. It was a very potent cocktail. Mathilda was so convinced she'd found her lost daughter that she approached me and commissioned me to paint the portrait.' He smiled ruefully. 'I thought my luck had changed but all she wanted, of course, was an excuse to find out more about Sarah from the only person available who knew anything of value.'

'But you didn't know that while you were painting her?'

'No. I did wonder why she was so interested in us both, what our parents were like, where they came from, if we had brothers and sisters, whether or not I got on with my in-laws. She didn't confine herself to Sarah, you see. If she had, I might have been suspicious. As it was, when she finally told me that Sarah was her lost child, I was appalled.' He shrugged helplessly. 'I knew she couldn't be because Sarah wasn't adopted.'

'Surely that was the first thing Mrs Gillespie asked you?'

'Not in so many words, no. She never put anything as directly as that.' He shrugged again in the face of the Inspector's scepticism. 'You're forgetting that no one in Fontwell knew about this child, except Jane Marriott, and Mathilda was far too proud to give the rest of the village a glimpse of her clay feet. She was looking for a private atonement, not a public one. The closest we ever came to it was when she asked me if Sarah had a good relationship with her mother and I said, no, because they had nothing in common. I can even remember the words I used. I said: "I've often wondered if Sarah was adopted because the only explanation for the disparity between the two of them in looks, words and deeds is that they aren't related." I was being flippant, but Mathilda used it to build castles in the air. Rather as you're doing at the moment, Inspector.'

'But she'd made up her mind before you started painting that portrait, Mr Blakeney. If I remember correctly she began consulting Mr Duggan about the will in August.'

'It was like a faith,' said Jack simply. 'I can't explain it any other way. She needed to make amends to the child who'd had nothing, and Sarah had to be that child. The fact that the ages, birthdays and mannerisms were pure coincidence was neither here nor there. Mathilda had made up her mind and all she wanted from me was the gaps filled in.' He ran his fingers through his hair. 'If I'd known sooner, then I'd have disabused her, but I didn't know, and all I achieved, quite unwittingly, was to fuel the belief.'

'Does Dr Blakeney know any of this?'

'No. Mathilda was adamant she never should. She made me promise to keep it to myself – she was terrified Sarah would treat her differently, stop liking her, even reject her completely – and I thought, thank God, because this way no one gets hurt.' He rubbed a hand across his face. 'I didn't know what to do, you see, and I needed time to work out how to let Mathilda down gently. If I'd told her the truth, there and then, it would have been like taking the baby away from her all over again.'

'When was this, Mr Blakeney?' asked Charlie.

'About two weeks before she died.'

'Why did she tell you, if she didn't want anyone to know?'

Jack didn't answer immediately. 'It was the portrait,' he said after a moment. 'I took it round to show it to her. I still had some work to do on it but I wanted to see what her reaction was so that I could paint that into the picture. I've had some amazing responses in the past: anger, shock, vanity, irritation, disappointment. I record them all beneath my signature so that anyone who understands the code will know what the subject thought about my treatment of his or her personality. It's a sort of visual joke. Mathilda's reaction was intense grief. I've never seen anyone so upset.'

'She didn't like it?' suggested Charlie.

'The exact opposite. She was weeping for the woman she might have been.' His eyes clouded in reflection. 'She said I was the first person who had ever shown her compassion.'

'I don't understand.'

Jack glanced across at the Sergeant who was still sitting staring at the floor. 'Tommy does,' he said. 'Don't you, my old friend?'

There was a brief pause before Cooper raised his head. 'The gold at the heart of the picture,' he murmured. 'That was Mathilda as she was in the beginning before events took over and destroyed her.'

Jack's dark eyes rested on him with affection. 'Goddammit, Tommy,' he said, 'how come I'm the only one to appreciate your qualities? Does anything escape you?'

When I told Father I was pregnant, he fainted. It was an extraordinary example of craven cowardice. Gerald, by contrast, was rather pleased. 'Is it mine, Matty?' he asked. Perhaps I should have been offended, but I wasn't. I found his delight in what he'd achieved rather touching.

Father is all for an abortion, of course, and not just because of the potential scandal. He says the baby will be even more of an imbecile than Gerald. I have refused. Nothing will induce me to go near a backstreet abortionist which is all Father is offering me. He says he knows of somebody in London who will do it for a small fee, but I don't trust him an inch and will not entrust my life to some incompetent woman with knitting needles and gin. In any case, if the child's as defective as Father's suggesting, then it will not survive long. Gerald is only with us in all conscience because his silly mother nursed him devotedly for years.

Every cloud has its silver lining. Gerald has never been easier to manage than he is at the moment. The knowledge that I am carrying his baby has wiped all memories of Grace from his mind. It means I shall have to marry to give the baby legitimacy, but James Gillespie is tiresome in his approaches, and will marry me tomorrow if I agree. Father says James is homosexual and needs a wife to give himself respectability, but as I need a husband for the same reason, I can no doubt tolerate him for the few months till the baby's born.

I have told Father to put a brave face on it, something the silly man is incapable of doing, and to let me and James have the use of his flat in London. Once the baby is born I shall return home. Father will stay at his club on the rare – now, very rare – occasions when he is sober enough to attend a debate at the House. He wept his drunken tears this evening and said I was unnatural, claiming all he had ever wanted me to do was be sweet to Gerald and keep him happy.

But it was Grace who introduced Gerald to sex, not I, and Father knows it. And how was I supposed to keep a sexually active imbecile happy? By playing bridge? By discussing Plato? Dear God, but I have such contempt for men. Perhaps I am unnatural . . .

Eighteen

JONES DRUMMED his fingers impatiently on the table. 'You told the Sergeant you were with an actress in Stratford the night Mrs Gillespie was murdered. You weren't. We've checked. Miss Bennedict said' – he consulted a piece of paper – 'she'd see you in hell before she allowed you near her again.'

'True.' He gave an amiable grin. 'She didn't like the portrait I did of her. She's had it in for me ever since.'

'Then why give her as your alibi?'

'Because I'd already told Sarah that's where I was, and she was listening when the Sergeant asked me.'

Charlie frowned but let this pass. 'Where were you then, if you weren't in Stratford?'

'Cheltenham.' He linked his hands behind his neck and stared at the ceiling.

'Can you prove it?'

'Yes.' He reeled off a phone number. 'Sarah's father's house. He will confirm that I was there from six o'clock on the Friday evening until midday on the Sunday.' He flicked a lazy glance at the Inspector. 'He's a JP, so you can be fairly sure he won't be lying.'

'What were you doing there?'

'I went on the off-chance that he had something I could show Mathilda that would prove Sarah wasn't her daughter. I knew I could talk fairly freely without him blabbing about it. If I'd approached her mother, she'd have been on the phone to Sarah like a shot and then the cat would have been out of the bag with Sarah demanding to know why I wanted proof she wasn't adopted. By the same token, she'd have asked me why I was going to see her father, so I told her I was staying with Sally to put her off the scent.' He looked suddenly pensive. 'Not the most intelligent thing I've ever done.'

Charlie ignored this. 'Did her father give you proof?'

'No. He said he hadn't got anything and that I'd have to talk to her mother. I was planning to bite the bullet and go the next weekend, but, by the Monday, Mathilda was dead and it didn't matter any more.'

'And you still haven't told your wife?'

'No.'

'Why not?'

'I promised Mathilda I wouldn't,' he said evenly. 'If she'd wanted Sarah to know what she believed, she'd have told her herself on the video.'

'Any idea why she didn't?'

Jack shrugged. 'Because she wasn't going to tell her in life either, I suppose. She had too many secrets which she thought would be exposed if she claimed Sarah as her own – and let's face it, she was right. Look what Tommy's unearthed already.'

'It would have been unearthed anyway. People were

bound to ask questions the minute they heard she'd left her money to her doctor.'

'But she wouldn't have expected the police to be asking them because she didn't know she was going to be murdered. And, as far as I can make out, from what Sarah has told me of the video, she did the best she could to warn Joanna and Ruth off putting in a counter-claim by dropping enough heavy hints about their lifestyles to give Sarah's barrister a field day if the thing ever went to court.' He shrugged again. 'The only reason either of them feels confident about challenging it now is because Mathilda was murdered. Whatever they've done pales into insignificance beside that.'

Cooper rumbled into life behind him. 'But the video is full of lies, particularly in relation to her uncle and her husband. Mrs Gillespie implies she was the victim of them both, but Mrs Marriott tells a very different story. She describes a woman who was ruthless enough to use blackmail and murder when it suited her. So which is true?'

Jack swung round to look at him. 'I don't know. Both probably. She wouldn't be the first victim to strike back.'

'What about this business of her uncle's feeble-mindedness? She described him on the video as a drunken brute who raped her when she was thirteen, yet Mrs Marriott says he was rather pathetic. Explain that.'

'I can't. Mathilda never talked to me about it. All I know is that she was deeply scarred by her inability to love and when I showed her the portrait with the scarring represented by the scold's bridle, she burst into tears and said I was the first person to show her any compassion. I chose to interpret that as meaning that I was the first person to see her as a victim, but I could have been wrong. You'll have to make up your own mind.'

'We wouldn't have to if we could find her diaries,' said Cooper.

Jack didn't say anything and the room fell silent with only the whirr of the tape to disturb the complete bafflement that at least two of those present were experiencing. Jones, who had approached this interview in the confident expectation that Jack Blakeney would spend tonight in a police cell, was falling prey to the same crippling ambivalence that Cooper had always felt towards this man.

'Why did you tell Mrs Lascelles this morning that you murdered her mother if you already had an alibi for the night Mrs Gillespie died?' he asked at last, rustling the papers in front of him.

'I didn't.'

'She says in this report that you did.'

'I didn't.'

'She says you did.'

'She said what she believed. That's a different thing entirely.'

Jones pondered for a moment. He had a nasty feeling that he would receive almost as dusty an answer to his next question, but he put it anyway. 'Why did you try to murder Mrs Lascelles?'

'I didn't.'

'She says, and I'm quoting, "Jack Blakeney forced me against the wall and started to strangle me. If Violet hadn't interrupted him, he'd have killed me." Is she lying?'

'No. She's telling you what she believes.'

'But it's not true.'

'No.'

'You weren't trying to strangle her?'

'No.'

'I have to tell you, Mr Blakeney, that according to this report she had the marks of a stranglehold on her neck when the car that answered the nine–nine–nine call arrived at Cedar House. Therefore someone did try to strangle her, and she says that someone was you.' He paused, inviting Jack to answer. When he didn't, he tried a different approach. 'Were you in Cedar House at approximately ten thirty this morning?'

'Yes.'

'Did you put your hand about Mrs Joanna Lascelles's throat?'

'Yes.'

'Is she justified in believing that you were trying to strangle her?'

'Yes.'

'Were you trying to strangle her?'

'No.'

'Then explain it to me. What the hell were you doing?'

'Showing you lot where you've been going wrong again. Mind you, it's not the most sensible thing I've done, and I wouldn't have done it at all if I hadn't been so pissed off by that jerk of an Inspector last night.' His eyes narrowed angrily at the memory. 'I don't give a toss about myself, matter of fact I rather hope he decides to prosecute and give me my day in court, but I do care about Sarah and I care very much indeed at the moment about Ruth. He treated them both like shit and I made up my mind then

375

that enough was enough. Joanna's past saving, I suspect, but her daughter isn't, and I want the poor kid free to put this bloody awful mess behind her.' He took a deep angry breath. 'So I sat up last night and did what you should have done, worked out who killed Mathilda and why. And believe me it wasn't difficult.'

Charlie did believe him. Like Cooper, he was beginning to find Jack irresistible. 'Mrs Lascelles,' he said with conviction. 'She's always been top of the list.'

'No, and I satisfied myself of that this morning. I agree she's quite capable of it. She has an almost identical personality to her mother, and if Mathilda could murder to get what she wanted, then Joanna could, too. You don't grow up in an atmosphere of extreme dysfunction and emerge normal at the end of it. But Joanna's relationship with Mathilda was very ambivalent. Despite everything, I suspect they were actually rather fond of each other. Perhaps, quite simply, their fondness was based on mutual understanding, the devil you know being more acceptable than the devil you don't.'

'All right,' said Charlie patiently. 'Then who did kill Mrs Gillespie?'

'I can't prove it, that's your job. All I can do is take you through what I worked out last night.' He took a moment to organize his thoughts. 'You've concentrated entirely on Sarah, me, Joanna and Ruth,' he said, 'and all because of the will. Not unreasonable in the circumstances – but if you take us out of the equation then the balance of probability shifts. So let's assume she wasn't killed for money and take it from there. Okay, I don't believe she was killed in anger either. Anger is a violent, hot-blooded emotion and her death was too well planned and too meticulous. Too symbolic. Whoever murdered her may well have been angry with her, but it wasn't done because someone's patience had finally run out.' He glanced at Jones who nodded. 'Which leaves what? Hatred? She was certainly disliked by a lot of people but as none of them had killed her before, why decide to do it then? Jealousy?' He shrugged eloquently. 'What was there to be jealous of? She was a virtual recluse, and I can't believe Jane Marriott stored her jealousy for years to have it erupt suddenly in November. So, at the risk of stating the obvious, Mathilda must have been murdered because someone wanted her out of the way.'

Jones had difficulty keeping the sarcasm out of his voice. 'I think we can agree on that,' he said.

Jack stared at him for a moment. 'Yes, but *why?* Why did someone want her out of the way? What had she done or what was she going to do that meant she had to be killed? That's the question you've never asked, not outside the context of the will at least.'

'Because I don't find it quite so easy, as you apparently do, to ignore it.'

'But it *is* just a will. Thousands of people make them every week and thousands of people die every week. The fact that Mathilda's was unusually radical becomes completely irrelevant if you absolve Joanna, Ruth, Sarah and me of her death. No one else is directly affected by the way she chose to leave her money.'

Cooper cleared his throat. 'It's a good point, Charlie.'

'All right,' he conceded. 'Why *was* she killed then?'

'I don't know.'

Charlie raised his eyes to heaven. 'God give me strength!' he growled savagely.

Cooper chuckled quietly to himself. 'Get on with it, Jack, before you give the poor man apoplexy,' he suggested. 'We're all running out of patience on this one. Let's take it as read that the will wasn't the motive and that neither the Lascelles women nor you and your wife were involved. Where does that leave us?'

'With Mathilda wearing the scold's bridle. Why? And why did it have half a hedgerow carefully entwined through it? Isn't that what persuaded you it wasn't suicide?'

Cooper nodded.

'Then the logical conclusion has to be that the murderer never intended you to think it *was* suicide. I mean we're not talking about a moron here, we're talking finesse and careful planning. My guess is that someone knew Mathilda thought Sarah was her daughter, knew that both Mathilda and Joanna had been conditioned by the scold's bridle in their childhoods, knew that Joanna was a florist and knew, too, that "scold's bridle" was Mathilda's nickname for Sarah. Hence the contraption on her head and the *King Lear* imagery. If you put all that together with the fact that Ruth was in the house that day, then the aim must surely have been to focus your attention on Sarah, Joanna and Ruth – Lear's three daughters in other words. And that's exactly what happened, even if it was the will that set you thinking along those lines because you mistook the symbolism for Ophelia's coronet weeds. You mustn't forget how close Mathilda played the will to her chest. As far as anyone knew, Joanna and Ruth were going to share the estate between them. Sarah's possible claim as the long-lost daughter was nothing but a wild card when the murder took place so, for the murderer, it came as a sort of bonus.'

Charlie frowned. 'I still don't understand. Were we supposed to arrest one of them? And which one? I mean, was your wife indicated because of the scold's bridle, was Joanna indicated because of the flowers, or was Ruth indicated because she was there?'

Jack shrugged. 'I'd say that's the whole point. It doesn't matter a damn, just so long as you focus your attention on them.'

'But why?' snarled Charlie through gritted teeth.

Jack looked helplessly from him to Cooper. 'There's only one reason that I can see, but maybe I've got it all wrong. Hell dammit!' he exploded angrily. 'I'm not an expert.'

'Confusion,' said Cooper stoutly, a man ever to be relied upon. 'The murderer wanted Mrs Gillespie dead and confusion to follow. And why would they want confusion to follow? Because it would be much harder to proceed with any kind of normality if the mess surrounding Mrs Gillespie's death wasn't sorted out.'

Jack nodded. 'Sounds logical to me.'

It was Charlie's turn to be lost in Cooper's flights of fancy. 'What normality?'

'The normality that follows death,' he said ponderously. 'Wills in other words. Someone wanted the settling of Mrs Gillespie's estate delayed.' He thought for a moment. 'Let's say she was about to embark on something that someone else didn't like, so they stopped her before she could do it. But let's say, too, that whatever it was could be pursued by her beneficiary the minute that beneficiary came into the estate. With a little ingenuity, you throw a spanner in the works by pointing a finger at the more obvious legatees and grind the process to a halt. How does that sound?'

'Complicated,' said Charlie tartly.

'But the pressure was to stop Mathilda,' said Jack. 'The rest was imaginative flair which might or might not work. Think of it as a speculative venture that could, with a little bit of luck, produce the goods.'

'But that brings us right back to square one,' said Cooper slowly. 'Whoever killed her knew her very well and, if we jettison the four who knew her best, then we're left with – ' he pressed his fingers to his eyes in deep concentration, 'Mr and Mrs Spede, Mr and Mrs Marriott, and James Gillespie.'

'You can do better than that, Cooper,' said Jack impatiently. 'The Spedes are simple souls who could never have dreamt up the *Lear* symbolism in a million years; Paul and Jane Marriott have avoided Mathilda like the plague for years so probably couldn't have found their way around her house, let alone known where she kept the Stanley knife; and, as far as I understand it, if what Duggan told Sarah is true, rather than trying to delay the processing of the will, James Gillespie is doing the exact opposite and pressing for the controversy to be settled so that he can lay claim to the clocks.'

'But there isn't anyone else.'

'There is, and I proved it this morning.' He hammered his fist on the table. 'It's Ruth's involvement that should have alerted you. Someone knew she was in the house that day and could therefore figure as a suspect. You've been chasing around in circles since you found out about it, but Sarah says you only learnt she was there because you received an anonymous letter. So who sent it?' He slammed his palm on the table at Cooper's blank expression. 'Who tried to rescue Joanna this morning?'

Violet Orloff opened her front door and stared at the piece of polythene-encased paper that Detective Sergeant Cooper was holding in front of him. He turned it round to read it aloud. '"Ruth Lascelles was in Cedar House the day Mrs Gillespie died. She stole some earrings. Joanna knows she took them. Joanna Lascelles is a prostitute in London. Ask her what she spends her money on. Ask her why she tried to kill her daughter. Ask her why Mrs Gillespie thought she was mad." Would we be right in assuming you wrote this, Mrs Orloff?' he enquired in his friendly way.

'Duncan did, but we were only trying to *help*,' she said breathily, looking from him to the tall figure of Charlie Jones behind him, the collar of whose thick sheepskin jacket was pulled up about his comfortably sad face. She took heart from their mutual lack of hostility. 'I know we probably ought to have come in person, but it's so *difficult*.' She gestured vaguely in the direction of the other part of the house. 'We are neighbours, after all, and Duncan does so hate unpleasantness.' She smiled tentatively. 'But when a murder's been committed – I mean, one can't expect the police to solve it if people who know things stay quiet. It seemed more *tactful*, somehow, not to get involved person-ally. You do understand, don't you?'

'Perfectly,' said Charlie with an encouraging smile, 'and we're very grateful to you for the trouble you took.'

'That's all right then. I *told* Duncan it was important.'

'Didn't he agree with you?'

She glanced cautiously over her shoulder, then pulled the door to behind her. 'I wouldn't put it quite like *that*,' she said. 'He's grown so lazy since we came here, won't stir himself, won't have his routines upset, can't bear what he calls aggravations. He says he's earned a peaceful retirement and doesn't want it *upset* by lots of bother. He's very unfit, of course, which doesn't help, but I can't help feeling that it isn't good to be so' – she struggled for the right word – '*unenterprising*.'

'Mrs Gillespie's death must have been a shock then, what with the police tramping about the house, and Mrs Lascelles and her daughter coming back.'

'He hasn't *enjoyed* it,' she admitted, 'but he did see there was nothing we could do about it. Don't get so het up, he told me. A little patience and it will all blow over.'

'Still, it must be very unsettling,' said Cooper, 'worrying about what's going to happen to Cedar House now that Mrs Gillespie's dead. Presumably it will be sold, but you won't have any control over who it's sold to.'

'That's just what *I* said. Duncan would go mad with noisy children next door.' She lowered her voice. 'I know one shouldn't take pleasure in other people's misfortune, but I can't deny it's a relief to have Joanna and Dr Blakeney at loggerheads over the will. They're going to court about it, you know, and as Duncan said, that sort of thing takes years.'

'And in the meantime the house will stand empty?'

'Well, *exactly*.'

'So it's definite that Mrs Lascelles intends to contest the will?'

'Oh, yes.'

'She told you that?'

She looked guilty again. 'I heard her and the doctor talking in the drawing-room. I don't make a habit of listening, not as a general rule, but . . .' She left the rest of the sentence unsaid.

'You've been worried and you needed to know what's going on,' suggested Charlie helpfully.

'Well, *exactly*,' she said again. 'Someone has to take an interest. If it's left to Duncan, we'll only know what sort of neighbours we've got when they're living next to us.'

'Like Mrs Gillespie, you mean. I suppose you knew a lot about her one way and another.'

Violet's mouth pinched disapprovingly. 'Not through choice. I don't think she ever realized just how piercing her voice was. Very *strident*, you know, and she was so convinced that her opinions *mattered*. I never really listened, to tell you the truth, but Duncan found her amusing from time to time, particularly when she was being rude on the telephone, which she was, often. She took people to task about the most *trivial* things and she thought they couldn't hear her, you know, unless she shouted. She was a very silly woman.'

Charlie nodded, as if in agreement. 'Then I'm surprised you didn't hear anything the night she died. She must have spoken to her murderer, surely?'

Violet's face flushed a dull red. 'She didn't, you know. Duncan never heard a sound.'

He pretended not to notice her embarrassment. 'And what about you, Mrs Orloff? Did you hear anything?'

'Oh, dear,' she wailed, 'it's not as though it's a *crime*

though you'd think it was the way Duncan carries on. I have a tot or two of whisky of an evening, really nothing very much. Duncan's a teetotaller and doesn't approve, but as I always say, where's the harm in it? Mathilda's done it for years – it's unnatural not to, she always said – and she drank far more than I do.' She dropped her voice again. 'It's not as though I'm an *alcoholic.*'

'Good *lord* no,' said Charlie effusively, picking up the loaded speech patterns. 'If I didn't drink enough to send myself to sleep every night, I'd be a nervous wreck come the morning.'

'Well, exactly,' came the repetitive refrain. 'But I do nod off in front of the television, and, of course, I *did* the night Mathilda died. Hardly surprising really since I spent the day in Poole with my sister, and I find that very tiring now. You see, I'm not as young as I used to be, and I won't deny I've been worrying ever since, did Mathilda call for help? Duncan *swears* she didn't but, you know, he's so anti getting involved in anything that he'd have persuaded himself it was just Mathilda being irritating.'

'Any idea what time you nodded off?' asked Cooper, showing more interest in the state of his shoes than in her answer.

'*Very* early,' she said in a whisper. 'We'd just finished supper and sat down to watch *Blind Date*, and the next thing I knew Duncan was shaking me and telling me I was snoring and it was annoying him because it was spoiling *Match of the Day*. Goodness, but I was tired. I went to bed and slept like a *log* till the morning, and I can't help feeling that if I'd only stayed awake, I might have been able to do something for poor Mathilda.'

And that of course was true.

Charlie gestured towards the door. 'May we talk to your husband now, Mrs Orloff?'

'Is that necessary? He won't be able to tell you anything and it'll just make him *grumpy* for the rest of the day.'

'I'm afraid it is.' He produced a paper from his pocket with an air of apology. 'We also have a warrant to search your house, but I assure you, we'll be as careful as we can.' He raised his voice. 'Bailey! Jenkins! Watts! Show yourselves, lads. We're ready to go.'

Quite bewildered by this sudden turn of events, Violet stood meekly to one side while Jones, Cooper and three DCs filed into her hallway. Behind their backs, she crept away with the stealth of a guilty person into the kitchen.

Duncan's small eyes watched the two senior policemen closely as they eased into the cramped living-room, but otherwise he showed remarkably little concern at this sudden invasion of his privacy. 'Forgive me if I don't get up,' he said courteously, 'but I find I'm not as mobile as I used to be.' He waved towards a delicate two-seater sofa, inviting them to sit down. They declined with equal courtesy, afraid of breaking it under their combined weight. 'I've met Detective Sergeant Cooper but I don't know you, sir,' he said, examining Charlie with interest.

'Detective Chief Inspector Jones.'

'How do you do.'

Charlie inclined his head in a brief salute. He was assailed with doubt as he looked at the fat old man in the oversized armchair, his huge stomach overhanging his thighs like the meat from a split sausage skin. Could such ungainly bulk have performed the delicate artistry of Mrs Gillespie's murder? Could he even have abstracted himself from this room without waking his wife? He listened to the shallow wheezing breaths, each one a battle against the smothering pressure of flesh, and recalled Hughes's description of the man who had used the key to open the back door. *His voice was all breathy like he had trouble with his lungs.* 'Was Mrs Gillespie aware that you knew about the key under the flowerpot?' he asked without any attempt at preamble.

Duncan looked surprised. 'I don't understand you, Inspector.'

'No matter. We have a witness who can identify you. He was there when you let yourself in one morning in September.'

But Duncan only smiled and shook his fat cheeks in denial. 'Let myself in where?' There was a sound above them as one of the DCs moved a piece of furniture across the floor, and Duncan's gaze shifted to the ceiling. 'What exactly is all this in aid of?'

Charlie produced the warrant and handed it to him. 'We are searching these premises for Mrs Gillespie's diaries or, more likely, the remains of Mrs Gillespie's diaries. We have reason to believe you stole them from the library of Cedar House.'

'How very peculiar of you.'

'Are you denying it?'

He gave a low chuckle. 'My dear chap, of course I'm denying it. I didn't even know she kept diaries.'

Charlie changed tack. 'Why didn't you tell my Sergeant on the Monday after the murder that Miss Ruth Lascelles had been in Cedar House during the afternoon? Or indeed that Mrs Jane Marriott had had a row with her in the morning?'

'How could I tell him something I didn't know myself?'

'If you were here, Mr Orloff, you could not have avoided knowing. Jane Marriott describes her confrontation with Mrs Gillespie as a screaming match and Ruth says she rang the doorbell because she left her key at school.'

'But I wasn't here, Inspector,' he said affably. 'I took the opportunity of my wife's absence in Poole to go for a long walk.'

There was a gasp from the doorway. 'Duncan!' declared Violet. 'How can you tell such lies? You *never* go for walks.' She advanced into the room like a small ship under sail. 'And don't think I don't know *why* you're lying. You can't be bothered to assist the police in their enquiries, just like you haven't been bothered all along. Of *course* he was here, and of *course* he will have heard Jane and Ruth. We *always* heard Ruth when she came back. She and her grandmother couldn't be in a room together without arguing, any more than she can be in a room with her mother without arguing. Not that I altogether blame her. She wants love, poor child, and neither Mathilda nor Joanna were capable of such an emotion. The only people Mathilda had any fondness for were the Blakeneys, you know, the artist and his wife. She used to laugh with *them*, and I think she even took her clothes off for *him*. I heard her in her bedroom, being very coy and silly, saying things like "Not bad for an old woman" and "I was beautiful once, you know. Men competed for me." And that was true, they *did*. Even Duncan loved her when we were all much younger. He denies it now, of course, but I knew. All us girls knew we were only second best. Mathilda played so hard to get, you see, and that was a challenge.' She paused for breath and Cooper, who was beside her, smelt the whisky on her lips. He had time to feel sadness for this little woman whose life had never blossomed because she had lived it always in the shade of Mathilda Gillespie.

'Not that it *matters*,' she went on. 'Nothing matters that much. And it's years since he lost interest. You can't go on loving someone who's rude all the time, and Mathilda was always rude. She thought it was funny. She'd say the most appalling things, and *laugh*. I won't pretend we had a close relationship, but I did feel sorry for her. She should have done something with her life, something interesting, but she never did and it made her bitter.' She turned a severe gaze on her husband. 'I know she used to *tease* you, Duncan, and call you Mr Toad, but that's no reason not to help find her murderer. Murder is inexcusable. And I can't help feeling, you know, that it was *particularly* inexcusable to put that beastly scold's bridle on her head. You were very upset when she put it on you.' She turned back to Charlie. 'It was one of her horrible jokes. She said the only way Duncan would ever lose weight was if he had his *tongue* clamped, so she crept up behind him one day when he was asleep in the garden with his mouth open and popped that horrid rusty thing over his head. He nearly *died* of shock.' She paused for another breath but this time she had run out of steam and didn't go on.

There was a long silence.

'I suppose that's how you put it on her,' murmured

Charlie finally, 'when she was already asleep, but I'd be interested to know how you gave her the barbiturates. The pathologist estimates four or five and she would never have taken that many herself.'

Duncan's gaze rested briefly on his wife's shocked face, before shifting to Cooper's. 'Old women have two things in common,' he said with a small smile. 'They drink too much and they talk too much. You'd have liked Mathilda, Sergeant, she was a very amusing woman, although the memory of her was a great deal more attractive than the real thing. It was a disappointment coming back. Age has few compensations, as I think I told you.' His pleasant face beamed. 'On the whole I prefer male company. Men are so much more predictable.'

'Which is convenient,' remarked Cooper to the Blakeneys in Mill House kitchen that evening, 'since he'll probably spend the rest of his life in prison.'

'Assuming you can prove he did it,' said Jack. 'What happens if he doesn't confess? You'll be left with circumstantial evidence, and if his defence has any sense they'll go all out to convince the jury Mathilda committed suicide. You don't even know why he did it, do you?'

'Not yet.'

'Doesn't Violet know?' asked Sarah.

Cooper shook his head, thinking of the wretched woman they'd abandoned at Wing Cottage, wringing her hands and protesting there must be some mistake. 'Claims she doesn't.'

'And you didn't find the diaries?'

'We never really expected to. He'd have destroyed them long ago.'

'But there's so much unexplained,' said Sarah in frustration. 'How did he get her to take the sleeping pills? Why did he do it? Why didn't Violet wake up? Why didn't he tell you Ruth had been there if he wanted her implicated? And then the bit I really don't understand – why on earth did Jane have a row with Mathilda that day?'

Cooper glanced at Jack, then took out his cigarettes. 'I can make a guess at some answers,' he said, planting a cigarette in the side of his mouth and flicking his lighter to the tip. 'Both Mathilda and Violet liked a tipple in the evening and they both drank whisky. I think the chances are it was Mathilda who first introduced Violet to it, made it respectable as it were in the face of Duncan's disapproval, but in any case Violet was certainly in the habit of dozing off in her armchair. The night Mathilda died, Violet went out for the count during *Blind Date* which comes on at six thirty or thereabouts, woke up briefly some time after ten o'clock, when Duncan shook her and told her she was snoring through *Match of the Day,* went up to bed and slept like the dead for the rest of the night.' He tapped ash into his cupped palm. 'That was definitely no doze. That was a barbiturate-induced stupor which is why Duncan leaving the room wouldn't have wakened her. I think he greeted Violet when she got home after a tiring day in Poole with a stiff whisky, laced with sleeping tablets, waited till she fell asleep, then trotted next door and used the same concoction on Mathilda. She kept the drink in the kitchen. How simple just to say: Don't stir yourself. Let me do the honours and get you a top-up.'

'But where did he get the sleeping pills from? He's on my list and I've never prescribed any for him or Violet.'

'Presumably he used the ones you prescribed for Mrs Gillespie.'

Sarah looked doubtful. 'When could he have taken them, though? Surely she'd have noticed if any were missing.'

'If she did,' he said dryly, 'then she probably assumed it was her own daughter who was responsible. With Mrs Lascelles's sort of dependence she must have been raiding her mother's drug cupboard for years.'

Jack looked thoughtful. 'Who told you?'

'As a matter of fact, you did, Jack. But I wasn't too sure what she was on until we searched the house yesterday for the diaries. She's not very good at hiding things, but then she's damn lucky she hasn't fallen foul of the police before. She will, though, now that the money's dried up.'

'I didn't tell you anything.'

Cooper tut-tutted. 'You've told me everything you know about Mrs Lascelles, right down to the fact that you, personally, despise her. I stood and looked at her portrait while we were discussing Othello and Iago, and all I could see was a desperately weak and fragmented character whose existence – ' he used his hands to depict a border ' – depends on external stimulation. I compared the pallid colours and the distorted shapes of Joanna's portrait with the vigour of Mathilda's and Sarah's and I thought, you've painted a woman without substance. The only reality you perceive is a reflected reality, in other words, a personality that can only express itself artificially. I guessed it had to be drink or drugs.'

'You're lying through your teeth,' said Jack bluntly. 'That bastard Smollett told you. Dammit, Cooper, even I didn't see all that and I painted the bloody picture.'

Cooper gave a deep chuckle. 'It's all there, my friend, believe me. Mr Smollett told me nothing.' His face sobered. 'But you had no business withholding that information, either of you, not in a murder enquiry.' He looked at Sarah. 'And you should never have confronted her with it the other afternoon, if you don't mind me saying so, Doctor. People like that are shockingly unpredictable and you were alone in the house with her.'

'She's not on LSD, Cooper, she's on Valium. Anyway, how do you know I confronted her with it?'

'Because I'm a policeman, Dr Blakeney, and you were looking guilty. What makes you think she's on Valium?'

'She told me she was.'

Cooper raised his eyes to heaven. 'One day, Dr Blakeney, you will learn not to be so gullible.'

'Well, what is she on then?' demanded Jack. 'I guessed tranquillizers, too. She's not injecting. I sketched her in the nude and there wasn't a mark on her.'

'It depends what you were looking for. She's rich enough to do the thing cleanly. It's dirty needles and dirty lavatories that cause most of the problems. Where did you look anyway? Arms and legs?' Jack nodded. 'The veins around her groin?'

'No,' he admitted. 'I was having enough trouble as it was, I didn't want to encourage her by staring at the damn thing.'

Cooper nodded. 'I found half a pharmacy under her floorboards, including tranquillizers, barbiturates, amphetamines and sizeable quantities of heroin and syringes. She's chronically addicted, I'd say, presumably has been for years. And, I'll tell you this for free, her mother's allowance alone couldn't possibly have funded what she'd got stashed away, and nor could fancy flower arranging. I think Duncan and Violet's anonymous letter said it all, Joanna is a high-class prostitute turning tricks to fund a very expensive habit, begun, I would guess, when she married Steven Lascelles.'

'But she looks so . . .' Sarah sought for the right word, 'unsullied.'

'Not for much longer,' said Cooper cynically. 'She's about to discover what it's like to live in the real world where there's no Mathilda to keep the coffers topped up. It's when you get desperate that you start getting careless.' He patted Sarah's hand. 'Don't waste your sympathy on her. She's been a taker all her life and, rather belatedly, her mother has forced her to face up to it.'

Of all absurd things, Gerald has developed a conscience. 'No more, Matty, please,' he said, bursting into tears. 'We'll go to hell for what we've done.' The ingratitude of the man beggars belief. Does he think I get any pleasure from being pawed by a drooling half-wit? It's Father's doing, of course. He lost his temper yesterday and started calling Gerald names. Now Gerald says he's going back to the slut down the road who first seduced him, and this time he says he'll marry her. 'Grace will give Gerry a baby, Matty,' he blubbered, 'and Gerry wants a baby.' Why, oh why, was my grandfather so stupid? How much more sensible it would have been to weather the embarrassment of certifying Gerald than to pretend to the world he was normal.

I sought out Father in the library, drunk as usual, and told him bluntly that Gerald wasn't playing any more. 'You're such a fool,' I stormed at him. 'Grace won't be bought off a second time. Don't imagine she hasn't guessed by now that she'll get more by marrying Gerald than by taking your bribes.' Father cringed away from me as he always does. 'It's not my fault,' he whined, 'it's your grandfather's fault. He should have mentioned me by name in his will instead of referring to Gerald's nearest male relative.' I could have murdered him then. The same old story, never his fault, always someone else's. But in one way he's right. Why did my grandfather create a trust to prevent his idiot first-born disposing of his wealth without clarifying that my father must inherit afterwards? And why did it not occur to him that Gerald might repeat the terms of the will parrot-fashion to any scheming little bitch who cared to listen? Grace must have worked out by now that Gerald is worth marrying just to produce a son who will inherit everything. I suppose my grandfather had no idea that imbeciles were so interested in sex nor, indeed, that they were capable of fathering children.

I made Father wear the scold's bridle all evening and he's promised to hold his tongue in future. Gerald, of course, whimpered in the corner, afraid that I would make him wear it, too, but I promised that if we heard no more talk of going to live with Grace, I would be nice to him. Now he is pliable once more.

How strange it is that these two, without a brain between them, can see the scold's bridle for the humiliation it is, while Duncan, who has some pretensions to intelligence, is disgustingly excited by it. For Gerald and Father it is a necessary penance for the sins they wish to commit. For Duncan, it is a fetish that unlocks his potency. He is invariably aroused by wearing it. But what a gutless worm he is. He begs me on his knees to marry him while he allows Violet and her parents to continue with the marriage arrangements. He is not prepared to risk losing her miserable dowry, unless he is first assured of mine.

I could never marry a man who takes pleasure in his own humiliation, for then there would be no pleasure left to me. I can only love them when they cringe. Still, it is odd how many men find cruelty attractive. Like dogs, they lick the hand that whips them. Poor Violet. I have planted fantasies in Duncan's mind that she can never satisfy. Well, well, what a very amusing thought that is. I really couldn't bear to see them happy. But then I can't bear to see anybody happy . . .

Nineteen

SARAH TOPPED UP their wine glasses and viewed the empty bottle with a wry look. 'Thank God my poison is legal,' she murmured. 'I know damn well I need an external stimulant to make the miseries bearable. Did you take her heroin off her, Cooper? She'll be in a desperate state if you did.'

'No,' he admitted, 'but you can keep that information to yourselves.'

'You're a very kind man,' she told him.

'I'm a realist,' he corrected her. 'If Joanna had murdered her mother then I was in a stronger position keeping what I knew up my sleeve than showing my hand before I had to. She would have been very vulnerable to police questioning if we could have charged her with possession and murder both at the same time.'

'You're such a bad liar,' said Sarah fondly. 'You're not going to charge her at all. Will you even tell her you know?'

But Cooper sidestepped that question. 'We were talking about how Duncan murdered Mathilda,' he said. 'So where were we?'

'With Mathilda being immensely suspicious when he

399

came through the back door uninvited and offered to top up her whisky,' said Sarah dryly.

'Oh, yes, well he wouldn't have gone that way. He'd have rung the front door bell. It was quite safe. Violet wasn't going to hear anything, not if she was snoring her head off in front of the television, and I'm sure he had a very convincing reason for knocking on Mathilda's door at seven o'clock on a Saturday evening. He did know a great deal about her life, after all, any bit of which he could tap into as an excuse. She would have to have been deeply paranoid to lock her door against a neighbour she saw almost every day.' Absent-mindedly, he tapped more ash into his palm then turned it upside down to scatter it on the floor. 'Once he'd given her the whisky, and watched her drink it, he made his excuses and left. He's a cautious man and he didn't know how effective the sedative would be, plus he needed to be sure Violet really was dead to the world and hadn't heard the bell ringing. Presumably if he'd found her semi-conscious, he'd have abandoned the project as being too dangerous and, by the same token, he wanted Mathilda well and truly under before he put the scold's bridle over her head.

'From then on, it would all have been very straight-forward. He checked on Violet, donned a pair of gloves, collected the appropriate weeds from the garden – he wouldn't have done that during daylight hours in case someone saw him and put two and two together when they heard about Mathilda's flower arrangement. Then he let himself in again, this time through Mathilda's back door, took the Stanley knife from the kitchen drawer, checked Mathilda was asleep, took the weeds, the knife and the scold's bridle upstairs where he left them on the dressing-table, filled the bath, then went back down to collect Mathilda. All he had to do was scoop her up in his arms, put her on the lift, take her upstairs and undress her.

'The time would have been approximately nine thirty, we think, which has made the pathologist very happy. He always favoured earlier rather than later, particularly as Mathilda wouldn't have died immediately.' He cast about in his mind again for the thread of where he had been. 'Right, so once he'd undressed her, he placed her in the warm bath, put the scold's bridle on her head, slit her wrists and then arranged the nettles and daisies in the head-band, probably using the sponge to wedge the gap. Then all he had to do was leave the whisky glass beside the empty sleeping-pill bottle, remove the diaries, wipe the key clean for safety's sake and replace it, before going home to Violet and the television. He undoubtedly took the poor woman to task the next morning over her drinking being so bad that she'd passed out the night before, or she might have told us earlier that she'd been asleep instead of going along with Duncan's story that there had been no sound from next door.' He massaged his chin. 'She's a very pliable woman and, in fairness to her, it obviously never occurred to her that he could have murdered Mathilda. I think she prompted him to write us the anonymous letter because she felt so guilty about letting Mathilda down.' He flicked a glance at Jack. 'She overheard her crying that time you went round to show her the painting, and she's convinced herself that if she'd only spoken to her then she might have prevented the murder.'

He saw the look of puzzled enquiry on Sarah's face, and

ploughed on relentlessly. 'As far as Ruth and Jane are concerned, Duncan didn't want to tell us about them being in Cedar House that day because he couldn't afford to draw attention to how much could be heard through the walls. But Violet gave him the perfect opportunity to involve Ruth when she overheard a row between Joanna and Ruth in their hall. She consulted Duncan about the wisdom of reporting it and, while he flatly refused to let her come in person, to avoid any unpleasantness, as he put it, he didn't object to an anonymous letter, although he insisted on wearing gloves to avoid us tracing it through the finger-prints. Violet thought that was *very* exciting,' he concluded with heavy irony.

'It's odd that Mathilda never mentioned hearing them,' said Jack. 'It's the sort of thing that would have driven her mad.'

'Mrs Orloff says she spoke very clearly and decisively, so perhaps she was a little deaf, and if she never heard them, it wouldn't occur to her that they could hear her. In any case, as soon as they realized just how much could be overheard, I suspect they tempered their own volume. It's interesting to watch them. He speaks just above a whisper and when-ever she gets excited, he frowns at her and she drops her voice.'

'I suppose that's how he found out about the key,' said Sarah slowly. 'When Mathilda told me where it was that day. He must have heard her.'

Cooper nodded.

'How did he know about the diaries?'

'According to Violet, she often used to talk to herself when no one was there, so I'm guessing she read them aloud. Otherwise, he stumbled on them by accident when he was looking for something else.' He frowned. '*He*'s not going to tell us, that's for sure. He's just sitting there at the moment denying everything and challenging us to give one good reason why he would suddenly want to murder a woman he had known for fifty years, when scarcely one cross word had been exchanged between them in all that time. And Violet supports him on that. She says Duncan is far too lazy either to take offence or give it, so Mathilda very quickly got bored with trying to provoke any sort of reaction out of him.'

'He's got you by the short and curlies,' remarked Jack with reluctant admiration. 'You won't get very far with "trying to delay the passage of the will" as a convincing motive for murder. Even if the Prosecution's prepared to run with it, I can't see a jury accepting it. Have you really no idea at all why he wanted her dead? Surely Violet must know something.'

'She's very distressed at the moment. The DCI hopes a little tender care from a sympathetic policewoman will help jog her memory, but, if you want my opinion, she's being genuinely honest when she says she doesn't know. She's a funny little person, seems to live in a world of her own most of the time, talks nineteen-to-the-dozen but doesn't listen. I suspect most of what went on inside Cedar House was just background noise to her.' He glanced from one to the other of them. 'All of which is why I'm here. I need to talk to Ruth. She mentioned that her grandmother wrote her a letter shortly before she died, and it occurred to me that there might have been something in there which might help us.'

'If it's the same one she told me about, then she tore it up,' said Sarah.

'Still, she'll remember what was in it. I really do need to talk to her.'

Sarah shook her head firmly. 'Not now, Cooper. She's paranoid about the police at the moment, what with last night, and Jack being carted off in handcuffs at lunchtime. Okay, I know none of it's your fault, but you've got to show her a little compassion.'

'Don't make me insist,' he begged. 'I really don't have a choice on this one. We can't hold Duncan indefinitely without some very concrete evidence and, once he walks, he'll be free to tidy up anything we've missed.'

She sighed and took one of his large hands in hers. 'Look, I'm going to tell you something that, strictly speaking, I shouldn't because it's Ruth's secret and not mine, but I'd trust you with my life, Cooper, so I think I can trust you with Ruth's.' She gave the hand a quick squeeze before releasing it to reach across for Jack's, her eyes creasing with affection. 'Why do you think this silly sod has been charging about like a bull in a china shop? He says what he's done is rational and sensible. You and I know it isn't. Rather belatedly, he's discovered that he has some very powerful paternal feelings which, because he's the generous soul he is, he does not intend to limit to his own offspring. He is acting in lieu of Ruth's dead father because he wants her to know that there is someone in this shitty world who loves her.'

Jack raised her fingers to his lips. 'Two people,' he corrected her.

She held his gaze for a moment. 'Two people,' she

agreed. She took her hand away and transferred her attention back to Cooper. 'Ruth is so vulnerable at the moment that if she's put under any more pressure, then I can guarantee she'll withdraw from reality in the way that Joanna clearly has done and Mathilda probably did as well. It's almost as if there's a self-destructive gene in the family that triggers the withdrawal.' She shook her head. 'Whatever it is, Ruth is not going the same way, not if Jack and I can prevent it. She's pregnant, Cooper. I know she doesn't look it, but she's almost at the legal cut-off point, and if she doesn't make up her mind very quickly about having the pregnancy terminated, then she'll have to go through with it. Jack was trying to buy her the peace and quiet she needs to reach a decision, because as yet she hasn't had the chance to do it.'

Cooper absorbed all this in grave silence. 'Are you helping her reach her decision?' he asked at last.

'I've given her all the information I can, but I don't like to say, do this or do that. It's her mother's role to give advice but Joanna doesn't even know about the rape, let alone about the pregnancy.'

'Hmm,' grunted Cooper, pursing his lips in deep thought. 'Well, I certainly don't intend to add to the poor girl's problems,' he said at last. 'I'm sure her grandmother wouldn't demand justice for herself before consideration for her granddaughter. If she was that way inclined she'd have reported Ruth for thieving when she was still alive.' He stood up and buttoned his coat about him, preparatory to leaving. 'But, if you'll forgive the impertinence, Dr Blakeney, you must take your responsibilities as her adopted mother, temporary or otherwise, a great deal more seriously. It's no good giving her information and leaving it up to her to decide, without making it very clear that you believe it's in her best interests to have an abortion. The chances are she'll scream and yell, say you don't love her and don't care tuppence for her feelings, but parenting is not about patting oneself on the back for being understanding and liberal, it's about guidance, education and training to help the child you love become a man or woman you can respect.' He nodded a friendly goodbye and made for the door, only to pause as he saw Ruth in the shadows of the hall.

'I've been listening,' she said, her wretched eyes full of tears. 'I'm sorry. I didn't mean to.'

'There, there,' said Cooper, gruff with embarrassment, pulling a large white handkerchief from his pocket and offering it to her. 'I'm the one who should apologize. I'd no business to interfere.'

Her eyes brimmed again. 'I don't mind about what you said. I was thinking – if only – you said you wished your children had had my opportunities – do you remember?'

He nodded. He had indeed said that, he thought with chagrin.

'Well, I was just thinking – I wish' – she gave him a watery smile – 'I wish I'd had theirs. I hope they appreciate you, Sergeant Cooper.' She took a letter from her pocket and gave it to him. 'It's Granny's,' she said. 'I didn't throw it away, but I couldn't show it to you because she talks about my stealing.' A tear splashed on to her hand. 'I really did love her, you know, but she died thinking I didn't, and that's almost worse than everything else.'

'Yes,' he said gently, 'I'm sure it is, because there's nothing you can do to mend it.'

'Not ever.'

'Well, as to ever – that I couldn't say. In this life, the best any of us can do is learn from our mistakes and try not to make them again. We're none of us infallible, Ruth, but we owe it to ourselves and to those around us to act with whatever wisdom we possess. Otherwise, how will mankind ever improve?'

She pressed her lips together to hold back the tears. 'And you think it would be wise for me to have an abortion?'

'Yes,' he said with absolute honesty, 'I do.' He placed his broad palm against her stomach. 'At the moment you're not quite old enough or tough enough to be mother and father to another human being, and you're too riddled by guilt over your grandmother, and what you see as your betrayal of her, to give this baby away to someone else.' He smiled rather shyly. 'That's not to say I expect you to agree with me or that I'll turn my back on you if you decide to have your baby. Dr Blakeney's quite right when she says it's your choice. But I'd rather see you pregnant when you've lived a little and found a man you can love who loves you, too. Then your babies will be wanted and you'll be free to be the kind of mother you want to be.'

She tried to thank him, but the words wouldn't come, so Cooper took her in his arms instead and held her tight. Behind them, Sarah turned a tear-streaked face to Jack. 'Remind me of this,' she whispered, 'whenever I get complacent. I've just learnt how little I really know.'

My dear Ruth [Mathilda had written], Your mother and I
have fallen out over a letter written by my uncle Gerald
Cavendish shortly before he died, making Joanna his heir.
She is threatening to take me to court over it because she
believes she can use it to overturn my father's will. She
won't succeed, but I have been unable to convince her of
that. She feels understandably aggrieved and wants to
punish me. I realize now there has been too much secrecy
within this family and so I am writing to you now to
acquaint you with the knowledge she already has, because I
do not want you to learn about it from her. She will not, I
think, tell you kindly. James Gillespie was not your
mother's father. Gerald Cavendish was. I realize how
shocked you will be by this information but I urge you to
do what I have done all these years and see it as something
that happened which should not be regretted. You may find
this hard to believe but, despite everything, I have always
been fond of your mother, as indeed I have been fond of
you.

I am faced now with a difficult choice. I am aware, my
dear, that you have been stealing from me for some
months. I am aware, too, that your mother has given up on
life and prefers the twilight world of drug dependency and
the casual relationships that give her the illusion of being
loved without the ties of responsibility. You are both
allowing yourselves to be abused by men and, in view of my
own history, I find that deeply disheartening. I realize I
have failed you, and have decided, therefore, to set you
both free to make your own decisions about your futures.

My intention is to make over a lump sum to you and
your mother on your eighteenth birthday, the amount to

be apportioned in the ratio 2:1, with your mother receiving double your share. Perhaps it is something I should have done a long time ago, but I was reluctant to give up what I have worked so hard for in the Cavendish name. As things are now, I see that a name is nothing unless the individuals who bear it stand above their peers, for it is not the accident of our births that makes us great but our individual characters. By setting you and your mother free to lead your lives as you choose, I hope to give you the chance to prove yourselves, just as others – those less fortunate – have already done.

In conclusion, should anything happen to me and you find yourself in need of a friend, then I urge you to talk to Dr Sarah Blakeney, my GP, who will give you nothing but good advice whatever the situation you find yourself in.

With love, Granny.

Cooper placed the letter in front of Detective Chief Inspector Jones. 'I've been asking myself where she was going to get the money from to give lump sums to Mrs and Miss Lascelles if she'd already made a will giving everything to Dr Blakeney.'

Charlie scanned the page rapidly. 'Did you come up with an answer?'

'I reckon it's on the video, if we'd only known what to look for. Do you remember when she was talking to Ruth towards the end and she mentioned her promise to leave the girl Cedar House before Ruth's behaviour of the last six months had persuaded her to change her mind? Okay, well immediately after that she went on to say something like: "You'd have had the choice either to sell up or stay but you'd have sold because the house would have lost its charms for you once the estate was approved." Or words to that effect.'

Charlie nodded.

'I assumed the phrase "once the estate was approved" referred to the goods and chattels being handed over to Joanna as part of her share.'

'Go on.'

'I think now she was talking about an estate of houses. She was planning to sell off the garden for development. How else could she raise a lump sum for the Lascelles women and still be able to leave Cedar House and its contents to Dr Blakeney? Just imagine the impact that would have had on Duncan Orloff. A man who can't bear the thought of noisy children next door sure as hell isn't going to sit tamely by and watch his garden turned into a building site.'

'Prove it,' said Duncan placidly. 'Name the developer. Explain why there's no correspondence with this mythical company. Good grief, man, she wouldn't even have got planning permission for such an enterprise. The days of unravelling the green belt are long gone. They're knitting it back together now just as fast as they can. There's electoral mileage in the environmental vote and none at all in speculative vandalism.'

All of which, thought Charlie gloomily, was true. It was

left to Cooper to bring a dose of common sense to the situation.

The following morning, after lengthy consultations with the local borough planning officer, he presented himself at Howard & Sons, building contractors of Learmouth since 1972. A middle-aged secretary, agog with curiosity at this unexpected appearance of a plain-clothes policeman in their midst, ushered him with some ceremony into the office of Mr Howard Snr.

Mr Howard, a thickset elderly man with a scattering of grizzled grey hairs, looked up from a set of plans with a frown. 'Well, Sergeant? What can I do for you?'

'I understand your company was responsible for the Cedar Estate development in Fontwell. It was built ten years ago. Do you recall it?'

'I do,' barked the other. 'What of it? Who's complaining?'

'No one, as far as I know,' said Cooper placidly.

He waved to a chair. 'Sit down, man. You can't be too sure about anything these days. It's a dog-eat-dog world where litigation's the name of the game and the only people who get fat are the solicitors. I had a letter this morning from a tight-fisted bastard who's refusing to pay what he owes because he says we're in breach of contract by putting in one less electric socket than the plans called for. It makes you sick.' He beetled ferocious eyebrows. 'So what's your interest in Cedar Estate?'

'You bought the land for it from a Mrs Mathilda Gillespie of Cedar House, Fontwell.'

'I did. Blood-sucking old bitch she is, too. Paid far more for it than I should have done.'

'*Was*,' Cooper corrected him. 'She's dead.'

Howard eyed him with sudden interest. 'Is that so? Ah, well,' he murmured without regret, 'it comes to us all in the end.'

'In her case rather prematurely. She was murdered.'

There was a short silence. 'And what does that have to do with the Cedar Estate?'

'We're having difficulty establishing a motive. One idea that suggests itself,' he declared ponderously, 'is that she was planning to continue her successful venture with you by selling off the rest of her garden for development. From consultations I've had with the planning department, I understand some sort of second phase has always been on the cards, but this would have made her very unpopular in certain quarters and might have inspired the murder.' He hadn't missed the gleam of interest in the sharp old eyes opposite. 'Have you had any recent correspondence with her on the subject, Mr Howard?'

'Only negative.'

Cooper frowned. 'Could you explain that?'

'She approached us with a view to going forward. We made an offer. She rejected it.' He grunted with annoyance. 'Like I told you, she was a blood-sucking old bitch. Wanted far more for the land than it's worth. The building trade's been through the worst recession in its history and prices have plummeted. I wouldn't mind so much if it wasn't down to us in the first place that she was even in a position to develop the damn thing.' He glared at Cooper as if Cooper were responsible for Mathilda's rejection. 'It was us who established the sodding outline permission on her garden ten years ago which is why we left access space on the south-east boundary. First refusal on the second phase if she decided to go ahead was part of the original contract and she had the gall to turn us down.'

'When was this? Can you remember?'

'The day she turned us down? Bonfire night, November the fifth.' He chuckled suddenly. 'I told her to stick a rocket up her arse and she hung up on me. Mind, I'd said many worse things first time round – I don't mind my Ps and Qs for anyone – and she always came back.'

'You saw her in person?'

'Telephone. She meant it, though, wrote a couple of days later confirming. Claimed she was in no hurry and was prepared to wait for the prices to go back up again. It's in the file, along with a copy of our offer.' The gleam of interest was back in his eyes. 'Still, if she's dead, her heirs might be interested, eh? It's a fair offer. They won't get better from anyone else.'

'Her will's being contested,' said Cooper apologetically. 'I imagine it will be some time before ownership of the property is proved. May I see her letter?'

'Don't see why not.' He pressed the intercom and demanded the Gillespie file. 'So who killed her then?'

'No one's been charged as yet.'

'Well, they do say planning disputes bring out the worst in people. Bit extreme to murder someone over it though. Eh?'

'Any murder's extreme,' said Cooper.

'A few houses more or less. It's hardly a motive.'

'People fear the unexpected,' said Cooper phlegmatically.

'I sometimes think that's the root cause of all murders.' He looked towards the door as the secretary popped in with an orange folder. 'The boat rocks and the only solution is to kill the person who's rocking it.'

Howard opened the file and selected a sheet from the top. 'There you are.' He handed it across.

Cooper examined it carefully. It was dated Saturday, November 6th, and typed. As Howard had said, it confirmed her refusal to proceed until prices improved. 'When did you say you got this?'

'Couple of days after the phone call.'

'That would have been a Sunday.'

'The Monday then, or maybe the Tuesday. We don't work weekends, not in the office at least.'

'Did she always type her letters?'

'Don't remember her ever doing it before.' He looked back through the file. 'Copper-plate script every time.'

Cooper thought of her letter to Ruth. That had been written in a beautiful hand. 'Have you any other letters from her? I'd like to compare the signatures.'

Howard licked a finger and flicked over the pages, removing several more sheets. 'You think someone else wrote it?'

'It's a possibility. There's no typewriter in her house and she was dead by the Saturday night. When could she have had it done?' He placed the pages side by side on the desk and squinted at the subscriptions. 'Well, well,' he said with satisfaction, 'the best laid schemes – you've been very helpful, Mr Howard. May I take these with me?'

'I'll want photocopies for my records.' He was consumed

414

with curiosity. 'Never occurred to me it wasn't kosher. What's wrong with it then?'

Cooper placed a finger on the typed letter's signature. 'For a start, he's dotted his "i"s' – he pointed to the others – 'and she hasn't. His "M" is too upright and the "G" runs on to the following "i".' He chuckled. 'The experts are going to have a field day on this. All in all it's a very cack-handed effort.'

'Bit of a fool, is he?'

'Arrogant, I'd say. Forgery is an art like any other. It takes years of practice to be any good.'

'I've a forensic team sifting through a dustbin full of Violet's old cinders,' Charlie told Cooper when he returned to the nick, 'and they tell me they've found the diaries. Or what's left of them at least. There's the odd scrap of paper but several quite substantial pieces of what they say is the calf-skin binding. They're still looking. They're confident of finding at least one scrap with her writing on it.' He rubbed his hands together.

'They might look for scraps of typed paper while they're about it, preferably with a Howard & Sons imprint,' said Cooper, producing his sheaf of letters. 'They made her a formal offer for her land on the first of November, and we certainly didn't find it when we went through her papers. The chances are Orloff swiped an entire file. Howard Snr has a stack of correspondence relating to Cedar Estate, and there wasn't a damn thing on the subject anywhere in the house. If there had been we might have twigged a bit sooner.'

'No one's fault but her own. I suppose she learnt never to trust anyone which is why she played everything so close to her chest. She said it all in her letter to Ruth, "there's been too much secrecy within this family". If she'd mentioned her plans to the solicitor even, she'd probably be alive now.'

'Still, we didn't ask the right questions, Charlie.'

The Inspector gave a dry laugh. 'If the answer's forty-two, then what's the Ultimate Question? Read *The Hitch Hiker's Guide to the Galaxy*, old son. It's harder to ask the right question than it is to come up with the answer, so don't lose any sleep over it.'

Cooper, who somewhat belatedly was trying to improve his reading, took out his notebook and jotted down the title. At the very least, it had to be more palatable than *Othello* which he was struggling through at the moment. He tucked his pencil back into his pocket and took Charlie through his conversation with the developer. 'It was six weeks of hard negotiating the first time before he and she could agree on a price. She used to horse-trade over the phone, apparently, rejecting every offer until he came up with one she could accept. Poor old soul,' he said with genuine feeling. 'Orloff must have thought his ship had come in when he heard her doing it the second time round. She made it so easy for him.' He tapped the typed letter. 'All he had to do was get rid of her and post that off the next day. Howard claims he and his sons lost interest immediately because he'd made it clear to her on more than one occasion that the bottom had dropped out of the market and he wasn't in a position to offer her any more.'

Charlie picked up the letter and examined it. 'There was

a portable typewriter on the desk in his sitting-room,' he recalled. 'Let's get the lads out there to make a quick comparison for us. He's put all his effort into forging her signature and forgotten that typewriters have signatures, too.'

'He'd never make it that easy for us.'

But he had.

'Duncan Jeremiah Orloff . . . formally charged with the murder of Mathilda Beryl Gillespie . . . Saturday, November sixth . . .' The voice of the Duty Officer droned on relentlessly, making little impact on Cooper who knew the formula off by heart. Instead, his mind drifted towards an elderly woman, drained of her lifeblood, and the rusted iron framework that had encased her head. He felt an intense regret that he had never known her. Whatever sins she had committed, it would, he felt, have been a privilege.

'. . . request that you be refused bail because of the serious nature of the charges against you. The magistrates will order an immediate remand into custody . . .'

He looked at Duncan Orloff only when the man beat his fat little hands against his breast and burst into tears. It wasn't his fault, he pleaded, it was Mathilda's fault. Mathilda was to blame for everything. He was a sick man. What would Violet do without him?

'Collapse of stout party,' muttered the Duty Officer under his breath to Cooper, listening to the rasping, anguished breaths.

A deep frown creased Cooper's pleasant face. 'By heaven, she deserved better than you, she really did,' he said to

Orloff. 'It should have been a brave man who killed her, not a coward. What gave you the right to play God with her life?'

'A brave man wouldn't have had to, Sergeant Cooper.' He turned haunted eyes towards the policeman. 'It wasn't courage that was needed to kill Mathilda, it was fear.'

'Fear of a few houses in your garden, Mr Orloff?'

Duncan shook his head. 'I am what I am' – he held trembling hands to his face – 'and it was she who made me. I have spent my adult life shunning the woman I married in favour of fantasies about the one I didn't, and you cannot live in hell for forty years without being damaged by it.'

'Is that why you came back to Fontwell, to relive your fantasies?'

'You can't control them, Sergeant. They control you.' He fell silent.

'But you returned five years ago, Mr Orloff.'

'I asked nothing from her, you know. A few shared memories perhaps. Peace even. After forty years I expected very little.'

Cooper eyed him curiously. 'You said you killed her out of fear. Was that what you fantasized about? Being so afraid of her that you could bring yourself to kill her?'

'I fantasized about making love,' he whispered.

'To Mathilda?'

'Of course.' He gathered his tears in the palms of his hands. 'I've never made love to Violet. I couldn't.'

Good God, thought Cooper with disgust, did the man have no pity at all for his poor little wife? 'Couldn't or wouldn't, Mr Orloff? There is a difference.'

'Couldn't.' The word was barely audible. 'Mathilda did

418

certain things' – he shivered like a man possessed – 'which Violet was offended by' – his voice broke – 'it was less unpleasant for both of us if I paid for what I wanted.'

Cooper caught the Duty Officer's gaze above Duncan's head, and gave a cynical laugh. 'So this is going to be your defence, is it? That you murdered Mathilda Gillespie because she gave you a taste for something only prostitutes could supply?'

A thready sigh puttered from the moist lips. 'You never had cause to be afraid of her, Sergeant. She didn't own you because she didn't know your secrets.' The sad eyes turned towards him. 'Surely it's occurred to you that when we bought Wing Cottage our solicitor discovered the outline planning permission on the remaining Cedar House land? We went ahead with the purchase because Mathilda agreed to a clause in the contract, giving us a power of veto over any future decision.' He gave a hollow laugh. 'I blame myself because I knew her so much better than Violet ever did. The clause was worth less than the paper it was written on.' Briefly, he pressed his lips together in an effort to control himself. 'She was obliged to tell me about her approach to Howard because she was going to need my signature on the final document, but when I told her that Violet and I would object to the proposed plan, which put the nearest house ten yards from our back wall, she laughed. "Don't be absurd, Duncan. Have you forgotten how much I know about you?"'

When he didn't go on, Cooper prompted him. 'She was going to blackmail you into signing?'

'Of course.' He placed his damp palms to his breasts. 'We were in the drawing-room. She left me for a couple of

419

minutes to fetch a book from the library, and when she came back she read extracts to me.' Distress wheezed from him in quickened breaths. 'It was one of her diaries – full of such terrible lies and obscenity – and not just about me – Violet, too – intimate details that Violet had told her when she was tipsy. "Do you want me to photocopy this, Duncan, and spread it round the village?" she asked. "Do you want the whole of Fontwell to know that Violet is still a virgin because the demands you made of her on your wedding night were so disgusting that she had to lock herself in the bathroom?"' – his voice faltered – 'she was very entertained by it all – couldn't put the book down once she'd started – read me pieces about the Marriotts, the vicar, the poor Spedes – everyone.' He fell silent again.

'So you went back later to read the others?' suggested Cooper.

Duncan shrugged helplessly. 'I was desperate. I hoped I'd find something I could use against *her*. I doubted there'd be anything of value in the early ones, simply because I'd have to find independent proof to challenge her, and, bar references to Joanna's drug addiction, Ruth's stealing and her belief that Sarah Blakeney was the daughter she'd had by Paul Marriott, the later ones were simply a catalogue of her dislikes. They were the product of a diseased mind, and she used them, I think, as a channel for expunging her poison. If she hadn't been able to express herself on paper' – he shook his head – 'she was quite mad, you know.'

'Still,' said Cooper ponderously, 'murder was an extreme solution, Mr Orloff. You could have used her daughter's and her granddaughter's problems against her. She was a proud woman. She wouldn't have wanted those made public, surely?'

The sad eyes fixed on him again. 'I never planned to murder her, or not till that Saturday morning when Jane Marriott went to see her. I intended to threaten her with divulging what I knew to Dr Blakeney. But as I told you, it was fear that killed her. A brave man would have said: "publish and be damned".'

He had lost Cooper. 'I don't understand.'

'She told Jane Marriott that things would get worse before they got better because she knew James had been reading her private papers – it never occurred to her it was me – then she went on to say that she had no intention of keeping quiet any longer.' He wrung his hands. 'So, of course, I went round the minute Jane left and asked her what she meant by "she had no intention of keeping quiet any longer"?' His face was grey with fatigue. 'She picked up the scold's bridle and taunted me with it. "Mathilda Cavendish and Mathilda Gillespie did not write their diaries for fun, Duncan. They wrote them so that one day they could have their revenge. They will not be gagged. I shall see to that."' He paused. 'She really was mad,' he insisted, 'and she knew it. I said I'd call a doctor for her so she laughed and quoted *Macbeth* at me. "More needs she the divine than the physician."' He raised his hands in a gesture of surrender. 'And I thought how all of us, who would be destroyed by her diaries, needed the divine more than the physician, and I made up my mind during that terrible afternoon to play . . . God.'

Cooper was deeply sceptical. 'But you must have planned

it all in advance because you stole the sleeping pills beforehand.'

He sighed. 'They were for me – or Violet – or both of us.'

'So what made you change your mind?'

'Sergeant, I am, as you rightly say, a coward and I realized that I could not destroy the diaries without destroying her as well. *She* was the poison, the diaries were only the outward manifestation. At least I have allowed all the others to keep their dignity.'

Cooper thought of the ones he cared about, Jack and Sarah, Jane and Paul Marriott; Ruth above all.

'Only if you plead guilty, Mr Orloff, otherwise this will all come out in court.'

'Yes. I owe Violet that much,' he said.

After all, it is easy to manipulate a man if all he wants is something as worthless as love. Love is easily given when it is the body that's invaded and not the mind. My mind can withstand anything. I am Mathilda Cavendish and what does Mathilda care when the only thing she feels is contempt?

> *Man, proud man,*
> *Drest in a little brief authority,*
> *Most ignorant of what he's most assur'd,*
> *His glassy essence, like an angry ape,*
> *Plays such fantastic tricks before high heaven,*
> *As make the angels weep.*

If angels weep Mathilda sees no sign of it. They do not weep for me . . .

Twenty

JANE MARRIOTT replaced the telephone receiver and held a shaking hand to her lips. She walked through to the living room where her invalid husband was dozing quietly in the bright winter sunshine which poured through the window. She sat beside him and took her hand in his. 'That was Sergeant Cooper on the phone,' she said. 'James Gillespie was found dead in his flat this morning. A heart attack, they think.'

Paul didn't say anything, only stared out across the garden.

'He says there's nothing to worry about any more, that no one need ever know. He also said' – she paused briefly – 'he also said that the child was a girl. Mathilda lied about your having a son.' She had told him everything after her return home from the surgery the day Sergeant Cooper had questioned her.

A tear squeezed from between his lids. 'I'm so sorry.'

'For James?'

'For – everything. If I'd known—' He fell silent.

'Would it have made a difference, Paul?'

'We could have shared the burden, instead of you bearing it alone.'

'It would have destroyed me,' she said honestly. 'I couldn't have coped with you knowing that Mathilda had had your child.' She studied his face closely. 'As time went by, you would have thought more of her and less of me.'

'No.' His marbled hand clutched at hers. 'She was in every sense of the word a brief madness so, even if I'd known about the child, it wouldn't have changed anything. I have only ever loved you.' His eyes grew damp. 'In any case, my dear, I think your first instincts were right, and that Mathilda would have killed the baby. We can none of us put any faith in what she said. She lied more often than she told the truth.'

'Except that she left her money to Sarah,' said Jane in a rush, 'and Sergeant Cooper said the baby was a girl. Suppose Sarah—?' She broke off and squeezed his hand encouragingly. 'Nothing's ever too late, Paul. Would it do any harm, do you think, to ask a few tactful questions?'

He looked away from her eager face and, in Cooper's earlier footsteps, traced the fickleness of fate. He had lived his life believing he was childless, and now, at the age of seventy, Jane had told him he was a father. But of whom? Of a son? Of a daughter? Or had Mathilda lied about this as she had lied about so much else? For himself, it hardly mattered – he had long since come to terms with being childless – but for Jane, Mathilda would always cast a long and spiteful shadow. There were no guarantees that Sarah Blakeney was his daughter, no guarantees even that the child, if it existed at all, would welcome the intrusion of parents into its life, and he couldn't bear to see Jane's hopes dashed in this as surely as her hope in his fidelity had been dashed. In the end, wasn't it better to live with the illusion of happiness than the awful certainty of trust betrayed?

'You must promise me you will never say anything.' He laid his head against the back of the chair and struggled for breath. 'If I am her father, then Mathilda never told her, or I'm sure she would have come here of her own accord.' His eyes filled with tears. 'She has a loving father already who has done a fine job – a very fine job – in bringing her up. Don't force her to choose between us, my dearest one. Rejections are such painful things.'

Jane smoothed the thinning hair from his forehead. 'Perhaps, after all, some secrets are best kept secret. Shall we share this one together and dream a little from time to time?' She was a wise and generous woman who, just occasionally, acknowledged that it was Mathilda's treachery that had given her insights into herself and Paul that she hadn't had before. After all, she thought, there was less to mourn now than there was to celebrate.

Joanna sat where her mother had always sat, in the hard-backed chair beside the french windows. She tilted her head slightly to look at Sergeant Cooper. 'Does Dr Blakeney know you're telling me this?'

He shook his head. 'No. I rather hope you'll make the first move by offering to drop your challenge to the will if she agrees to honour your mother's intentions as set out in her letter to Ruth. A little oil on troubled waters, Mrs Lascelles, goes a very long way and it's in everyone's interests to put this sad affair behind you and go back to London where you belong.'

'In Dr Blakeney's certainly, not in mine.'

'I was thinking more of your daughter. She's very young still, and her grandmother's death has distressed her a great deal more than you realize. It would be' – he sought for a word – 'helpful if you pursued an amicable settlement rather than a continued and painful confrontation. Barristers have a nasty habit of unearthing details that are best left buried.'

She stood up. 'I really don't wish to discuss this any more, Sergeant. It's none of your business.' The pale eyes hardened unattractively. 'You've been seduced by the Blakeneys just as my mother was, and for that reason alone I will not negotiate amicably with them. I still find it incomprehensible that you haven't charged Jack Blakeney with assault, or, for that matter, Ruth with theft, and I intend to make sure my solicitor raises both those issues with your Chief Constable. It's quite clear to me that Dr Blakeney, ably abetted by my daughter, is using her husband and you to pressure me into leaving this house so that she can gain vacant possession of it. I will not give her the satisfaction. The longer I remain, the stronger my title to it.'

Cooper chuckled. 'Do you even have a solicitor, Mrs Lascelles? I hope you don't because you're wasting your money if that's the sort of advice he's giving you.' He pointed to the chair. 'Sit down,' he ordered her, 'and thank your daughter and the Blakeneys for the fact that I am not going to arrest you now for the illegal possession of heroin. I'd like to, make no mistake about that, but as I said before it's in everyone's interests, not least your own, if Dorset is shot of you. I should, by rights, pass on what I know to the Metropolitan Police but I won't. They'll find out anyway soon enough because, even with the capital sum Dr Blakeney pays you, you'll be quite incapable of managing. There'll be no more monthly cheques, Mrs Lascelles, because there's no old lady left to terrorize. What did you do to her to make her pay?'

She was staring out of the window but it was a long time before she answered. 'I didn't have to do anything, except be her daughter. She assumed I was like her, and that made her afraid of me.'

'I don't understand.'

She turned round to fix him with her strangely penetrating gaze. 'I watched her murder her father. She was terrified I was going to do the same to her.'

'Would you have done?'

She smiled suddenly and her beauty dazzled him. 'I'm like Hamlet, Sergeant, "but mad north-north-west". You probably won't believe me but I was always more frightened that she would kill me. I've been sleeping quite well recently.'

'Will you go back to London?'

She shrugged. 'Of course. "When a man is tired of London, he is tired of life." Have you read Samuel Johnson, Sergeant? He was a great deal wittier than Shakespeare.'

'I will now, Mrs Lascelles.'

She turned back to the window and its wonderful view of the cedar of Lebanon that dominated the garden. 'I suppose if I fight Dr Blakeney you'll pass on what you know about me to the Metropolitan Police.'

'I'm afraid I will.'

She gave a low laugh. 'Mother was always very good at

blackmail. It's a pity you never met her. Will the Blakeneys look after Ruth, Sergeant? I wouldn't want her to starve.'

Which was, thought Cooper, the closest she would ever come to expressing affection for her daughter. 'They certainly plan to keep her with them in the short term,' he told her.

('Ruth will need all our emotional support,' Sarah had said, 'and that includes yours, Cooper, if she's to get through the abortion and Dave Hughes's trial.' 'And if Hughes is acquitted?' Cooper asked. 'He won't be,' said Sarah firmly. 'Three more girls have agreed to testify against him. Women have plenty of courage, you know, when they're not pinned to the ground with knives held to their throats.')

'And in the long term?' Joanna asked him.

'Assuming the will isn't challenged, then Dr Blakeney will set up a trust fund for Ruth at the same time as she makes you a gift of the money your mother intended you to have.'

'Will she sell off the garden to do it?'

'I don't know. She told me this morning that Cedar House would make rather a fine nursing home.'

Joanna gripped her arms angrily. 'Mother must be turning in her grave to think the old ladies of Fontwell will be looked after at her expense. She couldn't stand any of them.'

Cooper smiled to himself. There really was a beautiful irony about it all, particularly as the first customer would probably be poor, bewildered Violet Orloff.

*

Jack watched Sarah out of the corner of his eye as he sat at his easel putting the finishing touches to the portrait of Joanna. She was staring aimlessly out of the window towards the wooded horizon, her forehead pressed against the cool glass. 'Penny for them,' he said at last.

'Sorry?' She turned to glance at him.

'What were you thinking about?'

'Oh, nothing, just – ' she shook her head – 'nothing.'

'Babies?' he suggested, without the usual trace of irony.

She moved into the centre of the room and stared at the painting of Mathilda. 'All right, yes, I was, but you needn't worry. It wasn't in hopeful anticipation. I was thinking that you've been right all along and that having babies is a mug's game. They bring you nothing but heartache and, frankly, I'd as soon play it safe and spare myself the anguish.'

'Pity,' he murmured, rinsing his brush in turpentine and wiping it on the kitchen roll, 'I was just getting acclimatized to the whole idea.'

She kept her voice deliberately light. 'I can take your jokes on most things, Jack, but not where babies are concerned. Sally Bennedict destroyed any credibility you might have on the subject the day she destroyed your little mistake.'

He looked very thoughtful. 'As a matter of interest, am I being singled out because I'm a man or are you planning to lay that same guilt-trip on Ruth in years to come?'

'That's different.'

'Is it? Can't see it myself.'

'Ruth wasn't two-timing her husband,' she muttered through gritted teeth.

'Then we aren't talking about babies, Sarah, and whether

431

or not I have the right to change my mind, we are talking about infidelity. Two different things entirely.'

'In your book, maybe. Not in mine. Committing yourself to a person is no different from committing yourself to a belief. Why, if you couldn't bear to impregnate your wife, were you so unconcerned about impregnating your mistress?' Two spots of colour flared high on her cheekbones, and she turned away abruptly. 'Let bygones be bygones. I don't want to talk about it any more.'

'Why not?' he said. 'I'm having a hell of a good time.' He linked his hands behind his head and grinned at her rigid back. 'You've put me through hell these last twelve months. You yank me out of London without a "by your leave" or a "do you mind?". Stick me in the middle of nowhere with a "take it or leave it, Jack, you're only my shit of a husband".' His eyes narrowed. 'I've put up with Cock Robin Hewitt strutting his stuff about my kitchen, leering at you and treating me like something the dog threw up. I've smiled while mental midgets pissed on my work, because I'm just the bum who likes nothing better than scrounging off his wife. And on top of all that I've had to listen to Keith Smollett lecturing me on your virtues. In all that time only one person, and this includes you, ever treated me as if I were human – and that was Mathilda. But for her, I'd have walked out in September and left you to stew in your own complacent juice.'

She kept her back towards him. 'Why didn't you?'

'Because, as she kept reminding me, I'm your husband,' he growled. 'Jesus, Sarah, if I didn't think what we had was worth something, why would I have married you in the first place? I didn't have to, for Christ's sake. No one held a gun to my head. I wanted to.'

'Then why—?' She didn't go on.

'Why did I get Sally pregnant? I didn't. I never even slept with the horrible little bitch. I painted her portrait because she thought I was going places after the Bond Street dealer clinched my one and only sale.' He gave a hollow laugh. 'She wanted to hitch her wagon to a rising star, the way she's hitched it to every other rising star she's ever met. Which is what I painted, of course – a lazy parasite with pretensions to greatness. She has hated me ever since. If you'd told me she was claiming me as the father of her unwanted baby I'd have set you straight, but you didn't trust me enough to tell me.' His voice hardened. 'You sure as hell trusted her, though, and you didn't even like the bloody woman.'

'She was very plausible.'

'OF COURSE SHE WAS PLAUSIBLE!' he roared. 'She's a *fucking* actress, and I use the word advisedly. When are you going to open your eyes, woman, and see people in the round, their dark sides, their bright sides, their strengths, their weaknesses? Dammit, you should have let your passions go, clawed my miserable eyes out, slashed my balls – *anything* – if you thought I'd two-timed you.' His voice softened. 'Don't you love me enough to hate me, Sarah?'

'You bastard, Blakeney,' she said, turning round and raking him from head to toe with glittering eyes. 'You will never know how unhappy I've been.'

'And you have the nerve to accuse me of being self-centred. What about my unhappiness?'

'Yours is easily cured,' she said.

'It damn well isn't.'

'It damn well is.'

'How?'

'A little massage to ease the stiffness and then a kiss to make it better.'

'Ah,' he said thoughtfully, 'well, it's certainly a start. But bear in mind the condition's chronic and needs repeated applications. I do not want a relapse.'

'It'll cost you, though.'

He eyed her through half-closed lids. 'I thought it sounded too good to be true.' He dug in his pocket. 'How much?'

She cuffed him lightly across the head. 'Information only. Why did Mathilda have a row with Jane Marriott on the morning she died? Why did Mathilda cry when you showed her your painting? And why did Mathilda leave me her money? I know they're all related, Jack, and I know Cooper knows the answer. I saw it in his eyes last night.'

'No massage if you don't get the answer, I suppose.'

'Not for you. I'll offer it to Cooper instead. One of you is bound to tell me in the end.'

'You'd kill the poor old chap. He goes into spasms if you touch his hand.' He drew her down on to his lap. 'It won't make it any easier if I tell you,' he warned. 'In fact it'll make it harder. I know you too well.' Whatever guilt she felt now, he thought, would be nothing compared with the agonies of wondering if she had unwittingly conned Mathilda into believing she was adopted. And what would it do to her relationship with Jane Marriott? Knowing Sarah, she would feel duty-bound to tell Jane the truth, and push the poor woman away with a surfeit of honesty. 'I made Mathilda a promise, Sarah. I really don't want to break it.'

'You broke it when you told Cooper,' she pointed out.

'I know, and I'm not happy about it, any more than I was happy about breaking my promise to Ruth.' He sighed. 'But I really did have no option. He and the Inspector were convinced the will was the motive for Mathilda's murder and I had to explain why she made it.'

Sarah stared at Mathilda's portrait. 'She made it because she was buying her rite of passage into immortality and she didn't trust Joanna or Ruth to deliver the goods for her. They would have squandered the money while she trusted me to build the "something worthwhile in her memory".' She sounded bitter, Jack thought. 'She knew me well enough to know I wouldn't spend a bequest on myself, particularly one to which I felt I had no right.'

'She wasn't that cynical, Sarah. She made no secret of her fondness for you.'

But Sarah was still absorbed in the portrait. 'You haven't explained,' she said suddenly, 'why you went to stay with Sally that weekend?' She turned to look at him. 'But that was a lie, wasn't it? You went somewhere else.' She put her small hands on his shoulders. 'Where, Jack?' She shook him when he didn't answer. 'It had something to do with Mathilda's weeping and, presumably, her will, too, though you didn't know it at the time.' He could almost hear her mind working. 'And whatever it was required your absence for that weekend without my knowing where you were going.' She searched his face. 'But for all she knew she would live for another twenty years, so why tell you something now that wouldn't have any real impact until after she was dead?'

'She didn't intend to tell me. I was a very reluctant recipient of her confession.' He sighed. Sooner or later, he realized, Sarah would find out that he had stayed with her father and why he had gone there. 'A year or so after Joanna was born, she had a second daughter by Paul Marriott, whom she put up for adoption. For all sorts of reasons she persuaded herself that you were her lost daughter, and she told me she'd changed her will in your favour.' He gave a wry smile. 'I was so shocked that I didn't know what to do. Say nothing and let you inherit under false pretences? Tell her the truth and shatter her illusions? I decided to put the decision on hold while I went to see if your father had something I could show her.' He shook his head ironically. 'But when I got back Mathilda was dead, the police were searching around for a murder motive, and I was the only person who knew Mathilda had left you a fortune. It was a nightmare. All I could see was that you and I would be arrested for conspiracy unless I kept my mouth shut. We couldn't prove I hadn't told you about the will, and you had no alibi.' He gave a low laugh. 'Then out of the blue you offered me my marching orders and I realized the best thing I could do was grab them with both hands and leave you thinking I was a miserable bastard. You were so hurt and angry that, for once in your life, you didn't try to hide your emotions, and Cooper received a hefty dose of transparent honesty. You showed him everything from shock about the will to complete bewilderment that I'd been able to paint Mathilda's portrait without your knowing.' He laughed again. 'You got us both off the hook without even realizing what you were doing.'

'Thanks very much,' she said tartly. 'And what would have happened if I'd been overjoyed to see the back of you?'

His face split into an evil grin. 'Well, just in case, I took out an insurance policy by moving in with Joanna. She's better-looking than you so you were bound to be jealous.'

'Bollocks.' But she didn't elaborate on whether it was the looks or the jealousy that was evoking her scorn. 'Did Mathilda tell Jane she'd had Paul's child? Was that what the row was about?'

He nodded. 'But she told her it was a boy.'

It was Sarah's turn to sigh. 'Then I doubt it's even true. She could have fantasized a baby just as easily as she fantasized her uncle's suicide' – she shrugged – 'or had an abortion or smothered the poor little thing at birth. I think it just suited her to resurrect the fantasy in order to create a thoroughly guilty and embarrassed legatee whose strings she could pull after she was dead.' She turned back to examine the portrait again. 'She used and abused us all, one way and another, and I'm not sure I want to be manipulated by her any more. What do I say to Jane and Paul if they ask me why she left me her money?'

'Nothing,' he said simply. 'Because it's not your secret, Sarah, it's mine. Duncan did her one good service by destroying her diaries. It leaves you free to build a memorial to her in any shape or form you like. In ten years, Fontwell will see her only as a generous benefactress because there'll be no evidence to prove otherwise.' He cupped her face in his hands. 'Don't abandon her now, sweetheart. Whatever her motives were and whatever she did, she entrusted you with her redemption.'

'She should have entrusted it to you, Jack. I think she probably loved you more than anyone in her whole life.' Dampness glistened along her lashes. 'Does she deserve to have people think well of her?'

He touched her tears with the tip of his finger. 'She deserves a little pity, Sarah. In the end that's all any of us deserve.'

This is the diary of Mathilda Beryl Cavendish. It is my story for people to read when I am dead. If anyone finds it they should take it to the police and make sure Father is hanged. He made me do something wicked today and when I said I was going to tell the vicar, he locked me in the cupboard with the scold's bridle on my head. I WAS BLEEDING. He cries a lot and says it is Mother's fault for dying. Well, I think it's Mother's fault, too.

It was my birthday yesterday. Father says I am old enough and that Mother would not mind. She knew about men's needs. I am not to tell ANYONE or he will use the bridle. OVER AND OVER AGAIN.

Mother should never have done such things, then Father would not do them to me. I am only ten years old.

I HATE HER. I HATE HER. I HATE HER . . .

THE
Dark Room

'And we forget because we must
And not because we will.'

Absence
MATTHEW ARNOLD (1822–88)

'The idea of the False Self was put forward by R.D.
Laing, adapting some theories of Jean-Paul Sartre. The
false self was an artificially created self-image designed to
concur with expectations, while the true self remained
hidden and protected.'

Killing for Company
BRIAN MASTERS

1994

MAY

S	M	T	W	T	F	S
1	2	3	4	5	6	7
8	9	10	11	12	13	14
15	16	17	18	19	20	21
22	23	24	25	26	27	28
29	30	31				

JUNE

S	M	T	W	T	F	S
			1	2	3	4
5	6	7	8	9	10	11
12	13	14	15	16	17	18
19	20	21	22	23	24	25
26	27	28	29	30		

Prologue

WITH HER SHARP little face set in lines of dissatisfaction, the twelve-year-old girl sat up and searched for her knickers among the forest leaves. It had finally begun to dawn on her that sex with Bobby Franklyn wasn't all it could be. She put on her shoes and kicked him hard. 'Get up, Bobby,' she snapped. 'It's your turn to find the bloody dog.'

He rolled over on to his back. 'In a minute,' he muttered sleepily.

'No, *now*. Mum'll skin me alive if Rex gets home before me again. She's not stupid, you know.' She stood up and dug the heel of her shoe into his naked thigh, twisting it back and forth in a childish desire to hurt. 'Get up.'

'OK, OK.' He rose sulkily to his feet, tugging at his trousers. 'But this is pissing me off, you know. It's hardly worth doing if we have to go looking for the dog every time.'

She moved away from him. 'It's not Rex that makes it hardly worth doing.' There were tears of angry humiliation in her eyes. 'I should have listened to Mum. She always says it takes a real man to do it properly.'

'Yeah, well,' he said, zipping his fly, 'it'd be a damn sight easier if I didn't have to pretend you were Julia Roberts. What would your sodding Mum know about it, anyway? It's years since anyone gave her a good shagging.' He had few feelings for these girls beyond the purely animal, but he grew to hate them very quickly when they gave him lip about his performance. The urge to smash their jeering little faces in was becoming irresistible.

The girl started to walk away. 'I *hate* you, Bobby. I really *hate* you, and I'm going to tell on you.' She tapped her watch. 'Three minutes. That's as long as you can keep it up. Three lousy minutes. Is that what you call a good shagging?' She gave a triumphant glance over her shoulder, saw something in his face that alerted her to the danger she was in, and took to her heels in sudden fear. 'REX!' she screamed. 'RE-EX! He'll *kill* you if you touch me,' she sobbed, her small wiry body darting through the trees.

But it was Bobby who was going to do the killing. His anger was out of control. He threw himself at her back and brought her crashing to the ground, breathing heavily as he tried to get astride her thrashing legs. 'Bitch!' he grunted. 'Bloody bitch!'

Fear lent her strength. She scrambled away from him, crying for her dog, slithering and sliding in a flurry of decomposing leaves into a broad ditch that scored the forest bed. She landed on her feet, only yards from the huge Alsatian, who stood, hackles up and growling. 'I'll set him on you, and he'll rip you to pieces. And I won't care, and I won't stop him.' She saw with satisfaction that Bobby had turned white to the gills. 'You're such a CREEP!' she yelled.

And then she saw that Rex was growling at her and not at Bobby, and that what had drained the colour from her boyfriend's face was not his fear of the dog but stunned horror at what the dog was guarding. She had a glimpse of something half-unearthed and repulsively human, before panic drove her up the slope again in sobbing, wide-eyed terror.

Chapter One

SHE CLUNG TO sleep tenaciously, wrapped in beguiling dreams. It was explained to her afterwards that they weren't dreams at all, only reality breaking through the days of confusion as she rose from deep unconsciousness to full awareness, but she found that difficult to accept. Reality was too depressing to give birth to such content-ment. Her awakening was painful. They propped her on pillows and she caught glimpses of herself from time to time in the dressing-table mirror, a waxen-faced effigy with shaven head and bandaged eye – *hardly recognizable* – and she had an instinctive desire to withdraw from it and leave it to play its part alone. *It wasn't her.* A huge bear of a man with close-cropped hair and close-cropped beard leant over her and told her she'd been in a car accident. But he didn't tell her where or when. You're a lucky young woman, he said. She remembered that. Forgot everything else. She had a sense of time passing, of people talking to her, but she preferred to drowse in sleep where dreams beguiled.

She was aware. She saw. She heard. And she felt safe with the pleasant female voices that smoothed and soothed and petted. She answered them in her head but never out loud, for she clung to the spurious protection of intellectual absence. 'Are you with us today?' the nurses asked, pressing their faces up to hers. *I've been with you all along.* 'Here's your mother to see you, dear.' *I don't have a mother. I have a stepmother.* 'Come on, love, your eyes are open. We know you can hear us, so when are you going to talk to us?' *When I'm ready . . . when I'm ready . . . when I want to remember . . .*

ROAD TRAFFIC ACCIDENT:
Reported 21.45 approx 13.6.94 PCs Gregg and Hardy
   on scene at 22.04
Location: Disused airfield, Stoney Bassett, Hants
One vehicle involved. Black Rover Cabriolet automatic
Reg No: JIN 1X – vehicle written off
Driver: Miss Jane Imogen Nicola Kingsley
Unconscious and in need of emergency treatment
Driving licence gives date of birth: 26.09.59 and
   registered address: 12 Glenavon Gdns, Richmond,
   Surrey

Property tycoon's daughter in mystery pile-up

It was reported late last night that Jane Kingsley, 34, the fashion photographer and only daughter of Adam Kingsley, 66, millionaire chairman of Franchise Holdings Ltd, was found unconscious following a mystery car crash on the disused airfield at Stoney Bassett, 15 miles south of Salisbury. Mr Andrew Wilson, 23, and his girlfriend, Miss Jenny Ragg, 19, happened upon the scene by chance at 9.45 p.m. and immediately summoned assistance for the unconscious woman.

'The car was a write-off,' said Mr Wilson. 'Miss Kingsley's very lucky to be alive. If she'd been in it when it hit the concrete pillar, she'd have been crushed to death in the wreck. I'm glad we were able to help.'

Police describe Miss Kingsley's escape as a miracle. The car, a black Rover Cabriolet automatic, had collided head-on with a solid concrete stanchion, which was once the corner support for a hangar. Police believe Miss Kingsley was thrown through the open door of her car shortly before the impact.

'That pillar is the only structure still standing on the airfield,' said PC Gavin Hardy, 'and we don't understand yet how she came to hit it. There was no one else in the car and no evidence of another vehicle being involved.'

Jane's stepmother, Mrs Betty Kingsley, 65, was shocked by the news, which comes only days after the surprise cancellation of her stepdaughter's wedding. At home this morning in Hellingdon Hall, where she and Mr Kingsley have lived for the last 15 years, she wept bitterly and said she would blame Miss Kingsley's fiancé, Leo Wallader, 35, if Miss Kingsley didn't recover. 'He's treated her so badly.'

Police admitted this morning that Miss Kingsley had been drinking prior to the accident. 'She had a high level of alcohol in her blood,' said a spokesman. Miss Kingsley is unconscious in Odstock Hospital, Salisbury.

Chapter Two

SHE AWOKE ONE night with fear sucking the breath from her lungs. She opened her eyes and strained them into the blackness. She was in a dark room – *her dark room?* – and she wasn't alone. Someone – *something?* – prowled the shadows beyond her vision.

WHAT?

Fear . . . fear . . . FEAR . . .

She sat bolt upright, sweat pouring down her back, screams issuing in a tumult of sound from her gaping mouth.

Light flooded the room. Comfort came in the shape of a woman's soft breasts, strong arms and sweet voice. 'There, there, Jane. It's all right. Come on, love, calm down. You had a nightmare.'

But she knew that was wrong. *Her terror was real. There was something in the dark room with her.* 'My name's Jinx,' she whispered. 'I'm a photographer, and this isn't my room.' She laid her shaven head against the starched white uniform and knew the bitterness of defeat. There would be no more sweet dreams. 'Where am I?' she asked. 'Who are you? Why am I here?'

'You're in the Nightingale Clinic in Salisbury,' said

the nurse, 'and I'm Sister Gordon. You were in a car accident, but you're safe now. Let's see if we can get you back to sleep again.'

Jinx allowed herself to be tucked back under the sheets by a firm pair of hands. 'You won't turn the light off, will you?' she begged. 'I can't see in the dark.'

Query prosecution of Miss J. Kingsley /driving with 150mg per 100ml

Date: 22 June, 1994
From: Sergeant Geoff Halliwell

Miss Kingsley was thrown from her vehicle before it impacted against a concrete stanchion in one corner of the airfield. She was unconscious when she was found at 21.45 on Monday, 13 June, by Mr Andrew Wilson and Miss Jenny Ragg. Miss Kingsley suffered severe concussion and bruising/laceration of her arms and face when she was thrown from the car. She remained unconscious for three days and was very confused when she finally came round. She has no recollection of the accident and claims not to know why she was at the airfield. Blood samples taken at 00.23 (14.6.94) show 150mg per 100ml. Two empty wine bottles were recovered from the floor of the car when it was examined the following day.

PCs Gregg and Hardy had one brief interview with Miss Kingsley shortly after she regained consciousness, but she was too confused to tell them anything other than that she appeared to believe it was Saturday, 4 June, (i.e. some 9 days before the incident on 13.6.94) and that she was on her way from London to Hampshire. Since the interview (5 days) she has remained dazed and uncommunicative and visits have been suspended on the advice of her doctors.

11

They have diagnosed post-traumatic amnesia, following concussion. Her parents report that she spent the week 4–10 June with them (though Miss Kingsley clearly has no memory of this) before returning to Richmond on the evening of Friday, 10 June, following a telephone call. They describe her as being in good spirits and looking forward to her forthcoming wedding on 2 July. She was expected at work on Monday, 13 June, but did not show. She runs her own photographic studio in Pimlico and her employees say they were concerned at her non-appearance. They left several messages on her answerphone on the 13th but received no reply.

Interviews by Richmond police with her neighbours in Glenavon Gdns, Colonel and Mrs Clancey, reveal that she made an attempt on her life on Sunday, 12 June. Col. Clancey, whose garage adjoins Miss Kingsley's, heard her car engine running with the door closed. When he went to investigate, he found her garage full of fumes and Miss Kingsley half-asleep at the wheel. He dragged her outside and revived her, but did not report the incident because Miss Kingsley asked him not to. He and his wife are deeply upset that she has 'tried to do it again'.

Both Col. and Mrs Clancey and Mr and Mrs Adam Kingsley made reference to a Mr Leo Wallader who was until recently Miss Kingsley's fiancé. It appears he left 12 Glenavon Gdns on Friday, 10 June, after telling Miss Kingsley he couldn't marry her because he had plans to marry her closest friend, Meg Harris, instead. Mr Wallader and Ms Harris are unavailable for interview at the moment. According to Sir Anthony Wallader (father) they are currently travelling in France but plan to return some time in July.

In view of a recent MOT certificate on Miss Kingsley's vehicle, which tends to rule out malfunction, and the fact that the chances of hitting the concrete stanchion by accident are virtually nil, it seems clear that she drove her car into it deliberately. Therefore, unless she recovers enough of her memory to give an explanation of the events leading up to the incident, Gregg and Hardy incline to the view that this was a second attempt at suicide after a drinking session in her car. Mr Adam Kingsley, her father, has offered to pay the costs of the emergency services, meanwhile Miss Kingsley has been transferred to the Nightingale Clinic where she is receiving treatment from Dr Alan Protheroe. Mr Kingsley's solicitor is pressing for a decision on whether or not we intend to proceed against Miss Kingsley. My view is to do nothing in view of her father's willingness to pick up the tab, her disturbed state of mind and the fact that she chose such a deserted location. Please advise.

Chapter Three

HOW DRAB REALITY was. Even the sun shining through her windows was less vivid than her dreams. Perhaps it had something to do with the bandage over her right eye, but she didn't think so. Consciousness itself was leaden and dull, and so restrictive that she felt only a terrible depression. The big bear of a doctor came in as she toyed with her breakfast, told her again that she'd been in an accident and said the police would like to talk to her. She shrugged. 'I'm not going anywhere.' She would have added that she despised policemen if he'd stayed to listen, but he went away again before she could put the thought into words.

She had no memory of the first police interview at Odstock Hospital and politely denied ever having met the two uniformed constables who came to her room. She explained that she could not remember the accident, indeed could remember nothing at all since leaving her house and her fiancé in London the previous morning. The policemen resembled each other, tall, stolid men with sandy hair and florid complexions, who showed their discomfort at her answers by turning their caps in unison between their fingers. She labelled them Tweedle-

15

dum and Tweedledee and chuckled silently because they were so much more amusing than her sore head, bandaged eye and hideously bruised arms. They asked her where she had been going, and she replied that she was on her way to stay with her parents at Hellingdon Hall. 'I have to help my stepmother with wedding preparations,' she explained. 'I'm getting married on the second of July.' She heard herself announce the fact with pleasure, while the voice of cynicism murmured in her brain. *Leo will run a mile before he hitches himself to a bald, one-eyed bride.*

They thanked her and left.

Two hours later, her stepmother dissolved into tears at her bedside, blurted out that the wedding was off, it was Wednesday, the twenty-second of June, Leo had left her for Meg twelve days previously and she had, to all intents and purposes, driven her car at a concrete pillar four days later in a deliberate attempt to kill herself.

Jinx stared at her ugly, scarred hands. 'Didn't I say goodbye to Leo yesterday?'

'You were unconscious for three days and very confused afterwards. You were in the hospital until Friday, and I went to see you, but you didn't know who I was. I've come here twice and you've looked at me, but you didn't want to talk to me. This is the first time you've recognized me. Daddy's that upset about it.' Her mouth wobbled rather pathetically. 'We were so afraid we'd lost you.'

'I've come to stay with you. That's why I'm here. You

and I are going to confirm the arrangements for the wedding.' *If she said it slowly and clearly enough, Betty must believe her. But no, Betty was a fool. Betty had always been a fool.* 'The week beginning the fourth of June. It's been in the diary for months . . .'

Mrs Kingsley's tears poured down her plump cheeks, scoring tiny pink rivulets in her over-powdered face. 'You've already been, my darling. You came down a fortnight and a half ago, spent the week with Daddy and me, did all the things you were supposed to do, and then went home to find Leo packing his bags. Don't you remember? He's gone to live with Meg. Oh, I could murder him, Jinx, I really could.' She wrung her hands. 'I always told you he wasn't a nice man, but you wouldn't listen. And your father was just as bad. "He's a Wallader, Elizabeth . . ."' She rambled on, her huge chest heaving tragically inside a woollen dress that was far too tight.

The idea that nearly three weeks had passed without her being able to recollect a single day was so far beyond Jinx's comprehension that she fixed her attention on what was real. Red carnations and white lilies in a vase on her bedside table. French windows looking out on to a flag-stoned terrace, with a carefully tended garden beyond. Television in the corner. Leather armchairs on either side of a coffee table – walnut, she decided, and a walnut dressing table. Bathroom to her left. Door to the corridor on her right. *Where had Adam put her this time?* Somewhere very expensive, she thought. The Nightingale Clinic, the nurse had told her. In Salisbury. *But why Salisbury when she lived in London?*

Betty's plaintive wailing broke into her thoughts. 'I

wish it hadn't upset you so much, my darling. You've no idea how badly Daddy's taken it all. He sees it as an insult to him, you know. He never thought anyone could make his little girl do something so' – she cast about for a word – 'silly.'

Little girl? What on earth was Betty talking about? She had never been Adam's little girl – his performing puppet perhaps – never his little girl. She felt very tired suddenly. 'I don't understand.'

'You got drunk and tried to kill yourself, my poor baby. Your car's been written off.' Mrs Kingsley fished a newspaper photograph out of her handbag and pressed it into her stepdaughter's lap. 'That's what it looked like afterwards. It's a mercy you survived, it really is.' She pointed to the date in the top left-hand corner of the clipping. 'The fourteenth of June, the day after the accident. And today's date' – she pushed forward another newspaper – 'there, you see, the twenty-second, a whole week later.'

Jinx examined the picture curiously. The writhing mass of twisted metal, backlit by police arc lights, had the fantastic quality of surrealist art. It was a stark silhouette and, in the distortions of the chassis and the oblique angle from which the photographer had taken his shot, it appeared to portray a gleaming metal gauntlet clasped about the raised sword of the pillar. It was a great picture, she thought, and wondered who had taken it.

'This isn't my car.'

Her stepmother took her hand and stroked it gently. 'Leo's not going to marry you, Jinx. Daddy and I have

18

THE DARK ROOM

had to send out notices to everyone saying the wedding's been cancelled. He wants to marry Meg instead.'

She watched a tear drip from the powdered chin on to her own upturned palm. 'Meg?' she echoed. 'You mean Meg *Harris?*' *Why would Leo want to marry Meg? Meg was a whore. You whore . . . you whore . . . YOU WHORE!* Some horror – *what?* – lurched through her mind, and she clamped a hand to her mouth as bile rose in her throat.

'She's been out for what she can get as long as you've known her, and now she's taken your husband. You always were too trusting, baby. I never liked her.'

Jinx dragged her wide-eyed stare back to her stepmother. That wasn't true. Betty had always adored Meg, largely because Meg was so uncritical in her affections. It made no difference to her if Betty Kingsley was drunk or sober. 'At least Meg thinks I've something sensible to say,' was her stepmother's aggressive refrain whenever she was deep in her cups and being ignored by everybody else. The irony was that Meg couldn't tolerate her own strait-laced mother for more than a couple of hours. 'You and I should swap,' she often said. 'At least Betty doesn't play the martyr all the time.'

'When was this decided?' Jinx managed at last. 'After the accident?'

'No, dear. Before. You went back to London a week ago last Friday after Leo phoned you during the afternoon. Horrible, horrible man. He called every day, pretending he still loved you, then dropped the bombshell on the Friday night. I don't suppose he was at all kind in the way he did it either.' She held the handkerchief to her eyes again. 'Then on the Sunday, Colonel Clancey from next door rescued you from your garage before you could gas yourself, but didn't have the sense to ring us and tell us you needed help.' She swallowed painfully. 'But you were so cool about it all on the Saturday when you phoned home to tell Daddy the wedding was off that it never occurred to us you were going to do something silly.'

Perhaps she'd been lying ... Jinx always lied ... lying was second nature to her ... Jinx looked down at the newspaper clipping again and noticed amidst the wreckage in the photograph the JIN of the personalized number plate that her father had given her for her twenty-first birthday present. J.I.N. Kingsley. *Jane Imogen Nicola – her mother's names – the most hated names in the world. JINXED!* She had to accept it was her car featured there. *You got drunk ... Colonel Clancey rescued you ...* 'There's no gas in my garage,' Jinx said, fixing on something she could understand. 'No one has gas in their garage.'

Mrs Kingsley sobbed loudly. 'You were running your car engine with the doors closed. If the Colonel hadn't heard it, you'd have died on the Sunday.' She plucked at the girl's hand again, her warm fat fingers seeking the very comfort she was trying to impart. 'You promised him you wouldn't do it again and now he wishes he'd reported it to somebody. Don't be angry with me, Jinx.' The tears rolled on relentlessly in rivers of grief, and Jinx wondered, basely, how genuine they were. Betty had always reserved her affections for her own two sons and never for the self-contained little girl who was the product of Adam's first wife. 'Someone had to tell you, and Dr Protheroe thought it should be me. Poor Daddy's been knocked sideways by it all. You've broken his heart. "Why did she do it, Elizabeth?" he keeps asking me.'

But Jinx had no answer to that. *For she knew Betty was lying. No one, least of all Leo, could drive her to kill herself.* Instead she dwelt on the incongruities of life. Why did she call her father Adam while his wife of twenty-seven years called him Daddy? For some reason it had never seemed significant before. She stared past her stepmother's head to her reflection in the dressing-table mirror and wondered suddenly why she felt so very little about so very much.

A young man came into her room uninvited, a tall gangling creature with shoulder-length ginger hair and spots. 'Hi,' he said, wandering aimlessly to the french windows and flicking the handle up and down, before abandoning it to throw himself into one of the armchairs in the bay. 'What are you on?'

'I don't know.'

'Heroin, crack, coke, MDMA? What?'

She stared at him blankly. 'Am I in a drug rehabilitation centre?'

He frowned at her. 'Don't you know?'

She shook her head.

'You're in the Nightingale Clinic where therapy costs four hundred quid a day and everyone leaves with their heads screwed on straight.'

Oh, but her anger was COLOSSAL. *It wheeled around her brain like a huge bird of prey, waiting to strike.* 'So who runs this place?' she asked calmly.

'Dr Protheroe.'

'Is he the man with the beard?'

'Yeah.' He stood up abruptly. 'Do you want to go for a walk? I need to keep moving or I go mad.'

'No thanks.'

'OK.' He paused by the door. 'I found a fox in a trap once. He was so scared he was trying to bite his leg off to free himself. He had eyes like yours.'

'Did you rescue him?'

'He wouldn't let me. He was more afraid of me than he was of the trap.'

'What happened to him?'

'I watched him die.'

Some time afterwards, Dr Protheroe returned.

'Do you remember talking to me before?' he asked her, pulling up one of the armchairs and sitting in it.

'Once. You told me I was lucky.'

'In fact we've talked a few times. You've been conscious for several days but somewhat unwilling to communicate.' He smiled encouragement. 'Do you remember talking to me yesterday, for example?'

How many yesterdays were there when she had functioned without any awareness of what she was doing? 'No, I don't. I'm sorry. Are you a psychiatrist?'

'No.'

'What are you then?'

'I'm a doctor.'

The waxen image in the mirror smiled politely. *He was lying.* 'Am I allowed to smoke?' He nodded and she plucked a cigarette from one of the packets Betty had brought in, lighting it with clumsy inefficiency because it was hard to focus with one eye. 'May I ask you something?'

'Of course.'

'Wouldn't it have been courteous to tell me before I spoke to the policemen that the accident happened several days ago?' He had a rather charming face, she thought, a little weary, but lived in and comfortable. Like his sports jacket, which had seen better days, and the cavalry twill trousers that drooped at the hem where his heel had caught it. He was the sort of man whom, in other circumstances, she might have chosen for a friend because he seemed careless of convention. But she was afraid of him and sought refuge in pomposity.

He balanced his fountain pen between his forefingers. 'In the circumstances, I thought it better to let you speak the truth as you understood it.'

'What circumstances?'

'You had almost twice the legal limit of alcohol in your blood when you crashed your car. The police are considering whether to charge you but I think they may let the matter drop after this morning. They tend to be somewhat sceptical of a doctor's diagnosis, less so of the patients themselves. I could see no harm in wringing a little sympathy out of PCs Gregg and Hardy.'

Her reflection smiled at him in the mirror. 'That was a kind thought.' *She had never been drunk in her life because she had watched Betty stagger about the house too often to want to emulate her.* 'Could you pass me the ashtray?' '*You got drunk and tried to kill yourself . . .*' 'Thank you.' She placed it on the bed in front of her. 'What exactly has happened to me, Dr Protheroe?'

He leaned forward, clamping his large hands between his knees. 'In a nutshell, you left a car travelling at approximately forty miles per hour, gave yourself the sort of knock-out blow that would have felled an ox, then continued under your own impetus, grazing your scalp, eye and arms as you did so. The first miracle is that you're here at all, the second miracle is that you didn't fracture anything in the process and the third miracle is that you'll be as good as new before you know it. Once your hair grows back over the flaps of skin that had to be stitched, no one will know you've had an accident. The price you paid for all that, however, was concussion, one symptom of which is post-traumatic amnesia. You have been conscious but deeply confused for the last five days, and that confusion may persist on and off for some time to come. Think of your brain as a computer. Any memory that is safely filed has a good chance of reinstatement, but memories that you were too confused to store properly may never return. So, for example, despite the fact you were conscious, you're unlikely to recollect your transfer here from Odstock Hospital, or indeed your first interview with the police.'

She looked past him towards the gardens that lay beyond her window. 'And is pre-traumatic amnesia equally normal?' she asked him. 'I have no memory of the accident or what led up to it.'

'Don't be confused by the term "post". That's simply referring to amnesia after trauma. But with regard to what you don't remember before the accident, that's usually referred to as retrograde amnesia. It's not uncommon and seems to depend on the severity of the head injury. We talk about loss of memory,' he went on, 'when we should talk about *temporary* loss. Bit by bit you'll remember events before the accident, though it may take a little while to understand how the pieces fit together because you may not remember them in chronological order. You may also, although it's less likely, remember things that never happened, simply because your memory will have stored plans of future events and you may recollect the plans as real. The trick is to avoid worrying about it. Your brain, like the rest of your body, has taken a knock and needs time to heal itself. That's all this amnesia is.'

'I understand. Does that mean I can go home quite soon?'

'To your parents?' he asked.

'No. To London.'

'Is there anyone there who can look after you, Jinx?'

She was about to say Leo before she remembered that, according to her stepmother, he wasn't there any more. *Do me a favour, said the intrusive voice of cynicism,* Leo *look after you? Ha! Ha! Ha!* Instead, she said nothing and continued to stare out of the window. She resented the way this man called her Jinx, as if he and she were well acquainted, when her entire knowledge of him resided in an avuncular chat about a condition that was rocking her to her very foundations. And she

25

resented his assumption that she was a willing participant in this conversation, when the only emotion she felt was a seething anger.

'Your father's keen for you to remain here where he feels you'll be properly looked after. However, it's entirely your choice and, if you think you'll be happier in London, then we can arrange to transfer you as long as you understand that you do need to be looked after. In the short term anyway.'

Her reflection examined him. 'Is Adam paying you?'

He nodded. 'This is a private clinic.'

'But not a hospital?'

'No. We specialize in addiction therapy,' he told her. 'But we do offer convalescent care as well.'

'I'm not addicted to anything.' '*You got drunk . . .*'

'No one's suggesting you are.'

She drew on her cigarette. 'Then why is my father paying four hundred pounds a day for me to be here?' she asked evenly. 'I could have convalescent care in a nursing home for a fraction of that.'

He studied her as she sat like a dignified, one-eyed Buddha upon her bed. 'How did you know it costs four hundred pounds a day?'

'My stepmother told me,' she lied. 'I know my father very well, Dr Protheroe, so, predictably, it was the first thing I asked her.'

'He did warn me you'd take nothing for granted.'

The reflection smiled at him. 'I certainly don't like being lied to,' she murmured. 'My stepmother told me I tried to commit suicide.' She watched him for a reaction, but there was none. 'I don't believe it,' she went on dispassionately, 'but I do believe that Adam would pay a psychiatrist to straighten me out if *he* believed it. So what sort of therapy is he buying for me?'

'No one's lying to you, Jinx. Your father was very concerned that you should be in an environment where you could recover at your own speed and in your own way. Certainly we have psychiatrists on the premises, and certainly we offer therapy to those who want it, but I am precisely what I said I was, a doctor pure and simple. My role is largely administrative, but I also take an interest in our convalescent patients. There is nothing sinister about your being here.'

Was that right? It didn't feel right. Even the woman in the mirror found that one hard to swallow. 'Did Adam tell you I am very hostile to psychiatrists and psychiatry?'

'Yes he did.'

'Why does he think I tried to kill myself?'

'Because that's the conclusion the police have reached after their investigation into your crash.'

'They're wrong,' she said tightly. 'I would never commit suicide.'

'OK,' Protheroe said easily. 'I'm not arguing with you.'

She closed her eye. 'Why would I suddenly want to kill myself when I've never wanted to before?' Anger roared in her ears.

He didn't say anything.

'Please,' she said harshly. 'I would like to know what's being said about me.'

'All right, if you accept that there's a good deal of physical evidence to support the police theory, then the rationale behind it seems to be that you were upset by your broken engagement. Your last real memory is saying goodbye to Leo when you left London two and a half weeks ago to stay with your parents at Hellingdon Hall. You probably don't remember doing it, but you've repeated that memory several times – to the police and to my colleagues at Odstock Hospital – and they have concluded, possibly wrongly, that it's important to you to preserve a happy memory over the memory of the night a week later when Leo told you he was leaving you for your friend, Meg Harris.'

She considered this in silence for a long time. 'Then they're saying my amnesia isn't entirely physical. There's an element of face-saving in it. Because I can't bear to think of Leo rejecting me, I've wiped his shabbiness out of my mind and then gone on to forget my own weakness in being unable to face life without him.'

Her choice of words was fascinating. 'In substance, that's what your father's been told.'

'All right' – he saw tears glistening on her lashes – 'if I was so distraught about Leo deserting me two weeks ago that I had to wipe the whole thing out of my memory, then why am I not equally distraught learning about it all over again?'

'I don't know. It's interesting, isn't it? How would *you* explain it?'

She looked away. 'I was having too many problems adjusting to the whole idea of marriage. The only thing I feel now is relief that I don't have to go through with it. I'd say I wasn't distraught the first time.'

He nodded. 'I'm prepared to accept that. So, let's talk about it. Was the wedding your idea or Leo's?'

'The wedding was my father's idea, but if you're asking me whose idea it was to get married, then that was Leo's. He sprang it on me out of the blue a couple of months ago, and I said yes because at the time I thought it was what I wanted.'

'But you changed your mind.'

'Yes.'

'Did you tell anyone?'

'I don't think so.' She felt his scepticism as strongly as if he'd reached out and touched her with it. *Oh God, what a bloody awful situation this was.* 'But I'm sure Leo must have known,' she said quickly. 'Does he say I was unhappy about him leaving?'

Dr Protheroe shook his head. 'I don't know.'

She looked at the telephone on her bedside table. 'I know Meg's home number. We could phone him and ask him.' *But did she want to do that? Would Leo ever admit that it was she who didn't want to marry him?*

'At the moment he's not available. The police have tried. He's out of the country for a few weeks.'

Not available. She already knew that. *How?* She licked her lips nervously. 'What about Meg?'

'She's with him. I'm told they've gone to France.' He watched her hands writhe in her lap and wondered what complicated emotions had driven the other two to betray her. 'You were telling me why you changed your mind,' he prompted her. 'What happened? Was it a sudden decision or something that developed gradually?'

She struggled to remember. 'I came to realize that the only reason he wanted to marry me was because I'm Adam Kingsley's daughter and Adam's not poor.' *But was that true? Wasn't it Russell who had wanted to marry her for her money?* She fell silent and thought about what she'd said. ' "He that diggeth a pit shall fall into it," ' she murmured.

'Why do you say that?'

'Because you're going to ask me if Meg Harris's family is wealthy.'

He didn't say anything.

'They're not. Her father earns a pittance as a rural vicar.' She ground her cigarette into the ashtray and fixed a smile to her lips. 'So presumably Leo has discovered true love at last.'

'Are you angry with Meg? Your stepmother tells me you've known her a long time.'

'We were at Oxford together.' She looked up. 'And no, I'm not, as a matter of fact, but that's only because I'm finding it all rather difficult to believe at the moment. I only have Betty's word for it.'

'Don't you believe her?'

'Not often, but that's not an indication of an Electra complex. She's the only mother I've ever known and I'm very fond of her.'

He raised an amused eyebrow. 'What did you read at Oxford? Classics?'

She nodded. 'And a complete waste of time they were, too, for someone who was only ever interested in photography. I can do crosswords and decipher the roots of words, but apart from that my education was wasted.'

'What is that?' He gave his beard a thoughtful scratch. 'A defence mechanism against anyone who thinks you're over-privileged?'

'Just habit,' she said dismissively. 'My father finds my qualifications rather more impressive than anyone else does.'

'I see.'

She doubted that very much. Adam's pride in his only daughter bordered on the obsessional, which was why there was so little love lost between any of the inhabitants of Hellingdon Hall. How much did this doctor know? she wondered. Had he met Adam? Did he understand the tyranny under which they lived?

'Look,' she said abruptly, 'why don't I make this easy for you? I mean, I know this routine off by heart. How old were you when your mother died? Two. How old were you when Adam remarried? Seven. Did your step-mother resent you? I've no idea, I was too young to notice. Did you resent her? I've no idea, I was too young to know what resentment was. Have you any brothers or sisters? Two half-brothers, Miles and Fergus. Do you resent them? No. Do *they* resent *you*? No. How old are they? Twenty-six and twenty-four. Are they married? No, they still live at home. Do you love your father? Yes. Does he love you? Yes.'

Protheroe's laugh, a great booming sound that would bring reluctant smiles whenever she heard it, bounced around the room. 'My God,' he said, 'what do you do for an encore? Bite psychiatrists' heads off? I came to find out if you were comfortable, Jinx. As far as possible, I would like your stay here to be a happy one.'

31

She lit another cigarette. *He knew nothing.* 'I'm sure it will be. Adam wouldn't pay four hundred pounds a day unless he'd checked you out very thoroughly.'

'You're the one who'll be calling the shots, not your father.'

She flicked him a sideways glance. 'I wouldn't count on that if I were you,' she said quietly. 'Adam hasn't made his millions by sitting idly by while other people express themselves. He's a very manipulative man.'

Protheroe shrugged. 'He certainly seems to have your best interests at heart.'

She blew a smoke ring into the air. 'Show me his heart, Dr Protheroe, and I might believe you.'

Chapter Four

THE YOUNG MAN was in no hurry to get up. He lay on the bed, his limbs sprawled in satiated contentment upon the rumpled bedclothes, watching the woman button her blouse in front of the mirror. Her reflected eyes stared warily back at him. Despite his airs and graces, and his liberal use of 'please' and 'thank you', she knew exactly what she was dealing with here, and it terrified her. She'd seen every type there was to see – or thought she had – but this one was in a class of his own. This one was mad.

'You'll have to go now,' she said, trying to hide her nervousness. 'I've another customer due in a minute.'

'So? Tell him to go away. I'll pay you double.'

'I can't do that, love. He's a regular.'

'You're lying,' he said lazily.

'No, love, honestly.' She forced a smile to her sore lips. 'Look, I've really enjoyed this. It's years since I've come with a client. You wouldn't believe that, would you? A pro like me and it takes a man like you to give her something to remember.' She offered her raddled face to the mirror and applied eyeliner to her lids, watching him carefully while she did it. 'But it's a tough old world and I need my income just like any other girl.

33

If I tell him to bugger off, he won't come again' – she gave a wretched giggle – 'in every sense of the word. Know what I mean? So do us a favour, love, and leave me to my regular. He's not a patch on you, and that's God's honest truth, but he pays me weekly and he pays me handsome. OK?'

'Did I really make you come?'

'Sure you did, love.'

'You fat slag,' he said, surging off the bed with terrifying speed and hooking his arm about her neck. 'It'd take a bloody bulldozer to make an impression on you.' He levered his arm closed. 'I hate slags who lie to me. Tell me you're a lying whore.'

But she'd been on the game long enough to learn that you never told psychopaths the truth. She reached for his penis instead and set about rearousing him, knowing that if she came out of this alive, she'd be lucky. So far, his only real pleasure had been to beat her about the face while he reached his climax, and she knew he was going to do it again.

As he twisted his hand in her hair and yanked her backwards on to the bed, she had time to reflect on the awful irony of it all. She was so used to servicing old and inadequate men that when the voice on the phone had translated itself into an Adonis at her door, she couldn't believe her luck. God, but she was a stupid bitch!

Nightingale Clinic, Salisbury – 8.20 p.m.

The phone rang beside Jinx's bed, setting her nerves jangling with its insistent summons to a world outside that she wasn't sure she was ready to face. She was tempted to leave it until it occurred to her that it might be an internal call. *If she didn't answer it,* said the voice of paranoia inside her head, *then a little black mark would go down in a book somewhere and her mental equilibrium would be called into question.* She lifted the receiver and held it against her ear on the pillow. 'Jinx Kingsley,' she said guardedly.

'Thank God,' said a man's voice. 'I've had the devil's own job trying to find you. It's Josh Hennessey. I finally got through to your stepmother, who gave me this number. She says you're OK to talk but that you've lost bits of your memory.'

'Josh Hennessey?' she echoed in surprise. 'As in Harris and Hennessey? You sound so close. Where are you?'

He gave a rumble of laughter at the other end. 'The very same, except that it's all Hennessey at the moment and remarkably little Harris. She's buggered off to France and left me nursing the office. I'm in a call-box in Piccadilly.' He paused briefly and she heard the sound of traffic in the background. 'I'm damn glad the memory loss doesn't extend to your mates. There's a few of us eating our hearts out over this.' He paused again. 'We were really sorry to hear about your accident, Jinx, but your stepma says you're progressing well.'

She smiled weakly. Typical Josh, she thought. Always

35

we and never I. 'I'm not sure I'd agree with her. I feel like something the dog threw up. I suppose you know about Leo and Meg?'

He didn't say anything.

'It's all right, you don't have to spare my feelings. Matter of fact, I'm quite glad Leo found a good home.' *Was she telling the truth?* 'They're welcome to each other.'

'Well, if it's of any consolation to you, I can't see it lasting. You know Meg and her brief enthusiasms. She'll have some French guy in tow by the time she comes back, and poor old Leo will be on the scrap heap along with all the others. She's a two-timing bitch, Jinx. I've always said so.'

Liar, she thought. You adore her. 'She hasn't changed just because Leo prefers her to me,' she said. 'I don't bear any grudges, so why should you?'

He cleared his throat. 'How are you coping after the – well, you know?'

'You mean my suicide attempt? I don't remember it, so I'm fine.'

There was a short silence.

'Good, well, listen, the reason I phoned is that I've been trying to get hold of Meg for the last eight days and I'm getting zilch response from her answerphone. She swore on her sainted granny's grave that she'd call in for her messages every day but, if she's doing it, then she sure as hell isn't replying to any of them, and I'm going slowly ape-shit with all the work that's piling up. I've tried her brother and a few of her other friends to see if they know where she and Leo went, but they're as much in the dark as I am. You're my last hope, Jinx. Have you any ideas at all how I can contact her? Believe me, I wouldn't ask if I wasn't desperate. I've got a sodding contract here that needs her signature and I've got to fax it through post-haste.' He gave an angry grunt. 'I tell you, the way I feel at the moment, I could wring her neck. And Leo's, too.'

Jinx jabbed her fingers against the vein above her eye that was pounding and rushing like a swollen river. A strangely murky image had floated into her mind as he spoke, a meaningless, dark negative that relayed nothing to her at all except an intense frustration. She sought to hold on to it but, like a drowning man, it slipped away and left her cheated. 'Well, if it's France,' she said slowly, 'then they've probably gone to Leo's house in Brittany, but I'm afraid I can't remember the phone number, Josh, and I doubt he's got a fax either.'

'That doesn't matter. Do you know the address?'

She dug deep into her memory. 'I think so. It's Les Hirondelles, rue St Jacques, Trinité-sur-mer.'

'You're a brick, Jinx. Remind me to take you out to dinner one day.'

She gave a shaky laugh. 'It's a date,' she told him. 'Assuming I can remember to remind you.' She paused. 'Did you really want Meg's address?'

He avoided an answer. 'I could come and see you at the weekend,' he suggested. 'Or are you hibernating?'

'Sort of,' she said, unsure if she wanted to see anyone. 'I'm vegetating.'

'Is that a yes or a no?'

The vein above her eye throbbed mercilessly. 'It's a yes. I'd love to see you,' she lied.

For fifteen minutes paranoia held Jinx's hand. Ten times she had reached it out towards the telephone on the bedside table and ten times she had withdrawn it again. Her nerve had abandoned her along with her memory. She was afraid of eavesdroppers listening in. And what could she say that wouldn't sound foolish? At eight-thirty, as credits rolled on the television in the corner, she muted the sound, seized the telephone with sudden decision and dialled a number.

'Hello?' said a brisk voice that belied its eighty-three years.

'Colonel Clancey?'

'Yes.'

'It's Jinx Kingsley. I wondered – are you busy or can I talk to you for a moment?'

'My dear girl, of course you can talk. How are you?'

'Fine. You?'

'Worried,' he barked. 'Damned worried, if I'm honest. I feel responsible, Jinx. Daphne, too. We should have done more. Hold on a minute while I close the door. Bloody television's going full blast. Usual old rubbish, of course, but Daphne likes it.' She heard the receiver clatter on to their hall table, followed by the slam of a door and the distant yapping of Goebbels, their mild-mannered Yorkshire terrier. 'You still there?' he said a moment or two later.

38

She felt tears of affection pricking at the back of her eyelids. He made himself out to be so much more ferocious than his funny little dog and, in her mind, he was always Colonel Goebbels and the dog was Clancey. 'Yes. It's nice to hear you.' She paused a moment, unsure what to say. 'How's Goebbels?' She wondered why they'd called their dog that. *Was it something she knew and had forgotten, or was it something she had simply accepted as she had accepted all their other eccentricities?*

'Flea-ridden as usual. Daphne gave him a bath and he's looking like a mohair sweater. Absurd creature.'

She wondered if he was referring to the dog or to his wife. 'I'm worried about my plants,' she said, seeking neutral territory and remembering the Clanceys had her spare key. 'Would it be an awful bore for you or Mrs C to water them for me?'

'We go in every day, Jinx. Assumed it's what you'd want. Plants are fine, bit of cleaning up done. It's all ready for you as soon as you're well enough to come home.'

'That's very kind. Thank you.'

'Least we could do in the circumstances.'

There was an awkward pause while she sought for something more to say. 'Let me give you my phone number. I'm at the Nightingale Clinic in Salisbury.' She squinted at the dial. 'I don't know the code but the number's two-two-one-four-two-zero. Just in case anything unexpected crops up.'

'Got it,' he told her. 'And you say you're fine. Glad to hear it. Looking after you all right then, are they?'

'Yes.'

'Well, you sound cheerful enough.'

Another awkward pause. They spoke together.

'Best be going then—'

'Colonel—'

'Yes?'

'Please don't go, not yet.' She rushed her words. 'My stepmother said you rescued me from my garage. Is that true? She said I had the car engine running and you found me before I could – well – finish myself off.'

His voice grew gruff with emotion. 'Don't you remember?'

'No.' She swallowed painfully. 'I'm really sorry, but I don't. I don't remember anything – at least – not since I left to stay with my parents two weeks ago. Is Leo really not there any more? I don't know who else to ask – and I'm so, so sorry if it's embarrassing but I do need to be sure. They keep telling me ... things ... that don't make sense. They say I've got amnesia – that I got drunk and tried to kill myself. But – I just – oh, God ...' She clamped her hand over her mouth because tears were flooding her throat. *Hang up, you stupid woman.*

'There, there,' said his comforting elderly voice, 'no need for embarrassment. Good lord, I've had six-foot-tall men weep on my shoulder before now. Clear answers, eh, that's what you want. Your stepmother's a nice enough woman, I expect, but, if she's anything like Daphne, she'll have managed to confuse the message somehow. Not that I know all that much,' he warned. 'Never been one to poke my nose in where it's not wanted, as you know.'

'Quite. Best sort of neighbour always.' Odd, she

thought, how she picked up his shorthand when she spoke to him. Perhaps everyone did.

'Leo's been gone over a week, Jinx. Left the night you came home from Hampshire. Hope it's not an impertinence, but I'd say you're well shot of him. Never did like the cut of his jib much. You were far too good for him. Funny thing is, I spoke to you on the Saturday and you didn't turn a hair. "The bastard's jilted me, Colonel," you said, "and the only bugger is he beat me to it."' He chortled at the memory. 'And then, on the Sunday, there you were in your garage with the engine running. Fact is, it was Goebbels who spotted something was up. Parked himself in front of your garage door and barked his little head off.' He paused for a moment and she could picture him, fluffing his moustache and squaring his shoulders. 'Upshot was, pulled you out PDQ and got some fresh air into you. Should have done more, though. Called a doctor, got a friend round. Rather upset about that, to tell you the truth.'

'I wish you wouldn't be. Did I say anything? I mean, explain or something?' Her fingers tightened involuntarily around the handset. 'I just don't believe – well, you know. Not over Leo . . .'

'Matter of fact, I agree with you. Personally, thought it was an accident, garage doors slammed after you started the engine, that sort of thing. Not as though you had a hose pipe attached to the exhaust, is it? Truth is, you weren't feeling too clever afterwards, not surprising in the circumstances. But you can't have been in there very long. Back to normal in no time, cracking jokes and telling Daphne not to fuss. Even made a phone call to

41

some friends you were off to see. The old girl was all for a doctor but you wouldn't have it. "I'm perfectly all right, Mrs C," you said, "and if I don't get going I'll be late." Worst thing was, thought you were going to squash poor Goebbels, the way you hugged and petted him.' He gave a gravelly laugh. 'Hah! You said dogs were the only things worth having in your bed from then on.'

She dabbed at her cheeks. 'Then why does Betty think I was trying to kill myself?' Her voice was remarkably steady.

'On the principle that one swallow doesn't make a summer but two probably do, dear girl. Dare say it's our fault. Bobbies turned up a week ago, telling us you'd driven your car at a wall in what looked like a deliberate attempt at suicide, and did we know of any other attempts? So Daphne piped up about the garage and how you promised you'd be more careful in future, then told them what a rat Leo had been and, hey presto, conclusions being drawn all over the place. Silly old woman,' he said fondly. 'Practically ga-ga, though, let's face it, and awfully worried about you. Matter of fact, I did try to stem the breach by pointing out you weren't the type, but I might have been banging my head against the proverbial wall for all the good it did.' He cleared his throat. 'Must say, Jinx, talking to you now, more inclined than ever to think it's all nonsense. Never struck me as the type to throw in the towel.'

She couldn't speak for a moment. 'Thank you,' she managed. 'I don't think I am either. Will you give Mrs C and Goebbels a hug from me?'

'Certainly will. Coming home soon, I trust?'

'I'd like to but I'm bandaged to the hilt at the moment. You should see me, Colonel. I look like Boris Karloff in *The Mummy*.'

'Hah!' he harrumphed again. 'Kept your sense of humour, I see. Visitors keeping you chirpy, dare say.'

'No,' she said honestly. 'It's talking to you that's cheered me up. Thank you for getting me out of my car. I'll ring you the minute I'm demobbed and give you my ETA.'

'We'll be waiting for you, dear girl. Meanwhile chin up and best foot forward, eh?'

'Will do. Goodbye, Colonel.'

Jinx cut the line but held the receiver to her chest for several minutes as if, by doing so, she could maintain the link with him, for the comfort that the conversation had given her was all too ephemeral. Depression swept in behind it like an engulfing tide when it occurred to her that, of all the people she knew, the only one she had felt able to telephone was a man whose first name she was too shy to use. *Had she felt as lonely as this a week ago? Could she have done it? God help her if she had . . .*

'Your brother's come to see you, Miss Kingsley,' said a black nurse, pushing wide the half-open door. 'I've told him ten minutes. Visitors out by nine o'clock, that's the rule, but as it's your brother and he's come all the way from Fordingbridge, well – just so long as you don't make too much noise.' She noticed Jinx's pallor suddenly and clicked her tongue anxiously. 'Are you all right, my lovely? You look as if you've seen a ghost.'

'I'm fine.'

43

'OK,' she said cheerfully. 'Not too much noise, then, or my job will be on the line.'

Miles, exuding his usual boyish charm, took the nurse's hand in his and smiled into her face. 'I really appreciate this, Amy. Thank you.'

Her dark skin blushed. 'That's all right. I'd best be getting back to the desk.' She withdrew her fingers from his with clear reluctance and closed the door behind her.

'God,' he said, flopping into the armchair, 'she really thought I fancied her.' He eyed Jinx. 'Ma tells me you're back in the land of the living, so I thought I'd come and check for myself. You look bloody awful, but I expect you know that.'

She reached for her cigarettes. 'I'd hate to disappoint you, Miles.'

'She says you can't remember anything since the fourth. Is that true?'

She didn't answer.

'Which means it is.' He giggled suddenly. 'So you don't remember the week you spent at the Hall?'

She eyed him coldly as she felt for her lighter.

'You borrowed two hundred quid off me that week, Jinxy, and I want it back.'

'Bog off, Miles.'

He grinned. 'You sound pretty on the ball to me. So what's with this amnesia crap? You trying to get yourself off the hook with Dad?'

'What hook?'

'Whatever it is you've done that you shouldn't have done.'

'I don't know what you're talking about.'

44

He shrugged indifferently. 'Then why did you try to top yourself? Dad's been worse than usual this last week. You might have thought of that before you started playing silly buggers.'

She ignored him and lit a cigarette.

'Are you going to talk to me or have I wasted my time coming here?'

'I doubt you've wasted your time,' she said evenly, 'as I imagine seeing me was the last thing on your list.' She was watching his face, saw the flash of intense amusement in his eyes, and knew she was right. 'You must be mad,' she continued. 'Adam wasn't bluffing when he said you'd be out on your ear the next time. Why on earth do you do it?'

'You think you know everything, don't you?'

'When it comes to you, Miles, I do.'

He grinned. 'OK then, it gives me a buzz. Come on, Jinxy, a couple of hands of poker in a hotel bedroom, it's hardly major gambling. And who's going to tell Dad anyway? You certainly won't and neither will I.' He giggled again. 'I scored' – he tapped his jacket pocket – 'so no lectures, all right? I'm not planning to run up any more debts. The old bastard's made it clear enough he won't bail me out again.'

He was more hyped up than usual, she thought, and wondered how much he'd won. She changed the subject. 'How's Fergus?'

'About as pissed off as I am. A couple of days ago, Dad reduced him to tears. You know what my guess is? The worm'll turn when Dad least expects it and then it'll be your precious Adam who gets the thrashing.' He was fidgeting with the lapels of his jacket, brushing them, smoothing them. 'Why did you do it? He hates you now, hates us, hates everyone. Poor old Ma most of all.'

Jinx lay back and stared at the ceiling. 'You know as well as I do what the solution is,' she said.

'Oh, God, not more bloody lectures. Anyone would think you were forty-four not thirty-four.' He raised his voice to a falsetto, mimicking her. 'You're old enough to stand on your own two feet, Miles. You can't expect your mother to give you Porsches all your life. It's time to move out, find your own place, start a family.'

'I don't understand why you don't want to.'

'Because Dad refuses to ante-up, that's why. You know the score. If we want to live in reasonable comfort we stay at home where he can keep his eye on us. If we want out, we do it the hard way and graft for ourselves.'

'Then welcome to the human race,' she said scathingly. 'What the hell do you think the rest of us do?'

His voice rose again, but this time in anger. 'You damn well never had to graft. You stepped straight into Russell's money without lifting a finger. Jesus, you're so bloody patronizing. "Welcome to the human race, Miles." You piss me off, Jinx, you really do.'

She was dog-tired. Why didn't the nurse come back to rescue her? She stubbed out her cigarette and turned to look at him. 'Surely anything has to be better than letting Adam treat you like dirt. When did he last beat you?' There was something wrong with him, she thought. He was like an addict waiting for a fix, twitched, unable to sit still, fidgeting, fingering, eyes overbright. *Oh, God, not drugs . . . not drugs . . .* But as she fell asleep,

46

she was thinking that, yes, of course it was drugs, because self-indulgence was the one thing Miles was good at. If nothing else, his father had taught him that.

Odstock Hospital, Salisbury – 9.00 p.m.

The Casualty doctor was barely out of medical school and nothing in his training had prepared him for this. He smiled tentatively at the woman in the cubicle. It was worse than the Elephant Man, he was thinking, as he took his place beside the nurse whose hand the wretched woman was clutching. Her face was so swollen that she looked barely recognizable as a human being. She had given her name as Mrs Hale. 'You've been in the wars,' he said vacuously.

'My husband – belt . . .' she croaked through lips that could hardly move.

He looked at the bruising on her throat where the marks of someone's fingers were clearly visible. 'Is it just your face that's been hurt?'

She shook her head and, with a pathetic gesture of apology, raised her skirt and revealed knickers saturated with blood. 'He' – tears squeezed between her swollen lids – 'cut me.'

Three hours later, a sympathetic policewoman tried to persuade her to make a statement before she was transferred to the operating theatre for surgery to her rectum. 'Look, Mrs Hale, we know your husband didn't do this.

We've checked and he's currently serving eighteen months in Winchester for handling stolen property. We also know you're on the game, so the chances are that the animal responsible was one of your customers. Now, we're not interested in how you make your money. We're only interested in stopping this bastard doing the same thing to some other poor girl. Will you help us?'

She shook her head.

'But he could kill next time. Do you want that on your conscience? All we need is a description.'

A faint laugh croaked in her throat. 'Do me a favour, love.'

'You've got two fractured cheekbones, severe bruising of the throat and larynx, a dislocated wrist, and internal bleeding from having a hairbrush rammed up your back passage,' said the policewoman brutally. 'You're lucky to be alive. The next woman he attacks may not be so lucky.'

'Too right. It'll be yours bloody truly if I open my mouth. He swore he'd come back.' She closed her eyes. 'The hospital shouldn't have called you. I never gave them leave, and I'm not pressing no charges.'

'Will you think about it at least?'

'No point. You'll never pin it on him and I'm not running scared for the rest of my life.'

'Why won't we pin it on him?'

She gave another croak of laughter. 'Because it'll be my word against his, love, and I'm a fat old slag and he's little Lord Fauntleroy.'

48

Thursday, 23 June, Nightingale Clinic, Salisbury – 3.30 a.m.

As he did every night at about this time, the security guard emerged from the front door of the Nightingale Clinic and strolled towards a bench on the moonlit lawn. It was a little treat he gave himself halfway through his shift, a quiet smoke away from the nagging lectures of the nursing staff. He wiped the seat with a large handkerchief then lowered himself with a sigh of contentment. As he fished his cigarettes from his jacket pocket he had the distinct impression that someone was behind him. Startled, he glanced round, then lumbered awkwardly to his feet and went to investigate the trees bordering the driveway. There was no one there, but he couldn't rid himself of a sense that he was being watched.

He was a phlegmatic man, and put the experience down to the cheese he'd eaten at supper. As his wife always said: Too much cheese isn't good for anyone. But he didn't linger over his smoke that night.

Jane Kingsley was floating in dark water, eyes open, straining for the sunlight that dappled the surface above her. She wanted to swim, but the desire was all in her mind and she was too weary to make it happen. A terrible hand was upon her, pulling her down to the weeds below – insistent, persuasive, compelling – she opened her mouth to let death in . . .

She burst out of sleep in a threshing frenzy, sweat

pouring down her back. *She was drowning ... Oh, Jesus, sweet Jesus, somebody help her!* The moon beamed through a gap in her curtains, lighting a path through the room. *Where was she? She didn't know this place.* She stared in terror from one dark shadow to the other until she saw the lilies beside her, gleaming white and pure against the black of the carnations. Memory returned. *Jane was her mother ... she was Jinx ... Jane was her mother ... she was Jinx ...*

With shaking fingers, she switched on her bedside light and looked on things she recognized. The door to the bathroom, television in the corner, mirror against the wall, armchair, flowers – but it was a long time before the thudding of her heart slowed. She slid slowly down between the sheets again, as rigid and as wide-eyed as a painted wooden doll, and tried to stem the fear that grew inside her. But it was a vain attempt because she couldn't put a name to what she was afraid of.

Two miles away, in another hospital bed, her terror had its haunting echo in the battered face of a prostitute who had supped with the devil.

A case of 'caveat investor'?

If anyone needed a reminder that investments can go down as well as up, they received it yesterday when Franchise Holdings (FH), the property development group, suffered a temporary drop in the value of its shares, following a rumour that Adam Kingsley, 66, founder and chairman, was about to resign. FH has been a rare success story amidst the spectacular property group failures of the nineties.

The rumour was apparently generated by a remark made by Kingsley in a BBC interview on Tuesday night. Referring to his daughter Jane's recent car accident, he said: 'There are always times in one's life when one asks, has it all been worth it?' But Kingsley, nicknamed the Great White when he snapped up Charford Gordon Associates eight years ago, has now sunk his jaws into the BBC.

It is his policy to make private tape-recordings of interviews, and he has issued a typescript of the one on Tuesday. This includes a follow-up sentence which was edited out of the broadcast. 'This is not one of those times,' he went on to say. The matter is under investigation by the Broadcasting Complaints Commission.

However, the extraordinary episode has highlighted City fears about the long-term future of Franchise Holdings. As one analyst said: 'Adam Kingsley is a master juggler. No one knows how many balls there are in the air at any one time. Frankly, it's difficult to imagine who will catch them safely when he finally leaves the stage.'

Daily Telegraph – 23 June

Chapter Five

'LITTLE LORD FAUNTLEROY,' echoed a sceptical
sergeant the next morning. 'You think that's relevant, do
you?'

'Yes,' said WPC Blake stoutly. 'I reckon he's a lot
younger than she is and probably quite well spoken,
otherwise why would she have chosen that analogy? She
obviously thinks he'd make a far better impression in
court than she would.'

'It's not much to go on.'

'I know. So I thought – if I went through the files, I
might find someone else. The chances are high he's done
it before. If I could get two of them to support each
other' – she shrugged – 'they might find the confidence
to talk to us and give us a description. You should see
her, Guv.'

He nodded. He'd read the report. 'You'll be doing it
in your own time, Blake,' he warned, 'because there's no
way I'm going to explain to them upstairs why you're
shirking your other responsibilities to chase a prosecution
that doesn't exist.' He winked at her. 'Still, have a go and
see how you get on. I've been nicking Flossie's old man
for years. She never bears grudges. She's a good old soul.'

53

Nightingale Clinic, Salisbury – 10.30 a.m.

Jinx had been abandoned in an armchair by the window. 'Time you were up and about, dear,' coaxed a terrifying nurse with the hair of Margaret Thatcher and the nose of Joseph Stalin. 'You need to get some of those muscles working again.'

Jinx smiled falsely and promised to have a little walk later, then lapsed into quiet contemplation of the garden when the bossy woman had gone. Her ginger-haired visitor of yesterday – he of the fox obsession – made signs to her from a bench on the lawn, but she moved her head to stare in a different direction and he abandoned his half-hearted attempts at communication. She could see a wing of the building, projecting out at the far end of the terrace, and she guessed she was in a Georgian mansion, built for some wealthy family of two centuries earlier. What had become of them? she wondered. Had they, like the family who had built and inhabited Hellingdon Hall, simply faded away?

'Hello, Jinx,' said a quiet voice from the open doorway into the corridor. 'Can you stand a visitor, or should I make polite excuses and leave?'

Her shock was so extreme that her heart surged into frantic activity.

Fear ... fear ... FEAR! But what was there to be afraid of?

She recognized the voice and turned away from the window. 'Oh, God, Simon,' she said angrily, 'you gave me such a fright. Why on earth would I want you to leave?' She held a hand to her chest. 'I can't breathe. I think I'm having a panic attack. Don't you ever dare do that to me again.'

'I'd better call someone.'

'No!' She waved him inside and took deep breaths. 'I'm OK.' She leaned back, drawing the air into her lungs. 'I don't know why, but I'm really on edge at the moment. I keep thinking – no, forget it – it doesn't matter. How are you?'

Simon Harris stood half-in and half-out of the doorway, looking irresolutely down the corridor. 'Let me call someone, Jinx. I really think I should. You don't look at all well.' He had the fine-boned, rather ascetic face of the clergyman he was, and he was as different from his sister as chalk was from cheese. Meg would have told her: 'Sod it, sweetheart, be it on your own head. Don't blame me if you die.' Simon could only peer through his glasses with well-meant but impotent concern.

'Sit down, Simon,' she said wearily. *She wanted to scream.* 'I'm OK. Why wouldn't I want to see you?'

Reluctantly, he abandoned the doorway and made his way to the other chair. 'Because it struck me as I was walking along the corridor that I had deliberately shut my eyes to the potential embarrassment my visit might cause.'

Why do you always have to be so pompous, Simon? 'To you or to me?'

'To you,' he said. 'I'm more angry than embarrassed. I still can't believe my sister would steal her best friend's fiancé.'

'Well, I'm neither embarrassed nor angry, just very

lethargic and rather sore.' She eyed his dog-collar and cassock with disfavour. 'Mind you,' she grumbled, 'I don't go a bundle on the uniform. Couldn't you have worn jeans and a T-shirt like everyone else? They all think I'm suicidal as it is, so having a vicar visit me will destroy any credibility I've managed to salvage.'

He smiled, reassured by her feeble attempts at humour. 'No choice, I'm afraid. I'm doing an official stint in the Cathedral in approximately two hours so, if I wanted to visit you as well, I wasn't going to have time to change.'

'How did you know I was here?'

'Josh Hennessey told me,' he said, squeezing his knees with bony fingers. 'I managed to get through to Betty once during the week but she hung up as soon as I said who it was. The name Harris is *nomen non gratis* at Hellingdon Hall at the moment,' he finished ruefully, 'and I can't say I'm altogether surprised.'

'Then how did Josh persuade her? She knows quite well he's Meg's partner not mine.'

Simon pulled a face. 'He got the same treatment I did until he realized deception was the better part of valour. He lied, said he was Dean Jarrett and needed to talk to you urgently on business.'

Dean was Jinx's number two at the photographic studio and he played his homosexuality for all it was worth because it amused him. Jinx massaged her aching head. 'She must have been drunk as a skunk to fall for that. Josh doesn't sound anything like Dean.'

'*In vino* absolutely, but don't be too harsh on her. Josh says she sounded genuinely upset for you.'

Sudden irritation seethed in Jinx's soul. *Why shouldn't she be harsh on the silly woman? By what right did anyone suggest that she temper her scorn?* 'You will never speak about your stepmother like that again,' her father had said, when, at the age of ten, she had pointed out with genuine anxiety that Betty was so stupid she thought the moon orbited the sun and that Vietnam shared a border with America, which was why they were fighting a war there. 'She does nothing but paint her fingernails and go shopping,' she had told him severely.

But all she said now was: 'She was very sweet to me yesterday,' before plucking a cigarette from the packet on the arm of her chair and lighting it. 'So has Josh managed to track down Meg? I gather he's pretty annoyed with her for leaving him in the lurch.'

Simon shook his head. 'Not as far as I know, but I haven't spoken to him since last night.'

She studied his face through the smoke from her cigarette and saw he'd been lying when he said he wasn't embarrassed. He looked deeply uncomfortable – *almost as drained and wretched as she felt herself* – with his thin fingers smoothing and pleating the black serge of his cassock and his eyes looking anywhere but at her. Her irritation mounted. 'I couldn't give a toss about Leo,' she said harshly. 'If you want the truth, he was beginning to get on my nerves.' A tear glittered along her lashes. 'The only thing that's upsetting me is the embarrassment of everyone thinking I tried to kill myself over him.' She gave a hollow laugh. 'I don't envy Meg at all. Believe me, Leo will be absolutely insufferable if he thinks I couldn't bear to lose him.' *Oh, stupid, stupid woman! No one will believe the grapes weren't sour.*

Simon sighed. 'Dad and Mum don't know which way to turn. They felt badly enough before your accident, but afterwards – well . . .' He lapsed into silence. 'I don't know what to say to you, Jinx, except that I've never felt angrier with Meg than I do at the moment. God knows, she's no angel, but none of us thought she'd do something like this.'

'Like what?' She took quick nervous drags on her cigarette. 'All I've been told is that Leo said he wanted to marry her and that they then left for France. But does Meg want to marry *him*? If so, it'll be a first. She's never wanted to marry anyone else.'

'You really don't remember anything about it?'

'No,' she said grimly. 'I've made a prize arse of myself by telling everyone I'd be prancing up the aisle on July the second.' Tears threatened again. 'Look, it's not important. Tell me what's been happening in the world in the last week. Is everyone still killing each other in Bosnia? Is the Queen still on the throne?'

He ignored this and addressed himself to what she really wanted to know. 'Meg phoned Mum and Dad a week ago last Saturday and sprang on them that she and your fiancé had been having an affair for some time, that he wanted to marry her instead and that they were off to France until the fuss died down because they thought it would be more tactful.' He pulled a rueful face over the word 'tactful'. 'Rather predictably, she and Dad had a flaming row about it. He accused *her* of being shameless, and she accused *him* of being holier than thou as per usual. Result, they hung up on each other. Mum threw an almighty wobbly, screamed at poor old Dad that it was his fault because he would insist on preaching at her, then phoned me. My view was that if Leo was prepared to jilt *you* so unceremoniously, then he was probably a scoundrel and would abandon Meg just as unceremoniously, and Mum got on the blower to her and said she wasn't to go anywhere until they'd met him. Meg told her she was worrying unnecessarily and that she'd bring Leo down the minute they got back from France. And that's all we knew until we read about your attempted suicide.'

She flinched at the word 'suicide' but let it go. 'He wasn't a scoundrel, Simon. You're not old enough to use words like "scoundrel". He was a fucking scumbag.'

'I'm a vicar, Jinx.'

'So? I'm a millionaire's daughter who went to public school.' She rubbed her hands over her shaven scalp. 'Look, I don't care. They can shag each other to death as far as I'm concerned.' Tears flooded her throat. 'It's no big deal. I'd hate to lose Meg because of it. She's my friend, Simon.'

He felt ashamed in the face of such generosity, and as usual rushed to condemn his sister. Would Meg, he wondered, in the same circumstances, be as unjudgemental of the woman who had stolen her fiancé? 'Does it help if I say I don't believe you tried to kill yourself? Is that what's worrying you? What people are thinking?'

Jinx fished the newspaper clipping that Betty had given her from her pocket and stared at it. 'Except that it doesn't look like an accident, does it?' she said slowly, offering him the picture. 'They say it's a miracle I escaped.'

'Miracles do happen, you know.'

Not in her philosophy they didn't. 'Apparently I was drunk when it happened.'

'Does that matter?'

'Yes,' she said flatly, 'it does. To me, anyway.'

'Because of Betty's problems?'

'Partly.' She paused. 'No, it's more to do with my own self-esteem. I refuse to believe that I'd need to get drunk in order to kill myself.' She smiled faintly. 'You see, I'm a very proud woman, which makes me doubt I'd have given anyone, least of all Leo, the satisfaction of knowing I cared *that* much.'

'I believe you,' he said.

Tears flooded her eyes again, and she jabbed at them with the palm of her hand. 'Look, don't take any notice, OK? I'm tired, I'm pissed off and I wish to hell I was back in London.' She took deep breaths to bring her sorrow under control. 'Will you do me a favour? Tell Meg I'm happy for her, and that I don't bear any grudges. And tell your parents that I'm not about to end a damn good friendship because a bastard like Leo swaps horses mid-stream. Truly, Simon, I don't care.'

He nodded. 'I'll tell them,' he promised. 'You're very generous, Jinx.'

She listened to the screams of frustration that echoed off the walls of her mind. 'I wouldn't say it if it wasn't true,' she said carefully, glancing sideways at him. 'There's no generosity involved.'

He leaned forward, staring at the floor. 'You think you know a person and then something like this happens. She wasn't even remotely apologetic, just said these are the facts, stick them in your pipe and smoke them. It's caused the most unbelievable bitterness between the folks. Mum's blaming Dad for trying to force religion down Meg's throat for years, and he's blaming her for her frigidity.' He sighed. 'He's more upset than Mum is but I think that's because he's always been so fond of you. He can't understand why Meg would want to hurt you. I can't either for that matter.'

'I'm sorry,' she said inadequately, 'but I don't expect she meant to hurt anybody. You know Meg. *Carpe diem* and leave tomorrow to look after itself. She's always been the same.' She rubbed the side of her head where it was hurting. *Why did memories of Russell keep flooding her mind?* 'Your father must be very angry if he's saying things like that to your mother.' . . . *Russell and Meg . . . Meg and Leo . . .*

'They're just words,' he said, 'he doesn't mean anything by them, any more than poor old Mum means anything by striking out at religion.'

'But in a way they're both right, you know.' She felt very tired suddenly. 'Meg's never been comfortable in the role of vicar's daughter, and she's far too raunchy for your mother.' Her eyelid drooped in exhaustion as memories whirled effortlessly across her mind. 'It's your fault as much as anyone's.'

Russell dying . . . she had an affair with Russell, too, you know . . . you got drunk and tried to kill yourself . . .

His voice came across vast stretches of space. 'Why?'

'She couldn't compete with a saint, Simon, so she became a sinner . . .'

She lurched out of sleep with a sickening jolt and opened her eyes on Alan Protheroe. He was bending over her, and Jinx's immediate thought was that he must be Simon until relieved recognition told her he wasn't. She looked around rather vaguely. 'I was smoking a cigarette.'

He pointed to the butt in the ashtray. 'I put it out.'

'I had a visitor.'

'I know. Father Simon Harris. I gave him his marching orders. I was afraid he'd upset you.'

'He wouldn't dare,' she said with a twisted smile. 'He's an Anglo-Catholic priest.'

'And Meg's brother,' he said, taking the other chair. 'Do you like him, Jinx?'

She could feel the inevitable sweat drenching her back again. 'He's a sanctimonious prig like his father and mother, and he made his sister into a whore.' Her face turned towards this huge amiable man who was doing his best to care for her, and she felt an incredible urge to reach out and touch him. She wanted to curl in his lap, feel his arms about her, shelter, childlike, inside the protection of his strong embrace. Instead she withdrew to the other corner of her chair and wrapped her thin arms about her chest. 'I'm not sure why I said that.'

'Because you're angrier with her than you think you are.'

'Simon came to apologize.'

'For his sister's behaviour?'

'I suppose so.' She fell silent.

'Is he older or younger than she is?'

'He's a year younger.'

'Does Meg look like him?'

'Not really. She's very beautiful.'

'Do you like her, Jinx?'

'Yes.'

He nodded. 'You were dreaming just now, and they didn't look very happy dreams. Do you want to tell me about them?'

She didn't – *couldn't?* – answer. Even after ten years, the wound was still raw and she shrank instinctively from anything that might re-open it. Yet, there was an extraordinary need within her to convince someone – *anyone* – of how little Leo had really mattered to her. Do you like her? *Yes. Yes.* YES. *But why did it hurt so much to say it?*

'I was dreaming about a man I knew,' she said abruptly. 'He was beaten to death ten years ago, and I was the one who found him. He had an art gallery in Chelsea. The police think he disturbed some burglars because the place had been ransacked and several of the paintings stolen. We were supposed to be having dinner but he never turned up, so I went to the gallery to find him. There was blood everywhere. I found him in the store room at the back, but I didn't recognize him . . .' Her voice faltered and she held her fingers to her lips. 'He was still alive, but he couldn't say anything because his jaw had been smashed. So he tried to use his eyes to talk to me, but – I – couldn't understand what he

63

wanted.' She lived the terrible scene again in her mind, her shock, her revulsion, her inadequacy in the face of the bludgeoned bleeding mask that had once been Russell. 'And there was nothing I could do except call an ambulance, and watch him . . . I watched him die.' She fell silent. *Had Russell been in a trap, too?*

Protheroe didn't press her to go on. He was content to let her tell the story at her own speed, realizing perhaps that because it was so rarely told it was bound to lack fluency.

'I had nightmares about it for ages, so Adam packed me off to a hypnotherapist. But that just made everything worse. The man was a quack. He encouraged me to confront what disturbed me most about the incident and then put it into perspective, but all he actually succeeded in doing was exacerbating every feeling of guilt I had.' She fell silent again, and this time her face took on an introspective look as if she were revisiting rooms long closed.

Protheroe was more interested in what she hadn't said than what she had. He knew the details of the story already, both from what her father had told him over the phone and from reading the notes made by her psychiatrist. Why hadn't she mentioned, for example, that she and Russell Landy had been married? Or that the murder of her husband had caused her to miscarry at thirteen weeks? Why did she talk about being referred to a hypnotherapist when she had, in fact, been admitted to hospital in a state of near starvation, weighing under six stone, and with very severe depression? He ran his thumb down his jawline and pondered this last thought. She had referred to the therapist as 'he', yet the notes he had in his office were written by a woman.

He waited for another minute or two, then prompted her gently when it became clear she was lost in self-absorption. 'Did the psychiatrist at Queen Mary's Hospital help you at all, Jinx?'

'You mean the second one, Stephanie Fellowes?'

'Yes.'

She seemed to find her position uncomfortable and unlocked her arms to reach for the inevitable cigarette. 'When am I going to be allowed outside?' she demanded suddenly, flicking the lighter to the tip and eyeing him through the smoke.

'The sooner the better. We could go now if you like. I've a pretty good arm for leaning on and we can find ourselves a bench away from the madding crowd.'

She smiled faintly. 'No thank you. I'll wait till I can manage it alone.' She nodded towards her bathroom door. 'I've been to the loo a couple of times and had to crawl most of the way, so I'll practise in private for a bit. I'm not particularly keen to have you laugh at me.'

'Why would I want to do that?'

She shrugged. 'Not in front of me, perhaps, but I'm sure you could work it up into a good story for the golf club.' She mimicked his lower register. 'I say, chaps, have I told you the one about my pet hysteric who drove her car at a concrete pillar, survived by a miracle, then fell flat on her face when she tried to stand up?'

'Do you always ascribe such base motives to the people who care for you?'

'Stephanie Fellowes certainly thought so.' *But then I*

65

didn't trust her. She blew smoke rings into the air. 'You see, I'm not a willing guinea pig. I'd rather live with all my fears, depressions and obsessions than have clumsy people in hobnailed boots trampling about in my head.' She smiled without hostility. 'I presume she or my father has told you that I became so depressed I was starving myself?' She looked at him enquiringly and he nodded. 'Which one, as a matter of interest? Stephanie or Adam?'

He showed no hesitation about answering. 'Both. Stephanie sent me a copy of the notes she took at the time. Your father told me when you first came here.'

'Have you met him?'

'No. We spoke on the telephone.'

She nodded. 'That's how he does business. Technology, particularly the impersonal fax, was invented for Adam. He knows how intimidating it is to deal with somebody you never meet. I'd keep it that way if I were you.'

'Why?'

'No particular reason.'

'He seemed pleasant enough, and he's very concerned for you.'

She smiled to herself, and he wondered if she realized how provocative that smile was. As a character she was fascinating. She was determined to wean him away from her father, but in the most subtle of fashions – through innuendo rather than fact, through sympathy rather than honesty. And he knew he wasn't immune. There was something infinitely appealing about the combination of incisive intellect and physical weakness. Particularly for him, although she couldn't know that.

'So concerned that he hasn't been near me,' she pointed out.

'Then phone him and find out why not,' he suggested.

She shook her head. 'Adam and I never ask each other personal questions, Dr Protheroe.'

'Yet you always call him Adam. I assumed that meant you saw each other as equals.'

But that was clearly something she didn't want to discuss. 'We were talking about my alleged depression,' she said abruptly. '*Alleged* being the operative word.'

He abandoned the subject. 'You wanted to know whether it was Stephanie or Adam who told me you became so depressed that you were starving yourself,' he reminded her, 'and I said they both had. Shall we go on from there?'

'It happened the other way round. The depression developed because I wasn't eating, so when they took me into hospital and started feeding me I began to feel better.'

He thought it more likely that her improvement was due to anti-depressants, but he had no intention of arguing about it. 'Do you know why you weren't eating?'

'Yes.'

He waited for a moment. 'Are you going to tell me?'

'Maybe. If you tell me what Stephanie put in her notes.'

She would be satisfied with nothing less than the truth, he thought, although whether she would believe that what he told her *was* the truth was another matter altogether. 'The notes are in my office,' he said, 'so I can't quote her verbatim but I can give you the gist of

what she wrote. You were admitted with severe reactive
depression, following the murder of your husband and
the loss of your baby. Your symptoms were extreme – in
particular, loss of appetite and persistent insomnia. It was
clear to Dr Fellowes that you were very disturbed and
that your malnutrition was due not so much to a loss of
appetite as a refusal to eat, and she diagnosed you a
potential suicide. Your treatment consisted of a combination of drug and psychotherapy and, while she admits
that you were extremely hostile to the psychotherapy,
your condition began to improve quite markedly after
three to four weeks. As far as I recall you were discharged
fit after six weeks and, although you have consistently
refused to have your progress monitored at out-patient
attendances, Dr Fellowes regards you as one of her
successes.' He paused briefly. 'Or she did until I
requested your notes.'

Jinx frowned. 'I hadn't realized she thought I was
doing it deliberately.' She took a thoughtful puff of her
cigarette. 'It explains why you're all assuming suicide
now. *Pardus maculas non deponit*. The leopard doesn't
change his spots,' she translated idly, her eyes drifting
towards the window where a man was wandering across
the lawn. Fair hair, green sweater, brown cords. For a
fraction of a second she thought it was Leo, and her
heart lurched violently.

'If you weren't starving yourself for a reason, then
why were you doing it?'

She waited a moment before she answered. 'Because
the quack I saw first used hypnosis to unlock my nightmares, and turned me into a psychotic wreck in the

process.' She shrugged and stubbed out her cigarette. 'But a nightmare isn't so bad. Most of the time you don't remember details, and the relief of waking always outweighs the fears.' She used her fingertips to sweep the arm of the chair, something she would do again and again during the next few minutes. 'I wasn't getting very much sleep admittedly, but, other than that, I was coping pretty well in view of everything that had happened. At which point, enter my father.' She shook her head. 'You have to understand that he'd always loathed Russell, partly because we got married without telling him, but mostly because Russell was twenty years older than I was and had been one of my dons at Oxford. If my father referred to him at all it was always as "the twisted paedophile".' She dwelt on that for a moment. 'Anyway, about a week after the miscarriage, Adam had an attack of conscience – at least I assume that's what it was – and paid this extremely expensive therapist to counsel me through my double bereavement.' She took out another cigarette. 'If I hadn't been so shocked by it all, I might have realized he was a charlatan, but you don't think straight in situations like that. Do you know what flooding is?' She flung the question at him as she bent to the lighter.

Protheroe was taken by surprise. 'In psychiatric terms? Well, yes, it's a drastic method of dealing with fear. You force a patient to confront the thing he's afraid of, often without warning and usually with no means of escape. It's risky and not always successful, but when it works it's spectacular. It has its place in the treatment of phobias.'

'Do you use it here?'

'No.'

'Do you use hypnosis?'

He shook his head.

'Then what *do* you use, Dr Protheroe?'

'Nothing.' He smiled at her expression of disbelief. 'No tricks, anyway, and no short-cuts. We simply concentrate on restoring self-esteem, and most of the people who come here are halfway to winning the battle before they even walk through the door because they've already made up their minds they want to be free of whatever disturbs them.'

'One of your patients came in yesterday. He wanted to know whether I was on heroin or cocaine, so I presume he's a drug addict himself. He didn't strike me as being halfway to winning anything.'

'What did he look like?'

'Tall, skinny, long ginger hair.'

He looked pleased. 'Matthew Cornell. Well, that's an improvement. At least he's beginning to notice a world beyond smack, poppers and MDMA.'

'Is that why he came to my room uninvited, because you encourage your patients to notice each other?'

'I rely entirely on human nature,' he told her without a hint of guile. 'In the end, curiosity usually wins out. You're our newest resident, therefore you're of interest. I'm quite pleased Matthew found the courage to defy the restrictions.'

'What restrictions?'

'There's a huge notice outside your door saying Do Not Disturb.'

'I didn't know.'

'You should have looked.'

'If it's there, why did Simon Harris ignore it?'

He shrugged. 'Are you sure he did?'

'He came in.'

'Uninvited?'

'No, he asked me if he should make polite excuses and leave, but I could hardly say I didn't want to see him when he'd come all this way.'

'Why not?'

Because no one ever taught me how to say piss off. 'I won't be psychoanalysed, Dr Protheroe. I won't do group therapy. I won't join in. I won't play games.'

'Is anyone saying you must?'

'I know how it works.'

'I wonder if you do.'

'You were asking me about the hypnotherapist,' she said, ignoring this. 'He treated me for a phobia that I didn't have. All I had were feelings of guilt about letting Russell down. There was so much blood, and his face was completely raw and pulpy.' She pressed a hand to her bandaged eye, which had begun to ache. 'He wanted me to kiss him,' she said flatly, mechanically even, 'but I couldn't. And then I lost the baby, and there was more blood.' She paused. 'All I needed was a little time.'

He let her sit in silence for several minutes, relentlessly sweeping the chair arm and drawing on her cigarette. 'What did the therapist do?' he prompted finally.

She looked at him in surprise as if she thought he would have guessed. 'He put a raw steak on my face while I was in a trance and then woke me. It smelt of blood and dead meat, and I thought it was Russell come

71

back from the grave for his kiss. It was an awfully long time before I could eat something without being sick.'

'Good God!' He was genuinely shocked. 'Who was this man?'

She stared at him blankly for a moment. 'I don't remember his name.'

'Where was his office?'

But she couldn't remember that either. 'Somewhere in London,' she told him.

'OK, it doesn't matter.'

'You don't believe me, do you?'

'I've no reason not to.'

'How could I remember something so awful if it never happened?'

He didn't say anything.

'You think I've invented it,' she accused him. 'But why would I want to invent something that never happened?'

Perhaps because nobody's ever been charged with Russell's murder, he thought, for her guilt seemed rooted in a far more powerful anguish than her very natural reluctance to kiss the mutilated face of her dying husband.

Bodies found in Ardingly Woods

The remains of a man and a woman were discovered yesterday in Ardingly Woods in Hampshire. Cause of death has yet to be revealed but police are not ruling out foul play. 'We are asking for help in trying to establish their identities,' said a spokesman. 'Death is believed to have taken place ten to twelve days ago, but no one matching their descriptions has been reported missing.'

The man is described as 6'1", medium build, aged between 30–40, with straight blond hair. He was wearing fawn cotton slacks, a checked shirt and dark green ribbed jumper. The woman was 5'4", slim build, aged between 30–40, with short dark hair. She was wearing blue denim jeans and a navy blue T-shirt.

Police admit to being puzzled as to how the bodies came there. 'There are no reports of a car being abandoned in the area,' said the spokesman, 'and the woods are not on a bus route. We believe someone must have driven them there, and we are asking anyone who gave a lift to a couple answering these descriptions to come forward. It is possible that they hitched a ride from outside the county.'

Police have not ruled out a suicide pact, although they are concerned that neither body carries any form of identification. 'This is unusual,' said the spokesman. 'We would have expected to find a wallet or a handbag.' The woods continue to be searched for further evidence.

Mrs Mary Hughes, 73, who discovered the bodies with Pepita, her Jack Russell, is recovering at home, following a slight heart attack. She ran over a mile to the nearest telephone to alert police, and blames the attack on shock and over-exertion. 'I should have walked,' she said. 'I'm an old woman now and those bodies weren't going anywhere. There's no fool like an old fool.'

Wessex Post – 24 June

Chapter Six

THE REVEREND CHARLES Harris watched from his study window as the white Rolls-Royce – registration number KIN6 – pulled in through the vicarage gates and parked by the front door. The number plate said it all. By the strategic placing of a yellow-headed screw to break the six and turn it into a G, the word KING screamed out from both ends of the ostentatious vehicle. Not for the first time, he wondered how Jinx had remained so apparently unaffected by her vulgar family and, not for the first time either, he berated himself for being uncharitable.

His dismay grew when the chauffeur opened the back door and assisted Betty Kingsley out. Adam he might have coped with, but Betty was a different matter altogether, particularly when, as was clearly the case now, she had been hitting the bottle hard during the journey. With a sigh, he opened the door of his study and called to his wife. 'Caroline, we have a visitor. Betty Kingsley has just driven in.'

His wife appeared in the kitchen doorway, a look of apprehension on her thin face. 'I don't want to see her,' she said. 'I can't stand it, Charles. It was bad enough

75

talking to her on the phone. She'll just start screaming at me again.'

'I don't think we have a choice.'

'Of course we do,' she snapped, frayed nerves getting the better of her. 'There's no law that says we have to answer the door. We can hardly be blamed because Leo preferred our daughter.' The doorbell rang. 'Just ignore it,' she hissed at him. 'I won't be harangued by a common fishwife in my own home.'

But he was an old-fashioned man with old-fashioned manners. He shook his head in gentle admonishment and crossed the hall to open the front door. 'Hello, Betty,' he said kindly. She stank of gin and her lipstick was smeared at one corner. There was something infinitely sad, he thought, about the worn face covered in make-up and the plump body squeezed into a girlish dress. Growing old would always be something to fear because drink had addled whatever wisdom she had, and now there was nothing left to make her interesting.

She pushed past him belligerently to confront Caroline, bumping into a walnut card table as she did so and slopping water from the vase of flowers on to the polished surface. 'It's your slut of a daughter drove Jinx to kill herself, not me or her Daddy,' she grunted, jabbing her finger at the other woman. 'She'd never need to kill herself because of us. You've got me that riled, Mrs High-and-Bloody-Mighty. You think you can say what you like about me and mine, when the truth is it's your precious Meg deserves the blame.'

Caroline Harris glanced helplessly towards her husband. This is your fault, said her expression, so do something about it, but he gave an unhappy shrug and left her to fight the battle alone. 'I really can't see the point of discussing this,' she said in a voice that was pitched too high. 'Far too much dirt has been peddled already.'

'Yes, well, Meg always said you were a tight-arsed bitch who'd rather see everything swept under the carpet than have it aired in public.' She clutched at the table with a meaty fist and affected a classy accent. '"Oh, I say, I can't see the point of discussing this."' She took a deep breath. 'But you fucking well discuss it when it suits you. "Now, now, Betty, don't go blaming Meg for your own failings. Jinx needs a mother to talk to."' She slammed the table and set the vase rocking alarmingly. 'Well, she's got a bloody mother. Me.'

'But probably not the one she wants,' said Caroline icily. 'You were very offensive over the telephone, Betty. You called us murderers before you even knew if Jinx was dead. What did you expect me to do? Agree with you? Charles and I barely had time to digest the news that Leo had left Jinx for Meg before you were on the phone screaming abuse. It's been a terrible shock for all of us.'

'Where's the apology? The apology's what I'm after, missus, or perhaps you're too grand for that?' Tears welled in the heavily mascara'd eyes. 'You know what's being said? The wedding's off because Sir Anthony Wallader wouldn't have his son marry a Kingsley. And why? Because we're too bloody common.' She gulped her tears. 'But there's only one rotten apple in the barrel and I've a mind to make that public. Your Meg, who couldn't keep her knickers on if she was paid.'

Caroline Harris's lips thinned to an unattractive horse-shoe but, before she could say anything, the vicar intervened. He placed a hand on Betty Kingsley's arm and drew her round to face him. 'Is this true, Betty?' He smiled apologetically. 'We know so little, you see. Only what Meg told us over the phone and, in all conscience, that wasn't very much. Just that Leo preferred her to Jinx and they were leaving for a holiday in France.'

The woman's thick lips worked aggressively. 'Why should me and the boys take the blame for your daughter's screwing?' she slurred drunkenly. 'Adam says we've ruined Jinx's chances with our goings-on, but I can't see it myself. Leo's a right bastard – like his father – but we did nothing to upset the apple cart.' She took a deep breath. 'Not our fault,' she resumed after a moment. 'Meg's jealous, always has been. Sets out to bed anyone Jinx likes. Common is as common does. Bedded Russell, in case you didn't know.'

Charles turned a shocked face towards his wife but Caroline looked away and refused to meet his eyes. 'I didn't know,' he said. 'I'm sorry.'

Friday, 24 June, HO Forensic Lab,
Hampshire – 11.30 a.m.

Dr Robert Clarke, the Home Office pathologist, took pity on the three policemen and herded them out of the laboratory and into his office, peeling off his gloves and his mask as he did so. 'Not a pretty sight,' he agreed, opening his window to allow in the sweeter-smelling air of the busy road outside, 'but sealing both caboodles in body bags and spraying with Nuvanstykil is the only way to kill the maggots off and make what's left presentable enough to examine. Coffee?' he suggested.

The three men swallowed convulsively, and wondered how he could consider taking anything into his mouth after what they had glimpsed going on inside the bags. The stench of putrefaction still lined their throats, as it had done since yesterday when they had stood beside the ditch and stared in gagging repulsion at the pulsating white mass that had seethed turbulently amongst the pieces of clothing and decomposing body parts that lay there. They shook their heads vigorously.

'No thanks, Bob,' said Detective Superintendent Frank Cheever, wiping his lips with a handkerchief. He was older than the other two policemen, a fine-boned, rather studious-looking man with grey hair and pale blue eyes which he fixed unnervingly on the person he was talking to. He was something of a dandy and caused much amusement amongst his officers over what they considered his fetish for silk. He wore silk bow-ties, tucked matching silk handkerchiefs into his jacket breast pocket, and kept his expensive silk socks at permanent stretch by the use of sock suspenders. Rumour had it that he also wore silk underwear. 'But don't mind us,' he murmured, looking unhappily at the empty coffee mug on the desk, 'you go ahead.'

'I will.' The doctor stuck his head round the door,

waved the mug in the air and asked his secretary to bring
him a black coffee. 'It takes the taste away,' he said
insensitively as he settled himself behind his desk and
waved them towards some empty chairs. 'Now, let's see
what we've got.' He consulted some typed notes in front
of him. 'I won't bore you with the life history of
Calliphora erythrocephalus, which is the bluebottle we're
dealing with here, but in essence the time lapse in warm
weather between the laying of the eggs and the pupal
stage is some ten to eleven days. We found no pupa
cases, and the larvae at the time of the discovery were on
the way to being mature third-stage maggots, which
would suggest the eggs were laid some eight or nine days
before.' He tapped a calendar. 'Yesterday was the twenty-
third, so we're looking at the fourteenth or fifteenth as
likely dates for laying. Add another day or two for
Calliphora erythrocephalus to find the bodies and my
estimate for when death occurred would be the twelfth,
thirteenth or fourteenth, with Monday the thirteenth as
my first choice.' He beamed at his secretary who came in
with his coffee and a plate of chocolate biscuits. 'Sure
you won't join me, gentlemen?'

They became visibly paler. It occurred to Detective
Inspector Maddocks, a tall heavy-set man in his mid-
forties with a permanent scowl on his face, that Bob
Clarke was doing this on purpose, a kind of trial of
strength between the hard man of pathology and the
hard men of CID. He'd always suspected the little
bugger – Clarke was a miserable five feet six inches – of
having a chip on his shoulder. Now he was sure. There

was a horrible similarity between this cocky little scientist and the maths teacher who was the cause of his pending third divorce. *God, how he loathed arrogant little men!*

'All right, Jenny. Thank you.' Clarke dunked a biscuit into the cup and munched on it with pleasure. 'Their hands and feet were tied, as you know, so we've got two people quite unable to defend themselves. Cause of death was ferocious bludgeoning with a blunt instrument.' He pushed some X-ray photographs in Superintendent Cheever's direction with the flick of a finger. 'We took these before we put them in the bags. You see how both skulls have been fractured in several places. This one, in particular, shows a clear rounded depression in the woman's parietal bone. A long-handled club or sledge-hammer would be my bet, certainly something very substantial. Notice the break in the man's right clavicle which would imply a missed shot' – he made a downward swing with his hand – 'possibly glanced off the side of his head and landed with the force of a two-ton truck on the poor wretch's shoulder.' He shook his head. 'What we're looking at is two people on their knees with hands tied behind their backs and a maniac using them for target practice with something very heavy indeed. I think we can assume the first blows were delivered from behind because those are downward sweeps, and the blows that shattered the jaws and cheekbones were done after the bodies had toppled on to their sides. Imagine our maniac holding his hammer like a golf club and driving at both faces when they were on the ground. That should give you a good idea of what probably occurred.'

81

Cheever dabbed at his lips again as he examined the photographs. 'Where do you think it happened? In the ditch itself or at the top of the bank?'

'My guess would be on the bank. The sort of blows I envisage would have been harder to achieve in a confined space. No, I see him killing them at the top of the slope, then pushing the bodies over. It's not very pleasant to dwell on' – he dunked another biscuit in his coffee – 'but the golf-swing blows may have been his method of driving the corpses into a roll. Not that it would have worked very well,' he said thoughtfully. 'He'd have had to lay them out straight and give them a heave around their middles to really get them going.'

'What about those slide marks we found five yards down?'

Bob Clarke sorted out another photograph. 'Very interesting,' he said. 'Clearly made with a thin, hard heel. See here, quite deeply scored as if the wearer was sliding on one side with the heel digging in as a brake. But it's no more than an inch wide so I'd suggest it was a woman's shoe.'

'The female corpse was wearing trainers,' said Cheever.

'Yes. She couldn't have made marks like this, and neither could our male corpse. His heels are a good four inches wide. They weren't done all that recently either – you can see where the grass has started to sprout again in places – so the chances are there was either a woman present while the murder took place or someone else, who didn't report it, found the bodies before your old lady did.'

'If that's true,' said Cheever pensively, 'then it's conceivable they may be our wallet thief. The logical assumption is that the murderer removed anything that could identify them, but it's not beyond the bounds of possibility that someone else did the business.' He glanced towards his colleagues. 'What do you think?'

Gareth Maddocks gave a non-committal shrug, his narrowed eyes, sunk in folds of thick flesh, watching the pathologist's biscuit-dunking routine with disgust. 'You said it meant a woman might have been present during the murder,' he reminded him. 'Does that mean a woman could have delivered blows like this, or that she was there only as a witness to a man delivering them?'

Apparently oblivious to the other man's distaste, Clarke rubbed biscuit crumbs from his fingers and started in on his coffee. 'Assuming she had two people, incapacitated, on their knees in front of her and assuming a sledge- or club-hammer with a reasonable length handle, then any woman with the strength to swing the thing several times could inflict this sort of damage. But it's an unlikely *modus operandi* for a woman acting alone.'

'Not impossible, though?'

'Nothing's impossible, but, frankly, statistics and psychology are against you. It was a very physical crime, requiring energy and extreme savagery, neither of which are typical of female murderers. That's not to say there aren't some extremely savage and dangerous women about, but, in my experience, they prefer to conduct their murders within the four walls of a house, using a pillow over the face, poison, guns and knives even. I'd plump for a man or men, if I were you, with the possibility of a woman in tow who witnessed the whole event. It really is a pity there's been so little rain recently. A nice piece of soggy ground and I could have told you how many people were there, what they weighed and probably how tall they were.' He paused briefly. 'Of course you realize there'll have been a great deal of blood, and that's a brute to clean off, as you know. Your killer will probably have left bloodstains in the car he drove away in. I certainly feel those are areas worth concentrating on.'

'Tell us about the victims,' said Frank Cheever. 'We've got height, build and colouring. Anything else? What do their clothes say?'

'Ah, well, Jerry's having a field day with them.' Clarke pulled out another set of notes. 'It'll be a while before he can give you a full analysis but this is what he's come up with so far. These people weren't poor, quite the reverse in fact, Jerry says look at the wealthier end of the market. The woman first. Not much help from the jeans, which are stone-washed men's Levi 501s, but the T-shirt is American, made by a company called Arizona, and imported into this country by the Birmingham-based Interwear. Preliminary talks with them indicate that these T-shirts retail at fifty-five pounds from only ten stores throughout the country, all of which are centred in London, Birmingham or Glasgow. We're expecting a faxed list this afternoon, and Jerry will send it through to you as soon as it arrives, with precise details of the size, colour code and style that she was wearing.' He followed the notes with his finger. 'Her trainers are a Nike brand, retailing at eighty-five pounds, and her underwear, again not too helpful, is top-of-the-range Marks and Spencer. The point is, nothing that she was wearing was what you or I would call cheap, considering all her clothes are of the casual type.

'Now, the man. He's the better bet, by a long chalk. The pullover is dark green, Army-style with leather-patched elbows, designed by Capability Brown and retailing only through Harrods at a price of one hundred and three pounds.' He smiled at Frank Cheever's grunt of excitement. 'That's only the beginning, my friend. The shirt is a casual green/brown check from Hilditch and Keys in Jermyn Street, retailing at eighty-five pounds. Trousers by Capability Brown again, one hundred per cent lined cotton, with pleated front and button detail, colour described as taupe, and retailing out of Harrods for two hundred and fifty pounds. Socks by Marks and Spencer, shoes probably purchased in Italy because Jerry has no record of an importer who deals in that particular brand, but he's working on it. His best advice is that our chap has an account with Harrods and probably one with Hilditch and Keys as well. He has located some interesting fibres on both sets of garments which he believes are from the same carpet, probably a thick-pile, off-white Chinese rug, and some hairs which he suggests tentatively are cat hairs, but give him a few more days and he claims he'll be able to describe the room these two were in before they were taken to Ardingly Woods.'

'Anything else?' asked Cheever.

Clarke chuckled. 'Isn't that enough to be getting on with? Good God, man, we've had them less than twenty-four hours. What else are you expecting?'

'Some reasonable fingerprint impressions,' he said. 'You were doubtful yesterday, but perhaps you've had new thoughts today? If either of them have previous records, that's got to be the quickest route to identification.'

'Yes, well, I'll be in a better position to judge that when we've got them out of the bags.'

'What about the green nylon twine that was used to tie their hands and feet? Anything useful to say about that?'

'Not really. It's available in most garden centres, DIY stores and supermarkets. Impossible to break and takes years and years to wear through. The knots were standard grannies, repeated several times to stop them slipping, and they were very tight, so presumably the victims struggled to get out of them. That's an avenue worth exploring. How does one man tie up two healthy adults? And when did he do it? Before he transported them to Ardingly or after he got them there? If it was before, how did he get them to the middle of the forest? If it was after, why didn't one of them run away while the other was being trussed? I really think the most likely scenario is that you should be looking for two or more suspects.'

DI Maddocks rubbed his jaw in thought. 'Are you sure it was a hammer and not a heavy branch? If it was a branch, we could be looking at a rather more spontaneous attack. Our maniac – and I use the word advisedly – stumbles on a sleeping couple in the wood, renders them unconscious, ties them up and then bludgeons them to death before absconding with their money. Could it have happened like that?'

'Not with a branch,' said Dr Clarke amiably. 'Whatever made that neat hole in the woman's skull was cleanly and symmetrically shaped, very hard and heavy, and was probably at right angles to its shaft to penetrate so deeply. I wouldn't put my life on a sledgehammer, but I'd certainly put my savings on it.'

The third policeman, Detective Sergeant Sean Fraser, who was leaning against the wall by the open window, stirred into life. 'With respect, Guv'nor,' he said to Maddocks, 'if it had been a spontaneous killing, we'd have found a car somewhere. A guy who buys his clothes at Harrods isn't going to hitch a lift to Ardingly Woods for a snooze with his bird.' He crossed his arms and tapped his fingers against his leather jacket sleeve. 'It's interesting listening to the doctor's description of how it happened. Pick any war you like, and you'll have seen film footage of victims kneeling in front of open graves before they're dispatched with a shot in the back of the head to topple forward into the pit. I'd say it's a fair bet these two were executed.'

The others digested this in silence for a moment.

'What sort of execution are we talking about?' asked Superintendent Cheever finally. 'If it was a professional contract killing, we'd be looking at X-rays of bullet holes. You said yourself, a shot in the back of the head. I can't see a pro using a sledgehammer.'

'I've known gangs take each other apart with baseball bats, sir,' said Fraser, 'but, looking at what we've got, a man and a woman, mid-thirties to forties, I'd say it's a jealous husband we should be after. An execution of passion, that's my guess.'

Cheever punted the idea about his head. 'I still don't understand why no one's reported them missing. Well-dressed people don't vanish for two weeks without anyone noticing.'

'Unless it's their families who've done away with them,' said Maddocks. 'Perhaps we've got a Menendez situation on our hands – wealthy parents slaughtered by teenage sons out of greed for money or revenge for prolonged sexual abuse, depending on who you believe. It happens far too often for comfort. There was Jeremy Bamber – remember him? – did away with his entire family for the house and money and then tried to blame it all on his dead sister. Makes you wonder why any of us bothers to lumber ourselves with the next generation.'

Dr Clarke consulted his watch and stood up. 'Well, unlike you chaps, I don't earn enough to make it worth my children's while. A little kudos now and then for getting it right, that's my only real satisfaction for all the hours I put in on your behalf. Look for the bloodstains. Your individual, or more likely your duo or trio, will have had quantities of bright red haemoglobin splattered across their fronts. Someone, somewhere will have seen it and said: Ah!'

'Assuming Joe Public notices anything beyond his stomach and his prick,' said Maddocks sourly.

'All being well,' went on Clarke, opening the door, 'I should be able to pin-point their ages a little better for you by the end of the day, probably get some usable fingerprints and, in addition, tell you if the woman has ever given birth.' He ushered them into the corridor.

'But first I'll have to unzip those charming bags. Care to lend a hand, any of you?' He was chortling to himself as he headed for the lab.

'He's a miserable old fraud,' said Superintendent Cheever to the others. 'He earns twice as much as I do and puts in half the hours.'

The smell of death issued from the lab as the pathologist opened the door and went inside.

'I suppose you noticed,' said Maddocks, grinning at his boss while nodding towards the young sergeant, whose face had taken on an unhealthy hue under its thatch of blond hair, 'that the good doctor ate his biscuits without washing his hands.'

Nightingale Clinic, Salisbury – midday.

Jinx was standing in her bay window, leaning against the back of a chair for support. She was aware of the ginger head poked around her door for a long time before she said anything. 'Why don't you come in?' she said finally to the pane of glass in front of her.

'You talking to me?'

'There's no one else here.'

Matthew eased his thin frame through the gap in the door and joined her in her study of the garden. He found it impossible to stand still for very long and, out of the corner of her eye, she watched his nervous twitching with amusement. *God, he was unattractive.*

'Are you religious?' he asked bluntly.

'Why do you ask?'

'You had a vicar in here yesterday. Thought you might be one of the God squad.'

She flicked him a sideways glance, saw he was busy picking at the spots on his chin, and resumed her own scrutiny of the sunlit lawn and the people on it. 'He's the brother of a friend of mine. Came to see how I was. Nothing more sinister than that.'

He gestured towards a man on the right. 'See the guy in the checked shirt and blue trousers? Recognize him? Singer with Black Night. Used to shoot smack every two hours. Now look at him. And the guy next to him. Owns a freight company, but couldn't do the business unless he downed two bottles of whisky a day. Now he's dry.'

'How do you know?'

'I've done group therapy with them.'

'Did Dr Protheroe ask you to come and see me?' she asked cynically. 'Is this group therapy by the back door?'

'Do me a favour. The Doc never asks anyone to do anything, just sits back and rakes in the loot.' He kicked his toe at the carpet. 'The way I see it, the less he does, the longer we're here, and the better he's pleased. It's money for old rope, this lark.'

'He's obviously doing something right,' Jinx pointed out, 'or none of the patients would improve.'

Matthew ran a shaky hand around his stubble. 'Just keeps us away from temptation, that's all. There's no booze here, no drugs, but my guess is everyone looks for a hit the minute they leave. I'm sure as hell going to. Jesus, it's a bloody morgue this place. No excitement, no bloody fun, death by boredom. I'd fix myself now if I could lay my hands on something.'

She was suddenly tired of him. 'Then why don't you?'

'I just said, there are no drugs on the premises.'

'There must be some. I was offered a sleeping pill last night. Why don't you dissolve a few and shoot them?' she said evenly. 'It'd be a hit of sorts, wouldn't it?'

'Not the sort I want and where'd I get a syringe from?'

She glanced at him again. 'Then walk out. Go into town. Or are we prisoners here?'

'No,' he muttered, rubbing his arms as if he were cold, 'but someone would see. This place is crawling with security officers in case the proles get at the rich and famous. Anyway, what would I use for money? They take it off you when you first come in.'

Which presumably explained why she didn't have her handbag. There were a few clothes in her wardrobe, but no handbag. She had assumed it'd been lost in the crash.

'Well,' she said with idle sarcasm, 'if I was as desperate as you seem to be, then I'd go and mug some poor old woman for the money. I can't see what's stopping you.'

'You're just like everybody else,' he said angrily. 'Go and knock down old ladies, beat the shit out of a bank manager, steal some kid's piggy bank. Jesus, I'm not a criminal. All I want is one bloody hit. You should listen to the Doc some time. What's keeping you here, Matthew? You're over twenty-one, you know what you're doing, so go walkabout, phone your supplier, get him to bring you something. I bloody rang my old man and told him, the Doc's not trying to cure me, he's trying to encourage me, and this is what you're paying for.'

'What did your father say?'

'He said: "No one's stopping you, Matthew, so go ahead and do it." I don't know what the hell's wrong with everyone. How about that walk then? Do you fancy a walk?'

'I can't,' she said rather curtly. 'My legs aren't strong enough yet.'

'Yeah, I forgot. You tried to top yourself. OK, I'll get a wheelchair, then.'

'I suppose Dr Protheroe told you I was suicidal?' she said bitterly.

'Shit, no. Like I said, he doesn't do a damn thing. Everyone knows about you. You've been in the papers. Millionaire's daughter who tried to kill herself.'

'I didn't try to kill myself.'

'How would you know? The word is you can't remember a thing.'

She turned on him. 'You bloody little shit,' she said. 'What the fuck would *you* know about anything?'

He touched a surprisingly soft finger to the tears on her cheek. 'I've been there,' he said.

She was still standing in front of the window twenty minutes later, propped against the chair, when Alan Protheroe came in. 'I have a message for you from Matthew,' he told her. 'It goes something like this: "Tell the bird in number twelve that I've found a wheelchair but it's so filthy that I'm having to clean it. She probably wouldn't say no to some sodding lunch in the garden, so I've laid it on for her under the beech tree."' His amiable face broke into a grin. 'Does that charming invitation appeal at all, Jinx, or should I tell him I've ordered you back to bed? As before, he totally ignored the Do Not Disturb sign outside your door, so, in my view, he hasn't earned your company for lunch, and the chances are he'll bore you solid with constant reiterations of his urge to shoot smack. However, it's an entirely free choice.'

She smiled rather cynically back at him. 'I'm beginning to understand how you operate, Dr Protheroe.'

'Are you?'

'Yes. You work on the principle that people always do the opposite of what the figure in authority is telling them to do.'

'Not necessarily,' he said. 'I'm interested in encouraging each individual to establish his own set of values, and it's remarkably unimportant what triggers that process off.'

'Then you force us to make choices all the time.'

'I don't force anyone to do anything, Jinx.'

She frowned. 'Well, what am I supposed to do? Have lunch with Matthew or tell him to shove his head in a bucket. I mean, he's a patient, too. I wouldn't want to do the wrong thing.'

He shrugged. 'It's nothing to do with me. He'll clean the wheelchair till it shines, because he's made up his mind you're worth it. His brain's a bit one-tracked at the moment, because he's been doing drugs for years, but his father's a barrister and his mother's in advertising, and ten years ago he got three A-levels, so he can't be entirely stupid. It's a free choice, Jinx.'

'I wish you wouldn't keep saying that. In my philosophy, there's no such thing as a free choice, any more than there are free lunches. You always pay in the end.' She allowed him to see her dislike. 'And, as a matter of interest, if you're prepared to tell me so much about Matthew, then what have you told him about me?'

He arched an amused eyebrow. 'I said the bird in number twelve is streets brighter than you, went to Oxford to read Classics, and probably thinks you're a greasy-haired git who hasn't got the balls to go out and knock down an old lady for the sake of a hit. Which is pretty close to the truth, isn't it? He related most of the conversation you had with him.'

'Spot on,' she said tightly. 'I couldn't have put it better myself.'

'So, what do I tell him? That you'd like to have lunch with him in a wheelchair, or that you wouldn't?'

'You know I wouldn't.'

He tipped a finger at her. 'Then that's what I'll tell him.' With the briefest of waves he disappeared through the door.

'NO!' she shouted. 'COME BACK!' But he didn't come back, and, more angry than she could ever remember, she set off across the floor and thrust herself out of her own doorway. 'DR PROTHEROE!' she screamed at his retreating figure. 'DON'T YOU DARE SAY A WORD, YOU BLOODY SODDING BASTARD!'

He turned round and started to walk back. 'You *do* want to have lunch with Matthew?'

She waited until he had reached her. 'Not particularly,' she said quietly, 'but I will.'

'Why?' he asked curiously. 'Why do something you don't want to do?'

'Because you won't tell him "no" kindly. You'll tell him exactly what I told you, and I don't want you to do that. He's been nicer to me than anyone else and I think you might hurt him.'

'You're right on every count, Jinx.'

She gave a bored sigh. 'Oh, for God's sake. Look, I know what you're doing and I know why you're doing it. You're no different from Stephanie Fellowes. You want me to get out of this room, you want me to stop feeling sorry for myself, and you want me to start mixing again. But why can't you just say: Do it, please, Jinx, because it's good for you? Why involve that wretched boy in your silly games? He's not responsible for what's happened to me.'

Why couldn't she see that the room he wanted her to leave was the one in her mind? What was keeping her there?

'I agree, but I didn't involve him, he involved himself.' He tapped the Do Not Disturb notice that was taped to the wall beside her door. 'Don't you think it's a little patronizing to refer to him as a wretched boy, Jinx? He's twenty-eight and doesn't require protection from me or from you.' He grinned broadly. 'And one last point: as a matter of policy, I never instruct anyone to do anything. You either do things willingly, or you don't do them at all. My credibility's at stake here. I can't have people refusing. It would undermine everything I stand for.'

'Then please tell Matthew, thank you very much and, yes, I'd love to have lunch with him.' She reached up, tore off the notice, scrumpled it into a ball and threw it at him. 'As a good existentialist, Dr Protheroe, I'm sure you know why I did that.'

His thundering laugh boomed along the corridor as he walked away, tossing the ball into the air and catching it again. 'Because you enjoyed it,' he said over his shoulder.

She was wheeled around the gardens like a highly prized pig in a wheelbarrow, with her lanky escort showing her off with pride to anyone who was interested. She loathed every minute of it, spent the entire time chain-smoking and grinding her teeth at what she regarded as a Protheroe-inspired hijack. She perked up when, at the end of a tour of the boundary wall, they came to the main gate and paused by the gatekeeper's box. He glanced at them briefly through the window, then resumed his reading of the newspaper. Jinx gestured towards the unrestricted exit. 'Why don't we just keep going?' she suggested. 'You can get some smack and I can take a taxi home.'

'Sure,' said Matthew. 'You take it over then.'

She squinted up at him. 'Take over what?'

He made pushing motions with his hands. 'The wheels. It's no skin off my nose if you want to scarper. You're not my responsibility.' He squatted down beside her. 'But if you want out, why don't you just tell the Doc and phone for a taxi from your room?'

She shrugged. 'Probably for the same reason you don't.'

'Yeah,' he said. 'Reckon the guy from the band's got it about right. What he says is, when you've flung yourself into the ultimate abyss and you're still alive when you reach the bottom, it's probably worth asking yourself what the hell you're doing down there. So, do you want lunch? Or do you want out?'

'Both,' said Jinx, 'but I'll settle for lunch. You're not a rebel at all, are you?'

Matthew grinned. 'That depends,' he said.

'On what?'

'*Cui bono*? If it's me who gains, then I might be interested. What's the deal?'

'I don't know yet,' she said thoughtfully, 'but I'll tell you this for free. If you ever manage to kick the habit, you could make millions. You're even more manipulative than my father.'

'It takes one to recognize one,' he said, spinning her round. 'You're not exactly backward in that direction yourself. Hold tight now. Let's see how fast this contraption will go.' He bent down to press her back into the seat and, as he did so, she turned her head to smile at him.

The shock of *déjà vu* was so extreme that she flung her hand out instinctively and caught him a glancing blow across the face. *Meg and Russell ... Meg and Leo ... BLOOD ... whore ... whore ... WHORE ...*

Chapter Seven

AT THE OUTSET Bobby Franklyn had been careful with the four stolen credit cards, all of which carried the flamboyant signature that was so easy to copy. He had started in a modest way with purchases under thirty pounds to avoid incurring the inevitable telephoned checks, but after two days he was seduced by a leather jacket at one hundred and fifty pounds and caution gave way to greed. He sweated under the beady eye of the shop manager while the call for authorization was made, only to hit an adrenalin high when the jacket was handed to him and he knew that the cards had still not been reported missing. In the next five days, using each in turn, he bought goods to the value of six thousand pounds without, apparently, ever reaching any of the credit ceilings. He had yet to touch the woman's cards.

Of course, he grew careless. It was the nature of the beast to proclaim his cleverness and flaunt his new-found wealth, for there was no forward-thinking in Bobby's intellectual make-up, merely a childlike need to gratify immediate appetites and demonstrate that he was a cut above his peers. He strutted his stuff with increasing arrogance, provoking jealousy and resentment, and was

grassed up by an old school-friend, turned police informant, for a smoke and the price of a beer.

Friday, 24 June, Romsey Road Police Station,
Winchester, Hampshire – 12.15 p.m.

At about the same time that Jinx was considering
absconding, DS Sean Fraser tapped on the open door of
DI Maddocks's office. 'You remember what the Super
said about a third party nicking our couple's IDs and
money? Well, I took a look at the charge sheets for the
last week and came up with a cracker. It's too bloody
neat to be coincidence, Guv'nor. A lad by the name of
Bobby Franklyn was brought in this morning by the
uniformed boys. He lives on the Hawtree Estate, single-
parent family, five kids all running wild. He's the eldest.
Seems he's been using stolen credit cards to buy electrical
goods and clothes to the tune of six thousand quid in
five days. When they prised up the floorboards in his
bedroom they found four cards in the name of Mr Leo
Wallader and two in the name of Miss M. S. Harris. He
claims he found them in a carrier bag in the High Street,
but when Ted Garrety phoned through to find out when
they'd been reported missing he was told that, as far as
the companies who issued them are concerned, they're
still kosher. Ted's been trying to contact the two card-
holders. Wallader's registered address is 12 Glenavon
Gardens, Richmond, and Harris's is 43a Shoebury Terrace, Hammersmith. Two London numbers with no
answer at either end. What do you reckon?'

The permanent scowl on Maddocks's heavy face smoothed into alert interest. 'Is Franklyn still here?'

Fraser nodded. 'He's a nasty piece of work. Seventeen years old, and knows his rights. We've hauled him in before but this is the first time he's been old enough and bad enough to charge. According to Garrety, he had five televisions, half a dozen stereo systems still in their boxes beside his bed, and a quantity of brand new flashy clothing in his cupboard.'

'Does he have a brief with him?'

'A young woman from Hicks and Hicks. She's advised him to keep his mouth shut.'

The scowl returned. 'Miranda Jones, I suppose. If women stuck to what they're good at instead of muscling in on the male preserves, the world would be a better place.' He flicked a lazy glance at the young sergeant's prudish face. 'You'd agree with that, wouldn't you, Sean?' he goaded him, knowing that Fraser hadn't got the balls to contradict a superior officer.

Fraser stared at a spot on the wall above the Inspector's head and toyed briefly with the idea of thumping the bastard. He really hated Maddocks. He suspected the man's misogyny was pathological and put it down to the fact that Maddocks was in the middle of his third divorce. But it was no excuse, any more than it was an excuse for his apparent willingness to abandon the six children he had had along the way. 'She's better than some of the men they send, Guv.'

'OK, let's take a look at him,' said Maddocks, abandoning his sport to push his chair back and stand up. 'No chance he's our murderer, I suppose?'

Fraser stood aside to let him pass. 'I wouldn't think so, Guv. According to Ted Garrety, he has a reputation for liking little girls. A thirteen-year-old accused him of rape a couple of years back but no charges were ever brought because her mother removed her very speedily when it emerged how many other boys her daughter had slept with. The view is that Franklyn has all the makings of a paedophile, and give it another two to three years and we'll be banging the little sod up on a regular basis for child molestation. A type like that is deeply inadequate, so he'd probably rob two mature dead adults without a qualm, but I doubt very much he'd have the bottle to abduct them while they were alive.'

Which was a fair summary, thought Maddocks, as he examined the depressingly low-grade young man in the interview room who couldn't open his mouth without uttering obscenities and who fingered his crotch from beginning to end of the interview, apparently unaware he was doing it. He appeared unhealthy and unwashed with pinched, sharp features, eyes that looked anywhere but at the person to whom he was talking, and a sullen cast to his mouth. At times like this, the Fascist in Gareth Maddocks wondered why society tolerated such weasels within its midst.

'We have something of a problem here,' he murmured after Franklyn had replied 'no fucking comment' to the first three questions. 'I'm going to deal this one straight, Bobby, so that you know where I'm coming from. I think, then, you might decide to give me some answers. I'm not interested in your credit card fraud. As far as I'm concerned that's a separate issue. What I am interested in are the two people named on the cards, Mr Leo Wallader and Miss M. S. Harris, and the reason I'm interested is because I have two corpses I can't identify who were found in Ardingly Woods yesterday afternoon. Now, guesswork tells DS Fraser and myself that our couple could very well be Mr Wallader and Miss Harris and it would save us a great deal of time and effort if you could confirm that for us, Bobby. We think the chances are you stumbled on the bodies a week or so ago and did what any normal red-blooded male would do, and removed their wallets.' He smiled amiably. 'What the hell, eh? They were dead, not by your hand, no question about that, but they weren't going to need their credit cards any more, were they? How about giving us a break on this one? It really would help us to know who they are.'

'Sod off,' said Bobby. 'No fucking comment.'

Maddocks glanced towards the young solicitor. 'What say the Sergeant and I leave the room for five minutes and you discuss options with your client? It's worth pointing out, I think, that we might very well decide to bring additional charges against Mr Franklyn if and when we identify our dead couple as Wallader and Harris, and I should add that perverting the course of justice will be the least of them.'

Fraser watched Bobby's involuntary masturbation with marked distaste. 'If we're forced to go house to house on the Hawtree Estate, I wonder if we'll turn up someone else, a young girl perhaps, who was in the woods with Bobby.'

'There weren't no one wiv me,' said Franklyn in a rush, ignoring his solicitor's warning hand on his arm. *Shit, if they ever found out he'd screwed a twelve-year-old.*

'OK, OK, so I did find them two bodies and, Jesus, they were sodding 'orrible. Smashed bloody faces and bluebottles everywhere, but I was on me own. D'you fink I'd 'ave been able to lift them cards if I'd 'ad someone wiv me? Use yer fucking brains. They'd 'ave wanted an in on the goods, wouldn't they? But it was like you said, them two was dead and they wasn't gonna use their sodding cards again. Couldn't see no 'arm in taking them and doin' a bit of business.'

'You had a duty to report it, Bobby,' said Maddocks mildly, his habitual aggression cloaked in an encouraging smile which said: Don't worry about it, lad, we're men of the world, you and I, and we both know rules are made to be broken.

'Fuck that! It weren't none of my business. If I were a bit keener on you lot, then maybe, but you've never done me no favours so why should I do one for you? They was so bloody dead, you wouldn't believe. Couldn't see what difference it'd make to them if they was found a week ago or if they was found today. They'd still be dead, wouldn't they?'

Maddocks couldn't argue with that. 'Are you sure you were on your own, Bobby? If you had a girl with you we need to know now. It is important.' He was thinking of the skid marks on the bank, made by a woman's heel.

'Yeah, I'm sure.' He pondered for a moment. 'I'll tell you this for free. If a girl 'ad seen what I saw, she'd still be puking all over the sodding shop. I'm not thinking about it too much meself.' His skin grew even more unhealthy-looking. 'I 'ad to 'old me breath to search them. It was that bloody disgusting. Reckon there was a million bluebottles in that ditch. You gonna charge me? It weren't me what did them in. I don't do that kind of stuff.'

Maddocks glanced at Fraser, who shrugged. The lad's story certainly had the ring of truth. 'No,' said the DI, standing up. 'At the moment I don't intend to add any charges to those you're already facing, but we will want to talk to you again, Bobby, so I advise you very strongly to make yourself available. Neither DS Fraser nor I want the trouble of having to look for you.' He paused at the door. 'Just one last thing. Had there been any attempt made to bury the bodies?'

'You mean in a grave?'

'No, I mean had they been covered over with anything?'

'Only wiv leaves.'

'Well covered?'

'Yeah. Pretty well.'

'Then how did you know they were there?'

Franklyn's sharp little eyes shifted nervously. 'Because somethink 'ad been at the guy,' he said. 'A fox, maybe. The 'ead and top 'alf of 'is body 'ad been dug out, least that's what it looked like. I didn't know the woman was there till I started taking the leaves off 'im and found 'er 'ead beside 'is sodding legs. To tell you the truth,' he said, 'I wish I'd never seen them now.' He wiped his hands on his trousers. 'It's got me in bother and I'm not sure I cleaned myself properly afterwards. I've been worrying about that.'

Nightingale Clinic, Salisbury – 6.30 p.m.

Alan Protheroe looked in on Jinx later that afternoon and found her walking with gritty determination about her room. 'I'm not going out in a wheelchair again,' she told him angrily. 'I hadn't realized quite how sensitive I am to being stared at. It was a deeply humiliating experience.' She jabbed a finger at her bandages. 'When's this idiotic thing coming off my eye?'

'Probably tomorrow morning,' he said, wondering if it was only humiliation that had sparked her anger. It would be a while, he thought, before she felt confident enough to admit she remembered anything. 'You've an appointment at Odstock Hospital for nine-thirty. All being well, it'll be removed then.'

She came to a halt beside her dressing table. 'Thank God for that. I feel like Frankenstein's monster at the moment.'

His amiable face creased into a smile. 'You don't look like him.'

There was a short silence.

'Are you married, Dr Protheroe?'

'I was. My wife died of breast cancer four years ago.'

'I'm sorry.'

'Why did you want to know?' he asked her.

Straightforward curiosity. You're too nice to be running around free and most of your shirts have buttons missing. 'Because it's six-thirty on a Friday evening in June and I was wondering why you were still here. Do you live in?'

He nodded. 'In a flat upstairs.'

'Children?'

'One daughter at university, who's nineteen and very strong-minded.'

'I'm not surprised. You've probably been using her as a guinea pig for your theories on individual responsibility since she was knee-high to a grasshopper.'

'Something like that.'

She eyed him curiously. 'As a matter of interest, what happens when one of your patients chooses a wrong set of values? Acts in bad faith, in other words. I can't believe they all toe the existentialist Protheroe line. It's a statistical impossibility.'

He lowered himself into one of the chairs, stretched his long legs in front of him and clasped his hands behind his head. 'That's an extraordinarily loaded question but I'll have a stab at an answer. By "wrong" you presumably mean that they leave the clinic with the same problems they came in with? In other words, their time here hasn't persuaded them that another *modus vivendi* might be worth considering?'

'That's a very simplistic way of putting it, but it'll do, I suppose.'

He lifted an amused eyebrow. 'Then the simplistic answer is that my methods haven't worked for them, and they either remain as they are or seek alternative therapy. But they're usually the ones who discharge themselves within forty-eight hours because they didn't want to be here in the first place.'

Like me, she thought. 'You must have your share of back-sliders, though. I can't see Matthew sticking to the straight and narrow once he's away from here.'

'I think you're underestimating him. He's only been here two weeks, you know. Give him another month and then tell me he won't make it.'

She looked appalled. 'A month? How long am I supposed to stay here then?'

'As long or as short as you like.'

'That's not an answer. How long does my father expect you to keep me?'

'This isn't a prison, Jinx. I don't *keep* anyone.'

'Then I can leave tomorrow after the bandages have been removed?'

'Of course you can, subject to what I told you on Wednesday. You're still not physically fit, so I'd feel duty bound to inform your father that you'd discharged yourself.'

She smiled faintly. 'Does that mean I'm mentally fit?'

He shrugged. 'My impression, for what it's worth, is that you're as tough as old boots.' He leaned forward and studied her face closely. 'I'm having some difficulty squaring this rugged self-reliance of yours with the picture the police gave me of a heartbroken, vulnerable woman who drove her car at a wall.'

She pressed a fingertip to her eyelid to hide the awful rush of tears. 'So am I,' she said after a moment, 'but I've read the piece in the newspaper over and over again and I can't come up with another explanation.' She lowered her hand to look at him. 'I phoned Meg's answer-machine today. I thought if I could only talk to her and Leo, they could at least tell everyone that I wasn't upset about him going.'

'Is that something you can remember?'

'You mean, not being upset?' He nodded and she shook her head. 'No, I'm just so certain that it wouldn't have worried me.'

'Why?'

Because it didn't worry me last time. 'Because,' she said out loud, 'I didn't want Leo myself.' She looked away from him, fearful perhaps of seeing his disbelief. 'I know it sounds like sour grapes but I'm relieved I don't have to marry him. I can remember hanging around the studio till all hours just to avoid going home and spending cosy evenings with him, and I don't think it was cold feet about the wedding. I was beginning to actively dislike him.' She gave a hollow laugh. 'So much for rugged self-reliance. Why was I marrying someone I didn't like? It doesn't make sense.' She lapsed into a brief silence. 'It wouldn't be so bad,' she said suddenly, 'if I didn't have to keep shoring up my defences.'

'Against what?'

She pressed her fingertips to her good eye again to shut him out. 'Fear,' she said.

He waited a moment. 'What is there to fear?'

'I don't know,' she murmured. 'I can't remember.'

Romsey Road Police Station, Winchester, Hampshire – 7.00 p.m.

Events moved extraordinarily quickly once the bodies were given tentative names and addresses. A telephone call to the Richmond police uncovered the interesting information that 12 Glenavon Gardens had attracted the attention of another branch of the Hampshire police some ten days previously, following a road traffic accident involving Miss Jane Kingsley, the owner/occupier.

'You want to speak to a Sergeant Halliwell at Fording-bridge,' said the voice at the other end to Fraser. 'He asked us to make some enquiries about Kingsley because it looked to them like the RTA was a deliberate attempt to kill herself. The gist is, she was engaged to Leo Wallader, who lived with her in Glenavon Gardens for about two months before buggering off on the night of Friday, the tenth of June, three weeks before the wedding, to shack up with Kingsley's best friend. We talked to Kingsley's neighbours who mentioned another suicide attempt on the Sunday, the twelfth, and also to Wallader's parents by phone. The information we were given is that Wallader and his new girlfriend have scarpered to the continent until the fuss over the cancelled wedding has died down.'

'Any idea what the name of the girlfriend is?' Fraser held his breath.

'Harris. Meg Harris.'

Bull's-eye! 'Do you have an address for Wallader's parents?'

'Let's see, now. The father's Sir Anthony Wallader. Address: Downton Court, Ashwell, near Guildford.'

'What about Meg Harris's parents?'

'Sorry. She only came into it as the new girlfriend. We've nothing on her at all except her name.'

'OK, can you fax me everything you've got on this?' He read out the number. 'Within the next five minutes, if possible.'

'Will do. What's the story then?'

'Not sure yet, but we've got two bodies here that we think are Wallader and Harris. You'd better warn your chaps to expect us some time tomorrow. Cheers.'

He cut the line, flipped through a police directory and dialled Fordingbridge. 'Is Sergeant Halliwell still there?' he asked. 'Yes, I know it's late.' He drummed his fingers on the desk. 'OK, well this is urgent. Can you find him and ask him to call either DI Maddocks or DS Fraser in the Ardingly Woods incident room.' He rattled off the number. 'And make that a priority please.'

He gathered his notes together and made his way down the corridor to the fax machine, which was already printing the first of two pages being transmitted down the wire from Richmond. He skimmed both sheets before shouldering his way into Maddocks's office. 'Here's the Hampshire connection, Guv'nor. Leo Wallader was engaged to a Miss Jane Kingsley up until a couple of weeks ago. They were supposed to be getting married on the second of July, but Leo jilted her on the tenth of June for her best friend, Meg Harris.' He looked up. 'Miss Kingsley's father is Adam Kingsley of Franchise Holdings and the wedding was supposed to be taking place at Hellingdon Hall, which is where Kingsley Senior lives. It's a mansion to the north of Fordingbridge.' He handed Maddocks the sheets of paper. 'I've asked for a Sergeant Halliwell at Fordingbridge to give us a call. He's the one who requested this information when his guys hauled Miss Kingsley out of her car on the thirteenth of June, unconscious and drunk as a skunk. A suicide attempt, they reckon, following a previous one on the twelfth of June.' He tapped the Ordnance Survey map on the wall. 'According to the guy I spoke to in Richmond, the RTA was at Stoney Bassett airfield, which is' – he spread his hand across the map – 'two-thirds of the way between Ardingly Woods and Hellingdon Hall, say fifteen miles from the woods to the airfield and another seven from the airfield to the Hall. I've a real gut feeling about this one, Guv'nor. The geography's right, we've got skid marks on the bank made by a woman's shoe, and the Doc said a woman could have done it.'

Maddocks was an older and warier hand. 'Let's wait to hear from Halliwell,' he said.

Half an hour later they transferred to the Superintendent's office and brought him up to date on what they knew. 'I accept there's a remote chance that Wallader and Harris are sunning themselves on the Riviera,' finished Maddocks, 'either because Franklyn's lying to us or because our two bodies nicked the credit cards only to have them nicked again by Franklyn, but it's so damned unlikely that it's not worth considering. It explains why no one's reported them missing. According to Halliwell, Leo's family said they ran away to France to avoid the embarrassment of the cancelled wedding. So what do we do? Tell Sir Anthony Wallader we think his son's in the bath at the lab and ask him to make an identification? Or wait till we're sure the ID's accurate before we tell the families? We can probably lift some fingerprints from Harris's flat in Hammersmith, but Richmond say there's no way they can go back into Glenavon Gardens without alerting Jane Kingsley to the fact that something's up. Which could be a bad move if she's involved.'

Frank Cheever steepled his fingers on his desk and gazed thoughtfully out of the window. 'Did I ever tell you,' he said at last, 'that I began my career as a beat-bobby in London's Mile End?'

Maddocks and Fraser stared straight ahead. If he'd told them once, he'd told them a hundred times. Maddocks prepared to be bored. There was no merit in the old fool's reminiscences, beyond the one undeniably interesting fact that Cheever had been born a bastard to an East London prostitute. Even Maddocks had to admit that to work his way up through various police forces, while remaining married to the same woman for thirty-eight years, was an achievement for a boy who began life in the gutter.

'I was barely out of school,' he mused, 'and one of the first bodies I picked off the street was a black fellow who'd been bludgeoned within an inch of his life.' He thought about that for a moment. 'It turned out the poor wretch was engaged to the sister of an East End gangland boss and there was circumstantial evidence to show the future brother-in-law had done his dirty work himself. All my guv'nor needed was confirmation of identity but when the victim came round, he refused to co-operate and we had to drop it. I've never seen anyone look so scared. He was black as the ace of spades but he went white every time we mentioned a prosecution.' He looked from one to the other. 'The bastard who bludgeoned him was called Adam Kingsley. He wasn't prepared to have black blood in his family.' He fixed his pale eyes on Maddocks. 'But he got it anyway. The black fellow had more guts than Kingsley credited him with. He married the sister a week later, and went up the aisle on crutches to do it.'

Maddocks whistled. 'The same guy? This girl's father?'

Cheever nodded. 'He made a fortune out of buying up cheap properties with sitting tenants, then sending in his heavies to evict the wretched people in order to flog off the properties with vacant possession. He turned respectable in the sixties, probably about the time his daughter was born.' He stared out of his window into the darkness. 'All right,' he said, 'I suggest we tread carefully on this one. You and I, Fraser, are going to visit Sir Anthony Wallader tomorrow morning. We'll leave at eight sharp to be with him between nine and nine-thirty, and I want you to warn Dr Clarke that we may be bringing him back with us.' He turned to Maddocks. 'Meanwhile, Gareth, I suggest you split your team in two – half to concentrate on Meg Harris, the other half on Jane Kingsley. I want to know where they met, how long they've known each other, what sort of personalities they are. In particular I want to know about the relationship between Jane Kingsley and her father. OK? See what you can come up with by the time we get back.'

'But we don't approach Kingsley himself, presumably?'

'No.'

'What about the daughter? Halliwell says she's in the Nightingale Clinic in Salisbury suffering from the effects of concussion. Do we leave her alone as well? She has a drink-driving charge hanging over her head so we could get away with interviewing her on that without too much difficulty.'

'You think so, do you?' said Cheever dryly. 'Listen, my friend, this isn't the Samaritans we're dealing with, and you make damn sure Kingsley doesn't get a sniff of the questions you're asking. Understood? No one makes a move on that family until we know exactly where we are and what we're doing. If Jane is anything like her father, you handle her as delicately as you'd handle a snake. Of course you leave her alone. You leave them *all* alone.'

Saturday, 25 June, Downton Court,
Near Guildford, Surrey – 9.30 a.m.

Sir Anthony Wallader ushered the two sombre-looking policemen into the drawing room of his house and waved them towards empty chairs with a perplexed frown creasing his forehead. 'To tell you the truth, gentlemen, I've had it up to here' – he raised his hand to the side of his neck – 'with that wretched girl and her suicide attempts. I don't say I applaud my son in what he's done, but I do object to the way Philippa and I keep being dragged into something that is, frankly, none of our business. You do realize how long I've spent on the telephone to your colleagues round the country, not to mention the appalling conversation poor Philippa had with Jinx's stepmother. Philippa would insist on doing the right thing and sending her best wishes for Jinx's recovery, but Betty was as rude and offensive as one would expect from someone of her class and background.' He gave a shudder of distaste. 'She's the most objectionable creature, little better than the lowest East End tart, if I'm honest. God knows, we're well out of that family entanglement.'

Fraser, who knew Cheever's background, writhed quietly on behalf of his boss. The Superintendent merely nodded. 'It's not an easy situation, sir.'

'You're right, of course. And why should we be made to feel responsible for a grown woman's inability to deal with her emotions? Is this really so important that you can't wait for Leo to get back?' He sank on to the sofa and crossed one neat leg over the other, every inch the aristocrat. In different circumstances, Fraser might have been tempted to kick his arse. There was no sincerity, he felt, in Sir Anthony Wallader. 'Philippa and I barely know Jinx. Leo brought her down for the odd weekend but not enough for us to feel comfortable with her. She's a very clever girl, of course, but rather too modern for our taste.'

'In fact, we'd very much like to talk to your son,' said

Frank Cheever evenly. 'Do you have an address or telephone number where we can contact him?'

Sir Anthony shook his head. 'We haven't heard a word since they left. Not surprising really. They're embarrassed.' He clasped his hands over his knee. 'Us, too. We've been keeping our heads well down, as you can probably imagine. Not the done thing, jilting the bride four weeks before the wedding, but the trouble is we can't criticize him for doing it. Embarrassment tempered with relief is probably the best description of how we feel at the moment. She was quite wrong for him, took everything far too seriously, as amply demonstrated by these suicide attempts.'

Fraser was examining some family photographs on the table beside him. 'Is this your son, sir?' he asked, pointing to one of a tall, fair-haired man leaning against a Mercedes convertible with his arms crossed and a broad smile on his face. The family resemblance was strong. He had the same wide forehead as Sir Anthony, the same thick hair, the same elegant tilt to his patrician head.

'Yes, that's Leo.'

'Where exactly did he and Miss Harris say they were going, Sir Anthony?'

'They didn't. They just said they were taking the car across the Channel until the flak stopped flying.'

'You spoke to them in person?'

'Not face to face. Leo phoned on the Saturday morning to say the wedding was off, and that the best thing he and Meg could do was make themselves scarce.'

'Saturday being the eleventh of June?'

'That's right. Two weeks ago today.'

'And you haven't heard from him or Meg since?'

'No.' He swept his trousers with the palm of his hand. 'But I have to say that I can't see why any of this is important. It's hardly a hanging offence if your erstwhile fiancée makes an attempt on her life. Or is it now? I'm afraid the law makes less and less sense to me as I get older.'

Frank Cheever removed a folded piece of paper from his inside breast pocket and spread it out on his knees before passing it across to Sir Anthony. It was a photocopied montage of the credit cards that had been in Bobby Franklyn's possession. 'Do you recognize either of the signatures on this page, sir?'

Sir Anthony held it at arm's length. 'Yes,' he said after a moment, 'the top four are Leo's.' He half-closed his eyes. 'The bottom two are M. S. Harris, so presumably Meg's.' He shifted his gaze to the Superintendent. 'I don't understand.'

'I regret this very much, Sir Anthony, but we have reason to be very concerned for your son and Miss Harris. We came here because we hoped you could give us some idea of where they were and so assure us they were still alive.' He nodded towards the piece of paper. 'A seventeen-year-old boy was charged yesterday in Winchester with credit card fraud, and those six cards were in his possession. He informs us that he stole them a week ago from two bodies he found in Ardingly Woods, some two miles to the west of Winchester. It is my very sad duty to tell you that it is our belief the bodies are those of your son, Leo Wallader, and his friend, Meg Harris.'

Perhaps the information was too shocking to take in, perhaps, quite simply, it didn't make sense. Sir Anthony gave a surprised laugh. 'Don't be absurd, man. I've already told you. They're on the continent somewhere. What is this? Some sort of practical joke?' His brows snapped together angrily. 'That wretched man Kingsley's doing, I suppose.'

'No, sir,' said Cheever gently, 'not a practical joke, although for your sake I wish it were. We do have two unidentified bodies' – he glanced towards the smiling photograph – 'one male, aged between thirty and forty, six feet one inch in height with blond hair, and one female, aged between thirty and forty, five feet four inches in height, with short dark hair. While there is still a chance that the boy lied to us about how he came by the credit cards, I must warn you that it's very remote. Certainly the description of the male seems to fit your son, although we have still to compare the female with Miss Harris. As yet we have no description of her.'

Sir Anthony shook his head in denial. 'There must be some mistake,' he said firmly. 'Leo's in France.'

'Perhaps you can give us a description of Meg,' suggested Fraser.

'She came here once,' said the older man slowly, 'dropped in for lunch on her way back to London when Leo and Jinx were down for the weekend. Philippa took to her immediately. She was a nice girl, clearly besotted with Leo, a far better prospect in every way than Jinx. Good family, decent background. Philippa and I were pleased as punch when the boy phoned to say he was planning to marry Meg instead. The family comes from

119

Wiltshire, I believe. A pretty girl, dark hair, slim, always smiling.' He lapsed into silence.

'What sort of age—' began Fraser, but Cheever glanced across at him and made a damping motion with his hand.

Despair settled on Sir Anthony's face. 'This will destroy my poor wife, you know. Leo was the only one. We tried for more, but it wasn't to be.' He pressed a thumb and forefinger to his eyelids to hold back the tears. 'What was it? Some sort of accident?'

Cheever cleared his throat. 'We don't think so, no. The pathologist's view is that they were murdered.' He clamped his hands between his knees. 'I'm so sorry, Sir Anthony.'

He shook his head again angrily. 'No, no, this is outrageous.'

There was another long silence.

He raised a trembling hand to his forehead. 'Who would want to murder them?'

'We don't know, sir,' said Cheever quietly. 'They've been dead some time, perhaps as long as two weeks. At the moment we're looking at the thirteenth of June as the most likely date for when it happened.'

'That would be the day Jinx tried to kill herself,' he said flatly.

'So we understand.'

Sir Anthony's mouth worked. 'I suppose you know her husband was murdered?' he said harshly.

Frank Cheever leaned forward with a frown. 'You mean Miss Kingsley's husband?' This was news to him.

The other man nodded. 'She was Mrs Landy then. It

was nine or ten years ago. Her husband's name was Russell Landy. He was an art dealer in Chelsea.' He fixed Frank with a penetrating stare. 'He was clubbed to death with a hammer but his murderer was never found. Landy was so badly beaten that his face was unrecognizable. The newspapers described it as one of the most brutal killings anyone could remember. How was my son murdered, Superintendent? Will I be able to recognize him?' He saw the brief hesitation in the policeman's eyes, a shutter close on something horrific. 'Was he clubbed to death like Landy?'

Frank wiped a weary hand across his face. Good God, he was thinking. Could it be this easy? 'Death is never pretty, Sir Anthony, less so when several days have elapsed.'

'But was he clubbed to death like Landy?' There was anger in Wallader's voice.

'At this stage,' said Frank carefully, 'nothing has been ruled in or out. The pathologist hasn't had time to finish his examination and, until he does, it would be wrong to speculate, but I give you my personal assurance that I will pass on his conclusions to you as soon as possible after they have been reported to us.'

Whatever spark had fired Sir Anthony's anger extinguished itself as rapidly as it had ignited. He looked lost suddenly, as if the fact of his son's death had only just dawned upon him. 'I suppose you need me to identify the body.' He started to get up.

'There's no hurry, sir. I'd like you to take as much time as you need to talk it through with your wife. Please don't feel this is something you have to do immediately.'

'But it is,' he said abruptly, pushing himself from his chair. 'Philippa's out for the day doing her voluntary stint in the hospital so she won't even know I've gone. You talked about a remote chance,' he reminded the policeman with tears in his eyes. 'For my poor girl's sake, I'm praying for that.'

HO Forensic Lab, Hampshire – 11.45 a.m.

He stood, dry-eyed, over what was left of his son, now transferred to a clinically clean table, his torso discreetly veiled by white cotton sheeting. The hair, as thick and blond as it had been in life, was unmistakably Leo's and, dreadful though it was, there was still enough of the facial structure left for recognition.

His eyes sought out Dr Clarke. 'What should I tell my wife?' he asked him. 'I don't even know how to begin.'

Clarke looked down at the poor dead body. 'She'll need comfort, Sir Anthony, not truth. Tell her how peaceful he looked.'

Art Dealer Murdered

The battered body of Russell Landy, 44, was found in the stock room of his art gallery in Chelsea last night by his wife Jane Landy, 24. He was still alive when the ambulance reached him but died on the way to hospital. Mrs Landy, who is three months pregnant, is said to be deeply shocked. She had waited over an hour for him at Le Gavroche, where they were to have dinner together, but when he didn't arrive, took a taxi to the gallery to look for him. She was alone when she found him. Doctors say he had probably been attacked some 1–2 hours previously and might have survived had he been discovered sooner.

The gallery was ransacked and several of the more valuable paintings stolen. Police believe Mr Landy may have disturbed the robbers. A sledgehammer was recovered from the scene. Russell Landy was a relative newcomer to the art world. His gallery, Impressions, opened less than four years ago and specialized in the minimalist work of young painters such as Michael Paggia and Janet Hopkins.

Daily Telegraph – 2 February, 1984

Jane Landy Loses Baby

Two weeks after the murder of her art dealer husband, Russell Landy, Jane Landy has suffered a second tragedy. It was announced yesterday that she has lost the baby she was expecting. She is said to be distraught. Police are no nearer finding the murderer of her husband.

Daily Telegraph – 18 February, 1984

Landy Murder Mystery

Police admit to being puzzled about the murder of art dealer Russell Landy, 44, whose battered body was found two nights ago by his wife, Jane. 'The premises were broken into,' said a police spokesman, 'and some paintings were stolen, but we cannot account for the frenzied attack on Mr Landy. This sort of specialist robbery isn't normally associated with extreme and savage violence. Art thieves pride themselves on their professionalism.'

The police are asking dealers and collectors to watch out for the stolen paintings. 'If we can establish that robbery was the motive,' said the spokesman, 'it will assist us in our enquiries. At this stage, it is not clear whether the sledgehammer used to murder Mr Landy was already on the premises or was brought there by his attacker. Clearly we have to consider that murder may have been the intention all along.'

Jane Landy, 24, is the only daughter of Adam Kingsley, millionaire chairman of Franchise Holdings Ltd. He is said to be deeply upset by his son-in-law's death, despite declaring publicly after the wedding that Russell Landy was little better than 'a gold-digging cradle-snatcher'. Kingsley has two sons by his second marriage, Miles and Fergus, aged 16 and 14.

Friends of the Landys say Russell was a popular man with no enemies. 'He was an intellectual with a wonderful sense of humour,' said a close friend. 'I cannot understand why anyone would want to kill him.'

The stolen paintings have been valued at £250,000 but police believe they will be difficult to sell. Michael Paggia's work is well known in minimalist art circles but his appeal has a narrow base. His most famous work, Brown & Yellow, two large brown canvases on either side of a smaller yellow canvas, is currently on display at the Tate. It caused a furore when it was bought. One critic described it as: 'S**T & P**S'.

'It is very unclear,' said the police spokesman, 'why thieves would bother to steal paintings like this. Who would want to buy them?'

Daily Telegraph – 3 February, 1984

MEMORANDUM

To: ACC Hendry
From: Superintendent Fisher
Date: 9 August 1984
Re: Murder of Russell Landy – 1.2.84

Following our conversation of yesterday, I have asked
Andrews and Meredith to put together a summary of the
case for you. The salient points are these:

- None of the stolen paintings have materialized. Andrews'
  and Meredith's view, which I share, is that robbery was
  never the motive. Extensive enquiries have produced no
  witnesses to the break-in. (NB: Mrs Landy has made an
  insurance claim for compensation. The paintings were
  valued at £200,000 plus.)

- Landy's movements were traced for the three months
  prior to the murder but there is no evidence of anything
  remotely untoward in his background. His business was
  solvent, as were his personal finances, and bar some
  indications that he was an occasional cannabis smoker,
  he did not engage in any illegal activities. Despite
  questioning of friends, colleagues and relations, there is
  no evidence of a secret liaison. It seems highly unlikely,
  therefore, that he was killed by a jealous rival.

- He had several gay friends but extensive questioning of
  the gay community has convinced Andrews and Meredith

that he himself was not an active homosexual and that
this was not a 'gay' killing.

- He was on good terms with his wife. Friends describe
him as 'overly possessive of her' but there is no
evidence of domestic violence or cruelty. Her alibi for the
afternoon and evening of 1 February is solid. The only
time she was alone from midday onwards was when she
paid off the taxi which took her from the restaurant to the
gallery and entered the premises. She was alone when
she found Landy. Andrews and Meredith have taken
several opinions on the forensic evidence, all of which
support the original theory that Landy had been attacked
a minimum of one hour before she arrived at 21.05. With
the cab-driver's evidence of the time he dropped her, and
the logged 999 ambulance call, there is no question of
her having committed the assault herself.

- Her movements have also been traced for the three
months prior to the murder. Andrews and Meredith
looked specifically for evidence of an affair, but found
none. They also looked for evidence of a contract
between her and a third party to eliminate her husband
but, again, found none. Nor, it must be said, could
they discover a reason why she would want him
eliminated. Over a hundred friends and colleagues
have been interviewed and they all speak of an
amicable relationship between the two. There is some
indication that Mr Landy suffered periodic bouts of
jealousy but this was put down to the fact that he
was twenty years older than she was and not to any
infidelity on her part.

- There remains a continuing doubt over the role played by Mrs Landy's father, Adam Kingsley. All the evidence points to extreme hostility between him and Mr Landy. It is clear that he opposed the relationship from the outset and was deeply angry when the marriage took place without his knowledge. He refused ever to speak to his son-in-law, however phoned and was phoned by his daughter on a regular basis. Friends of hers say she was upset by the gulf between them, but refused to pander to either man's 'jealousy' and continued to relate to both on surprisingly easy terms. Her only proviso was that she would never talk about one to the other.

- After a prolonged investigation into Kingsley's movements in the weeks leading up to the murder and on the day of the murder itself, Andrews and Meredith have concluded that while it was not impossible for Kingsley to have committed the crime himself (he was in London that day and could have gone to Chelsea between a meeting in Knightsbridge which ended at 4.30 p.m. and another in the Edgware Road which began at 6.30 p.m.) they believe it to be unlikely. Kingsley refuses to give an account of his whereabouts between those two times, but independent enquiries, based on his movements in the preceding weeks, have elicited three witness statements which confirm he was with a prostitute in Shepherd's Market. This is a regular occurrence, and has been going on for many years.

- In the absence of any other explanation, Andrews and Meredith incline to the view that Kingsley took out a contract on his son-in-law's life. However, they have been unable to substantiate this view and, without any firm evidence to support it, see no way to proceed. Their suspicions are grounded in an analysis of Kingsley's character and background, which is briefly as follows:

1: He is known to have had extensive contacts with the London underworld since his early career. Born and brought up in and around the Docks in the 30s and 40s. Founded his fortune on black market racketeering during and after the war. Progressed to property scams in the 50s and 60s before 'legitimizing' his business under Franchise Holdings and expanding into full-scale development of office sites.

2: Began to amass an enormous fortune in the early 70s during the property boom. He has always had a reputation (unproven) for dishonest business practices but has twice won out-of-court settlements against newspapers who were foolhardy enough to suggest it.

3: Since Thatcher came to power he has been acquiring tracts of London's Docklands at deflated prices. To do this, he is known to be using his contacts in the underworld.

4: He has been married twice. His first wife, the mother of Jane Landy, died in 1962 of septicaemia. She was a middle-class doctor's daughter who was educated at private school, and Kingsley is said to have adored her. He remarried in 1967. His present wife, Elizabeth Kingsley, came from his own background and was a girlhood friend of his sister. It is thought he was engaged to Elizabeth in 1958 but broke the engagement to marry

his first wife. The second marriage has not been a
success. Mrs Kingsley has a drink problem and the two
sons from the marriage have been cautioned for petty
thieving, vandalism and car theft. The boys have been
educated privately at Hellingdon Hall since their
expulsion from Marlborough for possession of drugs.
Kingsley is known to adore his daughter.

In conclusion, I endorse Andrews' and Meredith's analysis.
Kingsley remains the prime suspect, although it is extremely
unlikely that he will have committed the offence himself. In
the absence of any witnesses to the break-in or the murder,
or indeed the stolen paintings coming to light, it is difficult to
see how we can proceed. Even were we given leave to
search Kingsley's numerous accounts for evidence of a
contract payment, it is very doubtful we would find it.

John

Chapter Eight

DI MADDOCKS AND his team had put together a substantial amount of information about Jane Kingsley in the short time they'd had, but had discovered nothing about Meg Harris or her parents. 'At the time of Miss Kingsley's car crash, a couple of PCs went out to talk to her parents,' he told Cheever. 'The stepmother, Mrs Elizabeth Kingsley, was tipsy and offered some vitriolic comments about Leo and Meg: They were both bastards but Meg was a snake in the grass and had set out to steal Jane's boyfriends since they were at Oxford together.' He looked up. 'BT can't help us. At a rough estimate, Wiltshire has over five thousand families called Harris living in it. If we had the father's initial it might help, or a profession even, but you say Sir Anthony doesn't know what her father was called.'

'No,' said Frank Cheever with rather more cynicism than was his wont. 'Despite his enthusiasm for her as an alternative daughter-in-law, he seems to know remarkably little about her.'

Maddocks eyed him curiously. Well, well, well, he thought, times they are a-changing. 'I've put two of our guys on to tracing Meg's next-of-kin through the university,' he went on, 'but then there's the other problem that Harris may not be her maiden name. I still say our quickest route is via the flat in Hammersmith, so Fraser and I are going up there this afternoon.'

'Understood. What about Jane Kingsley?'

'OK, first the Landy murder.' He pointed to some papers on the Superintendent's desk. 'That's as much as we've managed to get hold of on the case. It seems pretty comprehensive and there's a phone number you can call for an up-date. I guess you missed the Kingsley connection because she was calling herself Jane Landy in those days. Anyway, within weeks of her discharge from hospital following her treatment for depression, she negotiated an extremely favourable sale of his gallery and invested the lot in a photographic studio in Pimlico. She bought it out, lock, stock and barrel – premises, equipment and good-will. Until then, she'd been working part-time as a stand-in photographer when regulars didn't show.' His voice took on a note of reluctant admiration. 'She appears to have turned it into a success. Under the old management it was a run-of-the-mill enterprise, dealing in portraits of the local big-wigs' families, friends and pets. Under Miss Kingsley's management it's become a favoured studio for promotional work – actors, pop stars, fashion models, magazines. She's earned quite a name for herself in the trade.'

'Who's running it at the moment?'

Maddocks consulted his notes. 'A chap called Dean Jarrett. He's been with her from the beginning. She recruited him through an ad in the newspapers, asking for samples of work with a view to employment. She had over one thousand applications, interviewed fifty and selected one. The word amongst the professionals is he's brilliant and devoted. I got Mandy Barry to phone through and ask whether appointments and bookings were being honoured with Miss Kingsley in hospital, and the receptionist, one Angelica, was bullish and convincing about the studio's continued commitment. Loyalty to the boss was deeply felt and not feigned, according to Mandy.'

Cheever nodded. 'What else?'

'The house in Richmond was bought by Landy in eighty-one with an endowment mortgage of thirty thousand. On his death, the endowment paid off the mortgage and the house became Miss Kingsley's. She has shown no inclination to sell it. She gets on well with Colonel and Mrs Clancey who live next door and is well regarded by other people in the road. She lives quietly and unostentatiously and, bar the odd appearance of her father's Rolls-Royce, does not draw attention to herself. Interestingly, nobody referred to Landy at the time of Miss Kingsley's traffic accident, although some of them must have remembered him, but they were very ready to talk about Leo Wallader. The general view is that no one liked him very much and that he behaved badly, but Richmond police were left with the impression that her neighbours were more put out about missing a wedding at Hellingdon Hall than they were about Leo's shenanigans.'

'What about other boyfriends between Landy and Wallader?'

'Only what we've gleaned from the gossip columnists.

There've been two or three, but nothing lasting more than six months. Mind you, Wallader didn't make six months either. She met him in February and he was dead by June. Bit of a whirlwind romance, considering the marriage was scheduled for July.'

'What was the attraction?'

Maddocks shrugged. 'No idea, but Colonel Clancey said it was very clear to him and his wife that Jane was having cold feet about the wedding even if it was Leo who called it off. Claims he can't understand why she would want to top herself when he left.'

'Any ideas?'

'Only the obvious – that she killed them herself or witnessed the killing and then suffered a similar break-down to the one she had at the time of Landy's death. She's pretty damn weird, that's for sure. I mean, according to what we've found out, her favourite backgrounds for photographic shoots are cemeteries, derelict factories and grafittied subway walls.' He took a folded page that had been ripped out of a magazine from his pocket. 'If you're interested, that's her most famous photograph to date. It's that black supermodel standing in front of a filthy tiled wall with every obscenity you can imagine scrawled all over it.'

Cheever spread the sheet on his desk and examined it. 'Fascinating,' he said. 'She's quite an artist.'

'Well, I think it sucks, sir. Why put a beautiful woman against crap like that?'

'Where would you have put her, Gareth?' asked the other man tartly. 'On a bed?'

'Why not? Somewhere a bit more glamorous, anyway.'

The Superintendent frowned. 'It's a statement. I think it's saying that real beauty is incorruptible, never mind how profane or ugly the setting.' He pinched the end of his nose. 'Which is interesting, don't you think, in view of the ugliness of Landy's death? I wonder when she started using backgrounds like this in her work. There's something rather moving about the triumph of fragile human perfection over a wasteland of mindless filth.'

Maddocks decided the old man was going ga-ga. It was only a creased fashion photograph, not the *Mona Lisa*.

Hellingdon Hall, Near Fordingbridge,
Hampshire – 12.30 p.m.

Miles Kingsley shook his mother angrily then pushed her back on to the sofa. 'I don't believe it. My God, you're such a stupid cow. Why can't you keep your bloody great mouth shut? Who else have you told?' He glared across at his brother, who was skulking at the far end of the drawing room, feigning an interest in the leather-bound books his father had bought by the yard when they'd first moved into the Hall. 'Your neck's on the line, too, you little shit, so I suggest you wipe that smirk off your face before I slap it off.'

'Sod off, Miles,' said Fergus. 'If I had any sense I'd never have listened to you in the first place.' He kicked a Chippendale chair. 'It was your idea, for Christ's sake. Foolproof, you said. What can possibly go wrong?'

'Nothing *has* gone wrong. You'll see. Just a little more time, and we'll be free and clear with a sodding fortune.'

'That's what you said last time.'

Romsey Road Police Station, Winchester – 12.45 p.m.

Frank read the documents on his desk relating to the Landy murder, then dialled the contact number Maddocks had given him. DCI Andrews had been involved from the outset.

'The case was effectively closed at the end of 'eighty-five,' he said down the wire from Scotland Yard, 'when Jason Phelps was put away for the Docherty murders. Remember him? Clubbed an entire family to death for twenty grand on the instructions of Docherty's nephew. They both got four life sentences. We tried to persuade Phelps to confess to the Landy killing because it was a carbon copy of the Docherty murders, but we never got a result. There was no question he did it, though, and if we could have got him to spill the works, we'd have nailed Kingsley. *He* was the one we wanted.'

'Tell me about the daughter,' prompted Frank. 'What was she like?'

'I rather took to her, as a matter of fact. She was a good kid, deeply shocked, of course, and suffered a nervous breakdown afterwards. She kept saying it was all her fault but we never believed she had anything to do with it. Meredith put it to her that she was afraid her

136

father was responsible but she said no. A day or two later she lost her baby.'

'Did she ever suggest who might have done it?'

'An unknown artist whose work Landy had rejected. She said he could be very cruel in what he said and she was insistent that he'd told her a few days before the murder that he was being watched by some creep who'd come to the gallery. She didn't think anything of it at the time, because he treated it as a joke, but it certainly preyed on her mind afterwards. We checked it out, but there was no substance to it and we took the view that, if the watcher existed at all, it was as likely to be Kingsley's contract killer as an embittered artist.'

Cheever pondered for a moment. 'Still, it's something of a minefield. The only contact I've had with Kingsley was years ago when he beat his future brother-in-law to a pulp to warn him off the wedding. Now you're telling me he pulped his son-in-law *afterwards*? Why didn't he do it before?'

'That was his daughter's argument. She claimed Kingsley had done his best to get rid of Landy three years previously by having him sacked from his job, but had long since accepted defeat on the matter. Our view was that the pregnancy changed things. She admitted that she and Landy had been going through a rocky patch but that the baby had brought them together again, and we didn't think it was coincidence that the wretched man was murdered a week after she told her parents she was expecting. We guessed Kingsley was relying on the marriage failing and when he was presented with evidence that it wasn't, he signed Landy's death warrant.'

137

Cheever tapped one of the pieces of paper in front of him. 'According to the memo you faxed through, you and Meredith believed Kingsley adored his daughter. But we're talking about something much sicker than adoration, surely? I could understand it if Landy had been treating her badly and Kingsley wanted him punished, but from what you've said he acted out of jealous rage. There'd have to be a pretty powerful sexual motive behind actions like that.'

'In a nutshell, that's what we thought it was all about. Look, the man was very highly sexed, he was visiting the Shepherd's Market prostitute every week. The second marriage was a disaster because the poor creature he settled on wasn't a patch on the first wife and took to the bottle within a couple of years. Her sons never matched up to the first wife's daughter who, to make matters worse, is the spitting image of her dead mother. There's no evidence that Kingsley abused the child, but they lived alone together for five years before he married again, and we estimated the chances were high that he did. We had his psychological profile drawn up based on what was known of him, and it was very revealing. There was a heavy emphasis on his need to control through ruthless manipulation of people and events, and it was thought very unlikely that his daughter could have escaped unscathed.'

'Did you suggest it to her?'

'Yes' – a hesitation – 'more's the pity. We gave her the profile to read, and the next thing we knew, she was under the care of a psychiatrist with severe anorexia and

138

suicidal depression. We felt rather bad about it, to be honest.'

'Mind you,' murmured Frank thoughtfully, 'it's a typical reaction of an abused child who's suddenly forced to come to terms with a buried past.'

43a Shoebury Terrace, Hammersmith, London – 3.30 p.m.

Later that afternoon, Maddocks and Fraser entered Meg Harris's flat in Hammersmith. They were met at the door by two Metropolitan policemen and a locksmith, but dispensed with the services of the latter in favour of the spare key which a stout middle-aged neighbour produced when she saw the congregation through her window and issued forth to quiz them about what they were doing. 'But Meg's in France,' she said, countering their sympathetic assertion that they had reason to believe Miss Harris was dead. 'I saw her off.' She wrung her hands in distress. 'I've been looking after her cat.'

The men nodded gravely. 'Can you remember when she left?' asked Maddocks.

'Oh, lord, now you're asking me. Two weeks ago or thereabouts. The Monday, maybe.'

Fraser consulted his diary. 'Monday, June the thirteenth?' he asked her.

'That sounds about right, but I couldn't say for certain.'

'Have you heard from her since?'

'No,' she admitted, 'but I wouldn't expect to.' She looked put out. 'I can't believe she's dead. Was it a car accident?'

DI Maddocks avoided a direct answer. 'We've very few details at the moment, Mrs – er . . . ?'

'Helms,' said the woman helpfully.

'Mrs Helms. Do you know anything about Miss Harris's boyfriend?'

'You mean Leo. He's hardly a boyfriend, too old to be a boyfriend, Meg said. She always called him her partner.'

'Did he live here?'

'On and off. I think he's married and only comes to Meg when his wife's away.' She caught up with Maddocks's use of the past tense. 'Did?' she asked him. 'Is Leo dead too?'

He nodded. 'I'm afraid so, Mrs Helms. Would you have a contact address or telephone number for Miss Harris's parents, by any chance? We'd very much like to talk to them.'

She shook her head. 'She gave me the vet's number last year in case the cat fell ill, but that's all. As far as I remember her family lives in Wiltshire somewhere. She used to go down there two or three times a year for a long weekend. But how awful!' She looked shocked. 'You mean she's dead and her parents don't even know?'

'I'm sure we'll find something in the flat to help us.' Maddocks thanked her for the key and led the way down the stone steps to the basement flat, which was marked 43a and had terracotta pots, alive with busy Lizzies, cluttered about the doorway. He inserted the key into the lock and pondered the elusive nature of Meg's family. Even Sir Anthony Wallader, who claimed to know something about the Harrises, had no idea which part of Wiltshire they came from or what Meg's father did by way of a job. 'You'll have to ask Jinx Kingsley,' he told them. 'She's the only one left who knows.'

But, in the circumstances, the Hampshire police had preferred the more tortuous route of arriving at Wiltshire via Hammersmith.

A tortoiseshell cat greeted them with undisguised pleasure as they let themselves into the narrow hallway, rubbing its sleek head and ears against their legs, purring ecstatically at the thought of food. Fraser nudged it gently with the toe of his shoe. 'I hate to be the one to tell you, old son, but you're an orphan now. Mummy's dead.'

'Jesus, Fraser,' said Maddocks crossly, 'it's a cat, for Christ's sake.' He opened the door into what was obviously the living room and took stock of the off-white Chinese rug with its embroidered floral pattern of pale blues and pinks which covered the varnished floorboards in front of the fireplace. 'A cat and an off-white rug,' he murmured. 'The boffins will be even more unbearable after this.' He went inside, took a pen from his jacket pocket and manipulated the buttons on the answerphone.

'Hello darling,' said a light female voice. 'I presume you're going to phone in for your messages so ring me as soon as you can. I read in the newspaper today that Jinx was in a car accident. I'm very worried about what to do. Should I try and phone her? I'd like to. You were such

141

friends after all, and it seems churlish to ignore her just because ... well, well, enough said ... no more rows, we promised ... Ring me the minute you get this message and we'll talk about it. Goodbye, darling.'

'Hi, Meg, where the hell are you?' A man's belligerent voice. *'You swore on your honour you'd come into the office before you left. Damn it, it's Wednesday, there's a mound of sodding messages here and I can't make head nor tail of them. Who the fuck's Bill Riley? Most of them are from him. Ring me before you ring anyone else. This is urgent.'*

'Meg.' The same man's voice. *'Ring me. Immediately. Damn it, I'm so angry I feel like belting you one. Do you realize Jinx has tried to kill herself? I've had your wretched parents on the phone every day asking for news. They feel bloody about this and so do I. Phone, for Christ's sake. It's Friday, seventeenth of June, eight-sodding-thirty, no breakfast and I haven't slept a wink. I knew Wallader would be nothing but trouble.'*

'It's Simon.' A different, cooler man's voice. *'Look, Mum and Dad are going spare. You can't just bury your head in the sand and pretend nothing's wrong. I'm sure you know Jinx has tried to kill herself. It's been in all the newspapers. Mum says you're refusing to answer your messages, but at least ring me if you won't ring her. I'm going to visit Jinx, see how she's coping. One of us ought to show some interest.'*

'Darling, it's Mummy again. Please, please ring. I really am awfully concerned about Jinx. They say she tried to commit suicide. I can't bear to think of her being so unhappy because of you and Leo. Someone should talk to her. Don't forget how ill she was after Russell was killed.

Please ring. I'm so worried. I do hope you're all right. You're usually so good about phoning.'

'For your information, Bill Riley is now planning to sue us. He claims we're in breach of contract. Why the hell did you agree to work with him if you weren't prepared to see it through? Message timed at nine-thirty p.m., Thursday, June twenty-third. If I don't hear from you in the next twenty-four hours, consider our partnership terminated. I'm pissed off with this, Meg, I really am.'

'Hello, Meg.' A deeper woman's voice. *'It's Jinx. Look, I know this is probably politically incorrect'* – a low laugh – *'I ought to be ripping your first editions to pieces or something – but I really would like to talk to you. Things are a bit complicated this end – well, you've probably heard about it ...'* A pause. *'They say I drove my car at a concrete post – deliberately. Can you believe that? The bugger is I've lost my memory, can't remember anything since Saturday the fourth, so everyone's jumping to the conclusion that I was upset about you and Leo.'* Another laugh, rather more forced this time. *'It's the pits, old thing, which is why I need to talk to you both. You may not believe me, but I swear to God I am not harbouring grudges, so if you can bear the embarrassment, ring me on Salisbury two-two-one-four-two-zero. It's a nutters' hospital and I'm shit-scared of going round the bend here. Please ring.'*

The rest of the tape was blank.

Maddocks raised an eyebrow at Fraser. 'Genuine?' he asked. 'Or planted for the police to hear after they found the bodies?'

'You mean hers?' Fraser shrugged. 'I'd guess genuine.

The pissed-off partner made his last call two days ago, so hers must have been pretty recent.'

'How does that make it genuine?'

'Because she couldn't know when the bodies would be found. If it was a bluff, she'd have phoned sooner to make sure we got the message.'

Maddocks was more sceptical. 'Unless she's been following the newspapers.' He turned to a bookcase along the wall and plucked a book at random from the shelves. 'The reference to first editions was genuine. Look at this. A signed Graham Greene.' He ran his finger along the spines. 'Daphne du Maurier, Dorothy L. Sayers, Ruth Rendell, Colin Dexter, P.D. James, John le Carré. She's even got an Ian Fleming. I wonder who she's left them to.'

'Probably her friend Jane Kingsley,' said Fraser, opening a door to the right of the fireplace and disclosing a neat white kitchen with slate-grey worktops and pale grey units. He turned to the two London policemen. 'Do you fancy tackling this? Chances are there'll be papers in some of these drawers. I'll take her bedroom.'

He moved across the hallway to a door on the other side, clicked it open and surveyed the room. Like the rest of the flat, it was clean and meticulously tidy – so tidy, in fact, that he decided it was a spare bedroom and went to the only door he hadn't yet opened and found the bathroom. Apart from a pair of fluffy white towels that were folded with measured precision over the rail, there was nothing to indicate that the room had ever been used – no sponge, no soap, no toothpaste. He lifted the latch on the cabinet above the basin and stared thought-fully at the meagre contents. A bottle of disinfectant, a packet of Disprin and a clean tooth mug. Meg Harris was unreal, he thought. No one was this tidy, not even when they went away on holiday. And where was Leo's presence? Surely something should remain to show a man had lived there on and off. He lifted the lid of the laundry basket, but it was empty.

He retreated into the hall again where he noticed the cat's bed beneath a small radiator and wondered why Meg had bothered to keep a companion when she was clearly so house-proud that its movements had to be thoroughly restricted whenever she was absent. Tidiness appeared to be an obsession with her. Back in the bedroom, he opened the wardrobe and sorted through the few clothes hanging there. Only women's, he noted, no men's. The same was true of all the drawers. He searched for anything that might give a clue to the woman's personality, but it was like searching a hotel bedroom where a guest was staying just one night. Her clothes were neatly folded away, some odds and ends of costume jewellery and make-up lay in ordered rows in her dressing-table drawer, a small bowl of pot-pourri on the bedside table gave off a faint scent. But if there had ever been anything of a personal nature in that room she had taken it with her.

Maddocks looked up from a book as Fraser rejoined him. 'Last year's diary,' he said, 'but there's not a single phone number or address in it. Any luck your end?'

Fraser shook his head. 'Nothing. Just a few clothes. It

looks as if she took everything that mattered to her, which is odd if she was only going away for a couple of weeks. I couldn't find any suitcases.'

Maddocks abandoned the diary and stared about the living room with a frown. 'I don't get it. It's so damn clinical. Have you noticed there aren't any photographs about? I've been looking for an album but I can't find one. You'd think there'd be at least one photograph of her family, wouldn't you?'

'What about papers?' suggested Fraser. 'House insurance, mortgage details, a will? Where are they?'

Maddocks jerked his head towards a pine bureau in the corner. 'In there for what it's worth, but there's no will, just one folder with "house insurance" written across the front. There aren't even any letters, no indication at all who her friends were or what the family address is. It's bizarre. Most people have a few letters littered about the place.' He moved across to the kitchen door. 'What about you two? Have *you* found anything?'

The older man shook his head. 'Tell you what, sir, it reminds me of those cottages you rent in the summer. There's cutlery and crockery here and it's all clean, but there's no food anywhere, the fridge is empty, dishwasher's empty, new plastic bag in the pedal bin. Either she rented it and was about to move out or she was planning to move out and let it to somebody else.' He gestured towards a peg board on the wall. 'Even her notice board's empty but you don't do that when you're off on holiday. I'd say she's got another place somewhere.'

Fraser agreed with him. 'That's got to be it, Guv. It

doesn't make sense otherwise. Have you ever seen a flat as devoid of personality as this one is?'

'Why did she leave her first editions behind?'

'Because the insurance policy here probably specifies and covers the collection, which would make this the most sensible place to leave them unattended. What's the betting she moved all her personal stuff before the holiday, left the cat behind because she had a neighbour who would feed it, and was planning to come back for the books, the rest of her clothes and the cat on her return? She was moving in with Leo – it's the only logical scenario.'

'Goddammit,' said Maddocks ferociously, 'everything points to him moving in with *her*. If he had a place of his own, why the hell was he shacked up in Glenavon Gardens with the Kingsley woman? Frank'll go mad over this. It's my guess Jane Kingsley's the only person who knows anything.'

Nightingale Clinic, Salisbury – 3.30 p.m.

Minus her bandage and dressed in black jumper and trousers, Jinx sat on a bench in the shade of a weeping beech tree and studied the comings and goings on the gravel sweep in front of the clinic. She felt herself to be comfortably anonymous behind a pair of mirrored glasses, and for the first time in several days she allowed her tired body to relax.

The memory that she *had* known about Leo and

147

Meg's affair pierced her brain like a needle. *My God!* Leo himself had told her in the drawing room of his parents' house with Anthony and Philippa there as silent, horrified witnesses. She had screamed at them all – *why had she been screaming?* – and Leo had said: I'm going to marry Meg – *and she had been so, so shocked. Meg and Leo ... Meg and Russell ...* But when? When had Leo told her?

She wrestled with the memory, desperate to hold on to it but, like a dream, it started to fragment and fade and, in confusion, she took the bunch of flowers that was being pressed on to her lap and heard Josh Hennessey saying: 'Jinxy, love, are you all right?'

She had forgotten he was coming and stared up at his anxious face, smiling automatically while she knitted back the fabric of her subconscious and let the memory go. 'I'm fine,' she heard herself saying. 'Sorry, I was miles away. How are you?' *But, oh God, she'd been so angry ... she could remember her anger ...*

He squatted in front of her, his hands resting lightly on her knees, his eyes examining every inch of her face. 'Pretty bloody depressed if I'm honest. How about you?' He seemed to be looking for a reaction and was disappointed – *surprised?* – when he didn't get it.

She held a thin hand to her chest where her heart was beating frantically. *Something else had happened.* The knowledge weighed on her like a ton weight. *Something else had happened ... something so terrible that she was too frightened to search her memory for it ...* 'I'd describe myself as being in a state of suspended animation,' she said, breathing in jerky, shallow breaths. 'I exist, therefore I am, but as I can't think straight it's a fairly meaningless existence.' She thought how unattractive he looked, with fear and worry pinching his nose and mouth. 'I suppose if you're depressed, it means you haven't got hold of Meg.'

He shook his head, and she saw with dismay that there were tears in his eyes.

'I'm sorry.' She fingered the flowers on her lap, then laid them beside her. 'It was kind of you to bring these.'

He lowered himself to the ground and withdrew his hands. 'I feel so awful about this. Couldn't you have phoned, told me you were in trouble? You know I'd have come.'

'You sound like Simon,' she said lightly.

He ruffled his hair and glanced away from her gaunt, bruised face and shaven head. 'Simon's been on the phone almost every day. His parents are devastated, blaming each other, blaming Meg, wanting to do something to make up ... Well, I'm sure you can imagine how they feel. Simon tried phoning the Hall to find out where you were and got a mouthful of abuse. It's understandable, of course, but it didn't make things any easier.'

'I'm sorry,' she said again, 'but, oddly enough, Josh, it doesn't make it any easier for me either, to have everyone blaming themselves because I drove at a brick wall.'

He flicked her a quick glance but didn't say anything.

'Not that I did it deliberately,' she said through gritted teeth. 'That car cost me a fortune, and I can think of a hundred better ways of killing myself than writing off a perfectly good Rover.'

He plucked at a blade of grass. 'I spoke to Dean last

night,' he said uncomfortably. 'The poor chap was in tears, said if I managed to get hold of you, I was to tell you business is fine but please call him the minute you feel up to it. I gave him the number here, but he's afraid to call himself in case you're too unhappy to talk to him.'

It was hopeless. 'I'm not unhappy,' she said with a forced smile. 'I feel great. I'm looking forward to going home.' *Why was sympathy so unbearable?* 'Look, let's put these flowers in my room and then go for a walk.' *Stupid woman! Fifty yards would see her on her knees.*

'Are you sure you're up to it?' he asked, pushing himself to his feet.

'Oh, yes,' she said briskly. 'I keep telling you, I'm fine.' She set off ahead of him so he wouldn't see her face. 'Believe me, I don't intend to stay here very long. They've already said I'm mentally fit to go home, now all I need to do is prove I'm physically fit.' *Who the hell did she think she was kidding?* 'It's in here,' she said, putting one groggy leg over the sill of the french windows and hauling herself towards a chair.

The flowers slipped from her fingers on to the floor. She felt Josh's arms closing about her and saw murky images floating on the swollen river of her memory.

43 Shoebury Terrace, Hammersmith, London – 4.00 p.m.

Fraser rang the doorbell of number forty-three and asked Mrs Helms if Meg had given any indication that she intended to vacate her flat after her holiday.

'Not in so many words,' said the stout woman thoughtfully, 'but, now you come to mention it, there was a lot of coming and going shortly before they left. I remember saying to my Henry, it wouldn't surprise me if there was a change in that direction. Then she asked me to feed Marmaduke and it rather went out of my mind, except that she was insistent the poor creature shouldn't go into any of the rooms. Keep him in the hall, Mrs H, she said, thrusting a tin of cat food at me. What's going to happen to him now? Henry won't have him anywhere near, but then he's not well, you know.'

'We'll do our best to sort something out,' said Fraser, 'but in the meantime perhaps you could go on feeding the cat?'

'I won't let him starve,' she said grudgingly, 'but something ought to be done before too long. That stuffy hallway's no place to keep an animal.'

He agreed with her. 'You wouldn't happen to know what Miss Harris did for a job, would you, Mrs Helms?'

'Seems to me you know very little about her, Sergeant. Are you sure you've got the right person?'

He nodded. 'Her job?' he prompted.

'She called herself a headhunter. Used to be with a big consultancy firm in the City, then set up on her own about five years ago.' She spread her hand and made a rocking gesture with it. 'But it wasn't going too well from what I could gather. People are scared to give notice because of the recession, and you can't hunt heads when there are no vacancies to fill.'

'Any idea what her company is called?'

'No. We talked about Marmaduke and the milkman

151

from time to time but other than that' – she shrugged – 'we were just neighbours. Nothing special. Nothing close. I'm sorry she's gone, though. She never gave us any trouble.'

Fraser found himself dwelling on that last sentence as he walked the few yards to the DI's car. 'She never gave us any trouble' was the most depressing epitaph he had ever heard.

Nightingale Clinic, Salisbury – 4.00 p.m.

'What's the problem?' asked Alan Protheroe, reaching for Jinx's wrist and feeling for a pulse. He wondered who this man was and why he'd started so violently at the sound of the voice behind him.

'Well, look at her for God's sake,' said Josh in desperation, laying her slack head on the pillow and lowering her gently on to the bed. 'I think she's dying.'

'No chance. Built like a tank this one.' He let the wrist go. 'She's asleep.' He looked at the man's pinched nostrils and frightened eyes. 'You look in worse shape than she is.'

'I thought she was dying.' He leaned his hands on the side of the bed to steady himself. 'Now I feel sick. Jesus, I'm not sure I can take much more of this. I haven't slept in days, not since Simon Harris phoned to say Jinx was dead.'

'Why did he do that?'

'Because Betty Kingsley got rat-arsed and phoned

Meg's mother. Told the poor woman her daughter was a murderer.'

Alan gestured towards the terraced area beyond the windows. 'Let's go and sit outside. I'm Dr Protheroe.' He took the man's arm and supported him.

'Josh Hennessey.' He allowed Alan to lead him through the windows. 'One minute she said she was fine, the next her eyes rolled up and – wham!' He slumped on to a wooden bench and buried his face in his hands. 'I wish to hell she wouldn't keep pretending she's OK when she's not. She was the same when Russell was murdered. Kept saying: I'm fine, and then ended up in hospital.'

'You've known her a long time?'

He nodded. 'Twelve years. As long as I've known Meg. I'm Meg Harris's partner,' he explained. 'We run a recruitment consultancy.' He bunched his fists angrily. 'Or we did until she buggered off and left me high and dry with a bank manager baying for blood and work in progress with people I've never even heard of.'

Alan could feel the stress flowing off him in waves of anger and nerves. 'I see.'

'Do you? I sure as hell don't. Presumably you know Meg's hijacked Jinx's fiancé? I mean, have you any idea what that's doing to Meg's parents? First they get a phone call out of the blue to say Leo's jilted Jinx for her, then the next thing they hear is that Jinx has killed herself. Jesus! And on top of all that, I'm left in the bloody lurch, trying to run an office on my own, while Meg's farting about in France with a prize bastard.' His voice broke. 'I don't know what the hell's going on.' He rubbed his eyes. 'I'm so fucking tired.'

Alan watched him sympathetically for a moment or two. 'If it makes you feel any better, I think you're worrying unnecessarily on Jinx's account. All things considered, she's doing well.'

'Simon warned me she looked ill, but I wasn't expecting this.' He jerked his head towards her room. 'She's much worse than I thought she was going to be.'

'She probably isn't, you know. Look, she took a heck of a crack on the head and she's forgotten a couple of weeks out of her life, but that's all. She's a tough lady. Give her another week or two and she'll be good as new. It's only a matter of time.'

Josh stared at his hands. 'You've probably never seen her with hair. She's a bit of a stunner. Very Italian looking.' He touched a hand to his shoulder. 'Thick black hair to here, and dark eyes. I've always thought it's crazy her being on the business end of the camera when she should have been in the frame.' He fell silent.

'You sound fond of her.'

'I am, but my timing's lousy. When I was free, she was married. When she was free, I was married.' He looked away towards the trees bordering the lawn. 'Then I got divorced and Leo muscled in on the act. Do you reckon she still loves him?'

'She says she doesn't.'

Josh twisted his head to examine the older man's face. 'Do you believe her?'

'I do, yes.'

'Why?'

Alan shrugged. 'She isn't angry enough with Meg.' But *you* certainly are, he was thinking.

The Vicarage, Littleton Mary, Wiltshire – 4.00 p.m.

Charles Harris laid down his pen and folded his hands across the sermon he was writing. 'This has to stop, Caroline. You're working yourself into hysterics over nothing. Meg will phone when she's ready. And let's face it,' he added rather dryly, '"when Meg is ready" are the operative words. Judging by the frequency of her calls and visits in the past, you and I could go to hell and back without her even being aware of it. She's always been far more interested in whichever man she has in tow than she's ever been in us.'

Caroline looked at him with dislike. 'That's what you hate, isn't it? The men.'

'Don't be absurd,' he snapped. There were times when he had to restrain himself from hitting her. 'Must we go through this again?' he said, picking up his pen and returning to his sermon. 'I do have work to do.' He made a note in the margin.

'It shocked you to hear about her and Russell, didn't it?' she said spitefully.

'Yes, it did.'

'Your little Meggy in the arms of a man old enough to be her father. She loved him, you know.'

He kept his eyes on the page but found he couldn't write anything because his hand was shaking.

'Does it offend you to think of your daughter enjoying

155

sex with old men when she can't even bear to be in the same house with you?'

'No,' he said quietly, 'what offends me is her shabbiness towards her best friend. Between us, you and I created a monster, Caroline.'

Chapter Nine

JINX HAD RESUMED her vantage point under the beech
tree, dark glasses firmly in place, anonymity restored. To
observers, she was an object of curiosity, this thin, gaunt
woman who sat alone and used the protective fronds of
the hanging branches to hide behind. Almost, thought
Alan Protheroe, watching her from the french window in
his office, like a bird in a cage, for it was her loneliness
that impressed him most. He wondered if it was advisable
or possible to unlock the iron control that she exercised
upon her emotions, for he was doubtful that happiness
was a condition to which Jinx aspired. She couldn't bear
to be so vulnerable.

'I'm relieved,' she said when he'd asked her if she was
happy that her bandages had been removed. 'Only
children know how to be happy.'

'And were you happy as a child, Jinx?'

'I must have been. The smell of baking bread always
puts me in a good mood.' She smiled slightly at his frown
of puzzlement. 'My father wasn't always a rich man. I
remember being a small child and living in a two-up,
two-down in London somewhere. My mother did all her
own cooking and baked all her own bread, and I can't

157

smell warm bread now without wanting to turn somersaults.'

'Which mother was that? Your real mother or your stepmother?'

She looked confused suddenly. 'I suppose it was my stepmother. I was too young to remember anything my mother did.'

'Not necessarily. We begin to store emotions at a very young age, so there's no reason why you shouldn't remember happiness from when you were a toddler, particularly if it was followed by a period of unhappiness.'

She looked away. 'Why should it have been?'

'Your mother died, Jinx. That must have been an unhappy time for you and your father.'

She shrugged. 'If it was, I don't remember it. Which is sad in itself. Death should make an impact, don't you think? It's awful how quickly we forget and move on to something new.'

'But very important that we do,' he replied, 'otherwise we become like Miss Havisham in *Great Expectations* and sit for ever at an empty table.'

She smiled. 'If I remember my Dickens, poor old Miss Havisham was jilted by her fiancé on her wedding day and spent the rest of her life in her bridal gown with the remains of the banquet all around her. Hardly the most tactful parallel you could have drawn. In the circumstances, wedding plans are not a subject I particularly want to dwell on.'

'Then let's talk about something you *would* like to dwell on. What makes you feel alive?'

She shook her head. 'Nothing. I prefer the peacefulness of feeling nothing. For every up there's a down and I hate the sadness of disappointment.'

'Relationships don't have to be disappointing, Jinx. Far more often than not, they represent the sort of fulfilment most of us long for. Do you not think that's a goal worth pursuing?'

'Are we talking marriage and children, Dr Protheroe?' she asked suspiciously. 'Did Josh Hennessey tell you he fancied me?'

He chuckled. 'Not in so many words, but he seems fond of you.'

'He's far fonder of Meg than he is of me,' she said dismissively. 'Too fond, really. She treats him like a brother because business and pleasure don't mix, when all *he* wants to do is fuck her. Also, he was fond of his wife when he married her,' she added tartly, 'but he walked out on her four years later because he claimed she was boring. Is that the kind of fulfilling relationship you want me to have?'

'I doubt he'd find you boring, Jinx, but in any case, that's a side issue. What I think we're talking about is contentment.'

She gave a low laugh. 'Well, I'm a good photographer, and that makes me content. If I'm remembered for just one photograph, then that will be immortality enough. I don't need any other. It's a birth of sorts, you know. Your creation emerges from the darkness of the developing room with a similar sense of achievement as a baby emerging from the womb.'

'Does it?'

She shrugged again. 'I think so. Admittedly the only

birth I can compare it with was a rather messy business in the lavatory, but I imagine going to term and producing a living child is somewhat more rewarding. Yes, I'd say the sense of achievement in those circumstances is not dissimilar.' Her face was devoid of expression. 'By the same token, I imagine there's the same sense of disappointment when the result of your hard work is less than you'd hoped for. Works of art, be they children or photographs, can never be perfect.' She hesitated a moment. 'I suppose if you're lucky, they might be interesting.'

After that she had excused herself politely and walked outside, leaving Protheroe to wonder if she was talking about her own hopes of the child she had lost or her father's hopes of her. Although perhaps she was talking about neither. He reflected on the two unmarried brothers who still lived at home and who, if Jinx's closed expression when their names were mentioned was any guide, had little love for their intellectually gifted sister.

He was about to turn away from the office window and his contemplation of her seated, solitary figure when he noticed a man approaching across the lawn. *Now where the hell had he come from?* For no obvious reason, other than that he was responsible for Jinx's safety and she was clearly unaware that anyone was behind her, he felt a sense of imminent danger and, with a flick of his long fingers, turned the key in the lock and thrust the door wide. With farther to travel than the other, he raised his voice in a bluff bellow. 'There you are, Jinx!' he called. 'I've been looking for you.'

160

Startled, she turned her head, saw her younger brother first, then looked beyond him to Protheroe. 'God, you gave me a shock,' she said accusingly as they both drew close. 'Hello, Fergus.' She nodded a welcome. 'Have you two met? Fergus Kingsley, my brother – Dr Alan Protheroe, my existentialist shrink. You're a very bad liar,' she told Alan. 'You've been watching me for the last ten minutes, so why the sudden panic?'

He shook Fergus by the hand. 'Because I take my responsibilities seriously, Jinx, and for all I knew your brother was a stranger to you.' He folded his arms across his chest. 'As a matter of interest,' he said without hostility, 'which way did you come in? It's a rule of the Nightingale Clinic that visitors seek permission at the front desk before approaching our guests. It's a simple courtesy but an important one, as I'm sure you'll agree.'

Fergus reddened under the older man's stare. 'I'm sorry.' He looked very young. 'I didn't realize.' He gestured behind him to the other side of the lawn. 'I parked by the gate at the bottom and walked up.' He looked sullenly towards Jinx. 'Actually, I was going to do the thing properly, then I saw you under the tree.'

Jinx removed her dark glasses and squinted up at Protheroe with one blackened eye closed against the evening sunlight. 'I don't recall my consent being sought before. It's a perverse rule that operates at the whim of the director.'

He smiled affably. 'But a rule, nevertheless. I shall have to make sure it's properly enforced in future.' He nodded to them both. 'Enjoy your visit. If you want some tea, your brother can order it from the desk and have it sent out.' He raised a hand in farewell, then walked briskly back to his office.

Jinx stared after him. 'I think he's madder than some of his patients,' she said.

Fergus followed her gaze. 'He fancies you,' he said bluntly.

She gave a splutter of laughter. 'Don't be an oaf! The man's not blind, and they do let me look in a mirror from time to time.' She sobered suddenly and her eyes narrowed. 'Actually, I hate the way he's always watching me. It makes me feel like a prisoner.'

'Do you like him?'

'Yes.'

'Is he married?'

'He's a widower.' She frowned. 'Why so interested?'

He shrugged. 'You know what they say about psychiatrists and their patients. I was just wondering if he was going to be the next one in the Kingsley marriage stakes.'

'Do me a favour, Fergus,' she said crossly. 'I don't intend to stay here long enough to develop anything more than a passing acquaintanceship with the man.'

He leaned against the tree trunk. 'So you're planning to come home?'

'*Go* home,' she corrected him. 'Back to Richmond and back to the studio. Sitting around and doing nothing isn't what I'm best at.'

'Is that supposed to be a dig at me?'

'No,' she said mildly. 'Oddly enough, Fergus, I am more interested in my own problems at the moment than

I am in yours.' She studied his sullen face, which was so like Miles's to look at, but which lacked the charm that his older brother could switch on and off at will. 'Did you have a reason for coming?'

He scuffed the grass with his foot. 'I wondered how you were, that's all. Miles said you weren't too hot when he came, said you passed out when he was talking to you.'

'It's just tiredness.' She replaced her dark glasses so that he couldn't read the expression in her eyes. 'Miles told me Adam made you cry. Is that true?'

He reddened again. 'Miles is a bastard. He swore he wouldn't tell anyone. You know, sometimes I don't know who I hate more, him or Dad. They're such shits both of them. I wish they'd drop dead. Everything would be OK if they were both dead.'

It was the same childish whine she'd heard from him since he was five years old. Only the register of his voice was different. 'Presumably he belted you again. So what did you do to make Adam angry?'

'It wasn't me who made him angry. It's you being in this place.' He slid his back down the tree trunk to squat at the foot of it. 'He just went overboard and started screaming and yelling at everyone. Miles cowered in the corner, as per bloody usual, and Mum sat and blubbered. Well, you know what it's like. You don't need me to tell you.'

'But you must have done something,' she said. 'He might be angry about me and' – she gestured towards the building – 'all this, but he's never belted you without good reason. So what did you do?'

'I borrowed twenty pounds,' he muttered. 'You'd think it was a hanging offence the way he carried on.'

She sighed. 'Who from this time?'

'Does it matter?' he said angrily. 'You're as bad as bloody Dad. I was going to pay it back.' His mouth thinned unattractively. 'What nobody ever seems to recognize is that I wouldn't have to borrow money if Dad treated me like a human being instead of a slave. It's really degrading having to admit you're the son of Adam Kingsley when everyone knows you're earning peanuts. I keep telling him, if he'd only pay me a decent whack, I wouldn't have to resort to borrowing. I'm the boss's son. That should stand for something. Why do Miles and I have to start at the bottom?'

'You know,' she said with sudden impatience, 'if you called a spade a spade occasionally, you'd be halfway to earning Adam's respect. It's the lies that you and Miles tell that really fire him up. Can't you see that? You're a thief' – she fixed him with a scornful stare – 'and everybody knows it, so why bother with this garbage about borrowing? Who did you steal from this time?'

'Jenkins,' he muttered. 'But I was going to pay him back.'

'Then I'm not surprised Adam belted you,' she said tiredly. 'I wouldn't enjoy having to apologize to my gardener after my twenty-four-year-old son had stolen money from him. I suppose you thought Jenkins wouldn't have the nerve to say anything and that you'd get away with it. That's almost worse than stealing from him in the first place.'

'Oh, leave it out, Jinxy. I've had all this from Dad,

and you're both wrong, anyway. I really was going to pay him back. If he'd had a word with me, I'd have sorted it out, but, oh no, he had to go running to the old man and make a bloody mountain out of a molehill.'

Something fundamental snapped inside Jinx's head. She would always think of it afterwards as the blood bond that had tied her physically to a family that in any other circumstance she would have avoided like the plague. Suddenly, she found herself free to acknowledge that she didn't like them. More, she had only contempt for them. Ultimately, in fact, she agreed with what everyone knew Adam thought but had never put into words: Miles and Fergus were their mother's sons and, like Betty, saw Adam Kingsley only in terms of their meal ticket.

She smiled savagely. 'I'm going to tell you things that I've never told a soul in my life. First, I despise your mother. I always have done from the minute she came into our house. She's a fat drunk with an extraordinarily low IQ. Second, she married my father because she wanted to be a lady, and she had enough cunning to persuade him that, while she could never fill my mother's shoes, she could at least be a comfortable slipper for him at the end of a long day. He was lonely and he fell for it, but what he actually saddled himself with was a vulgar, money-grabbing tart.' She held up three fingers. 'Third, it might not have been so bad if she hadn't lumbered him with you and Miles. Even your names are an embarrassment. Adam wanted to call you something straightforward, like David or Michael, but Elizabeth wanted something befitting the sons of a rich lady.'

Her voice took on the accent of her stepmother. 'It has to be something posh, Daddy, and David and Michael are so common.' She drew an angry breath. 'Fourth, Adam finds himself father to two of the laziest, most unintelligent, most dishonest sons a man could have. Every gene you have has come to you straight from your mother. You are incapable, both of you, of contributing anything worthwhile to your family. Instead, you are only interested in bringing Adam and me down to your own shabby levels. Fifth, how the hell can you begin to justify stealing off a gardener who works day in day out to fund his very modest house and his very modest car while you, you little bastard' – she spat at him – 'swan around in your swank Porsche so that you can pick up any little tart who's stupid enough to think the Kingsley name means something? Will you explain that to me? *Can* you explain it to me?'

He stared at her. It was a shock to see his father mirrored in the set of her chin and the fury in her voice, but he had spent years playing on her conscience and, like Miles, he was a master at it. 'We've always known you were a snobbish bitch, Jinx,' he said idly. 'What the hell do you suppose it was like for Mum moving into a house with the perfect child already in residence and pictures of her perfect mother all over the walls? She says you were so condescending she wanted to slap you. I wish she had, as a matter of fact. If you'd been treated the way Dad's treated us, then maybe things would have been better for us all.'

'He didn't treat you any differently at the beginning from the way he treated me,' she said coldly. 'I can remember the first time he belted you because it was the first time you and Miles were reported for stealing. You were nine years old and Miles was eleven, and you stole money from the till in the village shop. Adam paid over a hundred pounds to Mrs Davies to hush the whole thing up, then took a strap to the pair of you to remind you what would happen if you ever did it again.' She shook her head. 'But it didn't work. You just went on doing it and he went on beating you, and it was me who had to try and calm him down because Betty was always drunk. Do you think I enjoyed any of that?'

He shrugged. 'I couldn't care less whether you did or not, and anyway you're exaggerating. Most of the time you were either at school or bloody Oxford, playing the family genius while Miles and I were being treated like Neanderthals. You should put yourself in our shoes once in a while. You know damn well he's always hated us. We only took that money from the shop because we thought he might notice us instead of mooning over his precious Jane.' His mouth took on a sullen cast. 'You don't know what it was like. When you were home for the holidays he was only interested in you and what you were doing, and when you were away he used to shut himself in his office with those bloody photographs of your mother.'

She saw that for what it was, the manipulative emotional blackmail of a selfish, twisted mind, but the habits of a lifetime die very hard and, as usual, she foundered on the hard certainty of Adam's obsession with her mother and herself. 'But why will you never help yourselves?' she asked him. 'Why do you go on doing what you know he hates? Why do you stay there and give him the opportunity to despise you? I just don't understand that.'

'Because it's my home as much as his and I don't see why he should push me out,' he said. 'It's all right for you. You got Russell's money. You were lucky.'

She experienced the strange sensation of a door slamming shut on a memory. For the briefest second, she had a glimpse of something remembered but it was as transient as a puff of wind on a summer's day and the memory was lost. *Had they had this conversation before?* 'You have some very warped ideas, Fergus. How can you regard anything to do with Russell's murder as lucky?' *Why did Russell keep intruding into every conversation? She had banned him from her thoughts for so long, but now she was being forced into thinking about him all the time.*

'Leave it out, Jinx. You weren't that fond of him and you ended up with all the loot.' But it was said without conviction, because he, like she, had lost the energy to continue an argument that was going nowhere. Where trust had been sacrificed, knowledge was all, and it mattered very little whether thoughts were spoken or unspoken when everyone knew where they stood. *Except* ... 'You're wrong to slag off poor old Mum,' he said with a half-hearted show of belligerence. 'She's gone out and batted for you, which is more than Dad's done since you've been in here. She's given the Walladers and the Harrises a pasting for the way Leo and Meg have treated you. She called Sir Anthony "a boil on the bum of society" and Caroline Harris "a tight-arsed bitch".'

Jinx lowered her head abruptly so that he wouldn't see the laughter in her eyes.

'OK, she was drunk,' said Fergus sulkily, 'but she meant well. Actually, Miles and me thought it was quite funny.'

So did Jinx . . . She had called Anthony a 'parasite' but how much more astute was Betty's judgement . . .

Romsey Road Police Station, Winchester – 7.30 p.m.

'You're going to have to let me talk to Miss Kingsley,' said Gareth Maddocks, dropping wearily into a chair. 'Seriously, sir, bar sitting by Miss Harris's phone and waiting for the damn thing to ring, I can't see how we're going to find out where her parents live.'

'Did you try Sir Anthony again?'

Maddocks nodded. 'He just keeps bleating Wiltshire at us. All this guff he gave you about what a relief it was when Leo took up with a nice girl like Meg amounts to sweet FA. The only thing she had going for her, as far as I can make out, was that she wasn't Jane Kingsley. The impression I get is that if Leo had turned up with some old slag from the local pub and announced his intention of marrying *her*, the Walladers would have jumped for joy.'

'Can't say I blame them,' said the Superintendent dryly. 'I wouldn't want Adam Kingsley for an in-law either.'

'Well, for what it's worth, his daughter sounds fairly

reasonable. She left a message on the answerphone. Nice voice, sense of humour, says she doesn't bear any grudges and wanted Meg to phone her.'

Frank raised an eyebrow. 'Have you got it with you?'

The DI reached into his pocket and took out a tape-cassette. 'We made copies at the Hammersmith nick, then took the original back to the flat.' He put it on the desk in front of him. 'Hers is the last message. I've listened to it several times now and I'm inclined to agree with Fraser that she has no idea Leo and Meg are dead.'

Cheever fingered the cassette for a moment, then picked it up, swivelled in his chair and pushed it into a tape-deck on the shelf behind him. He sat with bowed head, listening to the recorded messages, only stirring when Jinx's ended. He pressed *Rewind*, listened to hers again, then rubbed his jaw thoughtfully as he pressed *Stop*. 'She says she can't remember anything since June the fourth,' he pointed out.

'Which tallies with the Fordingbridge report,' said Maddocks. 'According to that, the concussion after the accident left her with amnesia.'

'Agreed, but it doesn't mean she didn't know about the deaths. Do you follow what I'm saying? She could have wiped the knowledge from her memory.' He tapped a finger on the desk. 'I think it would be extremely foolish to assume anything on the basis of this one recording.'

'I'm not arguing with you, sir, but it strikes me this is our best opportunity to question her without raising anyone's hackles, least of all her father's.' He leaned forward. 'Look, we are simply trying to trace the whereabouts of Miss Harris. Her credit cards have come into the possession of the police after the arrest of a thief, but repeated attempts to contact her at her address in London have failed to produce a response. Hammersmith police, concerned for her welfare, have entered the flat in order to trace her family and friends, only to discover that the flat has been cleared out. The one lead they came up with is Miss Kingsley because she was the only caller who left her telephone number. We have been asked by Hammersmith to interview Miss Kingsley with a view to tracing Miss Harris.' He spread his hands. 'Are you going to give me a shot at her on that basis? It's a legitimate approach.'

The Superintendent steepled his fingers on the desk in front of him and stared the other man down. 'You do realize I'll have your hide if you make a mess of it.'

Maddocks grinned. 'Trust me, sir.'

His eyes narrowed. 'I hate people who say that. Just make sure you get the consent of her doctor before you talk to her. In fact, you can go further, and ask him to be present while you put your questions. I do not want this force accused of bullying a sick young woman.'

'Do me a favour, sir,' said Maddocks plaintively, 'I wouldn't know how to begin. I like women.'

Frank's eyebrows beetled into a ferocious frown. It was common knowledge that Maddocks had been the subject of sexual harassment complaints by three different female officers, although, predictably, nothing had come of them. 'You've been warned,' was all he said.

Canning Road Police Station, Salisbury – 8.00 p.m.

WPC Blake stuffed a photocopy under the nose of the sergeant, as she came in at the end of her shift, and shook it vigorously. 'Read that, Sarge. It's a dead ringer for Flossie Hale's experience. Same MO, same refusal to talk, same injuries.'

He took it in both hands and placed it squarely on his desk. 'It may come as a surprise to you, Blake, but I have A-one vision. As yet, I do not require documents to be held half an inch from my eyes in order to read them.' He then scanned the page.

Incident report
Officers attending: PC Hughes and PC Anderson.
23.3.94. Disturbance reported 23.10 at
54 Paradise Avenue.
Woman banging on neighbour's door and causing a
nuisance.
On investigation, woman found to be in need of
urgent medical treatment. Severe bruising to the face
and lacerations of the rectum.
Name: Samantha Garrison. Known local prostitute.
Claimed assailant was her husband but believed to be
lying.
Refused to co-operate further.

'Have you followed this up with Hughes and Anderson?' he asked.

'Not yet.'

'Talk to them tomorrow.' He spread a broad palm across the sheet. 'Then have a word with Samantha, assuming you can find her, and keep me posted. Good girl. I think you could be on to something. Let's see you nail this bastard.'

Blake flushed a rosy-red. At twenty-one, she was still untouched by cynicism, so other people's approbation mattered.

Nightingale Clinic, Salisbury – 11.30 p.m.

Time had no relevance. An hour spent reading a book passed in a minute. A minute of agony lasted an hour. Only fear was eternal for fear fed itself. *Whose fear? Yours? Theirs? Ours? Mine? His? Hers? Everyone's.*

Even the dark was fearful.

Confusion . . . confusion . . . confusion . . .

Forget . . . forget . . . forget . . .

A moment of clarity.

Why am I here? What am I doing?

MEG WAS A WHORE! booms the great voice of reason. *My father made me evil.*

Chapter Ten

FOR VARIOUS REASONS, DS Sean Fraser was none too happy about accompanying Maddocks to the interview with Jane Kingsley, and he sat in gloomy silence in the passenger seat as the car headed for Salisbury. He had made himself a hostage to fortune by rashly promising his wife and two young daughters that he would take them to the beach at Studland that Sunday, and their tears and recriminations at the cancelled treat lay heavily on his conscience. His gloom was exacerbated by Maddocks's disgusting cheerfulness at the thought of a possible collar which he chose to express through a tuneless and repetitive rendering of 'The sun has got his hat on, Hip-hip-hip-Hooray . . .'

'Give over, Guv,' he said at last. 'It's worse than having a tooth extracted.'

'You're a miserable creature, Fraser. What's eating you, anyway?'

'It's a Sunday, Guv, so it's going to be a waste of time. You realize her entire family will probably be there visiting her, which means we won't get a look in, not unless we want Kingsley on our backs as well.'

'Nn-nn.' Maddocks gave a self-satisfied grunt. 'I sent

Mandy Barry over to chat up the nurses this morning and find out who's been visiting Jane and when. According to her, Kingsley hasn't been near his daughter since she was admitted, the stepmother's been in once and doesn't look like showing again, and the two brothers came independently and left in sulks. The word is there's no love lost between any of them, so the chances of them giving up their Sunday for her are non-existent.'

'You're round the flaming bend,' said Fraser angrily, seeing himself cast as co-conspirator in Maddocks's unorthodox methods. 'By the book, the Super said. He'll flip if he finds out you've had Mandy sneaking around behind people's backs.'

'Who's going to tell him?' said Maddocks carelessly. 'I'd be even more round the bend if I went in cold.' He swung the car on to the main road and accelerated up the hill. 'Look, lad, you've got to find some backbone from somewhere. You'll never get anywhere in this business if you can't act on your own initiative occasionally.' He broke into his tuneless dirge again.

Fraser turned away to gaze out of the passenger window. What really riled him about Maddocks was that the bastard was more often right than he was wrong. Initiative in Maddocks's vocabulary meant taking shortcuts and using methods that wouldn't stand scrutiny for a minute under the Police and Criminal Evidence Act, but he got away with it because, in his own terminology, 'he could smell guilt'. Privately, Fraser put this down to the fact that the Inspector was as ethically bankrupt as the people he arrested – he had heard more than one whisper that Maddocks had taken bribes in the past – but this raised troubling questions about the effectiveness of policemen and, as Fraser was a thoughtful man, the whole issue worried him. For there was an intrinsic absurdity about forcing the police to follow every rule, when criminal behaviour, which was dedicated to rule-breaking, remained unchanged.

Nightingale Clinic, Salisbury – 2.30 p.m.

Alan Protheroe listened to what the two detectives had to say with a frown creasing his amiable face. 'Presumably there's more to this than meets the eye,' he suggested. 'If the Hammersmith police only wanted the address of Miss Harris's parents, why didn't they telephone Miss Kingsley and ask her for it?'

'Because, in the message she left on Harris's answerphone, she refers to this clinic as a nutters' hospital,' said Maddocks easily, 'and, as I'm sure you know, there are rules governing the police in the way they question the mentally disturbed. So, before they approached her direct, Hammersmith asked us to find out why she was here, and we discovered very quickly from our colleagues in Fordingbridge that she had been admitted following a suicide attempt after her fiancé deserted her for Miss Harris. We have no desire to upset her unnecessarily, so it was felt that any questions should be asked by plain-clothes policemen.'

Alan took exception to his references to 'nutters' and 'the mentally disturbed'. More, he took exception to Maddocks himself, disliking the man's over-powering personality which thrust into the room like a bad smell. 'Why didn't you ring *me*?' he said suspiciously. 'I would have been happy to ask the questions for you.'

Maddocks spread his hands in a gesture of surrender. 'All right, I'll be honest with you, sir. The problem is not Miss Kingsley but Miss Kingsley's father. The orders from above are very clear. Do not give Adam Kingsley any excuse to sue the Hampshire police for alleged insensitivity towards his sick daughter. We haven't a clue what her reaction will be to questions about the woman who seduced her fiancé. For all we know, the mere mention of Meg Harris's name will have her climbing the walls, and we have enough difficulty paying our policemen without squandering the budget on court battles with a tetchy millionaire who's already worried about his daughter's state of mind.' He turned his hands palms down. 'And with good reason, it would seem. By her own admission, she's in a nutters' hospital and she's shit-scared she's going round the bend. Her words, sir, not mine.'

Fraser had to admire Maddocks's psychology. Whatever Protheroe's suspicions about their motives for being there, he was side-tracked into defending his clinic and his patient. 'I would prefer it, Inspector, if you ceased referring to the Nightingale Clinic as a nutters' hospital,' he said tartly. 'Jinx has a healthy cynicism about everything, coupled with a dry sense of humour. She was clearly joking. I have no concerns at all about her mental equilibrium. Nor, I am sure, has she. She has limited loss of memory following her accident, but is otherwise mentally acute.'

'Well, that's a relief,' said Maddocks. 'It'll be all right for us to talk to her then?'

'Assuming she agrees, then, yes, I see no reason why not.' He stood up and led the way to the door, noticing with interest that Sergeant Fraser appeared to find Detective Inspector Maddocks as uncongenial as he did. The body language spoke volumes, principally in the younger man's attempts to keep daylight between himself and his superior. He took them down the corridor. 'I think it would be better if I remained during the interview,' he said, tapping on the door of number twelve.

'I see no reason why not, sir, assuming Miss Kingsley agrees,' said Maddocks with derisory emphasis.

Jinx, in her turn, listened to the Inspector's explanation for being there. She sat in the chair by the window and, bar wishing the two policemen 'good afternoon' when they came in, said nothing until Maddocks had finished. Even then she didn't answer immediately, but eyed him in silence for a moment or two with curiously little expression on her pale face. 'Meg's parents live in a village near Warminster called Littleton Mary,' she said finally. 'Her father's the vicar there. I'm afraid I can't give you the telephone number because it's in my address book and I don't have that with me, but I should imagine it's in the book. Her father's initial is C for Charles and he and Meg's mother live in the vicarage.'

She reached towards the cigarette packet on the table, then changed her mind and left it where it was. She found herself reluctant suddenly to draw attention to the tremors in her hands, and doubted her ability to hold the flame steady long enough to light a cigarette. 'But Meg won't be there,' she continued in her deep voice. 'She's on holiday in France at the moment.'

'Well, that would explain why we've had difficulty contacting her,' said Maddocks, as if hearing this information for the first time. He glanced towards Alan Protheroe. 'In fact, Doctor, I really don't think we need keep you, not unless Miss Kingsley feels nervous at being left on her own.' He smiled down at her. 'Do you, Miss Kingsley?'

She shrugged indifferently. 'Not in the least.'

'Then thank you very much, sir. We won't be long.' Maddocks stood by the open door.

Alan frowned at him angrily, well aware that he was being rail-roaded. 'I'd rather stay, Jinx,' he said. 'I'm sure your father would expect me to.'

She gave her low laugh. 'I'm sure you're right, but as you keep trying to persuade me, Dr Protheroe, I call the shots, not my father. Thank you anyway. I think I can manage a few questions on my own.'

'Well, you know where I am if you need me.' He allowed himself to be closed out by Maddocks's firm hand on the door, but he wished he knew what the hell was going on. It was obvious that Jinx was as reluctant as the policemen to let him listen in on the conversation.

Inside the room, Maddocks beamed encouragingly at Jinx. 'Any idea which part of France, Miss Kingsley?'

She shook her head. 'No, but I can probably guess. I know the man she's gone with. His name's Leo Wallader and he has a cottage on the south coast of Brittany. The address is Les Hirondelles, rue St Jacques, Trinité-sur-mer. There is a telephone, but again' – she gave a small shrug – 'the number's in my address book.'

Maddocks nodded. 'But if you know she's in France,' he said with a puzzled frown, 'why did you telephone her London number?'

Jinx looked at him for a moment, then picked up her cigarette packet and tapped a cigarette into her fingers. Nicotine was more important than pride. She reached for the lighter but Fraser was there before her, holding the flame steady beneath the wavering tip. She thanked him with a smile. 'Meg can ring her answerphone and listen to her messages,' she said. 'I assumed that's what she'd do.'

'Who told you she was in France?'

'Her partner, Josh Hennessey.' She gazed at him through the smoke. 'He phoned me on Wednesday.'

Maddocks glanced towards Fraser to see if he'd written that down. 'And has Meg called you back, Miss Kingsley?'

'Not yet, no.'

'Is this Mr Hennessey in contact with her?'

'Not as far as I know. She didn't give him a contact number.'

He made a play of consulting his notebook. 'In fact we know about Mr Leo Wallader. He came up in connection with your car accident. I believe he was your fiancé until a couple of weeks ago?'

She blew a stream of smoke into the air and watched it ripple towards the ceiling. 'That's right,' she said evenly.

181

'But he preferred your friend Meg Harris and left you for her.'

She smiled slightly. 'Right again, Inspector.'

'So perhaps Miss Harris is embarrassed to phone you,' he suggested, 'despite your insistence in your message that you don't bear grudges.'

She tapped ash into the ashtray. 'To tell you the truth,' she said slowly, 'I can't really remember what I said.' She looked at him with an enquiring expression in her dark eyes.

'You talked about political incorrectness, said you ought to be ripping her first editions to pieces, told her you'd lost your memory after driving at a concrete post and asked her to phone you here if she could stand the embarrassment of talking to you. Does that ring any bells?'

'Only alarm ones,' she murmured. 'You were very precise in your introductory spiel. You said that Hammersmith police had listened to her messages, taken down this phone number and then asked you to contact me here for her parents' address. You made no mention of listening to the tape yourself.' She pressed the palm of her hand against the side of her head where a pain was beginning. 'So either you were there when they listened, or they made a copy which they sent on to you.'

'They faxed us a transcript,' said Maddocks. 'Why does that alarm you?'

'May I see the fax?'

He glanced at Fraser again. 'Did we bring it with us, Sergeant? The last time I saw it, it was on your desk.'

The young man shook his head. 'Sorry, Guv. I didn't

think we'd need it.' He turned to prop his notebook against the wall, hoping that his anger and unease were less obvious than they felt.

Jinx watched him for a moment. He was a poor liar, she thought, but then his complexion was against him. He was fair, like Fergus, and the blood ran too easily to his face. She felt a twinge of sympathy for him. He had a bully for a boss and she knew better than anyone that it took a peculiar kind of courage to stand up to bullies. 'As a matter of interest,' she said calmly, 'why didn't you phone Meg's business number and ask Josh these questions?'

'Because Hammersmith have been unable to locate it,' said Maddocks. 'As I explained at the beginning, she appears to be in the process of moving out. According to them, there's nothing left except a few first editions, some clothes and the cat.'

She turned to Fraser. 'So who's looking after Marmaduke?'

'The neighbour, Mrs Helms,' he answered obligingly.

There was a long silence.

'What exactly has happened to Meg?' asked Jinx quietly. 'I can't believe that Winchester CID would go all the way to London to search someone's flat just because her credit cards have been stolen.'

Maddocks, controlling an urge to show Fraser what a pillock he thought him, perched instead on the edge of Jinx's bed and leaned forward, hands clamped between his knees. 'It wasn't only hers that were stolen,' he admitted gravely, 'but Mr Wallader's as well. The registered address for his cards is 12 Glenavon Gardens,

Richmond, which was already in the Hampshire police file as a result of your accident. Richmond police were able to give us the address and telephone number of Leo's parents because they retrieved that information from your house following the crash. However, when we contacted Sir Anthony to discover where Leo and Meg have gone he couldn't tell us anything. And that worried us, because we couldn't understand why neither of them had notified the credit companies that their cards had been stolen. If they're in a cottage in Brittany, then perhaps that explains it, but I don't understand why Sir Anthony couldn't give us the address.'

She drew away from him into the back of her chair and tried to control the panic in her heart. *Something else had happened ... something so terrible that she was too frightened to search her memory for it ...* 'He doesn't know it,' she said in an uneven voice which came back to her through the thudding, racing blood in her ears. 'He knows very little about his son. Philippa, too.'

Maddocks's heavy face drew closer, his shrewd little eyes fixed on hers. 'Are you all right, Miss Kingsley?'

'Yes, thank you.' *Something else had happened ... forget ... forget ... FORGET!* 'As far as they're concerned,' she went on more steadily, 'his only capital assets are a few stocks and shares, when in fact he has the cottage in Brittany, a house in London, which he rents out to anyone who can afford it, and a condominium in Florida. There could be a great deal more, for all I know. Those are the three he told me about.'

'Do you know the address of the London house?'

They'd had a row ... Anthony and Philippa had been

there ... I want to marry Meg ... Meg's a whore ... She flicked her gaze back to Maddocks's face. 'Only that it's in Chelsea somewhere,' she said, licking her lips nervously. 'His solicitor could tell you. His name's Maurice Bloom and he has an office somewhere off Fleet Street. I'm sure you can find him through the Law Society.'

Maddocks checked to see that Fraser had taken down the name. 'Is there a good reason why he doesn't want his parents to know about his properties?' he asked her.

She thought about that. 'It depends on your definition of good. Yes, he has a reason and, personally, I think it stinks, but it makes sense to Leo.' She paused. 'I can't really tell you what it is without sounding bitter.'

'I think we need to know,' said the Inspector.

Did they? She was finding it hard to concentrate. *I said goodbye to Leo at breakfast ... we're getting married on the second of July ...* 'They're a type, not Philippa so much perhaps, but Anthony and Leo certainly.' Her voice sounded strangely remote again. 'You never pay for anything if you can get someone else to pay for you, you use other people's expertise to help you up the ladder, and you plead poverty all the time while making snide remarks about how wealthy everyone else is. It becomes very wearing very quickly for the person who's being bled, particularly when you know that the parasite you're supporting is rolling in it.' *Was she mad? These were the last people who should be hearing her confession. Talk to the doctor ... he wants your stay here to be comfortable ... it's a free choice ...*

Maddocks watched her eyes grow huge in a face made tiny by her lack of hair. He felt the pull of their attraction even while he was thinking: Got you, you murdering bitch. You really hated the poor bastard. 'And Leo did this to you?' he asked gently.

'Not immediately. He wasn't so crass. Actually, he was quite generous at the beginning. It was only when he moved into Glenavon Gardens that I realized what I'd saddled myself with.' She took deep breaths.

'There's no hurry, Miss Kingsley. Take your time.'

Memories of Russell's murder flooded her mind. *Take your time ... there's no hurry ... we know your father hated him enough to kill him ... we know your father's a psychopath ...* 'He's a believer in the what's-yours-is-mine principle,' she said in a rush to drown out the voices in her head, 'but without the reciprocity. He was just as secretive with me as he was with his parents. I only found out about his properties when Maurice Bloom phoned him at my house one day, and it was clear from his end of the conversation that he owned something in Florida. I was angry enough to make him tell me about it, because he had given me the impression he was in financial difficulties.' *So much so that, like Fergus, he had borrowed money from her handbag. God, she remembered now. It was the meanness that had finally got to her, the tax dodges, the obsessive secrecy surrounding his bank and credit card statements, the me-me-me of his lifestyle.*

'What sort of job did he have?'

She noted the past tense but let it pass. 'He called himself a stock broker but, as he never mentioned clients by name, I guessed he was playing the markets for himself.'

'Did he go out to work each day?'

He certainly went somewhere each day. 'He spends his time in the City.' *I want to marry Meg* . . . 'Keeping his finger on the pulse, as he calls it.'

'What sort of financial difficulties did he say he was in?'

'He said he'd lost everything on some bad investments but I think he was lying. He was always complaining about how badly off he was compared with me. He used to do the same with his father.'

'Yet you said his father's the same.'

She had let rip the day she decided to end it, told them all what she thought of them, called them over-privileged leeches whose only claim to respectability was that one of their ancestors had had the brains and the balls to earn a title. 'Anthony's certainly very mean. He never pays bills until the final demand arrives in the hopes the business may have gone under before he has to write the cheque.'

'If I understood you right, Miss Kingsley, you're saying Leo touches his father for money.'

She nodded but didn't say anything. *God, but they'd hated her for it. And triumphant Leo had told her he'd been having an affair with Meg, and that she was the one he wanted to marry. And the shock had been* ENORMOUS! *She remembered it all. Anthony's loathing . . . 'You're the daughter of a barrow boy . . . we never wanted you in this family . . .' Philippa's distress. 'Do stop . . . do stop . . . words can't be taken back . . .' Leo's sulk . . . 'I want to marry Meg . . . I want to marry Meg . . .'*

'Which is why he's never told him about these properties he owns?' Maddocks suggested. 'He doesn't want his father to know what he's actually worth.'

She nodded again. 'He was – *is*,' she corrected herself, 'obsessive about money. They both are.' She called her thoughts back from the past. 'One thing I can absolutely guarantee is that Leo would have his credit cards stopped the minute he realized they were stolen. And he certainly wouldn't leave for France without them.'

'So what are you saying?'

I'm saying Leo's dead. A picture flashed out of nowhere into her tired brain. A lightning image, sharply defined, but so brief that it was gone again before she could register what it was. *Meg's a whore . . . Meg's a whore . . . too many secrets . . . déjà vu . . . this has happened before . . .* 'God,' she said, pressing a bruised hand to her chest, 'I thought – just for a moment, I thought . . .' She looked blankly at Maddocks. 'What did you ask me?'

He hadn't missed the flicker of astonishment that swept across her face. 'I was wondering what conclusions you've drawn from the fact that Leo hasn't had his cards stopped?'

She pressed trembling fingers to her forehead. 'I feel awful,' she said abruptly. 'I think I'm going to be sick.'

Fraser bent down to look into her face. 'I'll get the doctor to you,' he said.

'The name of Miss Harris's company, that's the only other thing we need,' pressed Maddocks, getting to his feet. 'We can take it from there. You said her partner was Josh Hennessey. What's the name of her company?'

'Leave it out, Guv, for Christ's sake,' said Fraser angrily, pressing the bell beside the bed. 'Can't you see she's not well?'

'Harris and Hennessey,' she murmured. 'The number's

in the book beneath Meg's home number. M. S. Harris first, then Harris and Hennessey. I don't understand why you didn't call it before coming here.'

'Well?' demanded Maddocks of Fraser as he unlocked his car door. 'Why the hell didn't we?'

'Don't ask me, Guv. I went to Downton Court, remember. My recollection is that the Super instructed *you* to find out what you could about Meg Harris.'

'It's bloody Hammersmith's fault,' said Maddocks irritably. 'Goddammit, they've got the fucking telephone books in front of them.' He slid behind the wheel. 'What did you make of her?'

Fraser folded himself into the passenger seat and pulled the door shut. 'I felt sorry for her. She looks really ill.'

'Hmm, well, it didn't stop her running rings around you, did it?' He fired the engine.

'Or you,' said Fraser curtly. 'You set the alarm bells ringing, not me.'

But Maddocks wasn't listening. He thrust the car into gear and swung the wheel. 'I'll tell you something, she certainly didn't like Leo very much, or the parents either. You've met Sir Anthony. Would you say her description of him was accurate?'

'You can't tell much about a man when he's in shock. He's not poor, that's for sure.' He thought back. 'Matter of fact, I did think he was a bit of a pseud, but the poor bastard was about to be hit with his son's death, so I didn't analyse over much.'

'It's odd, though,' said Maddocks thoughtfully. 'If she despised them all as much as she claims she did, then why was she going through with the wedding? I mean, it was Leo who called it off, not her, and if he was so obsessive about money, why did he get shot of a Kingsley in order to hitch himself to a vicar's daughter? It doesn't ring true to me.' He gave Fraser a friendly punch on the shoulder. 'Well done, lad. Looks like you were right all along. She's our villain, no question about it. Now all we have to do is nail the bitch.'

Fraser had his doubts. She'd looked so damn good on paper, but the person, predictably, was a different matter. Could someone so frail have committed so physical a crime? 'She's not strong enough, Guv. There were two of them and Leo was over six feet.'

Maddocks slowed at the clinic gates. 'She's sharp as a tack. She used deception to kill them, not strength.' He pulled on to the road. 'And don't be seduced by that feeble-little-girl act either. Christ, I've never met such a calculating woman. She was one step ahead of us most of the time, and if she's suffering from amnesia I'll eat my hat.'

The Ragged Staff, Salisbury – 6.30 p.m.

WPC Blake, comfortably unobtrusive in jeans and a T-shirt, finally tracked Samantha Garrison to earth in a city centre pub. She was alone at the bar, a rather pathetic sight in a tight black strapless sheath that showed every one of her middle-aged bulges and encouraged her underarm fat to flow like soft lard over the sequined border. Limp hair hung like a damp curtain about her heavily made-up face and cheap scent rose in a thick miasma from her warm pores.

'Samantha Garrison?' she asked, slipping on to the neighbouring stool.

'Oh, Jesus,' sighed the woman, 'tell me you're not the filth, there's a love. I just don't need the aggro at the moment. I'm having a quiet drink in my local, all right? Do you see any customers because I sure as hell don't. Chance'd be a fine thing on a Sunday night in this miserable hell-hole.'

'I'm not here for aggro,' said Blake, catching the barman's eye. 'What are you drinking?'

Samantha eyed the half-pint of bitter that she'd been spinning out for the last forty minutes. 'Double rum and Coke,' she said.

Blake ordered a gin and tonic for herself, waited for the drinks to arrive, then suggested they adjourn to an isolated table in the window.

'You said no aggro,' Samantha reminded her. 'What do you want to say to me over there that you can't say here?'

'I want to talk about what happened to you on the twenty-third of March. I thought it would be less embarrassing if we were a little more private.'

A bleak expression settled over the painted face. 'I knew that one would come back to haunt me. What if I say I don't want to talk about it?'

'Then I'll be conducting a one-sided conversation which everyone will hear.' She glanced towards the barman. 'I'm trying to make things easy for you, Samantha. If you'd rather, we can go back to your house.'

'Gawd no. D'you think I want my kids reminding what happened?' She eased off the stool. 'Get your arse over here then but I'm not making no promises. It still gives me the sweats just thinking about it. I suppose it's what happened to that other girl that's got you on my back again.'

Blake took the chair opposite and leaned forward, elbows on the table. 'Which other girl's that?'

'The word is another one got done same as me.'

'It certainly looks like it.'

'Is she talking?'

'Not at the moment. She's too scared.'

Samantha took a huge swallow of her rum and Coke. 'Not bloody surprised.'

Blake nodded. 'We need one of you to help us. We're worried that if he does it again he might kill the next girl.' She examined the woman's face closely. 'Girl,' she thought, was quite the wrong expression. Flossie had given her age as forty-six and Samantha would never see forty again. There were other similarities, too. They were both plump, both blonde and both extremely heavy-handed with near-white face powder. 'How did he contact you, Samantha? Did he pick you up off the street, or do you advertise somewhere?'

'Listen, love, I said I wouldn't make no promises and I meant it.'

'Flossie called me "love". You call me "love". Look, please don't take offence, but you and she are very alike. I'd describe you both as "motherly".' She paused to collect her thoughts. 'The only reference Flossie made to her attacker was to call him Little Lord Fauntleroy, so I'm guessing he's much younger than both of you, probably well spoken and probably handsome, and I'm guessing, too, that he didn't choose either of you by accident. Judging by the fact that you and Flossie are of similar age and similar appearance, he was clearly looking for a specific kind of prostitute. Which means he must have picked you up off the street or he wouldn't have known what you looked like. Am I right?'

'I'm long past walking the streets, love.' Samantha sighed again. 'Look, get me another double rum and Coke, then maybe – just maybe – I'll tell you.'

'I'm not shelling out again unless it's a definite maybe,' said Blake firmly. 'This isn't official, you know, it's my own hard-earned money I'm using.'

'More fool you, dear. No one thanks you for anything these days.'

'How much did he pay you to keep quiet?'

'Forty,' said Samantha, 'but it's not the money, love. It was him. He promised me another going over if I opened my mouth, and I believed him. Still do, if it's of any interest to you. He was mad as a bloody hatter.'

'Forty,' Blake echoed in genuine astonishment. 'Christ! He must have money to burn. What do you normally charge? Ten?' No answer. 'So he's a *rich*, well-spoken, handsome young man?' Again no answer. 'Come on, Samantha, how did he know what you looked like? Tell me that at least. It means I can put the word out among the other girls to be careful in future.'

The woman nudged her glass towards the WPC. 'I

reckon you've got it back to front, love. I reckon he was expecting something young and pretty, and found a fat old slag instead. All I know is, he rang me on the number on my card – and the card's in that many shop windows I wouldn't know which one he saw – made an appointment to visit, climbed on to my sodding bed and went berserk. Claimed I was old enough to be his mother and that I'd no business to be advertising under false pretences. Now give us a fill-up, there's a good girl.'

Blake took the glass and stood up. 'So you think he's a regular round the prostitutes but only lashes out at the older ones?'

The heavy shoulders rose in a shrug. 'Thinking's never been my strong point, dear. If it had, I'd have been a brain surgeon. Mind, I reckon his father beats up on his ma. "Tell 'em your old man did it," he said, "and they'll believe you."'

Chapter Eleven

Sunday, 26 June, Nightingale Clinic,
Salisbury – 7.00 p.m.

THERE WAS NO pattern to Jinx's thoughts. Bits of remembered conversation plagued her weary brain. *Do your brothers resent you?* Yes, yes, YES! *You were so condescending she wanted to slap you* ... She had been seven years old. A baby, still ... *the perfect child already in residence with pictures of her perfect mother all over the walls* ... Was it her fault that her father had begun to despise his second wife within months of the wedding? *Relationships don't have to be disappointing, Jinx* ... She had never known one that wasn't. She had married Russell because she felt sorry for him and discovered too late that pity is a bad basis for marriage. Yet, without the wisdom to predict events before they happened, could anyone in her shoes have done better? *So what are you saying?* I don't know, I don't know, I DON'T KNOW! *Something terrible happened ... Russell's dead ...*

Dr Protheroe looked in on her at seven o'clock. 'How's it going?'

She was propped up on her pillows. 'I'm a mess,' she said honestly, feeling again that ridiculous urge to be plucked from the bed and held in the comfort of his arms. *Oh, God, she had never felt so alone.*

195

He leant over her and she could smell the soap on his hands. 'You told me the police hadn't upset you when the Sergeant called me in, but I think you were lying. What did they really want to talk to you about?'

She fixed on the hairs that were sprouting from his shirt where the button was missing, funny little black tendrils that poked out wickedly and made a mockery of his position as clinic director. Adam would have fired him a long time ago *pour encourager les autres*, but then Adam rated presentation above content, and Adam was a bully. 'They just wanted a few details about Meg,' she said. 'And they didn't upset me. I'm just very tired at the moment.'

He pulled the chair forward and sat in it. 'OK. So what's this mess you're in? Physical? Mental?'

A tear glittered along her lid. 'Life,' she said. 'I've made a mess of life, and I don't know how to put it right.'

What a very seductive combination it was, he thought, this switch from tough-minded independence in the company of policemen to tearful vulnerability when alone with her doctor. He wished he felt more confident that the tear was genuine. As Veronica Gordon, one of the nursing sisters, had said to him that morning: 'She has a way with her, Alan. I think it's those extraordinary eyes. They say one thing and her voice says another.'

'What do the eyes say?' he'd asked her.

'Help,' she'd said succinctly, 'but it's the one thing she never asks for.'

'Perhaps life has made a mess of you,' he suggested now.

'No,' said Jinx flatly. 'That's the excuse I've always

used, but it's not true. I allow things to happen instead of controlling them. Like this place, for example. I don't want to be here, but I am. And the only reason I stay is because my father will pursue me to London and put pressure on me to go home with him, and I want that even less than I want this.' She raised the sheet to her eyes to wipe away her tears. 'I'm only just beginning to realize how passive I am.'

'Why? Because you don't want to do battle with your father?'

'Among other things.' She sat up and linked her arms around her raised knees. 'Do you know that the only man I have ever been able to talk to on an equal basis is my next-door neighbour in Richmond, and he's in his eighties. I've been trying to remember all afternoon whether there's ever been anyone else and I haven't come up with a single person.'

'What about your people at the studio? Dean and Angelica. Surely you talk to them on an equal basis. As a matter of interest, have you called either of them since you arrived?'

He knew she hadn't. There had been only two calls out. And neither had been to her studio.

'There'd be no point. We only ever talk about work and I trust them to get on with it. Besides, I don't find it easy discussing my private life.'

He'd noticed. 'Josh? Can't you talk to him?'

She pulled a face. 'When I see him, which isn't very often. In any case, I usually end up apologizing for being Meg's friend. God knows why he ever went into business with her. She can be very unreliable at times.'

For the moment, he let Meg go. 'What about Russell?'

She stared beyond him out of the window. 'He was like my father. He was possessive, he was jealous and he thought I was wonderful.' She fell silent, lost in the past somewhere. He was about to prompt her again, when she continued of her own accord. 'It was a classic case of out of the frying pan and into the fire. The odd thing is, he was fine as long as we weren't married. It was ownership that changed him. He became like my father.'

'Why do you feel your father owns you, Jinx?'

'I don't. That's how Adam sees it. He thinks he can control us all.' She glanced at him. 'You, too, Dr Protheroe.'

He frowned. 'Because he's paying this clinic to look after you? That's hardly control.'

She smiled. 'But if push came to shove, whose interests would you put first? Your own and your daughter's, or mine and the other patients'?'

He found that amusing and gave a short bark of laughter. 'That's like asking me if I'd rather be the Archbishop of Canterbury or Jack the Ripper. Why should I be faced with such a dramatic choice?'

'Because if you do something my father doesn't like, you'll probably find yourself out of a job,' she said bluntly. 'Why do you think that, at the age of forty, Russell suddenly left a comfortable well-paid career in Oxford to buy a down-at-heel art gallery in London? Not through choice, believe me.' She smiled grimly. 'To coin a phrase, my father made him an offer he couldn't refuse.'

Interesting use of words, he thought. 'What was the offer?'

'Leave voluntarily, or leave in disgrace.'

'You'll have to explain, I'm afraid.'

'Adam doesn't play by civilized rules. He uses information to destroy people who get in his way.' She shrugged. 'He paid fifty thousand pounds for the information on Russell, and that's discounting what he paid his team of investigators to unearth the fact that it existed at all. He doesn't mess about.'

He hid his scepticism. 'Am I allowed to know what this piece of information was?'

She looked at him. 'You don't believe me, do you?' She could see that he didn't. 'Then it'll be your funeral, Dr Protheroe. Everybody underestimates Adam. He encourages people to believe they're dealing with a gentleman, when they're not. You see, he's not like Betty. You can't tell his origins by looking at him or speaking to him. He's far too clever for that.'

Protheroe felt he was being drawn once again towards a choice between her and her father, and chose to sidestep the issue. 'I neither believe nor disbelieve,' he said. 'I am merely wondering what Russell could have done that was so bad. Even ten years ago, and particularly at a liberal university like Oxford, leaving in disgrace seems a somewhat old-fashioned concept.'

'Not if you go to jail, it isn't.' She sighed. 'Russell went to Europe every summer on lecture tours. When he came back he'd bring upwards of fifty kilos of cannabis packed into the chassis of his car. It was a straightforward transaction. He made the collection in Italy and was paid on delivery in England. He used the money to fund his art collection. He had no conscience about it. His view was that cannabis was less dangerous than alcohol or cigarettes and that the Government was mad to criminalize its use. But the penalty for smuggling is prison. Adam offered him resignation or prosecution. Russell chose resignation.'

'Did you know he was smuggling drugs?'

She shook her head. 'Not till afterwards.'

'How did Adam find out?'

'According to Russell, he traced the contact in Italy and bought him off. Adam works on the principle that everyone has a chink in his armour, and if he keeps going long enough, he'll find it. I think what probably happened is that his people calculated the value of Russell's collection, realized he couldn't have afforded it on his salary, and started digging into the trips abroad.'

'Presumably it was Russell who told you about it, not your father.'

'Yes.'

'Did he explain why your father wanted him to leave Oxford?'

'To get him away from me.'

'Then why did Russell marry you, Jinx? Why didn't the blackmail hold good after he'd left? Presumably he was no keener to go to prison afterwards than he was before.'

She gave a hollow laugh. 'You sound as though you think I'm making this up.'

'Not at all. I'm just trying to understand.'

Again, she didn't believe him. 'I've told you before,
Dr Protheroe. We got married without my father's
knowledge. I persuaded Russell that Adam would back
off the minute I became Mrs Landy because, whatever
he might want to do to Russell, Adam would never drag
me in the mud. And I was right. He didn't.'

Alan pondered over that for a moment, thinking that
far from being passive, Jinx was describing herself as a
consummate manipulator. 'Didn't it ever occur to you
that your father would react the way he did?'

She frowned, but didn't say anything.

'If my maths is correct, Russell was only twelve years
his junior. Did you seriously think Adam would welcome
him as a son-in-law?'

'Of course not, but at the time Adam found out about
us there was no question of my marrying Russell. Look,
we were having a quiet little affair which was nobody's
business but our own.' She stared wretchedly at her
hands.

'Who told him?'

'My brothers.'

'And how did they know?'

She smoothed the sheet across her lap. 'Russell used
to write to me during vacations, and they opened one of
his letters and showed it to Adam. I should have expected
it, really. They were always looking for my clay feet.' She
paused. 'The irony is, my father's hated them for it ever
since. I think he knows that nothing would have come
of the affair if they hadn't drawn it to his attention.'

'Are you saying you wouldn't have married Russell if
you hadn't felt guilty about what your father did?'

She gave her faint smile. 'He was thoroughly miserable so, yes, Reader, I married him. Actually I was pretty miserable, too. I had another year at Oxford after he'd gone and it was just a series of tearful phone calls. I thought we'd both be happier if we made the thing official.'

'But you weren't?'

She didn't answer.

'How long were you married?' asked Protheroe.

She looked at him. 'Three years.'

'And you didn't enjoy it?' he persisted.

'I found it very stifling. He was afraid I was going to leave him for a younger man, and became jealous of everyone.' She seemed to think she was being disloyal. 'Look, it wasn't that bad. He was very funny when he was on form, and when I think of him now it's with affection. On the whole, the good times far outweighed the bad.'

Quite unconsciously, Alan echoed Fraser's thoughts of the day before. What a dismal epitaph on a dead husband. 'When I think of him now it's with affection.' But how clear it was to Alan that she tried not to think of him at all.

'As a matter of interest,' he asked curiously, 'did you approve of his smuggling?'

She picked at her fingernails. 'I shared his views on the idiocy of criminalizing cannabis. Or any drugs in fact. Black markets always undermine social orders. But I thought he was a fool to have done it. Someone was bound to find out about it sooner or later.'

'What sort of a lover was he?'

She gave a snort of laughter. 'I wondered when we'd get round to that. Sigmund Freud has a lot to answer for. Why do you give so much credence to the fantastic theories of a cocaine addict? I've never understood that.'

He smiled. 'I don't think we do any more, or not to the extent you're suggesting. Freud has his place in history.' He leaned back in the chair and crossed his legs, deliberately extending the space between them. 'But wouldn't you agree that the sexual relationship between a man and a woman is an integral part of the whole relationship?'

'No. I don't have sex with Eric Clancey and I get on better with him than anyone else.'

'He being your elderly neighbour?' She nodded. 'Yes, well, I was referring to relationships where there is a sexual content.'

'And you've had my answer. In my experience the best relationships have no sexual content whatsoever.' She reached for her cigarettes. 'In fact, Russell was a good lover. He knew which buttons to press – and when – and he was considerate and not overly demanding. Bed was one of the few places where we could communicate on a level playing field because it was only there that Russell could put aside his jealousy.' She lit a cigarette. 'There was no telephone in our bedroom so Adam couldn't reach me.'

Adam again. 'Was there any basis for his jealousy? Were you attracted to other men?'

'Of course,' she said honestly. 'In my shoes, so would you have been. The grass looked a great deal greener on the other side of the marital fence, but I never did anything about it.' She drew deeply on her cigarette. 'It was my father he was really jealous of. He recognized that Adam was as possessive as he was, and it frightened him. He was sure Adam would win in the end.'

'You told me the other day that you loved your father. Was that true or were you telling me what you thought I wanted to hear?'

'It was partly true.' She eyed him with sudden amusement. 'I never know whether I want to sit on his lap and be hugged by him, or dance a jig of freedom on his grave. I expect Freud would have found me fascinating.'

'Does he ever hug you?'

She shook her head. 'He hates demonstrations of affection. I kiss him on the cheek sometimes if I catch him unawares, but most of the time he won't even touch me.'

'Does he hug your stepmother?'

'No.'

'Your brothers?'

'No.'

'Do they hug their mother?'

'No. We're a very undemonstrative family.'

'Is there any love at all in that house, Jinx?'

'There's passion,' she said. 'They all fight like cat and dog for Adam's approval.'

'But you don't join in?'

'I don't need to,' she said dismissively. 'I already have it. Adam paid good money to transform his most intelligent child into something he could be proud of. The fact that I am incapable of making sensible decisions about my personal life is a minor irritation.' Angrily, she turned away from him, propping her chin on her hand and staring into the mirror. 'He made a lady out of me and he's besotted with her.'

'Is that why you call him Adam? To prove you aren't a lady?'

'I don't follow.'

'I assume it's a statement of equality. "You and I are no different, Adam. If you can't behave like a gentleman, then I can't be a lady." Something like that?'

She continued to stare into the mirror. 'You really do assume far too much, you know. In normal circumstances, I hardly think of Adam at all, and never in such analytical terms.'

'You said earlier that the best relationships were the ones without a sexual content,' he reminded her, 'yet you clearly don't have a good relationship with your father. Should I infer from that that you and he have had a sexual relationship?'

'No,' she said calmly, 'you should not infer any such thing. I will not allow you to foist some tacky child abuse theory on to me because it happens to be in vogue at the moment. Anyway, what would you know about any of this? I thought you said you weren't a psychiatrist.'

He could feel her anger. 'Why so defensive? Is it because you recognize that, but for his self-control, you and he might have had a sexual relationship? Perhaps the desire wasn't all one-sided.'

She closed her eyes suddenly. 'I really do urge you to remember what my father does to people he doesn't like, Dr Protheroe. You'd be quite mad to make an enemy of him.'

Now why, he wondered, did he get the feeling she was talking about herself?

With an effort of concentration she remembered Dean Jarrett's home telephone number. 'Dean?' she said when he picked up the receiver at the other end. 'Look, I'm really sorry to bother you at home—'

'Who is it?'

'It's Jinx.'

'Oh, my God!' screamed his well-remembered voice. She could picture him so clearly. The telephone was in the sitting room, an art deco excrescence, amongst all the other art deco excrescences in his vibrant and colourful living space. He would be lying on the *chaise-longue*, she thought, his peroxided silver head propped against the ornate tracery at the end of it, receiver in one hand, glass of champagne in the other. Dean performed even when he was alone, and she loved him for it because she couldn't do it herself.

'We've been worried sick,' he rattled on. 'I said to Angelica, Angelica sweetheart, supposing we've lost her? We didn't know what to do. Face the dread prospect of phoning that awful man who passes for your father and puts the fear of God into us, or sit tight and rely on you to come round eventually. You know he phoned and spoke to Angie, and he was most fearfully rude, all but called her a nigger, but he wouldn't say where you were. Just said you were unconscious in hospital and told us to get on with what we were paid to do. Then the fuzz came rushing round asking questions, and we nearly *died* of shock.' He floundered to a halt. 'Business is fine,' he went on more calmly after a moment. 'Don't you worry about the studio. Thank God, people have enough faith in yours truly to stay with us.'

She smiled. 'I know, that's why I haven't been worried.'

'You should have phoned,' he said. 'We've been that upset. We wanted to send you some flowers. Angelica's been sobbing her heart out, said someone ought to be visiting you.'

'I'm sorry. The trouble is' – she paused – 'well, to be honest, I'm only firing on about half a cylinder at the moment. I gave myself a hell of a crack on the head and ended up with galloping amnesia.' She forced a laugh. 'Can't remember much about the last three or four weeks. Silly, isn't it? Look, I'll give you the details of where I am, then you can get in touch when you want to.' She gave him the address and telephone number of the clinic. 'But I don't intend to stay here much longer,' she went on. 'As soon as I can find the energy, I'm hopping on the first train back to London.'

He clucked like a mother hen. 'Stay as long as you need. No sense in coming back before you're ready. Everything's tickety-boo this end, or it will be when I pass on the good news that I've spoken to you. Actually, my darling, you sound great even if the memory is a bit dicky. Is it worrying you?'

'Yes.' She took a deep breath. 'Have I spoken to either of you between the fourth of June, when I left for Hampshire, and now? Can you remember? I mean, did I phone you at all while I was with my parents or did I come in to work on the Monday after I got back? That would be the thirteenth.'

'No,' he said apologetically. 'That's what the police kept asking when they came to the studio. Had we seen you? Had we spoken to you? Did we know why you'd gone back to Hampshire on the Monday? And we told them the truth. Not a cheep out of you since Friday the third. Angelica phoned over and over again on the thirteenth when you didn't come in to work, and all she got was your answerphone. We were girding our loins to contact Hell Hall on the Tuesday morning when the devil himself phoned with the awful news that you were unconscious. Since which time we've been tearing our collective hair out.' He was silent for a moment. 'Do you really not remember anything since the fourth?'

She heard the note of concern in his voice. 'No, but it's all right,' she said with a light laugh. 'I've been told the important stuff, like the wedding's off, Leo's scarpered with Meg, and I tried to kill myself. I just don't remember any of it.'

'Well, for what it's worth, dear, neither of us believes the crash was deliberate. You were making it clear as crystal for a good week before you set off for the Hall that you'd made up your mind not to go through with the wedding. Angie and I assumed you were going to break the news to the old devil then, and call the whole thing quits. It came as a bit of a shock to find you hadn't.'

She stared at her reflection. 'Did I say I wasn't going through with it?'

'Not in so many words, but you were back to your

old sunny self again, and I said to Angie, well, thank God for small mercies, she's come to her senses and told Leo to get stuffed, and Angie agreed with me. Well, you know we never liked him. He's very pretty, of course, but he wasn't for *you*, Jinx. Far too interested in number one, and you want someone who cares for you, sweetheart. Let's face it, we all do.'

She laughed. 'How's George?'

'Unmentionable. He's left me for a Filipino chef.'

'I'm sorry. Are you surviving?'

'Of course. Don't I always? Now, tell me why you rang. I feel in my bones there was a reason, and it wasn't just to hear my dulcet tones.'

She raised her knees and propped her elbows on them. 'I want you to phone Leo's parents and say you need to contact Leo or Meg Harris as a matter of urgency.'

'With reference to what?'

Something terrible . . . 'Can you invent an excuse? Say you're an old school-friend of Leo's, that you're only in the country for a week and that you want to meet up with him. He went to Eton if they ask. I just want you to try and find out where they are without letting on you know me. Is that OK with you? I want to be able to talk to them and show there are no hard feelings. Could you do that for me?'

'Sure. What's his parents' number?'

'I don't know, but you can get it through Directory Enquiries because I did it myself once. It's A. Wallader, Downton Court, Ashwell, Guildford, and if *he* answers it's Sir Anthony and if *she* answers it's Lady Wallader. And Dean, whatever they say, you must ring me back tonight. Please. I don't care what they tell you, you must ring me back. OK?'

'No problem,' he said breezily.

The phone rang twenty minutes later. Jinx picked it up with trembling hands and cradled it against her face. 'Jinx Kingsley.'

'It's Dean,' he said carefully.

'They're dead, aren't they?'

There was a short silence. 'Why did you get me to make the call if you already knew?'

'But I didn't,' she said quietly. 'I guessed. Oh, God – and I was so hoping I was wrong. I'm sorry. I'm really sorry. I didn't know who else to ask. Who did you speak to?'

'His father. He was pretty upset.'

She rushed into self-justification. 'The police came this afternoon and asked me questions about them, but they wouldn't say why. And I thought, my God, they're dead and no one's telling me.' She chewed her lower lip. 'Did Anthony say what happened to them?'

There was another silence. 'Look, love, half an hour ago I thought you were unconscious, then I find you aren't. I don't know what to do. I phoned back because I promised I would, but let me talk to your doctor in the morning. It'd make me a damn sight happier, it really would.'

'No,' she said coldly. 'Tell me now.' She thought she heard his nervous finger rattle the receiver rest. 'And don't hang up on me, Dean, because I swear to God you'll be out of a job if you do.' *Oh Jesus! She sounded like her father . . . No matter how much she tried to deny it, his tyranny and passion were in her, too . . .*

'You don't have to threaten me,' he said in mild reproof. 'I'm only trying to do what's best.'

'I know and I'm sorry, but I'm slowly going mad here. I must know what's happened.' She waited but he didn't respond. 'OK,' she said abruptly, 'then I'm calling in your debts.' Her eyes narrowed. 'Just remember that the only reason anyone feels confident about you running the studio in my absence is because I've encouraged you to make a name for yourself along with me. I didn't have to do that. I could have done what everybody else does and put your work out under the studio's name. You owe me for that at least.'

'I owe you a great deal more, Jinx, which is why I'm shitting bricks this end. I don't want to make things worse for you.' He heard her indrawn breath. 'OK, take it easy, I will tell you, but you must promise me you won't do anything silly afterwards.'

'Do you mean try and kill myself?'

'Yes.'

'I promise,' she said wearily. 'But if I was desperate enough to want to do it, then giving my word in advance wouldn't stop me. It's only fair you should know that.'

Perversely, he found this honesty more reassuring than the pledge. 'Sir Anthony said Leo and his girlfriend had been murdered. Their bodies were found last Thursday in a wood near Winchester but the police think they were killed the week before.'

She clenched her fist against her heart. 'Which day the week before?'

211

'The Monday, according to Sir Anthony, but I'm not sure he knows. He really was very upset.'

Ice settled in a frozen block inside her. 'What else did he say?'

'Nothing much.'

'Did he mention me?'

He didn't answer.

'Please, Dean.'

'He said Leo had been engaged to a woman whose husband died the same way.'

She stared at her terrible image in the mirror.

'Are you still there?'

'Yes,' she said. 'I'm sorry I made you do it. It wasn't fair.'

'Don't worry about it.' But the line had gone dead and his words fell on deaf ears.

The Nightingale Clinic, Laverstock, Salisbury, Wiltshire

one page sent via fax (handwritten) to:
> *Adam Kingsley*
> *Hellingdon Hall*
> *Nr Fordingbridge, HAMPSHIRE*

Date: Sunday, 26 June 1994
Time: 20.30
Dear Mr Kingsley,

Is there any chance of your coming to the clinic tomorrow morning or afternoon for an informal chat about Jinx's progress? She is, as I am sure you are aware, a private person, and finds it difficult to talk about herself, but it would be helpful for me to have a clearer picture of her history and background. I have some problems understanding what compelled her to make an attempt on her life when she presents herself as a self-reliant and, in the circumstances of her tragic widowhood, well-adjusted personality. I would welcome your views on this. One idea I'd like to discuss is the possibility of a joint session where, under my guidance, you and Jinx can explore any rifts that may have developed between you. She is clearly fond of you, but retains a certain ambivalence following the death of her husband. I have tried telephoning but, in the absence of a reply, may I suggest that you call first thing tomorrow with a convenient time? Please be assured that I know how busy you are and wouldn't trouble you if I didn't believe it to be important.

With best wishes,

Alan Protheroe

HELLINGDON HALL
NR FORDINGBRIDGE
HAMPSHIRE

facsimile: 27.6.1994   09.45   * one page sent

Dear Dr Protheroe,

If the brief you were given is beyond your capabilities,
please advise me immediately. I understood my daughter
would be allowed to recover at her own speed and in her
own time.

Yours sincerely,

Adam Kingsley

Chapter Twelve

THE REVEREND CHARLES Harris and his wife came to
view the remains of their daughter together, but it was a
more harrowing identification than Leo's because Mrs
Harris was present. Frank Cheever had done his best to
persuade her to remain at home in the company of a
policewoman, but she had insisted on seeing Meg for
herself. She had worn her grief with calm composure
throughout the car journey but, faced with the terrible
sight of her daughter, she broke down. 'This is Jinx
Kingsley's doing,' she cried. 'I warned Meg what would
happen if she took Leo away from her.'

'Hush, Caroline,' said her husband, putting his arm
about her shoulders. 'I'm sure this has nothing to do
with Jinx.'

Her anger was immediate and terrible. 'You stupid
man!' she screamed, thrusting him from her. 'This is
your baby lying here, not some parishioner's child. Look
at her, Charles. Your Meggy, your darling, reduced to
this.' She held a fluttering hand to her lips. 'Oh, GOD!'
The word exploded from her with hatred. 'How can you
be so blind? First Russell. Now Leo and Meg.' She
rounded on Superintendent Cheever. 'I've been so

215

worried. From the moment she said Leo had left Jinx for her, I've been so worried. She's a murderer. She and her beastly father. They're both murderers.'

Calmly, Dr Clarke pulled the shroud over Meg's head, then took the mother's hand and tucked it into the crook of his arm. 'We have to leave now, Mrs Harris,' he said gently. 'Would you like to say goodbye to Meg before we go?'

She stared at him with drowned eyes. 'Meg's dead.'

'I know.' He smiled into the sad face. 'But this isn't a bad place. God is here, too.'

'Yes,' she said, 'you're right.' She turned and took a final look at the shrouded corpse. 'God bless you, my darling,' she whispered through her tears. 'God bless you.'

Frank Cheever watched Bob usher the wretched woman through the doors, and it crossed his mind that perhaps pathologists earned their salaries after all. He gestured awkwardly to Meg's father. 'I'm not as good at this as Dr Clarke,' he said apologetically, 'but if you'd like some privacy with your daughter . . .' He broke off.

'No,' said the vicar. 'God and Meg both know what's in my heart. I can't say any more to her than I've said already.' He led the way to the doors, then faltered. 'You really mustn't pay any attention to what Caroline said, Superintendent. Jinx would never have done anything to harm Meg.'

'Are you sure about that, sir?'

'Yes,' he said simply. 'She's rather a fine person, you know. I've always admired her courage.'

216

Nightingale Clinic, Salisbury – 10.00 a.m.

The telephone rang in Jinx's room, fraying her nerves with its jangling peal. She pushed herself out of the chair and reached reluctantly for the receiver. 'Hello,' she said.

'It's your father, Jane. I'm sending the car to collect you.'

Fear ripped through her like burning acid. *What did he know?* There'd been no mention of Meg and Leo in the papers or on the television news. Her fingers clenched involuntarily round the receiver, knuckles whitening under the strain, but her voice was calm.

'Fine,' she said, 'send the car by all means, it's no skin off my nose. I never wanted to be here in the first place. But I'm not coming home, Adam. I'll tell the driver to take me back to Richmond and, if he refuses to do that, then I'll call a taxi and go to the station. Is that what you intended to achieve by this phone call?'

There was an ominous silence at the other end.

'Leave things as they are or I promise I'll discharge myself.' Her voice hardened. 'And this time, you'll lose me for good. Do you understand, Adam? I'll take out an injunction to prevent you coming within a mile of my house.' She slammed the receiver down with unnecessary force, and sank on to the edge of the bed as the strength seeped like sawdust from her knees and thighs. She felt the beginnings of a headache sawing away behind her eyes, and squeezed her temples tightly with shaking fingers.

The flash of memory that burst in her brain was

blinding in its clarity. *Meg on her knees, begging . . . please . . . please . . . please . . .* She looked in confusion on her friend's terrified face, felt a corresponding rush of terror drive her own heart into a frenzy, before nausea sent her staggering into the bathroom to retch in agony into the lavatory. Shaking violently, she lowered herself to the tiled floor and, as she laid her cheek on the cold ceramic, she clung in desperation to the fact that, despite all her friend's faults, she had loved Meg Harris.

But it was an hour before the shaking stopped.

The White Hart Hotel, Winchester – 10.10 a.m.

'We know very little about your daughter,' said Superintendent Cheever to the Reverend Harris and his wife. 'As I explained, we had some difficulty finding you. There is almost nothing of a personal nature in Meg's flat, and we can only presume she was in the process of moving out of it.'

He had baulked at driving them to the police station and the sterility of an interview room, opting instead for a small upstairs parlour in a hotel near the mortuary, where Fraser and a WPC could sit unobtrusively in the background taking notes. He had abandoned the flamboyance of silk bow-tie and silk handkerchief in favour of sombre black, and he looked to be what he really was – an ordinary man in ordinary surroundings, unthreatening and rather kind. Mrs Harris sat hunched in an armchair beside the half-open window, a cup of tea, untouched, on the table next to her. Her husband sat on a hard chair next to her, clearly unsure whether to comfort her or leave her to come to terms with her grief alone, holding his own grief in check for fear of making things worse for her. Cheever felt sorry for both of them, but he reserved his deepest sympathy for Meg's father. Why was it, he wondered, that men were expected to disguise their feelings?

'She was going on holiday with Leo,' said Charles quietly, 'but she didn't say anything about moving out of her flat. Not to me anyway.' He looked irresolutely at his wife.

'She didn't tell you anything, Charles, because she knew you'd disapprove.' Caroline mopped her red-rimmed eyes. 'She had an abortion ten years ago. She didn't tell you about that either, did she? And why not? Because you'd have ruined her life for her.' She crumpled the handkerchief between her palms. 'Well, it's ruined anyway, but it might not have been if she'd been able to talk to you as a father instead of a priest. Everything had to be kept secret in case you preached at her.'

Her husband stared at her, the planes of his face bleached white with shock. 'I didn't know,' he murmured. 'I'm sorry.'

'Of course you're sorry. Now,' she added bitterly. 'I'm sorry, too. Sorry for her, sorry for the baby, sorry for me. I'd like to have been a grandmother.' Her voice broke on a sob. 'It's such a waste. It's *all* such a waste.' She turned to the Superintendent. 'We have a son, but he's never wanted to marry. He wanted to be ordained like his father.' Her eyes filled again. 'It's such a terrible waste.'

Cheever waited while she fought for control. 'You implied that you knew Meg was moving out of her flat, Mrs Harris,' he said at last. 'Could you tell us about that? Where was she going?'

'To live with Leo. He had a house. It made more sense for her to move in with him.'

'Do you know where the house is?'

'Somewhere in Chelsea. Meg was going to give me the address when she came back from France. Don't Leo's parents know?'

Frank side-stepped the question. 'They're very shocked at the moment.'

There was a painful silence.

'Have you met Sir Anthony and Lady Wallader?' Cheever asked next.

Caroline's mouth puckered tragically. 'We never even met Leo,' she said. 'How could we have met his parents? It was all so quick. We had an invitation to Jinx's wedding sitting on the mantelpiece, and then Meg phoned to say Leo wanted to marry her instead.' She shook her head in disbelief.

Charles stirred on his chair. 'She rang on the Saturday morning,' he murmured quietly, 'the eleventh, I believe, and I was rather upset by the news. I wondered what sort of a man Leo was to abandon his fiancée so close to the wedding in order to take up with her best friend.' He lifted his hands in resignation. 'She told me that she'd known Leo far longer than Jinx had, and that he'd only proposed to Jinx because of some silly row they'd had. "He wanted to spite me," she said.' He paused for a moment. 'I forget sometimes that she's a grown woman

– was a grown woman,' he corrected himself, 'and, yes, I can see now that I tended to preach, but it was so clear to me that this man was not to be relied upon, and I'm afraid we had a terrible argument about him. I said his behaviour was neither mature nor honourable, and that if he was prepared to treat Jinx so shabbily then Meg would be wise to have nothing more to do with him.' His voice faltered slightly. 'I'm afraid she hung up on me and we never spoke again, although I believe Caroline tried later the same day.' He turned to his wife. 'That's right, isn't it?'

She wrapped her arms about her thin body and hugged herself tightly. 'You know it is. You were listening.' She gave a shuddering sigh. 'She wouldn't hear me out either, but at least we didn't scream at each other. I said, why had she never mentioned him before if she'd known him so long, and she said there were a million things she'd never mentioned. It was her life and there was no rule that compelled children to tell their parents everything. I blame her father,' she said in a drained voice, turning her shoulder to freeze Charles out. 'She couldn't leave home quick enough to get away from him, so of course there were things we would never know.'

The Superintendent absorbed this in silence, careful to keep his face neutral. 'When did she tell you she was moving in with Leo?' he asked after a moment.

'During that telephone call. "We're going to live together until we get married," she said. "Leo has a house in Chelsea and I'm moving my stuff in now, but I don't want you to tell Dad because I can't take any more lectures." Then she said they were going to France until the fuss died down and that she'd phone her answer-machine regularly for messages.' She fingered her handkerchief, pulling out the crumples. 'She said we'd stop worrying once we met Leo, and promised to bring him down as soon as they came home. And I said, what about poor Jinx? And Meg said Jinx would survive because she always has. Then we said goodbye.' She held the handkerchief to her eyes.

To Frank's ears, this description of Meg was an unflattering one and he wondered if Mrs Harris was aware of the picture she was painting. 'Tell me about Meg,' he invited. 'What was she like?'

Her sad face brightened. 'She was a beautiful person. Kind, thoughtful, very loving. "Don't worry, Mummy, I'll always be here," that's what she used to say.' The tears welled again. 'She was so intelligent. She could do anything she set her mind to. "I'm going places," she always told me. Everyone adored her.'

Frank turned to the vicar. 'Is that how you saw her, sir?'

Charles glanced at his wife's rigid back. 'She had faults, Superintendent, we all do. She was a little self-centred, perhaps, rather too careless of other people's feelings, but, yes, she was a popular girl.' He folded his hands in his lap. 'Our son Simon could give you a better idea of what she was like. He's worked in various London parishes over the years and saw far more of her than we did. As Caroline told you, we effectively lost her when she went to university. She used to come down two or three times a year, but other than that we had very little contact.'

'Is he still in London, sir?'

'No, he was given a parish of his own two years ago. It's a village called Frampton, ten miles to the north-east of Southampton.' He lifted the cuff of his cassock to look at his watch. 'But he'll be at the vicarage in Littleton Mary by now. I thought it would be easier for us if he came up.'

'Easier for you, you mean,' said Caroline unsteadily, swinging round to face him. 'You think he's going to take your side.'

Charles shook his head. 'There's no question of anyone taking sides, Caroline. I hoped we could support each other.'

Her cheeks blazed suddenly. 'There's been too much secrecy. I can't stand it any more.' She reached out a claw to clutch at the Superintendent's sleeve. 'I knew we'd lost her,' she said. 'I prayed we'd only lost her to Leo, but in my heart of hearts, I knew she was dead. I kept asking myself why Jinx had tried to kill herself.' Her eyes rolled alarmingly, and Frank glanced towards the WPC for assistance, but Caroline went on in an unsteady voice: 'She did the same thing after Russell was murdered, you know, but that time she tried to starve herself to death. If it hadn't been for her father, she'd have succeeded. This is Jinx's doing, Superintendent. She won't have her men taken away from her.'

'You're talking nonsense, Caroline,' said her husband severely.

'Oh, am I?' she snapped. 'Well, at least I'm not a hypocrite. You know the truth as well as I do. We're talking about jealousy over Meg, Charles, something you know all about.'

He pressed his hands to his face and breathed deeply for several seconds. 'I really don't think I can continue, Superintendent,' he said unexpectedly. 'I do apologize. Can I urge you to talk to Simon? I'm sure he's the best person to give you an objective view of this sorry business.'

Fraser, who was sitting a few yards apart, looked up and caught Cheever's eye. 'Sorry business' was a peculiarly cold-blooded way to describe a brutal murder, but then it hadn't occurred to either of them at that stage how much the Reverend Charles Harris had disliked his daughter.

Nightingale Clinic, Salisbury – 1.00 p.m.

'Are you busy, Dr Protheroe?'

He glanced up from his desk to find Jinx hovering, poised for flight in the doorway, a look of indecision in her dark eyes. 'We're very informal here, you know. You can call me Alan if you want.'

The idea of anything so intimate appalled her. 'I'd rather stick with Dr Protheroe, if you don't mind.'

'Fine,' he said indifferently. 'Come in then.'

She stayed where she was. 'It's not important. I can come back later.'

He gestured towards a vacant armchair. 'Come in,' he

said again. 'I could do with a break from the paperwork.'
He stood up and walked around the desk, ushering her
in and shutting the door behind her. 'What's up?'

With her escape route barred, Jinx accepted that the
die was cast. She crossed the parquet flooring but, instead
of sitting down, took up a position by the window and
gazed out across the garden. 'My father phoned to say
he wants me out of here. I wondered why. Do you
know?'

'No,' he said, resuming his seat and swinging round
to look at her back.

'Did you phone him about the police visit?'

'No.'

She turned round to study his face closely, then
nodded in relief. 'Then I don't understand,' she said.
'Why does he want me to leave?'

'I suppose it may have something to do with the fax I
sent him.' He reached inside his top drawer and removed
both the fax in question and the reply he had received
that morning. 'Read them,' he invited. 'My extraordinarily anodyne letter is typical of a hundred more on file,
so why should your father find it threatening?'

She perched on the edge of the armchair and read
both pieces of paper before handing them back to him.
'What was your brief?' She chewed nervously on the side
of her thumb.

'What he says. To let you recover at your own speed.
He didn't want psychiatrists meddling.'

*Why not? What was there to fear from psychiatrists this
time? What did Adam think she could tell them? What
could she tell them?* 'Then it must be your invitation to

225

talk about Russell's death,' she said slowly. 'Wild horses wouldn't make him do that, and certainly not with me present.'

'What's he afraid of?'

'Nothing.'

Why did she keep lying to him? he wondered. And why this need to protect her father when it was so very clear she thought he'd murdered her husband? 'There must be something, Jinx, or it wouldn't require wild horses to drag it out of him,' he said reasonably.

'There's nothing,' she insisted. 'It's just that, as far as Adam's concerned, Russell didn't exist. His name's never mentioned. The episode is forgotten history.'

Protheroe mulled this over. 'You obviously think your father views your tragedy as a "forgotten episode",' he said thoughtfully. 'But is that how you see it, too?'

She didn't answer.

'Tell me about your father's background,' he suggested next. 'Where did he come from?'

She spoke in quick, jerky sentences. 'I only know what Betty's told me. Adam never talks about his past. He was born in the East End of London. He was the third of five children. His father and two older brothers were merchant seamen – and all died when their ships were sunk in the North Atlantic. His younger brother and sister were evacuated to Devon while he remained with his mother to face the blitz. His education was minimal. He learnt more from the black marketeers working out of the docks than he ever learnt in school. By the end of the war he had amassed a list of contacts abroad and enough

226

money to set up as an importer. The first goods he shipped in were silks, cottons and cosmetics – they arrived on his seventeenth birthday. He doubled his money overnight by flogging the lot on the black market, and he's never looked back. He began life as a crook – knew the Kray twins very well. That's all I know.'

He believed her. If Adam Kingsley was anything like she described him, he was a man who compartmentalized every aspect of his life. *Rather like his daughter*. It would be interesting to discover whether he, too, closed doors on dark rooms and threw away the keys. The chances were high that he did. 'As far as Adam's concerned, Russell didn't exist,' Jinx had said.

'What happened to his mother?' Protheroe asked now.

'I don't know. He didn't have much to do with her after he married my mother. As far as I can make out, neither family approved of the marriage.'

'And the brother and sister? What happened to them?'

'They went back to London after the war, presumably to live with their mother. The only thing Adam has ever said on the subject is that he's always regarded them as strangers because he and they grew up apart.'

'Does he still feel like that?'

She slipped down into the chair and laid her head against the back of it. 'He hasn't spoken to either of them for over thirty years. Uncle Jo emigrated to Australia and hasn't been heard of since, and Aunt Lucy married a black man. My father severed all his ties with her the day she walked up the aisle.'

'Because her husband was black?'

'Of course. He's a racist. Betty used to know Lucy quite well when they were all younger. She told me once that Adam tried to stop the wedding.'

'How?'

With shaking fingers, she lit a cigarette. 'Betty was very drunk. I'm not sure she was telling the truth.'

'What did she say?'

She took quick pulls on the cigarette, considering her answer. 'That Adam tried to scare Lucy's fiancé off with a beating,' she said in a rush, 'but that Lucy went ahead and married him anyway. It might be true. He really does hate black people.'

Alan watched her for a moment. 'How do you feel about that?'

'Ashamed.'

He waited. 'Because your father's a bully?' he suggested.

She could taste hot, sweet bile in her mouth and drew in a lungful of smoke to mask it. 'Yes – no. Mostly because I should have sought Lucy and her family out years ago and made a stand – but I never did.'

Veronica Gordon was right about the eyes, he was thinking. What the hell was going on inside her head that she could look so frightened and sound so composed? 'Why not?'

She turned her face to the ceiling. 'Because I was afraid the whipping-boys would be punished if I did.'

'Meaning your brothers.'

'Not necessarily. Any whipping-boy will do,' she said flatly. 'If I'd sought out my aunt, then Betty would have been taken to task because she knew Lucy as a child and would have been accused of being the instigator. But it's more often the boys than not.'

'Are we talking literally or metaphorically? Does your father physically beat your brothers?'

'Yes.'

'So was Russell another whipping-boy, do you think?' he asked mildly.

He caught her unawares and she stared at him in shock. 'My father didn't kill him,' she said, her voice rising. 'The police ruled him out very early on.'

'I was talking metaphorically, Jinx.'

She didn't answer immediately. 'I don't think you were,' she said, lowering her gaze, 'but it doesn't make any difference anyway. Russell was never punished for my shortcomings.'

'No,' he agreed. 'I suspect you were punished for his.' He toyed with his pen. 'How much do you know about your mother? Why did both families disapprove of the match, for example?'

'Her people were middle class and my father's were working class. I presume it was straightforward snobbery on her side and inverted snobbery on his, and I don't suppose it helped that he made money out of black marketeering.' She was silent for a moment. 'I know he adored her.'

'Did he tell you that?'

'No, he never talks about her.'

'Then how do you know?'

'Because Betty told me. Her name was Imogen Jane

Nicholls, she was the only child of a doctor, privately
educated, and very much a lady, and he has photographs
of her all over his office walls.'

He thought of the name on Jinx's file cover. Jane
Imogen Nicola Kingsley. 'Do you look like her as well?'

'Of course I do,' she said with a kind of desperation.
'Adam set out to re-create her.'

He couldn't fault the desperation – it was there in her
voice – but he doubted it had anything to do with her
mother. 'Even your father can't perform miracles, Jinx,'
he said with a touch of irony, as he watched the ash on
her cigarette lengthen and curl. 'I suspect that little
scenario is more in your stepmother's mind than his. We
all need ways of coming to terms with a partner's
indifference. None of us is immune from pride.' He
nudged the wastepaper basket towards her with his toe.
'You should know that.'

The Vicarage, Littleton Mary, Wiltshire – 1.15 p.m.

Fraser watched Cheever's courteous and sympathetic
handling of this devastated family with a far more willing
admiration than he had felt for Maddocks yesterday. The
Superintendent knew as well as he did that there were
some strange undercurrents at work, but never for one
moment did he pressure either of the Harris parents into
saying what they were.

They drove in convoy back to Littleton Mary, with
Mrs Harris and a motherly WPC in the leading car, and
himself, Cheever and Mr Harris in the one behind. There

was little conversation. The vicar clearly found talking difficult, and the Superintendent was content to leave him to his thoughts. Where 'initiative' was Maddocks's watchword, 'patience' was Cheever's.

In retrospect, of course, Fraser had to ask himself whether Maddocks's insensitive approach wouldn't have been more appropriate, for it was Cheever's willingness to take his time that gave rise to the events that followed. Maddocks would have squeezed every last drop of information out of them, irrespective of the trauma they were suffering, and Charles could not have conspired with Simon to keep the information about Meg and Russell's affair to themselves. But would justice have been better served, Fraser always wondered, if they'd known about it then instead of later?

As they drew up behind the other car in the vicarage driveway, Charles Harris touched a hand to his dog-collar as if seeking reassurance. 'Could I suggest that I have a quick word with Simon first?' he said rapidly. 'Just to explain why you're here, then perhaps you could talk to him outside, away from his mother? It's important you get a clear picture of Meg, and I'm afraid you won't get that if Caroline is listening.'

The Superintendent nodded. 'I'll ask WPC Graham to take Mrs Harris inside. Sergeant Fraser and I will wait here.'

It was five minutes before Simon emerged, his thin face looking very drawn. He ushered them round the corner of the house to some chairs grouped about a table on the lawn. 'Dad's asked me to tell you about Meg,' he said, sitting down, 'but I'm not sure . . .' He took off his glasses abruptly to pinch the bridge of his nose. 'I'm sorry,' he said, struggling for composure. 'It's all been a bit of a shock.' He breathed deeply over the tears that were crowding his throat. 'I'm sorry,' he said again.

'That's all right, sir,' said Frank. 'Would it be easier if we asked you questions?'

Simon nodded.

'Your father says you worked in London for several years and saw more of Meg than they did. Perhaps you could tell us something about her lifestyle. Did she have many friends, for example? Did she go out a lot? Did she enjoy discos, pubs, things of that sort?'

'Yes,' said Simon, 'all of those. She loved life, Superintendent.' He wiped his eyes with the sleeve of his shirt, then put his glasses back on. 'She had a very happy personality, people always enjoyed being with her.'

Frank twisted his chair against the sunlight. 'That's how your mother described her,' he said, 'but your father seemed to have reservations. Why is that, do you think? Did he and Meg not get on?'

Simon's expression was unreadable because the sun was reflecting off his lenses, and Frank wished he'd had the sense to position him better at the beginning. 'No, Dad and Meg got on fine,' he said, but his tone was too flat and lacked conviction. He was silent for a moment. 'Look, perhaps it would be simpler after all, if I just told you what Dad's asked me to say. He's worried you've fixed on Jinx Kingsley as a suspect because of what happened to Russell.' He took off his glasses again and laid them on the table, fishing in his trouser pocket for a handkerchief to blow his nose. 'It's not much fun this,' he said by way of apology. 'I've been so angry with Meg for the last two weeks, and now – well, you never expect anyone to die.' He took a deep breath to steady himself. 'The irony is it's my job to comfort people in this position, tell them it's the whole history of their love that matters, not the two small weeks of anger.' He blew his nose. 'But it's only when you experience it yourself that you realize how patronizing that is.'

'We can only do our best, sir,' said Frank, giving the man's shoulder an awkward pat. 'In this job, we run up against it all the time. Such sadness everywhere and no easy answers.'

Oddly enough, Simon seemed to find this trite response rather comforting, perhaps because it proved to him that he wasn't alone in offering banalities by way of consolation. He rested his hands on the table and toyed with his glasses. 'The reason Dad didn't want Mum listening to this,' he said, 'is that she never really knew what Meg was like. She knew Meg had a lot of boyfriends but she assumed the relationships were fairly casual.' He corrected himself immediately. 'Well, of course, they *were* casual, but casual in Meg's terms, not in my mother's. I suppose you'd describe Meg as promiscuous, except that that gives a false impression of her because we tend to use it pejoratively only where women are concerned.' He gave an uncertain smile. 'I don't really know how to explain this to you without setting up prejudices in your minds. You had to know Meg. She was very innocent in an odd sort of way. She loved having fun.'

Fraser raised his head. 'It sounds to me as though

you're saying she enjoyed sex, sir, but didn't want the commitment of a relationship. Is that so unusual these days?'

'No,' said Simon with relief, 'but I'm sure you can appreciate what my mother would think if she ever found out. She's very strait-laced.' He fell silent.

Fraser waited a moment. 'In fact, sir,' he said when Simon didn't continue and the Superintendent gave him the nod, 'your mother gives the impression that it's your father who's strait-laced. She refers to his preaching and the fact that Meg couldn't leave home fast enough to get away from him. She talks about the fact that they had arguments and that he was always lecturing her over the phone. She also knew about Meg's abortion, which your father clearly didn't. Are you sure she's as ignorant as you suggest?'

Simon nodded unhappily. 'Yes, but I'm afraid you'll have to take my word for it. Mum likes to think she knew what sort of life Meg led, but it's not true. In fact, Meg only ever lied to her because she didn't want to upset her.'

'So was the abortion a lie?'

'No, that did happen. But she didn't tell Mum about it until they had their row over Leo. It's one of the reasons I was so angry with her. If she'd only come down and talked to them in person, instead of giving them ultimatums over the phone about the fact that it was her life and she could do what she liked with it, then they might not have taken it quite so badly.' He raised his glasses off the table and swung them from side to side, watching the pendulum motion with absorbed fascination. 'She said a lot of things that I'm sure she regretted afterwards.'

Fraser glanced at the Superintendent before asking his next question.

'Are you saying her announcement about her relationship with Leo caused friction between your parents?'

Simon squeezed the bridge of his nose again. 'It's been a nightmare,' he said after a moment. 'I think the trouble was that Meg knew she was behaving badly so she set out to defend her position right from the word go. Dad, of course, homed straight in on her betrayal of Jinx, and Mum homed in on the fact that she must have been sleeping with Leo. If only she'd just apologized and left it at that.' He looked bleakly at the Sergeant. 'We never do, though, do we? It's human nature to justify ourselves.'

'What did she say?'

'I only know what she told me afterwards. She phoned me about lunchtime, but by then I'd had Mum on the phone in floods, so I was pretty angry as well.' He held the handkerchief to his eyes. 'We all said things we wish we hadn't, and now it's too late.' He breathed deeply through his nose to calm himself. 'As I understand it, she said Dad was a sanctimonious hypocrite who lusted after anything in a skirt, including her and Jinx, but hadn't got the balls to do anything about it, and Mum was a frigid prude who couldn't bear the thought of anyone enjoying sex. Meg said she'd told her about the abortion to prove there was at least one woman who didn't see babies as the only reason for having intercourse.' He caught the look of interest that flashed in Fraser's eyes.

'I'm telling you what she said, Sergeant,' he murmured tiredly, 'I'm not saying it's true. She was defending herself, so she went for their weaknesses. My mother is a prude, in so far as she deplores modern sexual practices, but she's not frigid. My father is extremely fond of Jinx because she shares his interest in the Classics, but he doesn't lust after her. If Meg had telephoned from France or if Jinx hadn't driven her car into a wall, the storm would have blown over in a day or two. As it was, my parents were left blaming each other for what they see as their fault – namely Meg's cavalier theft of her friend's fiancé, and Jinx's resulting suicide attempt. You really must understand what an impossible situation they found themselves in. Jinx's family wanted scapegoats – not unreasonably in the circumstances – but the only scapegoats available were my wretched parents. They've had to put up with some fairly strong abuse, so it's hardly surprising they feel responsible.'

Fraser nodded as he turned back through the pages of his notebook. 'Did you know about your sister's abortion before your mother did?'

'Yes.'

'When did she have it?'

'A long time ago. After she came down from Oxford. She was very much more careful after that.'

'Do you know who the father was?'

'No. I don't think she did either.'

'Did she tell you about it at the time?'

He nodded. 'I drove her to the hospital to have it done.'

'Did you approve?'

For the first time, Simon smiled. 'It didn't matter whether I did or I didn't.'

'But you must have had an opinion, sir.'

'Funnily enough, no. Where Meg was concerned, I never gave opinions. She wouldn't have listened to them.'

Fraser found the page he was looking for. 'You said: "It would be simpler if I just told you what my father wants me to say. He's worried that you've fixed on Jinx Kingsley as a suspect." Could you expand those remarks, sir?'

Simon nodded. 'Apparently my mother keeps accusing Jinx of murdering Meg and Leo, and he's afraid you'll believe her.' He looked enquiringly at the other man, but got no reaction. 'But Jinx wouldn't have done it. She and Meg were more like sisters than friends.'

'Even more reason to be angry, then, when Meg stole her fiancé,' suggested Fraser. 'Are you saying that wouldn't have upset Miss Kingsley?'

'She says not. I went to see her on Wednesday and she was very bullish about it, asked me to tell Meg she bore them no resentment and said she wished everyone would stop worrying about it.'

'Miss Kingsley's suffering from amnesia, sir. How can she know what she felt at the time?'

'I don't know, Sergeant, but I believe her and so does my father.' He leaned forward to emphasize his point. 'We've known her for years, and we can't accept she's a murderer. She certainly didn't murder Russell. She was with Meg that afternoon. Meg was her alibi.'

The Superintendent nodded thoughtfully. 'You said

your father took Meg to task for her betrayal of Jinx. Am I right in thinking that's why you were angry with her as well?'

'Yes. Jinx didn't deserve to be treated so shabbily. She's been through hell one way and another, but she's never allowed it to sour her. She's very generous.' He jerked his head towards the parish church across the road. 'Helped Dad out with his steeple fund five years ago, persuaded her father to stump up for a Romanian orphans' charity I'm involved with. She's a very fine person.'

Frank smiled agreement. 'You have a high opinion of her.'

'Very.'

'Rather higher, perhaps, than you had of your sister? People who love having fun tend to be somewhat selfish and egocentric. Quite often, they're the black sheep of the family.'

Simon looked at him. 'Yes,' he said simply. 'Meg was certainly that.'

Chapter Thirteen

Monday, 27 June, Nightingale Clinic,
Salisbury – 1.15 p.m.

ALAN SENSED THAT Jinx felt she had revealed too much of herself. He wondered if this was his last chance to learn what he could about her. 'You told me your father wants you to leave, but you didn't say what you intend to do about it.'

She propped her chin on her hand and gazed at him with a troubled expression, but there was something studied about the whole gesture. 'I said I'd discharge myself back to Richmond and then take out an injunction to stop him ever interfering again unless he left well alone. Now I'm worried sick.'

He gave a surprised laugh. 'Why? I couldn't have advised better myself. You must be allowed the freedom to make your own choices.'

'I wish you'd try to understand,' she said helplessly. 'It's not my freedom that's likely to be curtailed, it's yours. If Adam thinks you suggested the injunction . . .' She gave a small shrug and didn't finish the sentence.

'You're worrying unnecessarily,' he said. 'What can he possibly do to me?'

'He hasn't built his empire on charm, Dr Protheroe.

If he's going to do something, he'll do it quickly. He won't want you putting any more unpleasant ideas in my head.'

'I can only repeat,' he said, eyeing her curiously, 'what can he possibly do to me?'

'That's what Russell said.' She stood up abruptly. She might have added – *and Leo, and Meg* – but she didn't.

Alan put through a telephone call to Matthew Cornell's father. 'No,' he assured him, 'Matthew's doing well. I wondered if I could pick your brains on an unrelated matter.'

'Go ahead.'

'What do you know about Adam Kingsley of Franchise Holdings?'

'I'm a criminal barrister,' Cornell reminded him. 'Not a stock broker.'

'Which is why I called you,' said Alan. 'I've been told he began life as an East End crook, and I wondered if there was any truth in it.'

'I see.' There was a short pause. 'All right, rumour has it he was active alongside the Krays and the Richardsons in the fifties and sixties, but kept a much lower profile and turned legitimate as soon as he could. He was never charged with anything because he adopted the Mafia *cuscinetto* system and erected buffers between himself and the violence his thugs meted out. But that is all hearsay, Protheroe, and not for public consumption. He's won damages in the past against two newspapers foolish enough to put that into print.'

Alan doodled on the pad in front of him, wondering how to frame his next question. 'How does he conduct business now?'

'Why? Are you thinking of investing in Franchise Holdings?'

'Maybe,' Protheroe lied.

'There's the odd hint from time to time that he's used unorthodox methods to acquire property and land in the London Docks, but it's pure speculation. I'd say he runs as clean a ship as the next man. Matter of fact,' he admitted, 'I've a small sum invested in him myself.'

'What about social skills? He was described to me as someone to be wary of in personal dealings. Would you agree with that?'

'What you'd expect from an East End boy made good.' Cornell sounded intrigued. 'I wouldn't want to get in too deep with him. Put it this way, he's not called the Great White Shark for nothing. If you work on the principle that he uses lawyers now as his buffers instead of hired muscle, then you'll probably have some idea of his *modus operandi.*'

'What does that mean exactly?'

'*Plus ça change, plus c'est la même chose.*'

'Are you saying: Once a Mafia boss, always a Mafia boss?'

An amused laugh floated down the line. 'No, Protheroe, *you're* saying it. I can't afford a slander suit.'

'Josh? It's Jinx. Are you busy or can you talk for a minute?'

'What is it?' He sounded hostile, she thought.

'Meg's dead.'

There was a silence. 'I know,' he said.

She was shivering with cold and her expression had a curiously vacant look, as if she were waiting for something. 'Who told you?'

'Simon rang,' he answered guardedly. 'They're both dead, Meg *and* Leo. How did *you* know, Jinx? Have you started to remember things?'

'No,' she said abruptly, 'I guessed. The police came here asking questions about them. What else did Simon say?'

'Nothing much, only that his mother's going out of her mind. She wants to know where Leo's parents live, so he called me.'

'Did you tell him?'

'I said I didn't know, so he's trying Dean Jarrett.'

It was her turn to hold the silence. 'You know quite well where they live,' she said at last. 'I remember telling you myself when Leo and I first got engaged. The wedding will be a nightmare, I said, Surrey gentry versus Hampshire parvenus, with each side trying to score points. And you laughed and asked which part of Surrey the Walladers came from. Downton Court, Ashwell, I told you.'

'I don't remember.'

He was lying, she thought. 'Why didn't Simon ring me?'

Another silence.

'I'm sorry,' she said.

'What for?'

'Meg's death. She was your friend as well as mine.'

'Is that what you called to tell me?'

Her grip on the telephone was so brittle that her fingers hurt. 'I wanted to know what people are saying, Josh. Do Meg's parents think I killed her? Does Simon?'

'What makes you think they were murdered?' he asked.

'I'm not a bloody fool, Josh.'

'No one's saying anything,' he said. 'Not to me, anyway.'

She didn't believe him. 'Why are you afraid of me?' she asked, addressing the fear she heard in his voice. 'Do *you* think I did it?'

'No, of course I don't. Look, I have to go. The police are due here any minute, and I'm trying to find out how the business stands with one partner dead. I'll ring back later when things calm down.' He cut the line and left her listening to empty silence. *Someone else she couldn't trust? Or someone as scared as she was?*

She replaced the receiver carefully, doubts seething in her tired brain. Was anything he said true? And why was he afraid of her? Because he thought her memory was coming back? She went to lie on the bed and stared at the ceiling, knowing that safety lay in remembering nothing, but knowing, too, that she must eventually remember something. However much her father might want what was locked inside her head to remain there for ever, she knew it was an impossibility. If Alan Protheroe didn't prise the truth out of her with his sympathetic existentialism, then somebody else would. And they wouldn't do it kindly either.

Tears stung her eyelids. Common sense told her it would be suicidal – she dwelt on that thought for a moment – to relay memories that no one believed. For this time there was no Meg to give her an alibi.

'There's a gentleman to see you, Dr Protheroe,' said his elderly secretary, popping her head round his office door. 'A Mr Kennedy. I told him you were busy but he says he's sure you can find time to talk to him. He's a solicitor, representing Mr Adam Kingsley.' She pulled a face. 'He's very insistent.'

Alan finished the notes he was writing. 'Then you'd better show him in, Hilda,' he said.

A small, thin man with spectacles and a pleasant smile entered the room a few seconds later and shook Protheroe firmly by the hand. 'Good afternoon,' he said, proffering his card and taking the chair on the other side of the desk. 'Thank you for seeing me, Dr Protheroe. Did your secretary explain that I'm here as Mr Adam Kingsley's representative?'

'She said something to that effect,' agreed Alan, examining the little man, 'but I can't imagine why Mr Kingsley feels he needs to send a solicitor.' *Jesus Christ!*

Mr Kennedy smiled. 'I am instructed to remind you of the assurances you gave my client when you undertook the care of his daughter.'

Alan frowned. 'Say again,' he invited.

The little man sat back in the chair and crossed his legs. 'Mr Kingsley is fond of his daughter, Dr Protheroe, and very concerned for her welfare. He asked you to take her in as a convalescent patient because, following the prolonged enquiries he made earlier this year, with a view to his wife becoming a patient at this clinic, he was satisfied that Jane would find the atmosphere here more congenial than the clinical surroundings of a hospital. In particular, he was keen to ensure that Jane would not feel pressured into taking part in any sort of psychiatric therapy that would remind her of her previous unfortunate experiences. To which end he asked you – as a doctor and not a psychiatrist – to take charge of her convalescence and leave her to recover at her own speed and in her own time.' He smiled his pleasant smile again. 'Would you agree that that is a fair summary of the faxed letter he sent you on the twentieth of this month?'

'I would, yes.'

'And is it equally fair to say that, in your telephone conversation with my client following receipt of his faxed letter, you made the very precise statement: "You have my assurance that your daughter will not be pressured, Mr Kingsley, and will certainly not be expected to engage in any form of therapy unless she chooses to do so."'

'I may have said something along those lines, but I can't vouch for the preciseness of the statement.'

'My client can, Dr Protheroe. He is a cautious man and insists on having tapes made of every conversation that relates to his affairs. That is word for word what you said.'

Alan shrugged. 'All right. To my knowledge, those assurances have been honoured.'

Kennedy removed a folded piece of paper from his pocket and consulted it. 'You sent my client a faxed letter

245

last night in which you state: "One idea I'd like to discuss is the possibility of a joint session where, under my guidance, you and Jinx can explore any rifts that may have developed between you." May I ask if Miss Kingsley gave you permission to suggest this to her father? In other words, has she chosen to engage in such an activity?'

'Not yet. I thought it more sensible to seek his agreement first. There seemed little point in putting the idea to Jinx if her father wasn't prepared to take part.'

'Nevertheless, Dr Protheroe, simply by suggesting a form of therapy, you have gone against my client's express instructions to leave his daughter to recover at her own speed. It is also clear from other statements in your fax that you have been encouraging Jane to talk about events that Mr Kingsley asked you very specifically not to mention because he felt they would upset her.' He quoted extracts from the letter: ' "She finds it difficult to talk about herself." "I have some problems understanding what compelled her to make an attempt on her life." "She retains a certain ambivalence following the death of her husband." '

Alan shrugged again. 'I don't recall your client instructing me to keep his daughter in solitary confinement, Mr Kennedy. Had he done so, I would most certainly not have agreed to take her.'

'You will have to explain those remarks, I'm afraid.'

'Jinx is an intelligent and articulate young woman. She is able and willing to participate in conversations. The only way to stop her talking would be to isolate her from everyone in the clinic. Is that what her father wants?' His eyes narrowed. 'To stop her *talking*?'

The little man chuckled. 'About what?'

'I don't know, Mr Kennedy.' He balanced his pen between his fingers. 'But then I'm not the one who's worried. Your client is.' *Who the hell was pulling the strings here? Adam or Jinx?*

'My client's concerns are entirely related to his daughter's welfare, Dr Protheroe. He believes firmly that any rehashing of the past will be to Jane's disadvantage, a point emphasized for him this morning when she threatened him with an injunction over the telephone. He feels, quite reasonably, that this abrupt return to her previous antagonism is due to your refusal to abide by his wishes.'

Alan considered that for a moment. 'Shall we get to the point?' he suggested. 'Is Mr Kingsley looking to control every minute of his daughter's life or does he want excuses not to pay?'

'I am instructed to remind you of the assurances you gave my client when you undertook the care of his daughter.'

'If you're referring to pressure and unwanted therapy, then there's no argument between us. Jinx has been subjected to neither.'

'Yet you state in your fax: "She finds it difficult to talk about herself."' He looked up. 'The clear inference is that you have sought to persuade her to do just that.'

'This is absurd,' said Alan angrily. 'I wrote to Mr Kingsley because I assumed he had his daughter's welfare

247

at heart and, as Jinx's doctor, I believe it to be in her best interests to seek a rapprochement with her father. However, if his only response is to send a solicitor to spout gobbledegook, then obviously she is right and I am wrong. Her father is only interested in manipulating and controlling her, and little good can come from a meeting.' He squared the papers on his desk. 'Presumably there's some sort of implied threat in these repeated instructions of yours. Would you care to tell me what it is?'

'Now you're being absurd, Dr Protheroe.'

'This is all beyond me, I'm afraid.' Alan studied the solicitor with a perplexed frown. 'I really have no interest in playing games with my patients' well-being. If Mr Kingsley is seeking excuses not to pay, then I shall discuss the matter with Miss Kingsley herself. I have no doubts at all she will wish to honour the obligations her father entered into on her behalf. Please tell your client that I have strong reservations about his reading of his daughter's character. She is far less anxious than he appears to be about reliving her past experiences. In addition, I cannot agree with the police presumption that she attempted suicide.' He leaned forward. 'You may also tell him that, in my professional opinion, it is Mr Kingsley who represents the greatest threat to Jinx's peace of mind. There is an ambivalence in her attitude towards him which can only be resolved by a clearing of the air between them, particularly in relation to her husband's death and to what she perceives as Mr Kingsley's obsessive and continued need to interfere in her life. However, in the face of his obvious unwillingness to talk to her, a clean break by means of an injunction would seem to be the only alternative.' He placed his hands flat on the desk and pushed himself to his feet. 'Good-day, Mr Kennedy. I trust you will have the courtesy to convey *my* views with the same assiduous detail with which you have just conveyed your client's.'

The solicitor beamed as he, too, rose to his feet. 'No need, Dr Protheroe,' he murmured, patting his breast pocket. 'I have it all on tape. I believe I told you that Mr Kingsley insists on having taped records made of every conversation relating to his affairs. I know he will be interested to hear everything you've said. Good-day to you.'

The phone rang on Alan's desk ten minutes later, and he picked it up with ill humour.

'I've a Reverend Simon Harris for you, Dr Protheroe,' said Hilda. 'Do you want to speak to him?'

'Not particularly,' he grunted.

'He says it's important.'

'He would,' said Alan sarcastically. 'It'll be a red-letter day when someone doesn't think what they have to say is important.'

'You sound cross,' said Hilda.

'That's because I am.' He sighed. 'All right, put him through.'

Simon's voice came on the line. 'Dr Protheroe? Do you remember me? I'm a friend of Jinx Kingsley. I came to visit her on Thursday.'

'I remember,' he said.

'I find myself in a somewhat invidious position,' said the younger man in a voice that was clearly troubled. He paused briefly. 'Has Jinx told you that Meg and Leo are dead, Dr Protheroe?'

Alan raised a hand to his beard and smoothed it automatically. 'No,' he said.

'They were murdered, probably on the same day that she tried to kill herself.'

Alan stared across the room at a print of Albrecht Dürer's *Knight, Death and Devil*, and thought how appropriate it was that he should be looking at that. 'I'm so sorry, Mr Harris. You must be very upset.'

'We've not had much time to be upset,' said Simon apologetically. 'We had the police here until an hour ago.'

'I'm sorry,' said Alan again. 'What makes you think Jinx knows?'

'Her assistant told me.'

'You mean Dean Jarrett?'

'Yes.'

'How does he know?'

Simon sighed. 'Apparently the police visited her yesterday and she guessed something was wrong. She rang Dean during the evening and persuaded him to phone the Walladers for confirmation.' He paused again. 'She knew before we did, as a matter of fact. My parents weren't told until ten o'clock last night and only made the formal identification this morning. My mother's very bitter about it. She's blaming Jinx for Meg's death.'

Alan wondered what else his patient had withheld from him. 'Why are you telling me this?' he asked.

Another hesitation. 'As I said, I find myself in an invidious position. My father, too.' He cleared his throat. 'It's difficult to think straight when you're shocked – well, I'm sure you know that—' He broke off abruptly. 'Sir Anthony Wallader is going to *The Times* with accusations against Jinx and her father, egged on by my mother. It's understandable. They're both very upset, as you can imagine – well, of course we all are.' He blew his nose. 'I've no idea how much the newspapers are likely to print, but it could be very bad, especially if the tabloids get hold of it. My mother's not very well – she's . . . that is . . . Dad and I felt Jinx should be protected from the worst of it – it's little better than a kangaroo court – and I didn't know who else to phone. I thought she'd have told you – about their deaths anyway.' His voice broke with emotion. 'I'm sorry – I'm so sorry.'

Alan listened to the quiet tears at the other end of the line. 'I wouldn't worry too much,' he said with a calm he didn't feel. 'Jinx is an extraordinarily tough young woman' – *even he hadn't realized till now just how tough* – 'and I'm confident it's only a matter of days before her memory returns in full and she's able to set minds at rest.' He thought for a moment. 'Presumably we're talking about speculation and not fact? If there were any evidence against Miss Kingsley the police would have confronted her by now. Am I right?'

Simon fought for composure. 'As far as I understand it, yes, but we've been told very little. Sir Anthony's known since Saturday morning and he said that Leo had been bludgeoned to death . . . The same way Russell Landy was.'

251

'Does Jinx's father know Meg and Leo are dead?'

'I don't think so. Dad and I think their intention is to hit Jinx while she's vulnerable, but we can't see justice being done that way.'

Alan was curious. 'You're being very generous to her, Mr Harris.'

'Things aren't as straightforward as they might seem,' Simon said tightly. 'We're worried about my mother, and we don't want Jinx's suicide on our conscience. She'll be under a lot of pressure when the news breaks and what she's tried once, it seems likely she could try again.'

'Well, on that score at least I don't think you need worry,' said Alan slowly. 'If I had any doubts at all about her mental equilibrium you've just laid them to rest. Thank you for letting me know, Mr Harris.'

He said goodbye and replaced the receiver with a thoughtful frown. What on earth was going on here? Did Adam Kingsley know? Is that why he'd sent Kennedy? *God almighty!* Were he and the clinic being dragged into some sort of conspiracy to pervert the course of justice? 'SHI-IT!' he roared at Dürer's *Knight, Death and Devil*. Why the hell had he agreed to take the bloody woman in?

He sought out Veronica Gordon, the sister in charge. 'I've had it up to here,' he told her, chopping at his throat. 'I'm going AWOL for a few hours. If there's an emergency, get Nigel White to deal with it.' He thought for a moment. 'But if it's an emergency concerning Miss Kingsley, call me on the mobile. No,' he corrected himself, 'we'll go one step further where she's concerned. I want her checked every half-hour without fail. Got that? A physical check by you or one of the nurses every thirty minutes, and if you're worried at all, page me. OK?'

Veronica nodded. 'Any particular reason?'

'No,' he growled, 'just a safety precaution. Her father sent his blasted solicitor over to give me an ear-bashing, and he's put the wind up me. I don't want to be sued for negligence if she takes it into her head to do something stupid.'

'She won't,' said the woman with confidence.

'Why are you so sure?'

'I've watched her. Everyone does exactly what she wants, including you, Alan, and people like that don't hang up their boots lightly.'

'She's already had one go.'

'Balls!' said Veronica with an amiable grin. 'She may want her Daddy to think she did, but if it had been a serious attempt she'd be dead. My guess is there were a lot of hidden agendas at work when she threw herself out of her car, and a little fatherly sympathy was one of them. Mind you,' she added thoughtfully, 'she didn't research the science of movable objects hitting solid Tarmac very thoroughly. I'm not convinced severe concussion and amnesia were part of the original equation.'

Alan shrugged. 'It may not be part of the endgame either. You don't have to be Einstein to fake amnesia, Veronica.'

She looked at him in surprise. 'Are you saying she's a fraud?'

'Not necessarily,' he lied. 'I was merely stating a fact.'

'But why would she bother with anything so elaborate unless she had something to hide?'

'Perhaps she does.'

Fergus was leaning against Protheroe's Wolseley when the doctor emerged into the warm late afternoon and approached across the gravel. He gave a perfunctory nod towards the older man and ran a hand over the bonnet. 'I thought it might be yours,' he said. 'I noticed it when I visited Jinx the other day. Do you want to sell it?'

Alan shook his head. 'I'm afraid not. We've been together too long to part so easily.' He put the key into the lock. 'Have you seen Jinx, or are you on your way in?'

'Just waiting. She's wandering about the garden somewhere. Miles has gone looking for her. Did Kennedy give you a roasting then?'

'Is that what he's employed to do?'

'It depends on Dad's mood. I told him you were pretty high-handed with me on Saturday, so I thought maybe he'd ordered his Rottweiler in to remind you who foots the bill. I also told him I reckoned you had the hots for Jinxy.' He peered at Alan out of the corner of his eye, judging his reaction. 'Dad was bloody cross about it, so I'm not surprised he sent Kennedy over.'

Alan gave a snort of amusement. 'I doubt you have the bottle to tell your father anything, Fergus.' He pulled the car door open. 'As a matter of interest, how did you know Kennedy was here?'

'I saw him leave.' He yawned. 'Miles wants to meet you. I promised I'd keep you here till he got back.'

'Another time perhaps.'

'No, now.' Fergus caught at his arm. 'We want to know what's going on. Does Jinx remember something?'

'I suggest you ask her.' Alan looked down at the restraining hand. 'You're welcome to come and talk to me any time you like, just so long as you make an appointment first. But at the moment' – he placed his hand over the young man's and prised it off his arm – 'I've more important things to do.' He smiled amiably and eased in behind the wheel. 'It's been nice meeting you again, Fergus. Give my best wishes to your mother and brother.' He shut the door and gunned the Wolseley into life, before spinning the wheel and roaring away down the drive.

When Sister Gordon did her rounds at nine o'clock that evening, she found Jinx standing by her window watching the remnants of the day burn to crimson embers. 'Isn't it beautiful?' Jinx said without turning round, knowing by instinct who her visitor was. 'If I could stand and look on this for ever, then I would have eternal happiness. Do you imagine that's what Heaven is?'

'I guess it depends on how static you want your Heaven to be. Presumably you've watched this develop from a simple sunset into glorious fire, so at which point would you have stopped it to produce your moment of eternal happiness? I think I would always be wondering if the moment afterwards had been more beautiful than the one I was stuck with, and that would turn the experience into a hell of frustration.'

Jinx laughed quietly. 'So there is no Heaven?'

'Not for me. Bliss is only bliss when you come upon it unexpectedly. If it lasted for ever it would be unbearable.' She smiled. 'Everything all right?'

Jinx turned away from the window. 'Exactly the same as it was half an hour ago, and the half-hour before that. Are you going to tell me now why it's so important to keep checking on me?'

'Perhaps the doctor's worried that you've been over-exerting yourself. You put the fear of God into me this afternoon with that wretched walk. It was too far and too long.'

'It wasn't, you know,' said Jinx idly. 'I spent most of the time hiding.' She smiled at the other woman's surprise. 'I saw my brother coming and dived for cover in one of the outside sheds.' She glanced back towards the window. 'Dr Protheroe told me he was expecting a visit from my father,' Jinx lied easily. 'So do you know if Adam ever came? I thought he might pop in afterwards to visit me.'

'I believe his solicitor came,' she said, plumping up the pillows and smoothing the sheets, 'but I don't think your father did.'

Jinx pressed her forehead against the glass. 'Why hasn't Dr Protheroe been to see me?'

'He's taken himself off for a few hours' R and R. Poor fellow,' she said fondly, wishing as she often did that she hadn't saddled herself with Mr Gordon. 'He has a lot on his mind one way and another, and no one to share his problems with.'

Jinx wrapped her arms about her thin body to stop the shivering. *Did he have Leo and Meg on his mind? And was it Kennedy who'd told him?*

Sister Gordon frowned. 'You've been at that window too long, you silly girl. Quickly now, into your dressing gown and into bed. No sense catching pneumonia on top of everything else.' She clicked her tongue sharply as she opened the dressing gown and slipped it over Jinx's shoulders. 'You were lucky that young couple arrived when they did on the night of your accident or you'd have started pneumonia then.'

'It was certainly convenient,' said Jinx impassively.

Tuesday, 28 June, Nightingale Clinic, Salisbury – 12.05 a.m.

The Wolseley swung through the clinic's gates, its head-lamps scything a white arc across the lawn. It was after midnight and Alan slowed to a crawl to avoid waking the patients with the crunch of wheels on gravel. He felt no relief about coming home, no sense of welcome at his journey's end, only a growing resentment that this was all there was. The temporary euphoria that a bottle of expensive Rioja over a meal of langoustines in garlic butter had given him had evaporated during his careful drive home to leave only frustrated depression. What the hell was he doing with his life? Where was the satisfaction in ministering to a clutch of rich bastards with over-inflated egos and no self-control? Why hadn't Jinx told him Meg and Leo were dead? And why couldn't he get the damn woman out of his mind?

He drummed an angry hand on the wheel, only to wrench it in alarm as the lights picked out the white flash of a face, inches from the nearside wing, disembodied against the blackness of the trees bordering the drive. *Shit! SH-I-IT!* His heart set up a sturdy gallop as he slammed his foot on the brake and brought the crawling car to an almost instantaneous halt. Half-hourly checks, he'd said, and she was out here dodging bloody cars.

'Jinx,' he called, fumbling open the door and hauling himself out and upright with a hand on the car roof. 'Are you all right?'

Silence.

'Look, I saw you.' *God help him if he'd hit her.* He used the red light thrown by his rear lamps to scan the grass verge behind the car, but there was no huddled body there. 'I know you can hear me,' he went on, staring into the trees, searching for her. He walked round to lean against the passenger door. Sooner or later she would have to move and he'd see the flash of the white face again. 'I think you're a fraud, Jinx. The amnesia's crap and I don't believe for one second that you tried to kill yourself. It was a set-up, pure and simple, designed to get your father on your side, and it sure as hell worked, even if you probably did yourself rather more damage than you intended. So are you going to tell me what it's all about?' He waited. 'I should warn you I'm feeling pretty bloody ratty at the moment, and my mood isn't improved by hanging around in my own sodding drive because one of my patients wants to play silly buggers. But don't expect me to give up tamely and leave you here. You move one muscle, girl, and I'll catch you. So are you going to show yourself or are we going to wait this out till daylight? Your choice.'

There was a blur of movement, so quick and so close that he was completely overwhelmed by it. He lurched to one side but pain exploded in his shoulder as the solid metal head of a sledgehammer tore his arm from its socket. He ducked away from another arcing blow and scrambled round the bonnet of the car towards the open door of the driver's seat. With an instinct born of desperation, he threw himself behind the wheel and slammed the door. But as he reached across his chest to force the gear clumsily into reverse, the sledgehammer burst through the windscreen towards his face.

Amy Staunton looked at her watch. 'What's Dr Protheroe want half-hourly checks for anyway?' she grumbled. 'The girl's been fast asleep since ten o'clock.'

'Ours not to question why,' said Veronica Gordon. 'Ours just to do or die. Finish your tea. I can't see five minutes making much difference here or there.'

He didn't know if it was sweat or blood that was pouring down his face. As the car accelerated backwards, he only knew that he was in agony. With a sense of unreality he watched the figure – *a man* – vanish into the darkness before the Wolseley's back-end piled into a solid oak tree. *What the hell was going on?*

The door handle of number twelve rattled and the door was pushed half-open as the black nurse looked into the pitch darkness inside. She heard something and, with a start of fear, she felt about for the light switch. 'Are you all right, love?' She flooded the room with light, glanced at the bed where Jinx was threshing her sheets into a tumbled mess, then looked towards the french windows where the curtains flapped in the breeze. Tut-tutting impatiently, she crossed the room to close and lock the windows, then went to the bed and placed a gentle hand on the woman's forehead.

As though galvanized by an electric shock, Jinx sat bolt upright in the bed, mouth sucking frenziedly for air. *She couldn't breathe . . . Dear God, she couldn't breathe* . . . She clutched at her throat in a vain attempt to dislodge whatever was blocking her airway. *But it was earth, filthy acrid earth . . . and it was killing her . . . NO-O-O!* She flung herself off the bed and burst through the bathroom door, wrenching at the cold water tap in the basin and ducking her head under the icy water. She drew in breath on a gasp of shock and let the sweet, sweet water wash the taste of death away.

'Oh, good God, girl,' screeched the nurse, 'what's got into you? You being sick? What you been taking? What you doing with your clothes on? You was fast asleep last time I checked.'

Jinx slumped to the floor and stared at her from red-rimmed eyes. 'It was a dream, Amy,' she whispered. 'Only a dream.'

'Ooh, you're a wicked girl. I've never had such a fright in my life. You just wait till I tell Dr Protheroe. I thought you'd done for yourself good and proper.' She beat her chest. 'I could have had a heart attack. And why did you open your windows? Top panes only after nine o'clock, that's the rule. What you been up to?'

Jinx curled into a ball on the tiled floor. 'Nothing,' she said.

Bodies in Wood Identified

It was confirmed last night by Hampshire police that the two bodies discovered in Ardingly Woods near Winchester on Thursday have been identified as Leo Wallader, 35, of Downton Court, Ashwell, Guildford, and Meg Harris, 34, of Shoebury Terrace, Hammersmith, London. Police are treating their deaths as murder.

Information about the identity of the two victims came from Leo's father, Sir Anthony Wallader, 69, who is angry about what he calls police apathy over the affair. 'I identified my son's body on Saturday morning,' he claims, 'but have had no contact with the Hampshire police since. They tell me my son and his girlfriend were murdered some two weeks ago, yet there is no urgency to the enquiries. I have been contacted by Meg's mother, who lives in Wiltshire, and she is as upset by the police lethargy as I am. We feel it may have something to do with the fact that both sets of parents live outside the county. If this was a Surrey police investigation I would have more confidence.'

It is no secret that Leo Wallader was engaged to Jane Kingsley, daughter of Adam Kingsley of Hellingdon Hall, Hampshire, Chairman of Franchise Holdings, but the wedding was cancelled when Leo announced he wanted to marry Jane's friend, Meg Harris.

Subsequently, Miss Kingsley was involved in a mysterious car crash on a disused Hampshire airfield. Police believe this to have been a failed suicide attempt. Despite testing positive for alcohol when she was rescued from her car, Hampshire police have still failed to charge Miss Kingsley with any offence.

Jane Kingsley's first husband, Russell Landy, was clubbed to death 10 years ago with a sledgehammer but his murderer was never found. Hampshire police refused to comment on how Leo Wallader and Meg Harris died, but Sir Anthony said both victims had been brutally bludgeoned. 'It was terrible to see,' he said. 'I dread to think how Mrs Harris feels.'

'We have very little to go on at this stage,' said Det Supt Cheever of Hampshire police, 'but we are pursuing every lead we have. I am sorry Sir Anthony feels as he does but I can assure him we are leaving no stone unturned to discover his son's killer.'

Supt Cheever said he could not confirm that a sledgehammer had been used to murder the couple. 'The bodies lay undiscovered for some ten days,' he said, 'and it is always difficult in those circumstances to be precise about how and when the victims died.'

The Times – 28 June

Chapter Fourteen

Tuesday, 28 June, Nightingale Clinic,
Salisbury – 1.00 a.m.

THE TWO CONSTABLES surveyed the shattered windscreen and the crushed Wolseley boot with unfeigned disgust. It was parked forlornly by the front door where Alan had driven it when he realized that, without some very prompt action, his dislocated shoulder would require reduction under general anaesthetic at the nearest Casualty department. He had blared the horn with all the vigour of the angels and archangels sounding the last trump, and had sobbed with relief when the night security officer had emerged to rescue him, and Veronica Gordon, using strong hands and a steady nerve, had guided the bones back into place. Even so, it had been a close call. After fifteen minutes, the joint had been so swollen that the pain was unbearable.

'That's criminal,' said one policeman, lighting the damage with his torch. 'How many times did you say he hit it, sir?'

'Only once,' said Alan, cradling his left elbow in the palm of his right hand, unconvinced that the sling he was wearing was reliable. 'I smashed the back in when I was reversing away from him. I'm rather more interested in the fact that he had at least two swipes at me.'

'Still, sir,' said the other ponderously, 'he seems to have done more damage to your car.'

'Remind me to show you some pictures of dislocated joints thirty minutes after the event,' he said dryly, 'then tell me he did more damage to my car.' He led the way inside and into his office, padding wearily to his desk and hitching a buttock on to the edge. 'I suppose it's occurred to you he might still be out there.'

'Highly unlikely, sir, not with all the activity that's been going on.'

The police car had arrived within ten minutes of the 999 call and, following Dr Protheroe's description of events, namely that he had glimpsed a face in his headlights and had stopped to investigate, the policemen worked on the logical assumption that an intruder had come with the intention of burglary and the doctor had had the misfortune to get in his way. A thorough check of all the doors and windows, however, had failed to find any signs of a break-in.

'We can't fault your security, sir,' said the larger of the two constables with a perplexed frown, 'which makes me doubt this fellow had cased the clinic very thoroughly. If he was planning a burglary, he can't have known how difficult it was going to be to break in. So are you sure you didn't recognize him? Otherwise I don't understand why he bothered to attack you. He clearly hadn't committed a crime at that point, not unless he entered and left by the front door, which your security officer says is impossible because he's been at the reception desk since ten o'clock.'

266

'I'm sure. In any case I was beginning to think I'd made a mistake about seeing anyone at all until I felt the hammer brush my arm. I had no idea he was so close to me. I certainly didn't hear him, but, as I'd left the car engine running, that wasn't really surprising.'

'And you can't think of any reason why someone would want to attack you?'

Alan shook his head. 'Unless he knew I was a doctor and thought I had drugs in the car. I've been racking my brains but I can't think of anything else.' There would be time enough tomorrow, he thought, to decide whether it had been Jinx's face he had seen in the headlamps, or whether his imagination had put her there because she had been on his mind.

'An ex-patient, perhaps, who would recognize your car?'

'I wouldn't have thought so. It's one of the first things I make clear when they arrive. We have a limited supply of drugs on the premises and they're always locked away in that safe over there.' He jerked his head towards the solid Chubb in the corner. 'They certainly know I never carry anything in my car.'

The constable lowered himself on to a chair and took a notebook from his pocket. 'Well, let's get some details down. You say he ran away after smashing the windscreen, so you must have had a pretty good look at him then.'

Alan plucked a Kleenex from a box on his desk and dabbed at his face, which was still bleeding from where tiny shards of glass had embedded themselves in his skin.

'Not really. I was having a hell of a job trying to find reverse with my right hand, so I was concentrating on that.'

'Will you describe him for me, please?'

'He was a bit shorter than I am – say about five ten or eleven. I suppose you'd describe him as medium build – he certainly wasn't fat – and he was dressed in black.'

The policeman waited for him to continue, pencil poised over notebook on knee. When he didn't, he looked up. 'A slightly fuller description would be more helpful, sir. For example, what skin colour was he?'

'I don't know. I think he was wearing a ski-mask. All I saw was a man dressed in black from head to toe wielding a sledgehammer.'

'Fair enough. Then perhaps you could give me some details of his dress. What was he wearing on his top?'

Alan shook his head. 'I don't know.' He saw impatience in the constable's eyes. 'Look,' he said with a flash of anger, 'it's very dark. I get out of my car and the next thing I know some bastard is trying to make mincemeat out of me. Frankly, taking in the minutiae of his dress is the last thing on my mind.'

The policeman waited a moment. 'Except that you must have taken in a few more details when you were back in the car and he was running away.'

'It happened very fast. All I can tell you is that he was dressed in black.'

'It's not much to go on, sir.'

'I'm aware of that,' said Alan testily.

There was a short silence. 'Yet you're very sure it was a man. Why? Did he say something to you?'

'No.'

'Could it have been a woman?'

'Maybe, but I don't believe it was. Everything about him – body shape, strength, aggression – told me it was a man.'

'You wouldn't be so convinced if you saw some of the women we deal with, sir,' said the constable with heavy humour. 'There's no such thing as a weaker sex these days.'

Alan took a deep breath. 'Look, would it be a problem if we left all this till tomorrow? I'm pretty tired and my shoulder's giving me hell.'

The constables exchanged glances. 'I can't see why not,' said the one who had remained standing. 'The place seems secure enough and, without a good description, there's not much we can do tonight anyway. We'll have one of the plainclothes lads come and talk to you tomorrow. Meanwhile, sir, you might make a list of where you've been today and who you've spoken to.' He gave a courteous nod. 'It was a good bet that anyone coming back after midnight was more likely to be a doctor than a visitor or patient. So for what it's worth, I think your theory about drugs is the most likely explanation.'

Alan stopped at the nurses' room on his way to bed. 'Everything all right?' he asked.

Veronica Gordon, the only occupant, looked at his bloodied face. 'Are you trying to play the martyr?' she demanded. 'Is that why you won't let me do something about those cuts?'

'You're too ham-fisted, woman,' he growled. 'I'd rather do them myself, quietly and gently, in my own time. Any problems?'

'Good lord, no,' she said tartly. 'Why would there be problems when a house full of insecure drunks and drug addicts get woken in the middle of the night by security officers and policemen tramping about the gravel and shining torches through their windows? For your information, Amy and I are being run off our feet. She is currently responding to the three bells that rang just before you came in.' A light began flashing on the board at her elbow. 'There's another one. They're all too nosy for their own good. They want to know what's going on.'

'What about Jinx Kingsley? Are you still running the half-hourly checks?'

She swung the night register round for him to look at. 'Fast asleep, and has been since ten o'clock. Matter of fact, she's the only one who hasn't given us any trouble. Amy checked her just before you started blaring your horn but it's not recorded because we haven't had time, not with all the hoo-ha going on. I've popped my head in once since then, but she's out like a light. Do you want us to go on with it?'

'Yes,' he said thoughtfully. 'Just in case. It makes me feel easier, knowing where she is.'

It wasn't until after he'd gone that Veronica was

struck by the inappropriateness of what he'd said. She intended to mention it to Amy Staunton, but it went out of her mind when the demands of another bell sent her off down the corridor. Had it not, and if Amy had been encouraged to tell her that Jinx was fully dressed, she, like Sergeant Fraser, often wondered afterwards how different the end result might have been.

Jinx's waxen cheeks lost their last vestiges of colour when Alan Protheroe entered her room before breakfast the following morning, his left arm supported in a sling and his face scarred with tiny cuts and scratches. 'Did Adam do that?'

He was visibly taken aback. Whatever reaction he'd expected from her, it certainly hadn't been that. 'Why would your father want to break my windscreen?'

'He wouldn't,' she said rapidly. 'Forget I said it. It was silly. Is that what happened? Is that why the police were here last night?'

He smiled. 'There now, and I was reliably informed you slept through the whole thing.'

'I did.'

'Then how do you know the police were here?'

'Matthew told me. He came in half an hour ago.'

God damn bloody Matthew! He seemed to spend more time in this room than he did in his own. 'Did he say what it was all about?'

Jinx shook her head. 'He's on a trawl to see if anybody else knows.'

She was a great liar because she understood the

importance of being plausible. 'I see.' He perched on the end of the bed. 'And you couldn't tell him because you don't know.'

She held his gaze for a moment before looking away. 'That's right.'

'The police think it was an intruder after drugs.' He examined her exhausted face. 'For someone who slept through it all, you don't look very rested.'

She forced a cheerful smile. 'It's my skinhead look. It doesn't do me any more favours than it does your average convict. But it's not really designed to, is it? Hair is the original fashion accessory.'

'Are you cold?' he asked her. 'You're shivering.'

'It's nerves.'

'Why are you nervous of me, Jinx?'

'I'm not.'

'Then what *are* you nervous of?'

'I don't know,' she said. 'I can't remember.'

He grinned broadly. 'I had a dream about you last night. I dreamt I was lying on my back on a cliff edge when a hand came up, grabbed my ankle, and started to pull me towards the brink. As I was sliding over, I looked down and saw your face staring up at me, and you were smiling.'

She frowned. 'Is that supposed to mean something?'

'Yes,' he said, standing up. 'It means you were pulling my leg.'

It was a Detective Constable Hadden of the Wiltshire police who took up where the two uniformed policemen had left off the previous night. He was a bluff middle-aged man who was there to pay lip-service to police procedure but without any obvious intention of pursuing the matter further. Rather to Alan's annoyance, he arrived with the newspaper which put paid, for the moment anyway, to Alan's attempts to substantiate what Simon Harris had told him over the telephone.

'Frankly, sir,' confided DC Hadden, pushing his ample bottom into the sculptured recesses of the leather sofa, 'I'm inclined to go along with the junkie theory, unless you've remembered anything overnight that points to something more concrete. You see our dilemma. We'd have more success looking for a needle in a haystack than scouring the countryside for this man you've described. It would be different if you could give us a name or if he'd stolen something – there'd be a slim chance of tracing him through the goods – but as it is' – he shook his head – 'needle-in-haystack stuff, sir. I'm sure you understand the problem.'

'Then this list I made of the people I spoke to yesterday was a complete waste of time,' Alan snapped irritably. 'I could have had another half-hour in bed, which would have done me rather more good than attempting to assist the police in an inquiry they aren't even interested in.' He snatched the list from the coffee table and prepared to roll it into a ball.

'Now I didn't say that, sir,' said Hadden, holding out his hand for the piece of paper. 'We will, of course, look at any information you give us but the report of last night's incident emphasizes very strongly that you did not believe the attack was personal. Perhaps you've reconsidered?'

Alan shook his head. 'What I said was, I can't think of anyone who would want to have done it, but I did make the point that the man took another swing at me even after I'd shut myself in the car. If drugs were what he was after, why didn't he give up then?'

Hadden glanced down the list as he spoke. 'Because these types don't act logically, sir, as I'm sure you know. His mind was set on whatever you had in the car, so he smashed the windscreen to get at it. Hospitals lose thousands of pounds' worth of stock every week. Sooner or later, someone was bound to think a place like this was worth a hit.' He thumbed the corner of the page. 'Mr Kennedy, solicitor to Adam Kingsley,' he read slowly. 'Would that be Adam Kingsley of Franchise Holdings?'

Alan nodded.

The transformation from bored indifference to alert interest was startling. 'May I ask why his solicitor came to see you, sir?'

'Mr Kingsley's daughter is a patient here.'

'I see.' The detective frowned. 'Why send his solicitor? Is there some dispute between you?'

'Not that I'm aware of.'

'Then what did you talk about? Was it an amicable discussion?'

'Perfectly amicable. We discussed Miss Kingsley's progress.'

'Is that normal, sir? Discussing a patient's progress with her father's solicitor?'

'Not in my experience, no, but Mr Kingsley's a busy

man. Perhaps he trusts his solicitor to keep confidential information confidential.'

The other man's frown deepened. Clearly, he found the episode as inexplicable as Alan had done. 'Have you met Mr Kingsley himself?'

'No. We correspond by fax and telephone.'

'So you can't say what sort of a man he is?' Alan shook his head. 'There's a Fergus Kingsley on your list. Would that be a relation?'

'The younger son. Miss Kingsley's half-brother.'

'And was your conversation with him amicable?'

He thought of Fergus's hand on his arm. The gesture had been annoying, but not hostile. 'Yes, it was amicable.'

DC Hadden folded the page and stuffed it into his pocket. 'You said your guy was carrying a sledgehammer. No question about that?'

'None.'

'OK.' He stood up. 'We'll see what we can do, sir.'

Alan raised an enquiring eyebrow. 'Why the sudden change of heart? Two minutes ago you were quietly going to drop the whole thing, now you're raring to go. What's Kingsley got to do with this?'

Hadden shrugged noncommittally. 'I seem to have given you a false impression, sir. The Wiltshire police take all assaults seriously. Presumably, if we need to come back to you, we'll find you here. You're not planning to go away in the next day or so?'

'No.'

'Thank you for your help. I'll be off then.'

Alan watched him leave, then, with a thoughtful frown, reached again for the newspaper. The piece about Leo and Meg was on an inside page and, when he read it, he understood why mention of sledgehammers in the context of the name Kingsley had galvanized so indolent a man as DC Hadden into activity.

Romsey Road Police Station,
Winchester – 10.00 a.m.

An hour later and twenty miles away in Winchester, Frank Cheever listened to what his oppo in Salisbury told him over the telephone and smiled for the first time in twelve hours. It had been a bastard of a night, beginning with the call from *The Times* seeking confirmation of identity and continuing with a bombardment from other journalists demanding to know if the implications in *The Times* piece had any basis in fact. Sir Anthony Wallader, it seemed, had been very specific in his accusations against Kingsley and his daughter and, while none of the newspapers was foolish enough to print his statement verbatim, they had all followed *The Times*'s lead by mentioning Landy's death and quoting Frank's own refusal to specify whether a sledgehammer had been used. They had also flirted with Wallader's other accusation that Kingsley was using his influence to suppress the investigation in his home county of Hampshire, leaving their readers to tease out all the damning implications.

Frank's ears were still smarting from a deeply critical

276

dressing-down by the Chief Constable for his failure to keep Sir Anthony and Mrs Harris informed of developments. Frank had pointed out, but to no effect, that Meg's body had not been formally identified until a few hours previously and that Sir Anthony's complaint to the newspapers was very specific, namely that Hampshire police had not immediately arrested and/or charged Adam or Jane Kingsley. The Chief Constable was unimpressed by such niceties of distinction. Frank should have addressed the Wallader and Harris concerns at the outset and never allowed this climate of distrust to develop.

'It must have occurred to you that the two sets of parents would get together. Why on earth didn't you go back to the Walladers the minute the Harrises had left? Of course they're going to suspect the worst if we can't be bothered to keep them informed. I'm organizing a press conference for this afternoon and I expect you to have pacified both families in the meantime. No one is to be left in any doubt at all that Hampshire police are pursuing this inquiry with vigour and commitment, irrespective of who may or may not be involved.'

Frank glanced at his watch as he replaced the receiver. Sir Anthony and Lady Wallader were due in less than ten minutes. The Harrises had declined the invitation, but had agreed to see Detective Superintendent Cheever in their home at midday. The press conference was scheduled for three-thirty. He picked up the telephone again and ordered DI Maddocks into his office immediately.

'Sir,' said Gareth, presenting himself sixty seconds later, as anxious not to annoy the Superintendent as Frank was anxious not to further annoy the Chief

Constable. The pecking order had been viciously active since seven o'clock the previous evening.

'I've had a call from Salisbury. Dr Alan Protheroe at the Nightingale Clinic was attacked last night with a sledgehammer. He avoided serious injury by raising the alarm and attracting help but, and this is the interesting bit, Salisbury say Protheroe had a visit from Kingsley's solicitor yesterday afternoon. I want you to go to Salisbury, take Fraser with you, talk to Detective Superintendent Mayhew and a Detective Constable Hadden and then go on to the Nightingale Clinic to interview Dr Protheroe. Get me a complete run-down of his day, the names of everyone he spoke to and what was said. The solicitor's visit cannot be coincidence.'

Sir Anthony Wallader was in no mood to be placated. He denounced the Kingsleys as murderers, repeated his accusations of police lethargy, demanded to know why Russell Landy's death had gone unpunished, insisted that if the police had done their job over that, then Leo and Meg would still be alive. He seemed unable to contain his grief or deal with it, and three days had brewed in him an anger that needed to lash out at anyone who could be blamed for his loss. Lady Wallader, by contrast, sat with bowed head and said nothing.

Frank, too, sat in silence until the storm abated.

'Please accept my apologies for any insensitivity that I and my team have shown you and your wife, Sir Anthony,' he said quietly. 'Our difficulty was tracing Meg's parents and, as I'm sure Mrs Harris told you, it wasn't until yesterday morning that they were able to make the formal identification. Clearly, I should have telephoned you immediately afterwards to acquaint you with developments and I regret intensely that I did not.'

'At the very least, someone should have been sent to comfort my wife. Why wasn't that done? The Reverend Harris tells me you sent a policewoman to support *his* wife.'

'We did offer support and counselling, sir, but if you remember you said it would only make it worse to have strangers in your house.'

'Well, I'm not going to let it rest. I'm making an official complaint. In my view you should be taken off the case immediately and replaced with someone more competent.' Tears gathered in his eyes. 'My son has been murdered and what are you doing about it? Nothing. Any more than anything was done after Russell Landy's murder.'

'I do assure you, sir, we have done a great deal in the few days we've had. For example, we've located your son's London house where we expect to find most of his and Miss Harris's possessions.' He checked the time. 'A team of detectives was due in there this morning, accompanied by your son's solicitor. We have in addition requested the French police to enter his house in Brittany although, as it seems clear he and Meg died without ever leaving England, we are not hopeful of anything material coming back across the Channel. There is also the condominium in Florida, but, again, we think it unlikely that a search will bear fruit.' He paused for a moment, pretending not to see the hurt bewilderment on the older man's face. 'We are still trying to locate his two cars. His solicitor is sure that one of them, at least, is in the garage of the Chelsea house and he has given us the address of another garage in Camden which Leo rented for several years. Mr Bloom has agreed to take the detectives there after they have finished in the house. There are, in addition, two safety deposit boxes, which we will apply to search, and several bank accounts that may tell us something when we can gain access to them. I regret that these efforts had to be delayed until today, but we were only given Mr Bloom's name on Sunday afternoon. We contacted him yesterday and arranged for the searches to be made this morning.'

'But this is outrageous,' spluttered Wallader. 'We should have been told all this immediately.'

'In fact, this information was only confirmed for us late yesterday afternoon in a fax from Mr Bloom's office,' said Frank. 'It took some time to assemble because of the complexity of your son's affairs.' He folded his hands in front of him. 'I do regret the turn events have taken, sir. Please believe that Mr Bloom had agreed to accompany me to Guildford after the searches of your son's premises in order to clarify and explain what he knows of Leo's estate. Wrongly perhaps, I thought it would be more appropriate for you to hear the details from a solicitor. It seems your son had considerable assets which, from the little you were able to tell us on Saturday, I gather you and your wife knew nothing about.'

Lady Wallader looked up at Cheever. 'He had a flat in Kensington which he had to sell in 'eighty-eight to pay off his debts,' she said tiredly. 'He lost everything in the stock market crash and had to live in rented accommodation in Kew for five years until he met Jinx and moved in with her.'

Frank consulted the fax from Bloom. 'Would that be a flat in Kensington Garden Road?'

She nodded.

'It makes up part of his estate, Lady Wallader, together with three flats in Kew and two in Hampstead. His list of properties is as follows: a five-bedroomed house in Chelsea, which was let until April of this year, at which point he instructed Bloom and his agents to keep it vacant; the flat in Kensington, which is currently empty but with instructions to let; two flats in Hampstead, which are currently let; a three-storeyed house in Kew, which was converted to three flats four years ago, all of which are currently let; a house in Brittany, which is let during the holiday season when Leo himself doesn't require it; and a condominium in Florida, which is let year-round to holiday tenants. Off hand, can you remember where he said his rented flat was?'

'The Avenue, Kew,' she whispered.

'Tremayne, The Avenue, Kew?' he asked her.

'Yes.'

'He bought the entire property eight years ago for two hundred and eighty thousand pounds, Lady Wallader. Perhaps you misunderstood what he meant by rented accommodation.'

'No,' she said. 'He led us both to believe he was finding it difficult to make ends meet, but I knew he was lying. If I hadn't, I might have done what he asked and lent him some money.' She stared at him with red-rimmed eyes. 'Was it Jinx who gave you Mr Bloom's name?'

'Yes,' he told her.

'Does that mean she's better? I spoke to her step-mother on the telephone and she told me Jinx had lost her memory. I was very sorry to hear that.'

'I understand it's only partial amnesia, Lady Wallader. Two of my detectives spoke to her on Sunday, and most of what she can't recall relates to events in the two weeks preceding her accident.'

'How bloody convenient for her,' said Sir Anthony furiously. 'You realize she's probably lying.'

Frank ignored him. 'Did you like her, Lady Wallader?'

'Yes, I did,' she said quietly. 'But she was angry the last time we saw her and I guessed Leo was up to his tricks again. It's difficult to be objective about your children, Superintendent. For all their sins you go on loving them and, however much you wish they *would*, the sins don't go away.'

Her husband's hand descended on her arm in an iron grip. 'You're being disloyal,' he said angrily.

There was a short silence.

'I'm telling the truth, Anthony,' she said quietly. 'It doesn't mean I loved Leo any less. You know that.' She ignored his hard fingers digging into the flesh of her arm.

'The only truth that matters now is that your son was murdered,' he grunted. 'Do you want his murderer to get away with it?'

She looked at him. 'No,' she said, 'which is why it's important that the Superintendent knows the truth.'

'You're hurting your wife, Sir Anthony,' said Frank calmly.

The haggard face turned blankly towards him.

'Your hand, sir. I think you should remove it.'

Obediently, he unclenched his fist.

'Tell me why Jinx was angry the last time you saw her.'

'Oh, because she'd had enough of his lies and deceits,' said Lady Wallader matter-of-factly. 'Like every other girlfriend Leo ever had. In the end they all discovered that the charm and the good looks disguised a very selfish personality.' She glanced briefly at her husband. 'He couldn't share, you see, even as a child. He became quite violent whenever another child borrowed something of his, so in the end we took him to a psychologist who diagnosed a personality disorder. She told us there was nothing we could do about it but that he would probably learn to control his aggression better as he got older.'

'And did he?'

'I suppose so. He stopped using his fists, but I can't say hand on heart that he felt any less angry inside about having to share what he had. He was very immature.'

'Miss Kingsley described him as excessively secretive. Is that how he solved the problem, do you think? By refusing to divulge what he was worth.'

'Yes.' She gestured towards the fax. 'Well, clearly that's true. We had no idea he owned so many properties. I did recognize that he was much better off than he said he was, but not to this extent. I'm sure we must seem very gullible, Superintendent, but life with Leo was so much calmer when he was allowed to keep his secrets.'

Frank waited a moment. 'You said Jinx had had enough, Lady Wallader. Does that mean it was she who called off the wedding?'

It was her husband who answered. 'No,' he said firmly. 'She was very abusive to us all, though to what purpose remains a mystery. At no point did she say she wouldn't go through with it. It was Leo who told her there wasn't going to be a wedding when she finally stopped shouting.'

'Did he explain why?'

'He said he'd been having an affair with Meg Harris and was going to marry her.'

'And what was Jinx's reaction?'

'Shock,' he said. 'It was the last thing she'd expected and she stared at him in complete shock.'

'Would you agree, Lady Wallader?'

She looked up. 'Yes,' she admitted, 'I would. She didn't say anything, but she clearly hadn't expected a response like that. I got the impression she was very angry but I think she was more angry with Meg than Leo. It's difficult now to say for certain. We were all very distressed and, frankly, Anthony and I were relieved when they left.'

'When was this?'

'It was the bank holiday weekend at the end of May.'

Cheever frowned. 'Yet, according to the evidence we have, the last thing Miss Kingsley remembers is saying goodbye to Leo on June the fourth when she set off to stay with her parents. Why was he still in her house a week after he said he was planning to marry her best friend?'

'We don't know,' said Sir Anthony. 'They left our house furious with each other, then Leo telephoned later that evening to ask us not to say anything to anyone until he gave us permission. But he didn't explain why and he didn't call until nearly two weeks later. It was the Saturday, June the eleventh, and he said he and Meg were making themselves scarce until the fuss died down.' His brows drew together in an angry frown. 'I accept Leo had his faults but he was a damn good catch for the daughter of an East End crook. My view is she wasn't going to let him go that easily. She flared up the May weekend for no good reason and then changed her mind. That's how I see it. Kept him with her till she went to Fordingbridge, then lost him back to Meg while she was away. I mean to say, if she was planning to back out of the whole thing, then why didn't she tell her father to send out cancellation notices during the week she spent at the Hall? That would have been the obvious time to do it. You see, it doesn't add up.'

'Yes,' said Cheever slowly, 'I see your point.'

Chapter Fifteen

WHEN ALAN PROTHEROE summoned Jinx to his office to break the news of Meg and Leo's deaths, she drew away from him into the corner of the wide leather sofa in his office, a distant expression on her gaunt face. He wondered if she was even listening or if, like so much in her life, she was choosing to blank out what she didn't want to hear. She, for her part, refused to be soothed by the sympathy in his voice or the look of compassion in his eyes, both of which she felt were false. Dr Protheroe was not a man to take on trust, she thought.

'Bar the identities of the two bodies, I doubt many of the other details in the newspaper are true,' he finished quietly. 'It reads to me as if Leo's father has made some sweeping statements in a moment of grief which he will probably come to regret, but I'm afraid we can expect another visit from the police and I didn't want you to hear about this from them.'

She favoured him with a tight little smile. 'I've known since Sunday night. But you knew that already, didn't you?'

He nodded.

'Who told you?'

287

'Simon Harris. He phoned yesterday afternoon. He wanted to warn me that the story would break today.'

A look of relief crossed her face. 'Simon?' She searched his face. 'Why would he bother to do that?'

'I think he and his father feel this sort of treatment' – he tapped the newspaper on his lap – 'isn't justice. He talked about his mother and Sir Anthony whipping up a kangaroo court.'

'Caroline doesn't like me at all,' she said disconsolately. 'For some reason she's always blamed me for Meg's behaviour. She thinks Meg fell into bad company. I suppose she looked at Adam and decided like father like daughter.'

'It's not uncommon. We all blame other people for our children's failings.' He paused. 'Why didn't you tell me the police visit upset you?'

She rubbed her eyes. 'I don't trust the police,' she said, 'but it's a form of paranoia that I'm not particularly happy about. I might have been imagining things. There was no sense in worrying you unnecessarily until I knew for certain.'

'You could have told me yesterday.'

'Yesterday I was paranoid about what my father was planning.'

He raised his hands in a gesture of despair. 'How am I supposed to help you if you keep everything to yourself?'

'You're a very arrogant man,' she said without hostility. 'Hasn't it occurred to you that I might not *want* your help?'

'Of course,' he said curtly, ' but that doesn't mean I

have to stop offering it. Do you think my other patients want my help any more than you do? They begin with good intentions but, within hours, most of them are climbing the walls to get out for their next fix. The only arrogance I see is on your side, Jinx.'

'Why?'

'You think you're clever enough to outwit me, the police and your father combined.'

She shifted her gaze back to his. 'I'm certainly contemptuous of fools who shut themselves away in their ivory towers and close their eyes to the madness outside,' she snapped. 'Russell was murdered. For ten years I avoided any sort of serious involvement. Then, when I thought the dust had settled, I let myself go and fell for Leo. Now he's dead, too, along with the only real friend I've ever had. So precisely what sort of help are you offering me? Help in remembering the deaths of my husband, my friend and my lover?' She looked very angry. 'I like it the way it is. I don't want to *remember* anything. I don't want to *know* anything. I don't want to *feel* anything. I just want to be allowed to take surrealistic photographs where all my repressed fears and desires jostle for expression in an idiosyncratic juxtaposition of purity and corruption.' She bared her teeth at him in a ferocious smile. 'And that's a direct quote from a review of my work in the *Sunday Times*. It's pretentious rubbish, but it sounds great.'

He shook his head impatiently. 'You know perfectly well it's not rubbish. I've looked at some of your published work, and that same theme appears over and over again.' He leaned forward. 'You seem to see the world in extraordinarily stark terms. Black and white. Good and evil. For every kindness, a cruelty; for every positive, a negative. Why are there no grey areas for you, Jinx?'

'Because perfection can only exist in an imperfect setting. In a perfect setting it becomes ordinary.'

'So it's perfection that fascinates you?'

She held his gaze for a moment but didn't reply.

'No,' he said, answering for her, 'it's *im*perfection that fascinates you. You're more attracted by the black than by the white.' He studied her face closely. 'The backgrounds to your pictures are always more compelling than the subjects, except in the few instances where you've turned the idea on its head by making ugliness the subject and beauty the setting.'

She shrugged. 'I expect you're right. Black humour certainly appeals to me.'

'As in *schadenfreude*?'

'Yes.'

'You're wrong, woman. You experience anguish on behalf of others while the only person you laugh at is yourself.' He quoted her own words back at her. 'My education was a waste of time. The *Sunday Times* writes pretentious rubbish about my art. I won't get out of bed in front of you because you'll turn me into a golfing club joke.' He paused. 'Are you laughing at Leo now? You should be if you enjoy *schadenfreude*. There's no blacker joke than the timely comeuppance of someone who's done you wrong.'

'I can think of several,' she said flatly. 'Like when you wake up one morning in a police cell and remember it was you who dealt the death blow. That's going to be a gut-wrencher when it happens. Ho! Ho! Ho! We'll all be splitting our sides.' She looked towards the window, cutting herself off, symbolically extending the space between them.

'I don't think that's very likely to happen.'

'Somebody killed them. Why shouldn't it have been me?'

'I'm not quibbling over whether or not you did it, Jinx. I'm quibbling with your waking up in a police cell one morning and remembering it was you. *That's* what's unlikely. Amnesia doesn't vanish overnight, so you'll know long before the police arrest you whether they've got good cause to do it.' He watched her. 'Have they?'

She continued to stare out of the window for several seconds before finally, with a sigh, turning back to him. 'I keep seeing Meg on her knees, begging,' she said, 'and last night I remembered going to her flat and feeling terrible anger because Leo was there. I have nightmares about drowning and being buried alive, and I wake up because I can't breathe. I can remember feeling strong emotions.' She fell silent.

'What sort of emotions?'

'Fear,' she said. 'It hits me suddenly and I start shivering. I remember fear.'

These revelations had come at him so suddenly that he wasn't ready for them, and he experienced a terrible sadness for she seemed to be remembering an over-whelming guilt. 'Tell me about Meg,' he prompted at last.

'She was begging, holding her hands out. Please,

please, please.' Her eyelashes glittered with held-back tears.

'Was she begging from you?'

'I don't know. I just keep seeing her on her knees.'

'Where were you?'

'I don't know.'

'Was anyone else there?'

'I don't know.'

'OK, tell me what you remember about going to Meg's flat and finding Leo there.'

'I just had this image of Leo opening the door to me, and I knew it was Meg's flat because Leo was holding Marmaduke. Marmaduke's a cat,' she explained. 'The funny thing is I heard him purring, but the rest of it was completely static, like a photograph.'

'But you remember feeling angry with Leo.'

'I wanted to hit him.' She pressed her lips together. 'That's really what the memory *was*, not the picture so much as a sense of incredible rage. It came to me suddenly that Leo had made me furious and then I saw him in Meg's doorway.'

'Do you know when that was?'

She pondered deeply. 'It must have happened after June the fourth because that's the last thing I remember – saying goodbye to Leo. He came into the hall and said: Be good, Jinxy, and be happy . . .' She lapsed into another thoughtful silence.

'What did *you* say?'

'I don't know. I just remember what *he* said.'

He pulled forward a notepad and pen. 'Give me a run-down of the day before. What sort of day was that?'

She spoke with confidence. 'I was at work. We were doing some publicity shots of a new teenage band. It was tough to come up with anything original because they were deeply uninteresting and horribly pleased with themselves. Four clean-cut young men with flashing white teeth and hairless chests, who thought they were so pretty we could just take a few snap-shots and every pre-pubescent girl in the country would swoon.' She laughed suddenly. 'So I told Dean to needle them a bit and, after three hours, we ended up with some brilliant shots of four extremely angry young men glowering into the lens.'

Alan chuckled in response. 'What did Dean say to them?'

'He just kept calling them "his pretty little virgins". They got pissed off very quickly, especially as we kept them hanging around for a couple of hours while we fiddled with lights and lenses. They really hated us by the end of it but we got some good pictures as a result.'

'So you developed the film straightaway?'

'No. We had some location work in the afternoon and we were running out of time, so we grabbed some sandwiches and left.' She paused in sudden confusion. 'I went straight home afterwards.' She stared at him. 'So when did I see those photographs?'

'Well, let's not worry about that for the moment. Was Leo there when you got home?'

'No,' she said slowly, 'but he wasn't supposed to be.' Her eyes lit with sudden excitement. 'I remember checking the rooms to make sure he'd really gone and then I felt a sense of absolute peace because I'd got the house to myself again.' She clapped her hands to her face. 'I remember. He wasn't there, and I was *pleased*.'

Protheroe wondered why she hadn't noticed the glaring inconsistency. *Or perhaps the inconsistency was part of the game.* 'So how did you celebrate?'

Her eyes gleamed with sudden amusement. 'I drank two pints of beer, ate baked beans out of a tin, smoked ten cigarettes in half an hour, watched soaps on the telly and had fried eggs and bacon in bed at half-past ten.'

He looked up with a smile. 'That's very precise.'

'I was making a statement.'

'Because they were the things Leo disapproved of?'

'A mere fraction of them. His view of how women should behave was modelled on his mother, and she's kept herself in clover by constant appeasement of a chauvinistic husband.'

He arched an interested eyebrow but didn't pursue the issue. 'So what did you watch on television?'

'Wall-to-wall soap. One after the other. *EastEnders. The Bill. Brookside.*' She smiled. 'Then I couldn't stand it any more, so I watched the news. Soap operas are pretty bloody boring when you haven't a clue what's going on.'

'Why didn't you watch *Coronation Street*?'

'It wasn't on.'

'Are you sure about that?'

'Positive,' she said. 'I went through the *Radio Times* and picked out the soaps deliberately. If it *had* been on, I'd have watched it.'

He stroked his beard thoughtfully. 'I'm not much of an expert, admittedly, but I'm sure *Coronation Street* goes out on a Friday, and you say you remember this as being Friday the third of June.' He eased gingerly out of his chair, his shoulder protesting at the movement, and went to the desk. 'Hilda,' he said into the intercom, 'can you rustle up a *Radio Times* from somewhere and bring it in? I need to know which days of the week *don't* have *Coronation Street*, but *do* have *EastEnders, The Bill* and *Brookside.*'

Her giggle rattled tinnily down the wire. 'There now, and I always thought you preferred the intellectual stuff.'

'Very funny. This is important, Hilda.'

'Sorry, well, I can tell you without the *Radio Times*. *Coronation Street* is Mondays, Wednesdays and Fridays. *EastEnders* is Mondays, Tuesdays and Thursdays. *The Bill* is Tuesdays, Thursdays and Fridays, and *Brookside* is Tuesdays, Wednesdays and Fridays. So, if you don't want *Coronation Street* but you do want the others, then that means Tuesday.'

'Good lord!' said Alan in amazement. 'Do you watch them *all*?'

'Most days,' she agreed cheerfully. 'Anything else I can help you with?'

'No, that's fine, thank you.' He returned to his seat. 'Did you hear that?' he asked Jinx. 'You appear to be remembering a Tuesday and not a Friday, and it does seem a little unlikely that Leo would have returned for breakfast immediately after he had packed his bags and gone.'

She stared unhappily at her hands.

'I wonder if you're quite as clear about Saturday the fourth as you think you are. You remember saying goodbye to Leo and you're very specific about the day and the date, but do you know why? What happened to fix Saturday the fourth in your mind?'

'It was in my diary for ages,' she said. 'Week at the Hall, beginning June the fourth.'

'And you were definitely leaving for the Hall when you said goodbye to Leo?'

'Yes.'

'So how many suitcases were you carrying?'

She stared at him in confusion.

'Did you have *any* suitcases?' he asked.

'I know I was going to see my father,' she said slowly.

He waited. 'And?' he prompted at last.

'My bag was hanging on the back of the chair.' She stared into the past. 'It's a small leather pouch on a long strap. I slung it over my shoulder and said, I'm off now.' She frowned. 'I think I must have put the suitcases in the car the night before.'

'Is that what you usually did?'

'It's the only thing that makes sense.'

'I wonder if it is.' He took a diary out of his jacket pocket. 'Let's work forwards,' he suggested, 'beginning with what you know to be true. Tell me about the first time you met Leo.'

The Vicarage, Littleton Mary,
Wiltshire – 12.15 p.m.

Simon Harris answered the door and looked in some dismay at Frank Cheever. 'We – that is, my father and I—' He broke off as the sound of shouting erupted from the window to the right. 'My mother's not very well, I'm afraid. She can't really come to terms with what's happened. We'd like her to see the doctor but she won't have him near her. The problem is she's making some very wild accusations, and we're worried – well, frankly, she's accusing Dad of some terrible things and we – that is I—' He fell silent as Mrs Harris's voice rose to a scream, her words carrying clearly through the open window.

'How dare you deny it? Did you think I didn't know how you lusted after her? Did you think she wouldn't tell me what you did to her? She couldn't wait to get out of this house, couldn't wait to get away from you. You made her what she was and you dare to accuse her now of weakness. You disgust me. You've always disgusted me.'

Charles Harris said something in a murmur which wasn't audible.

'Of course I'll tell the police. Why should I protect you when you never protected her? You disgusting man.' Her voice rose to a scream again. 'CHILD ABUSER!' There was the sound of a door slamming, followed by silence.

Frank looked at Simon's shocked face. 'None of that would be admissible in court, sir. I couldn't possibly swear that it was your mother I was listening to and not a radio programme, so please don't worry unnecessarily. As you say, she's overwrought and we all say things we don't mean when we're angry.'

'But you heard it.'

'Yes.'

'It's completely untrue. My father has never abused anyone in his life, and certainly not Meg. It's my mother who has the problem.' Anguish pinched his already drawn face. 'This is so awful. I keep asking myself, why? What have we done to deserve it?'

Frank was spared an answer by the door opening behind Simon's back and his father putting an arm round the young man's shoulder and drawing him inside. 'Come in, Superintendent. You find us in turmoil, I'm afraid. Grief is often the most selfish of emotions.'

Nightingale Clinic, Salisbury – 12.30 p.m.

Alan smiled encouragingly as Jinx showed her first signs of faltering. 'You're doing very well. We can check all this with Dean later, but you've taken me up to Friday, the twenty-seventh of May without any hesitation at all.' He consulted his diary. 'The following Monday, May the thirtieth, was a bank holiday. Does that help at all? You're unlikely to have gone to work so maybe you took the opportunity for a long weekend away.'

'Friday was the last day of the *Cosmopolitan* fashion shoot,' she recapitulated slowly. 'Dean had tickets to a rock concert at Wembley and he had to meet his lover at five o'clock at the tube station, so he left me to develop the films. I wanted to get it done because . . .' She paused at the same place she'd paused before. 'I know it was urgent,' she said, 'but I can't remember why.'

'There were only four working days the following week because of the Bank Holiday Monday,' he pointed out, 'and you were spending the week after that at Hellingdon Hall. Perhaps you realized you were running out of time.'

She stared into the middle distance. 'Miles and Fergus came,' she said suddenly. 'It was after Angelica had left and they kept hammering on the studio door until I let them in. There was a cab-driver with them, demanding money. They were both pissed. They said they'd lost all their cash gambling, couldn't go home and needed beds for the night. I said why hadn't they gone to Richmond and waited for me there, and they said they had, but Leo had refused to pay the taxi fare and told them to come to the studio instead and make me pay for it. Which I did.' She took out a cigarette and lit it, watching the blue smoke spiral from its tip for a second or two before going on.

'I can remember now,' she said in a strange voice. 'I made them some coffee and told them to wait in the reception area till I'd finished what I was doing, but Miles was so drunk that he barged in on me in the dark room and let the light in.'

'What happened then?'

'The film I was working on was completely buggered, so I did what my father does and beat the shit out of him.' She gave a hollow laugh. 'I chased him into the studio and started hitting him with a plastic chair. I was *so* angry. And then Fergus came lurching in to find out what was going on, so I hit him as well. But the person I really wanted to have a go at was Leo. It was the last straw, sending them on to me when he knew I was up to my eyes in work.'

'How did he know?'

'Because when Dean left I phoned to tell him. We were going to his parents' for the weekend and he wanted to leave on the Friday evening. So I rang to suggest that he go on his own and leave me to follow on the Saturday, but he said he had things to do himself so it didn't matter.'

'And it was after the phone call that he sent Miles and Fergus on to you?'

She nodded.

'What happened then?'

'I made up my mind to call off the wedding. It was the money more than anything, the fact that he wouldn't pay their taxi fare.' Her lips thinned angrily. 'He'd been scrounging off me for so bloody long, and he wouldn't even pay one miserable taxi fare, and I thought, I'm mad. What the hell am I doing tying myself to this selfish bastard who doesn't give a toss for anyone except himself?' She looked at Alan. 'So I packed it in for the evening, got the boys into the car and went back to have it out with him. And he wasn't there.' She shrugged. 'So I ordered a pizza, made the boys eat some, and sent them to bed to sleep it off.'

There was a short silence.

'Weren't Miles and Fergus angry when you hit them?'

'I think they were too shocked.' She thought back. 'The funny thing is I lost my temper with Fergus the other day and I thought it was the first time I'd ever done it but it was nothing to the anger I felt that night. I remember screaming at them so much that I had a sore throat the next morning.' She smiled slightly. 'I didn't hit them very hard. It was the fact that I did it at all that shocked them. Miles burst into tears and said I was just like Adam, and I thought: For the first time I understand why Adam does it.'

'And why is that, Jinx?'

She looked at him. 'Because you're so bloody tired, you're working so bloody hard, you've tied yourself to a worthless parasite, and two immature drunks come along and ruin everything you've done because they think it's funny. I could have killed them all that night, every one of them. I got no sleep because I was so angry, and all I could think about was what hell the next week was going to be because I'd have to work late to catch up. And I kept worrying that the ruined film was the only film that was any good, and how was I going to explain to *Cosmopolitan* that we'd have to do the shoot all over again.'

'Did Leo come back that night?'

'If he did, I didn't hear him. I bolted the front and back door on the inside, so he couldn't get in.' She brushed imaginary fluff from her sleeve. 'He came back at lunchtime on the Saturday.'

'Were Miles and Fergus still there?'

She nodded. 'We were all in the kitchen when he came in through the back door. They couldn't go unless I lent them some money for the tube fare back to Miles's Porsche, which was parked outside a casino somewhere, but I was refusing to shell out any more. I said they could walk for all I cared, or phone Adam and explain what they'd been doing. He'd already told them that if they persisted with the gambling he'd cut them out of

301

his will.' She closed her eyes and touched her fingertips to her eyelids as if she had a pain there. 'So Leo offered to drive them and they all left.'

There was another silence.

'And what did you do then?' asked Alan.

'I don't know,' she said. 'I can't remember anything after they left. I think I must have gone to sleep.' She lowered her hand and looked at him with a kind of despair.

The Vicarage, Littleton Mary, Wiltshire – 12.30 p.m.

They sat in the drawing room in deep discomfort. Caroline Harris was crouched on the sofa, misery etched into every line of her face. Charles sat as far away from her as he could, while Simon perched unhappily on a stool. Frank, overheated and tired, was offered a deep leather armchair which hurt his back.

'We've located Leo's house in Chelsea,' he explained, 'and, according to the information phoned through before I left, there are several boxes and suitcases on the premises which appear to belong to your daughter. Preliminary searches have uncovered a photograph album which shows several snap-shots of Meg and Leo together, taken in July 1983.' He addressed his question to Mrs Harris. 'Were you aware they had known each other for at least eleven years?'

Her lips thinned to a narrow line. 'No,' she said.

'Was she a secretive person, Mrs Harris?'

The woman glanced spitefully at her husband. 'Not with me. She told me everything. It was her father she kept secrets from.'

'That's not true,' said Simon.

Frank glanced at him. 'You'd say she *was* secretive.'

'Very. She didn't want anyone to know anything about her life, least of all Mum or Dad. Particularly Mum, in fact. She knew how much Mum hated sex so she didn't tell her until recently how many men she slept with, and she only did that because she was angry.' He closed his eyes to avoid looking at his mother's pain. 'She loved sex, saw it as a healthy expression of life, love and beauty, and couldn't bear to have it treated as something dirty and disgusting.'

'You wanted her, too, Simon,' said Caroline in a whisper, 'just like your father. Never mind she was your sister. You think I didn't notice? I saw how you looked at her.'

A dull flush rose in Simon's face. 'It was you who made her uncomfortable,' he said quietly, 'not Dad. Everything she did was the opposite of what you've done. She got herself a decent education, she rejected God, she loved sex, she stayed single, she dived into London life to get away from the sterility of village rectitude. She experienced more in her thirty-four years than you will experience in a whole lifetime.' Tears glittered in his eyes. 'She didn't strangle life, she glorified every minute as if it were her last. I wish to God the rest of us could do the same.'

There was a desperate and terrible silence.

Frank cleared his throat. 'One of the photographs has

a somewhat cryptic caption underneath it. It reads' – he consulted a notebook – ' "Happiness AA". I'm told Meg is sitting in Leo's lap on a beach.' He looked up. 'Do you know what AA stands for? It seems unlikely that Automobile Association or Alcoholics Anonymous would fit the bill.'

Simon looked towards his mother but she had retreated into some internal world and was rocking herself tenderly on the sofa. 'After Abortion,' he said quietly. 'Married couples always talk about their lives BC – Before Children. Meg always referred to life after her abortion as double-A time. She said she'd never realized before just how awful it would be to have children and she thanked God she'd discovered early on that she wasn't cut out to be a mother.'

'Was Leo the father?'

'I don't know. She never told me who it was, and I didn't ask.'

'Did you know about Leo before your parents did?'

'Not by name. I knew she had a long-term lover who came and went between her other affairs. She was very fond of him, called him her old stand-by. I presume that was Leo if she'd known him eleven years.'

'Did she ever say why she didn't marry him?'

Simon shrugged. 'She said once that he was permanently broke, but the truth is I don't think she wanted to get married. She certainly didn't want children.' He glanced towards his father. 'She always felt that I fitted into our family better than she did, and she was afraid of bringing a child into the world who didn't belong. She said it wasn't fair.'

'It can't have been Leo,' said his father. 'Surely she wouldn't describe a man with a house in Chelsea as permanently broke.'

Frank Cheever tucked his notebook into his pocket. 'In fact, sir, he had several properties both in this country and abroad, but no one knew about them, not even his parents. He made a habit of pleading poverty when, according to his solicitor, he was worth a very tidy fortune. Miss Kingsley describes him as a parasite who was obsessively secretive about money. His mother describes a disturbed young man with a pathological dislike of sharing. He wasn't a straightforward character by any means, so it's highly probable he did give your daughter the impression he had no money.'

'How very tragic.' Charles Harris looked distressed. 'One tends to think the type doesn't exist any more, certainly not amongst the young. I suppose we must blame Dickens for creating so extreme an example that the rest pass unnoticed.' He saw the Superintendent's perplexed expression. 'Scrooge,' he explained. 'Misers. People who need to hoard wealth but can't bring themselves to spend it. You come across them in the newspapers from time to time, old people who've died in shocking squalor only to leave a fortune behind.' He folded his hands in his lap. 'As I say, it's not something one associates with youth, but presumably a miser is a miser all his life. Poor Leo. What a sad, sad state of affairs.'

His wife began to scream. It was a piercing terrible sound that curdled sympathy and frayed nerves.

Nightingale Clinic, Salisbury – 12.45 p.m.

'Let's try a different tack,' suggested Alan. 'You said you and Leo were supposed to be staying with his parents for the weekend. Have you any recollection of doing that or was the whole idea abandoned when you decided you weren't going to marry him?'

Jinx's expression cleared. 'No,' she said, 'we did go. I had a row with them. I seem to have had rows with everyone that weekend.'

'It's not surprising. You were under a lot of pressure. The wedding was only a few weeks away and you were having second thoughts about going through with it.'

'But why did I go down there with him if I knew I wasn't going to marry him?' It was a puzzle, but not one she thought Protheroe could solve.

He recalled her acceptance of Matthew Cornell's invitation to lunch. 'Presumably they were expecting you, so perhaps you thought it was the polite thing to do.'

'Yes,' she said in surprise. 'I didn't think it would be fair to Philippa not to go.'

'Tell me about the row.'

'I remember it so clearly,' she said. 'It was after lunch on the Monday and I blew my stack when Leo asked his father for some money and Anthony said he was a bit short because he'd been forced to pay for some building work he'd had done.' She shook her head. 'The job had been completed six months before and he was angry because the builder had gone to a solicitor.' She pulled a rueful face. 'I'd been holding myself back for twenty-four hours, and I went berserk. I called him every synonym for skinflint I could think of, then turned on Leo and let rip at him. Poor Philippa looked mortified, and I was sorry about that because she'd always been so sweet to me.' She sighed. 'I wish I'd had the sense not to go in the first place. It wasn't a very dignified display. I kept spitting saliva all over the place because I couldn't get the words out fast enough.'

'Was that when you told Leo it was all off?'

A look of irritation crossed her face. 'I never got the chance. I just made an awful lot of noise, screaming and yelling and calling them names. I don't know what I thought I was doing really, except getting all the poison out of my system. It was Leo who said he wasn't going through with it.' She gave a small laugh. 'He said he'd been having an affair with Meg, and was planning to marry her instead.' She looked at him. 'I did tell you I wouldn't have wanted to kill myself over Leo and Meg. Do you believe that now? I can remember my relief when he said it. Thank God, I thought. I'm off the hook.'

'But it must have been a shock.'

'I suppose it was. I never thought she'd do it again, not after what happened to Russell.'

He was lost. 'Do what again?'

She looked at him rather blankly. 'It was history repeating itself,' she said impatiently, as if it was something he ought to have known. 'Meg was having an affair with Russell when he was murdered.'

Mystery surrounds murdered couple's relationship

Hampshire police revealed this afternoon that the murdered couple, Leo Wallader, 35, and Meg Harris, 34, had kept their eleven-year-old relationship secret from their families. 'It is not clear at this stage,' said Detective Superintendent Cheever, leading the investigation, 'why secrecy was important, but we hope that by publishing photographs of them someone may come forward who knew them as a couple.'

Further mystery surrounds Leo Wallader's estate, which has been valued at over one million pounds. 'He told friends and relations that he was in financial difficulties,' said Det Supt Cheever, 'and it came as something of a surprise to everybody to discover how much he was worth.'

Sir Anthony Wallader, Leo's father, who accused Hampshire police yesterday of lethargy, refused to comment on his son's financial affairs. 'My wife and I are too upset to talk to anyone,' he said. In the absence of a will, Sir Anthony and Lady Wallader, as next-of-kin, will inherit their son's fortune. Sir Anthony is believed to have a substantial fortune in his own right.

Det Supt Cheever agreed that Hampshire police were unhappy about the accusations of lethargy. 'We have been working very hard to find Leo and Meg's murderer,' he told journalists, 'but cases like this are never easy. The length of time that the couple knew each other clearly puts a different emphasis on what has happened here, and we need to establish why they felt it important to keep their friendship secret.'

He went on to say that he recognized the pressure both families were under and regretted any insensitivity Hampshire police may have shown. 'We have a tendency to assume,' he admitted, 'that the families of victims understand we are working hard on their behalf. Clearly this is not always recognized, and we will make sure there is no misunderstanding in future.'

Southern Evening Echo – 28 June

Chapter Sixteen

Tuesday, 28 June, Nightingale Clinic,
Salisbury – 12.50 p.m.

ALAN PROTHEROE WIPED a weary hand across his face, then pushed himself out of his chair and wandered restlessly towards the window. Could he, hand on heart, say he believed anything Jinx told him? *When what she claimed to remember could be as fantastic as she chose because there was no one left to contradict her.* There were three dead people, and all three were intimately connected with this one woman. Logic dictated that she must know something about their deaths. Logic also dictated that her father knew something, or why had he put her in here with such very precise instructions concerning her care? Adam was as anxious as she was, it seemed, that her memories lie dormant.

'I'm not sure I can believe that,' he said with his back to her. 'You described Russell to me only a couple of days ago as possessive and jealous. You said your marriage was stifling. Now you tell me he and your best friend were having an affair. That doesn't quite square, does it?'

'Russell believed in double standards,' Jinx said reasonably. 'If he was capable of cheating the customs, do you not think he was equally capable of cheating his wife?'

'That's hardly an answer, you know. Obsession with one woman doesn't usually lead to philandering with others. Surely the two are mutually exclusive?'

'It depends what sort of obsession you're talking about. Russell was far more obsessed with himself than he was with me. I was little better than a trophy that he could show off to his middle-aged friends, the child bride who adored him so much she forsook fortune and fame to marry him. Meg was a different kind of trophy, the one that proved to him he was still sexually active and attractive at forty-plus. But we had no more value to him than the paintings in his collection. He liked owning things.'

He turned round. 'My problem is I have to take your word for that. Sadly for Russell, the dead can't speak for themselves.'

'Is there a reason why you shouldn't take my word?' She said it without hostility but there was anger in her eyes. 'Suddenly you're a policeman, yet ten minutes ago you only wanted to help.' She made as if to get up. 'This is just a professional exercise for you, and I'm hungry, anyway. I want some lunch.'

He refused to be intimidated. 'Don't be so childish,' he said sharply. 'Healthy scepticism and a wish to help are not mutually exclusive, Jinx. Arguably, the one strengthens the other. Convince the sceptic and you will have a stronger ally for the future. Perhaps if you changed your mind-set *vis-à-vis* the police in that area, you could shed your paranoia and make a positive attempt to help them find Meg and Leo's murderer. Or are you as disinclined to do that as you were to have Russell's murderer named?'

She looked at him with dislike. 'I'll phone Colonel Clancey and ask him to post Russell's diaries and letters to you. I keep them in my bookcase at home. For what it's worth, the entry on the day we got married went like this: "Felt and looked great. Wore black velvet suit and white satin shirt. Speech afterwards was a triumph of wit and erudition. What a pity there were so few guests to enjoy it." I interpret that as self-obsession but then, admittedly, I'm an arrogant woman and I was put out that his bride didn't rate a mention.'

'Still, I'm surprised you didn't mention the affair before. It's a little odd, don't you think, that Meg should have slept with both Russell *and* Leo. Was she in the habit of stealing your men friends?'

'If you want to be strictly accurate about it, I stole them from her. She had a six-month fling with Russell, got bored with him and introduced him to me. She did the same with Leo, told me he was a business acquaintance and said he and I would get on like a house on fire. It was only later that I realized business acquaintance meant lover.'

'Didn't it upset you to get her cast-offs?'

'Everybody's somebody's cast-off. In some ways it's easier if you know your predecessor because then you know you're not competing with Superwoman.'

He resumed his seat. 'You're avoiding the question. Were you upset?'

'Only in retrospect. Meg was a great deal more

311

attractive than I am and completely careless of other people's feelings, particularly men's. She had no qualms about taking up with someone, then dumping him two or three months later for somebody else. The trouble is, I'm less adept at that so I got lumbered with the jerks when it suited her.'

'But she took up with them again later when *that* suited her.' He shook his head in genuine bewilderment. 'If this is true, Jinx, then I can't understand why you describe her as the only real friend you've ever had.'

'I'm not doing this very well,' she said, surprisingly sanguine about his disbelief. 'You'd have liked Meg.' She marshalled her thoughts. 'Look, when I say I got lumbered with them that doesn't mean I hold her responsible for what happened afterwards. She kept telling me not to marry Russell, said I was mad to tie myself down at twenty-one, but by then it was too late. I couldn't just abandon him after what Adam had done, and that wasn't Meg's fault.'

Alan was highly doubtful that Meg Harris was a woman he would have liked. If Jinx had said one thing that was true, it was her admitted inability to make sensible decisions about her personal life, particularly where her choice of friends was concerned. She appeared to be completely blind to their character flaws, and he wondered if she realized that it was only the egocentric personality that seemed to attract her. Was this because she found it difficult to differentiate between self-centredness and self-confidence? She had so many mixed feelings about her domineering father that it wasn't surprising she found people impossible to read. 'I suppose it wasn't Meg's fault either that she had an affair with Russell after he was married?'

She looked at him for a moment. 'Not entirely, no. Presumably Russell had some say in it.' She shrugged. 'Anyway, they were very discreet. I didn't find out about it till after he was dead and by then it was water under the bridge.'

'Who told you?'

'No one. She wrote him some letters which he'd hidden amongst a stack of old exam papers in the attic at Richmond. They were rather sweet,' she said, remembering. 'The sad thing is, I think she really did love him, but she couldn't bear the thought of being tied to one person. She was terrified of ending up in a country backwater like her mother and being the dutiful wife.'

'Did you ever talk to her about Russell?'

'No.'

'Why not?'

'I couldn't see the point.'

'Did the police know about it?'

'If they did they never mentioned it.'

'Why didn't *you* mention it?'

'Because I didn't find the letters until a year later and by then the case was effectively closed.' She plucked at her lower lip. 'I don't think you realize what it's like to be part of a murder inquiry. It's not a very comfortable experience. I'd have needed something much stronger than a couple of faded love letters to make us all go through that terrible mill again.'

He leaned forward. 'So for the next nine years you pretended nothing had happened and then you learnt about her and Leo and you were afraid history was about to repeat itself.'

She didn't say anything. Perhaps she realized how thin it all sounded, and how odd her own behaviour must seem in the circumstances.

'So what did you do, Jinx?'

'I thought it would be better if no one knew, so when we got back to London, I told Leo to phone his parents and make sure they didn't say anything until he gave them the go-ahead. I said I needed to speak to my father first.' She propped her chin in her hands and stared wretchedly at the carpet. 'But I can't remember if I spoke to Adam or not, so I don't know whether—' She broke off abruptly.

'You don't know whether you gave him a reason to have them murdered.'

53 Lansing Road, Salisbury, Wiltshire – 1.15 p.m.

WPC Blake inserted her foot in Flossie Hale's door and refused to remove it. 'I'm not going away until you talk to me,' she said firmly, 'so you may as well let me in.'

After a second or two the pressure against her foot lessened and the door swung open. Flossie regarded her without enthusiasm from a face rainbow-hued with healing bruises. She clasped an old candlewick dressing gown across her broad chest with a plaster-encased forearm, looking twenty years older than her forty-six years. 'What do you want?'

'Just a chat. How are you feeling now?'

'So-so.' She gave a wheeze of bitter amusement. 'Still a bit tender when I sit down, but I'm surviving.' She led the way into a tiny sitting room stuffed with overlarge furniture. 'You might as well take a seat,' she said ungraciously, propping her plump arms on a television set and leaning her weight on it. 'By rights I should be in my bed, but I can't say I fancy it much at the moment. I tried to persuade the hospital to keep me in a bit longer but they turfed me out for some old boy with piles.' She gazed disconsolately at the young policewoman. 'I suppose life's pretty grim for everyone these days.'

Blake nodded. 'It seems that way. I only ever hear hard-luck stories.'

'I wouldn't mind so much if I didn't pay my taxes. You're entitled to expect something for all the money you shell out.'

Privately, WPC Blake thought it highly unlikely that Flossie had ever declared an income in her life, but she nodded sympathetically. 'I agree with you, which is why I'm here. Part of what you should expect in a civilized society is peace of mind and safety, and until we find the man who assaulted you, I'm afraid you won't have either.' She ignored the expression of stubborn resistance that settled on Flossie's face and took her notebook from her handbag. 'You're not the only prostitute he's beaten up. There was another one three months ago and he was just as vicious with her. She says he paid her forty pounds. Was that what he paid you?'

'It may have been,' Flossie said grudgingly.

'She also said she thought he was expecting someone young and attractive and took against her when it turned

315

out she was old enough to be his mother. Was that your experience?'

She shrugged. 'It may have been,' she said again.

'She advertises in telephone boxes and shop windows. I think that's how you get your customers, too, isn't it?'

'Maybe.'

'OK, well, I've done a bit of leg-work in the last couple of days around the girls who advertise the same way, and, while no one else seems to have suffered in quite the way you and the other woman did, three of them gave me a description of a well-spoken handsome young man who became aggressive during his climax.' She consulted her notebook. 'One described him as twisting his hand in her hair and almost pulling it out by the roots. Another said he hit her about the face with her own hairbrush, and the third said he pulled her wig off, then got so angry with her he stuffed it into her mouth. She said he apologized afterwards and paid her an extra ten pounds for her trouble.' She looked up. 'All three girls are in their twenties but they all agreed he had a thing about hair and hairbrushes. Does this sound familiar, Flossie?'

She sighed. 'Seems you've been working overtime, love. Go on then, what's the description?'

Blake read it out. 'Height, about five feet eleven. Slim, muscular build, with hairs down the centre of his chest. Good-looking, boyish face with dark blonde, slightly curly hair, possibly highlighted at the sides, and blue or grey eyes. No facial hair. One girl suggested he plucked his eyebrows because they were very fine and nicely shaped. Clothing varied between a dark suit and white shirt to Levi's and white T-shirt. They all described him as clean, well spoken and probably the product of a public school. Is that about right, would you say?'

'He looked as if butter wouldn't melt in his mouth, but, God, he was a vicious little brute.' She touched a hand to her bruises. 'I'll tell you something, he couldn't sustain himself for half a second. All the shouting and yelling and hitting he went in for was his way of pretending he could keep it up. It didn't occur to me the first time round – I mean, let's face it, you don't feel much when you've been on the game as long as I have. But the second time around he never even got it in he came so quick. And he didn't half punish me for that. It wasn't just that I was old enough to be his mother – though I guess that had something to do with it – mostly it was because he was inadequate.'

'Is there anything you can add to the description?'

She shook her head. 'Sorry. He was very good-looking, beautiful really, reminded me a bit of Paul Newman in *The Hustler*. Not that that'd mean anything to you. You're too young to remember it.' She paused for a moment. 'But there were some odd things he said. "It's not my fault, my father made me evil." That was one of them. And then when he was leaving: "I never had to kill a woman before."'

'Before what?'

Flossie regarded her morosely. 'I guess he meant he'd beaten up on lots of girls but that none of them had died.' She shivered suddenly. 'Gawd, he was mad, one of them split personalities. Looked like a little angel when he arrived and turned into a zombie with staring great eyes the minute he got a hard on. Bloody miracle he hasn't killed someone yet, that's my view.'

Blake agreed with her. 'Any idea how he got here? Car? Did he walk?'

'I don't know. I just wait for the bell to ring and let them in.' She frowned. 'Mind, he did have some car keys with him. I remember him fishing them out of his pocket when he left. He had a really nice jacket on, tight fit, padded shoulders, and he pulled his keys out and held them in his palm while he told me to keep my mouth shut.' She screwed her forehead in concentration. 'There was a black disc on the key-ring. It was hanging down between his fingers and I remember staring at it because I didn't want him to think I was staring at him.' Her eyes gleamed suddenly. 'It had an eff and an aitch on it in gold lettering, same initials as mine, which is why I noticed them. You know what? I reckon FH are the little sod's initials!'

Nightingale Clinic, Salisbury, Wiltshire – 1.30 p.m.

There was a tap on the door and Hilda poked her head inside. 'I'm sorry to bother you, Dr Protheroe, but there's a Detective Inspector Maddocks and a Detective Sergeant Fraser here. I've told them you're busy but they say it's too important to wait.'

'Five minutes,' said Alan.

The door opened wide before Hilda could answer, and Maddocks pushed past her into the room. 'It is important, sir, otherwise I wouldn't insist.' He stopped when he noticed Jinx. 'Miss Kingsley.'

Alan frowned angrily. 'Since when did being a policeman give you the right to barge, uninvited, into a doctor's consulting room?'

'I apologize, sir,' said Maddocks, 'but we've already waited fifteen minutes and we *do* need to talk to you rather urgently.'

Jinx stood up. 'It's all right, Dr Protheroe. I'll come back later.'

'I'd rather you stayed,' he said, looking up at her with a clear message in his dark eyes. 'I can't help feeling this is very poor psychology.'

'For whom?' she asked him, with a mischievous glint in her eye. '*Illi intus aut illi extra?*'

He dredged through his Latin for a translation. The insiders or the outsiders, he decided. 'Oh, *illi extra*, of course,' he said with a barely perceptible nod towards Maddocks. '*Caput odiosus iam maximus est.*' His odious head is already maximum size, was what he hoped he'd said.

Jinx smiled at him. 'If you recognize that, Dr Protheroe, then I don't think it's poor psychology at all. It means you hold the advantage. In any case, I really am starving so, with apologies for desertion, I think I'll go and find myself some lunch.' She gave him a brief nod then slipped past Fraser and Hilda, who were standing irresolutely by the door.

'All right, Hilda, thank you very much.' He gestured towards the sofa. 'Sit down, gentlemen.'

'May I ask what Miss Kingsley said to you?' enquired Maddocks as he took a seat.

'I've no idea, I'm afraid,' said Alan amiably. 'It was all Greek to me.'

'You answered her, sir.'

'I can run that stuff off by the yard,' he said. '*Vos mensa puellarum dixerunt habebat nunc nemo conduxit.* I haven't a clue what it means but it always sounds intelligent. What can I do for you?'

Maddocks, silently admitting defeat, eyed *The Times* which was folded neatly on the coffee table. 'Presumably you've read that?'

'I have.'

'So you know that Mr Leo Wallader and Miss Meg Harris are dead.'

'Yes.'

Maddocks watched his face closely. 'Does Miss Kingsley know?'

Alan nodded. 'I told her after I read it.'

'What was her reaction, sir?'

He stared the Inspector down. 'She was very shocked.'

'Did you also tell her that the man who attacked you last night was wielding a sledgehammer?'

Alan thought about that. 'I can't remember,' he said honestly. 'I mentioned the disturbance to all my patients this morning, but I really can't recall whether I gave precise details or not.' He eyed Maddocks with curiosity. 'Why?' he asked. 'Do you see a connection between the assault on me and the deaths of Mr Wallader and Miss Harris?'

Maddocks shrugged. 'We certainly find it interesting

that Miss Kingsley and a sledgehammer appear to be the only common factors between three murders and a vicious assault,' he said bluntly.

'The third murder being Miss Kingsley's first husband.'

'Yes.'

'Well, I'm afraid I don't follow your logic. Let's say, purely for the purposes of argument, that there is a connection between the murder of Russell Landy and the murder of Mr Wallader, and that the connection is Miss Kingsley's attachment to both men. Marriage in the first instance and marriage plans in the second. And let's go on to say – again purely for the purposes of argument – that because Mr Wallader changed his mind and decided to marry Miss Harris instead, someone decided she also had to die. How does the assault on me fit into this hypothetical scenario? I have known Miss Kingsley as a conscious and functioning individual for a week. We have a doctor/patient relationship. I am neither married to her, nor engaged to marry her. I have not slept with her, nor do I have plans to sleep with her. I know none of her friends and she knows none of mine. She is a paying guest under my roof who is free to leave whenever she chooses.' His eyes narrowed in speculation. 'Have I missed something that makes this spurious connection even halfway believable?'

'Yes, sir,' said Maddocks evenly. 'Coincidence. It's not something that we, as policemen, can readily ignore. Our experience shows that where there's smoke there's fire.' He smiled slightly. 'Or, to put it another way, where there's Miss Kingsley there's also a sledgehammer.'

'Are you suggesting she wields the damn thing herself?'

'I'm not suggesting anything at this stage, sir. I am merely drawing your attention to the coincidence. You would be foolish to pretend it doesn't exist.'

'Well, it certainly wasn't Jinx who took a swing at me last night. She's not big enough or strong enough, and, judging by the build and the height, it was a man.'

'We understand you had a visit from her father's solicitor yesterday.'

'It wasn't him either, Inspector. He's a tiny little chap with dainty feet and hands. I'd have recognized him immediately, ski-mask or no ski-mask.'

Maddocks smiled. 'I was thinking more in terms of Mr Kingsley himself. Perhaps you said something to the solicitor that his boss didn't like?'

'I wouldn't know. I've never met Mr Kingsley so I've no idea what he looks like.' He thought for a moment. 'In any case, I'm sure it was a young man, and Mr Kingsley's sixty-six.'

'What about Fergus Kingsley? He's on your list.'

Alan nodded. 'Yes, he was about the right size. So was the waiter who served me at dinner, but my conversations with both were perfectly friendly and I can't see either of them taking the trouble to hang around the clinic waiting to belt me.' *But was that right? He had run up against Fergus twice now, and neither time had he felt comfortable with him.*

Maddocks saw the sudden thoughtfulness in Protheroe's expression. 'Tell me what you and Fergus Kingsley talked about,' he invited.

322

'Nothing very much. He was waiting beside my car when I came out. He expressed an interest in buying it, as far as I remember, then asked me to meet his brother. I explained I was in a hurry and suggested we leave it to another time. Then I left.'

Fraser looked up with a frown. 'But you weren't in a hurry, sir. According to the report we've seen, you decided to go for a drive and treat yourself to a decent meal because it's some time since you've had an evening off.'

Alan gave another amiable chuckle. 'So I made a polite excuse and left. Is that so odd? I'd spent a long time talking to his father's solicitor, I was hungry and I had promised myself a slap-up meal. At the risk of sounding churlish, I didn't particularly want to spend another half-hour making small-talk with a total stranger.'

'You've never met Miles Kingsley then?'

'No.'

'But both brothers have visited their sister here.' It was a statement rather than a question and Alan wondered how Maddocks knew.

'As I understand it, Miles came last Wednesday at about nine o'clock when I was off duty. Fergus came on Saturday.'

'So they both know their way around.' Another statement.

Alan frowned. 'Fergus spoke to Jinx in the garden, so presumably he could find his way back to the tree they sat under, and Miles, who saw her in her room, could probably find his way back there. Does that amount to knowing their way around? I wouldn't have thought so.'

'I was thinking more in terms of the layout of the driveway, sir.'

'Oh, for God's sake!' Alan snapped impatiently. 'Any moron can wait in the bushes near a gate in the hopes of someone driving in. You don't need to be acquainted with a place to follow a car going at five miles an hour, which is all I was doing because I didn't want to wake the patients by crunching the gravel.' He sighed heavily. 'Look, unless you've got something a little more concrete to put to me, I really can't see the point of continuing. My own view is that you should put your suspicions to Miss Kingsley herself, to her father and to her brothers.' He nodded towards *The Times*. 'In fact, *if*, as you are implying, there is such a strong link between all three murders, I share Sir Anthony's and Mrs Harris's surprise that you haven't done it already.'

'You're very defensive of this family, sir. Is there any particular reason for that?'

'Such as?'

'Perhaps you're more partial to Miss Kingsley than you pretend and perhaps that's why someone saw fit to attack you with a sledgehammer.'

Alan smoothed his jaw reflectively. 'But wouldn't I have had to have *told* someone I was partial to her to provoke such a response?'

'Not necessarily, sir. You looked pretty matey to me when you were spouting Greek at each other. Perhaps someone else sussed that your feelings aren't quite as reserved as you say they are.'

Alan's booming laugh brought a responsive twitch from Fraser's lips. 'I'm afraid I was teasing you, Inspector, when I said it was all Greek to me.' He stood up. 'I am doubtful, *ipso facto*, whether any conclusion you've drawn can be relied upon. Now, if you'll excuse me, I have patients to see.'

Outside, Maddocks scowled angrily as he reached into the car for the handset. 'Put me through to Detective Superintendent Cheever,' he grunted into the mouthpiece, 'and tell him it's urgent, girl. DI Maddocks, and I am at the Nightingale Clinic in Salisbury.' He drummed his fingers impatiently on the roof. 'Yes, sir. No, look, we've run into a spot of bother here. The doctor's playing hard to get and the whole set-up stinks. He and the girl were having a very cosy little chat when we arrived and our view is he knows a damn sight more than he's telling. Yeah, Fraser agrees with me.' He glared at the Sergeant, demanding support. 'No, I think we should talk to her now. We're on the spot, she's seen us and she knows Wallader and Harris are dead. If we leave it any longer she'll have a solicitor in tow guarding her interests. Matter of fact, I'm amazed her old man hasn't parked one here already, although maybe he's set the doctor up as watchdog.' His eyes gleamed triumphantly. 'Will do, sir.' He listened for a moment. 'Yes, got it. Letters from Landy . . . abortion 'eighty-four . . . Wallader or Landy the father.'

He replaced the handset and grinned at Fraser. 'We've been given the chance to show a bit of initiative, lad, so let's grab it with both hands. And whatever happens I don't want that arrogant jerk of a doctor around. So no by-your-leave on this, OK?' He nodded towards the path round the corner of the building that led on to the terrace. 'We'll go this way.'

Jinx was sitting in her armchair, watching the local news on the television, and didn't notice the two men approaching. She felt their shadows blot out the sun on the back of her shaven head as they stepped quietly across the threshold of her open french windows, and she guessed immediately who it was. Unhurriedly, she used the remote to switch off the television, and twisted round to look at them. 'There's a rule here that visitors seek permission before they impose themselves on patients. I don't think you've done that, have you, Inspector?'

Maddocks strolled in and perched himself on her bed as he'd done before. 'No,' he said bluntly. 'Does that mean you have objections to helping the police?'

'Several,' she said, 'but I can't imagine it'll make any difference.' She smiled coldly. 'Not to you anyway.' She glanced up at Fraser with a look of enquiry. 'It might make a difference to your partner.' She examined the younger, pleasanter face closely. 'No? Ah well, we can't all have principles, I suppose. It would be a dull, dull world.'

'You're very sharp for someone with memory loss,' said Maddocks.

'Am I?'

'You know you are.'

'I don't,' she said. 'I'm the first person I've ever met who's suffered from amnesia so I've no yardstick by which to judge it. However, if you're interested, you don't become a zombie just because a few days of your life are missing.' She gave him an amused smile. 'I don't suppose you remember every woman you've rogered, Inspector, particularly if you were tanked up when you did it, but it hasn't done you any harm, has it?' She reached for a cigarette. 'Or perhaps it has and that's why you accuse me of being sharp.'

'Point taken,' he said affably.

She flicked the lighter to the cigarette and eyed him through the smoke. 'Freud would have enjoyed that,' she remarked idly.

He frowned. 'What?'

She gave a low laugh. 'Your somewhat unfortunate remark following so closely on my description of your rogering habits. Freud would suspect that that's what your lady friends say to you at the moment *coitus* occurs.' She heard Fraser's snort of amusement. 'It's not important, Inspector.' She lapsed into silence.

Maddocks was not amused. 'We have a few questions to ask you, Miss Kingsley.'

She watched him but didn't say anything.

'About Leo and Meg.' He waited. 'We understand Dr Protheroe has told you they're dead.'

She nodded.

'It must have been a shock.'

She nodded again.

'Well, forgive me for saying this, Miss Kingsley, but the shock didn't last very long, did it? Your fiancé and your best friend have been bludgeoned to death with a sledgehammer, their faces smashed in just as your husband's was, and you're sitting here quite calmly, smoking a cigarette and cracking jokes. It's about the most unconvincing display of grief that I've ever seen.'

'I'm sorry, Inspector. Would it make you feel better if I did the little-womanly thing and wept for you?'

He ignored her. 'About as unconvincing, frankly, as this amnesia rubbish.'

'I'm sorry?' She compressed her lips into a savage smile. 'I'm afraid I've quite forgotten what we're talking about.'

Maddocks glanced at Fraser, who was grinning to himself. 'We're talking about the deaths of three people, Miss Kingsley, all of whom were closely associated with you and all of whom have been brutally murdered. Russell Landy, Leo Wallader and Meg Harris. In addition, we are talking about a violent attack on Dr Protheroe last night which, but for his own quick thinking, would have resulted in a similar bludgeoning to that received by your husband, your fiancé and your best friend. Presumably he told you he was attacked with a sledgehammer?' He flung the question at her, watching for a reaction.

'He didn't,' she said quietly.

'How do you feel about that?'

'Fine,' she said. 'I don't expect Dr Protheroe to tell me everything.'

'Doesn't the fact that a sledgehammer was used worry you just a little, Miss Kingsley?'

'Yes.'

'Then tell me now that you find the situation amusing, because I sure as hell don't, and neither do the two heartbroken mothers whose maggot-ridden children were dug out of a ditch last Thursday.'

She drew on her cigarette and stared past him. 'I'll tell you whatever you like, Inspector,' she said with an odd inflection in her voice, 'because it won't make any difference.' She shifted her gaze back to him. 'You will still twist everything I say.'

'That's nonsense, Miss Kingsley.'

'*Experto credite*. Trust one who has been through it.' She flashed him a faint smile. 'You're no different from the last lot. They also wanted to prove my father was a murderer.'

329

Chapter Seventeen

Tuesday, 28 June, Nightingale Clinic,
Salisbury – 2.30 p.m.

FRASER MOVED INTO Jinx's line of vision. He pulled forward the second armchair and sat in it, hands clasped between knees, his face less than a metre from hers. *Grab the initiative, the DI had said.* And Fraser, at least, was intelligent enough to recognize that they wouldn't get anywhere with intimidation. But then, unlike Maddocks, he didn't feel he had anything to prove, not against women anyway.

'We really are trying to keep an open mind,' he assured her, 'but what we find difficult to ignore is the similarity in the method of killing and the fact that the three victims, although separated by ten years, were all known to you. We are not talking about passing acquaintances here, Miss Kingsley, we are talking about the two men who have probably been closest to you during your life and the woman whom your parents described at the time of your accident as your best friend.' He smiled ruefully. 'Do you see the problem we have? Even to the most impartial observer, your involvement with all three people would appear significant.'

She nodded. *Jesus wept! Did he think she was a moron?* 'I understand that. It appears significant to me, too, but for the life of me I can't tell you why. I've gone over it again and again and I keep coming up against the brick wall of Russell's murder.' She stubbed out her cigarette to avoid the smoke blowing into his face. 'The reason that was never solved is because the London police concentrated on me and my father. We were both ruled out of direct involvement because we both had alibis. I was then ruled out of indirect involvement because there was no obvious reason for me to want Russell dead. My father, on the other hand, had loathed him and made no secret of it, so the police convinced themselves that he'd ordered a contract killing and they abandoned the search for anyone else. But supposing they were wrong? Supposing my father had nothing to do with it, where is the significance then in my knowing all three victims?' She looked earnestly into his face. 'Do you understand the point I'm making?'

'I think so. You're saying that if someone else entirely killed Russell, then there may be an unknown link between the murders.'

'Yes, and if you make the same mistake the London police made, then that unknown person will get away with it again.'

'It's a little hard to accept, Miss Kingsley. We've been sent detailed accounts of the Landy case and there's no hint of a mystery person in the background.'

She shook her head vigorously. 'There *is*. I kept telling them about this artist Russell was rude to. He mentioned twice that he'd seen him hanging around the gallery, and he said if he came again he'd report him to the police. Then he was murdered.' She spread her hands in a pleading gesture. 'I am sure that's the man you should be looking for.'

'It was mentioned in the report but the view seems to be that, if the man existed at all, he was more likely to be your father's contract killer than a resentful artist. It would be different if you could have supplied the police with a description or a name but, as I understand it, you couldn't give them any information at all.'

'Because I didn't know anything. All I could tell them was what Russell told me. An artist came to the gallery with some bad paintings, Russell told him they were bad, the man became abusive and Russell ordered him out. He never mentioned it at the time, but he did tell me on two occasions later that he'd noticed a man watching the gallery and he thought it was this same artist.' She sighed. 'I know it's not much but no one was even remotely interested in following it up. They were all so hooked on my father having done it.'

'With reason, don't you think?'

She didn't answer.

'He made no secret of his dislike for your husband.'

'Oh, I know all the arguments. I listened to them often enough at the time. My father knew the right contacts in the underworld for a contract killing. He's ruthless, he's tough, he began life as a black marketeer, and he's thought to have made millions through dodgy business practices, although no one's been able to prove it. He has the credentials of a home-grown Mafia god-father, with the same blind loyalty to family, for whom the death of a hated son-in-law would be a natural way to solve a problem.' She smiled bleakly. 'I was even shown a psychological assessment of him, based on facts known to the police, in which he was portrayed as a psychopath with a phenomenal sex drive. This, apparently, was why he visited prostitutes because, as I was the real object of his desire, he was unable to satisfy his animal needs properly.'

Fraser waited for a moment. 'And you don't think any of that's true?' he prompted.

'I don't know,' she said honestly, 'but I don't see that it matters. The police squeezed that character assessment for all it was worth, but they still couldn't link Adam with Russell's death. Doesn't that mean Adam probably had nothing to do with it?'

Fraser shook his head reluctantly. 'It might mean he paid a great deal of money to put distance between himself and the murder.' But he, too, found the black saucer eyes in the white face compelling and he tried to soften the blow a little. 'That's not to say I've a closed mind on the matter, Miss Kingsley. It was a botched job for a contract killing. Russell was still alive when you found him, so his murderer was damn lucky to get away with it, and so was whoever hired him.'

Her tongue moistened her dry lips before, abruptly, she pushed herself back into her chair and clapped her hands over her nose and mouth. 'I should have thought about this a long time ago,' she said in a muffled voice. 'God, I've been a fool.' She took her hands away. 'My father's a perfectionist in everything he does,' she said, 'and so are the people he employs. None of them would have dared do a botched job. Adam would have skinned them alive.'

Fraser eyed her curiously. 'Meaning you think he was capable of ordering Russell's murder, but didn't in fact do it?'

'Yes.' She leaned forward again. 'Look, my father was in London that day, so his alibi always had holes in it. He wouldn't pay to distance himself only to end up being compromised. Plus, as you said, Russell was still alive when I found him and might have survived if I'd got there earlier, but Adam would never employ anyone who was so incompetent that the victim was still conscious an hour after he'd been attacked.'

'Perhaps the killer was interrupted?'

'No,' she said in excitement. 'Don't you see? If Adam had ordered the killing he would have given instructions for Russell to be killed anywhere but the gallery. He knew I had the only other key, so knew I was the most likely person to find the body, unless somebody happened to go round the back and saw the stock-room window had been smashed.' She saw his scepticism. 'Oh, please, Sergeant,' she begged him, 'hear what I'm saying. The police said Adam was so besotted with me that he became pathologically jealous of Russell. But if that were true, he'd have had Russell killed as far away from me as possible, certainly not left alive and bleeding to death where I would probably be the one to find him. The last thing he'd have wanted was for me to have a nervous breakdown and retreat into my shell. Don't you think?'

Fraser was impressed with this argument. 'Did you make that point to the London police?'

'How could I? I've only just thought of it. Look,' she

said again, 'I know it seems odd, but when something that awful happens to you, you block it out as soon as you can or you go mad. Before my breakdown I never had time to think it through properly, there was the police, the funeral, the miscarriage . . .' She faltered slightly. 'And then when I came out of the hospital, I made up my mind to shut it away and never, never get it out again. It's only since my accident that it's started to come back. The nightmares, seeing Russell on the floor, the blood . . .' She faltered again but this time didn't go on.

Maddocks had listened to the exchange with growing scepticism but he spoke gently enough. 'The police weren't wedded to a contract killer, Miss Kingsley. They always recognized that your father might have wielded the sledgehammer himself. Let's say he went to the gallery, and he and Russell had a row. Do you think he'd care then whether you found the body or not? He'd be saving his own skin, and high-tailing it out as fast as he could.'

Jinx turned to look at him. 'You can't expect to have it both ways, Inspector. If Adam is the organized criminal you all claim him to be, then he would have arranged for the mess to be cleared up. And he wouldn't have left Russell alive.' She pressed her palm to her temple. 'He doesn't make mistakes, Inspector.'

'He beat a negro half to death,' said Maddocks idly, 'who went on to become your uncle. Perhaps that was another mistake. Perhaps he meant to kill him, too.'

Jinx dropped her hand into her lap and clasped it tightly over the other. She was feeling extremely unwell but knew Maddocks would exploit it if she said anything. She concentrated on Fraser, willing him to respond.

'Let's say you're right, Miss Kingsley,' the Sergeant said after a moment, 'and that there's another link between the three murders. Have you any idea what – or who – it might be?'

'The only one I can think of is Meg,' she told him gravely. 'She was as close to Russell and Leo as I was.'

Maddocks stirred again. 'Closer,' he said bluntly. 'According to some letters and diaries found in Leo's house, your friend Meg Harris was having an affair with your husband at the time of his death and also jumped in and out of bed regularly with your fiancé. One of them – and it's clear from entries in her diary that she didn't know which – was the father of a child she aborted shortly after Landy was murdered.'

There was a brief silence before colour flared in Jinx's cheeks. 'No wonder she was so upset when I lost my baby,' she said slowly.

Maddocks frowned. 'You don't seem very surprised about the affair.'

'I knew about that,' she said, 'but I didn't know she'd had an abortion. Poor Meg. She must have felt guilty if she thought hers had been Russell's child as well.'

'So this is something else you withheld from the London police?'

She held his gaze for a moment. 'How could I tell them something I didn't know? It was long after Russell was dead that I found out about the affair.'

'Ah,' he murmured, 'I think I could have predicted that. Did Miss Harris tell you?'

'No.' She repeated what she'd told Alan Protheroe, about the letters in the attic and her reluctance to re-open old wounds. 'But perhaps if I had said something, Meg and Leo would still be alive,' she finished bleakly. 'It's so much easier to be wise after the event.'

'Yes,' said Maddocks thoughtfully. 'Things do seem to take a very long time to germinate in your mind, don't they? Who else knew about this affair?'

'I don't think anyone did. I told you, they were very discreet.'

'Did you tell your father about it?'

'When I found out, you mean?' He nodded. 'There was no point.'

'Anybody else?'

She shook her head. 'Only Dr Protheroe. I told him this morning.'

Maddocks nodded. 'Did you and Miss Harris ever discuss Landy's murder?'

'Once or twice, before I went into hospital,' she said unevenly. 'We discussed it before, but never afterwards.'

'Did she say who she thought might have done it?'

She rested her cheek against her hand and tried to picture scenes in her mind. 'It's so long ago,' she said, 'and neither of us was very inclined to dwell on it, but I think she went along with the initial police view because that was the only one that was reported in the papers. A robbery that went wrong. As far as I know, that's what most people still believe.'

'So she never knew that both you and your father were under suspicion?'

She pretended to think about that. *Everyone knew, you bastard . . . every damn friend I ever had knew . . . why the hell do you think I've been so fucking lonely for the last ten years? . . .* 'I had to supply the police with a list of our friends, most of whom were Russell's, but Meg was on it as a friend of mine, and I do remember her telling me that the police were asking about the relationship between Russell and Adam.' She frowned suddenly. 'You know, I remember now. She did make one rather odd comment. She said: "They will keep asking for information but I'm sure it's better to let sleeping dogs lie. There's been so much pain caused already."'

'What did she mean by that?'

'At the time, I probably thought she was talking about Russell and Adam's relationship, saying she couldn't see the need to supply any more details. But now I think she might have been referring to her affair with Russell. I know the police dug very hard for evidence of something like that, on the principle he might have been killed by a jealous husband.' She paused for a moment. 'But she knew I didn't know about the affair, so perhaps she didn't want to hurt me unnecessarily by revealing it to the police.'

'It must have upset you when you finally found out about it,' said Fraser.

She turned to him with visible relief. 'I know it sounds callous, but in fact it made me feel better. Russell and I hadn't been getting on for months before he died, and I'd always felt guilty about it. It's awful to have someone die on you when you know you've made them unhappy.

I kept thinking, if only I'd done this, or if only I'd done that' – she gave a troubled smile – 'and then I was let off the hook by a couple of love letters.'

Maddocks watched her performance with cynical objectivity. The story was too pat and too well polished and he saw Dr Protheroe's hand at work behind the scenes. 'So let me get this straight, Miss Kingsley,' he said acidly. 'Number one: at the time of Russell Landy's death, you and he were not getting on but you told the London police you were. Number two: you believed your father was capable of putting out a contract on your husband but defended him anyway. Number three: Russell and your best friend were having an affair but you knew nothing about it, and she did not reveal it to the police. Number four: she aborted the child she had conceived either by your then husband or the man who later became your fiancé, but neither you nor the London police were ever told about it. Number five: when you discovered your friend and your husband had been having an affair, you kept the information to yourself. Number six: your best friend, who'd had an affair with your husband and knew that your husband had been murdered, nevertheless proceeded to resurrect an old affair with your fiancé and so persuade him to abandon you for her. Number seven: he and she were subsequently murdered in an identical fashion, though in a different location, to the way your husband was murdered.' He arched his eyebrows. 'Is that a fair summary of what you've told us?'

'Yes,' said Jinx honestly. 'To my knowledge, that is accurate. Assuming the abortion and the way Meg and

Leo were murdered to be true. Those are the only two things I didn't know.'

He nodded. 'All right, then I have one last question on the Landy murder before we talk about Wallader and Harris. According to the reports we have, you were ruled out of direct involvement because you had a cast-iron alibi. Who gave you the alibi?'

'It was Meg,' she said. 'I spent the afternoon and early evening with her and then she drove me to the restaurant for seven-thirty. I waited there about an hour and, when Russell didn't show, I took a taxi to the gallery. Isn't that in the report?'

Maddocks ignored the question. 'Wouldn't it have been simpler to phone the gallery?'

'I did. There was no answer. So I phoned home but there was no answer there either.'

'Then why assume he was at the gallery? Why bother to take a taxi there?'

'Because it was on the way home.'

'But you paid off the taxi before you went inside.'

'It was nine o'clock at night and the driver wouldn't let me leave the cab without paying. I think he was afraid I was planning to leg it down the nearest alleyway. He said he'd wait five minutes and if I wasn't back by then, he'd go. As it was, I was back within two, screaming my head off. The driver dialled nine-nine-nine while I sat with Russell, then he waited outside till the ambulance arrived. That's why the police had no trouble tracing him afterwards to support my story.'

Maddocks chuckled softly. 'You have an answer for everything, don't you?'

She studied him with a remarkably cool gaze. 'All I'm doing is telling you the truth, Inspector.'

'And let's face it, girl, you've had ten whole years to get it right.'

One of the security staff at the clinic, Harry Elphick, after learning about the assault on Dr Protheroe, made a detour on his departure to check the outhouses near the staff parking places. He remembered some weeks back seeing a sledgehammer in one of them, and it occurred to him that it might be worth a second look. He reasoned, quite logically, that the most likely person to take a swipe at Dr Protheroe was one of the more aggressive junkies in his care, and he went on to reason that, because the Nightingale was not a prison, then any observant patient had the same opportunities as he to notice the sledgehammer. Harry would have considered it naïve rubbish to assume that none of them would bother to attack Dr Protheroe because they knew he didn't carry drugs in his car. Harry, ex-Army and past his middle years, had little time for the sort of over-privileged dregs that Dr Protheroe treated, and it was with some satisfaction that he opened an outhouse door and, after a cursory search, found a sledgehammer with red Wolseley paintwork ground into its head.

'When did you first discover that Leo and Meg were having an affair?'

Jinx stared at her hands for a moment before reaching

for her cigarette packet. 'When I came round a few days ago. My stepmother told me.'

Maddocks frowned. 'Are you saying that's the first you knew about it?'

She leaned back in her chair to light a cigarette. 'I don't know,' she said. 'I can't remember anything much from before the accident.'

'What *do* you remember?'

She stared at the ceiling. 'I remember saying goodbye to Leo at breakfast on the morning of June the fourth. I was coming down to Hampshire to stay with my parents for a few days.'

'That's a very precise memory.'

'Yes.'

'When did you find out they were dead, Miss Kingsley?'

She toyed with another lie, then thought better of it. She was too fond of Dean to drop him in this bastard's shit. 'Sunday,' she said. 'I knew you were lying about what had happened to them so I asked a friend to phone the Walladers. Anthony told him they were dead and the friend rang me back to tell me.'

'Which friend?'

'Is that important?'

'It depends whether you want me to believe you or not. This friend might confirm that you were genuinely shocked when you heard the news. Otherwise I'm having some difficulty trying to understand how a woman whose best friend and fiancé have been brutally butchered can retain such extraordinary composure.'

'My number two at the studio, Dean Jarrett.'

'Thank you. Were you upset when your stepmother told you Leo had left you for Meg?'

She shook her head. 'Not particularly. I was more relieved than upset. I think I made it clear to you on Sunday that I had severe doubts about Leo. I am sure in my own mind that I had no intention of marrying him, irrespective of whether he was having an affair with Meg.'

'Then why did you try to kill yourself?'

'I wish I knew.' She smiled suddenly. 'It seems very out of character for someone with extraordinary composure.' She flicked ash from her cigarette. 'So out of character that I don't think I did.'

'You were drunk and you drove your car at full speed towards the only structure of any substance on a deserted airfield. What other explanation is there?'

'But I didn't kill myself,' she pointed out.

'Because you were lucky. You were thrown clear.'

'Perhaps I *threw* myself clear,' she said. 'Perhaps I didn't want to die.'

'Meaning what, precisely?'

Her eyelashes grew damp·but she held the tears in check. 'I don't know, but I've had far more time to think about this than I have about Leo and Meg, and it seems to me that if *I* wasn't trying to kill myself, then the only other explanation is that someone *else* was trying to kill me.' She abandoned any attempt to persuade Maddocks and turned instead to Fraser's more open face. 'It would be so easy. My car was an automatic. All anyone would have to do was aim it at the post, put it into *Drive*, wedge the accelerator at full throttle and then release the handbrake. If I was unconscious and belted in, I'd have been crushed in the wreckage. That might have happened, don't you think? It's a possibility, isn't it?'

'If you'd been belted in, how could you have been thrown clear?'

'Then maybe I wasn't belted in,' she said eagerly. 'Maybe the idea was to have me go through the windscreen. Or maybe I came round in time and released myself.'

He would have liked to believe her, but he couldn't. 'Then this hypothetical murderer would have seen what had happened and finished you off. He couldn't afford to leave you alive if he'd just tried to kill you.'

From her pocket she took the newspaper clipping that Betty had given her and pressed it into his hands. 'According to this I was found by a young couple. He wouldn't have had time to finish me off if he saw them coming.'

'Look, Miss Kingsley,' said Maddocks, 'I hate to be cruel, but facts are facts. According to your neighbours in Richmond, this wasn't the first time. Your first attempt was on the Sunday. Whether you like it or not, indeed whether you remember it or not – and by your own admission you have a habit of blocking out anything that disturbs you – something so terrible happened that you primed yourself with Dutch courage and then had a second go at finishing it all.'

Something terrible happened . . . 'I've never been drunk in my life,' she said stubbornly. 'I've never wanted to be drunk.'

'There's always a first time.'

She shrugged. 'Not as far as I'm concerned, Inspector.'

'You had consumed the equivalent of two bottles of wine when you had your accident, Miss Kingsley. The bottles were found on the floor of your car. Are you telling me you can absorb that amount of alcohol without being what the rest of us would term drunk?'

'No,' she said. 'I'm saying I would never have *wanted* to drink that much.'

'Not even if you had done something you were ashamed off?'

She fixed him with her steady gaze. 'Like what?'

'Been party to a murder perhaps?'

She shook her head. 'Do you not see how illogical that argument is? As I understand it, Meg and Leo's bodies were found near Winchester, which means that whoever murdered them must have worked out some fairly complicated logistics. I can't find out from the newspapers whether they were killed in the wood or taken there after they were dead but, whichever it was, someone went to a great deal of trouble to get them there. But why would anyone go to those lengths if they were so ashamed of what they'd done that they then tried to kill themselves? It doesn't make sense. On the one hand, you're describing a very calculating personality who set out to get rid of two people; on the other, you're describing a weak personality who may have struck out in a moment of anger but was then so appalled by what he'd done that he tried to make amends by killing himself.'

'You really have given this a lot of thought, haven't you?'

The huge black eyes filled again. 'As you would have done, if you were in my place. I'm not a fool, Inspector.'

Maddocks surprised her by acknowledging this with a nod. It was on the tip of his tongue to say, 'Point taken,' but he checked himself in time. 'There's no logic to murder, Miss Kingsley, not in my experience anyway. It's usually the last people you'd expect who do it. Some of them show remorse early, some of them show it when they're convicted, and some of them never show it at all. Believe me, it is not uncommon for a calculating individual to plan a murder, carry it out, dispose of the body, and then have an attack of conscience. We see it over and over again. There's no reason why this case should be any different.'

'Then you might as well clap the handcuffs on me now,' she said, 'because I can't defend myself.'

Nothing would give me more pleasure, sweetheart. 'There's no question of that,' he said affably. 'As Sergeant Fraser said, we are pursuing various lines of enquiry, and this is just one of them. However, I'm sure you realize how important it is that you give us some indication of what went on in the two weeks prior to your accident and the deaths of Leo and Meg. Unfortunately, you seem to be the only person left who can shed any light on the matter.'

She drew on her cigarette with a worried frown. 'What about Meg's friends? Have you spoken to any of them? Surely they can tell you something.'

'Acting on the information you gave us, we spoke to

Josh Hennessey yesterday. He told us that the first he
knew about Leo and Meg getting together was a phone
call from Meg on Saturday, June the eleventh. She told
him your wedding was off, that she and Leo were leaving
for France but that she would pop into the office before
she left to bring him up to date with her side of the
operation. She never showed and he never heard from
her again. He also gave us the names of some of Meg's
close friends. We spoke to a couple of them, Fay Avonalli
and Marian Harding, and they told us the same story.'

'But didn't you ask Josh about her and Leo's relationship before that? I mean, he and Meg have worked
together for years, he knows everything about her, so
presumably he knew about the affair.'

It was Fraser who answered. 'He gave us the name of
one man who featured seriously for two or three months
at the beginning of this year, but he said Meg had hardly
mentioned Leo at all, and he was surprised when she
phoned to say they were planning to get married. He
said Leo had been around for years, and they had an off-
and-on relationship which resurrected itself whenever
they were both at a loose end. But he'd never known
them to stick together for more than a month or two
because Meg always got so irritated with Leo's' – he
sought for a suitable word – 'selfishness. He said he told
her she was mad to think it would be any different this
time, and gave the relationship a month to run. He also
told her she was a prize bitch and that the only reason
she wanted Leo was because he was marrying you.' He
smiled sympathetically. 'According to him, Meg was
jealous of you. Apparently, she resented you inheriting

Russell's money on top of the money you will inherit from your father. She said Jinx always lands on her feet, while she ended up in the cesspit.'

'Which is true in a funny sort of way. All Meg ever wanted was enough ready cash to give her the good times. She said it was so unfair that she had a vicar for a father when penury was the one thing she loathed. She couldn't understand why I didn't touch Adam for money at every opportunity.'

Fraser echoed Protheroe's scepticism of earlier. 'I'm surprised you liked her.'

'I don't have many friends. In any case, she was fun. I suppose it was a case of opposites attracting. I take life too seriously. She gloried in it. She's the only person I've ever known who lived entirely for the present.' A tear fell on to her cheek. 'I was far more jealous of her than she was of me.'

'So would you say your jealousy extended to anger over her stealing of your men friends?' asked Maddocks.

Jinx stubbed out the butt of her cigarette. 'No,' she said tiredly, 'it didn't. I'm sorry, Inspector, but I really don't think there's anything more I can tell you.'

Alan Protheroe was waiting by their car when they rounded the corner of the building. 'I trust, gentlemen, that you showed Miss Kingsley rather more courtesy than you showed me when you pushed your way into my office.' His eyes narrowed. 'I have extreme reservations about these bully-boy tactics of yours.'

'We had a little chat, sir,' protested Maddocks, 'which

you could have joined at any time, had you or Miss Kingsley wished it.'

Alan shook his head in irritation. 'You're a type, Inspector, and it's not a type I admire or even believe should be in the police force. Do you really need reminding that Miss Kingsley was in a coma less than a week ago? Or that your colleagues at Fordingbridge believe she has twice tried to kill herself?'

'It's a funny business that suicide attempt.' Maddocks nodded towards Fraser. 'She told the Sergeant here she thought someone was trying to kill her. What's your reading of it, Doctor? Attempted suicide or attempted murder? Does Miss Kingsley strike you as the suicidal type? I can't see it myself.'

'But attempted murder *convinces* you?'

Maddocks grinned. 'I'd say that was a clutching at straws to lay the blame on someone else.'

'So what are you left with if it was neither?'

'A little piece of theatre, I think. She's one hell of an actress, this patient of yours, but then I'm sure you know that already.'

Alan nodded abruptly towards the front doors. 'One of my security staff has something to show you. My view is it should be handed to the Salisbury police, who I understood were dealing with the assault on me, but they appear to be passing the buck to you.' He led the way inside and gestured towards the sledgehammer, which was lying on top of the reception desk with a polythene bag neatly attached to its head. 'Harry Elphick,' he said, introducing the security officer. 'He found it in one of the outhouses. It has flakes of red paint on the metal which might have come from my Wolseley.'

Maddocks smiled appreciatively. 'Good man, Harry. What made you go looking for it?'

Harry, who prided himself on his judgement, recognized a good'un when he saw one. 'Well, sir, it was like this. Begging the doctor's pardon, I don't set as much store by the youngsters here as he does.' He launched into a rambling account of his reasoning processes, finishing with: 'So, as I always say, when you're looking for an answer, look for the obvious, and the obvious in this case is that one of the little tykes on the premises thought he'd chance his arm.'

Maddocks glanced towards Alan with a malicious smile. 'Or *her* arm,' he murmured. 'I hadn't realized until Miss Kingsley stood up in your room just how tall she is. Five feet ten would be my guess.'

Nightingale Clinic, Salisbury – 10.00 p.m.

Veronica Gordon heard the commotion from the front hall as she was sipping her cup of tea in the staff sitting room. She walked out and frowned angrily at the sight of Betty Kingsley trying to wrestle free of Amy Staunton. 'Black bitch,' Betty was shouting. 'Get your hands off me. I want to see my daughter!'

'What on earth is going on?' Veronica asked icily, laying a hand on the older woman's collar and yanking her back with surprising strength. 'How dare you speak to one of my nursing staff in those terms? I won't tolerate it, not from anyone, and most especially not from a drunk.' She looked very angry. 'What a disgraceful exhibition. Just who on earth do you think you are?'

Betty's face grew sullen as she shook the hand off. 'You know who I am,' she said aggressively. 'I'm Mrs Adam Kingsley and I've come to see my daughter.' But she was wilting visibly in the face of the sister's sobriety and superior aggression.

'That's out of the question,' Veronica snapped. 'It's ten o'clock at night and you're in no condition to talk to anyone. I suggest you go home and sober up, and come back again tomorrow morning in a rather more presentable state than you are in at the moment.'

Betty's eyes bulged in her powdered face. 'My husband's going to hear about this. You've got a right nerve talking to me like that.'

'What an excellent idea. Why don't we phone Mr Kingsley now? I'm sure he'll be delighted to hear that his wife has engaged in a drunken brawl with a nurse at the Nightingale Clinic.'

Tears coursed down the grotesque face. 'I need to see Jinx,' she wept. 'Please let me see my daughter.' But she seemed to realize that tears weren't going to win her any sympathy, so she took a deep breath, patted her hair and pulled her coat straight. 'There you are. That's better, isn't it? I won't cause no trouble, not if you let me see her.' She dabbed her eyes and fixed a pathetically roguish smile on her lips. 'Cheerful as anything. Don't take no mind of what I said earlier.' She patted Amy's arm. 'I didn't mean anything by it, dear. I've got a cruel mouth sometimes. Are you going to let me see Jinx? Please, it's that important.'

Veronica mellowed a little. 'What is so important that it can't wait till tomorrow, Mrs Kingsley?'

'Meg and Leo,' she said. 'Me and the boys read they'd been murdered but her Daddy's refusing to do anything about it. Seems to me someone should give the poor kid a cuddle, even if it is only me.'

Veronica agreed with her, and if she thought it a little odd that Betty had waited twelve hours and got herself drunk before she put the idea into practice, she didn't say anything. Instead she sent Amy down to find out if Jinx was still awake, before escorting Betty to number twelve and leaving the two women together with the door wide open. 'I'll be just along the corridor,' she informed them. 'You have fifteen minutes, Mrs Kingsley, and I do not expect to hear any raised voices. Is that understood?'

Betty waited till she'd gone then gave a disparaging sniff. 'She's a right bitch, that one.' She staggered to a chair and collapsed into it, staring morosely at her stepdaughter who was already in bed. 'I suppose some-one's told you Meg and Leo are dead.'

Jinx hid her dismay. 'Who brought you, Betty?'

'I made Jenkins do it.' She waved a meaty hand towards the door. 'He's waiting outside.'

'Does Adam know you've come?'

'Course not.' She shook her head. 'He's in London. The shares have been sliding all day. He's trying to repair the damage.'

'I saw it on the news.'

'Oh, my, my. You're a cool one. Always were.' She blew her nose. 'D'you know why they're sliding? Because Leo's dead and Russell's dead, and fingers are pointing.'

Jinx watched her for a moment. 'It won't affect you or the boys,' she said calmly. 'The company's sound and Adam won't let the slide continue indefinitely. Your shares will go back up again, so you won't lose out.'

'And how's your precious Adam going to stop the slide?' she hissed, her little eyes like flints. 'You tell me that. There's me and the boys worrying ourselves sick, while you and your daddy behave as if nothing's happened.'

'If necessary, he'll resign.' A small frown creased her forehead. 'You know that as well as I do. It's what he's always said he would do in a crisis.'

'And where will that leave us?'

'With all the shares Adam gave you ten years ago.'

Betty took out a compact and floured her ravaged face. 'No,' she said tightly, 'it'll leave me with no home to call my own. It's not ours, remember, belongs to the company. An asset. That's what they call it, isn't it? Did you think of *that* when you brought this crisis on our heads? If your daddy resigns we lose the Hall. The boys'll be out of a job, and none of us'll have a roof over our heads. What've you got to say to that?'

'I'd say it means you've sold your shares and you're afraid Adam's going to wash his hands of you.' Jinx rested her head against her pillows. 'And about time, too. He deserves better than three dead-weights who know only how to drag him down. You should all be standing by him, instead of whingeing about what's going to happen to you.' She smiled to herself. 'Do you know what? When you came in, I thought, my God, one of them has come to hold my hand. One of them has come to say, we believe in you, Jinxy. We know you must be going through hell, but we're here for you. What a mug, eh? Why on earth should I have imagined for one minute that you or your good-for-nothing bastards could change the habits of a lifetime?'

'Don't you call my sons bastards.'

'Why not?' said Jinx, pressing the bell beside her bed. 'It's what they are. You've never been a wife to my father.'

Betty's eyes filled with tears again. 'I hated you the first time I saw you.'

'I know. You always made that very clear.'

'You hated me, too.'

'Because you were so stupid.' She turned to Veronica Gordon, who had appeared in the doorway. 'My stepmother's leaving,' she said.

'I did my best,' said Betty. 'I wanted to love you.'

'No, you didn't. You wanted to displace me. Jealousy is a disease with you. You knew damned well that Adam loved me far more than he would ever love you.'

She smiled coldly, and Veronica found herself reassessing every opinion she'd ever had of the young woman. This was no dewy-eyed victim, she thought.

MEMO

From: Det Supt Cheever
To: CC
Date: Wednesday, 29 June, 1994
Re: Wallader/Harris

Detailed below is all relevant information, as of 09.00 hours today.

- Despite extensive enquiries, we can find no witnesses to an individual wearing bloodstained clothes in the vicinity of Ardingly Woods on 12/13/14 June. No weapon has been found. Reports of several cars in the area, but no effective leads. (NB: Forensic examination of Jane Kingsley's car reveals no bloodstains.)

- Wallader's and Harris's personal effects have been located at 35, Eagleton Street, Chelsea.

- Wallader's two cars have been located. One at Eagleton Street and the other in a rented garage in Camden. Harris's car was located in the street outside number 35. All three cars are undergoing forensic examination today, but a preliminary examination revealed nothing of significance.

- A reading of Harris's diaries, in conjunction with the evidence of friends and relations, suggests that Harris and Wallader had an ongoing, if spasmodic, sexual relationship for some 11 years. In addition, it is now clear

356

that Harris was sexually involved with Russell Landy both before and during his marriage to Jane Kingsley.

- There is evidence that Harris had an abortion in February, 1984, some five days after Landy's murder, although it is unclear who the father was. Some indication that it may not have been Wallader or Landy. Her diaries reveal a promiscuous personality, as borne out by her brother's evidence.

- There remain question marks over the Harris family. Clear indication of tension. Neither Simon nor Rev H had much time for Meg, with both expressing preference for Jane Kingsley (bizarre in the circumstances); Mrs H, on the other hand, seems overly fond of Meg and angry/jealous (?) of Jane.

- A twenty-five-year-old psychological assessment of Wallader, supplied by his mother, describes a child with a severe personality disorder.

- The Walladers mention an argument on Monday, May 30, during which Leo claimed he planned to marry Meg instead. He phoned later that evening to warn his parents not to say anything until he gave them the go-ahead. In the event, the go-ahead was not given until Saturday, June 11, although Sir Anthony and Lady W cannot account for the delay.

- Current estimate of Wallader's wealth, held in property, stocks and shares, and gold: £1.1 million. According to his solicitor, Wallader consistently refused to make a will so there is none in existence.

- Harris informed her parents of events on Saturday, June 11. On the same day she also phoned her business partner and two friends with the information. We can find no one who was privy to the facts prior to Saturday, June 11. She told her business partner she would be in the office on Monday, June 13. (NB: Harris's diary entries are erratic. There are empty weeks, followed by a day, or days, fully recorded. There are no entries after Monday, May 18, and no mention of Leo Wallader, by name, since December, 1993, when she writes that after all these years she has finally introduced Leo to Jinx.)

- According to her partner, she did <u>not</u> visit her office on Monday, June 13.

- NB: Entry in Harris's diary, following Kingsley's marriage to Landy, reads as follows: 'Since becoming unattainable, Russell is so much more attractive.' Echoed, in April, 1994, by the following: 'Jinx tells me she is taking the plunge again. I knew I would live to regret that introduction.'

- According to Mr and Mrs Kingsley's statements of Tuesday, June 14 (following Jane Kingsley's accident), they were informed by telephone of their daughter's cancelled wedding on Saturday, June 11. This is supported by the evidence of Colonel Eric Clancey who stated, also at the time of the accident, that Jane Kingsley told him about her changed wedding plans on June 11.

- The evidence of Mr and Mrs Kingsley (taken after the accident) is that Jane spent the week from Saturday, June 4 to Friday, June 10 at Hellingdon Hall. She appeared to be in good spirits, made no mention of the row with Leo and discussed preparations for the wedding as if it were going ahead.

- Jane Kingsley's own evidence in an interview conducted 28.6.94 is that she cannot remember anything since June 4. She admits to knowing about Harris's affair with Landy, though claims she only learnt about it after Landy's death. She claims not to remember being told about Wallader and Harris but this is disputed by the Wallader parents' testimony, which states Leo told her on the afternoon of Monday, May 30 (i.e. prior to memory loss from June 4). DI Maddocks is convinced she remembers more than she says, and this would seem to be borne out by the above.

- Miss Kingsley admits she believes her father could have ordered Landy's death but does not believe he did so. She can offer no evidence in support, other than her own conviction that he would not have allowed her to find the body. There is some merit in this argument if Kingsley is fond of her.

- A possibly related incident occurred at the Nightingale Clinic during the night of Monday June 27. Dr Protheroe, the clinic's director, was attacked by an intruder with a sledgehammer. Miss Kingsley has been a patient of his for some ten days, and in addition Dr Protheroe was visited by Kingsley's solicitor during the afternoon of June 27.

- Protheroe escaped relatively unscathed, however the weapon was found later in an outhouse at the

MINETTE WALTERS

Nightingale by a member of the security staff who states it belongs to the clinic. This is supported by preliminary forensic tests which have found no blood/hair/tissue on the hammer head but some paint from Protheroe's car, which was badly damaged during the assault. This would suggest his assailant was well acquainted with the layout of the clinic grounds and points to a past or present patient, or possibly a visitor. Protheroe described his attacker as male, 5′ 10″ or 5′ 11″ and of medium build. The assailant was dressed in black and wearing a ski-mask or similar.

- Miss Kingsley is 5′ 10″ and slim build. However (1) the attack was at night, (2) DI Maddocks is of the opinion that Protheroe is doing his utmost, for whatever reason, to protect his patient, (3) Miss Kingsley could have worn padding. One pointer that may be worth considering, assuming the incident to be related to the Landy/Wallader/Harris murders, is that Miss Kingsley is unquestionably weak following her accident and Protheroe had little trouble fighting off the attack. Dr Clarke does not rule out a woman being capable of the attacks on Wallader and Harris. In addition, the heel marks on the bank near where the bodies were found do seem to imply that a woman was present at the scene.

- Re: the Landy murder. Miss Kingsley's alibi for the afternoon and early evening of February 1, 1984, was supplied by Miss Harris. In light of the new evidence that Harris and Landy were having an affair, and that Miss Kingsley may have known about it, this alibi is not as straightforward as it appeared at the time. Worth a

360

second look. NB: Harris's diary says nothing on the subject, indeed does not mention Landy's murder at all.

IN CONCLUSION:

1. Meg Harris clearly made a bid to win back both men after they had made serious commitments to Jane Kingsley. We only have Kingsley's word that she knew nothing about this and/or did not bear a grudge.

2. It appears Wallader and Harris did not reveal their proposed marriage plans until shortly before they were due to leave for the relative safety of France.

3. Jane Kingsley, too, saw fit to keep the secret.

4. Their killer probably drove them to Ardingly Woods in his/ her own car.

5. On the most likely date of Wallader/Harris's deaths, Kingsley drove her car at a concrete stanchion only some 20 miles from Ardingly Woods.

6. Shortly after Kingsley's admission to the Nightingale Clinic, Dr Protheroe was attacked with a similar weapon to Landy/Wallader/Harris.

The investigating team is concentrating its efforts on uncovering the movements of Wallader/Kingsley/Harris between May 30 and June 13. All relevant parties will be re-questioned with a view to establishing a timetable of events.

Yours
Frank

City worries about Franchise Holdings

There was a sharp drop in the value of Franchise Holdings (FH) Ltd shares yesterday, following the identification of one of the bodies found in Ardingly Woods last Thursday as Leo Wallader. Until recently, Wallader, a 35-yr-old stock broker, was engaged to Adam Kingsley's daughter, Jane, and the market has reacted to press speculation linking this murder to the murder of Kingsley's son-in-law, Russell Landy, ten years ago.

Concerns have been expressed for some time about who will succeed Adam Kingsley to the chairmanship, and it is these concerns that are fuelling the present crisis. Adam Kingsley has a reputation for hands-on management and, without his driving force, there are doubts about the future of Franchise Holdings.

A spokesman for the company said this afternoon that investors are being panicked by irresponsible press coverage. 'There is no question of Adam Kingsley stepping down,' he said. 'Our investors have done well by us and will continue to do well for many years to come.'

However, City analysts are more sceptical. 'Franchise Holdings is a one-man band,' said a source. 'If Kingsley goes, the collapse in confidence will be catastrophic. Frankly it will be a miracle if he can weather the present storm. The fear is that any investigation into Kingsley's affairs will uncover financial irregularities. The funding of some of his early acquisitions has never been adequately explained. It would be different if there was an obvious successor.'

Kingsley's sons, Miles, 26, and Fergus, 24, were expelled from public school for possession of drugs, and have been cautioned in the past for vandalism and theft. They are regulars at the various London casinos and at race meetings.

THE DARK ROOM

Adam Kingsley's daughter, Jane, 34, who owns and manages a successful photographic studio in South London, was married to Russell Landy for three years before his murder. Police have re-opened the file since the death of her fiancé.

Daily Mail – 29 June

363

Chapter Eighteen

WPC BLAKE NOTED the thunder clouds on DC Hadden's face as he pushed past her and shouldered his way through the double-doors. 'What's up with Hadden?' she asked the sergeant as she leaned her elbows on the front desk.

'Politics,' he grunted, preoccupied with some notes he was writing. 'He reckons the DCI has given away the best case he's ever had.'

'Who to?'

'Hampshire police. He handed over a prime piece of evidence last night on the Ardingly Wood murders and Hadden's furious about it. Claims he's the one who cracked the case and now no one's going to credit him with it.'

'What was the evidence?'

'The sledgehammer that was used to attack the doctor up at the Nightingale on Monday night,' the sergeant told her.

Blake watched his busy pen for a moment. 'So what's the connection with Ardingly Woods? Sledgehammers come two-a-penny on building sites. What's so special about this one?'

'The dead man's fiancée is a patient at the Nightingale, and she appears to be in the habit of losing husbands and lovers to death by bludgeoning.' He glanced up from his notes. 'Jane Kingsley, daughter of Adam Kingsley. It's been all over the newspapers for the last couple of days.'

'I've been busy.'

He pushed a tabloid towards her and stabbed a double column with his pen. 'Hampshire gave a press briefing yesterday. It's all there.'

Blake took the paper and read the piece rapidly. 'Well, I can see why Hadden's pissed off,' she remarked, laying it back on the counter. 'Who do you reckon did it?'

He shrugged as he signed his name. 'All I know is I wouldn't want to be employed by Franchise Holdings if they arrest Adam Kingsley. According to the business pages the shares are sliding already, and that's just on *fears* he might have been involved.' He straightened up. 'How are you getting on with the Flossie Hale assault?'

'Not bad.' She gave him a run-down of what she'd discovered. 'He was carrying a key-ring with a black disc embossed with a gold F and H. Flossie thinks they might be his initials but I'm not keen to put that in the description in case she's wrong. What do you think?'

He stared at her thoughtfully for a moment or two then picked up the newspaper and leafed through the pages impatiently, looking for the business section. Inset into the article on Franchise Holdings was a picture of the company's logo – entwined initials against a black background. He showed it to her. 'Something like that?'

'What are you, Sarge,' said Blake in amazement, 'a bloody magician?'

Nightingale Clinic, Salisbury – 9.30 a.m.

The floor around Jinx's feet was awash with newspapers when Alan Protheroe knocked on her door at nine-thirty. 'I ordered the lot,' she said with a weak smile. 'Have you seen what's happening?'

He nodded. 'I watched the breakfast news. The shares started sliding again as soon as the market opened.'

'Poor Adam, it's very unfair,' she said bitterly. 'They've been dying to cut him down to size for years and now they've been given the chance.' She clenched her hands in her lap. 'You know what makes me maddest of all? It's this garbage about no obvious successor. It's a cheap way to parade the family failings. Three of the present board are perfectly capable of taking over if anything happens to Adam, and the City knows it. There was never any question of Miles, Fergus or I stepping into his shoes. He wouldn't have it. He's worked too hard to watch his children destroy what he built.' She sighed. 'Well, we're destroying it anyway, between us. It wouldn't matter a tuppenny damn what I'd done if either Miles or Fergus could stand up and be counted.'

'What have you done, Jinx?'

'How about this for starters?' she said sarcastically. 'I managed to choose three murder victims as husband, fiancé and best friend. It does rather imply there's something rotten in the state of Denmark when three corpses litter the doorstep, don't you think?'

'Yes.'

There was a short silence. 'Do you know why I hated Stephanie Fellowes so much, and why I wouldn't engage in any of her psycho-crap?' said Jinx coldly. 'Because she couldn't believe I had nothing to do with Russell's death. Did she put that in her notes?'

'No.'

'Are you putting your scepticism in your notes?' *Would it hurt so much if she liked him less?*

'No.'

'But you are keeping notes?' He nodded. 'Then what are you writing about me, Dr Protheroe?'

'They're just private ones.' *The sexual fantasies of a man going mad from celibacy . . . OK, so Russell pressed the right buttons but did he turn you on? . . . What are you like in bed, Miss Kingsley? . . .* 'Yesterday, for example, I wrote: "It's a pity Jinx doesn't smile more. It suits her." '

She promptly frowned. 'Instead of saying "yes" just then, why couldn't you have said: The odds against you or your family being involved aren't good, Jinx, but they do exist? What makes you think I'm so fucking hard that I don't need reassurance, even if it is from a bastard like you?'

He grinned. 'Because you'd probably have torn strips off me for being patronizing. We both know you're not a fool and we both know you're up against it. All I can do, in the absence of something concrete to work on, is to point out the pitfalls. It's up to you how you choose to negotiate them.'

'It's patronizing to say smiling suits me.'

'It wasn't intended to be, but if that's how you choose to see it, then so be it.'

'I hate existentialism.'

'Sure you do,' he said. 'Which is why you're such a master of it.' He touched the newspapers with the toe of his shoe. 'What will happen to Franchise Holdings?'

'If they can't stop the slide, then Adam will resign,' she said matter-of-factly. 'He certainly won't stand idly by while receivers are sent in. In fact, if you've any spare cash, now's the time to gamble on some shares. They're a bargain at the moment. I guarantee the price will start back up again the minute the panic subsides.'

'What about the rumours of financial irregularities?'

'I'm betting there aren't any, or none that can be proved. Adam once said that if "Nipper" Read of Scotland Yard couldn't get anything on him then no one could.'

'Are you going to buy some shares?'

Her eyes gleamed wickedly. 'I already have. I phoned my stock broker this morning. He's selling everything in my portfolio to buy into Franchise Holdings.'

'What if you're wrong and you lose the lot?'

'It'll be in a good cause,' she said. 'At least I'll know I nailed my colours to the mast when it really mattered.'

'Is the motive really as pure as that?'

She looked at him suspiciously. 'What's that supposed to mean?'

'Veronica Gordon tells me your stepmother came last night. I just wondered if there was a little malice mixed in with the altruism.' Veronica had been shocked by

369

Jinx's cruelty, far more than she had by Betty's drunkenness: 'I think I've underestimated her, Alan. My guess is, she's as ruthless as her father.'

'What sort of malice?'

'The sort that jumps up and down and says: Look at me, Adam, I'm supporting you. Look at her, she's not.'

Jinx lit a cigarette. 'Chance would be a fine thing, wouldn't it? Will I ever get the opportunity to do that? I don't remember Adam coming here, but perhaps that's something else I've forgotten.'

'Have you invited him?'

She gave her faint smile. 'I didn't invite Simon Harris, but he still came. I didn't invite Miles or Fergus, but they came. Why does Adam require an invitation, Dr Protheroe? Surely loving fathers visit their sick daughters as a matter of course.'

'Perhaps he's afraid of rejection, Jinx.'

'I doubt it. If he were, he wouldn't be so quick to reject everyone else.' She returned to his questioning of her motives. 'In any case, malice would be redundant where Betty's concerned. She's burnt her boats and she's drowning, and I'm not going to lift a finger to help her.'

Then why do you look so sad? he wondered.

14 Glenavon Gardens, Richmond,
Surrey – 10.30 a.m.

The re-questioning of everyone connected with Jane Kingsley, Leo Wallader and Meg Harris was planned as a rolling programme throughout that Wednesday, with questions specifically geared to building a clear picture of their movements and whereabouts each day from the Bank Holiday Monday through to the evening of Monday, 13 June.

DS Fraser was assigned to London and interviews with the Clanceys, Josh Hennessey, Dean Jarrett, and Meg's neighbour Mrs Helms. He began with the Clanceys in Richmond, first explaining the purpose of the questions and then taking them back to Monday, 30 May, two weeks before Jinx's car crash. 'We understand from Leo's parents that he and Jinx returned to London some time during the late afternoon–early evening. Can you confirm that?' As he spoke, he tickled Goebbels's ears. The tiny little dog had stretched itself along his knees, chin hanging over the edge, and Fraser, thoroughly seduced, was grateful that Maddocks wasn't there to pour scorn on this simple affection.

Colonel Clancey pursed his ancient lips. 'I remember seeing Jinx on the Saturday morning but not on the Monday,' he said at last. 'I was in the garden and she came out to talk to me. She was hopping mad, far as I recall. Her two brothers were sleeping off hangovers upstairs, and Leo hadn't come home the night before. She asked me if I knew where he'd gone because they were supposed to be going down to Guildford together, and I said I hadn't seen him for a couple of days.' He glanced briefly at his wife. 'I also said,' he went on firmly, 'that she was making a mistake with Leo and she said, don't worry, Colonel, I've already come to that conclusion myself. Then she went back inside and a little while later Leo himself showed up.'

'You never told me you said that,' said Mrs Clancey.

'Thought you'd be angry,' he barked. 'You were always so keen on her marrying again.'

'Nonsense. It was you kept telling her she owed it to society to have babies. A woman like you with brains and initiative, you kept saying, you've got a responsibility to pass on the genes. Can't be doing with all these teenage nitwits producing hundreds while the clever people don't produce any. End up with idiots running the planet.'

Hastily, Fraser forestalled the development of this argument. 'When did you next see either of them?'

'I saw them leave together on the Sunday morning,' said Daphne helpfully. 'Jinx was wearing a baseball cap because Leo would insist on driving his car with the top down, and I remember thinking how much prettier she'd look in a straw bonnet.'

'Why was she going away with him if she'd already decided he wasn't for her?' asked Fraser thoughtfully.

'She has lovely manners,' said Mrs Clancey.

'The Wednesday after,' said the Colonel baldly, who had been thinking hard. 'We were in the garden, six o'clockish, G&T time anyway, and Jinx came down the path from the garage' – he gestured towards the window – 'runs along the fence, don't you know? She was happy as a sandboy, singing her head off, and I called out: "Who's won the jackpot?" And she popped her head over the top and said: "How's tricks?"'

'Yes,' agreed Daphne, 'and I said: "You're obviously looking forward to your week in Hampshire," and she said: "Got it in one, Mrs C. A change is as good as a rest."'

372

Fraser waited for a moment while Goebbels turned on his back and offered his tummy for scratching. 'Was that all?' he asked, crooking a sly finger and plucking at the golden fur.

They nodded simultaneously.

'You didn't ask her about Leo and how the weekend went?'

The Colonel looked offended. 'Good lord, no,' he said. 'None of our business. Doubt she'd have told us anyway. Private sort of person, Jinx.' He scowled at Goebbels, whose erect penis was showing pinkly through his fur. 'Filthy little beast. Kick him off if it upsets you.'

Fraser, who hadn't noticed, smiled weakly and uncrooked his finger. 'Did you see Leo that day?'

'No. Matter of fact' – the Colonel paused for thought – 'I don't recall seeing him at all after the Saturday morning. Hadn't really considered it, to tell you the truth, but now you ask . . .' He looked enquiringly at his wife. 'Do you remember seeing him?'

'For me it was the Sunday,' she reminded them.

The Colonel snorted impatiently. 'Afterwards, woman, afterwards.'

'Well, I wouldn't expect to see him, not as a general rule,' she said, addressing her remarks to Fraser. 'He never went out of his way to be particularly pleasant. The odd "good morning" once in a while, and that was the most one could expect. I think he resented us because we'd known Russell and he was afraid we were making comparisons, but we didn't like Russell very much either, and it was a bit of a disappointment to find Jinx had picked the same type again.'

Her husband fixed her with a basilisk glare. 'The question was, you silly old thing, did you see him after the Sunday?'

She smiled absent-mindedly. 'I don't think I did, no.'

'Not even during the week Jinx was away?' Fraser prompted.

'Definitely not,' barked the Colonel fluffing his moustache, 'but then he wasn't supposed to be there. Jinx popped in on the Friday night – that'd be June the third – to say *she* was off to Hampshire in the morning and *he'd* be spending the week in Surrey. She said not to bother about watering the house plants but yes, please, put some water on the garden when I had the hose running. Back the next Sunday, she told us.'

Fraser frowned and leant down to flick through some papers he'd placed on the floor beside his chair. 'I was under the impression she came back on the Friday, June the tenth.'

'Well, yes, matter of fact she did. Not that we knew until the next morning. Came looking for me on the Saturday – that'd be the eleventh – and said: "Guess what, Colonel, the wedding's off as of last night. The bastard's jilted me, and the only bugger is he beat me to it."' He pursed his lips again and frowned. 'And let me tell you, Sergeant, she was pleased as punch about it, looked as if a weight had been taken off her shoulders. Then she went back inside to phone her father, telling me to keep my fingers crossed that he wouldn't make her pay for the cost of the cancelled wedding.'

'According to her parents, she came home earlier than she'd planned after a phone call on the Friday afternoon.

When she got here, she caught Leo packing his belongings, at which point he told her he was going to marry her best friend and left. The implication was that he had been here all the time.'

'No,' said the Colonel stoutly, 'and I'm damn sure he didn't put in an appearance on the Friday either. I was in the front garden all afternoon so I'd have seen his car.'

'Are you sure about that?'

'I certainly am. We have a strict routine. Tuesdays and Fridays, the front garden; Mondays and Wednesdays, the back; Thursdays, shopping. Never varies.'

Fraser glanced towards Daphne Clancey, who nodded. 'Never varies,' she agreed. 'I blame the Army for it.' A sly smile crept around her mouth. 'I blame the Army for a lot of things.'

Fraser chewed the inside of his lip in thought. 'Why didn't you tell the Richmond police this when they interviewed you after Jinx's accident?' he said.

'Because they were only interested in why Jinx would want to kill herself,' the Colonel pointed out. 'So Daphne told 'em Leo jilted her and, before I could explain that she didn't seem too unhappy about it, Daphne starts weeping and wailing about the incident on the Sunday. False conclusions being drawn all over the place, if you ask me.'

'What's your explanation for the incident on Sunday, sir?'

'It was an accident,' he said. 'Door blew shut. Goebbels was on to it like a shot. Me, too, for that matter. Hauled her out of the garage and she was right as rain in no time.'

'The silly old fool nearly killed himself,' said Mrs Clancey fondly. 'Jinx is no lightweight in all conscience.'

Fraser nodded again. 'Did she give you an explanation after you got her out of the garage?'

'Just agreed it must have been an accident,' said the Colonel, 'then begged Daphne to stop fussing. "I'm all right," she said.'

Fraser had observed the outside of the garage when he arrived. Like the Clanceys', which was separated from it by a narrow pathway beside the four-foot wall that divided the properties, it was part of a two-storey side elevation at the rear of the house with access from inside. The front doors faced each other under discreet porches halfway between the corners of the houses and their garages, leaving an enviable stretch of ground between the gates and the front elevations. Jinx's was full of shrubs and small trees, masking the ground floor of the house from the road; the Clanceys' was rather more formal with rose beds around a small area of lawn. After all, thought Fraser, it wasn't surprising Tuesdays and Fridays were given over to its care. A view of the back garden through their sitting-room window showed an area of equivalent size.

'Did Miss Kingsley drive off in her car after you rescued her?' he asked Colonel Clancey.

'Not immediately.'

'But she did go out?'

He nodded. 'She made a phone call first, then shooed us out, saying she was fine.'

'Who was she phoning?'

'No idea. Made the call from her bedroom. Whoever

she was going to visit, presumably, needed to explain why she was delayed.'

'Do you think it was wise to let her drive in the circumstances?'

'Matter of fact, no, but there wasn't much we could do to stop her.'

'Did she come back later?'

The Colonel looked at his wife. 'Couldn't say, to be honest, but I would imagine so. She wasn't one for staying out.'

Fraser tugged one of Goebbels's ears. 'So were the garage doors bolted or unbolted when you went to see why Goebbels was barking?'

'Unbolted,' said the Colonel.

'Oh, Eric!' scolded his wife. 'Where's the sense in lying? It won't help Jinx. They were bolted,' she told Fraser. 'Eric looked through the garage window, saw what was happening, and came to me for the spare key. Frankly, it's a mercy she hadn't bolted the front door as well, otherwise he'd have had a terrible job getting in.'

The old man pushed himself out of his chair and moved across to gaze out over the garden. 'Known Jinx since she first moved in here with Russell,' he said shortly. 'Thirteen, fourteen years, give or take a year. She's a fine woman, a little remote, perhaps, too independent sometimes, thinks she can do anything a man can do, then finds she's not as strong as she thought she was – rescued her once from under a bag of cement because it was too damn heavy for her.' He paused on a low chuckle. 'Wedged under it like a great floundering crab – haven't laughed so much in years.' He paused again. 'Saw her through that terrible business over Russell, watched her put her life back together again and make a success of her photography. And with no help from her father, I might add. She wouldn't have it. "I'll make it on my own, Colonel, or not at all." That's what she said.' He turned round with his beetling white brows drawn together in a ferocious frown. 'Woman like that doesn't commit suicide, or even think about doing it. And if she did, she'd do it right. She'd have run a hosepipe from the exhaust and plugged the gaps in the window where it came in. Wouldn't rely on the fumes in the garage to kill her.'

'Perhaps she wanted to be rescued,' suggested Fraser.

The Colonel snorted derisively. 'Then she'd have wept her heart out afterwards and told us how unhappy she was,' he argued. 'Seems to me, the important question is why. Before anyone knew Leo and Meg were murdered, the police latched on to Jinx's unhappiness at losing Leo as the reason. Two suicide attempts when you're depressed make some sort of sense.' His eyes narrowed. 'But what's your thinking now that you know Leo's dead? You suggesting she knew about the murders and tried to kill herself afterwards?'

Fraser thought about this for some time, his eyes searching the old man's face closely. It was a good point, he admitted to himself. There was an inherent paradox if the first suicide attempt happened before Meg and Leo were murdered, because it was a peculiarly complicated psychology that led you from suicidal despair to murderous anger and back to suicidal despair again.

He cupped his hands around the little dog, turned

him over and set him on his feet on the floor, then he picked up his notes and sorted through them. 'I spoke to her yesterday,' he told them. 'She talked about her car crash, said she didn't think she'd been trying to kill herself.' He isolated a page. 'She said: "It seems very out of character." Then she went on: "If I wasn't trying to kill myself, someone else must have been trying to kill me."' He looked up. 'Did you see anyone come to her house that Sunday? Did you hear anyone? Did you notice anything when you let yourself in through the front door?'

Colonel Clancey shook his head regretfully. 'No,' he admitted.

Fraser felt oddly disappointed. 'OK,' he said, 'then let's move on to Monday, June the thirteenth.'

'*I* did,' said Mrs Clancey, with a faraway look in her eyes. She drew them back from whatever memory she was observing to gaze with fixed concentration on the Sergeant. '*I* did,' she repeated. 'How very strange, I'd forgotten all about it. I was so worried about Eric having a heart attack when he was pulling Jinx out of her car that it quite went out of my head.' She leaned forward, her pale old eyes suddenly alight with excitement. 'Goebbels went into the house with Eric,' she said, 'and I could hear him barking his little head off. Well, of course, I thought he was with Eric, but the next thing I knew he was rushing up the path from the back garden, barking and snarling as if he were looking for someone. Well, you know the noise dogs make when they're after an intruder. He must have jumped out of the window in the drawing room, and *that* means,' she said firmly, 'that someone had jumped out before him, probably when Goebbels first raised the alarm. Certainly the drawing-room window was open when we took Jinx inside. I closed it myself when she was making her phone call.'

'Well done, old thing,' said the Colonel approvingly. 'Bound to be what it was all about. Some bastard was trying to do away with her. Nothing else makes sense.'

'Then why didn't Jinx tell you that?' said Fraser reluctantly. 'She wasn't suffering from amnesia then.'

'Made a big fuss of Goebbels, you know, after I told her he was the one who alerted us to what was happening. Nearly squashed the poor little bugger.'

'Still . . .' The whole scenario was idiotic, Fraser told himself, but he felt drawn to continue. 'Look, you don't put a conscious person in a car and start the ignition in the hopes of them being silly enough to sit there until they die? She'd have to be unconscious.'

'She said her head was hurting.'

'Then someone must have hit her first. So why didn't she report it to the police?'

There was another silence.

'Because,' said Mrs Clancey stoutly, 'she knew the person very well and couldn't believe they had meant to hurt her. No harm had come to her, after all, and Eric went on and on about it being a silly accident. It's human nature to assume the best, you know.'

'*Or*,' said Colonel Clancey reflectively, 'she had more important things to do than answer police questions. As I said, very independent woman, Jinx. Probably thought she had the situation under control. I mean, who was the telephone call to? Seemed perfectly straightforward at the time, but now – well worth looking into, I'd say.'

Fraser made a note. 'When did you next see her?'

The old man looked at his wife. 'I don't remember seeing her again. The next we knew the police were banging on our door on the Tuesday, telling us she was in hospital.'

Fraser eyed them both thoughtfully. 'Your neighbour tried to commit suicide and you didn't check up on her?'

'Suicide wasn't mentioned until the Tuesday,' said the Colonel sharply. 'Far as we knew, it was a silly accident. Kept an eye out, naturally, but there was nothing untoward happening. Weren't going to make a nuisance of ourselves when the poor girl probably felt like a prize ass.'

Harris and Hennessey, Soho, London – 12.30 p.m.

Josh Hennessey, who, despite his threats on Meg's answerphone to withdraw from the partnership, was still working to keep the business alive, greeted Sergeant Fraser with little enthusiasm. 'I've already told you everything I know,' he said, ruffling his hair into a crest and staring sourly at the man in front of him.

Fraser explained the purpose of his visit. 'If you have a business diary,' he suggested, 'it might speed things up a little. I need as accurate a timetable of Meg's movements as possible.'

With bad grace Hennessey took a book from his desk drawer and rustled through the pages. 'OK, these are

Meg's appointments. Monday, May thirty: nothing. It was a bank holiday, Tuesday, May thirty-one: blank. But it's crossed through with a blue pencil so that means she'll have been working in her office.'

'Do you remember her being here, sir?'

'No,' said Josh curtly. 'It was three weeks ago and Meg and I have worked together for years. How am I supposed to remember one day amongst thousands? In any case, if I was out I wouldn't have known.'

'Were you out?'

He glanced at the diary. 'According to this I was in Windsor, recruiting.'

'Are the blue lines reliable? Would she cross a day through even if she hadn't been in the office?'

'Yes, if it suited her.'

'Go on.'

'Wednesday, June one: ten o'clock, Bill Riley, 12 Connaught Street. All day meeting. Thursday—'

'One moment, sir,' Fraser broke in. 'Did she keep that appointment?'

'It's crossed through which, in theory, means it was dealt with.' He shrugged. 'OK, yes. Considering the amount of time I've spent since on that one customer, she was probably there until midnight sorting out his personnel problems. Mind you,' he admitted grudgingly, 'it's keeping us afloat at the moment. Precious little else is.'

'Fair enough. Thursday,' he prompted.

'Thursday, June two: blank in the morning, meeting with bank manager at three-thirty. Both crossed through.'

'Would that be the partnership's bank manager or her personal bank manager?'

'Probably the partnership's. We've been through a rough patch during the recession and Meg has fairly regular meetings with the bastard who holds our loans. *Had*,' he corrected himself bleakly. 'I keep forgetting she's dead. Friday, June three: blank but crossed through. Monday—'

'I'm sorry to keep interrupting, sir, but have you any idea what she did over the weekend of the fourth and fifth?'

'We had a business relationship, Sergeant, as I explained the last time I spoke to you. What she did at weekends was a closed book to me, unless it involved the partnership. Monday, June six: ten o'clock, Bill Riley again. Crossed through. Tuesday—'

'Perhaps it would be easier if I just made a photocopy,' said Fraser. 'I suspect it's a waste of both our time to go through it like this if there's nothing you can add to the written entries.'

Hennessey pushed the book across the desk. 'There's nothing. I checked after the last time you lot came, and bar a couple of meetings with Riley and the bank manager's demands for a business plan on the tenth, she seems to have spent most of that week skiving. You're farting about in cloud-cuckoo-land, frankly, if you think there's anything I can tell you.'

'You're being very unhelpful, sir,' said Fraser mildly. 'Do you not want your partner's murderer found?'

Josh reached for a pack of cigarettes at the side of the desk. 'I thought I'd kicked this fucking habit until all

383

this happened. Now I'm back with a vengeance.' He lit a cigarette and tossed the match into an ashtray, gazing moodily at the twists of smoke that rose from the spent head. 'I don't know what I want, Sergeant. Meg was a good friend. Jinx is a good friend. Heads you win, tails I lose.'

'Why do you say that?'

'Because I can read,' said Josh curtly. 'The newspapers are full of it and, unless they're way off beam, you're aiming to arrest Jinx or her father because of the way Russell died.'

'Did you know Russell?'

'Not very well. Jinx brought him to the office a couple of times when Meg and I were still with Wellman and Hobbs.'

'Did he ever come to see Meg without Jinx?'

Josh shook his head. 'Not that I remember.'

'Did you know she was having an affair with him?'

Josh drew heavily on his cigarette. 'Not at the time. I heard about it afterwards.'

'Who told you?'

Josh didn't answer immediately. 'I don't remember,' he said flatly. 'Either Meg or Simon, I should think.' He seemed to make up his mind. 'It was Meg. She was really cut up about Russell's death, kept bursting into tears for no apparent reason, so I asked her why and she told me.'

Fraser didn't believe him. 'I think it was Miss Kingsley who told you.'

Josh looked at him for a moment. 'I don't remember,' he said again. 'It was a long time ago.'

Fraser gave a pleasant smile. 'It's not particularly

384

important, but we're trying to tie up a few loose ends. Can you recollect how soon after Russell's death she told you?'

'Look, I haven't said it was Jinx, OK?' Fraser was fascinated by Hennessey's hands, which seemed to have a life of their own, twitching, plucking, always fidgeting.

'Understood. Can you remember when you first heard about it, sir?'

'I think it was after she lost the baby.'

'Thank you,' said Fraser easily. 'I don't need to keep you much longer. I'd be grateful if we could just run over the last conversation you had with Meg, which I believe was the telephone call to your home on Saturday, June the eleventh. According to what you told us before, she said Leo and Jinx's wedding was off, that she was going to marry him instead, that they were leaving for France on the Tuesday but that she would pop in before then to bring you up to date with office affairs.'

'That's right.'

Fraser consulted the business diary. 'Yet, according to this, she returned to the office on the Friday afternoon following an appointment with the bank manager. So why didn't she tell you then? That's a bit odd, isn't it?'

'Too bloody right, it's odd,' he growled. 'Dammit, I get this phone call out of the blue saying she's pissing off to France, leaving me to hold the fort till she gets back. I gave her absolute hell and told her I'd swing for her if she didn't get in here and sort her desk out before she left.'

'So it was your idea and not hers that she come in on the Monday?'

Josh frowned as he thought back. 'Probably. I was damned angry about her leaving me in the lurch without any warning. Who the hell's going to have confidence in a business where one partner buggers off at the drop of a hat? I sank every cent I own into this sodding venture.' He shook his head. 'Does it make a difference?'

'It might,' said Fraser. He paused to think about it. 'Perhaps you made her feel guilty enough to keep them hanging around longer than they meant to.'

'I don't get it.'

'Meg made all her phone calls on the Saturday morning,' said Fraser slowly. 'I wonder if the idea was to make the announcements and then leave for France immediately. Let's face it, she knew better than anyone what had happened to Russell Landy.'

'Are you saying they'd still be alive if I hadn't laid a guilt trip on her?' asked Josh harshly.

'I don't know, sir. I think we need some idea of where they were on the Monday before we come to any conclusions. I mean, it's you who put pressure on them to delay their departure.' Fraser looked at the other man closely before continuing. 'And as things stand, I only have your word for it that she and Leo didn't come here as promised.'

Chapter Nineteen

Wednesday, 29 June, 53 Lansing Road, Salisbury,
Wiltshire – midday

FLOSSIE HALE EXAMINED the newspaper clipping of
the Franchise Holding emblem. 'Oh, yes,' she said, 'no
question, that's the key-ring all right.' Next she turned
her attention to the grainy faxed photograph of Miles
and Fergus Kingsley in the members' enclosure at Ascot
and, after a brief hesitation, planted her finger on a face.
'That looks like him, but it's not a very good picture, is
it, love? I don't recall his hair being as dark as that. The
jacket's similar.'

'What about the man next to him?'

She held the page away from her, half-closing her
eyes, as if looking at an impressionist painting. 'The
trouble is you don't look at their faces much, not when
they're punching you. You're too scared. Yes,' she said
with sudden decision, stabbing at Miles again, 'that's him
all right. Little bastard. I said butter wouldn't melt in his
mouth. Who is he then?'

'His name's Miles Kingsley.' WPC Blake retrieved the
photograph and tucked it into her bag. Samantha Garrison had also picked out Miles and, if neither woman had
been quite as decisive as Blake would have liked, she put
it down to the poor quality of the photocopy and

postponed her niggling concerns over whether or not this could ever result in a successful prosecution. If Flossie had been more co-operative at the start, allowed them in to dust for fingerprints or let them take swabs, they would have had something more concrete to work on.

'Well, I don't understand it,' the older woman was saying. 'How'd you turn what I told you into a blooming photograph of someone with the initials MK?'

'Just luck, Flossie. He's a bit of a playboy, this creep. If you're interested, the photograph was faxed through to us from *The Tatler*. You got done over by one of society's best. His dad's a multi-millionaire.'

Flossie shook her head. 'It makes you wonder what the world's coming to. What's he doing trawling Salisbury for cheap old tarts like me if he can afford the high-class ones in London?'

Blake couldn't answer that.

The Studio, Pimlico, London – 1.00 p.m.

Dean Jarrett was effusively helpful. 'Well, of *course*, dear,' he told Fraser, ladling out the charm while sussing him coolly from the corner of his eye. He thought this policeman looked less of a homophobe than most, might even, if the friendly smile was anything to go by, be tolerably sympathetic towards Jinx and her bizarre entourage at the studio. Certainly, he had taken Angelica's pink hair in his stride and appeared unfazed by Dean's flirting. 'I can give you a blow-by-blow account of everything Jinx did from Tuesday the thirty-first until Friday the third. But after that it's a complete no-no, I'm afraid. She was at Hell Hall the next week, and we didn't hear a dicky bird out of her – didn't expect to, of course, because she was on her hols – and then she did a vanishing trick on us. Angelica phoned and phoned on the Monday, when she was supposed to be here, and all she got was Jinx's answerphone.'

'That would be the thirteenth of June?'

'It would. And then, on the Tuesday, we heard the awful news that the poor mite was unconscious in hospital somewhere. I suppose you've seen her. Is she all right?'

His face contorted itself into a moue of concern, and Fraser nodded reassuringly, even if he did find the expression less than sincere. 'She seems fine. A bit hazy about what happened, but otherwise very alert and very composed.'

'Isn't she *amazing*?' said Dean. 'Quite my most favourite lady.'

'Yet you haven't been to see her,' said Fraser dispassionately, 'or not as far as we know. Is there some reason for that?'

The moue vanished abruptly. 'Yes, well, unlike the Josh Hennesseys and Simon Harrises of this world, who both tell me they've inflicted themselves on her, I prefer to wait for an invitation. Imagine the awfulness of feeling like death and having well-meaning friends impose themselves on you. Jinx is a very private person. Half the time I think she's completely ignorant of how much we all adore her, the other half I retreat into my little shell because I'm afraid the truth is we bore her rigid.' He sighed. 'In any case I didn't know where she was for ages. Her brute of a father wouldn't tell me.'

'Still, I'm surprised she wasn't worried about the studio.'

Dean gave a squeak of distress. 'How crushing you are, Sergeant. Don't you feel the poor darling has rather more pressing concerns at the moment than leaving her business in the hands of the second best photographer in London?'

Fraser's lips twitched. 'What did you think of Leo?'

'He was absolutely *dire*. A real leech, but could Jinx see it? Well, you know what the trouble is, she's blinkered when it comes to a pretty face. Falls for the outside, and forgets that what's underneath is more important. It's her father's fault. He looks like an old vulture and he's always been so damn distant with her that she assumes a pretty face means a pretty personality.' He rolled his eyes to Heaven. 'I hate to say it, because he's a very rude man, but I actually think Adam Kingsley is probably worth ten Leo Walladers. If the number of phone calls he's made, checking up on me and Angelica, is anything to go by, he cares about Jinx a great deal more than she's ever given him credit for. My *God*, if we'd thought about letting things slide – which we haven't – he'd have been round here tearing our innards out.'

Fraser grinned. 'You've met him then?'

'I was introduced the first time he paid one of his terrifying visits,' said Dean with a shudder, 'as was Angie. But as I'm gay and she's black, it was hardly the social event of the century. He washed his hands afterwards in case he'd caught something. On all subsequent visits, he has grunted rudely in our direction and swept through to talk to Jinxy in private.'

'Why are his visits terrifying?'

'Because he insists on bringing his tame gorilla with him.' Dean rolled his eyes again. 'Says he's the chauffeur but since when did chauffeurs need fifty-four-inch chests? The man is there to make mincemeat of anyone who dares say boo to the boss.'

'That's not so unusual these days, you know. A bodyguard-cum-chauffeur. Most millionaires have them. You said Mr Kingsley's distant, but would you also say he's fond of Jinx?'

'Yes, in a brooding sort of way. He never touches her, just sits and stares at her as though she were a piece of Dresden china. I get the feeling he can't really believe she's his. I mean he's common as muck, after all, and she's such a lady, and the only other two children he had are A-one arseholes.' He thought for a moment. 'Fond isn't the right word. I think he idolizes her.'

'How does she feel about that?'

'Loathes it, but then you have to understand that he's not idolizing Jinx, he's idolizing the person he thinks she is. I mean, you'd have to be mentally deficient to see Jinx as Dresden china. A piece of good solid Staffordshire pottery that bounces when you drop it and retains its integrity through a thousand washes, that's a better analogy.'

'Why doesn't Jinx put him straight?'

'She's tried, dear, but there's none so blind as those who will not see. She was going to marry Leo Wallader, for God's sake. What better demonstration could there be of flawed judgement and appalling taste? Not that her father could see it, of course. Leo had blue blood in his veins, so he must have been a cut above the rest of us.'

Fraser smiled. 'Tell me about Tuesday, May the thirty-first,' he invited.

'That was a very busy day. We had a teenage band here all morning who thought they were the bee's knees. Their record company wanted some publicity shots and it was like drawing blood from a stone to get them to do anything other than simper into the lens.' He thought for a moment. 'OK, in the afternoon we did some location work round Charing Cross station for a television company. Atmospheric stills for a documentary on homelessness. We clocked off about six, because Jinx wanted to get home in reasonably good time.'

'Did she say why?'

He shook his silver head. 'But she was in a brilliant mood all day and, when I asked her if we could thank Leo for it, she said: "In one respect, I suppose you can." So I said: "Don't tell me, darling, he's finally come up trumps in the rogering department." And she said: "Don't be absurd, Dean, Leo would need to be face down on a mirror to do that." And I thought, thank God, she's finally seen the light, but, for once, I was far too tactful to say it.'

Fraser grinned again. 'Wednesday, June the first,' he prompted.

'Let me think now. All right. I spent the morning developing and printing contact sheets. There was some undeveloped film left over from the previous week, and the two projects from the previous day. Jinx caught up on a mound of paperwork in order to clear it before she went on holiday. Wednesday afternoons are always reserved for portrait work, and I think we had five or six families that day. Then we grabbed supper at about half-six, before going back to Charing Cross to finish the location work there. They wanted twilight and night-time shots as well, so we didn't clock off that day until about ten-thirty.'

'And how was her mood on Wednesday?'

'The same. Happy, sunny, brilliant. Angie and I were quite persuaded she'd given Leo the boot, but she didn't say she had, so we guessed she was hanging fire till she could tell her old man during her holiday. You've got to realize we'd been walking on egg shells for God knows how long. The mere mention of Leo's name brought glowering looks and an abrupt change of conversation. Then suddenly, out of nowhere, she's her old sweet self again.'

'And you put that down to the fact that she'd decided not to marry him after all?'

Dean nodded. 'More than that, sweetheart, I put it down to the fact that he wasn't *there* any more, and certainly not in her bed. For the first time in weeks, she actually *wanted* to go home. Take the Thursday. She had me working like a slave all morning and, come the afternoon, she suddenly looks at her watch and says: "Do me a favour, Dean, and mind the shop. There's a few things I need to do at home, and tomorrow we're out all day." You could have knocked me over with a feather. She'd been avoiding the place like the plague ever since Leo got his knees under her table.'

'Why?'

Dean tut-tutted impatiently. 'Because she realized she couldn't stand him, of course, but she didn't know how to admit it. Her father's fault again. He'd really gone to town on the wedding preparations, invited half of Surrey and Hampshire, and Jinx was too embarrassed to say anything. I mean, there were a couple of Cabinet ministers coming, and you don't tell them to bog off without a few qualms, do you?'

Fraser chuckled. 'I've never had the chance. Could be fun, though.' He paused. 'It makes sense if he wasn't there. She and he had a blazing row on the Bank Holiday Monday, and the logical thing would have been for him to move out immediately.' Pensively, he pulled at his lip. 'But she claims he was there on the following Saturday morning, June the fourth, when she left for Hellingdon Hall, remembers their farewells as fond ones.'

Dean shrugged. 'Then Leo must have undergone a character transplant in the meantime. I swear to God, if the sight of blood were a little less sickening, I'd have bopped him on the nose several times. He was a complete slime-ball.'

'So what are you saying?'

'That Jinx is telling fibs about the fond farewell.'

'You think they had a row?'

'No. I'm guessing she didn't want anyone to know he'd gone, so pretended fond farewells that never happened. I mean, if we always had to tell the truth about our relationships, we'd be wobbling jellies with no self-esteem. I lie all the time about mine – keep some lovers going long after they've deserted me.'

'It's a pity you didn't tell the police all this at the time of her accident,' said Fraser in mild reproof.

'Well, I would have done, if they'd been remotely interested in anything prior to Friday, June the tenth, but all they wanted to know was had we seen or heard from her since her return from Hampshire. I did say that we were a teensy-weensy bit surprised to hear she'd only cancelled the wedding on the Saturday after she got back from Hell Hall, when we were sure she'd made up her mind two weeks earlier, but they said it was Leo who had jilted *her*, and as I couldn't prove any different, there wasn't much more to be said.'

'OK, then there's just Friday the third left to cover. Anything unusual happen that day?'

'Just a wall-to-wall fashion shoot in London's Docklands. We began at eight-thirty and went right through to seven o'clock in the evening without a break. Jinx dropped me off with all the cameras and equipment at the studio around seven-thirty, blew me a kiss and said: "It's all yours for a week, so be good." And I haven't seen her since.'

'Have you spoken to her?' asked Fraser idly.

'Just once, on the telephone.'

'When was that?'

'Sunday night.'

'Who called who?'

'She called me.'

'At home?'

Dean nodded.

'It must have been important then,' said Fraser.

'Oh, it was,' said Dean. 'It was my thirtieth birthday and she knew I'd have died a *thousand* deaths if I hadn't spoken to her, never mind she's flat on her back in hospital and suffering galloping amnesia.' He beamed engagingly. 'As I said, she's quite my most favourite lady.'

Fraser flicked over a page or two of his notebook. 'Odd,' he said. 'According to her, she asked you to phone the Walladers to find out whether Leo and Meg were dead. She never mentioned your birthday. Can *anything* you've said be relied upon, sir?'

Romsey Road Police Station, Winchester – 1.00 p.m.

The call from Salisbury came through to the incident room as Detective Superintendent Cheever was briefing the team he'd picked to conduct interviews at Hellingdon Hall that afternoon. He listened for five minutes, with only the odd interjection to show he was interested, then he said: 'And the prostitute is certain of her identification?' A longish pause. 'You've got two of them who swear it's him. Yes, we're planning to interview the whole family this afternoon. No, he's never entered the frame at all.' Another long pause. 'Because he was sixteen when Landy got done, that's why. OK, OK. We all know ten-year-olds do it now.' He compressed his lips into a thin, frustrated line. 'Well, how quickly can she get here? Half an hour. Yes, all right, we'll hold on. Yes, yes, yes.

We've had cars stationed outside since yesterday afternoon. The whole family's there, including Kingsley. He drove back from London this morning.' He listened again. 'No, we won't steal her blasted thunder.' He slammed the phone on to the rest and glared at the assembled detectives. 'Damn!' he growled.

'What's up?' asked Maddocks.

'Miles Kingsley has been beating up on prostitutes in Salisbury. The DCI there says he has all the hallmarks of a classic psychopath.'

'Where does that leave us?'

Testily, Cheever fingered his bow-tie. 'High and dry for the moment. They're sending a WPC over with what she's managed to get on him. I suggest we put everything on hold till she gets here.' He steepled his hands in front of his face. 'This is what's known as a spanner in the works, gentlemen. Why in God's name should Miles Kingsley have murdered his sister's husband, fiancé and friend? Can any of you make sense of that?'

'You're jumping the gun, sir,' protested Maddocks. 'So the bastard beats up on prostitutes, that doesn't make him a killer.'

'You still favour Jane for the murders then?'

'Of course. She's the only one with a motive for all three.'

'And her father, knowing what she's done, protects her?'

'That's about the size of it. After Landy's death, she's bundled off to a psychiatric unit while Dad takes the flak himself because he knows the Met will never be able to prosecute him. This time, she's shoved into the

Nightingale, following a fake suicide, and we're told, hands off, because she's got amnesia. Meanwhile Dad's solicitor is busy on a crisis limitation exercise with the clinic's administrator. She's guilty as sin. Her father knows it and so does Dr Protheroe.'

'That's a hell of a conspiracy theory and it's full of holes, anyway. If the doctor's protecting her why did she go for him on Monday night?'

'Because she's off her bloody rocker, sir.'

'She's a psychopath, in other words.'

'Sure she is.'

Frank lowered his hands and smiled sarcastically. 'The Met said her father was a psychopath. Salisbury say her brother's a psychopath. You say she's a psychopath. It's beginning to look like an epidemic, and I don't buy that, Gareth.'

Maddocks shrugged. 'What would you buy, sir?'

'One psychopath, maybe, but not three. I suggest two of them have been tarred with the brush of the other.'

The announcement that Adam Kingsley had resigned in favour of his number two, John Normans, was released through Franchise Holdings' London headquarters at twelve o'clock. At one o'clock on the BBC television news, video footage of the gates of Hellingdon Hall formed a backdrop to the news story. 'Adam Kingsley reached his decision this morning amidst the peace and quiet of this palatial eighteenth-century house on the edge of the New Forest, although it is unlikely he will be here for very much longer. Hellingdon Hall is a regis-

tered asset of Franchise Holdings and sources say it will
be sold off to recoup some of the losses of the last few
days.'

Incident Room, Romsey Road Police Station, Winchester – 1.45 p.m.

The message over the radio crackled with excitement.
'Listen, sir, a Porsche, registration number MIL 1, has
just left Hellingdon Hall by the tradesman's entrance,
and it's piling off up the road at about a hundred miles
an hour. We're following but it's definitely not old man
Kingsley. Do we go back to the Hall or do we continue?'

'Who's your back-up?'

'Fredericks at the trade entrance, and half a dozen
uniformed local chaps at the front gate, keeping the
paparazzi in order. But the place has been dead as a dodo
all morning, sir. This is the first action we've seen.'

'All right, continue,' said Frank Cheever, 'but don't
lose him. It's probably Miles Kingsley, and I want to
know where he's going. Fredericks, are you hearing me?
Stay alert, and if anyone else comes out notify me
immediately. Understood?'

'Will do, sir.'

The first radio burst back into life. 'He's turning on
to the A338, Guv'nor. Looks like he's heading for
Salisbury.'

43 Shoebury Terrace, Hammersmith, London – 2.00 p.m.

Fraser's last port of call was Meg's neighbour in Hammersmith, Mrs Helms. She greeted him with surprising warmth, rather as she might an old friend, and took him into the front room. 'My husband,' she said, waving her hand towards a pathetic husk of a man who was sitting with a blanket across his knees and gazing forlornly on to the quiet street. 'Multiple sclerosis,' she mouthed. She raised her voice. 'This is Detective Sergeant Fraser, Henry, come to talk to us about poor Meg.' She went back to her whisper. 'Just ignore him. He won't say anything. Hardly ever does these days. It's a shame, it really is. He used to be such a busy little soul.'

Fraser took the armchair that Mrs Helms indicated and, for the fourth time that day, explained the purpose behind his questions. 'So, have you any idea what Meg did over the bank holiday weekend?' he asked.

She greeted this with a girlish squeal. 'I couldn't begin to say,' she declared. 'Goodness me, I can't even remember what *we* were doing that weekend.'

Fraser glanced towards her husband, thinking that if his mobility was as poor as it appeared to be, then the chances of them *not* being there were fairly remote. 'Perhaps you had family come to visit?' he suggested. 'Does that jog any memories? Meg wouldn't have been at work on the Monday.'

She shook her head. 'Every day's the same. Week

days, weekends, holidays. Nothing varies very much. Now, if you could tell me what was on the television, that would help me.'

Fraser tried a different tack. 'It's a fair bet that Leo was here during the nights of Friday, May the twenty-seventh, possibly Monday, the thirtieth, and very probably Tuesday, the thirty-first. In fact, he may well have been in residence for the rest of that week *and* the week after. Does that help at all? In other words, did you notice him around more than usual? Before when I spoke to you, you said there was a lot of coming and going shortly before they left for France.'

'Well, I certainly noticed he was in and out rather more often than normal, but as to whether he was living with her . . .' She shook her head. 'Dates don't mean anything to me, Sergeant. And how on earth would I know if Leo stayed on a particular night? Frankly, Meg's love-life was of no interest to either of us, and why would it be? We've enough troubles of our own.'

Fraser nodded sympathetically. 'Leo had two very distinctive Mercedes convertibles, one black with beige leather upholstery, and the other white with burgundy seats. We think one or other would have been parked outside whenever he was there. Do you remember seeing either of them at any point in the two weeks before they left for the holiday in France?'

She gave her girlish squeal again. 'I wouldn't know a Mercedes from a Jaguar,' she said, 'and I never notice cars, full stop, unless they're blocking my way. Dreadful invention.'

Fraser gave a quiet sigh of frustration. Mrs Helms's

epitaph of a few days previously – *she never gave us any trouble* – came back to haunt him afresh. What a pity, he was thinking, because if she *had*, then Mrs Helms might have taken a little more notice of her. He looked disconsolately towards her husband. 'Perhaps Mr Helms saw something?' he suggested.

She shook her head vigorously. 'Wouldn't notice a double-decker bus if it was parked in his lap,' she said *sotto voce*. 'Best not to bother him, really. It makes him anxious if he's bothered.'

But Fraser persisted, if only to reassure himself that he had left no stone unturned. 'Can you help me, Mr Helms? It is important or I wouldn't press the point. We have two unsolved murders, and we need to establish why and when they happened.'

The thin face turned towards him and regarded him without expression for several seconds. 'Which day was the second?'

'Of June?'

The other nodded.

Fraser consulted his diary. 'It was a Thursday.'

'I had a hospital appointment on the second. I came home by ambulance and the driver noticed the Mercedes. He said: "That's a new one, not seen that here before," and I told him it belonged to downstairs and had been there two or three days.'

Fraser leaned forward. 'On and off or permanently?'

'It was there each night,' he managed with difficulty, 'but not always during the day.'

'Can you remember when it left for good?'

It was clear he had difficulty articulating words, and Fraser waited patiently for him to resume. 'Not sure. Probably when they went to France.'

Fraser smiled encouragingly. 'And would you be able to say which day that was, Mr Helms?'

The man nodded. 'Clean sheets' day. Monday.'

'Goodness me,' said Mrs Helms, 'do you know he's right. I'd just stripped the beds when Meg came with the cat food. Dumped the sheets in Henry's lap while I went out to talk to her. There now, and I'd quite forgotten.'

'That's grand,' said Fraser. 'We're making real progress. Did they leave together in the Mercedes?'

Mr Helms shook his head. 'I didn't see. Anthea pushed me and the sheets into the kitchen.' There was a look of irritation in his eyes and Fraser thought, you poor bloody sod, I bet she sorted the sheets on your lap as if you were a mobile laundry basket.

'Did you happen to notice when Meg's car went? It's a dark green Ford Sierra. We've found it since in a street in Chelsea.'

'The Friday evening. Both cars went. Only the sports car came back.'

'With both Meg and Leo in it?'

'Yes.'

'Which makes sense. They were clearing the decks before they left on holiday.' He drummed his fingers on his knee and addressed his next question to Mrs Helms. 'Did Meg give any indication on the Monday that they had postponed their departure for any reason?'

She pulled a face. 'Not really. She just rang the doorbell, thrust the key and the food at me and said they were off to France. Very odd, I thought.'

'Did anything else strike you as odd?'

'Not really,' she said again. 'She hadn't done her hair, and her eyes were rather red, so I thought she might have been crying, but I put it down to a lover's tiff.'

'Anything else?'

'Well, saying Marmaduke had to be kept a prisoner in the hall was a bit odd. She'd never done that before. Poor little fellow, it's no way to keep a cat.'

Fraser frowned and flicked through his papers. 'Last time we spoke,' he murmured, isolating a page, 'you said Meg was insistent that Marmaduke shouldn't go into any of the rooms.'

'That's right.'

'But just now you said she wanted him kept prisoner in the hall.'

'Well, yes. Same difference.'

'Can you remember her actual words, Mrs Helms?'

'Oh lord. It's nearly three weeks ago.' She screwed her face in concentration. 'Let me see now. It was all over in half a second. "You remember I said we were going to France, Mrs Helms?" That's how she began. Well, of course, she'd never said anything of the sort but I was too polite to say so. "And you promised you'd look after the cat?" she said next. Which annoyed me because I hadn't. I'd have said so, too, except she shoved the key and tin at me, and never gave me a chance to answer. "The cat's imprisoned and will want to get out. Please be careful how you open the doors. I don't want any more damage done." And that was all she said. And that's what I've done, though for the life of me I can't imagine why it was necessary. Damage never worried her before.'

'She said "the cat" and not Marmaduke?' The woman nodded. 'And you were outside on the doorstep?'

'That's right. She wouldn't come in.'

He pictured the little porch under the basement steps and realized then what had happened. Someone had been down there, listening, he thought. He tapped his pencil against his teeth. For Leo, read lion, read cat. 'Leo is imprisoned. Please be careful. I don't want any more damage done.' *Jesus!* What despair Meg must have felt, knowing her only chance resided in this irritatingly stupid woman. But if he were honest, would anyone have understood so cryptic a message?

'OK.' He turned back to Mr Helms. 'What did they do on the Saturday and Sunday? Do you know? Did you notice anyone coming to the door?'

His mouth worked. 'Her friend came,' he blurted. 'The tall one. Saturday night.' He raised a weak hand and dropped it on to his thigh. 'Banged on the door. Said: "You must be mad. What the hell are you doing?"'

'Was it a woman?'

'Yes.'

'Jinx Kingsley?'

'Tall, dark. Drives a Rover Cabriolet. JIN 1X.'

'When did she leave?'

But Mr Helms shook his head. 'Anthea likes television. I'm not allowed to sit here all the time.'

'I should think not,' said his wife sharply. 'The neighbours would get quite the wrong idea if you did. They'd say I was neglecting you.'

Fraser flicked the man a sympathetic glance. 'Not to worry,' he said. 'Did you happen to notice any other visitors?'

But Mr Helms had told him all he could.

'We're on our way now,' said Detective Superintendent Cheever on a mobile link to his colleague in the Wiltshire police. 'It looks as if he's heading for the Nightingale. Got that. You'll send back-up to the clinic? Agreed. We'll only talk to him about the murders after you've charged him on the assaults. No, Adam Kingsley's on hold at the moment. I'm more interested in hearing what Miles has to say.'

Nightingale Clinic, Salisbury, Wiltshire – 2.30 p.m.

Miles stormed through Jinx's open french windows and flung himself into the vacant armchair with the sullen expression of a thwarted five-year-old. 'I suppose you've heard what he's done?'

'You mean his resignation?'

'Of course I mean his resignation,' he said in a mimicking falsetto. 'What the hell else would I mean?' He drummed his feet on the ground. 'God, I'm so angry. I don't know which of you I'd rather strangle at the moment. You realize you've buggered everything between you?'

'No,' she said calmly, lighting a cigarette. 'I can't say I do realize that. What exactly is buggered, Miles?'

'FOR CHRIST'S SAKE!' he yelled, his eyes narrowing to unattractive slits. 'We've lost everything, the house, everything.'

She gazed at him through the drifting smoke. 'Who's we?' she murmured. '*I* haven't lost anything. The shares have risen ten points since Adam resigned, which means I've already made a tidy paper profit on my morning's investment alone. I hope you're not going to tell me you sold your shares, Miles. When Adam gave them to us, he said: Sell everything else but don't sell these. You should have had more faith in him.'

'I had to,' he said through gritted teeth. 'Fergus, too. We borrowed money on the back of the damn things and the bastard we were in hock to made us sell out to cover the debts.'

She shrugged. 'More fool you.'

He was as tightly strung as a new bow. 'Oh, Jesus, if you knew how much I hated you – it's all your fault this has happened . . .' His voice carried a tremor of despair.

She arched a sardonic eyebrow. 'How do you make that out?'

'Russell – Leo – they were both shits.'

'What's that got to do with anything?'

'If you'd picked someone halfway decent, we wouldn't be in this mess.'

She watched his knuckles turn white as he gripped the

arms of the chair. *After all, what did she really know about this brother of hers?* 'You were only sixteen when Russell was murdered,' she said slowly. 'Betty swore you and Fergus were at the Hall all day.'

He stared at her with hot, angry eyes. 'What the hell are you talking about?'

'I thought – never mind.'

'You thought I did it?' he sneered. 'Well, sometimes I wish I had. The old man would have bent over backwards for me after that. I'd have done it for free, too, because I'd have enjoyed doing it. I loathed Russell. He was almost as arrogant and patronizing as you are.' He surged out of his chair in one violent movement and trapped her in hers by leaning over and gripping the arms. 'It cost Dad a packet to get rid of him, you silly bitch, and another packet to do for Leo and Meg. And now Fergus and I are in the shit because of it. The police are parked all round the Hall, just waiting to arrest him, and the minute they do, Mum, me and Fergus will be out in the sodding street. We're wiped out – don't you understand? Mum, too – she sold her shares months ago. There's nothing left.'

'You've still got your jobs,' she said, gazing steadily up at him so that he wouldn't guess how frightened she was.

He threw himself petulantly back into his chair, his anger spent. 'God, you're so naïve,' he said. 'John Normans won't keep us on. We're only there because of Dad. *You* know that. Everybody knows it. Christ, it's not as though either of us is even needed. All I have to do is make sure the site security contracts are kept up to date.

Any moron could do it.' He banged his fist against the chair arm. 'I get a moron's salary because of it. Do you know what I do? I engage the night watchman and put my signature to the standardized contract that comes off the sodding word processor.'

'Then why aren't you doing it now?' she asked him. 'Surely this is the time to prove that you're worth keeping.'

His anger flared again. 'You stupid, patronizing BITCH!' he screamed. 'IT'S OVER! Dad's made sure you're OK, because you're his fucking darling, but he's dropped all the rest of us in it. Can't you get that into your thick skull?'

She blew a stream of smoke towards the ceiling and watched the patterns it made in the draught from the open windows. 'How do you know Adam had Russell killed?' she asked quietly.

'Who else could have done it?'

'Me,' she suggested.

Miles looked amused. 'Little Miss Perfect. Come off it, Jinxy, you haven't got the guts.'

'And you think Adam has?'

He shrugged. 'I *know* he has.'

'How?'

'Because he's bloody vicious, that's how. Look at the way he treats me and Fergus.'

She formed her lips into an approximation of a smile. 'I want proof, Miles, not impressions. Can you *prove* Adam had Russell killed?'

'I can prove he *wanted* him killed. He said afterwards that Russell had got what was coming to him. Your precious husband was shafting your best friend. Dad hated him for it.'

'What did he say when he heard about Leo and Meg?' Even to Jinx her voice sounded strangely remote.

Miles shrugged again. 'That he hoped your memory loss was permanent, then he shut himself in his office and called his solicitor. He's paranoid about you starting to remember things, so we reckon you saw something you shouldn't have done.'

She stared at the opposite wall. 'You said it cost him a packet. How much exactly?'

'A lot.'

'How much, Miles?'

'I don't *know*,' he said sulkily. 'All I know is it comes damned expensive.'

She shifted her gaze lazily to look at him. 'You don't know anything, do you? You're talking about what you *wish* Adam had done, not what he actually did. I suppose it makes you feel better to think of your father as a murderer.' She laughed suddenly. 'You know, I really feel quite sorry for you. Presumably you've spent the last ten years justifying all your shabby little deceits against Adam's guilt, so how the hell are you going to cope when it turns out he's whiter than white?' A movement at the windows caught her eye and, as she looked enquiringly towards the two uniformed policemen blocking the light, there was a peremptory knock on the door behind her. She frowned as WPC Blake walked in uninvited. 'Can I help you?' Jinx said politely, looking beyond her to Superintendent Cheever, Maddocks and Alan Protheroe, who were standing in the open doorway.

Blake glanced at her briefly before transferring her attention to the brother. 'Miles Kingsley?' she asked.

He nodded.

She proffered her warrant card. 'WPC Blake, Wiltshire police. Miles Kingsley, I have reason to believe you can assist us in our enquiries into the grievous bodily harm and indecent assault of Mrs Flossie Hale on the evening of the twenty-second of June last, at number fifty-three, Lansing Road, Salisbury—'

'What the hell are you talking about?' he broke in angrily. 'Who the fuck's Mrs Flossie Hale? I've never even heard of the bitch.'

Chapter Twenty

LITTLE LORD FAUNTLEROY, thought Blake, was a good description of Miles Kingsley, with his clean-cut face and his wide-spaced blue eyes. They weren't the sort of looks that attracted her – she preferred her men rougher and tougher – but she could imagine Flossie finding them appealing. 'She's a prostitute, Mr Kingsley. She was brutally attacked on the evening of the twenty-second. She has identified you as her assailant, as has Mrs Samantha Garrison, another prostitute, who suffered a similar assault on March the twenty-third.'

He frowned angrily. 'They're lying. I've never been to a prostitute in my life.' He rounded on Jinx. 'What the hell's going on? Is this something Dad's set up?'

'Don't be an oaf,' she snapped. She looked at the policewoman. 'How could they identify him? Did the assailant give a name?'

Blake ignored her. 'I think it would be better if we discussed the whole matter at the police station. Mr Kingsley, I am requesting you to accompany me—'

'Look, you sour-faced cow,' said Miles, surging aggressively to his feet, 'I don't know what your game is—'

'Sit down, Miles,' hissed Jinx through gritted teeth, grabbing his arm and forcing him into his chair again, 'and keep your mouth shut.' She took a deep breath. 'You say you have reason to believe my brother can assist you, so please will you explain what those reasons are. In particular, how both women came to identify their attacker as my brother.'

Blake frowned. 'I'm not obliged to explain anything, other than to say we have a positive identification of the man two women say attacked them. We would like him to answer some questions on the matter and to that end we are asking him to accompany us to the police station. Do you have a problem with that, Miss Kingsley, bearing in mind the assaults were serious enough to put both women in hospital?'

'Yes,' she said curtly, 'I think Miles should refuse to go with you. You obviously have nothing more concrete than this inexplicable identification or you'd have come with an arrest warrant.' She glanced at Maddocks. 'My guess is, you're trying to pick us off one by one to answer questions on Meg and Leo's murders. I'm even doubtful if these prostitutes exist.'

Miles sneered. 'That's the stuff, Jinxy. Give 'em hell.'

The young policewoman eyed him curiously for a moment then addressed herself to his sister. 'I'm Wiltshire police, Miss Kingsley, and I've spent the last week investigating the attack on Flossie Hale. She's forty-six years old. She sustained severe injuries to her head, face and arms and, but for her own courage in getting herself to hospital, would have died in her bed. She has identified your brother as the man who injured her. I will admit that the publicity surrounding the death of your fiancé and your best friend led indirectly to her identification of him, but that's as far as the connection goes. I am not interested in you or your relationship with the Hampshire police. I am merely interested in preventing any more women suffering as Flossie did.'

'OK,' said Miles cockily, leaning back in his chair and stretching his legs in front of him, 'then arrest me. You won't get me any other way. Have you any idea what sort of fuss my father's likely to kick up about this? Sacking will be the least of your worries once his solicitor gets on to it.'

Jinx pressed fingers to her throbbing head. 'Shut up, Miles.'

'No, I bloody well won't,' he snapped, whipping round to look at her. 'You bug me, Jinx, you really do. You can say anything you like because you're so fucking clever, but not stupid Miles. He's got to sit here with his mouth shut.' He slammed his fist into his palm. 'Jesus, I wasn't even in Salisbury on the twenty-second and I can prove it.'

'You visited your sister here at nine o'clock last Wednesday night, Mr Kingsley,' said Maddocks bluntly. 'Last Wednesday being the twenty-second of June, and the Nightingale Clinic being in Salisbury. Both your sister and the staff on duty will testify to that. Mrs Hale was attacked at eight-fifteen, which would have given you plenty of time to sort yourself out before you presented yourself here.'

His face took on a pinched look. 'OK, so I forgot. It's no big deal. I drove straight here from Fordingbridge.

My mother and brother will swear I was at Hellingdon Hall till eight-thirty.'

Blake looked at Jinx. 'Is that what he told you when he got here?'

She didn't answer.

Miles darted her a frightened glance. 'Tell them I told you.'

'How can I? I don't remember you saying it.'

'The nurse said it when she brought me in. Here's your brother from Fordingbridge. You must remember that.'

'I don't.' She could only remember him saying he'd been gambling that night. *But had he?*

'Oh shit, Jinxy,' he begged, 'you've got to help me. I swear to God I never hurt anyone.' He reached out a hand and clutched at her arm. 'Please, Jinx, help me.'

Meg is a whore . . . please . . . please . . . please . . . help me, Jinx . . . such fear . . . oh God, such terrible fear . . .

'I'll talk to Adam and ask him to send Kennedy out,' she said shakily. 'Just don't say anything else till he gets there. Can you do that, Miles?'

He nodded and stood up. 'As long as you don't let me down.'

Blake put a firm hand on his arm and steered him towards the windows. 'This way, Mr Kingsley. We've a car waiting outside.'

'What about my Porsche?'

She held out her hand. 'If you'll give me your keys, I'll have one of these officers drive it for you.' She nodded towards the two Salisbury policemen. 'He can follow along behind us.'

Miles fished them out of his pocket and thrust them into her palm with bad grace. She looked at the fob – a black disc with gold lettering – then led him away.

With shaking hands, Jinx reached for her cigarette packet off the arm of her chair, then retreated to the dressing table and its firm, supportive edge. She looked briefly towards Alan Protheroe, who was leaning against the wall by the door, then turned her attention to Frank Cheever. 'I recognize you from the television,' she told him, lighting a cigarette with difficulty. 'You gave a press conference the other day, but I'm afraid I can't remember your name.'

'Detective Superintendent Cheever,' he told her.

She glanced at Maddocks. 'Then you're here to talk about Leo and Meg?'

Frank nodded.

'And you think Miles might have done it because of what happened to these wretched women?'

'It's a possibility.'

She nodded. 'In your shoes, I'd probably say the same.'

'And if the roles were reversed and *I* were in your shoes, what would I say then?'

She stared at him rather strangely for a moment. 'I think you'd be too busy stifling the screams inside your head to say anything at all.'

Frank watched her. 'Are you well enough to talk to us, Miss Kingsley?'

'Yes.'

'You don't have to,' said Alan sharply. 'I'm sure the Superintendent will give you time to recover.'

That amused her. 'They kept telling me that when Russell died. It meant I could have ten minutes to compose myself before they started in again.' She took a pull on her cigarette. 'The trouble is, you never recover from something like that, so ten minutes is just time wasted and, as I need to phone my father, I'd rather get this over and done with as quickly as possible.'

'Please,' said Frank, gesturing towards the telephone. 'We'll go outside while you do it.'

She shook her head. 'I'd rather wait till you've gone.'

'Why?' asked Maddocks. 'The sooner your brother has a solicitor with him the better, wouldn't you say?'

'Oddly enough, Inspector, I'd like to work out what I'm going to say first. My father will be devastated to hear his son's been accused of a brutal sex attack. Wouldn't yours? Or is that something he's come to expect from you?' She turned abruptly to the Superintendent again. 'Miles didn't kill Russell, so if the same person went on to kill Leo and Meg, then it wasn't Miles.'

'Do you mind if we sit down?' he asked.

'Be my guest.'

The two policemen moved across to the chairs, but Alan remained where he was. 'Why are you so sure he didn't kill Russell?'

She thought deeply for several seconds before she answered, and then she did so elliptically. 'It's rather ironic, really, considering I've just told him to keep quiet until he has a solicitor present. You see, I'm not convinced solicitors always give good advice. I consulted one after Russell was murdered,' she told them, 'because it became clear to me that I was at the top of the list of suspects. He persuaded me to be very circumspect in how I answered police questions. Do not volunteer information, keep all your answers to the minimum, avoid speculation, and tell them only what you know to be true.' She sighed. 'But I think now I'd have done better to say everything that was in my mind because all I achieved was to raise the level of suspicion against my father.' She fell silent.

'That's hardly an answer to my question, Miss Kingsley.'

She stared at the floor, taking quick, nervous drags at the cigarette. 'We were talking about Russell's death before you came in,' she said suddenly. 'Miles told me he's always believed my father was responsible, which means he and Fergus could indulge in petty deceit after petty deceit without a second thought. Nicking twenty quid off the gardener or forging their mother's cheques counts for nothing against the enormity of murder.' She looked up. 'But what Miles believes – indeed what anyone believes – is confined by his own prejudices, and in this instance it is very important that you understand how desperate my brother has always been to feel superior to his father.'

'Does he have proof of your father's complicity in your husband's murder?'

'No, of course he doesn't, because Adam wasn't involved.'

'But presumably you can't prove that any more than

your brother can prove he was.' He smiled without hostility. 'Truth is a disturbingly elusive phenomenon. All I, as a policeman, can do is accumulate the available facts and weigh them in the balance. In the end, I hope, truth carries weight.'

'Then why do so many policemen only hear what they want to hear?'

'Because we're human and, as you said yourself, belief is confined by prejudice.' He gestured towards Maddocks. 'But I think we're both professional enough to stay objective about what you tell us, so I hope that gives you the confidence to speak out.'

She drew on her cigarette and gazed steadily at Maddocks. 'Would you agree with that, Inspector?'

'Certainly,' he said, 'but you're asking for miracles if you expect us to take everything you say on trust. For example, explain this to me. How come you never resorted to petty theft as a way of getting back at your father? Surely I'm right in thinking you, too, have always believed he was guilty of Landy's murder? What was *your* revenge, Miss Kingsley?'

'Rather too subtle for you to understand,' she said curtly before returning to her previous point. 'If you're willing to be objective, then why were you so dismissive of everything I told you yesterday?'

His smile didn't reach his eyes. 'I don't recall being dismissive. I do recall challenging some of the statements you made. But then you're a suspect in this case, too,' he pointed out, 'which means that anything you say will be subject to scrutiny. Is that unreasonable, do you think?'

'No, but I'd be interested to know if you've pursued

any of the suggestions I made to you. For example, have you looked for another link between the three murders? Have you examined the possibility that someone was trying to kill me on the day of my accident?'

'These things take time,' he said. 'We can't work miracles, Miss Kingsley.'

'But are you even *trying*, Inspector?' She turned to Cheever. 'Is anyone?'

The Superintendent, who was ignorant of both suggestions because they had not been relayed to him, answered honestly. 'Not to my knowledge, no, but if you can persuade me they are worth pursuing, then I shall certainly do so. Why do you think someone was trying to kill you?'

She glanced towards Protheroe, seeking support, but he was staring at the floor. 'Because of a series of negatives,' she said flatly. 'I'm not the type to kill myself. I didn't want to marry Leo. I never get drunk. I didn't kill Russell, so can't imagine I'd have killed Leo or Meg either. And the car crash clearly wasn't an accident. I can't think of another explanation for what happened to me bar attempted murder. And I keep thinking, what if I *had* died? Would you have looked for anyone else in connection with Leo and Meg's deaths? Wouldn't you all just have said to yourselves: That explains everything, she must have killed Russell as well?'

'Do you remember anything at all about the crash, Miss Kingsley?'

She looked away. 'No,' she said, her face devoid of expression.

He studied her for a moment, unsure if he believed

421

her. 'Well, I'm quite happy to go through all the documents relating to it to see if there's anything we've missed, but I should warn you I'm not very optimistic. Even if you're right, I don't see how we'll ever be able to prove it.'

'I realize that, but the important thing is that you don't dismiss it as a possibility. You must see what a different light it sheds on the whole thing? I keep coming back and back to it in my mind. If someone tried to kill me, then that means *I'* – she pressed her hands to her chest – 'must know who murdered Leo and Meg, even though I can't remember it. And it also means that *that* someone is the missing link, because whoever the person is probably murdered all three.' She regarded him anxiously. 'Do you follow?'

'Oh, yes,' he said, 'I follow very well. It's an interesting hypothesis, but it doesn't help us very much unless you can suggest a name.'

And if I suggest a name, what then? Do you have any proof, Miss Kingsley? 'What good is a name if I can't give you any evidence?'

The Superintendent shrugged. 'It would give us a starting point.'

But she was only interested in the endgame and she doubted whether the police could ever deliver a result. *Truth is a disturbingly elusive phenomenon . . . presumably you can't prove that . . . policemen accumulate the available facts and weigh them in the balance . . . what was your revenge, Miss Kingsley?*

'Yesterday,' Maddocks reminded her, 'you argued that it was Meg who linked the three murders.'

'And I still believe that's right,' she said, turning back from long corridors that led nowhere. 'Look, I spent all last night thinking about it.' She drew on her cigarette before stubbing it out in the ashtray. 'I haven't been sleeping too well,' she explained. 'I don't blame you for seeing my relationship with Russell and Leo as the focus for what's happened, but Meg's relationship with them was just as strong. Last night, I kept coming back to the thinking at the time of Russell's murder, which was that my father killed him because he didn't like him. I remember one of the policemen saying to me: Whoever killed him hated him because it was done with such rage. And that set me wondering if the rage was jealous rage.' She gave her troubled smile. 'But not jealousy over me,' she said. 'Jealousy over Meg.'

There was a short silence.

'We've read her diaries,' said Frank Cheever. 'At a rough estimate, she slept with fifty different men in the last ten years. Even by today's standards, she would be described as promiscuous.'

'Only because she had a very hedonistic view of sex. Why say no, if you both want to do it? In some ways she had a very masculine approach to life. She could love them and leave them and never turn a hair while she did it.'

'But surely you must see the flaw in your argument? If someone was so jealous that they were prepared to kill her lovers, then we should have fifty corpses on our hands instead of two.'

It was Alan Protheroe who answered. He had stood with bowed head, listening intently to Jinx's reasoning, but now he looked up. 'Because Russell and Leo were the only two lovers she really cared for,' he pointed out. 'By the sound of it, the rest meant nothing at all. Jinx told me the letters Meg wrote to Russell were very moving, and the newspapers talk about an eleven-year relationship between her and Leo. If someone else was in love with her, then it's those two men who represented the threat, not the fifty or so others who came and went as regularly as clockwork.'

'Why kill Meg as well?'

'For the same reason jealous husbands kill their wives when they find them *in flagrante delicto* with other men. On the face of it, it's illogical. If you love a woman enough to be jealous, then how can you summon the hate required to kill her? But emotions are never logical.'

'Then why wasn't she killed when Russell was killed? Why only kill her over Leo?'

Alan shrugged. 'For any one of twenty reasons, I should think. A desire to give her a second chance. A belief that Russell was a sort of Svengali who'd influenced her against her will. Simple logistics – she wasn't with him the day of the murder. Myself, I'd probably pick the Svengali option because that would explain why she had to die this time. If she'd known Leo for eleven years then it must have been clear to anyone who knew them both that she was an equal party to all decisions made. You need to find out who else knew about the affair with Russell. Isn't that the key?'

DI Maddocks cleared his throat. 'I could almost buy this theory if it wasn't for one small snag. Like Superintendent Cheever says, we've read her diaries, or what there is of them, and nowhere is there a mention of another man who lasted longer than three or four months. So who is this mysterious lover? You knew her better than anyone else, Miss Kingsley. Do you know who it is?'

'No,' she said, 'I don't.'

Maddocks was watching her carefully. 'So give us a handful of likely candidates, and leave us to ferret out what we can.'

'Ask Josh,' she said, evading the question. 'He knew her men friends far better than I did.'

'We'll do that. Did he also know her women friends better?'

'Probably.'

'Did she have many?'

Jinx frowned, unsure where he was leading. 'A few close ones, like me.'

'That's what I thought.'

She flicked him a puzzled glance. 'Why is it important?'

He quoted her own words back at her. '"Why say no if you both want to do it? Meg had a masculine approach to life."' He held her gaze. 'I wonder if this jealous lover was a woman, Miss Kingsley?'

Canning Road Police Station, Salisbury – 3.30 p.m.

Blake showed Miles into an interview room. 'You can wait here till the solicitor comes, although I may have to move you if the room's needed by someone else.'

'How long are you planning to keep me here?'

'As long as it takes. First we wait for the solicitor, then we ask you questions. It could be several hours.'

'I don't have several hours,' he muttered, glancing at his watch. 'I need to be out of here by five at the latest.'

'Are you saying you don't want to wait for the solicitor, Mr Kingsley?'

He thought rapidly. 'Yes, that's what I'm saying. Let's get on with it.'

Nightingale Clinic, Salisbury – 3.30 p.m.

'Which way?' asked Maddocks as he turned out of the clinic gates. 'Salisbury CID or back to Winchester?'

'Stoney Bassett airfield,' grunted the Superintendent. 'Young Blake will keep Miles on ice till we get there. Let's face it, he's not going anywhere in a hurry.'

Hellingdon Hall, Fordingbridge, Hampshire – 3.30 p.m.

Betty put down the extension in her bedroom and dragged herself to her dressing-table stool, pools of sweat gathering under her arms and drenching her corset at the back. She thrust her fat face at the mirror and desperately applied powder in an attempt to repair the ravages of time and her husband's neglect. She listened for his footsteps on the stairs, knowing that it was over. This time there would be no reprieve for her or the boys. As usual, she turned her resentment on the first Mrs Kingsley, whose ghost had defied every attempt she had ever made to lay it. It wasn't fair, she told herself. All right, so no one had ever promised her a rose garden, but no one had warned her that marriage to Adam would be a bed of thorns either. 'Hello, Daddy,' she said with desperate gaiety, as the door was flung open, 'it's been a bugger of a day one way and another, hasn't it?'

Stoney Bassett Airfield, New Forest, Hampshire – 4.15 p.m.

They stood on the bleak, heather-strewn plain where broken Tarmac runways, covered in weeds, were all that remained of the wartime airfield. 'What are we looking for?' asked Maddocks, careful to keep his tone neutral. He could happily have kicked his boss from here to eternity. Like Fraser yesterday, a few clever words and a troubled smile had made him doubt the girl's guilt and, for the life of him, Maddocks couldn't see how she did it.

Frank pointed to the concrete stanchion which reared up like a single broken tooth some yards from where they were standing. 'We'll start there,' he said. 'Presumably, that's what she drove at. How wide would you say it was?'

'Nine feet square,' guessed Maddocks.

'Interesting, don't you think?' murmured Frank.

'Why?'

'I thought it was much narrower. You've seen the

photographs. The car appeared to be wrapped around it like a metal fist.' He cocked his head from side to side, studying different angles. 'It must have impacted on one of the corners and the arc lights threw everything else into shadow.' He moved forward to prowl around the structure.

'What difference does its size make?' asked Maddocks, following him.

The Superintendent squatted down to examine an area of gouged and heavily scarred concrete on both faces of one corner. 'If you were driving at a nine-foot-wide wall with the intention of smashing into it, wouldn't you head straight for the middle? Why aim for one end?'

There was shattered glass from the windscreen still littering the ground, and intermittent tyre traces to a point fifty metres back where the car had obviously been sitting until, at maximum revs, she had released the brake to hurl it and herself at the concrete structure. Frank spent ten minutes walking back and forth across a broad expanse of area around the stanchion, then he returned to stand and gaze at the burnt rubber marks where the tyres had spun before biting into the Tarmac. He crouched down and followed the line the car had taken. 'She was absolutely square to the middle of that wall when she set off,' he said, 'so how come she ended up wrapped around the right-hand corner?'

'Hit a pot-hole and lost control?' suggested Maddocks.

'Except there isn't anything big enough, not on this stretch. That's what I was checking for. She could have driven at any of the three sides that face on to the Tarmac but she chose the one with the best approach. If she was intent on killing herself, then there was nothing to stop her driving in a dead straight line.'

'She changed her mind at the last minute,' said Maddocks. 'Didn't fancy it so much when she saw the wall rushing towards her and tried to pull out of it.'

'Yes, that's a possibility.' He turned with his back to the wall and surveyed the area that would have been behind the car. 'Why didn't she start further off and use the greater distance to build up her speed? Why sit here and rev up the engine?'

'Because it was dark and she needed to see the wall.'

'It was ten o'clock on one of the longest days in the year. She could have seen that thing two, three hundred yards away.'

'All right, then, she parked herself here, sat staring at the wall while she drank herself stupid, then suddenly made up her mind to do it. Look, sir, I know what you're getting at. You're saying that attempted murder isn't out of the question. Someone got her drunk – though I have to say that's a mystery in itself – picked the best piece of ground for the car to stay in a straight line, made it near enough to the stanchion to preclude too much divergence from the track, stuck her unconscious in the driving seat, put the car into *Drive*, wedged the accelerator flat down with one of the empty bottles, and released the brake. At which point, brave Miss Kingsley comes out of her drunken stupor, sees what's happening, tries to steer clear, realizes she can't make it so throws herself out of the open door.' He gave a sour smile. 'Apart from the fact that you'd do yourself a hell of a lot of damage, leaning in to release the handbrake of a car on full throttle, why on earth didn't he finish her off when she threw herself out?'

'You wouldn't use the handbrake,' said Frank, 'you'd use the foot brake with some sort of brace – a piece of two by four, maybe – a sledgehammer, even' – he lifted a teasing eyebrow – 'between the metal frame of the seat and the pedal, with a rope attached. Then you'd wedge your throttle and use the rope to yank the brace away. The other alternative would be to chock the tyres and not use the brakes at all.' He gestured towards the ground. 'But I think it'd be obvious if chocks had been used.'

'And the fact that he didn't bother to finish her off?' muttered Maddocks sarcastically.

'Perhaps he thought he had,' said the Superintendent mildly, 'or perhaps he didn't have time to check.' He was silent for a moment. 'Would you care to explain to me why this little exercise is making you so angry?'

'Because she's guilty as hell, sir. The whole thing was a set-up to get her old man's sympathy. I can't see it makes a blind bit of difference which approach she chose, how far away she was when she started, whether chocks were used, or when she was found. She was in control of the car from the moment she set off.'

Frank scuffed his foot over the broken surface of the Tarmac. 'She could have torn the skin off her face throwing herself out of a speeding car on to this. Why not choose something less painful?'

'Because she likes drama,' said Maddocks dismissively. 'Anyway, she didn't tear the skin off her face. She's not going to be permanently disfigured once her hair grows and the bruises fade. All things considered, she came off very lightly. Too lightly for attempted murder or genuine suicide, wouldn't you say?'

Canning Road Police Station, Salisbury – 4.45 p.m.

'Look,' said Miles angrily to the two police officers sitting opposite him, 'how many times do I have to tell you? I've never been to a prostitute in my life. Why would I need to? Jesus, I had my first lay when I was fifteen.' He banged his fist on the table. 'I don't know any Flossie Hale and I don't know any Samantha Garrison, and if I wanted to shaft a forty-six-year-old – which I bloody well don't – I could shaft Dad's housekeeper for free. She'd probably pay me if I asked her. She's had the hots for me for years.'

'You have a very high opinion of yourself, Miles,' said the Sergeant.

'Why shouldn't I?'

'No reason, except that men who talk big tend to be better in theory than they are in practice.'

'What do you expect me to do? Burst into tears and say I'm so fucking inadequate I need to pay some old slag to give me a good time? Do me a favour.'

'Is that what you'd do if you felt you were inadequate?' asked Blake.

Miles shrugged and lit a cigarette.

She turned to the tape-recorder on the table. 'Mr Kingsley's response was a shrug.'

'Like hell it was,' said Miles furiously. 'Mr Kingsley's response is, I'm not fucking inadequate so I wouldn't fucking well know what I'd fucking do if I was.' He yelled into the microphone. 'Have you fucking well got that?'

'Calm down, Miles,' said the Sergeant wearily. 'You'll break the machine if you keep shouting at it. Why don't you just tell us where you were and what you were doing on the night of the twenty-second?'

'You've asked me that same sodding question a hundred times and I've given the same sodding answer a hundred times. I was at home till eight-thirty, when I left to visit Jinx.'

'And we don't believe you. Tell me, will the randy housekeeper lie for you, the way you claim your mother and brother will?'

'I never said they'd be lying.' He looked at his watch. 'Oh God! Look, I've got to get out of here. Are you going to charge me or not? Because if you're not, then I want out.'

'Why? What's happening at five o'clock that's so important?'

'I owe money, you moron,' said Miles through gritted teeth, 'and I need to buy a bit more time. That's what's happening at five o'clock. Why the hell do you think I went to see Jinxy? OK, so we shout at each other a bit but she's always come through in the past.'

There was a tap on the door and a second WPC looked in. 'I've got a Mr Kennedy out here, Sarge. He says Mr Kingsley's his client.'

'Show him in. Tape stopped at four fifty-one p.m.'

Kennedy looked at Miles with dislike, refused the chair that was offered him and, instead, placed two photographs on the table. The first showed Miles entering a hotel foyer, the second showed him getting into his Porsche. 'My client's sister informs me that you are enquiring into an assault on a prostitute in Lansing Road, Salisbury, at around eight o'clock on Wednesday, June the twenty-second. Is that correct?'

'Yes,' agreed Blake.

Kennedy tapped the photographs, indicating the printed times and date in the bottom right-hand corners. 'My client, Miles Kingsley, entered the Regal Hotel, Salisbury, at five-thirty p.m. on Wednesday, June the twenty-second. He returned to his car at eight forty-five p.m. that same evening and drove to the Nightingale Clinic to visit his sister. While at the Regal he spent three and a quarter hours in room number four-three-one, leaving it only once to meet a man in the lobby.' He placed another photograph on the table, of Miles, head down, talking to someone whose back was to the camera. 'That was at seven o'clock. He remained with this man for three minutes before visiting the gentlemen's lavatory in the lobby. He returned to room four-three-one at seven-fifteen. He was followed, photographed and watched from midday until midnight on June the twenty-second by one Paul Deacon, who can be contacted on this number and at this address.' He placed a card beside the photographs. 'I trust this clears my client of any suspicion in connection with the assault in Lansing Road.'

Blake looked from the photographs to Miles's drained, white face. 'It would certainly seem to,' she agreed.

Kennedy smiled coldly at his client. 'Your father's outside, Miles. I suggest we don't make him wait any longer than we need to.'

Miles shrank into his seat. 'I'm not going,' he said. 'He'll kill me.'

'Your mother and Fergus are with him. I'm sure they'll both be very pleased to see you.' He gestured towards the door. 'Your father's most aggrieved by all of this, Miles, and he gets very angry when he's aggrieved, as you know. You wouldn't want your mother and brother to bear the brunt of his anger, would you?'

Miles looked terrified. 'No,' he said, lurching to his feet. 'It was my idea. Mum and Fergus were just trying to help. I thought, if we put the shares up as collateral, we could get out from under once and for all. So it's me he should blame, not them.'

Blake watched the young man pull the remnants of his courage together and thought he was braver than she'd given him credit for. But what the hell sort of man was Adam Kingsley to inspire such fear in his twenty-six-year-old son?

Chapter Twenty-one

Wednesday, 29 June, Nightingale Clinic,
Salisbury – 5.00 p.m.

DR PROTHEROE STOOD in Jinx's open doorway, watching her. She was speaking on the telephone, body rigid with tension, fingers clenching the receiver, shoulders unnaturally stiff. Her father, he guessed, for he doubted anyone else could elicit so much nervous energy. He remembered another woman standing in just this way, listening to a voice at the other end of the line. His wife, hearing her own death sentence. *I'm so sorry, Mrs Protheroe. How long? It's difficult to say. How long? Twelve months – eighteen, if we're lucky.*

Jinx watched him while she spoke. 'What's wrong?' she asked as she replaced the receiver.

He shook his head. 'Nothing. I was thinking of something else. Bad news?'

'No, good,' she said dispiritedly. 'They've let Miles go.'

'With or without charges?'

'Without.' She climbed on to her bed and sat cross-legged in the middle of it. 'Kennedy was able to prove he was somewhere else.'

'You don't seem very happy about it.'

'Adam was on his mobile. I could hear Betty crying in

435

the background. I think the sword has finally snapped its thread.'

'Are we talking about the sword of Damocles?'

She nodded. 'Adam's had it hanging over their heads for years. The trouble is . . .' She lapsed into one of her silences.

'They were too stupid to realize it,' he suggested.

She didn't say anything.

'So what was Miles really doing that night?'

She pressed her hands flat on the counterpane, then released them, apparently intrigued by the depressions they'd made. 'Cocaine,' she said suddenly. 'In between gambling his non-existent fortune away. He and Fergus are in hock up to their eyeballs.' She was silent for a moment, stroking and pummelling the bed. 'Adam paid off fifty thousand pounds on their gambling debts in March, and he said if they ever gambled again he'd throw them out and disinherit them. He's had them watched for the last four weeks.'

Alan took up her favourite position against the dressing table. 'Why?'

'Because Betty sold the last of her shares halfway through May and he guessed it was to cover their losses.'

'So why didn't he make good his threat then?'

She smiled rather grimly. 'I imagine he wanted to know who he'd be dealing with when the boys failed to pay up.'

'They're over twenty-one,' said Alan dispassionately. 'He's not responsible for their debts.'

'You're back in your ivory tower again,' she said, two spots of angry colour flaring in her cheeks. 'Do you honestly believe anyone would bother to take Adam Kingsley's sons to the cleaners if they didn't think they'd get their money? You've seen what Miles is like. Now imagine what he and Fergus will have said about Adam and Franchise Holdings while high on cocaine. There'll be a video somewhere full of damaging allegations.'

Alan folded his arms. 'He can't have a worse press than he's had in the last couple of days, so what does it matter what your brothers might have said?'

'It would have mattered four weeks ago,' she said through gritted teeth. 'Four weeks ago he was planning a society wedding and he couldn't afford any scandal, not if his precious Jinx was to have her day. Miles was right. It *is* my fault. If I'd had the sense to tell them I didn't want to go through with the bloody thing, well . . .' She fell silent again.

He watched her for a moment. 'As a matter of interest, why didn't he kick them out at twenty-one and tell them to fend for themselves?'

She didn't answer immediately. 'Because they'd have done this, anyway,' she said at last. 'If he'd turned them loose, he'd still be expected to pay their debts. I think he hoped that by keeping them close he could check their worst excesses.' She bent her head so that he couldn't see her expression. 'They've always wanted to throw his money in his face the way I do, but get-rich-quick schemes were all they could think of.'

Was that her subtle revenge, he wondered, pissing publicly on what her father valued most, his self-made wealth?

'He's making good his threat now,' she went on flatly.

'He's going to turn them off without a penny and divorce Betty.'

'Do you blame him?'

'No.'

'What will happen to them?'

'I don't know. I doubt he can leave Betty penniless because the courts won't allow it' – she pressed her forehead into her clasped hands – 'but I'm not sure about Miles and Fergus. He says he doesn't care any more.'

She was more upset than he would have expected. If she had any love for her stepmother and her two brothers, she had always hidden it well. 'There is a bright side,' he said after a moment. 'If your father's had them watched for the last four weeks, then one thing you can be sure of is that neither of them is guilty of the murder of Leo and Meg, or for that matter responsible for the attack on me.'

'I never thought they were,' she muttered at the bed.

'Didn't you?' he said, injecting surprise into his voice. 'They've always struck me as likely candidates. They're self-centred, not overly bright and very used to getting their own way, usually through you or their mother. I can imagine both seeing murder as a solution to a problem.'

'It never occurred to me,' she said stubbornly.

Of course it didn't, because you've always known who the murderer is. 'I wish you'd tell me why you don't trust me,' he said, in a carefully impassive voice. 'What have I ever said or done to make you feel you can't?'

She rested her chin on her hand and regarded him as

438

impassively. 'How do you know it wasn't me who attacked you?'

He took the sudden switch in his stride. 'It didn't look like you.'

'Matthew says it was dark, the person was dressed in black and the only description you could give was five feet ten and medium build.'

'How does Matthew know what I said?' asked Alan.

'Everyone knows.'

'Veronica Gordon,' he murmured. 'One of these days that woman's going to talk herself out of a job.' He watched her curiously for a moment. 'Look, there are plenty of compelling reasons why it couldn't have been you. You're too weak to wield a sledgehammer. You've no reason to want to attack me. You didn't know when I was coming back, and I'd ordered half-hourly checks to be made on you before I left. If you'd been out of your room, Amy or Veronica would have noticed.'

'Except that I *was* out of my room.'

He made no attempt to pretend surprise.

'After Sister Gordon did her nine o'clock rounds,' she went on, 'Amy took over. I was in bed with my light out the first time she came. The second time, I was in the bathroom in darkness, and she didn't bother to check whether the pillow I'd stuffed down the bed was me or not. After that, I got dressed and went outside. I was wearing black jeans and a black jumper. I'm five feet ten, and before the crash I weighed nine stone, so my clothes can easily take some padding.'

'Go on,' he said.

'I wanted to know why Adam had sent Kennedy over,

439

so I thought I'd waylay you. I waited under the beech tree until I was so tired I couldn't wait any longer, then I went back to bed and fell asleep with my clothes on. I was having a nightmare when Amy found me. I'm amazed she didn't report it. She was scared stiff I'd been doing something I shouldn't and might be held responsible.' She examined his face. 'Or perhaps she did report it and you haven't told me.'

He shook his head. 'No.'

'Then obviously she trusts me more than she trusts you, Dr Protheroe.'

He lifted an eyebrow. 'Is that what this was? A lesson in who's trustworthy and who isn't?'

'More or less,' she said, refusing to look at him. 'You already knew I was outside – Matthew heard you calling my name – but you've never mentioned it, not to me anyway.'

Damn Matthew to hell and back! He was going to shred the little toe-rag the first chance he got. 'Only because I realized I'd made a mistake. I thought I saw you at the side of the road as I drove in but, as it wasn't you who attacked me, I saw no point in mentioning it. Does that set your mind at rest?'

'No,' she said bluntly. 'You talk about trust as if it can be had for the asking. Well, it can't, not when you're up to your neck in it. All I know for certain is that my father's paying you to look after me, that for some reason he sent his solicitor over to talk to you on Monday afternoon, and that shortly afterwards you ordered half-hourly checks on me before disappearing.' A glint – *of humour?* – appeared in her eyes. 'Then, when you finally reappear, you're attacked with a sledgehammer and the police come down on me like a ton of bricks.'

Thoughtfully, he scratched his beard. 'You've run those facts into a related sequence when my interpretation is there's no relation between them at all.'

'Why did Kennedy come and see you then?'

'Assuming there were no hidden agendas at work, to remind me that I promised your father you wouldn't be subjected to therapy you didn't want. Kennedy taped our conversation and, as I haven't heard anything since, I've concluded that I said the right things in response and not the wrong things.'

'What did you say?' she shot at him.

'I suggested it was Adam and not you who didn't want you remembering anything.' He noted her alarmed expression. 'I also said he'd misread your character entirely and that he was worrying unnecessarily about any rehashing of Russell's murder because you didn't share his anxieties on the subject. Mind you, at that stage I was unaware that Meg and Leo were dead, or that you knew about it.' Her alarm deepened. 'If I had, I'd have been even more forceful in my remarks on his misreading of your character because I've never met anyone, man or woman, who is as self-reliant as you are.'

She plucked at the counterpane. 'It's something you learn very quickly when you find yourself on the wrong end of a murder inquiry,' she said. 'You never stop watching your back.'

'Yet you're so adept at getting everyone else to watch it for you,' he said mildly. 'Amy, for one; Matthew, for another.'

She smiled grudgingly. 'Poor Amy is watching her own back. She's terrified of getting the sack, but you can't use what I've told you as an excuse. You're my doctor and everything I've said was said in confidence.' She changed tack. 'According to Matthew, the police think the sledgehammer that was used to attack you belongs to the clinic. Is that right?'

'What a mine of information that young man is.'

She ignored that. 'Is he right?'

'Yes.'

'Is there any doubt about it?'

'I don't think so. One of our security officers went looking for it because he knew we had one. It was abandoned in an outhouse with paint from my Wolseley on the head.'

She sat in deep thought for several seconds. 'Could your security officer have been mistaken?' she asked suddenly. 'I mean, it seems such an odd thing to leave to chance. How could he rely on a sledgehammer being here?' She searched his face eagerly. 'He must have brought one with him. It doesn't make sense otherwise.'

He found himself moved by the terrible yearning in her amazing eyes. Were Matthew and Amy as easily moved? 'Meaning there's another sledgehammer out there somewhere?'

She nodded.

'OK. If it's there, I'll do my best to find it, but wouldn't it be easier just to tell me who *he* is?'

Her face took on a closed expression. 'Whoever hit you.'

He straightened with a sigh. 'No, Jinx, it was whoever

tried to kill me.' *You're not the only one watching your back at the moment.* 'Think about that.'

Matthew Cornell was lounging against the front porch, smoking a cigarette, when Alan went outside. Alan toyed with the idea of tearing his arms off, then abandoned it as a non-starter. All in all, he was growing increasingly fond of his ginger-haired convert.

'How's it going, Matthew?'

'Pretty good, Doc. How's the shoulder?'

'So-so.' He eased the muscles gently. 'Could have been a lot worse.'

'Yeah. You could be dead.'

Alan watched him out of the corner of his eye. 'Any ideas who might have done it? One theory is it was a junkie after drugs.'

'That's not the way I heard it.'

'Is it not?'

'There's only one person in the frame and it sure as hell isn't a junkie.'

'You mean Miss Kingsley.'

'She's the only one with sledgehammers in her background.' He ground his cigarette out under his heel.

'Except she doesn't fit the bill. It was a man I saw in my headlights.'

'You sure, Doc? You've got a loud voice and I was sitting by my window Monday night, having a quiet smoke. I didn't get the impression you thought it was a man.'

'And you told her all about it the next morning.'

Matthew grinned at him. 'Didn't seem fair not to. It's a mean old world, Doc, and how was I to know you weren't going to tell the police? I knew she was out there. She lit up her face every time she had a fag. I was watching her for about an hour before you came back and got clobbered. You should remember where my room is, upstairs on the corner, with windows facing both ways.'

'Are you saying you saw everything that happened?'

'Not everything. I watched Jinx for a while, then some time later I heard you calling and looked out the other window. I saw your car parked, then – wham! – your windscreen exploded and I saw a silhouette against your headlights as you roared backwards and piled into the tree.' He lit another cigarette. 'I thought, shit, what the fuck is going on and what the fuck do I do about it? And by the time I'd made up my mind, all hell was breaking loose. You were driving up to the front door, blaring your horn, and all the lights were coming on. So I reckoned I'd keep my head down and see what panned out.'

'Thanks very much,' said Alan tartly. 'I could have been dead by the time you came to a decision. You're required to act in good faith, you know, not stick your head in the nearest bucket.'

He grinned again. 'Yeah, well, I thought it was only your windscreen that'd been smashed, not your shoulder, and no one dies of a broken windscreen. You should have lights along the drive, then maybe I'd have seen a bit more.'

Alan glared at him. 'So all you saw was a silhouette,'

he growled, 'and you don't know any better than I do who it was.'

'That's about the size of it.'

'Are you planning to elaborate, or is that all I get?' he said curtly. 'It may have escaped your notice, but I suffered an unprovoked attempt on my life two nights ago and I'm not keen for a repeat experience.'

Matthew blew a stream of smoke into the air. 'It was hardly unprovoked, Doc. The way I remember it, you were threatening to stay there all night till Jinx showed herself. You're too convincing, that's your trouble. The bastard believed you.'

Alan had forgotten that. 'So what was he doing there?'

'Waiting.' He flicked him a sideways glance.

'What for?'

Matthew shrugged. 'For whatever he came here to do.' He saw thunder clouds gathering on the doctor's face. 'Look, Doc, I can guess, same as you can, but that's not to say either of us'd be right. Personally, I can't see that scarecrow in number twelve murdering anyone, therefore there's some maniac wandering around out there, trying to shove the blame on to her. Strikes me he'll be shitting bricks in case she spills the beans, so my guess is he was waiting to have another go at her.'

Alan considered this for a moment. 'That can't be right. You said she was out there for an hour and you saw her face every time she lit a cigarette. If you saw her, then he must have seen her, too, so why not finish her off then?'

Matthew looked down the drive towards where Alan had stopped his car on Monday night. 'Because he didn't expect to find her outside. She'd have screamed her head off if he'd crept up on her under the tree.'

'Not if he'd hit her from behind. She wouldn't have had time to scream. *I* didn't.'

'Jesus, Doc,' said Matthew severely, 'you don't have much imagination, do you? He wasn't going to make it look like murder, not after he went to so much trouble to fake suicide last time. He was going to trap her in her room, slit her wrists or string her up from the bathroom door, and you'd have had a suicide on your hands next morning, and the cops would have rubbed their hands and closed their files. My guess is, he's been waiting for days for an opportunity to slip inside and do the business, but he's up against it here. He probably didn't reckon on so many people being on the premises at night. You've got good security, Doc, but then you need to with the sort of fees you charge.' He grinned. 'There are too many rich bastards in here who'd do their nuts if intruders could walk in and out as they pleased.'

'Why did he have the sledgehammer if he didn't plan to hit her with it?'

Matthew shook his head in exasperation. 'You're no psychologist, are you? It's the tool of his trade, Doc, and the rule is, you carry the tools with you just in case. Look at the Yorkshire Ripper, he carried his hammer and chisel with him wherever he went. You should study a bit. This guy's an organized nutter, and your average organized nutter doesn't go out unprepared.'

'Except we're not talking about a serial killer.'

'You reckon? Three murders look like a series to me.'

'Come on, Matthew, there was ten years between

them, two of the victims were men and one was a woman, and all three victims were linked to Jinx Kingsley. That's not a typical pattern for serial killing.'

'Not yet maybe,' said Matthew, 'but I'd say his control's really slipping now, wouldn't you? There were nine years between Jeffrey Dahmer's first and second murders, then in the next four years he committed another fifteen. Will you still be saying this guy isn't a serial killer when the next poor sod gets bludgeoned to death?' He saw Alan's scepticism. 'Anyway, who's to say what he's been doing between then and now? I'll lay money on the fact that he's found some other way to work out his aggressions. You should talk to my Dad. He's represented creeps like this at trial. They're bloody clever and bloody manipulative, and I'll tell you this for free, if I were Jinx, I'd have amnesia too.'

'All she has to do is give his name.'

'Which means it'll be her word against his. Get real, Doc. She's number one suspect, so it stands to reason she's going to try and throw suspicion on someone else. That's the name of the game as far as the police are concerned. She needs proof, and my guess is, there is none. I'd say she's desperately buying time at the moment until she can remember something that will nail the bastard.'

'She couldn't be any worse off than she is now.'

Matthew flicked his butt on to the drive. 'You're forgetting she's been through this once with Russell. She already knows what happens when no one's convicted of a crime. The victim's nearest and dearest live with the guilt for ever and tear each other apart in the process.

Suspicion's an evil thing, Doc. I know. I've been there. My old man's accused me of some terrible things in the past, not because he knows I've done something, but because he's *afraid* I've done it.'

'So has she told you who it is?'

'There'd be no point. What could a junkie do? It's her father she needs to tell. He's the only guy with the clout to sort this bastard out once and for all.'

Alan frowned at him. 'You haven't suggested that to her, have you?'

'Jesus Christ! Do me a favour!'

'You have to act in good faith, Matthew, and that usually means acting within the law.'

Matthew grinned. 'I know what good faith is, Doc.'

But did he?

The Nightingale employed two gardeners, who were packing up for the evening and who both agreed there had been a sledgehammer in the tool sheds prior to the assault on the doctor. 'I used it myself a week or two back,' said one. 'When I was replacing the fencing posts near the bottom gate.'

'Do you remember where you put it when you'd finished?' asked Alan.

He nodded towards the younger man. 'Tom here took it back on the trailer, same as always.'

Alan turned to the lad. 'Do you remember which shed you put it in?'

There was a moment's silence. 'I didn't put it nowhere,' said Tom, shuffling feet that were too big for him. 'I borrowed it out to my dad to do some building work back home. There weren't no harm. We've only used it here once in six months, and Dad's looking after it like it were his own.'

Romsey Road Police Station, Winchester – 7.15 p.m.

Frank Cheever found the note from his secretary when he returned to his office later that evening, following a fruitless trip to Salisbury after his bird had already flown. 'We couldn't hold him,' said Blake. 'And, if you're interested, the solicitor gave us another photograph as he was leaving.' She handed it over. 'I think it was meant for you and not for us. He said to remind anyone who was interested that it takes a minimum of five hours to drive from here to Redcar, and another five hours to drive back again.'

The Superintendent looked at a picture of Miles and Fergus laying bets on a racecourse. The time was 3.10 p.m.; the date was June the thirteenth and the venue, according to a handwritten piece on the back, was Redcar in Cleveland. 'How did Adam Kingsley know Meg and Leo were murdered on the thirteenth?' he grunted suspiciously. 'We don't know for sure ourselves when they died.'

'Because the thirteenth was the day his daughter faked her suicide,' said Maddocks impatiently.

'Dr Protheroe phoned,' said the note. 'The sledge-hammer found at the Nightingale Clinic on Tuesday is not the one Harry Elphick saw before the assault. Dr

Protheroe has interviewed the gardeners and has established that the clinic's hammer has been on loan to a Mr G. Stack for the last two weeks and is still in his possession. Address: 43 Clonmore Avenue, Salisbury. He suggests this rules Miss Kingsley out of suspicion as far as the attack on himself is concerned and further suggests that you test the sledgehammer in your possession for Leo's and Meg's blood. If it proves positive, he believes this will absolve Miss Kingsley of their murders. There is no way (he asked me to underline 'no' twice!) she could have brought the murder weapon with her to the Nightingale as she was semi-conscious when she arrived by ambulance and has not left the premises since. (Dr Protheroe insisted on the following PS) Why am I expected to do DI Maddocks's work for him? I am tempted to say that, had the matter been left to the Salisbury police, the above facts would have been unearthed yesterday afternoon.'

Frank tossed the note to Maddocks. 'Well?' he demanded.

Maddocks read it with a frown. 'Not my fault, sir. I can only pursue one line of enquiry at a time.'

'Meaning what precisely?'

'Meaning that you never gave me the chance to follow up. The weapon was handed over to us yesterday afternoon, sir, and I've been chauffeuring you all today. Anyway, Bob Clarke's already given it a clean bill of health. There's no blood on it, only paint.'

'Well, it's a pity you didn't establish ownership yesterday afternoon,' said Frank sharply. 'It might have saved us today's wasted exercise.'

'Hardly, sir,' said Maddocks with careful emphasis,

'you'd have been even more inclined to pursue Miles Kingsley if you knew the hammer had come in from outside.' He looked at the note again. 'I'd like to know what set Dr Protheroe asking questions of the gardeners. He was listening when Elphick told me he'd seen the sledgehammer before and, believe me, it didn't occur to him any more than it did to me or Fraser that the old boy had got it wrong.' He put the paper on the desk. 'What's the betting the girl put him up to it after you and I left this afternoon?'

'What are you suggesting now? Some sort of conspiracy theory?'

'I'm just commenting on the way we're being dripfed information that seems to suit a certain party.'

Frank folded himself into his chair and reached for the telephone. 'Find out if DS Fraser's back and send him down to my office.' He leaned back to look at Maddocks. 'Go on,' he invited.

The DI shrugged. 'It's gut instinct. She's our murderer. You see, I've always wondered how I'd do it if I ever wanted to get rid of someone. The received wisdom is you keep it simple, engineer a reasonable alibi and deny everything, but she couldn't do that because of Russell's murder. The police were bound to draw parallels, and whatever method she used to do away with Leo and Meg, she would still be in the firing line.' He stroked his jaw. 'So she's done what I would have done. She's made herself the obvious suspect by tying Leo's and Meg's murders to Russell's ten years ago, and my guess is she's just waiting for the right moment to prove beyond a shadow of a doubt that the alibi Meg Harris

gave her then is rock solid. Which will leave us floundering because we've bust a gut to tie the three murders
together.'

'Are you saying she didn't murder Russell but did
murder Leo and Meg?'

Maddocks nodded. 'Yes. Look, you've read the Met
reports. Landy's murder was a contract killing, carried
out by one Jason Phelps on the instructions of Adam
Kingsley. There was never anyone else in the frame. All
this garbage about Adam not allowing Jane to find the
body comes from her, and, dammit, she's had a hell of a
long time to come up with excuses. She says herself that
her brothers have always believed her father was responsible, and that's pretty obvious, frankly, from the way
they behave. You don't grow up normal if you think
your father's a ruthless murderer. And look at the wife.
Drunk as a skunk by ten o'clock in the morning according to Fordingbridge. We're talking major family breakdown here, and the idea that the daughter's immune
from the madness is crazy.' He paused to collect his
thoughts, nodding briefly to Fraser as he entered the
room. 'I think she's telling us the truth about Russell. At
the time of his death, I think she knew nothing about his
affair with Meg. I also think she knew nothing about the
murder and was genuinely shocked by it. But I'd argue
that ten years of living with the knowledge that her father
ordered it and got away with it has left her as damaged
as she claims her two brothers to be.'

Nightingale Clinic, Salisbury – 7.15 p.m.

Sister Gordon was insistent. 'Doctor's orders, Jinx. He wants you moved to a room upstairs.'

'Why?'

'Good grief, girl,' she said irritably, 'do you question everything? How would I know? As usual, no one's bothered to tell me anything.'

Jinx glanced towards her french windows. 'I'd rather be in a room I can get out of if I have to.'

'Yes, well, perhaps that's what's worrying the doctor,' said Veronica tartly, who had been putting snippets from the rumour factory together with Alan's peculiar remark on Monday night and his sudden decision to move Jinx to a room upstairs. 'I expect he'll feel safer knowing you've only got one exit.'

Romsey Road Police Station, Winchester – 7.25 p.m.

'There's a chance she did know about Meg's affair with Russell at the time of the murder,' said Fraser slowly. 'According to Hennessey, she told him about it after she lost her baby but, if you remember, *her* story was that she found some love letters in her attic a year later.'

Maddocks put his hands on the Superintendent's desk and leaned forward belligerently. 'I'm sure that's not the only lie she's told us. I swear to God, sir, she's leading us all by the nose.'

'Why would Meg Harris give her an alibi?'

'Because she convinced her she was innocent. Dammit, she's all but convinced you and you hardly know her.'

'Five minutes ago you were arguing she didn't kill Russell.'

'Five minutes ago there was no evidence she knew about the affair, but you'll never get a better motive for murder than straightforward jealousy. Dammit, everything else I said stands. Even better if it was precious Jane who got away with Russell's murder, she could tie the other murders to it and say: "But the Met have proof I wasn't involved. They know it was my father."'

'There's still no evidence she knew about the affair *before* the event,' Fraser pointed out. 'If Hennessey's telling the truth, then we only have hearsay evidence that she knew about it at the time of her miscarriage, and that was two weeks *after* the murder.'

'Is there any reason to think he isn't telling the truth?' asked the Superintendent.

Fraser shook his head. 'No, but I wouldn't want to rely on him in a witness box. He's pretty hyped up at the moment, swings from anger against Meg for leaving him in the lurch, through anguish when he remembers she's dead, to a sort of sullen protection whenever Miss Kingsley's name is mentioned. I think he thinks Jane is responsible, but I also think he blames Meg for provoking her into it. My guess is he was fond of them both and doesn't know who to blame.'

Frank drew a doodle on a pad in front of him. 'How fond?'

'He's known them both a long time.' He consulted

his notebook. 'He was working with Meg at a company called Wellman and Hobbs when Jane was married to Russell.'

'I meant, was he sleeping with either of them?'

Nightingale Clinic, Salisbury – 7.30 p.m.

Fergus shouldered his way into Jinx's new room and stood aggressively over Matthew. 'I want to speak to my sister,' he said, jerking his head towards the door.

Matthew leaned forward to stub out his cigarette in the ashtray on the coffee table. 'I assumed the whole point of your being given another room was to stop aggressive visitors barging in,' he told her. 'I'll bet it was that old fool Elphick who told him where you are.'

'You heard me,' said Fergus. 'On your bike.'

Matthew ignored him. 'Is he dangerous, or are you happy to speak to him in private?'

'I think I'm safe enough on my own.'

'I'll be down the corridor. A good scream should fetch me back.' He raised his skinny frame off the bed and squared up to Fergus. 'I hope you're going to behave like a gentleman, Mr Kingsley.'

'*Piss off,*' said Fergus.

Matthew smiled gently before bringing his knee up with the speed of an express train into the young man's crotch and pushing him backwards against the wall. 'Never judge a book by its cover,' he murmured. He cocked a finger at Jinx. 'Sorry, but your brother's a creep. I'll see you around.'

Jinx waited till he'd gone, then looked down on the slumped, defeated shoulders of her baby brother. 'Where's Miles?' she asked him.

'Outside in the car,' he said tearfully. 'Dad gave him a hell of a beating then threw us out.'

'What about Betty?'

'She's in the car as well,' he said shamefacedly. 'Look, I know it's a lot to ask, but we need a place to stay. We've pooled our petrol in one car, and we've enough to get to Richmond. Miles and Mum said you'd never agree but, well . . .' He flushed. 'Well, I said you might and it was worth a try.'

She let him stew in his own discomfort for several seconds. 'I'll crucify you all if you do a damn thing in that house I don't like,' she said crossly. 'That means no mess, no gambling, no drugs, no drunkenness, and you bend over backwards to be nice to the Clanceys. Do you understand?'

He nodded. 'We'll need a key.'

'Try saying: Thank you, Jinx, you're a sodding brick. We owe you one.'

'Thank you, Jinx, you're a sodding brick. We owe you one.' He smiled sheepishly. 'We'll still need a key.'

'The Clanceys have one. I'll phone them and ask them to give it to you when you arrive. There's probably enough food in the freezer to keep you going till I get back.' She glared at him. 'And you're not to run up phone bills. And you're not to tell Adam where you are. I won't have my house turned into a war-zone. Got that?'

'Sure.' He rose. 'I knew you'd be OK about it.'

'It won't be for ever, Fergus.'

'I know. Hey, we'll take care of the house, I promise. I'll make sure Miles and Mum behave. And no phone calls. We'll lie low till you get back.'

She nodded.

He paused by the door. 'To be honest with you, I wasn't really sure you'd say yes. You're not so different from Dad, you know. I guess you were right the other day. You got the good genes and we got the bad ones.' He checked himself in case she changed her mind. 'But, look, I'm grateful. You won't regret this, honestly.'

She smiled suddenly. 'I know I won't. I'd have had far more to regret if you hadn't asked me, Fergus. I was really afraid this afternoon that I was never going to see any of you again.'

He looked surprised. 'Why?'

'I didn't think you'd bother with me if Adam chucked you out.'

'That's what we thought about you,' he said. 'I guess we never learnt to trust each other. That's pretty sad, really. I mean, if you can't trust family, who the hell can you trust, Jinx?'

Chapter Twenty-two

SUPERINTENDENT CHEEVER GAVE a small shake of his
head as he replaced the receiver. 'They've tailed Fergus's
Porsche, containing Fergus, Mrs Kingsley and Miles,
from the Nightingale Clinic to Jane's house in Richmond,' he told Maddocks and Fraser. 'The old boy next
door has just let them in, switched on the lights and left.
They've got several suitcases between them, and as many
boxes stuffed with bits and pieces as they could cram into
the Porsche. According to the tail, they look like staying
for the duration.' He tapped his pen thoughtfully against
his teeth. 'That's interesting, don't you think?'

Maddocks prowled irritably towards the window. 'It's
all over the news that Kingsley Senior's about to lose
Hellingdon Hall, so I guess he's told the three of them
to bugger off. She's given them a roof over their heads.
What's so odd about that? She's their sister.'

'I said interesting, not odd,' snapped Frank, pulling
off his bow-tie and slapping it on the desk. He unbut-
toned his shirt collar and ran his finger round the inside.
'Obviously Jane's family doesn't share your low opinion
of her. Would you move into her house, believing what
you do about her?'

459

'Miles and Fergus lived under their father's roof long enough, believing he was a killer. Same difference, wouldn't you say?'

'No.' Frank jabbed his finger angrily at the air. 'There's no comparison. If Kingsley's responsible, then he's kept a healthy distance between himself and the killings. If the daughter's responsible, then she's done them herself and she's bordering on the insane. So I repeat, would you move into her house if you had doubts about her?'

Fraser cleared his throat. 'Look, sir, with the best will in the world this isn't getting us anywhere. The truth is we need more evidence or it'll be a re-run of the Rachel Nickell murder inquiry, or the Russell Landy one, if it comes to that.'

'Jesus, Fraser,' said Maddocks, rounding on him furiously. 'How the hell did you pass your sodding sergeant's exams?' He raised his hands to Heaven. 'More evidence, he says. Where do you expect us to find it, for Christ's sake? We've put everything under the microscope – Ardingly Woods, Leo's possessions, Leo's house, his cars, his garage, Meg's possessions, her flat, her car, Jane Kingsley's car. Zilch. Zero. Nothing. We've got a heel mark on a bank which may or may not have been made by a woman's shoe, and we might be able to argue that, because Miss Kingsley's clothes were disposed of by the hospital after the accident, some of the blood on them might have been Leo's and Meg's.' He paused to draw breath. 'It's not much, I agree, but what we have in abundance is circumstantial evidence pointing in one direction, and one direction only. Towards the woman who had both motive and opportunity. I say we go with that and persuade her to talk.'

'Explain why the blood on her clothes failed to get into her car,' said Frank. 'Bob Clarke's team have taken it apart and there's not a spot in there, not even her own.'

'She was wearing a jacket when she was found. She put that on over her bloodstained clothes when she got into the car.'

'That's fantasy, not evidence. Explain how the sledgehammer got to the Nightingale Clinic on Monday night.'

'It was a set-up, courtesy of her father. Get me off the hook, Daddy, and Daddy obliges. Fake attack on Dr Protheroe with pristine sledgehammer and finger points to an outsider being involved.'

Frank jerked his chin at Fraser. 'Your turn,' he said curtly.

They'd been round this circle a hundred times already and, with a sigh, Fraser set out on it again. 'OK, the DI reckons she's manipulating events because she's guilty. I think she's manipulating them because she's innocent and scared. I'm guessing Leo left her on the night of Monday, May the thirtieth, to move in with Meg and I'm also guessing that she didn't give a shit about losing him. What concerned her was how her father was going to react. I think she was terrified of him because she shared her brother's view that he'd had Russell murdered. But no one could prove it, so she did her best to keep her distance from him and cut him out of her life. All she achieved in the process was to ratchet up his rather peculiar obsession with her. Dean Jarrett describes Adam as sitting staring at her as though he couldn't believe she was really his. My guess is, she became so paranoid about it that she persuaded Leo and Meg to leave for an indefinite stay in France in case her father reacted badly to the news of Leo's desertion.'

Frank drew a Cupid on the pad in front of him and stabbed an arrow through its heart. 'Except that the ideal time for them to go was June the fourth, the day she went down to stay at the Hall. Why wait till the following weekend?'

'Because they didn't share her paranoia. Look, as far as they were concerned, Russell was killed by a burglar.' He glanced at Maddocks, saw his sardonic smile. 'We're talking about two very egocentric personalities here, and that's on the word of their own families. Self, self, self, in other words. Leo thought principally in terms of money and possessions; Meg thought principally in terms of money and sexual gratification. Do you seriously believe either of them would dwell on the death of Miss Kingsley's husband? Meg was probably upset for a while but, as I recollect, her diary recorded her going to bed with a complete stranger less than a month later, and there's no evidence Leo even *knew* Russell. Frankly, if they ever thought about him at all, it was almost certainly in terms of a burglary gone wrong.'

He went on. 'The only one haunted by the wretched man's death was his widow, but even she got over it eventually. Sure, she's kept herself to herself rather more than most, but she's made an independent life, refused any help from her father, who she suspects is a murderer, and she's come out on top at the end of it. Then the nightmare starts all over again. She embarks on another attempt at marriage, only to find that Leo's no different from Russell and that she's making another mistake.' It was his turn to smile maliciously at thrice-married Maddocks. 'Which isn't so unusual in all conscience. People tend to be attracted by the same type every time. What is unusual is that her first marriage ended in murder instead of divorce, and Meg was involved with both men.'

'So she goes ape-shit and kills for a second time,' said Maddocks.

'You still haven't explained why they didn't leave on the fourth,' Cheever reminded him wearily.

'Because they couldn't go until the eleventh, sir. Meg had a business to keep afloat and Leo had investments to look after. The eleventh was the earliest day they could leave.'

'You're guessing again.'

'Yes, but it makes sense. Look, Jane is privately convinced her father had her husband killed, probably because the police profile persuaded her. She may even suspect he knew about the affair with Meg, which would have given him a motive. But when she tries to convince Meg and Leo, they're highly sceptical. However, they feel guilty enough about their own affair to humour her. They agree to keep the whole thing under wraps until they can leave for France – and that probably suits them anyway, because they know they'll be castigated when the news leaks out. Meanwhile, Jane has to face the week in Hampshire with her family. If she doesn't go, questions will be asked. If she does, she has to pretend the wedding's still on. So she pretends. She returns to London on the Friday for the mythical row when Leo tells her he's going to marry Meg, all three make their phone calls on the Saturday morning and Meg and Leo scarper.' He paused. 'That was the plan, anyway.'

'Then Josh Hennessey persuades Meg she's being a first-class bitch and they delay their departure till the Monday,' Frank said, driving another arrow through his Cupid's heart. 'Which brings Jane scurrying round on the Saturday night, asking them why the hell they're still there.'

'It's as plausible as the Guv's scenario, sir.'

'What about the business in her garage on Sunday?' demanded Maddocks. 'How does that fit in?'

'How does it fit in with *your* scenario?' countered Fraser.

'It was a fake, like the second one. The more attempts she made, the more protective her father would become.'

'With respect, Guv, that's bullshit,' snapped Fraser. 'Like Colonel Clancey said, if she wanted people to believe it was suicide, then she'd have wept all over him and his wife. Plus, she's done her damnedest to persuade us since that she's not the suicidal type. It doesn't add up. And another thing. You keep harping on about this protection her father's supposed to be giving her. Well, where the hell is it? He's not been near her. He's far more interested in salvaging his precious business.'

'He's paying four hundred quid a day to a corrupt quack to let her pretend she's an amnesiac. I tell you, if we could get her in here for questioning, she'd spew the lot before you could say Jack Robinson.'

Frank listened to this heated exchange with ill temper. 'I'm going home,' he said abruptly. 'We'll pack it in and sleep on it.' He started to lift his jacket off the back of his chair, then paused. 'Why did she tell Fordingbridge that the last thing she remembered was saying goodbye to Leo on the fourth of June if he wasn't even in her house?' he demanded of Fraser. 'And don't tell me she was manipulating events when she was semi-conscious, because I'll hit you from here to Salisbury and back if you even try.'

'No, sir, I'm not.' He glared at Maddocks, who was smirking. 'Look, there's no question she was concussed and there's no question, either, that she thought the accident happened on the fourth. I'm sure, to that extent, her amnesia was genuine. It may still be, for all I know. But I've done a bit of reading, and I'm guessing that story's what's called confabulation. In other words, she made it up. It was the story she was going to tell her father when she saw him on the fourth, the one she probably rehearsed all the way down in the car and then delivered convincingly. Leo's fine. I kissed him goodbye over breakfast. He sends his regards. The fact that it wasn't true is neither here nor there. It remained in her memory as something that happened because she knew that's what she had to say to her father when she saw him.'

'So her father's our murderer?'

'I'd say it's a probability, sir.'

Frank stood up, thrusting his arms into his jacket sleeves. 'You're right about one thing, Sergeant,' he said acidly. 'This is a carbon-copy of the Landy case. We have the same two suspects, and no likelihood of bringing a prosecution against either of them unless someone finds me some evidence.'

Thursday, 30 June, Hawtree Estate, Winchester – 3.30 a.m.

The child's screams rent the air as they had done every night for the last two weeks. In the kitchen, Rex started barking. 'CINDY!' yelled her mother, thrusting her arms into her dressing gown and storming across the landing to throw open her daughter's bedroom door. 'I've had enough.' She seized the child and shook her furiously. 'Either you tell me what this is all about or I'm taking you to the doctor. Do you hear me? DO – YOU – HEAR – ME? I can't stand it any longer.'

Nightingale Clinic, Salisbury – 6.30 a.m.

Alan Protheroe slept badly that night. At six o'clock he finally gave up the struggle, rolled out of bed with a groan, dressed and went for a jog in the grounds of the clinic. It had rained during the night and the grass was sodden under his feet. Water oozed through the fabric of his trainers, his cheek hurt where the shards of glass had cut the skin, and his shoulder ached with every step he took. *What the hell was he doing?* Jogging was for masochists, not for cynical middle-aged doctors who knew that death was as random and unfair as Government health policies.

With a sense of relief at a decision made, he hobbled to a bench on the terrace and sat down to view the misty landscape. Far away, beyond the clinic boundaries, low hills rose purple against the pale summer sky. Closer in, the majestic spire of Salisbury's beautiful cathedral showed above the myriad greens of the tree-tops. He viewed it, as ever, with weary pessimism. Perhaps it could survive the terrible encroachment of man and man's devices, but he doubted it.

'You look very thoughtful,' said Jinx, slipping on to the seat beside him.

She was dressed in black with a dark woollen hat pulled low over her forehead. He studied her wet shoes for a moment before nodding towards the spire. 'I was pondering man's destruction,' he said, 'and whether when it comes to it, as it surely will, he will destroy himself or his artefacts first.'

'I don't suppose it matters much,' she said, following his gaze. 'Nature will overrun whatever we leave behind, so our artefacts will cease to exist whether we destroy them or not.'

'It's rather depressing, isn't it?'

She laughed. 'It won't happen if man learns to live within his means, and if he can't learn, then he doesn't deserve his place on the planet. I have no sentimental attachment to mankind as a species. On the whole, I'd say we're one of the nastier by-products of natural selection.'

She pointed to the trees around the boundaries. 'They do nothing but good. We do nothing but harm.'

'They have no choice,' said Alan.

'Yes,' she said slowly. 'Free will is a bugger, isn't it?'

They sat in silence for a while.

'Nice hat,' said Protheroe finally.

'Matthew lent it to me to keep my head warm.'

He decided not to ask her if she had had it on Monday night. 'Where have you been?' he said instead.

'Walking.'

'You're very brave. According to Matthew, the place is crawling with would-be killers. I can't believe he hasn't alerted you to that threat when he took so much trouble to alert me.'

She nodded. 'Has he also told you about the fox in the trap, the one that was biting its own leg off to try and escape?'

'No.'

'It died of fright. I don't want to die of fright.'

'So you went for a walk to prove you're not afraid.'

'Yes.' She flicked him a quick glance, then resumed her study of the cathedral spire. 'But I couldn't sleep anyway. Matthew's bath wasn't very comfortable.'

'They rarely are,' he murmured. 'Is there a particular reason why you were trying to sleep in Matthew's bath?'

'Of course there was. I'm not in the habit of doing anything without a reason.'

'Are you going to tell me what it was?'

'His bathroom door has a lock on it.'

'I see.'

Another silence.

'So where was Matthew?'

'Probably in my bathroom, unless he was brave enough to sleep in my bed.'

He waited. 'Are you going to explain,' he said at last, 'or am I expected to go on racking my over-tired and rather addled brains?'

'I'm his surrogate fox. He's become very bossy in the last couple of days, and I blame existentialism for it. He thinks assuming responsibility means taking control.' She turned to look at him and her quiet laugh fanned the hairs on his cheek.

Oh, God, he thought, *think of ice-packs, Protheroe. She's a patient, for Christ's sake.*

Stoney Bassett Airfield, New Forest,
Hampshire – 7.30 a.m.

There was a roar of sound as the car, which had been parked in the same place since dawn, sped across the Tarmac and smashed on full throttle into the scarred concrete pillar. There was no survivor. Nor was there a convenient courting couple to effect a rescue. The car burst into flames almost on impact, probably because it was packed with open petrol cans, and by the time a passing motorist saw the smoke and called the fire brigade, the only occupant – the driver – was dead.

Romsey Road Police Station, Winchester – 9.00 a.m.

'You'd better read this,' said Frank, poking a statement across his desk with the tip of his pen. 'A Mrs Hanscombe and her daughter Cindy came in at four o'clock this morning to get Cindy's worries off her chest. Apparently, she's been having nightmares for two weeks and her mother felt the sooner she came clean, the sooner the family would get a decent night's sleep.'

> It was Tuesday, June 14th. Me and Bobby
> Franklyn found the bodies after we'd done it in the
> woods. I ran away from Bobby and slid down this
> bank. I was that scared. Rex, my dog, had dug in
> the ditch and I saw this dead person. I think it was
> a man. Bobby said he'd stick me in there with him
> if I ever said a word, but I can't stand it no more. I
> keep dreaming the man's going to get me. No, I
> didn't know the ditch was there. I dug my heel in
> to stop myself sliding. I was afraid Bobby would
> catch me at the bottom. I hate Bobby Franklyn.
> He's no good at anything. I'm twelve years old.
> Yes, he knows that.
>
> Signed: *Cindy Hanscombe*
>
> Parent's signature: *P. Hanscombe*

Maddocks read it slowly. 'So where do we go from here?' he asked.

'We go back to the beginning,' said the Superintendent. 'I want a second search made of Ardingly Woods, and I want all the water dragged within a mile radius. I also want the statements of every sighting in that area on June the thirteenth re-examined and, if necessary, we go door-to-door again to jog memories. There's a sledge-hammer and some bloodstained clothing out there some-where, and I want them found.'

'What about the Kingsleys, sir?'

Frank nodded towards the door. 'You heard me, Inspector. We start again and, this time, we do it the hard way.'

Canning Road Police Station,
Salisbury – 10.30 a.m.

'Flossie is adamant the key-ring had the Franchise Hold-ings emblem on it,' protested Blake. 'She says it was identical to the one Miles was carrying.'

'She also said Miles was the man who assaulted her,' the Sergeant reminded her. 'She's hardly the most relia-ble witness, is she?'

'I accept that, but she insists the two men were not dissimilar, and there must be something in that or she and Samantha would have blown me away when I showed them the photograph.'

'What's your point, Blake?'

'There's got to be a Franchise Holdings connection or why would he have a key-ring?'

'Come on! The bastard's married to someone who works there. He was given it during a promotion. He found it in the street. It's a big organization, Blake. You'll be interviewing people into the twenty-first century.'

'Not necessarily. I thought I'd give it one shot and if that doesn't work I'll abandon it.'

He looked at her suspiciously. 'Jane Kingsley, I suppose.'

'She's on our doorstep, Sarge. We'd be mad to miss out.'

Nightingale Clinic, Salisbury – 11.30 a.m.

Jinx was standing by her window when Blake tapped on her open door and pushed it wide. 'I saw you arrive,' she said, without turning round. 'I thought Miles was in the clear.'

'He is, as far as I'm concerned. I can't speak for my colleagues, though,' she said honestly. 'I'm afraid he's quite likely to face gambling and narcotics charges as a result of the information your father's supplied.'

Jinx turned round. 'I suppose that means you've been given the name and address of anyone Miles has been in contact with in the last four weeks?'

Blake nodded. 'I'm afraid so. A Mr Paul Deacon came in this morning at our request and supplied us with copies of everything he had, including photographs.'

'So Fergus is implicated as well?'

Blake nodded.

Jinx smiled rather bleakly. 'I should have expected it,

really. My father wouldn't miss an opportunity like that to get the blood-suckers off his back.' She flopped into an armchair and lit a cigarette, proffering the pack to the policewoman. 'Do you smoke?'

'No thanks.' Blake took the other chair. 'I could be speaking out of turn, Miss Kingsley, but a prosecution isn't always a bad thing. It depends on your brothers. It might be just the sort of shock they need to pull themselves together.'

Jinx sighed. 'You're wasting your time if you've come to talk to me about Miles and Fergus. I truly do not know anything about what they've been doing and I don't want to know. As far as I'm concerned it's a closed book.' *You're not so different from Dad . . . as far as Adam's concerned, Russell never existed . . . it's a closed book . . .*

'I haven't. That's a different case now, and I'm not involved with it.' She took a photograph of a Franchise Holdings key-ring out of her handbag and showed it to Jinx. 'Do you recognize this?'

'Yes.'

'Could you tell me what it is?'

'You know exactly what it is. It's Miles's key-ring. You took it off him yesterday.'

'How do you know it's Miles's?'

Jinx touched a spot on the black embossed disc in the photograph. 'The diamonds are in different places. It's how we tell them apart. It was my stepmother's idea. Think of the disc as a watch face with the Franchise Holdings logo the right way up. Adam's diamond's at two o'clock, mine's at four o'clock, Betty's is at six o'clock, Miles's at eight o'clock, and Fergus's at ten o'clock. That's the one you took off Miles yesterday.'

Blake couldn't hide her surprise. 'We thought it was a bit of glass. It must be pretty valuable then.'

Jinx smiled. 'I think each one cost about three thousand pounds. The disc is jet and the letters and rim are gold. Betty commissioned them two years ago from a jeweller in London for her and Adam's twenty-fifth wedding anniversary. She said it was something we should all celebrate.' The smile became rueful. 'It was a nice idea until Adam saw the bill. After that all hell broke loose.'

'Presumably there's a cheaper version in plastic which your father's employees use?'

'I suppose there may be. I've never seen one, though. Betty always told me she thought this up for herself. She wanted something unique to the five of us.' She frowned suddenly. 'Why do you want to know?'

Blake debated with herself. 'Oh, what the hell!' she said suddenly. 'I guess Flossie got it wrong again.' She sighed as heavily as Jinx had done. 'One of the reasons we thought your brother was involved in the assault on Flossie Hale was because she said her attacker had a key-ring just like this. She remembered it because the initials were the same as hers, and when we showed her the Franchise Holdings logo, she identified it immediately. So we then showed her a photograph of your two brothers, and she picked out Miles. I accept she made a mistake over that, but she was adamant this morning that this, or one exactly like it, is the key-ring the man was carrying.' She shrugged. 'I'm sorry. It looks like I've wasted your time.'

'Have you made that public?' asked Jinx, in a detached tone of voice, as though she didn't care what the answer was.

'About the key-ring? No. It's been a low-priority investigation because the prostitutes didn't want to talk.'

'What are the chances of this man still having the key-ring on him?'

'Pretty good, I would think.'

Jinx closed her eyes suddenly, and Blake thought she saw tears on the lashes. 'I gave mine away,' she said in an unsteady voice. 'I didn't think there was much to celebrate, not after my father lost his temper. In any case, he paid for it, and I made a vow a long time ago never to accept anything from him again.' She pressed her finger-tips to her eyelids before lowering them to look at the young policewoman. 'The irony is, when I gave it away, I said I hope it brings you luck.' She ran her tongue round dry lips. 'But I think the luck must have stayed with me.'

'Who did you give it to, Miss Kingsley?'

'A vicar. He's Anglo-Catholic and he said the F could stand for Father. Father Harris. He has a parish in a village called Frampton. He's better looking than Miles,' she said in a strained voice, 'but they aren't unalike. Simon's thinner and not so dark. His sister confused them once so you mustn't blame the prostitutes for getting it wrong.'

Blake listened to the tremors in her voice. 'Would the sister be Meg Harris? Your friend who was murdered?'

'Yes.'

'Did this Simon have something to do with that?'

Jinx's eyes grew huge. 'I think I'm going to be sick,' she said. 'I'm so sorry.'

Blake moved her feet rapidly as vomit sprayed across the carpet.

The Vicarage, Frampton, Hampshire – 12.25 p.m.

Blake drew to a halt beside the other police car and switched off her engine. 'What's going on?' she called to a uniformed copper by the front door. 'Is the vicar in there?'

'Not as far as I know.'

'Do you know where he is?'

'Last I heard, he was stinking to high heaven of roast pork on Stoney Bassett airfield.'

To whom it may concern:

I don't believe in God but I have stood with the Host in my hand every Sunday and professed belief on behalf of others. I wonder sometimes if it would have been different if I had believed, but I don't think so. If God exists, He had no power to change what He had ordained, that I must be brother to Meg. There is no greater torment than to love a woman you can't have.

People will say I am mad. Perhaps I am. Yet it's a strange madness that brings meaning to the actions men say are wicked and confusion to those they condone. They say I'm a good priest, yet I stumble in black night before the altar of God's flesh and blood, and only see clearly when Man's flesh and blood is warm between my hands. Then I understand that sacrifice is necessary if the dark rooms of the mind are to be cleansed, for purpose takes over and what I do becomes inevitable. I am alive. I see truth.

It starts again **CONFUSION**

Meg became a **WHORE** *but I knew why and forgave her. She said, better a generous whore than a spiteful wife. She was open and honest and hid nothing from me. There was no* love *only physical gratification and excitement, until*

SECRECY

terrible uncertainty   where is god   god sleeps   but not

477

Russell. Russell laughs and his laugh breaks into my head, smashing my brains   smashing   smashing   Meg loves

russell simon hates god

Remembering is painful. I understand why Jinx prefers to forget. I have always hated Jinx. She made Meg jealous. What were Leo and Russell to my sister till Jinx made them desirable? Nothing. Little men of little worth, unJinxed. She turned them into gods and sent them back to Meg. With Jinx there is always

secrecy & SPITE unJinxed Meg is an honest whore

confusion *again. Awful, terrible   danger   danger* danger *forget, forget   whores   young whores   old whores   You're wicked where's my hairbrush naughty boy   smack   smack   I hope that hurts   don't you look at your sister like that again wicked*

wicked   wicked

GOD the father made simon dEVIL

Where are they? Not in Hammersmith. The birds have flown because Jinx made them   it was a SECRET *but simon made Jinx tell kill   kill   kill   no* WEAPON

god loves Jinx   miracles for her not for simon

she is SAVED

she follows simon to leo's house and simon says gods will be done amen

But why does god save Jinx? Three times simon tried to kill her and three times god saved her. He didn't save Meg or Leo. They tried to save themselves with

lies

you don't want the cat to die, Simon   you love the cat let me go to hammersmith and feed the cat   let the cat live   the cat's imprisoned

she means leo   leo's imprisoned in simon's boot   dead already

*   like jinx imprisoned in a box in chelsea, buried alive in her coffin, dead if Meg disobeys*

no one sees no one hears   she begs for life   too late   too late

please SIMON   *pretty please simon   simon says* NO

   forget forget forget forget forget forget forget forget forget

simon says sorry

Epilogue

DETECTIVE SUPERINTENDENT CHEEVER and DS
Fraser waited in silence while Jinx read the letter that
Simon Harris had left behind on his desk before setting
out to take his own life. It was a chilling document, not
least because the sickness it revealed was echoed nowhere
else in his house, except, perhaps, in a single cassock
which, although it had been cleaned, still showed positive
where blood had splattered the front. Despite this and
the letter, however, there was considerable unease about
Simon's suicide, particularly in respect of the open petrol
cans that had turned his car into a fireball, destroying all
chance of forensic analysis, and the extraordinary order
in his life that was in such contrast to the apparent
disorder in his mind.

The police had not been able to discover a single
parishioner in Frampton who found their vicar's homi-
cidal tendencies even halfway credible. 'He was a sweet
man.' 'Nothing was ever too much trouble for him.'
'Father Harris wouldn't hurt a fly.' 'He was the hardest
working priest we've ever had.'

There was circumstantial evidence to show that he
had been absent from the vicarage from lunchtime on

Sunday, 12 June, to the morning of Tuesday, 14 June, but it hardly stood up to close scrutiny. 'I noticed Simon's car wasn't outside on the Sunday or Monday night,' said his next-door neighbour, 'but he used to park it in his garage sometimes, so it may have been in there. I don't remember seeing him after morning service but that wasn't unusual. We're busy people and we don't keep track of each other's movements. The car was certainly there on Tuesday morning. I had a form for him to sign and I had to walk round it to reach the front door. No, I didn't notice anything odd about him. He was in his usual good spirits.'

Caroline Harris, quite destroyed by the disasters that had overtaken her family, swore that Simon had been with her and Charles on the Sunday and Monday night. She also claimed that he had been staying with them on June the twenty-seventh, when Protheroe was attacked. But when her husband was asked later to corroborate these stories he shook his head. 'No,' he said quietly, 'I'm afraid neither is true.' He had read his son's letter without obvious emotion and handed it back to Cheever with a request that his wife should never see it. 'I blame myself,' he said. 'I should have realized how damaging it was to grow up in a house where the sexual act was viewed as something degrading and disgusting. Selfishly, I thought it was only I who was affected but, clearly, Meg confused it with love and Simon confused it with hate . . .'

To begin with, Flossie Hale and Samantha Garrison were doubtful that Simon was the man who assaulted them. 'He didn't wear glasses, you see,' said Flossie, studying the photograph of the earnest young vicar, 'and he was better looking.' But when shown a snap-shot of a younger smiling Simon minus spectacles and in casual clothes, they were more confident. 'Little Lord Fauntleroy,' said Flossie triumphantly, 'and he's not so different from the first one I picked out either. Same eyes. It's the innocence. Gawd, I'll remember never to be taken in by pretty blue eyes again.'

DI Maddocks was liaising with the Metropolitan police in an attempt to discover whether any London prostitutes had suffered similar assaults to Hale's and Garrison's during the five years that Simon had worked there. If they could establish a prolonged pattern of criminal assault on prostitutes, it would ease police doubts over the meagre evidence pointing to Simon's involvement in the murders of Landy, Wallader and Harris. For, as Maddocks said to Cheever when he'd read Simon's letter: 'Someone beat the crap out of him to make him write this, sir. It's got bloodstains on it.'

Frank watched Jinx lower the letter to her knees. 'As you see, Miss Kingsley,' he said, 'there are one or two questions left unanswered. We're still looking for the weapon, but there was a cassock in his house that appears to have bloodstains on it. However, it will be some time before we can say definitely that the blood was Meg's and Leo's. The likely scenario is that he removed the cassock after he killed your two friends, which would explain why we had no reported sightings of someone wearing bloodstained clothes. We believe he probably used the same method to kill your husband, donned his cassock in other words, to keep the blood off his clothes.'

She looked paler and more drawn than ever, he thought, and the hand that held the letter shook violently. 'I don't wish to upset you further, but we would be grateful for any details you can give us.'

She glanced towards Alan Protheroe for support, then nodded.

'Perhaps we could begin with Saturday, the eleventh of June, the day you phoned your father to tell him the wedding was off. Do you remember that day, Miss Kingsley?'

'Most of it, yes.'

'Do you remember going to Meg's flat in the evening and being angry when she or Leo opened the door to you?'

Jinx nodded.

'Could you tell me about that? We assume they were supposed to be long gone, so what made you think they were still there? Why did you go?'

'To collect Marmaduke and take him home with me,' she said simply. 'I couldn't believe it when I saw Leo's car parked outside. I was furious.' Tears welled in her eyes. 'I'd gone to so much trouble and they just thought I was being paranoid.'

'So you had a key to Meg's flat?'

She shook her head. 'I was supposed to collect it from the neighbour. But I could see Leo in the sitting room, so I hammered on the door instead and let rip at them.' She dabbed miserably at her eyes. 'I wish I hadn't now. It was the last time I really spoke to either of them and I was so bad-tempered. You see, I knew they were in danger. I had this feeling all the time that something terrible was going to happen.'

Frank waited a moment till he felt she was back in control of herself. 'What happened then?'

'Meg gave me this big spiel about Josh and how badly she was behaving towards him. She said it was my fault, that I was using Russell's murder as a stick to beat her and Leo with because I wanted to make life as uncomfortable for them as I could. We really did have an awful row.' She looked at her hands. 'Well, that's not relevant any more. I bullied them into going to Leo's house in Chelsea until Monday. I said, at least they'd be safer there than in Hammersmith because I was the only other person who knew the address.'

'Did they go?'

'Yes.'

'What time was that?'

'I think it was around midnight. Meg insisted on leaving the flat spick and span so that prospective purchasers wouldn't be put off when they went round it.'

'So she was selling it?'

'Yes,' said Jinx again. 'I was going to put it with an estate agent as soon as they left for France. That was part of the deal. Meg's business needed an injection of cash, and I promised to try and raise it through the sale of her flat if she and Leo would agree to make themselves scarce for a while. The plan was for me to explain it to Josh after they'd left . . .' She faltered. 'But Meg got cold feet when she spoke to him on the phone on Saturday and decided to postpone the trip so she could tell him in person.' She licked the tears from her lips. 'Josh threatened to pull out of the partnership unless she gave him a few guarantees about her commitment, and they'd been going through such a rough patch recently that she believed he'd do it unless she took the trouble to calm him down.'

Frank studied her bent head curiously. 'I have some problems understanding why they were prepared to go along with all the secrecy, Miss Kingsley, particularly if, as you say, they thought you were being paranoid.'

She stared at him rather bleakly for a moment. 'Meg had done the dirty on me twice. She was in no real position to argue. In any case, Leo was on my side. He was cock-a-hoop about being in France when the news broke. The last thing he wanted was to face the embarrassment of a cancelled wedding. He'd have gone immediately if Meg had been free to leave.'

'Why wasn't she?'

'She had a client she didn't want to lose, and a couple of meetings with the bank manager. She said he'd pull the plug on the business if she tried to cancel them. The earliest she could leave was the eleventh.' She fell silent.

'Then she reneged at the last minute?'

Jinx nodded. 'She only agreed to go along with it in the first place because Leo was in favour, but the minute Josh came down on her like a ton of bricks she dug her heels in, kept calling me neurotic and absurd.' The tears ran down her cheeks again. 'I think she wanted to say she was sorry afterwards, but she was too afraid of Simon to look at me. It was very sad.'

'I understand.' He waited again. 'So they left for

Chelsea at about midnight on the Saturday? Are you sure they went there?'

'Oh, yes. I followed them. Leo parked in the garage, and I watched them both go inside. Then I went home.'

'What about the cat? What happened to him?'

'We stuck with the original plan, but delayed it until Monday. We left poor old Marmaduke in the hall with some food and the cat tray, but he was only going to be there for thirty-six hours at the most. I would collect the key from the neighbour, rescue Marmaduke, and explain about the flat going on the market. Meg was supposed to call them the minute she got to France, tell them I was kosher and ask them to let me in.'

'But why was it so necessary to keep Mr and Mrs Helms in the dark?' asked Fraser. 'You can't have suspected them of being involved in Russell's death.'

'Of course not.' There was a long silence. 'I thought it was my father we needed to be afraid of,' she said at last, 'and I couldn't be sure how much he already knew about Leo and Meg's affair. I know he found out about Meg and Russell because Miles told me afterwards. That's one of the reasons I thought he might have had Russell killed.' She rubbed her head. 'Leo swore his parents wouldn't have said a word to anyone, but' – she raised her hands in a small gesture of helplessness – 'Adam has a way of finding out. If Mr and Mrs Helms knew anything in advance, they would tell the first person who asked them. In fact, Meg said it was worse, that Mrs Helms wouldn't wait to be asked, she'd stand on the street corner and broadcast it to the world.'

'Why weren't you worried about Leo parking his car

in Shoebury Terrace if you thought your father was having him and Meg watched?' asked the Superintendent.

She lifted her head to look at him and for the first time he understood some of the agonies she had been through. 'I was. I tried to persuade him to leave it in Richmond but he wouldn't go along with it. He said that was taking the whole thing to ridiculous lengths. But, you see, I knew what had been done to Russell and they didn't. I spent a nightmare week at the Hall, worrying myself sick. I made Leo phone every day to let me know they were all right and to make my family think everything was normal. Then he phoned on the Friday afternoon to say they were leaving first thing the next morning, and it was safe to come back and make the announcements. And I thought, thank God, it's all over. I've made a complete idiot of myself, but I don't care.' She held a handkerchief to her eyes. 'I can't explain it because I don't believe in second-sight or precognition, but I knew the minute Leo told me he wanted to marry Meg that they were going to die. It was like having cold water thrown over me.' She looked wretchedly towards Alan. 'So I put two and two together and came up with Adam and, if I hadn't, then maybe, just maybe, they'd still be alive.'

'No,' he said. 'It would have made no difference. At least Adam was a terrifying enough prospect to force them to listen to you. They'd have been dead a week earlier otherwise.'

She held out Simon's letter. 'Except that I made them

keep the secret,' she said, 'and that's why he killed them. It was the secrecy that made him do it.'

'No,' said Alan, who had read the letter before he took the two policemen to Jinx's room. 'He was a very disturbed man, Jinx. It was his illness that made him do it, and nothing you could have done would have stopped that.'

'The doctor's right, Miss Kingsley,' said Superintendent Cheever. 'The only person who might have guessed that Simon murdered Russell was Meg. She was closer to him than anyone else, in all conscience. If it never occurred to her to be afraid of him, then there's no reason why it should have occurred to you.' He paused. 'Did she ever show any fear of him?'

'Not in the way you mean. She's been afraid *for* him as long as I've known her. If only Simon were more like me, she always said, he'd be OK. She was worried that he was becoming a bit of a loner. He never seemed to have any friends. I remember her saying once, he never plays at anything except being a priest.'

'Didn't it occur to her he might be ill?'

Her expression clouded. 'She asked me once if I'd noticed anything odd about him, and I said: What sort of thing? I think he pretends, she said. I'm sure he hates our parents, Mother in particular, but he never says anything unkind about her or to her. I'm the exact opposite. I'm always rude about her because she's a square peg in a round hole and won't do anything to change it, but I'm actually quite fond of the old bag, and all right, Dad's a sanctimonious old buzzard, but I wouldn't have him any different.' She pressed her lips into a thin line to stem her tears. 'She wondered if I'd ever got the impression that Simon hated them but, as I never had, she let it drop. I know she always thought he was far too withdrawn, but I think she put that down to religious fanaticism. I'm sure it never occurred to her that he had anything to do with Russell's death.' She laced her fingers nervously. 'Well, it never occurred to anyone.'

'That's very clear, thank you. Let's move on. Tell us about the Sunday afternoon and this incident in your garage. What was that all about? Presumably the reference he makes in his letter to the birds having flown, and the phrase "it was a secret but Simon made Jinx tell" had something to do with it?'

Her hands began to tremble so violently again that she gripped them in her lap until the knuckles shone white. 'It's what he says. I told him where they were. He knew they'd left Hammersmith, you see, because Meg didn't answer the phone.' She stared at Cheever in desperation. 'It was – he thought they'd gone to France – but he made me – I was the only one who knew.' She brought herself back under control with an effort. 'He came after lunch to apologize for what Meg had done,' she managed. 'He said he'd prayed for me during services that morning but realized prayers weren't enough and he needed to come and commiserate in person. So I laughed' – her voice broke again – 'and said there was nothing to commiserate about. I said if anyone needed commiseration it would be poor old Meg in a few months' time when she discovered she'd tied herself to a mean, self-serving bastard.' She swallowed painfully. 'I shouldn't have laughed. I think he guessed I'd known about it for a while. He was so angry – kept talking about secrets – called Meg a whore . . .' She tailed off into a long silence.

'What did he do then?' asked Frank gently.

She shook her head.

'I think it might be easier if I tell you,' said Alan. 'When the news came through yesterday that Simon was dead, Jinx told me as much as she could remember of what happened.' He squatted down and pressed a warm, protective hand to the nape of her neck. 'Would you like me to do that, Jinx?'

She looked into his face, for a moment, then looked away again. Why couldn't he see what he was doing to her? She was far too emotionally disturbed to survive an Alan Protheroe undamaged. She wished he would take his hand away. She wished he would go to the other side of the room. *Oh, God, she wished* . . . 'If you're allowed to,' she said curtly.

The Superintendent nodded. 'I have no problem with that, Doctor.'

Alan straightened. 'Then I think it's important you understand how terrifying it is to be confronted with an individual whom you've known for years as a mild-mannered non-entity, but who, without any warning at all, becomes dangerously psychotic. This was Jinx's experience that Sunday afternoon. It's difficult to say what Simon's diagnosis would have been if he'd ever been examined, but it seems clear that he was suffering from some very extreme paranoid disorder, probably of a sexual origin, either centred on his mother or his sister, or both. I think this hatred he had of God may well have been a more general hatred of any dominant male figure because he seems to have seen the sexual act as a degenerate exercise. Only whores enjoyed it, therefore for a man to enjoy it he must either employ whores or make respectable women miserable.' He looked enquiringly at the Superintendent. 'Which may have been something his mother instilled in him. If she persuaded him that nice women found sex disgusting, then he would have had a very ambivalent attitude towards it in later life, particularly if his adored sister flaunted her libido while he curbed his by choosing voluntary celibacy within the Anglo-Catholic church.'

'His mother clearly has problems in that area but I doubt she set out deliberately to destroy her son.'

'I'm sure she didn't, and I'm sure there were other factors involved. For example, he hated being laughed at. That seems to have been one of the triggers of his paranoia. It may have been why he chose to enter the church, because he was more likely to be taken seriously inside it than he was outside. Another clear trigger was secrecy. As long as he knew what was going on, or thought he did, he could keep his paranoia under control, but the minute he discovered he had good reason to be paranoid, then the control deserted him. It's interesting what close tabs he kept on everything. Jinx says he used to phone her or Josh quite regularly, and I suspect he continued to do that after Meg and Leo were dead. He certainly phoned me to try and find out what information I had.' He rubbed his shoulder thoughtfully.

'One of the complicating factors of a paranoid disorder,' he went on, 'is that, while it may impair your functioning on certain levels, particularly where relationships are concerned, your thinking remains clear and orderly and you can function normally within your job and the wider social environment. Which is why I told you it was important to recognize what Jinx was suddenly faced with that Sunday, and equally important that she recognizes it, too.' He looked down at her bent head. 'She's been terrified of Simon ever since she started to remember what happened, but I'm afraid she feels she didn't do enough to protect Meg and Leo. Isn't that right, Jinx?'

She didn't answer, and Fraser, for one, thought he was being surprisingly insensitive.

'She went into the kitchen to make some coffee, and she thinks Simon must have hit her on the head while she was doing it, but she doesn't remember the blow. What she does remember is coming round to find herself lying on the floor with her hands tied to her feet behind her back. Simon then put a polythene bag over her head and said he would smother her if she didn't tell him where Meg and Leo were. She couldn't breathe and she believed him. So when he took the bag off her head, she told him the Chelsea address. The next thing she remembers is being pulled out of her car by her neighbour. She didn't know how long she'd been there, how long it took her to clear her head, or find the number of Leo's house in Chelsea, but by the time she phoned to tell Meg that Simon had just tried to kill her, Simon was already there. Am I right so far, Jinx?'

Silence.

'She was given a straightforward choice,' Alan went on. 'Simon said: Leo is in the same position you were in. In other words, he will be dead of asphyxiation in two minutes. Meg is tied up but can speak into the phone if I hold it to her mouth. If you do what I tell you, they will live. If you don't, they will die.' He brushed the back of her head with his fingertips. 'She chose to help them live. She clung, as we would all have done, to the Simon she knew best. The vicar, the man who loved his sister, the man to whom she'd given her expensive key-ring for luck. It was her tragedy, and Meg's, that they had only ever known and learnt to trust Simon's false self, while his true self, the damaged self, had remained hidden. We all protect parts of ourselves – God knows it's not unusual – but for most of us, the hidden self isn't dangerous.'

Jinx wiped her tears away. 'I should have told Colonel Clancey. He's always been the best friend I've ever had.' She sucked in her anguish on a sob. 'I know some people think he's eccentric and stupid, and they make fun of him behind his back, but he would have made it all right.' Her mouth worked as she sought for words. 'I did it all wrong. I told the Clanceys everything was OK when it wasn't. I thought, if I just do what Simon says – because, you know, we used to play that game all the time, Simon Says. But it was just arrogance – I thought I knew the right thing to do.'

Fraser glanced at Protheroe for a permission he didn't need. 'It's not arrogance to believe a threat, Miss Kingsley, particularly if you knew what Simon was capable of. I'm no expert admittedly, but it sounds to me as if you acted out of love, and I'd say that does you credit.'

Alan nodded. 'He said there wasn't much traffic because it was a Sunday, and that she had twenty minutes to drive her car to Leo's house in Chelsea. If she wasn't there in twenty minutes, he'd know she'd spoken to the police and he would kill Meg and Leo. Then he put Meg back on.'

'And Meg asked you to do as he said?'

Jinx nodded.

'What happened when you reached the house?'

Alan took over again when she didn't say anything. 'She saw Leo briefly through an open doorway. He was lying on the floor and, from the way she describes him, he had probably died of asphyxiation before she got there, so whatever was done to him afterwards was done to disguise that fact. At least she gave Meg a chance to live by arriving when she did. Simon promised he wouldn't hurt them because he never killed women. All he wanted to do was talk. He sat them beside each other against the wall, tied their hands and feet in front of them, and talked for hours. So long, in fact, that Jinx felt he was beginning to calm down.'

'And?' asked Frank Cheever, when neither of them spoke.

'Meg offered to have sex with him,' said Alan into the silence. 'She thought that's what he was after. It probably was, but he didn't want to be reminded of it.' He shook his head. 'To be honest, I shouldn't think it mattered a damn what Meg said. Whichever role she chose – sister, mother, lover, friend – he would still have gone off the deep end.' He glanced at Jinx's fluttering hands. 'But there's nothing Jinx can tell you about what happened to Meg and Leo after that,' he went on. 'Simon went berserk at that point, grabbed Jinx by the ankles to pull her away from Meg, then put a polythene bag over her head and taped it to her neck. All she remembers is Meg screaming and drumming her heels on the floor before she lost consciousness.'

There was another silence. 'Can you tell us what happened to you, Miss Kingsley?' asked Frank. 'Or would you prefer Dr Protheroe to do it?'

Her huge eyes searched his face, looking for understanding. 'I truly don't remember very much,' she said unsteadily, 'except that I woke up at some point. There was a hole in the bag where my mouth was and, because my hands were crammed up under my chin, I was able to make the hole bigger. But that's all I could do. I was wedged into a sort of box and every time I tried to move it was so painful I gave up.' She plucked at her lip. 'I thought he'd buried me alive, and I just wanted to die.' She paused, lost in some private hell. 'Then the engine started and I knew I was in the boot of my car. The funny thing is, I felt better knowing that. It didn't seem so frightening.' She gave an odd little laugh. 'But he was so angry,' she said. 'He kept kicking me and saying, get up, get up. He couldn't understand why I wasn't dead. You should be dead. You should have died in your garage and you should have died in your boot. Why does God love you?'

'Where was that?' asked Frank.

She looked at him blankly. 'I don't know. Somewhere outside. I woke up and I was lying on the ground, but I couldn't move because I was so stiff. There was a black dustbin bag round me and it smelt because I'd' – she glanced at Alan – 'I think I must have been in it for hours.'

'So do you know what time it was?'

'No, but it was getting dark.'

'Do you remember him giving you something to drink?'

'I think so. He talked about sacrifices,' she said in some confusion, 'and Jesus.'

'Which is probably when you drank the wine, although if you'd been there for hours then you were probably very dehydrated, and I doubt you drank as much as your blood sample implied. What happened next?'

She stared down at the letter, which she'd abandoned in her lap. 'I don't remember anything else.' She crumpled the photocopy into a tight ball. 'I don't remember anything else,' she said on a rising note of alarm. 'I think I remember him putting me into the car seat, but after that – I don't remember anything else.'

'That's fine,' said Frank with a smile of encouragement. 'I think we can work out the rest. You obviously have a very strong will to live, Miss Kingsley. I envy you your courage, and whichever guardian angel is watching over you, because I can't believe that courting couple arrived by accident.' He watched her for a moment. 'Dr Protheroe tells me Simon came to visit you the day after you regained consciousness. Did you know then that he was responsible?'

'No.'

'When did you remember?'

She kept her head down. 'Yesterday morning,' she said, 'when the policewoman asked me about the key-ring.'

'Not before?'

She didn't say anything.

'Did you tell your father that Simon had murdered Meg and Leo, Miss Kingsley?'

Her head snapped up, eyes huge with surprise. 'No, of course I didn't. Why would I do that?'

Cheever nodded. 'Your brothers? Your stepmother?'

'No.'

Alan Protheroe frowned. 'Why do you ask, Superintendent?'

Frank Cheever gave a small shrug. 'Just tying up loose ends, Doctor. We don't want accusations floating around afterwards about the' – he sought for a word – '*convenience* of Simon Harris's suicide. One might almost say the poetic justice of how he met his end. Our problem is there's only this letter and the bloodstains on the cassock linking him to the murders and, as the cassock had been cleaned recently, it may not produce the material evidence we're looking for. We assume Simon took Leo and Meg in his own car to Ardingly Woods but, as it was completely burnt out yesterday, we're very doubtful of being able to prove anything from a forensic examination. We've also examined your car, Miss Kingsley, and I have to tell you there's nothing to show you spent twelve to eighteen hours in the boot.'

'There wouldn't be,' said Alan. 'Not if he wrapped her in black polythene before he put her in there.'

'I accept that, but it's a problem nevertheless. It would've helped if you had been able to identify him as your attacker.'

Alan nodded towards the crumpled photocopy in Jinx's hands. 'But you've got a written confession. Doesn't that count for anything? Presumably you've verified that it's Simon's handwriting?'

'Certainly we have, but the original is being tested at the moment for the blood and mucus stains on it. We believe Simon was bleeding from his nose when he wrote it. And that means he may have been coerced into doing it.'

'By whom?'

'We don't know, sir, which is why we're interested in finding out when Miss Kingsley began to remember and whether she told anyone about it.' He glanced at Jinx. 'It would be very unfortunate if doubts about Simon's guilt began to circulate.'

Alan rubbed his jaw aggressively, his fingers rasping through the thick stubble. 'Are you suggesting Jinx is lying about what happened, Superintendent?' he demanded. 'Because if you are, then I begin to understand why she has such a low opinion of Britain's policemen. Goddammit, man, imagine if the murdering little bastard was still alive, and she tried to tell you he was guilty. She wouldn't stand a chance. You'd still be sitting there smugly, giving us this garbage about lack of evidence. Well, thank God she didn't remember before is all I can say, because she'd have been signing her own death warrant by naming him. He was obviously a psychotic with paranoid delusions, but he was quite clever enough to convince you of his innocence while he did away with the woman he held responsible for his murderous binges.'

Cheever shrugged. 'You've encapsulated our dilemma rather well, sir. Personally, I have no doubts that Miss Kingsley is telling the truth. I am also hopeful that we will find other prostitutes in London who will identify Simon Harris as the client who assaulted them, which, in turn, will point to a pattern of serial criminal behaviour. However, in the short term, we have a rather timely suicide on our hands which, in view of Harris's undoubted cleverness, to which you yourself referred, and his past determination to throw the blame on Miss Kingsley, raises rather too many doubts for comfort. I am sure Miss Kingsley does not want this story to run and run, any more than we do' – he turned his attention to Jinx and held her gaze with his – 'so anything she can tell us now that will result in the coroner bringing in an unequivocal verdict of suicide would be helpful.'

Jinx nodded. 'I understand,' she said, glancing towards the open notebook on Fraser's lap. She thought for a moment. 'I did not remember anything until the policewoman asked me about the key-ring yesterday, then it all came back to me in a rush and I was violently sick, as she will testify. I have been told since that Simon had been dead for some hours before I gave her his name. Because I did not remember who tried to kill me,

I could not tell anyone who it was. Dr Protheroe, whom I trust implicitly and whom I would have told had I been able to remember, will testify that at no time did I ever give him a name or even hint at a name. Had I been able to remember, I would, of course, have told the Hampshire police. From the outset of the investigation they have made it clear to me that, while I was a suspect, media speculation would not be allowed to cloud their judgement. As a result, I have always had confidence in Superintendent Cheever and his team and have given them all the time and assistance I could.'

She looked enquiringly at Frank, saw the tiny encouraging lift of his eyebrows and went on. 'I believe Simon, through his telephone calls to my friends, my doctor and my relations, learnt that the Hampshire police had refused to take anything at face value and realized he would be arrested the minute my memory returned. I have known him a long time, and knew him to be very fond of his parents. It is my own conviction that he would have done anything to avoid putting his mother and father through the trauma of his trial, and I am saddened but not surprised that he took his own life.'

'I doubt he'd want his colleagues or his parishioners to be subjected to that sort of trauma either, do you?' Cheever prompted.

'I knew him to be a very dedicated clergyman,' she resumed obediently, 'who must have been appalled, when lucidity returned, to realize that the burden of his guilt would fall on the people who loved him. He was an ill man, not a bad one.'

Cheever held out his hand to her as he stood up. 'It's hardly appropriate to say this, Miss Kingsley, but I've enjoyed crossing swords with you. I'm only sorry we had to meet in such tragic circumstances. You may be required to appear at the inquest but, if you give your evidence there as clearly as you've just given it to us, there shouldn't be a problem. In my experience, a little generosity goes a long way. Suicide is always easier to accept if there's a good reason for it.'

'I know,' she said, shaking his hand. 'If Simon had made my car crash look like an accident, then I'd have been a little more worried. You see, I could always accept I might have killed Meg and Leo. They really did behave like bastards. I just couldn't accept I'd kill myself.'

His eyes twinkled. 'So you weren't quite as indifferent as you led us to believe?'

'I have my pride, Superintendent.' She smiled suddenly. 'After all, I am Adam Kingsley's daughter.'

Fraser turned the car into the main road. 'So what's the verdict, sir?' he asked. 'Do you still reckon she got her old man to take Harris out?'

'I do,' said the Superintendent mildly. 'She was afraid it would be her word against Simon's, didn't trust us to believe her, so turned to her father to sort something out.'

'Well, I'm not so sure. She strikes me as being dead straight, sir.'

'But, as she said herself, Sean, she's Adam Kingsley's daughter.'

'With respect, sir, I don't see what difference that makes.'

'You would, if you'd ever met the breed.' Frank looked out of the window on to sunlit countryside. 'They're effective. They get things done.'

'They weren't too effective when Landy was murdered.'

'People rarely are when they're at cross purposes.'

'How come?'

'I suspect *he* became convinced that she killed Russell, and *she* became convinced that he did. If they both learnt about the affair afterwards, then they both knew there was a motive for the other one to commit the murder. Divided they fell, united they stand.'

'It seems odd that Miss Kingsley didn't tell the police, though. You'd think she'd want her husband's murderer punished, and, let's face it, it's not as though she's very fond of her father.'

'You think so, do you?'

'She certainly doesn't go out of her way to express affection for him.'

Cheever smiled but kept his thoughts to himself.

'So are you going to charge Adam Kingsley with Simon's murder, sir?'

The Superintendent closed his eyes and let the sun warm his face. 'I don't think I heard you right, Sergeant. Did you say something about a murder?'

'Isn't that what you reckon . . .' Fraser broke off.

'Yes?'

'Nothing, sir.'

Nightingale Clinic, Salisbury – 12.45 p.m.

Matthew Cornell opened his eyes to find Alan Protheroe looming over him where he lay sprawled on a bench in the clinic gardens. 'Hi, Doc.' He shielded the sun's glare with a raised hand, then swung his legs off the seat and sat up, lighting a cigarette.

Alan lowered himself on to the vacant piece of bench. 'The police have come up with a bizarre theory about Simon Harris's suicide,' he said in a conversational tone. 'They seem to think Jinx might have given his name to her father in order to have him dealt with once and for all.' He glanced sideways. 'However, she's persuaded them that she didn't remember anything until yesterday morning, which means neither she *nor* any of her friends here could have passed the information on to Adam Kingsley.'

Matthew looked straight ahead. 'Why are you telling *me*?'

'Because I know how you like to keep abreast of the facts.'

The young man turned to grin at him. 'Plus, as an existentialist, you want to be sure I continue to act in good faith. Isn't that right?'

'I couldn't have put it better myself, Matthew.'

'Well, I reckon good faith is all about justice.' Matthew turned the cigarette between his fingers. 'Have you ever wondered what a murderer's victims would demand if their voices hadn't been silenced? At the very least they would ask to be heard as loudly as their killers, wouldn't they?'

'There's a difference between justice and revenge, Matthew.'

'Is there? The only difference I see is that justice comes damned expensive. If it didn't, my father couldn't afford to keep me here.'

Half an hour later, Alan stood with Jinx at her window and watched a tall, well-built man in an immaculate suit emerge from the back seat of a Rolls-Royce. 'Your father?'

'Yes.'

'You've never explained why you call him Adam.'

'What makes you think there is an explanation?'

He smiled. 'Your expression every time the subject comes up.'

She watched the tall figure disappear from view into the building. 'I wanted to punish him, so I did what God did and cursed Adam for allowing his wife to seduce him.' She turned to Alan. 'I was seven years old. I've called him Adam ever since.'

'You were jealous of Betty?'

'Of course. I didn't want to share my father with anyone. I adored him.'

Alan nodded. 'In spite of everything, I suspect you still do.'

'No,' she said, 'I'm long past adoration. But I do admire him. I always have done. He achieves while the rest of us get by.'

'Well, I hope you recognize that he's making the first move,' said Alan casually. 'Will you be generous to him?'

'If I'm not, the clinic won't get paid.' She smiled slightly at his expression. 'Don't go sentimental on me, Dr Protheroe. The one thing you can be sure of is that my father will never change. He'd sue if he thought you'd deliberately poisoned my mind against him.'

'So what happens now?'

'I'm discharging myself. I'm not your patient any more. I think we say goodbye.'

'Where will you go?'

'Back to Richmond.'

'Does your father know Miles and Fergus are there?'

'Not unless they've told him.'

'If they need a good barrister, then don't forget Matthew's father. I'm told he's one of the best.'

Jinx smiled and tapped her pocket. 'Matthew's given me his card. I thought I'd use the gains I've made on the Franchise Holdings shares to pay his fees. Matthew says they'll be exorbitant.' She shrugged. 'Then, with luck and a little emotional blackmail, I may persuade Adam to acknowledge Betty and the boys again once it's all over.'

'You don't think it might be better to let Miles and Fergus fight this battle alone?'

'Probably.'

'Then why don't you?'

'Because they're my brothers,' she said, 'and their mother's the only one I've ever known. It's worth another try, don't you think?'

'It depends whether you believe in the triumph of hope over experience.'

'I do. Look at me. Look at Matthew.'

He nodded. 'Matthew's very fond of you, Jinx.'

'Yes.' She listened for footsteps approaching down the corridor. 'But only because I have the same black eyes as his dying fox. He wants to train as a vet when he leaves here. Has he told you that?'

Alan shook his head.

'He's a sucker for wounded animals. People, he can take or leave.'

'He's not so different from you then.'

She gave a little jump as Adam's footsteps sounded at the top of the stairs. 'On the whole,' she said in a rush, 'I'm not quite so prepared to leave them as I used to be. Perhaps my judgement's improving.'

'That's good.' He smiled down at her. 'The Nightingale's achieved something then.'

'Except that I don't think it was the Nightingale.' She crossed to the door and stood with her back to it. 'I don't always look like something the dog threw up, you know. You'd be amazed what a little hair does for me.' She hesitated. 'I – er – I suppose you wouldn't like to look me up in a month or two when I'm more presentable?'

He shook his head. 'Not really.'

She blushed with embarrassment. 'It was just a thought, Dr Protheroe. Rather a stupid one. Sorry.'

There was a loud knock on the door. 'Jane, are you in there? It's your father.'

Alan lowered his voice. 'The name is Alan, Jinx, and who the hell needs hair? I only ever fantasize about bald women.'

Another knock. 'Jane? It's your father.'

Her eyes gleamed. 'I'll be with you in ten minutes,

Adam,' she called. 'There's something I have to do first. Can you wait in the foyer for me?'

'Why can't I wait in there?'

The Nightingale's administrator lifted an eyebrow. 'I'll be psychotic in two months,' he murmured. 'It does a man no good to keep his feelings zipped up as tightly as this. I'm in considerable pain here.'

Jinx was shaking with laughter as she quietly locked the door. 'It's a woman's thing, Adam,' she called to him in a quivering voice. 'You'd only be embarrassed.'

'Oh, I see. Well, no rush,' said her father gruffly. 'I passed Dr Protheroe's office on my way in. I'll have a word with him while I'm waiting.'

'You do that,' she said, wiping the tears from her eyes. 'You'll like him, Adam. He's your sort of man. Straight as a die and larger than life.'